the soul sacrifice

academy of magical creatures book six

MEGAN LINSKI & ALICIA RADES

We the authors acknowledge that the United States of America is a country formed on stolen land. We respect and honor the indigenous peoples who have lived here for centuries, and we recognize there is still much work to do to make reparations and heal the damage caused to the many indigenous nations who were first here, both in the past and today.

May we remember the atrocities once committed, create a better world in the present, and look forward together for our future.

A special thank-you to our sensitivity reader Kris Riley of the Cherokee tribe for her invaluable feedback on indigenous life and culture, as well as her commentary on living with chronic illness.

This book features conversations in American Sign Language (ASL). ASL is a unique language that uses hand gestures to communicate. ASL has its own rules for grammar and syntax, and does not follow the same rules as English. However, all conversations in ASL (shown in italics) have been translated to English for ease of reading. In the United States, approximately 48 million people are affected by hearing loss.

ONE

Running from a rolling boulder wasn't exactly how I pictured my new year to begin, but here I was, hauling ass to avoid being completely squashed under the weight of another booby trap— second one of the day, actually.

"Fucking dammit, Baine!" My breaths came in long gasps as I pumped my arms. The temple hallway was long and made of stone. There were no windows, and the only light we had came from a singular torch that Professor Baine was carrying. My eyes glanced everywhere for an exit, but I didn't see a spare door. The thunderous rolling of the boulder behind us grew closer and closer, picking up speed.

The hallway sloped downward. Eventually, the boulder would roll faster than we could run.

Baine wheezed for air. Though he was in shape from crawling around in temples lately, he was no spring chicken. Old man was starting to slow up.

My eyes focused on a door at the end of the hallway. If we made it there, we could escape— though it was still twenty feet away, and the boulder was right on our heels.

With a desperate glance back, I saw with horror the boulder was going to crush us any second. We didn't have time to make it to the door before the giant rock smashed us flat. My powers reached out for something, anything that could save us. Miraculously, the Toaqua magic flowing through my veins caught something.

There was an underground water system nearby, just beyond the wall that closed us in. We were in the bottom of the temple. It wasn't much, but it was our only shot.

I threw my hand in front of me like I was smacking something. The wall up ahead burst. A burst of water blasted open the brick on our right side and went clear through to the left.

As the wall exploded, I grabbed Baine and yanked him to the side. His torch went out as it splashed into the water. We ducked into the crevice the blast had made, though water continued to pour down through the hole I created and soaked our clothes.

We had to press together as the boulder rolled by. I held my breath. The rock scuffed us and ripped my pant leg, but it didn't hurt us. I heard the rock smash against the end of the hallway with a colossal *boom,* shaking the walls.

The water pouring from the hole I'd made trickled down the long hallway. It'd soon flood in here. Needing some reprieve, I pried Baine off and stumbled into the open space. I leaned over my knees and heaved, taking deep breaths.

I heard the sound of a lighter. Baine had lit another torch from his pack and held it high, so we could see. The water ebbed out of the hole, already filling up to our ankles.

One more mistake. One fucking more—

"Looks like we triggered another Nivita trap," Baine breathed. He leaned against the wall to steady himself and catch his breath.

"Oh, gee, no shit," I responded sarcastically. I spat and forced myself to stand up. "Guess that wasn't the right way, huh?"

Baine narrowed his eyes. "What are you implying?"

"I'm asking if you know where you're going." I sounded frustrated, but my patience was at its limit. I'd been away from my wife and newborn for a week and a half, and it'd been nothing but setting off traps and hitting dead ends with my dear old father-in-law.

"Of course I know where I'm going!" Baine said, flustered. "We can't be too far."

I'd heard that one before. When we'd gotten here, Baine had accidentally found a Fire wall Koigni trap and ended up burning his ass. *His literal ass.* I had to shield my eyes so I didn't have to watch him put cream on it once we were safe, as we hadn't brought any Anichi or healing Familiars along.

We'd had a week to recover after the battle in *Hok'evale* before Baine insisted getting the *Azaimperiai* was of absolute importance and the search had to begin right away. He told us the *Azaimperiai* could be found in the abandoned Anichi temple in Kinpago— the one where Sophia had summoned Showana Harjo to discover more about the prophecy. Baine had wanted to go alone, but all of us worried if we let something as important as this be left up to Baine, something would go wrong. We'd eventually harassed him enough that he agreed to take one other person. I more or less told him it was going to be me.

Lucky me, right?

"I sacrificed time with my daughter to be here with you," I spat. "I'd ask you not to waste it."

"You didn't *have* to come, you know," Baine said resentfully. "I work best on my own."

"I didn't trust you to come back with the *Azaimperiai* in one piece." I wiped my forehead. "Come on. We need to keep moving."

"*Excuse me?* I am in control of this expedition, sir!" Baine blustered.

He didn't have control of shit. As we wandered up the sloping hallway, I took deep breaths. I'd barely had time to feel well after my fight with the Task Force a few weeks ago, and my magic was still weak. Not to mention running around in this crappy temple and sleeping on hard stone wasn't doing wonders for me. My body was starting to give out. It wouldn't be long before I'd be forced to return to *Hok'evale* and get some rest. We had days left to find this thing, if that.

"I'm going to ask you again. Are you *sure* this is where it is?" I asked.

"Of course it is!" Baine exclaimed. "I wouldn't have brought us here if I wasn't absolutely sure."

Didn't put a lot of stock in that. "Let's go over what you know. You think the *Azaimperiai* is here because—"

"Because this is the only place it *could* be." Baine cut me off, his words an irritated jumble. "The Anichi would never hide the *Azaimperiai* in a place that wasn't sacred. They would consider such an object revered by the ancestors and want it in a location that honored it, and protected it from those who would try to steal it."

"And you're insistent it's in this particular temple."

"Correct. There are few Anichi temples left in the world, all of which I've explored— except for this one." Baine held up a finger. "I've never searched this temple because I considered it ransacked by the other Houses.

Each House has traps set up here to prevent each other from investigating the temple; therefore, most of it has already been explored. I'd believed that if the *Azaimperiai* was here, it'd been long discovered by now. However, I had a thought. If the other Houses have put their mark on this place, why wouldn't Anichi?"

"And you think there's a hidden passage to a secret room somewhere containing it, most likely guarded by an Anichi booby trap."

"Yes. Nothing else makes any sense." Baine sounded so confident, like he'd bet his life on us finding the *Azaimperiai* today.

I just wanted to get the hell out of here, so I could see Sophia and my kid.

"And what if it's in one of the temples that's either disappeared or destroyed?" I asked.

Baine let out a breath. "Impossible. It must be here."

"You're going on a hunch," I argued. "You have no proof."

"Proof!" Baine exploded. "Of course I have proof. The *moglyn* Thalassa killed is all the proof we need."

Moglyn was the technical term for the sea worm we'd fought in the ocean battle weeks ago. It'd been a monstrous creature hundreds of feet long, with thousands of teeth. Thalassa had defeated it, but nearly lost her life in the process. According to Baine, *moglyn* were supposed to be extinct — which is why the appearance of this one was so strange. They only existed in underwater reservoirs beneath blessed ground— mainly, the site of Anichi temples.

The rider on its back had been bonded to it and was working for the Elders, which meant the creature had to come from somewhere around Kinpago. This was the only Anichi temple nearby, and Baine had a theory there was a *moglyn* pod in the temple near the *Azaimperiai*.

But it was just that. A theory. We had no definitive answers.

We left the hallway and entered into a giant amphitheater, one we'd been coming in and out of all week to use as a base. Baine put the torch into a holder and yanked out maps, propping them on the folding table we'd brought. I collapsed onto my cot and tried not to fall asleep.

My mind whirled. We'd been here forever. Was this actually going anywhere?

I heard a dragon's cry from above. It was Julian checking in. Julian was outside the temple, waiting for us to come out. He was hiding from the Task Force in the forest around the temple, but still, it made me uneasy to keep him exposed for so long.

As Baine fussed over the maps, I said, "You've looked at those a million times. It's not going to change anything."

"Look, there's only one corridor we haven't tried." Baine circled the map and pointed. He walked over to me, shoving the map in my face. "*That's* where we have to go. If it's not there, we have nowhere else to look."

Thank the ancestors. Not getting the *Azaimperiai* would be really shitty, but at this point, I just wanted to go home.

We took another twisting hallway downward. I kept my eyes peeled, but luckily, we didn't run into any booby traps... yet.

Baine noticed my impatient stature. "I understand you're in a hurry to get back to your new wife, but she'll be there," Baine went on. He made a romantic, weird sound. "I remember what it was like to be young and in the honeymoon phase."

"I've been with Sophia for over two years." On and off, granted, but never stopped loving her besides.

Baine gave a *psh*. "Nothing when you've loved someone for a lifetime."

"You've barely been back with Doya for a month!"

That is, if he *was* back with her, which I was pretty sure he was. After we'd found out Baine and Doya were Sophia's biological parents, it'd all been very weird. They acted like a couple, but never really told anyone what they were. As far as I knew, the relationship didn't have any labels.

Baine didn't confirm or deny. Instead, he turned to his favorite topic lately, which was blithering on about how hot Doya was. "You know, some women only get more beautiful with age. Eleanor, for example. She's like a fine wine. Her hair's the color of wine. And her thighs. Eleanor has wonderful thighs, you know. I think that's my favorite part of her."

I gave a long, drawn out sigh. "Okay, I *really* didn't want to ask this, but you keep going on about it and I'm done with wondering. Are you and Madame Doya hooking up again?"

"What is *hooking up?*" Baine adjusted his glasses, confused by the phrase.

Fucking A. This guy taught college kids, for ancestors' sake.

"I mean, when I see her carriage parked in front of your house all the time, are you two doing unmentionable activities?" I asked.

Baine's face remained blank.

I facepalmed and shouted, "*Sex!* Are you guys banging again!?"

Baine frowned. "I hardly see why it's appropriate to ask."

"Well, you keep talking about her," I said crossly. He hadn't shut up about the woman since we'd been here.

"If it's so *dire* to know, then yes. We are *hooking up*." Baine puffed out his chest. "And I'm happy to report I've still got it."

"Fucking fantastic. Glad you float her boat."

We reached the end of the hallway. It was a dead end. There was no door leading to another place.

It was strange. Why would the Anichi build a passage to nowhere?

Unless this was a place only the Anichi were supposed to know about. I began looking for clues. I knelt to the ground, trying to find some sort of button or lever.

Baine stood back from the wall and surveyed it. He ran his hands over the bricks. "Hmm... there must be some kind of—"

Baine didn't finish his sentence, because he tripped over me. His boot connected with my face, and he went flying. I gasped as Baine kicked me in the eye, and I fell against the ground. Baine himself toppled over. As he landed, I heard a small *click*.

The wall before us opened. It was the hidden door we were looking for. Baine clambered to his feet. I remained on the ground, holding my eye. It was watering profusely and pounded in pain.

Baine beamed. "Look at that! We found the secret door!"

"Great. Only thing you had to do was blind me," I growled.

Baine scowled. "Quit being so dramatic. Come on."

I got to my feet and slowly drew my hand away from my eye, though it still watered and twitched. I didn't think Baine had given me a black eye, but it still hurt.

The secret door led to a large room a hundred feet across. The room was bare of artifacts or statues, unlike the other rooms in the temple. I searched for the *Azaimperiai*, but it wasn't there.

"Look," Baine stated. "The *moglyn*."

The giant worms slithered in and out of the open area, through holes connecting to the room. There were three or so, all differing in size. Though they were terrifying, they didn't seem hostile. They ate dirt and moved along the floor with no attention to us.

"We're getting close." Baine's voice picked up in excitement. "Hurry."

We took another twisting hallway, until it felt like we were at the lowest point of the temple itself. The ancient Anichi really wanted to hide this thing.

Finally, the tunnel ended, opening into a circular room. There was a white glow inside. As we entered, I saw that the white glow was coming from an Anichi shield. Unlike the others I'd witnessed, this one was visible.

It wrapped around a tomahawk suspended in thin air, hovering tantalizingly before us, just daring us to take it. I wasn't sure how the shield remained in place with no Anichi here to sustain it. It must be some kind of deep magic.

Baine's eyes sparked with greed and desire. "The *Azaimperiai!*"

It was a short distance away, but there was a problem. A creature stood guarding it. The animal had fluffy white fur, long legs, a body and ears like a hare's, with big blue eyes and a thin tail that ended in a fan. It was at least twelve feet tall standing on its hind legs.

I think I'd learned about these at Orenda Academy. They were Anichi creatures, mammals called warbels. They lived underground, ate plants and were known for being more or less harmless. It was thought they were extinct, but as we had learned, most Anichi creatures had survived the war in years prior. I didn't think the creature would attack us.

Baine, though, didn't use his head. He was so amped up about getting the *Azaimperiai* he was willing to barge through anything in his way. Baine ran toward the creature, holding the torch aloft as a weapon and giving a wild yell. He went to swing it, but the animal turned around and whacked Baine with its massive tail.

Baine went flying and slammed against the wall. The torch skidded to the side.

Baine groaned. I walked over, trying to contain my irritation. "Calm down. It's not going to hurt us," I scolded. "It's just here to watch the *Azaimperiai.*"

"That thing?" Baine burst. He got up and shoved the torch in a nearby holder. The warbel gave a mew.

"Look around you. There's no Anichi to sustain the shield. That means the warbel is doing it," I said.

"That doesn't make sense. How did this particular creature survive decades to protect it?" Baine spat.

"It didn't. Warbels live in colonies," I said. "There are probably more down here. I bet Showana Harjo tasked them with defending the *Azaimperiai*, and they've done it through the generations. We just arrived on this one's shift."

Baine huffed. "My life's work right in front of me, and I'm being prevented from obtaining it by an oversized rabbit."

I walked toward the shield. "We have to break it somehow."

But we couldn't get close. When we got near the shield, the warbel hopped in front of us, planting in our way and raising its tail as a warning.

We tried to come at it from different sides, but the warbel was too fast. We couldn't get around it. Though the warbel didn't outright attack, it wasn't letting us through, either. We could use brute force, but that didn't mean the shield would fall, and there wasn't enough water in the air down here to be useful to either of us. Both of us carried a small canteen to in case of emergencies, but it wouldn't be enough to fight the warbel. I could stop its heart, but I didn't like killing things if I didn't have to, and the warbel seemed innocent.

"It's a puzzle, like most of the temple's traps," I said. "We just have to figure out the solution."

"And how, pray tell, do we do that?" Baine snapped. He was in a crabby mood.

I ran a hand through my hair as I thought, remembering my time in the temple with the group when we'd gone to speak to Showana Harjo. "Well, every House trap has a certain trait attached to it. The Toaqua traps are about leadership. The Nivita traps are about using intelligence, and the Yapluma traps are about mind games. Koigni traps center around bravery. We just need to discover what trait the Anichi trap is testing."

"Neither of us are Anichi. How do you expect us to come up with a solution?" Baine complained. He wiped sweat from his brow as he drank from his canteen.

"We'll find a way." My eyes were still fixated on the warbel, who tilted its head at me.

"It's useless. We might as well give up," he bitched.

"Okay, *Grandpa*." Now he was getting on my nerves. We'd found the thing he'd wanted so badly, and he wanted to throw in the towel and run away because we had an obstacle to face?

Baine sent me a glare. "You'll be old one day too, you know."

"Chances of that aren't stellar." I walked in a circle around the room. The warbel followed me, blue eyes keenly observing my actions.

Baine frowned. "Don't say that, Liam. You're a good man. You're kind, and caring, and you protect the people around you. You still have a long life to live."

"Personality traits don't extend your lifespan, sorry."

Baine blinked. "Have you considered the option you might not die as young as you think?"

That made me pause. To get the chance to see my daughter grow up— it was something I hadn't dared to dream of.

And there was a reason for that. I had a rare disease that was barely under control. My life expectancy was up in the air— and thinking about dying of old age instead of young in some hospital bed felt like wishing on a star. I'd already been in some bad situations because of my health, some of which I wouldn't have pulled out of without healing magic. I didn't know how many more times I could tempt fate and get away with it.

I sighed. "I'm counting my blessings by enjoying the years I've got. Nobody is ever promised anything. Especially not me."

"You need to stop this thinking that you're fated for an early death. It's not helping you in the long run," Baine stated. "Why, I'd thought years ago I'd be killed in some cave-in while exploring, and it hasn't happened yet! I've been through plenty of scraps and tight situations, and I've always survived. Perhaps you will as well."

I turned away. "Maybe."

"Liam." Baine proceeded toward me. "You're going to survive this war, and you'll have a long life afterward. You must accept that."

"Accept what? That I might, just *maybe*, last long enough I'll get to walk my daughter down the aisle? Don't get my hopes up." I dropped my head.

Baine put a hand on my shoulder. "We have to do our best with what the ancestors have given us. And I believe your time is far from over. You're not close to being done. You have many years ahead of you, and I want you to have faith in that."

His words brought me a small smile. If Baine believed I had more time than I had allotted myself, who was I to argue that?

He was right. I needed to stop putting myself on a time limit and start focusing on what mattered most— which was living. To constantly believe I was going to die young... I wasn't just hurting myself, I was being selfish by not considering other people. I'd done a lot of work breaking through my negative attitude over the years, but it still looked like I had a ways to go.

"Thanks," I replied. "I guess... I should stop being so hard on myself."

Baine nodded in agreement. The warbel gave a croon, and just like that, the light in the cave dimmed as the shield vanished completely.

Baine gasped. The warbel moved aside, and my eyes widened in shock. It hit me. Anichi's trait was compassion. Baine had broken the shield by being compassionate toward me— and I'd shown compassion by being kind toward myself.

"We did it!" I shouted. The warbel bowed its head.

Baine didn't waste any time. He ran toward the *Azaimperiai*, snatching it out of the air it suspended on. His gaze was revered, jaw dropped. He held the tomahawk like a holy object, completely sucked in to the historical significance of the artifact.

"I've got it," Baine whispered. "After all these years, I've finally got it."

I looked over his shoulder. It was just like what I'd seen in the drawings. The tomahawk was no longer than my forearm, decorated with feathers and still sharp. Small, unreadable runes, like the ones on Sophia's Spirit Totem, covered the handle.

It seemed like such a simple thing— but I wasn't fooled. I knew the kind of power that this object held, the power to control the ancestors themselves.

To be honest, it scared me. No one should ever have that kind of power, no matter what they intended to use it for.

Baine handed the *Azaimperiai* to me. The object was much lighter than I expected, though to my surprise, I didn't feel the pulsing magic within that it clearly held.

But this object wasn't meant for me. I wasn't Anichi, and I couldn't use it. The *Azaimperiai* belonged to Sophia.

As I gave the ax back to Baine, he stuck it securely in his pack. "Very good. Now let's get back home, so we can give this to Sophia, and she can use it to end this—"

The floor beneath us began rumbling. Dust fell from the ceiling, and bricks tumbled from above. Baine gaped, looking around as the circular room crumbled around us.

The trap wasn't over yet. The Anichi had set up a final test, just in case someone managed to get past the shield.

The warbel gave a nervous start and ran off. It hopped out the secret door, its long tail vanishing behind it.

"We have to get out of here!" I shouted, but my cries were already being swallowed up by the sound of falling stone. We made a run for it. The secret door was only a few feet away, but as we reached it, the door caved in, blocking off our only exit.

A huge rock hurtled from the ceiling and struck Baine in the leg. He gave a cry and fell to the floor, landing on his pack. His leg twisted at an odd angle, and he clutched at it in pain.

I dove out of the way of the falling rocks, dodging the debris and covering my head. Eventually, they stopped coming. The rumbling in the cave subsided and ceased completely, but by this time, there was no way out.

My heart pounded furiously in my chest. The one torch we had was starting to dim. Baine's leg was broken, and the oxygen within the room was slowly draining. Baine screamed as he held his broken leg.

"Julian!" I cried, but my shouts echoed back to me. I doubted my dragon could hear me through the heaps of stone piled over top of us. He could get us out, but only if he knew we were down here— and I didn't have a mental connection with him to alert him to our predicament.

There was no way out. We were completely trapped.

sophia

TWO

I stood on a cliff at the edge of the world. The expansive darkness of space spanned in front of me. Below was nothing but a dark abyss. My newborn daughter was swaddled in a soft pink blanket and wrapped tightly in my arms. I could feel the heat of massive flames on my back, but she seemed unaffected— like she didn't notice the world was burning.

Ava-Marie's eyelids fluttered, but she didn't wake. Her chin bobbed up and down, as if she was searching for milk. She looked totally at peace, like her mind was in another place— in the Ancestral Lands with the rest of them.

A single tear streaked my cheek and fell onto her swaddle. "I'm sorry, Ava," I whispered, my voice cracking. "I'm sorry I couldn't save the Hawkei."

She didn't respond, just snuggled deeper into my arms.

My chest became heavy as I turned from the cliff to look behind me. The world blazed with flames of my own making. They were red-hot and blinding, and the smoke billowed high above my head for miles. There was nothing left but destruction.

"I'm sorry," I whispered to the earth. I pulled my daughter closer and tilted my body backward—

Until we both fell from the cliff and into the abyss below.

I woke with a start, my heart racing and my body covered in a sheen of sweat. I crossed a hand over my chest to reach for my daughter, but my fingers touched fur instead. Esis stirred at my side. I gasped and shot upright in bed. "Ava!"

"Shh..." a voice came from the other side of the dark bedroom. Doya stepped out of the shadows so I could see her in the light of the rising sun. She rocked my daughter in her arms. "She's all right. She's sleeping."

"I want to hold her," I said quickly, my voice wavering. My hands shook as I held them out.

Doya sat on the edge of the bed and gently placed my daughter in my arms. Ava-Marie was as calm as she was in my dream. She barely wiggled when I cradled her to my chest.

Esis awoke from his slumber and moved closer to me. He started to drift off again within moments. I felt blessed to have him by my side, when so many other Familiars had gone missing. We didn't have any clues on where to find them.

"Did you have another nightmare, Sophia?" Doya asked.

I nodded solemnly. It wasn't the first strange dream I'd had since Baine announced he'd found the *Azaimperiai* and left with Liam to find it. I thought my nightmares were over now that I'd accepted my past.

But these new ones were a different kind of terrifying. Instead of reliving the past, I was playing out scenarios for the future.

"Do you think they may be messages from the ancestors?" Doya theorized. She spoke gently, as a mother should. I was still getting used to the way she treated me now that she'd admitted she was my birth mother. Sometimes it felt like she was overcompensating for her transgressions.

I took a deep breath and settled into the bed, letting my heart rate slow. "I don't think the ancestors are talking to me. I'm not a *naderei*. I think... it's like I'm trying to tell *myself* something."

"What was the dream about?" Doya inquired.

I sighed and told her the details I could remember.

Doya pressed her lips together. When she made that expression, I could see the old Doya coming through, reminding me she was the same woman as before. She'd just allowed her defensive walls to fall.

"Perhaps you're afraid you cannot fulfill the prophecy," she suggested.

"Maybe..." I said thoughtfully as I gazed down at my daughter's sleeping form. "But I don't *feel* scared. My husband and *pataa* will find the *Azaimperiai*. I will use it to win the war. I'm ready."

Doya frowned. "Are you ready because you *want* to be, or because you *have* to be?"

The room went silent for several beats as I contemplated her words. "I want to save the Hawkei— whatever it takes."

Doya nodded, as if that was the answer she expected of me. I was, after all, her daughter. She shouldn't expect anything less.

I brushed my fingers over Ava-Marie's soft skin in the following silence. I spoke slowly, choosing my words carefully. "I think what scares me is I still don't know *how* I'm meant to fulfill this prophecy. Showana said I must be willing to die to save the Hawkei. And I am, because it means protecting my daughter and my family. But what if I choose the wrong moment, and all is lost? I just don't want to make the wrong choice."

Doya's face fell, and though she tried to hide it, I saw the guilt lurking behind her eyes. "We're all afraid of making the wrong choice, Sophia."

She didn't say it, but I knew she was talking about her choice to give me up. She'd saved my life, but we'd lost so much time together.

"I just wish I knew what to do," I said. "I don't want all of this to be for nothing."

"It won't be," Doya assured me.

I sighed. "Do you know anything else, anything you learned as an Elder that could help?"

Doya pressed her lips together and shook her head. "I'm afraid not. I'd have told you by now if I did."

"What about the other half of the Koigni prophecy?" I questioned.

"The only information it gives is to find the *Azaimperiai*, which we already know."

"What's the exact wording?" I asked, rocking Ava-Marie back and forth.

Doya took a breath. "Our piece states; *The fated Koigni child, born in the Summer Solstice in the Year of the Dragon shall bring glory to the greatest House. The most powerful relic the tribe possesses will serve to fulfill her destiny.*"

I pressed my lips together. "I suppose that's not useful, unless there's a hidden meaning. You should tell Imogen. Maybe she can investigate."

Doya shifted on the bed. "I don't believe she'll find anything, Sophia. The most powerful relic *is* the *Azaimperiai*. We've known what it meant since the day the prophecy was given."

"But the Koigni never found it," I pointed out thoughtfully. "You were looking for it all this time."

"Yes," Doya confirmed. "The Koigni had spies searching for generations."

"That's why you sent Naomi after Amelia in Utah," I said. "You thought she had a lead."

"I did," Doya admitted. "I knew the prophecy was getting closer and closer to coming true. I noticed Amelia sneaking around and sent Naomi to follow her. Naomi discovered she was seeking out an object from the ancestors. I didn't know it was the Spirit Totem at the time, until you told me. I thought it might be the *Azaimperiai*. I believed Toaqua had found it and sent a student to retrieve it, to throw us off so we wouldn't be suspicious. I was covering my bases as a Koigni Elder. You have to understand, Sophia. I never wanted to hurt your sister. I just wanted to do what was right by the tribe."

My lips tightened, and my brow furrowed as I considered her words. I knew she was telling the truth, but my knee-jerk reaction still kept me questioning her at times.

Doya sighed. "Don't make that face, Sophia."

I raised my eyebrows. "What face?"

"That hard look you get when you're thinking," she said. "You look so much like me."

I chuckled lightly. "Well, I *do* get it from you."

Sunlight spilled in through the bedroom window, illuminating her features.

"Everyone says we look so much alike," I remarked. "I'm not sure I see it."

Doya frowned. "If you look at the pictures from before I had you, you would. After you were born, I had surgery on my nose. I told myself it was to cure a deviated septum, but the truth is, Sophia, I was trying to distance myself from you as much as possible— to disguise we were related if you ever returned. I'm sorry."

Her apology felt real, and it settled deep in my chest, warming my heart.

"What matters is that you're here now," I said.

Doya leaned over, until she was looking down on my sleeping daughter. "Yes. And I have no plans to leave you or Ava ever again."

"Thank you—" I started to say, but I was cut off by the sound of a piercing dragon's cry from outside. It was so loud it shook the bed. Pebbles from the rocks that made up my bedroom wall crumbled and clattered to the cave floor. Esis shot to his feet and squealed.

My eyes went wide, and I shot a glance at Doya. "It's Julian! Liam must be back."

I scrambled to get out of bed. Doya gently took my daughter from my arms. I wore only a nightgown, but I threw on a bathrobe and a pair of shoes and rushed out of the room. Esis scurried alongside me at my feet.

Jonah burst out of his room, and Squeaks followed behind. Jonah's hair fell around his shoulders, and his shirt was backward, like he'd just tossed it on. Imogen's room was empty, as she'd spent last night at Cade's.

"Was that—?" Jonah started.

"Julian?" I finished for him. "Liam's back!"

The two of us hurried through the living room. Naomi perked her ears from where she was lounging on the couch. We passed by Doya's Familiar and into the cool January air. Squeaks squawked from behind us, and Esis made a sound that seemed like an attempt to mirror Julian's cry.

We raced down the front steps and into the canyon that enclosed the village of *Hok'evale*. Julian had landed in the center of the road. His leathery wings folded onto his back, but there was no rider with him.

My stomach plummeted. "Liam!?"

The dragon let out a roar and reared his head upward, repeating the frantic gesture over and over again. Squeaks pounded her hooves into the ground. The hippogriff appeared wild.

Jonah came to a halt at my side. He breathed deeply, trying to catch his breath. "Squeaks says Julian's trying to tell us Liam's in trouble."

"I got that," I replied.

My husband's companion cocked his head and cried out again. I didn't need the Familiars to translate. I knew we had to go looking for my husband and *pataa*. Something terrible must've happened to them.

"We have to help them!" I said quickly.

Jonah wasted no time jumping onto Squeaks. I took a step toward Julian, but hesitated a moment and looked back toward the house. Doya stood there, looking slightly frightened. Ava-Marie was still soundlessly asleep in her arms.

"Sophia, you can't go," she insisted. "You risk exposing yourself to the Task Force."

My heart fell. "I have to. They're my family."

"But what about Ava?" Doya asked.

"You can take care of her until I get back," I suggested. "Liam and Baine could be hurt. They might need my healing magic."

Doya couldn't argue with that. I'd have expected her to fight to come with us for Baine's sake, if it weren't for her granddaughter in her arms.

"Come back safe," she insisted.

"I will," I promised.

I reached up for the spines on Julian's back. It was a feat in itself to pull myself onto him, considering I still wasn't back to normal after my labor. But I couldn't stay behind when my husband was out there, possibly hurt. Esis scurried up Julian's back and settled in front of me.

Jonah gave a loud whistle, and we were off. Julian pumped his wings, and Squeaks followed closely. My heart hammered as I left my daughter behind. I hadn't left her side in a week. I didn't think it'd be so soon.

Cold air whipped by my face as we flew over *Hok'evale* and outside of the Anichi shield's boundaries. Usually, the shield would keep invaders out and residents in, but Julian had a free pass from Luana to come and go as he pleased.

The flight from *Hok'evale* to the Hawkei reservation usually took some time, but I was so frightened, the miles seemed to fly by under us. Julian remained high, so if the Task Force was looking for us they'd only see his shadow amongst the clouds.

"What do you think happened?" Jonah asked over the rush of the wind.

"I don't know!" I shouted back. "I just hope they're okay."

Julian flew us over the forest. In the distance, I could make out the highest point of the Anichi temple. Julian circled the pyramid once, then dropped us off at the entrance. Squeaks landed beside us, and Jonah jumped off her back.

We hurried inside the temple— except Julian, because he didn't fit through the doorway. Inside, the ceiling was massively tall. It looked exactly like the last time we'd been here, except two cots had been set up, and supplies were scattered around them. I could tell which cot was Baine's and which was Liam's just by the mess of belongings. Liam's sleeping bag had been rolled up nicely, while Baine's was hanging across the floor.

"Their packs are gone," Jonah noted, looking over the campsite. "They could be anywhere. There are so many tunnels and caverns, it could take us weeks to search them all."

I forced my worry out of the way and went into leadership mode. Liam wasn't here, which made it my job now. "Let's look for clues. Esis, see if you can pick up any scent trails."

Esis scurried toward one of the doorways that split off from the main room. Squeaks joined him and inspected each tunnel. Jonah went through

Liam's stuff to search for hints. Squeaks began tossing items every which way with her beak, not really paying attention to what she was doing.

I started picking through Baine's things. There were granola bar wrappers and trash everywhere that had spilled from a garbage bag nearby. A change of clothes had been piled in a heap with his bedding, and a bunch of different maps were stacked on top. I started going through the maps, but they were so disorganized I could hardly make sense of them. Most of them were covered in scribbles that must've meant something to Baine but made zero sense to me.

As I looked through the maps, Esis continued around the room. He yelped like he caught a trail, but huffed a moment later. My guess was Liam and Baine's scent was everywhere.

"I've got nothing. I can try searching with my Air—" Jonah suggested, but I cut him off with a gasp.

"Hold on. I think I found something!" I cried.

Jonah leaned over my shoulder and looked down at the map.

"This tunnel here is circled." I pointed.

"Are any of the others?" he asked, looking through the stack.

"I didn't see any," I said. "I think we should start here."

"Agreed."

I used my Anichi powers to guide us with my light. We followed the map down various tunnels, but it was a maze in here. Baine had scribbled over the map so much it was hard to follow.

We came to a split in the tunnels, and I had to check the map again. "What do you think this means?" I asked Jonah, pointing to a spot covered in ink.

Jonah pressed his lips together thoughtfully. "I think we have to go this way."

He pointed to the left. His guess was as good as mine, so I followed him. I thought we were making good progress... until the sound of shifting stones met my ears.

All it took was a split-second. One moment we were walking along down the tunnel, my light illuminating the way. The next, rocks shifted beneath our feet, and the ground fell away to reveal a deep, dark pit.

My stomach dropped to my toes, and Esis screamed so loudly his cry filled the entire hall. I scrambled backward with my Familiar, but Jonah wasn't so lucky. He and Squeaks had been several steps ahead of us, and when the stone crumbled into the pit, so did they. Jonah's arms flung upward as he fell, reaching desperately for something to catch him. But I couldn't make it in time. In less time than I could react, he and Squeaks were gone.

"Jonah!" I screamed, my heart twisting in my chest.

When the ground stopped rumbling, I inched closer to the pit, my pulse pounding so hard it made my hands shake.

"Jonah!?" I wailed.

I expected to hear the sound of their bodies hit the ground, but the pit was so deep I heard nothing. I shone my Anichi light down it, but all I saw was blackness.

My jaw dropped. I was so shocked I could hardly move. I couldn't have lost Jonah so easily!

"No. No, no, no," I cried, backing up from the pit.

Esis howled down the pit for Squeaks, but no one responded. Finally, he turned to me, his lips turned into a deep frown. He crawled into my lap, and I cradled him in my arms, feeling deeply sad and alone in the quiet temple. I fixed my eyes forward on the wall, trying to process how quickly it had happened. Jonah had only been standing next to me less than ten seconds ago.

"They can't be gone," I told myself. I refused to believe I was alone down here.

"*Relax*, Sophia," Jonah's voice responded.

Hope surged in my chest. I looked upward to see Jonah rising from the pit. He stopped in mid-air and hovered there. Squeaks flapped her wings, and the two flew out and to safety.

"Jonah!" I cried, rushing forward to throw my arms around him. "Ancestors, I thought I lost you."

Jonah blew a puff of air. "Pft. You think this temple could get rid of me that easily? Or did you forget I could fly?"

"For a second," I admitted.

"Don't worry," he said. "Nothing's taking down the Storm Lord. But I think we went down the wrong tunnel."

"Agreed," I said. "Let's try the other one."

Jonah and I backtracked and took the right-hand tunnel. We walked— carefully, so we wouldn't trigger any traps— until we came to the spot circled on the map.

My stomach dropped when I saw what was in front of us. The path had been completely blocked by a huge pile of stone that reached all the way to the ceiling.

"This can't be it!" I exclaimed. "We must've missed a tunnel on the map."

Jonah's face fell. "I think it is, Sophia."

I gaped at him a moment, not wanting to believe Liam might be beyond the cave-in. "But—"

He placed a hand on my shoulder. "I think this is what Julian was trying to tell us about."

Jonah approached the pile of stone and started heaving them out of the way with Squeaks' help.

"Liam!" I cried, praying for an answer. "*Pataa?*"

There was nothing but silence in response. My heart slammed against my rib cage.

"Liam, we're here. If you're back there, please answer us!" I called.

My guts sank. If this was the reason Julian came to us, it might already be too late. They might've been crushed under the stone. Or suffocated.

No. I couldn't let my daughter grow up fatherless.

"Liam!" I wailed, falling to my knees.

Jonah grunted as he heaved aside a huge boulder, but as it slammed to the ground and rolled to the side, I swore I heard something. I went breathless, but Jonah didn't notice. Esis grabbed pebbles and moved them out of the way.

"Shh!" I hissed.

Jonah groaned as he cleared another stone, and Squeaks tossed another out of the way.

"Quiet!" I said. "I think I heard something!"

Everyone stopped, and the tunnel went silent. I listened intently, but the noise was gone.

"Liam!?" I screamed again.

A beat passed, and nothing came. Then, a muffled but hopeful cry came from beyond the rock.

"*Pawee!*"

I shot to my feet and rushed forward, grabbing for any stone I was strong enough to move. "Hang on, Liam! We're coming for you!"

Jonah's face paled in the light coming from my hand. "Squeaks! Help me with this one!"

The two rolled away a huge piece of stone, while I moved the smaller pieces. My heart beat frantically, and sweat broke across my entire body. I feared what we would find behind the cave-in.

After what seemed like a lifetime of moving rock, Jonah pushed away another stone, revealing a hole large enough to crawl through.

"Let me through!" I insisted.

"It's all yours." Jonah held a hand out and helped me climb the rock pile until I reached the crawlspace. I squeezed myself through, and Esis followed behind me.

"*Pawee?*" I heard Liam's voice before I saw him.

I shone the light from my palm around the room. Rubble was everywhere, and the air was stale from the dust.

Finally, my light passed over Liam. He sat slumped against the wall, half-leaning on one of the fallen pieces of stone. His face was pale, and he looked weak.

I stumbled over piles of rocks to reach him. "Liam, are you hurt!?"

Before he could answer, I grabbed his face in my hands and pulled him into a passionate kiss. Heat pooled in my belly as I ran my tongue over his lips. We drew away from each other, breathless.

Liam groaned and pushed himself upright. "Forget about me. Help Baine."

My eyes darted over to where Liam had looked. Baine was sprawled across the floor. A large stone covered in blood lay beside him, and his leg was twisted at an odd angle. Baine's eyes were closed; he was totally out of it.

Esis was already at his side. He placed his hands over the wound on Baine's leg, and the skin started knitting itself together.

"Ancestors!" My stomach twisted. I hurried over to my *pataa* and leaned over him. His skin was ashen, and he didn't move.

"Is he—?" I started. I reached for Baine's hand and squeezed it, to see if he would respond.

"He's alive," Liam said through labored breaths. "Broken leg, though. It took everything I had to move the rock off him. He passed out at the first sight of blood."

I breathed a sigh of relief. Baine was already stirring as Esis used his healing magic. Esis was far better than me at healing, so I let him work on Baine, while I turned to Liam.

"Let me help you," I insisted.

Liam grabbed my hands before I could place them on his chest. "Save your energy in case Baine needs it."

I shook my head firmly. "Esis can heal a broken leg. You're going to need your strength to get out of here."

"She's right," Jonah cut in. He'd made it through the crawl space and looked out of breath. Squeaks couldn't fit through, but I could hear her pacing on the other side of the rocks.

Liam hesitated a few moments. Finally, he sighed. He brought my hands forward, splaying them across his chest.

He didn't say anything, but that simple act meant everything. Liam was accepting my help.

I closed my eyes and turned my focus inward. I searched for the calm energy deep within my belly. It was easy to find now, thanks to Luana's lessons. I drew the Anichi energy outward, until a gentle buzz filled my palms. I pushed tendrils of magic further, channeling them into Liam's body. The magic was like an extension of myself. I could feel everything it did.

I directed my magic through his skin, down to his bones and into his organs. His disease was familiar to me now. It smelled smoky, like burning incense, and tasted mildly sour. I instructed my magic to warm, as if melting away the symptoms— but that wasn't the only problem. Deep within his leg, and up in his shoulder, my magic hit a block and resisted. As if I could see inside his body with my own two eyes, I knew which injuries he'd sustained. Liam had torn his hamstring and pulled a shoulder muscle trying to move the rock off Baine's leg.

I focused my magic at the sites of injury and felt the muscle healing. The block fell away, and I continued to explore. The biggest problem was he was weak and dehydrated. I did what I could about the weakness and directed my magic to boost his systems. Glucose entered his cells to give him strength. It'd help for a while, but there wasn't any more I could do until he ate, drank, and slept.

I drew away. "Better?"

Liam's features seemed brighter. "For now."

"You need to rest and have a good meal," I told him.

"I know," Liam groaned. He eyed me up and down. "*Pawee*, why aren't you dressed?"

I shrugged. "We were in a hurry."

Liam nudged me and gestured to Baine. Esis stepped back, as if admiring his handiwork. Baine stirred, then lifted a hand to press it to his head.

He groaned. "Oh, my."

Jonah reached out for Baine's hand and helped him sit up. "Great to see you awake, Professor."

Baine groaned again and glanced around the room. I realized how dim it was and made my Anichi light brighter, so we could all see each other.

"Are you okay, *pataa?*" I asked.

Baine looked better, though his pants were ripped, and there was still blood all over his leg. He moved his leg and said, "Much better. I assume I have Esis to thank?"

Esis chittered proudly. Baine reached over to scratch him behind the horns, and Esis cooed. I knelt beside Baine and pulled him into a hug.

"I'm glad you're both all right," I said.

"What happened here?" Jonah questioned. "If the temple's this dangerous, you should come home."

I gaped at him. I was the last person who wanted Baine or Liam to get hurt, but we couldn't give up. "What about the *Azaimperiai?*"

Baine got a big smile on his face and reached for his bag. "We found it."

"What?" Jonah squeaked.

Baine pulled out a decorated tomahawk. "We found the *Azaimperiai!*"

"Ancestors!" I cried, my heart pounding. This was a miracle! "We can restore Anichi's magic! We'll win the war!"

Baine's cheesy smile only grew. "It's quite exciting, isn't it?"

I reached out for the tomahawk, but Liam placed a hand on my shoulder to stop me.

"Perhaps we should get home before we test it out," he suggested. "We don't know how it works, and I'm not sitting around waiting for another cave-in."

"Good idea," I agreed. "Let's get out of here, before any of us set off another booby trap."

"Impossible," Liam deadpanned. "Baine's set them all off already."

Baine frowned as he got to his feet. "I hardly think I'm the only one to blame."

Liam chuckled and nudged Baine with his elbow. "Relax. I'm only joking."

"Amazing," Baine said, adjusting his glasses.

"What is?" I asked.

Baine cocked an eyebrow. "Your husband has a sense of humor."

Jonah laughed. "Ooh, Liam. That's a burn."

"Shut up," Liam mumbled.

I laughed, feeling relief wash over me now that we'd found them. It appeared that the two had bonded while they'd been away.

Getting out of the temple was easy, though we spent a good fifteen minutes helping Baine pack up his stuff. I felt at ease as Liam and I climbed onto Julian's back and I snuggled into my husband. I felt like we'd been away from each other for months. Inhaling his pine scent put me at ease. I closed my eyes and felt myself drifting off.

Liam grabbed on to me tightly. "Soph, you okay?"

I snapped to attention. "Fine. Still recovering from labor, but I'm all right."

Liam grabbed one of Julian's spines and said, "Let's get home to our baby."

We took off to the skies again. Squeaks was slow, since she had to haul Jonah *and* Baine, but we made it back to *Hok'evale* in one piece.

As soon as we landed in the canyon, the front door to our house flung open. Imogen and Sassy rushed out, followed by Luana and Amelia. Sierra fluttered on Luana's shoulder, and Kiwi flew above us.

Doya stood in the doorway. Ava-Marie was in her arms, and Naomi was close behind. Liam slid off Julian's back, then helped me down.

"What happened!?" Imogen cried.

"A minor mishap," Baine said with a wave of his hand.

Liam scoffed and rolled his eyes. "Minor. Yeah."

"What matters is we found the *Azaimperiai*," Baine rushed to say.

Imogen's eyes went as wide as saucers. "You did?"

I didn't hear his response, because Amelia came up to me and squeezed me as tight as she could. "Sophia!" she scolded. "Why didn't you come get us? We could've helped."

"I don't know," I admitted. "It all happened so fast."

She glanced down to my robe and boots. "Yeah, I can see that. You must be freezing."

Should we talk about this inside? Luana asked in sign language.

"Yes," I agreed, signing back to her.

We'd all spent enough time with Luana that everyone knew enough sign language to understand her now. We turned to walk back to the house, where we could talk about the *Azaimperiai* in private. Imogen held her arm out to Luana, and they looped their elbows together to stay warm.

We entered the house. Doya helped me get settled into the couch before she placed Ava-Marie back into my arms. My heart melted all over again when I touched her, like it was the first time. I didn't think I'd ever get sick of holding her.

Liam collapsed beside me and draped an arm around my shoulder. He leaned over and cooed at Ava-Marie, poking her tiny little nose as she looked up at him in wonder. Esis sat at my feet.

"I'm so glad you're back," Doya said quietly to Baine as everyone got situated.

Baine leaned over and pecked her on the lips, as if forgetting the rest of us were there to witness. I was getting used to the two of them being my parents, but it still shocked me every time they showed any PDA. It was like I forgot they'd actually screwed to bring me into existence.

Jonah cleared his throat, and Baine snapped back to attention. "The *Azaimperiai*, Professor?"

Baine straightened. "Right. Yes. We got it."

He pulled the tomahawk from his bag and held it up for everyone to see. "This is what we've been searching for."

Doya stared at it like Baine was holding the moon in his hands. Her eyes were filled with wonder I'd seen only when she held her granddaughter.

But this was different, too. It wasn't full of love, but disbelief.

"I can't believe you've found it... after all this time," she said breathlessly.

Baine puffed out his chest. "Well, it was no easy feat."

Liam groaned at Baine's obvious boasting. "Yeah, it only took fifty booby traps and a broken leg."

Doya's face paled. "You broke your leg?"

"No harm done," Baine claimed. "Esis was there to heal me. I'll tell you about it later."

"Don't forget the part where you passed out at the sight of blood," Liam teased.

Baine frowned. "I did not *pass out*. I, uh— was merely resting my eyes."

Has Sophia had a chance to use it? Luana asked.

Not yet, I signed.

"Let's try it," Amelia suggested, signing as she spoke.

"I don't even know how to use it." I tried to sign the best I could one-handed, since the other was holding Ava.

"I'll take her," Liam offered.

I almost didn't want to give her up, but Liam looked so entranced by having her in his arms. He loved her so much, and he'd been gone for two weeks. He deserved to hold her. I passed her off, and the expression he got when he brought Ava-Marie close made me melt.

"None of us know how to use it," Imogen pointed out. "But that shouldn't stop us from trying."

"Yeah, I want to see what happens," Jonah added.

Baine held the *Azaimperiai* out to me. I hesitated a moment before asking, "I'm not going to hurt anyone, am I?"

"I don't imagine so," Baine said. "You should be able to control the magic within it."

"Okay. I'll try. But we should probably go outside," I suggested.

Everyone followed me out the back, where we were secluded in a small garden. Rock walls sloped on all sides of us and opened to the expanse of the sky above. Liam stayed back by the door with Ava-Marie, since we didn't know what might happen with my magic. It might be too much to control.

"Everyone ready?" I asked.

"Ready!" Imogen nodded eagerly.

I took the artifact from Baine's outstretched hand. I expected something to happen, like wind swirling around me, or the cave rumbling, but everything was still.

"What do you feel?" Doya asked.

I shook my head, struggling to come up with an answer. "Nothing."

Baine furrowed his brow. "Nothing? But you're the chosen one."

"I know that," I practically snapped. "But I don't feel any magic in it."

Jonah pressed his fingers to his lips. "Could it be the wrong one?"

"No," Baine insisted. "All the ancient Hawkei texts speak of this particular object."

"Maybe it's a decoy?" Amelia offered.

Baine shook his head, looking utterly perplexed. "Absolutely not. The way it was guarded confirms what it is."

"Then what does this mean?" I asked.

"Perhaps it's protected," Doya theorized. Her eyebrows knit together tightly, like she was thinking hard. "Maybe the magic was sealed inside, to keep it from being tracked down."

"Then how do we break the seal?" Liam asked. He stepped forward once he knew it was safe.

Doya pressed her lips together. "I'm not sure. This type of magic is difficult— even beyond what most Elders can do."

"So, we've hit another dead end?" Jonah asked.

Imogen shifted her weight between her feet. "It's just a bump in the road, right?"

The crease between Baine's eyebrows deepened. "Yes. This is merely a delay. We'll figure it out."

"You don't know what this means?" I asked. "You're supposed to be an expert on these types of ancient artifacts."

"I am," Baine assured me, though he seemed bothered. "I can get it to work eventually."

"Luana?" Imogen nudged her in the side and signed. "You haven't said much. Any ideas?"

Luana scrunched up her face in thought. *I'm not certain. If this is the true Azaimperiai, I think it's simply a matter of figuring out how to tap into its magic. I don't see why tapping into such a powerful object would be easy, but it should be doable.*

My heart sank. She made it sound hopeful, but I'd feared this might happen— that finding the *Azaimperiai* wouldn't be the end of our journey. We still had to figure out how to use it.

I was ready to do whatever it took. I just didn't know what our next move was.

"Too bad this thing doesn't come with a manual, huh?" I said, trying to ease the twisting sensation in my gut.

"We'll figure it out," Amelia assured me.

"I hope so." My throat was getting tight. I handed the tomahawk back to Baine and said, "Excuse me a moment."

I could feel everyone's eyes on me as I walked back inside the house. I went down the hall and into my bedroom, shutting the door behind myself.

At my dresser, I pulled out the compass Haloke had given me. According to legend, the compass was gifted to the wives of Toaqua chiefs from the ancestors. It'd been passed down for generations. It was said to lead you to whatever you needed when you were lost.

I slumped onto the bed in defeat. "Ancestors," I whispered, staring down at the compass. There were no cardinal directions, and the needle did not move. "We're at a loss for answers. We found the *Azaimperiai*, but we don't know how to use it. Tell me where I need to go to fulfill the prophecy. Where's the answer we need?"

The needle on the compass began to move. At first, I was hopeful— until it made a complete three-sixty rotation. The rotation began to speed up, until it was going round and round in a circle so fast it became blurry.

I huffed. It wasn't the first time the ancestors had refused to answer me through the compass. I wasn't even sure it worked.

A light knock sounded at the door, and Liam stepped inside. Ava wasn't in his arms; he'd come alone.

"Hey, *pawee*," he said gently, taking a seat beside me. "We'll figure out the *Azaimperiai*. You know that, right?"

I dropped my gaze to my hands. "I hope so, but Liam..."

"What is it, Soph?" He wrapped an arm around my shoulder.

I gazed up at him, and my voice wavered. "I'm scared."

He tilted his head to the side. "Scared of what?"

"I'm scared of a lot of things," I admitted. "Familiars are still missing, and I feel responsible for finding them. We can't win this war without them."

"That's not on you," Liam assured me. "We have people looking for them. We'll find them."

"It's not just that." I sighed. "This morning, I had a dream that I couldn't save the Hawkei. I woke up worrying I'd make the wrong choice with the *Azaimperiai*. But it doesn't call out to me, Liam. It's supposed to, right? Because I'm the chosen one?"

"Yes, but there has to be another explanation," he said.

"That's what scares me. I think I know what my dream was trying to tell me now."

"What, *pawee*?"

I sighed and looked back down to my hands. "Maybe I can't save the Hawkei. Maybe I'm *not* the chosen one."

"But you *are*," Liam insisted. "*The fated Koigni child, born on the summer solstice in the year of the Dragon*. You're the only one who fits the bill, Soph."

I shook my head solemnly. "But I'm not. Remember there was another girl born that same night. Lucy and Anthony's daughter, Charlotte."

Liam looked taken aback. "What are you saying, *pawee*?"

I swallowed. "I'm saying... maybe the *Azaimperiai* was meant for *her*."

Liam looked deeply contemplative. "That can't be right. She's not around anymore, Soph. Which makes you the only one."

I didn't quite believe him. My inability to get the *Azaimperiai* to work today had me convinced the ancestors had saved the wrong child. They should've spared Charlotte, not me. She was the real chosen one... I was just a backup. Because it was in my hands, and not hers, the *Azaimperiai* was useless.

I frowned. "Regardless, I just hope to the ancestors we can save the Hawkei. Before it's too late."

We'd come too far only to lose everything.

Liam

THREE

Ava-Marie's cries woke me up early in the morning. I rolled out of bed. Sophia was still deep in sleep beside me, though her face twitched, as if searching for a way out of her nightmares.

It'd been a week since we'd found the *Azaimperiai,* and we hadn't gotten any farther ahead.

It was quite frustrating. Sophia and I both felt stuck.

I stopped by the crib. Ava-Marie was hungry. She moved her head from one way to another, looking for food. Her eyes fixed on my face as I leaned over.

"Hey there, sweetheart." I picked her up. This resulted in more wailing. I ducked out before she could wake Sophia up, and I took Ava-Marie to the kitchen.

I got a bottle from the fridge and warmed it up before I fed her. She sucked down the milk greedily, keeping her eyes locked on mine.

She was the most precious little thing. When she was finished eating, I ran a finger along the edge of her face. She grabbed it with her tiny hand and squeezed, making a loud noise.

My heart became over full. I couldn't stop watching her. Everything she did seemed like the most interesting thing in the world. I'd seen and performed incredible magic, but she was the most incredible thing of all.

As I changed her diaper, she made a face. When something unpleasant was happening, Ava-Marie developed a habit of scrunching up her nose and looking unimpressed.

I laughed. "Cut it out. You look like me when you do that," I whispered. She scrunched her nose up again.

After I'd slipped her into a new onesie, she fell asleep in my arms. I was still having a hard time letting her go. If I was holding her, it was like I could protect her from the world and all its problems. Once she was out of my reach, there was only so much I could do to defend her from how messed up everything was.

And I knew how awful the world could be. Thinking of the things her mother and I had experienced... it churned my stomach imagining it could happen to our child.

I set her back into the crib, where she drifted into a peaceful slumber.

We were still working on getting her to sleep through the night. I felt like it was going to be a long road. Ava-Marie was a pretty fussy baby. Most nights, she slept on and off for two hours at a time before one of us had to take her. Last night was the first time she'd finally slept six, and thank the ancestors for it, because I was ridiculously tired.

My Water Council was handling things in my absence. I'd requested some time off, to find the *Azaimperiai* and bond with my new baby, but I had to go back to work eventually. We were in the middle of a war, and every day counted.

I just hoped I worked up some stamina by then, because this exhaustion wasn't doing me any favors.

Jonah emerged from his bedroom with Squeaks. "Look at you, up bright and early."

"The baby was hungry. What about you? It's the weekend. Usually you sleep until noon."

Jonah froze, before he eased up and said, "Oh, you know... just making pancakes."

Something was up. "Um, okay."

As I drank my morning coffee— something that was necessary with an infant— I watched as Jonah knocked things over and fumbled around while cooking breakfast.

"Is there something on your mind?" I asked, already knowing the answer.

"Yeah," Jonah said casually, though it sounded fake as shit. "But we can talk about it when the girls get up."

On cue, Sophia and Imogen emerged from their bedrooms. Sophia still looked sleepy. She had huge bags under her eyes and was carelessly dressed. Her hair was in a bun, and she had no makeup. She had on a sweatshirt of mine that was so big on her, it fell to her knees. She wore it like a dress, which gave off that *hot new mom* vibe. Sexy.

Esis was tucked into the sweatshirt pocket. He stuck his head out of it and trilled.

Imogen laughed when she saw Sophia. Imogen was wearing a rainbow pair of leggings, with a tie-dye sweater and fuzzy boots. I was happy to see that her sense of fashion had come back— something she'd lost while battling her nightshade addiction a few months prior. Sassy waltzed beside her, adorned with a matching rainbow tie.

"Ancestors, Sophia, put on some pants." Imogen giggled and slid into the seat next to me.

"Pants are for losers," Sophia grumbled. "I have a newborn. I give no fucks."

"Glad to see I'm rubbing off on you. Pancakes?" Jonah shoved a glass of orange juice in Sophia's face. She took the mug and chugged it down.

I eyed her. "You gonna make it?"

"I'll be fine. My schedule just needs time to adjust." Sophia smiled and gave me a morning kiss. "Thank you for taking care of the baby."

"Of course."

Jonah placed the pancakes on the table. Imogen bit her lip. Sassy nervously grumbled at Squeaks, who paused working through her stack of pancakes to look up.

As Jonah carefully sat down, my irritation broke. "Okay, what's going on?" I asked. "You two are acting like a bomb is about to go off."

Sophia perked up. Jonah looked at Imogen. They shared the same anxious expression.

"There's kinda something we wanted to talk to you about," Jonah said slowly. He took a deep breath. Several seconds passed before he said, "Jake asked me to move in with him."

"And Cade asked me to come live at his apartment," Imogen stated.

I didn't know what to say. The four of us had hardly parted from each other's sides for the past twelve months. We'd been shoved in the Biyami dorms together, forced to go on the run, and then lived as a unit ever since.

"You guys wanna move out?" Sophia asked. I caught a hint of sadness in her tone.

I shared her sentiment. It felt like the team was breaking up or something.

"Cade is really helping me with my recovery," Imogen began. "He's been wonderful. And I know you guys are supportive, but I think my chances of avoiding relapse are better if I'm in a place where all my attention can be on building a new life."

Cade had been over here a lot. To be honest, it'd been kind of annoying. We only had so much space in the house, and he'd been in the way while we were taking care of Ava-Marie more than once, though it always made me feel guilty when he and Imogen had to hole up in her room to get some privacy.

"You guys have your own lives. You have a kid now. You deserve to have a home of your own," Jonah stated. "We don't know how long this war is going to go on, and Jake and I are getting serious. We want to spend as much time together as we can, before..."

Jonah dropped off, and I knew he feared what he thought was inevitable. *Before it's too late.*

"Do you guys want to leave because we had a baby?" Sophia asked. "I know she cries, but she'll get better. She's still so young."

Imogen shook her head. "No. Jonah and I both *adore* Ava."

Jonah gushed. "She's my little cutie!"

"We just think it'd be better for her if you two had your own space," Imogen continued. "You're married now. Ava-Marie should have her own room, and you two might want to have more kids."

"Well, we weren't thinking about having more until the war was over," I said. My reserve failed as I saw the logic of the situation. "But I guess you're right."

"The thing is... we all have our own significant others now. And our own lives," Imogen said. "I think it's safe now to start living them. We've been afraid to separate because we worried about what would happen if we did. But we don't have to worry about that anymore."

She was right. We didn't.

Sophia teared up, and she gave a sniff. Imogen reached across the table and started wiping her tears away. "Sophia! You didn't think we'd all live together forever, did you?"

She gave a tearful giggle. "Kind of."

"Shit, that'd have to be a big house," I mused.

Jonah wiped at his eyelids. "Ancestors, don't cry, bitch. You'll make me ruin my eye makeup."

Sophia got up from her chair. She threw her arms around Jonah and squeezed him tight. Esis was squished between the both of them and gave a yelp.

"I'm going to miss you guys so much!" she bawled. I shushed her, so she wouldn't wake the baby sleeping in the other room.

"For fuck's sake, woman, we're moving down the street; we're not going off to war!" Jonah blushed when he realized the poor choice of words, and I gave him a filthy glare.

"We're still going to hang out and see each other all the time," Imogen vowed. "We promise."

Sophia let go of Jonah and wiped her face with the sleeve of my hoodie. "It just... it feels like everything is coming to an end."

"It's not ending. It's a new beginning!" Imogen burst. She slung an arm around my shoulders. "Nothing's going to change."

I got what she was saying— but at the same time, I disagreed with her. Everything *had* changed. I'd been feeling it in my bones since the morning Ava-Marie was born. The only reason I wasn't fighting it was because I knew it was unavoidable. Jonah and Imogen deserved to be happy, like Sophia and I were. It wouldn't be right to hold them back from that.

I smirked at Jonah. "How's that celibacy vow going to work if you two are living together?"

Jake had told Jonah weeks ago he didn't want to have sex until they were married. Hard to do when you were sharing a bed every day and there was plenty of time to be alone.

"He still wants to keep it," Jonah said. "He's *very* serious about it. I bet we can make it until then."

"Right. You let me know how that goes." I snickered.

Jonah drew himself up. "You don't think I can do it?"

Imogen smiled. "Well... you can be a bit of a horndog."

"A *bit*?" I asked incredulously.

Sophia waggled her eyebrows. "It's easy to keep a purity vow when you don't live together. Cohabitating, on the other hand..."

Jonah narrowed his eyes. "You guys will be swallowing your words on my wedding night."

"You'll be too busy swallowing something else to notice!" Imogen cracked. The girls burst out laughing, and Esis chirped.

Jonah scowled. Squeaks gave him a playful nudge, and he scratched her head before he said, "Yeah, yeah. We'll see who's laughing in the end."

I made a skeptical noise and took another sip of coffee. Jonah was right — we'd see.

❦

IMOGEN AND JONAH spent the rest of the day moving their things out to their respective new homes. It didn't take long. Almost everything we had was lost when Orenda Academy burned, and none of us had gathered that much stuff in the meantime. We had almost everything moved by lunchtime.

As they were packing up the last of their things, Luana came by. I was helping Jonah load a few boxes onto Julian's back as she approached. She carried something in her hands— the cradleboard I'd woven for Sophia. It was finally finished, adorned with strands of beads Luana had sewn into it.

She presented it to me outside the house. *It's all done!* she signed.

"It looks amazing. Sophia's going to love it," I said, signing as I spoke. She nodded, and we headed back in.

Sophia was carrying Ava-Marie in one arm. She'd changed into a pair of jeans and a t-shirt. Esis ran beside her feet, looking under counter tops and furniture for anything Imogen and Jonah might've accidentally dropped.

She got a broad smile when she saw the cradleboard. "What's this?"

"It's a cradleboard. I wove it for you. Luana decorated it with beads," I explained. "Now you can carry Ava around on your back while leaving your hands free."

"Oh my gosh. It's beautiful," Sophia said, running her hand over the cradleboard.

"It's adjustable, so you'll be able to use it when she gets bigger," I said. "It'll last for her first year."

I grabbed a swaddling blanket from the bedroom. I'd made that, too, a few weeks ago. It was decorated in alternating shades of red and blue, woven in traditional Hawkei style.

I unfolded the blanket on the couch, and Sophia handed Ava-Marie to me. I swaddled Ava tightly in the blanket while Sophia slipped the straps of the cradleboard over her shoulders.

Ava-Marie wiggled in the tight bundle. I went to put her inside the cradleboard, but Esis was already snuggled inside.

"Not for you," I snapped. "Get down."

Esis sent me the finger, then wriggled out of the cradleboard. I slipped Ava-Marie in, and nearly died of cuteness. She looked so adorable, swaddled up in that blanket and tucked into the cradleboard.

Sophia adjusted the cradleboard straps. "It's pretty comfortable. I kind of love it."

Ava looks cozy, too, Luana signed. Ava-Marie made a loud noise before giving a yawn.

The front door clicked open. Ezra and Stevie had dropped by for a visit. Ezra sauntered in just fine, but I noticed Stevie walked a little slower—almost at a crawl. Her face sagged, and I could tell with each stiff movement she gave her muscles were bothering her. Even the bow in her ponytail looked like it was drooping.

I couldn't blame her. She'd done some badass magic at the battle a few weeks ago, and she was still recovering. I was more or less feeling the same.

Ezra caught sight of Ava-Marie in the cradleboard and brightened. "Aw. She looks like a little burrito," Ezra said. He tickled Ava-Marie's cheeks, and she stared.

"Only you would compare your niece to food." Stevie laughed, before she put a hand to her side and winced. Ezra and I both caught it, but her eyes were pleading not to mention anything.

"Speaking of food..." Ezra said. "Mom's throwing a moving out party for Imogen and Jonah."

"How did Haloke hear about that?" Imogen asked, peeking her head out of her room. "Jonah and I just decided this morning."

"My mother knows *all* the best gossip," Ezra said. "Word didn't take long to spread once y'all started moving boxes out of the house."

I rolled my eyes. That was the downside of living in a small, tight-knit community. People talked.

Stevie stretched. "I was hoping you guys could come, so we could get some practice in."

"Stevie..." Ezra groaned. They'd had this talk this morning, I bet.

"I haven't touched my powers in weeks, Ez. I'm fine," she snapped. "You don't have to baby me."

He frowned, but I sent him a look, and he didn't object. As much as Ezra wanted to protect Stevie, he had to let her do things on her own.

Sophia looked thoughtful. "Liam and I haven't had much time to work on our magic, with the baby. We're out of practice. This would be a good way to start warming up our powers again without pushing ourselves too far."

"Then let's do it." Stevie led the way. Julian flew off to deliver the boxes to Cade and Jake, while the rest of us walked to the beach.

It was a nice day for a Northern California winter, sixty-five degrees or so. There was a seventeen year-old kid playing frisbee with Katie and Christian on the beach. He was skinny and short. At his side was a dog, an English Whippet running up and down the shoreline.

The boy waved to Stevie and beamed as we came near, before the frisbee sailed by. His dog Familiar jumped up and did a backflip, making an impressive catch. "Hey, guys. What's up?"

"My brother, Teagan," Stevie introduced. "Liam, this is the first time you guys have met."

He was one of the people who had Combined Magical Suppression Syndrome, like me. He seemed like a nice guy.

"How you doing, man?" I shook his hand. He had a firm grip and callused hands.

Teagan shook back. "It's an honor to meet you, Chief. Just trying to get some practice in."

"He plays professional frisbee. He thinks that makes him cool," Stevie teased. She ruffled his hair, and Teagan shoved her off with a smile.

"Liam, Liam!" Katie and Christian came running up the beach. Katie panted as she said, "Teagan is *so cool*. He taught me to do this thing. Watch!"

Teagan threw the frisbee. Katie ran and caught it behind her back. She waved and held it up in the air, while Christian's face dropped.

"Hey, he taught me that, too!" Christian argued.

"Enough, you two." I gave Teagan an apologetic smile. "I hope they're not bothering you."

"Nah." Teagan caught the frisbee as Katie threw it back. "They're all good. It's nice to have someone to practice with, seeing as how Butterfingers over here can't catch a frisbee to save her life."

"Screw you," Stevie laughed. Teagan smiled and flung the frisbee behind his back, so his dog could catch it again.

We wandered down the shore. As I watched Teagan, I had the thought he looked really athletic and healthy— especially compared to me and his sister. CMSS didn't seem to affect him as badly... at least on the outside. Or maybe he was just having a good day. I didn't know.

Mom was in the house, busy cooking. Doya sat on the porch swing, while Naomi soaked up the sun. Jackson laid by her side on a blanket, playing with toys.

Doya was always around lately. Normally, I would've complained about it, but she was actually a lot of help with the baby, so I kept my mouth shut. Baine was nowhere to be seen. He was probably doing research, trying to figure out why Sophia couldn't get the *Azaimperiai* to work.

I'd done everything possible to avoid bringing the *Azaimperiai* up to Sophia. She'd worked with it every day this week, and hadn't once been able to harness its power... or even feel it.

Incredibly depressing. Not enough to get us to stop, though. We'd hit road bumps before, and we always figured them out.

Or at least, I fucking hoped so.

I took Ava-Marie out of the cradleboard. Doya held her arms out, as if she was entitled. Though I hated her, I trusted her with my kid, and that was all that mattered. I handed Ava-Marie off to Doya without a word, so the baby would be safe in the shade. Esis remained behind to lounge beneath the umbrella. Our group backed off to a safe distance. Ezra and Teagan were already tossing water balls back and forth. Sophia and I faced each other.

"Why don't we spar?" she asked.

"We've never done that before," I said warily. "Sure we aren't going to hurt each other?"

Sophia scoffed. "I'm not going to touch you. Unless you're scared you can't keep up."

Oh, that was it. "You're in for it." I commanded a jet of water to rise from the ocean before I shot it at her. Sophia ducked to the side, away from the jet, and sent a fireball racing my way.

I summoned a shield of water to halt the fireball in place. The fireball collided with my shield, but it didn't fizzle out at once. It hit the water and sizzled against it, burying itself within the waves and trying to get to me. I gritted my teeth and forced the surrounding water to submerge the fireball, putting it out, but it wasn't an easy task.

I let my shield drop, and Sophia took advantage. She shot fireball after fireball at me, trying to throw me off my guard. I used whips of water to fling them away, and they sailed into the ocean. Sophia changed tactics, and summoned her Fire to shoot blazing jets out of her palm, twelve feet in length. I had to duck, though I could feel the fire's intense heat inches above me.

A wave rose from the ocean and crashed over the jet streams, putting the fire out— but Sophia was already waiting for me. She scrunched her nose up in concentration, and the Fire emerging from her palm became a dragon made of flames. The creature moved, and it belted out smoke.

Holy fuck. I'd never seen her do *that* before.

I think it was surprising to her, too, because a flash of shock took over her face before it was replaced by confidence. She advanced the dragon on me. I backed away a few steps before calling water from the ocean— a lot of it. I forced my magic to make the water take shape. It morphed into a sea serpent. The two reptiles charged and waged war. Steam rose around the beach as the elemental creatures fought, but even as I put all my focus into channeling magical energy into my Water serpent, the Fire dragon got the advantage, and it delivered a killing blow to my sea serpent that sent the water splashing into the sand.

Sophia smirked at me. I scowled. My wife was stronger than I was. She was totally kicking my ass.

She bounced a fireball in her hand. "You might as well give up. You're not gonna make me scream."

"Funny, that hasn't been my experience in the past."

Her mouth dropped open. "You're a dick!"

I snickered as she sent the fireball sailing toward my head, but I ducked and threw back a water ball of my own. We sent fire jets and water balls whizzing at each other at the same time. Our magic collided, creating spectacular fireworks. I was sweating with the effort of keeping up with her. Ancestors, she was good.

Sophia held her Fire back. She was breathing hard, which made my pride feel a little better— at least this wasn't too easy for her.

I decided to get on the offensive before she had any other ideas. My magic became a column of water, twirling around her like a snake. I meant to box her in, so she'd have nowhere to go and surrender. Sophia switched from Fire and to Spirit magic before I knew what was going on. My assault was stopped when Sophia created a shield, and the column of water burst. She shot out her light to blind me, and as I cringed away, she tossed a ball of light that raced toward me and collided into my chest.

The blow flung me backward a few feet, and I smashed into the sand. Ow. She hadn't exactly *hurt* me, but that didn't tickle.

I knew when I'd been beat. I lay flat on my back, staring up at the sky.

Sophia rushed over. "Oh my gosh, I'm sorry," she gushed. "I didn't mean to hit you that hard."

"Well, you did," I wheezed.

Though she was apologetic, she still smirked. "So, had enough?"

I sat up with a groan. "Yeah. I'd say so."

Sophia helped me to my feet. When the fight was over, Esis left the shade and raced to the shoreline.

Julian had returned by this point. The red dragon landed in the water, sending waves crashing onshore. One of them soaked Esis. His flat expression told me he was getting tired of Julian's shit.

I got an idea. "Hey, why don't you try intrafusion?" I suggested. "Maybe if you can siphon power from other creatures, it'll help you harness the magic inside the *Azaimperiai*."

Sophia blinked. "I don't know why I didn't think of that. How's it done?"

I wasn't sure if it would work. The only people besides my Anichi students who had mastered intrafusion were myself and Baine. But Sophia was Baine's daughter, and she had Anichi blood, so I didn't see why she didn't stand a fighting chance.

"Okay. You know how you can pull energy from Esis? Try it with Julian," I said. "Reach out until you can feel his magical power, then siphon it off for yourself. It's just like drawing from a crystal with transference."

The dragon came onshore. He held his snout out to Sophia, and she stroked his ruby scales. "Hm. Okay."

The moment she said that, Julian yelped in surprise. He jumped backward. Through our connection, I felt his magic be drained by Sophia. My mouth fell open in shock.

"Um... *okay?*" I repeated. "Sophia, you just did that with no effort at all."

"What? Is it like, hard?" she asked. Esis copied her blank look.

"*Is it hard.* What the fuck?" I facepalmed. "Soph, my students have been taking *weeks* to master intrafusion. You just did it in seconds."

"I don't know anything about intrafusion. I know you can do it, and I know the basics, but that's about it." She scratched her head. "I don't see why it's so difficult."

She let go of Julian's power, and I felt it flood back into him. I took a deep breath. "Fine. Then try on me. See if you can take my powers."

She cocked her head. "But we don't know where your power comes from. I know you have Julian now, but you don't have a Familiar. It might work differently."

"Yeah, I get that, but just try," I said. "I want to see if it's possible."

Sophia glanced at Esis. "Well, all right. It's your funeral."

Sophia reached out with her magic and wrapped her power around my own, yanking it backward toward her. The result brought me to my knees. Like, her magic touched me, and *wham.* Down I went. I fell face-down in the sand. I felt my powers come rushing back into my body when Sophia let them loose.

"Fuck, Liam!" I heard her footsteps on the sand as she hurried over. I was still reeling. By then, the rest of the group around the area had stopped to watch. I felt all eyes on me as Sophia helped me to my feet.

"You pack quite a punch, *pawee*," I gasped. It felt like she'd socked me in the gut.

"Ancestors, Sophia. Did you really do that?" Imogen gaped. Jonah had a similar expression.

Ezra hissed with laughter. "Liam fell like a sack of potatoes."

"Shut up, Ez," I growled. He was still chortling.

While I was recovering my breath, Sophia said, "I don't get it. Everyone makes intrafusion sound impossible, but it's the easiest magic I've ever done. It's like picking up something light and putting it across the room."

"Maybe we just haven't hit your limit yet." I finally got my breath back, though I put a hand on Julian to steady myself. "We should try something else."

I looked around. Squeaks' curious gaze got my attention. "Let's see if you can interrupt the connection of bonded partners," I offered. "Try cutting off Jonah's bond to Squeaks."

"*Excuse me?*" Jonah objected. Everyone ignored him. Sophia turned to face Jonah. We all watched in interest. Jonah was a pretty powerful Elementai. I figured it'd be difficult for Sophia to take that much power without a struggle.

Squeaks' mouth abruptly fell open. Jonah snapped his fingers, trying to conjure lightning. When it didn't work, his mouth fell open in shock. "Hey, what the hell?"

Sophia laughed. She shot her hand into the air, and lightning crackled across the sky. "You're not the only one who can conjure lightning, you know."

"No fair! Give my powers back, you ho!" Jonah complained.

"Don't stop," I encouraged. "See how far you can spread it."

By this point, Doya had come forward with Ava-Marie, Naomi prowling at her side. Sophia turned in a circle, her eyes locking with each person in turn. The sand Imogen was manipulating slumped into a pile, and Sassy leapt out of the way. Doya took her free hand and flicked her wrist, but nothing happened.

I couldn't believe it. Sophia was able to interrupt every magical connection in the area, all at once. Ezra, Stevie, Teagan, Doya, Imogen, Jonah... none of them were able to use magic or connect with their Familiars.

"Hey, what gives?" Ezra asked. He waved his hands at the water, but it didn't move. Stevie wiggled her fingers at an incoming wave. I noticed, quite impressed, that the wave did move, but only slightly.

Sophia conjured Fire in her hand. The column was twelve feet tall and shot out of her hand like a fountain. She sustained it with an easygoing smile. When she finally put it out, the air still smelled like smoke.

"This is fucking amazing, Soph," I said in awe. "Do you know how much power you've got running through you right now?"

"It's not just me. Esis is holding most of it." Sophia gestured to Esis, and he puffed his chest up proudly. "I'm more or less directing it."

"Esis can handle it, too?" Stevie asked in amazement. "But— he's so little!"

Sophia shrugged. "I don't know. It's easy for him. He's like... playing with it. We can toss it back and forth without breaking a sweat."

"You're telling me you're not even struggling to hold all that magical energy?" I asked in surprise. I'd taken the energy of only two Elementai at once— Elder Poole and Elder Malison— and it'd nearly killed me.

She shook her head. "No. It has no effect on me."

"Soph, I think that's why you're special," I said. "You can store, use and transfer more magical energy than anyone else. It's what makes you super powerful."

Sophia snapped her fingers, and I guess the magic went back to the people it belonged to, because Imogen was able to shift the sand again, and Ezra could make a water ball. Sophia picked up Esis and said, "It's a good theory. One that explains a lot."

And left a lot of questions. It didn't make sense why Sophia couldn't use the *Azaimperiai*. If she was capable of using power like this, she should be able to harness what was inside the tomahawk easily.

We were overlooking something. I wasn't sure what it could be, but there was some vital detail that had slipped us by. Sophia failing to use the *Azaimperiai* had nothing to do with how strong she was, I was certain. We'd fucked up along the way somehow.

"You're able to do more than you were before," I said. "You were always strong, but this is insane."

Sophia ran a hand through her hair before she sent a quick glance back at our daughter. "I was afraid to show my magic before. I was scared of my own abilities and what I could do. I didn't want to hurt anyone."

She took a breath and kept her gaze locked on Ava-Marie. "But I'm not afraid anymore, because I want to be as strong as I can for Ava. I'm not afraid to hurt someone to defend her. I'll kill someone to protect my daughter. As far as I'm concerned, my powers can be unbound."

"That's a good thing," I encouraged. "You shouldn't be scared of what you can do."

"I'm not anymore." She bit her lip. "Not since the night Ava was born."

"What do you mean?" I wasn't sure what she was getting at.

"I don't know, Liam. There was something weird about that birth." Sophia scuffed her foot in the sand, then she looked at me. "I know it was my first time, but it wasn't natural. That labor... it's hard to explain. It just didn't feel right."

My stomach bottomed out. I hated talking about this. We'd barely brought it up since Ava-Marie had been born, because Sophia knew it made me upset. "I know you almost died. Ava, too. But it's okay now. You both made it through."

"That's not what I'm talking about. You weren't there, so you couldn't feel it," she protested. "It was almost... supernatural."

Sophia shook her head, like she was coming out of a stupor. "All I know is that I'm different now because of it. I feel stronger. It's like once I gave birth, there's no holding back my magic."

A shiver ran up my spine, but I pushed it away and said, "I just wish we had answers as to why you're so powerful."

"I have blood from three different Houses," Sophia said. "That has to count for something."

"I know some of it's gotta be your mixed blood. But there are other mixed-House children we know about, and none of them are as strong as you," I pointed out. "There have got to be other factors."

Sophia shrugged. "Maybe."

Mom called to say lunch was served. She placed food out on the picnic tables outside the house. Doya handed Ava-Marie off to Sophia, and she sat down. I worked on getting plates around for the both of us while Sophia put a bonnet on Ava to keep her head from getting sunburned.

Sophia chewed on her lip. "There's something else. The thing is... I tried feeling out Ava-Marie's magic when I was siphoning power off of everyone else, and it just wasn't there. At least, not what I could feel. I thought I'd be able to feel Koigni magic, if she inherited Fire, or Anichi magic, if she inherited Spirit... I even figured my powers would clash with hers if she was Toaqua, but there was nothing there."

"Ava's a baby. Her powers won't awaken until she's of age," Jonah objected.

"It doesn't matter. It still lives in her blood... or it should," I mused. "Sophia should be able to feel her magic."

There was a bout of silence, before Christian spoke up. "Maybe your baby's just not magical."

"Christian!" Mom snapped.

"What?" Christian whined. "It could be true!"

Doya came forward. She looked down at Ava-Marie when she spoke. "When you were born, Sophia, I did the same thing. I used my magic to try to feel your power, to determine if you were Koigni or Toaqua. I felt nothing. I assumed no magic lived inside of you, because of your mixed blood."

Doya's eyes locked on Sophia's. "I was wrong. It took me many years to realize I couldn't feel your powers because your abilities went far beyond my own."

"That's just not possible. No one is stronger than Sophia," Jonah objected.

Ezra jerked his head toward Ava-Marie. "Well, you might've found her."

Ezra's words were ominous. More than that, they were terrifying. If Doya's theory was correct, and Ava-Marie would someday grow to be even stronger than Sophia was... people would want to use her. They'd come after her. And what was more, I didn't think Sophia and I were equipped to deal with that kind of magic. We certainly couldn't rein it in. Sophia's magic was a frightening thing to handle sometimes. I couldn't imagine if Ava-Marie had powers beyond that.

It made my insides turn to water. "All right, enough talking about scary-ass shit," I said, and that was the end of it— though Doya noticeably kept her eyes on Ava-Marie as we ate.

Ancestors, this was sickening. As much as she'd supposedly *changed*, Doya still had a thing for power. I didn't like the thought of her using my daughter to obtain that.

Lunch was almost over by the time Maddie shuffled out of the house. She was so pale. I figured she never got any sun these days.

Drew had come out a half-an-hour ago and was playing frisbee with Teagan. He shot a glance at Maddie, but nothing beyond that.

He still lived with my Mom, but to be honest, I didn't know if he and my sister were still together. They didn't really act like a couple anymore. But then again, Maddie had ceased to act like a person altogether.

Maddie eyed the food with slight disgust. She only took a few spoonfuls of pasta salad before she sat down.

"You need to eat more than that," Mom objected, eyeing Maddie's lithe form. Her clothes hung off her bones.

"I'm *fine*, Mom," Maddie snapped. She nibbled at her food, but wasn't really eating. She didn't look at us.

"Maddie, mind your manners," I said sternly. Fuck, my little sister's attitude was so over-the-top.

Maddie jumped right up from her seat and rounded on me. It took one little comment like that to create an explosion. "Fuck you, Liam! You think now that Dad's gone you can take his place and—?"

Maddie gasped, and she cut-off mid-sentence. Her eyes rolled in the back of her head, and her legs buckled. Her body went limp. She began convulsing, mumbling words in Hawkei so quickly I didn't have time to memorize what was said.

"Mads!" Ezra scrambled to catch her. He caught her before she fell to the ground. She shook in his arms as she continued to whisper unknown things.

Sophia clutched Ava-Marie to her chest. Imogen started, and Jonah reeled backward. Mom hustled to Maddie's side and knelt beside her, summoning a strand of cool water from the ocean and running it over Maddie's forehead. Doya observed with wide eyes; like she'd hoped one day she'd get to witness something like this, and was regretting that wish completely.

Stevie wrapped her arms around Teagan. Drew just stood there and watched helplessly, like this was something he'd watched again and again.

"What's happening?" Sophia asked fearfully. Ava-Marie started crying, and Jackson followed suit.

"She's having a vision," I choked out. Ancestors, it was terrible when Maddie got like this. She'd only done this a few times in front of me, but it was always awful to watch. It was like she was having a seizure. Ezra laid her carefully on her back as her body continued to jerk.

Eventually, the convulsions ceased, and Maddie stopped speaking in riddles. Her eyes fluttered open, and Mom helped her sit up.

Esis didn't move from Sophia's side. He put a paw on Ava-Marie's head and stroked her hair as he observed Maddie's quaking form with big, blue eyes. The rest of the Familiars had backed off to give Maddie space. Their body language acted like something about the whole thing was unnatural.

Maddie shivered. As she took in Ezra's features, her skin went pale. She began to gag. She fell to her hands and knees and retched, but nothing came out.

When she was done, she threw her arms around Ezra and held him tight. He hugged her back, because he didn't know what else to do. She sobbed into his shoulder, not letting him go for long minutes.

Mom rubbed her back gently. "What did you see, darling?"

Maddie's voice came out ragged. "Nothing... you want to know."

Mom's expression was crestfallen. I got up from the table and knelt by her side. Maddie dared to look up from Ezra's shoulder. When she did, she caught sight of Esis caressing Ava-Marie, and burst into tears all over again.

"If you tell us, we can help," I said, though I couldn't promise such a thing. We had enough trouble interpreting one prophecy. Maddie's visions were something she couldn't even understand.

"You can't help with this." She angrily wiped at her face. "There's nothing I can do... there's nothing anyone can do."

Ava-Marie and Jackson began crying louder. I persisted. "Whatever you saw, we can turn it around. Prophecies have loopholes. You said so yourself."

"You don't understand!" Maddie cried. "The things I've seen— you don't know what the price is going to be. We're going to win this war, but it's going to come at a great cost. Us winning is worse than us losing!"

A pit formed within me and sucked my spirit down to hell. What could be so terrible we'd rather lose to the Elders than win?

"If that's true, tell us how to avoid it." Ezra grabbed her shoulders. "We can stop this."

Maddie shook her head. "You don't understand. There's *nothing* we can do about this. I've tried thinking of options, and every alternative just leads to more pain. And if I tell you anything— it'll only make everything worse. I just can't take this anymore."

Maddie stumbled to her feet and wrenched herself away from Ezra. She ran off into the house, slamming the door behind her.

Mom wearily got up from the ground and wiped a few stray tears from her eyes. She picked Jackson up and bounced him to soothe his wails.

Ancestors, I felt bad for her. I knew she was having a difficult time with Maddie. The rest of us— even the younger kids— had managed to patch ourselves together and move on after we'd fled Kinpago.

Maddie had not. Whatever Oleander had done to her, it made her mind remain back there, in a place too agonizing for words to describe.

"I'll check on her," Ezra offered. He strode after Maddie and shut the door quietly. I sighed and returned to my seat. Ava-Marie was settled now, though she still let out small noises of upset.

I rubbed my face. Sophia turned. "Is she going to be okay?"

"I'm not sure," I responded. This was such a fucked-up situation. "I don't know how to help her."

"Maybe you should try talking to her," Sophia suggested.

"Talk to her how? You can't say one word without her losing her shit!" I pointed out.

Sophia laid a hand on my shoulder. "I used to know someone like that," she said kindly. "And he turned out pretty damn good."

She had me there. "I took a long time to get better," I admitted.

"Yeah, but you did. And so will Maddie," Sophia encouraged. "She was there for you in your tough times. Maybe she just needs proof you aren't going to back down from being there, no matter how much she tries to push you away."

Sophia knew me so well. "I know you're right." I stood. "Give us a minute. Maybe Ezra and I can talk some sense into her."

I hadn't even gotten onto the porch steps, though, before I heard Ezra let out a strained cry. "*Maddie!*"

Fuck. His voice sounded shocked— and deeply upset.

I already knew what had happened. Didn't have to guess. I entered Maddie's room. Ezra was standing in the doorway. Maddie had dropped something sharp. She yanked her sleeves down, though a trickle of blood ran down her wrist. The color from her face faded as she saw I was another witness.

I grabbed Ezra by the collar and hauled him out before he could have a major freak-out. I closed the door behind us. Ezra's eyes were calculating, adding things up.

"Calm the fuck down," I told him. "She doesn't need this right now."

Ezra took deep breaths. "Did you know about this?" he asked nastily.

My tone was regrettable. "I found out a few years ago. I didn't tell anyone. She'd gotten better."

"She's obviously not *better* now!" Ezra hissed.

"Hey, guys." Drew had followed us in. His look was haunted. He knew what we were fighting about.

"How long has this been going on, Drew?" I asked.

He didn't need to ask what I meant. "A while. Since you brought us to *Hok'evale.*"

My heart dropped. That was months ago. Ezra's hands were balled into fists. "And you didn't tell us?"

Drew's tone was cold. "I helped Maddie the best way I could."

Ezra was still fuming. "We gotta do something. I—"

"You'll do nothing. I'm going to talk to her," I said.

"But—"

"I'll *handle it*, Ez." I didn't give him any room to argue. I left him and Drew behind in the hallway as I entered Maddie's room.

She was sitting on her bed, her face in her hands. I sat beside her, close enough we weren't touching but near enough she knew I was there. "We should probably talk about this."

"What's to talk about?" Maddie's voice came out muffled. She raised her head, and her bloodshot eyes connected with mine.

"Come on, sis. You need help. You haven't been okay since..." I took a breath. "I've been where you are. I know how it feels."

"This is different from your situation, Liam."

"Not that much different."

"No, it is. You can't comprehend what I feel because you're not a *naderei*. I know who lives. I know who dies," she began. "The outcome of this war isn't going to be anything any of us want, but there's no way to fix what's been done. Too many variables are racing toward the worst possible scenario."

She swept her hair back from her eyes. "And I can't handle knowing that people I love are going to die."

Maddie looked up to the ceiling. "That's why I do this. It makes my gift stop. The more I hurt, the less the visions come. The more pain I feel, the easier it is to get them to go away. If I can't do anything to change the future, I'd rather not know it at all. And if the only way to stop my visions is to do this... it's worth it."

"It's not," I insisted. "Maddie, you've got to look at your powers in a different light. You've always hated them, but maybe if you stopped fighting against them and tried to interpret them instead, you'd have better luck handling them."

She took a quivering breath. "It was easier with Eirakari. She helped me. I was doing so well, until Oleander took her away from me. She was helping me to understand my visions. Now that she's gone, I'm lost."

"We'll find her. We'll bring back the missing Familiars."

"And what if you can't?" Her gaze was burning. "You're the chief of Toaqua, but you only have so much power. Being chief didn't save Dad from dying. I couldn't save him. I don't know if I can save you, either."

My gut wrenched. "Just because something happened to Dad doesn't mean it'll happen to me."

"Don't you get it? It's my fault that Dad died," Maddie cried. "I was the one who ran off that night, looking for Drew. Dad was still at Orenda

Academy because of me. I could've foreseen his death. I could've saved him. I've seen other people die. I should've seen his death, too."

She sniffled and turned away. "But I didn't. I was too wrapped up in dating Drew."

"You can't blame yourself for that. It was Dad's time to join the ancestors," I said.

"That's just something people say to make themselves feel better," she shot at me. "It's not true."

"It is, though." This was hard to talk about. But I swallowed the lump in my throat and continued on, because my little sister needed me. "I've done a lot of thinking about those we've lost. When it's your time to go, nothing will be able to change it. Dad's moved on to the Ancestral Lands. He's at peace. And I don't think he'd want you to blame yourself for loving Drew."

Maddie threw her hands up. "What has our relationship done for Drew? Oleander tortured him because he loves me. How can I ask someone to suffer like that for me?"

"Sophia wouldn't ask me to endure torture for her, but I'd do it, a thousand times over," I told her firmly. "Drew knows the consequences of being with you. And he's willing to take them."

"Sometimes I just wonder if it's better to be alone."

"Been there, done that." I shook my head. "It doesn't work. And the more you try to push Drew away, the stronger your connection's going to get."

She swallowed. "I just don't want to hurt him. He cries every time I have a new scar."

"Pushing him away is only hurting him more," I pointed out. "Keeping him out will hurt you and him. He wants to help."

"I've been getting intense visions for months," Maddie choked out. "Ever since the end of your trial. These are different— usually I'll just get a sense about something, you know... space out for a bit. I'll see a glimpse, a picture, then it'll go away. These aren't like that. It's like watching a movie on fast-forward and trying to remember it all."

"Did you foresee anything that's happened recently?" I asked.

"You're not getting it. These visions aren't about the present. They're about the future, *decades* away!" Maddie exclaimed. "And I can't make heads or tails of them."

"Let's talk it out, then," I offered. "Maybe you need a new perspective."

Maddie took a breath. "It's like... take you and Sophia, for example. The first time I met her, I had a vision of you two at your wedding. It was like a photograph. That's how all my visions of the near future are."

She bit her lip. "But these new ones are different. They happen *years* down the line, and I don't have time to record them before something else pops up. I just don't know *why* I'm getting them now, when they're not useful to our cause. I need information that'll stop what's coming in a few months, not stuff decades away."

"Mads, Showana Harjo made the prophecy a very long time ago. She wasn't connected to this war, but the information she gave us is helpful to us now," I said calmly. "She was probably frustrated that her visions didn't give her any direction on how to save the Anichi when Koigni was destroying them. But in a way, they did, because the Anichi are still alive, and we're helping them now. Even though it wasn't in Showana's lifetime, her prophecy is making a difference today."

"Yes, but I need information that's going to help us right away!" she shouted. I shushed her, and her voice quieted.

"Maybe you should start writing this stuff down," I suggested. "Just in case an Elementai in the future needs it."

"If there are any Elementai left after this," she said glumly.

"You say that your visions are absolute. That there's no way around them, or a way to change what is coming. But you told me yourself prophecies are interpretations," I said. "They're based on our choices, different possibilities on the paths we walk."

"Prophecies can be changed and interpreted. But that's what makes this stuff so hard," Maddie insisted. "You and Sophia were destined to be together. That's why I saw the two of you in my vision. But futures can be altered if *significant events* take place. For example, if you had been convicted during your trial and killed, your destiny wouldn't have come to pass."

"So maybe your visions of the war aren't as clear cut as we thought," I offered. "There might be a way to stop what's coming."

Maddie seemed downhearted. "No, Liam. There's not. This will end in a big battle. And no matter how that battle is fought, it comes out the same way every time. Nature demands a balance."

"If you think that way, why do you believe there's something you could've done to save Dad?" I asked.

"Dad was *one person*. I might've been able to change certain circumstances around his death," Maddie explained. "What's coming is so big, one person doesn't have power over it. Even if I was to explain, no one would believe me... they'd say it wasn't possible."

I grew frustrated. "Can you at least give me a hint? Some sort of clue?"

Maddie gave me a sad look. "If I told you now, you wouldn't have the strength to go through with what's necessary when it's time."

A shiver ran through me. She was speaking of making a sacrifice.

I stood. "Either way... I think you need to go to therapy, Maddie. You need to deal with what's been bothering you. You have to make a choice to live. You told me once that I was destined for incredible things, and so are you. But you have to decide to get better if you're going to live your life."

Maddie stared at the carpet. "I just need time. Let me be for now."

Maddie swept away from me and out of her room, where she squeezed past Ezra and avoided Drew.

As she walked out onto the porch, Ezra frowned. "Did you get through to her?"

"Barely," I said. "I think we can all agree she shouldn't be alone right now."

"I'll watch her," Ezra volunteered.

"And me," Drew offered. "I won't leave her side."

A silent understanding passed between us that we'd be here to help Maddie, no matter what. But there was only so much we could do, if she didn't want to help herself.

Maddie's words haunted me. *If I told you now, you wouldn't have the strength to go through with what's necessary when it's time.*

Showana said Sophia would lose her life. She'd have to give herself up in order to save the tribe.

I'd never be strong enough for that. Maddie knew it. That's why she was holding off on telling me the truth. She knew I'd do everything in my power to avoid what was inevitable. If the time came for Sophia to sacrifice herself, I'd interfere. I would fight to save Sophia's life, and I'd doom the Hawkei forever.

If I had to make the choice between Sophia and my people— I couldn't do it. Not even as chief.

My wife or the Hawkei? I'd pick my wife. Every. Damn. Time.

And that's what my sister was so terrified of.

I felt helpless watching Maddie seize. I had healing magic, and yet there wasn't a thing I could do to help her. Afterward, I couldn't get the images of Maddie's features out of my head— the way her eyes rolled backward and her body convulsed. I wished there was more I could do.

What would you have done? I asked Luana on Monday.

I was still on maternity leave and taking a break from my Anichi sessions, but Luana usually came by to help me with Ava-Marie in the morning.

I've never seen a naderei *experience a vision,* Luana admitted. *But I don't believe any healing magic could've helped her at that moment. The best you can do is give her space and let the vision reveal itself.*

I don't think that helps her. Liam made it sound like she gets worse the more visions she has, I signed.

Luana looked thoughtful. *She's a* naderei. *She was chosen, as were you and I. The ancestors wouldn't give her visions without reason. Perhaps the problem is not with the visions, but with the way she views them.*

My heart sank for Maddie. I couldn't imagine being in her place, seeing things I didn't want to see, keeping secrets I didn't wish to keep.

Except... I realized I *had* been in her place before. I'd never had a vision, but I'd experienced flash-backs and hid my pain from others because I thought I had to be strong for them.

But Maddie couldn't hold it together anymore. She was crumbling, and it was easy for the rest of us to see. Liam kept saying we had to give her time, but I feared if we didn't do something, she wouldn't have much time left.

That afternoon after Luana left, I placed Ava-Marie in the cradleboard, bundled us up and left to visit Maddie. Esis followed closely at my feet. When we arrived, Haloke was folding laundry with the help of her britnai housemaid, Beatrice.

"Sophia," she greeted pleasantly when I walked in the door. "What a wonderful surprise!"

"Hi." I smiled back. "Is Maddie around?"

"She's in her room," Haloke said.

Of course. Maddie didn't go much of anywhere these days.

Ava-Marie squirmed and let out a light peep, then yawned. Haloke set down the towel she was folding and came over.

"Look at my beautiful granddaughter," she sang. "Do you mind if I hold her?"

"Not at all." I helped her pull Ava-Marie out of the cradleboard. She was still so fragile. "Would you actually mind watching her for a bit? I came to visit Maddie."

"Of course I will," Haloke said, staring down at Ava-Marie. She started talking to Ava in a high-pitched voice. "I'll watch my granddaughter any time. Yes, I will!"

"Thank you." I started toward Maddie's room, but Haloke stopped me. Her gaze seemed concerned.

"Sophia? If you could get Maddie to eat something, that would be a miracle."

I offered a smile, but it was forced. "I'll see what I can do."

I grabbed an apple off the counter on my way to Maddie's room. Esis stayed behind to play with Ava-Marie. I knocked lightly on Maddie's door.

She groaned. "I'll eat later, Mom. I'm not hungry."

I cleared my throat. "Um, it's me. Sophia."

Maddie's voice came out clearer. I heard her footsteps padding across the room. "Sophia?"

The door swung open. I shuddered at the sight of Maddie. Her sweatshirt hung off her form, and her eyes were dark and sunken in. It was as if everyone had completely ignored her for months, but I knew that wasn't true. Haloke, Drew, and everyone else had done whatever they could to help. But you couldn't save someone who didn't want to be saved.

I wasn't giving up. I had to try.

Maddie eyed me curiously, and she pursed her lips. "What are you doing here? Where's Ava?"

"She's playing with your mom. I just came by to visit."

Her gaze narrowed. "Are you sure you didn't come to ask about the prophecy?" she bit. "Because I can't tell you anything."

I reeled backward. "What? No. I came because you're my sister-in-law and I wanted to see how you were doing."

Her features softened. "Oh, well... I guess you can come in."

Maddie turned away from me but left the door open. I stepped into the room. I noticed something strange. I couldn't put my finger on it right away. The room was spotless; I was sure Haloke or Beatrice had been cleaning up after Maddie. There weren't any strange smells or weird drawings on the walls that would've sent off immediate red flags. The room seemed... positively bland.

And that's when I noticed what was strange about it. There weren't any pictures on the walls, no keepsakes on the dresser. Maddie's room was completely void of personality, as if no one had been living there at all these last few months. It was completely off for a teenage girl to have no decoration whatsoever in her room.

I looked to Maddie, who seemed nothing more than a shell of a human being, and I realized why. Maddie hadn't really been living.

She slumped to the bed. "Well...? You're here. What do you want?"

I sighed and sat beside her. "Can we talk?"

Her lips tightened, and she glanced down to the apple in my hands. "Did Mom make you bring me that?"

I nodded lightly and pressed it into her hands. "You should try to eat something."

Maddie dropped her gaze, but she didn't throw the apple at me, so that was a good sign.

I sighed. "Look, the truth is, I came because I thought I might be able to help," I admitted.

Maddie frowned, and she didn't meet my gaze. "I know healing magic worked for Liam when he was depressed, but it's not going to work for me."

"I'd like to try," I said. "It won't heal you completely, but it might help clear your mind."

She shook her head firmly. She spoke quietly, but her tone was harsh. "This isn't anything like what Liam went through. You don't know. Nobody knows."

"You don't have to tell me," I assured her. "But eventually, you're going to have to tell someone. We can't help you if we don't understand what's truly wrong and where those wounds lie. Believe me, bottling it up inside only makes those wounds fester."

Maddie blew a puff of air. "Believe *you?* What would you know? You're perfect."

She wasn't mean about it. In fact, she spoke like she... admired me.

"I'm *far* from perfect, Maddie," I promised her. "I will never be able to understand what you went through with Oleander, or what you go through daily being a *naderei*, but I *do* know something about pressure. I was chosen by the ancestors, too."

Maddie stared down at the apple, but her features changed, like she was considering what I had to say.

"I've been on the run, Maddie," I reminded her. "I've watched people be gutted and burned alive in front of me. People I loved. When you were Oleander's prisoner, I was fighting PTSD. I can never pretend to know what it's like for you, but I'm not perfect, either."

Maddie's eyes glistened, and she finally lifted her gaze to meet mine. She didn't say anything, but I could see I was getting through to her.

"We've all been through a lot," I said.

"That doesn't make what I've gone through any less valid," she growled.

"No, it doesn't," I said gently. "I don't wish to invalidate you in the slightest. Please understand that. Your pain is very real, and don't let anyone tell you differently. But realize that you are not alone, and your mom, Drew, and your siblings may understand you more than you realize."

Maddie's eyebrows knitted together in thought. After a few beats, she asked, "H-how'd you do it? Get over your PTSD?"

I shook my head. "Some days, I'm still not sure that I have. But it's better— much better— than it was. I don't feel like it owns me anymore."

Her eyes started to water. "How'd you get your ownership back?"

I paused for a moment. There was no easy answer. "I made a choice. I chose to face my issues instead of running away from them. I chose to accept what happened to me, and work through my problems."

Maddie bit her lower lip. "You make it sound so easy."

"It's not," I assured her. "It is the hardest thing in the world. But you don't have to do it all at once."

Maddie furrowed her brow, like she'd been expecting an instant cure.

"Take one step today, one step tomorrow, and so on," I said.

"I just want to wake up one day and all this will be over," she whispered.

I sighed and placed a gentle hand on her back, rubbing up and down. "I do, too, Mads."

Maddie dropped her head and sniffled. "Did you go to therapy like Liam did?"

The question halted me in my tracks, and my guts sank. I didn't know why I'd never thought about it until now. Maybe it would've made things easier.

"No," I admitted. "And it was a big mistake— especially after seeing how much it helped Liam."

"Yeah, Mom won't stop reminding me," Maddie groaned. "I just can't get on board with talking to a stranger about this."

"Then talk to someone you trust," I said. "I didn't have a licensed therapist, but I had Liam. I had my friends. When I opened up to Liam, it was like... like a huge weight lifted off my shoulders. I think that's what helped me the most."

Maddie wiped at her eyes, and her voice cracked. "I just don't want to burden anyone with this."

"Mads," I said gently, reaching out to pull her chin up. She gazed at me with glistening eyes. "Nobody thinks you're a burden. Sharing your fears will not burden others; it will allow them to help. But don't do this for them — do it for *you*."

"I-isn't that selfish?" she stammered.

I shook my head. I wished I could make her see, but I couldn't. She had to go through the journey herself to learn the lessons. "Have you ever heard the saying, *you can't pour from an empty cup?*"

Maddie nodded lightly, though she had a thoughtful look on her face.

"Your cup's empty, Mads," I said softly.

I wasn't sure if she would take it as an insult or not. I didn't mean it that way. I only wanted to show her that other people were there— that we could pour from our glasses to fill hers.

Her expression remained static for several moments. I held my breath, awaiting her response.

I expected her to either snap at me and throw me out of the room, or to admit that I was right. What she did instead was so unexpected it made me jump.

Maddie burst into tears and threw her arms around my neck. I stiffened for a second as her wails filled my ears, but I relaxed a moment later and hugged her back.

"I *am* an empty cup!" she cried. She didn't sound offended. It was more like she was finally admitting it to herself.

"Hey, Mads, it's going to be okay," I told her, rubbing her back.

She said something else, but I couldn't make it out. I didn't speak as I sat there embracing her. I just held her to let her know I was there for her— no judgements. Maddie's shoulders shook, and her tears soaked my shirt. I took deep breaths, and it was only a few minutes before her cries slowed and her breaths began to match mine.

Finally, Maddie drew away, wiping at her eyes. "I'm sorry. I feel ridiculous crying in front of you."

"Don't," I said, reaching up to wipe the tears. "Let it out, Mads. It's okay."

She sniffled, then nodded.

"Would it be okay if I tried healing you now?" I asked.

She seemed scared— but she nodded. "O-okay," she agreed, her voice cracking.

Maddie set the apple aside, and I took her hands in mine. I guided the calm energy of my healing magic into her body.

My magic resisted before I even had a chance to explore. I could feel the mental illness seeping its poison into every cell of her body. The illness smelled like a damp basement, but felt dry— as if it was sucking the life right out of her. It tasted bitter.

"Are you doing it?" Maddie asked.

"I've never healed anything like this before," I admitted. "I'm trying to find the source."

It was hard, because there was no definitive wound to heal. It was a lot like Liam's disease, but with his, I could target it down to his immune system. With Maddie, her illness permeated every system, and none of it was working properly.

My magic tingled over her forearms, and I felt the sharp sting of the cuts across her arms. The surface wounds were easy to heal. I started using my magic to heal them, but Maddie jerked away.

She cradled her arms to her chest. "Don't heal those. I need them."

I furrowed my brow. "Are you sure?"

Her gaze was firm. "I'm sure," she said.

"Okay, I'll leave them," I agreed. It wasn't my job to judge her. I didn't understand why she wanted to keep the scars, but I needed her to feel like I was here to support her, not question her.

Maddie put her hands back in mine, and I filled her with my healing magic again. I searched her head for signs of the mental illness, but I couldn't see within her mind. All I knew was things weren't quite right with her body's systems, from hormone production to the beat of her heart.

I started by healing the pain and inflammation in her joints, then focused on her lungs. I did all I could, then funneled my magic into her immune system. I hoped it would help the fatigue and clear her mind.

When I drew away, Maddie took a deep breath. "Am I better?"

"Not completely. I can't heal everything," I said.

Maddie dropped her gaze in disappointment.

"Your body's not quite right, Mads," I admitted. "I'm still learning what everything means, but I can tell some of it is hormonal, and a lot of it is malnourishment. I'm not saying eating something will cure you, but it will help."

Maddie pushed a strand of hair behind her ear. "Thank you for the help."

"I'm glad to hear that," I said. "That's what sisters are for."

Maddie forced her lips up into what could be considered a smile. "I think I need some time to think over what you said."

"That's fair." I stood to give her space. "If you need anything, Liam and I are always here. Understand?"

She nodded. "I know."

I paused at the door and looked back to her. She tugged at her sleeves and balled them into her hands. I wasn't quite sure I had helped, or if she was just saying that to get me to leave. But as I shut the door, I swear I heard her take a bite of the apple.

It wasn't much, but it was a step in the right direction.

I DIDN'T HEAR from Maddie the rest of the week, but Liam stopped by after work one day and said Maddie had left her room. I took it as a good sign.

On Saturday, I was startled awake by the sound of the front door shutting. As my eyes opened, I wondered why Liam would leave so early without saying goodbye. But Liam groaned beside me, and I realized he hadn't even awoken.

"Liam!" I hissed, shaking him. My heart pounded, and my eyes darted over to Ava-Marie sleeping soundlessly in her crib.

"W-what?" Liam asked, rubbing his eyes.

"I heard something," I whispered. "I think someone's in the house."

Liam's eyes sprang wide open. He went to go sit upright, but he groaned at the stiffness in his joints. Esis grumbled as Liam tugged the blanket.

After a beat, Liam relaxed. "No one would get inside," he claimed. "Julian keeps watch on us."

I didn't know who would be stupid enough to try to break in with a dragon guarding the door, but dumber things had happened before. "I *swore* I heard something," I pressed.

Just then, the sound of footsteps sounded outside the door. Liam stiffened beside me.

"Stay here!" he hissed, jumping out of bed. He stumbled, as his joints hadn't had time to loosen up yet. He reached for the glass of water on the nightstand and created a water ball in his hand.

Heart pounding, I got out of bed and tiptoed to the other side of the room to Ava-Marie's crib. She let out a light coo as I picked her up.

"Shh..." I whispered. I cradled her close to my chest and pressed myself into the corner, holding my breath.

The footsteps got louder, and Liam reached cautiously for the door. He raised the water ball in his hand, then yanked the door open.

I gasped when I saw a tall, shadowy figure in the doorway. Liam didn't hesitate a second. He threw the water ball straight at the intruder's face, and the man went down.

"*Ow!* What the hell?" a familiar voice whined.

Liam and I dropped our shoulders in unison. It was only Jonah.

"Fuck, man! I'm sorry!" Liam yelped. He rushed forward to help Jonah to his feet. Jonah clutched his face, and blood streamed out his nose.

"Jonah!" I scolded. "You scared the crap out of us!"

"*Me?*" he squeaked. "I'm not the one who attacked like a wild animal!"

Liam sighed. "You should've announced yourself."

"I didn't want to wake you," he said.

"Too late." Liam slumped back into the room and sat on the bed. "What are you doing here?"

Jonah wiped his nose in the doorway. "I'm looking for Baby. I woke up this morning, and the poor little hippogriff was gone. I thought he might've gotten confused and come back here."

Esis' ears perked up. We'd saved Baby after liberating the child camps a few months ago.

"Squeaks doesn't know where he is?" I asked, shocked. "She's basically his mother. She coddles him twenty-four-seven."

"I know, which is why it's weird," Jonah said. "He never leaves her side."

"It's very unlike him," I agreed. "We'll help you look."

"Thanks, guys," Jonah replied. "Sorry to barge in."

Liam rolled his eyes. "Sorry, not sorry. Knock next time."

Jonah wiped the last bit of blood from his face. "I won't make that mistake twice. I'm going to head up the block and see what I can find. Are we still on for the Hall of Records today?"

"Yes," Liam said. "Gotta gather as many clues as we can to win this war."

"I'll meet you there," Jonah said. "Send Julian to find me if you locate Baby."

"We will," I assured him.

After Jonah left, Liam sighed and started changing. "Baby couldn't have gone too far. He's growing bigger every day. He should be easy to spot."

"Agreed. We'll find him."

I changed, and Liam helped me strap Ava-Marie to my body. Esis wanted to copy Ava, so he jumped on Liam's back and clutched his coat, like he was getting a piggy-back ride.

"Hey, what's the deal?" Liam protested. "You're choking me. Not cool, Esis."

I laughed as Liam spun in a circle, trying to get Esis off of him. Esis grinned proudly that he'd found a spot Liam couldn't reach. Liam outsmarted him and slipped out of his jacket, dropping Esis onto the couch. I laughed. Ava-Marie watched on with interest as Esis tried to unbury himself from the coat. Finally, he popped his head out from under it and crossed his arms at Liam.

Liam tried to play along, but he couldn't help it when a smile broke across his lips. "Fine, Esis. You win. But no piggy-back rides."

Esis seemed to consider it a win either way, because he got to ride on Liam's shoulder.

We left the house and started down the street, calling Baby's name. Julian flew above us to get a better view. There weren't a lot of people out this early in the morning, but no matter how much we called, Baby didn't seem to hear us. Or, he didn't respond, at least.

We walked halfway to the beach when Liam slowed his steps and turned to me. "There's got to be a better way to search for him, right?"

"What do you want to do? Put up posters?" I asked, half-serious.

Liam pressed his finger to his chin. "We've just gotta think. Where would a hippogriff go?"

"I don't know," I admitted. "Baby was always either at home or with Squeaks."

"He's older now," Liam pointed out. "Maybe he feels safer exploring on his own."

I frowned. "That might be true, but until we find him, I'm still worried. You don't think someone could've come and taken him, do you? He's not the first Familiar to have gone missing."

Liam shook his head. "If anyone's stealing Familiars out of *Hok'evale*, an unbonded, teenage hippogriff with a missing wing would be the last one anyone would target."

"True—" I started to say, but I cut off when I heard the sound of familiar voices around the corner.

We stopped when we spotted Imogen and Trace on the next street. Their two fox Familiars were playing with each other at their feet. They were standing in front of a café and looked deep in conversation. They didn't notice us.

"I'm sorry I didn't tell you right away," Imogen said to her brother. "I guess I should've known news would travel fast in this small town."

Liam and I slunk back around the corner. We didn't mean to eavesdrop, but we didn't want to interrupt, either. This was pretty awkward.

Trace reached out and placed his hands on Imogen's shoulders, forcing her to look at him. "Imogen, I'm not mad you didn't tell me you moved in with Cade."

Imogen tilted her head to the side. "You're not? I thought you'd... I don't know... think it was weird."

Trace shrugged. "I did a little, at first. When Cade came to *Hok'evale* and told me what had been going on between you two, I admit I didn't really like it. But now that I've seen you two together, I think you're a perfect pair."

Imogen sounded shocked. "Really?"

"Im, if you're waiting for me to tell you I'm okay with this, don't," Trace assured her. "It's not my call to make whether you two should be together or not. But if it *was* up to me, I'm glad you two chose each other. Cade's a great guy."

"Yeah, he is," Imogen said softly.

"I love you both, Im," Trace continued. "So don't feel like you have to hide your relationship from me. And when he *does* ask you to marry him, I better be the first to know."

My jaw dropped, and Liam and I exchanged a wide-eyed glance.

"Oh my gosh, Trace!" Imogen squealed. "Is he planning to ask me? What did he tell you?"

"N-no," Trace stammered. "He didn't tell me anything. I just meant... I hope you two work out."

Imogen's voice calmed. "I do, too."

The two went silent after that. Liam and I peeked around the corner to see they were in a tight embrace.

Imogen drew away and breathed a heavy sigh. "That makes me feel so much better."

"Wait," Trace said. "You didn't know I approved of you two?"

Imogen dropped her gaze. "Not really. You never said anything."

"Im!" He sighed. "I didn't realize I had to say it explicitly. I thought it was obvious!"

"Not to me," she replied.

Trace nudged her in the shoulder. "Ancestors, Im. You're so smart, but sometimes..."

"Sometimes, what?" she teased, narrowing her eyes at him playfully.

He shrugged. "Sometimes I wonder."

"Watch it," she warned. "Or you'll be eating your words before sundown."

Trace rolled his eyes at her. "We'll see about that."

He threw his arm around her shoulder and messed up her hair, like they were kids again. She laughed. It was really refreshing to see from Imogen.

"Stop it," she chuckled. "Let's get serious. We have to find Baby."

Before Trace could respond, Imogen looked up and spotted Liam and me. She rushed over instantly. "Hey, you guys! Did you hear about Baby?"

"Yeah," Liam answered, sticking his hands in his pockets. "We've been out looking for him for half an hour."

"I'm so worried," Imogen said, but she didn't sound worried. She spoke in a high-pitched voice and tickled Ava-Marie's nose while she spoke. She was still riding the high of the thought of her and Cade getting engaged.

"Us, too," Liam said. "I hope he'll show up—"

"Um, guys," I cut him off. All eyes turned to me.

While Liam spoke, the door to the café opened. A guy my age stepped outside. I recognized him as Nicholas, a Koigni guy who'd been in some of my classes at Orenda Academy. A hippogriff the size of a pony followed behind him. It took me a second to notice the missing wing. Baby strutted with pride, like he was king of all hippogriffs or something. He didn't look in danger at all, but rather glowed with pleasure. If hippogriffs could smile, he'd be beaming.

"Mystery solved. I found him." I pointed toward Baby, and everyone drew a collective breath of surprise.

I started toward him. "Hey, Nicholas!"

Nicholas stopped and turned his head. He looked a little surprised to see me approaching. "Hey, Sophia. What's up?"

"Um... this is our hippogriff," I said. "Where'd you find him?"

Nicholas looked flustered. His gaze shot between Baby and the rest of us. He raked his hands through his hair, then shoved them in his pockets, like he didn't know what to do with them. He stepped closer to Baby, like he was protecting him. "Oh, wow. This is kind of awkward. Um... he and I sort of... bonded last night."

Nicholas bit his lip, like he expected us to fight for Baby. Instead, Imogen let out a high-pitched squeal.

"Ancestors, Baby! You bonded!" she cried. She rushed forward and threw her arms around Baby's neck. Baby squawked proudly and threw his head upward, like he was celebrating.

"That's great, man," Liam said. "Congratulations."

Just then, I heard the sound of a hippogriff crying down the block. I looked to see Squeaks running so fast around the corner that she lost her balance and skidded into the middle of the street. Luckily, there were no carriages going by at the time, so she only knocked over a stack of boxes. Sassy barked and jumped up and down, as if we hadn't all noticed Squeaks totally face-plant.

Squeaks righted herself, just in time for Jonah to trip over his own feet behind her. He fell into her, and the two ended up in a heap on the ground.

Trace and Liam breathed a collective sigh, then went to help Jonah and Squeaks to their feet.

Jonah's hair was in disarray, and he breathed heavily. "We heard Baby!"

"Everything's okay, Jonah," I assured him. "Baby's fine. He left home last night because he bonded!"

Jonah's jaw dropped, and tears welled in the corners of his eyes as he took in Baby's proud stance. "Aw... my little Baby... all grown up."

Nicholas looked really uncomfortable as Jonah came forward and hugged his Familiar.

"Jonah, a little space?" I suggested. "Baby's bonded now." To be honest, he and Imogen were being kind of rude by touching someone else's Familiar.

Jonah cleared his throat and stood up straighter. "Right. So, you're the lucky guy?"

Nicholas nodded. "I guess I am."

"Well, congratulations," Jonah said, reaching out to shake Nicholas' hand. He shook it back and seemed to relax. "Mind if I give you some advice?"

"Have at it," Nicholas said.

While Jonah started talking to Nicholas about Baby's likes and dislikes, and how to properly care for a hippogriff, Squeaks stepped forward and bowed her head to Baby. It looked like they were having a conversation—perhaps saying goodbye. Baby bowed his head back, and the two pressed their foreheads together. Squeaks looked proud, but equally sad— like a mother dropping her kid off at college or something.

"Let's give them a moment," Liam suggested.

Ava-Marie started fussing then, so Liam and I attended to her to make sure she was warm enough.

"I think she's hungry," I said. "I'll feed her once we get inside."

Liam whistled to Jonah. "Hey, guys. We're gonna head to the Hall of Records. We have to get Ava out of the cold."

Jonah saluted him. "No problem. I'll be just a minute."

I rocked Ava-Marie back and forth until Jonah and Imogen were ready to go. Trace waved goodbye, and the rest of us headed off to the Hall of Records with our Familiars.

The Hall of Records was nothing more than a room above the town's main library. I didn't know why I expected tall shelves and endless tables like the library back at Orenda Academy, but I was shocked by how small it was. The room wasn't much bigger than our living room, but it was beautiful. There were dark shelves lining the perimeter, with high arched windows made of stained-glass above them. Huge beams stretched across the ceiling, and sconces were set between every bookcase.

I was surprised to see many of the book cases empty of books, with Anichi sculptures of magical creatures set to fill the space. Chief Cauac wasn't lying when he said they didn't have much in their Hall of Records.

There were only two tables set in the room. When we arrived, Luana was sitting at one of them. A guy with god-awful lime-green hair sat across from her. I stopped dead in my tracks when we entered the room, because the green hair was so bright it was impossible to miss.

When the man turned, I nearly choked on my own breath. Liam actually *did* choke, and started coughing to cover it up.

"B-Baine!?" he cried between coughs.

Baine furrowed his brow. "Are you okay, Liam? Why are the four of you staring at me like that?"

Baine shot a glance at Luana, as if she could explain. *Your hair*, she signed. She looked like she was trying really hard not to laugh.

Sierra fluttered over and landed on Baine's head. It was hard not to laugh when the luna moth blended in so well she might as well have used invisibility.

"Sick style," Imogen said proudly.

"What did you *do*?" Jonah asked, looking disgusted.

Baine brushed his fingers through his hair. "A minor mishap. I tried to color my hair, but I must've gotten the chemicals mixed up."

"Color your hair?" Jonah asked, then wiggled his eyebrows. "For someone special?"

Baine opened his mouth, then closed it, then opened it again. "As a matter of fact, yes. Eleanor always did like my natural color."

"Yes, I can see why," Liam deadpanned. "Green is very flattering on you."

The four of us couldn't contain ourselves. We burst into a fit of laughter. Baine just huffed and turned back to his book.

"It's okay, *pataa*," I said, stepping forward to pat him on the shoulder. "Ava loves it. See?"

I pulled Ava-Marie out of the cradleboard, and she smiled at Baine.

"Well, at least someone does," he said. "But no matter. Let's forget about my hair. We have work to do."

"What is it we expect to find?" Jonah asked. He walked over to one of the bookshelves and pulled a folder down.

"I'm not entirely sure," Baine admitted. "What we really need is a clue on how to work the *Azaimperiai*. Beyond that, I have no specifics."

"We'll know when we see it," Liam said. He turned to Luana and signed, *Find anything yet?*

She shook her head. *Nothing useful. I've been too distracted by Baine's hair.*

We all started laughing again, but Baine hadn't seen her sign.

Imogen turned to the nearest bookcase and took a book off the shelf. "Well, I guess we have to start somewhere."

She and Sassy got settled at one of the tables next to Jonah. I took my feeding cover out of the diaper bag and slipped it over my head to breast-feed Ava-Marie. Meanwhile, Liam brought over a stack of books for us to start with. Esis grabbed one of the books and dragged it across the table, then used two hands to open it, struggling like he was lifting weights. It was funny to watch.

I was just finishing feeding my daughter when the door opened again. I turned to see Jake walk through, followed by his Familiar, Sabor. Both of them moved slowly and looked exhausted, though Jonah's expression brightened when he took Jake in.

"Sorry I'm late," Jake said. "I meant to be here sooner, but something came up."

"What's wrong?" Imogen asked.

Jake raked his fingers through his hair and sat down. "We had a break-through on the nightshade case."

Imogen's spine straightened. "What'd you learn?"

Jake took a deep breath. "Do you want to hear the good news or the bad news first?"

"Lay it on us either way," Jonah said.

Jake shook his head. "The good news is we know how nightshade was getting into *Hok'evale*. The bad news? It was one of my own officers."

Jonah gasped. "No way. Which one?"

Jake's lips tightened. "Anton."

Jonah's eyes narrowed. "I always knew there was something off about that guy."

"Wait," I said quickly. "He's the one who led my team at the child camps."

Jake's frown deepened. "That's the one. He thought Black Ivy could strengthen our soldiers and help us win this war, but he knew I'd never approve of it."

"Of course not!" Liam exclaimed. "Look at the side effects."

"Exactly," Jake agreed. "He went behind my back to trade unicorn hair and other magical items with the Miriamic Coven for the nightshade. The supply traveled through our soldiers and onto the streets. According to my intel, the coven called off the deal a few weeks ago. *Hok'evale's* been surviving on the last of supply they had left, but it's dwindled to the point there's not enough to go around. One of my soldiers on withdrawal finally caved and outed his dealer, who outed *his* dealer, who led me to Anton."

Imogen shook her head. "I'm *so* glad I'm off that stuff. The withdrawals have been hell."

"I've got a handful of soldiers headed to rehab right now," Jake said.

"If you need to go deal with that, you can," Jonah offered. "We've got this handled."

"No." Jake sighed. "I'd rather be here with you right now. I need a break."

"Are you allowed a break?" Liam teased.

Jake shrugged. "Hey, you're the Toaqua chief. I could ask you the same question."

"I'm still on paternity leave for another week. Either way, what we're doing here is important," Liam said. "That is... if we find anything."

Imogen flipped a page. "This library may be small, but we *do* have a lot of information to read through."

"Then let's get started," Baine said.

The Hall of Records went silent after that. We were all so wrapped up in our own files and books that no one spoke for hours. Ava-Marie fell asleep against my chest, but Jonah kept groaning from the table next to us so it was hard to concentrate.

After what must've been the fifteenth time Jonah groaned, Liam burst.

"Jonah, would you stop that? I can't hear myself think!" Liam hissed in a whisper.

Imogen breathed a sigh. "Finally, someone said it."

Jonah gaped, like he had no idea what they were talking about. "I'm sorry. I didn't mean to. I'm just not finding *anything*."

"Me, either," Jake added in a bored tone.

"It's going to take time," Baine assured all of us. "But if we can find even *one* piece of information to help us in this war, this research will be worth it."

I agree, Luana signed.

"Okay, but how is this ancient book on Anichi architecture going to help us?" Jonah asked, waving it around.

Baine adjusted his glasses. "Architecture has many significant symbols, Mister Chanee. It's possible that the Anichi of old hid sacred messages in their architectural designs, just as they did in their sculptures and other artworks—"

"Okay, okay, big guy," Jonah stopped him. "I don't need a lecture. I was being rhetorical."

Baine scowled. "Forgive me. Usually when someone asks a question, they want it answered."

"Hey, Grandpa Baine," Jonah scolded loudly. "There's no reason to get all snippy with me."

Ava-Marie wiggled in my arms. Before I could calm her, she started wailing.

"Great," Baine huffed. "You've woken the baby."

"Calm down. Both of you," I snapped. I stood and rocked Ava-Marie from side to side. "I know we're all irritated we can't find anything, but we need to keep trying."

"Sorry," Jonah mumbled. "I... I think I'm just hungry."

Jake shot a nervous glance at Ava-Marie, who was still crying. "Yeah... maybe we should go grab some take-out."

Imogen cocked an eyebrow. "Is someone scared of the baby?"

"Pft," Jonah breathed. "Jake? He *loves* babies."

"It's true," Jake agreed. "But I also love food, and we're going to need some if we're going to be here all day. Even the Familiars are getting antsy."

He was right. Squeaks and Sabor were pacing around the room, and Esis patted his belly at the talk of food. Ava-Marie was still crying really loud, and no amount of rocking her seemed to help.

"Liam!" I pleaded. "I don't know what's wrong."

"Here, let me take her," he offered.

As soon as she was in his arms, Ava-Marie settled. She cooed as he held her close.

Ancestors, Ava-Marie was *such* a daddy's girl. If I couldn't get her to calm down, he always could.

"Jake, Jonah, you guys grab some food. We'll hold down the fort here," Liam said.

Watching Liam take care of our baby was a major turn-on. He was such a hot dad. Seriously, I wanted to make *more* babies with him.

After Jake and Jonah left with their Familiars, Ava-Marie grew quiet again. Liam held her in his arms and started flipping through his book. "Take a break, Sophia. I've got her."

"Thanks," I said. I really didn't want to let Ava-Marie out of my arms, but I knew I couldn't be attached to her at all times. I stood to stretch out my legs, and the room got really quiet again. I paced near the bookshelves, eyeing the stacks of folders and books there.

I stopped when a pile of files caught my eye. They were tattered around the edges of the pages, with burn marks scorched onto them. The ones on top were more burnt than others. I pulled the stack down and started thumbing through them.

"What'd you find?" Liam asked curiously.

"I don't know," I admitted. Some pages were older and written in quill and ink, while others looked to be typed on a typewriter. There were lists of names, all connected by various lines. "I think it's a genealogy chart. I wonder why they're burnt up."

Luana looked intrigued by the files I found. *You're right. They are genealogy charts. Most of the Anichi's charts were destroyed in the war. The records didn't make it to* Hok'evale.

Then what are these? I asked.

They're the most recent records, she answered. *The library caught fire about ten years ago. These were the files that made it.*

Barely, I signed back.

I'm sorry, Sophia, Luana said. *That's why I couldn't track your lineage.*

Baine leaned over and eyed the names as I flipped through the delicate pages. Imogen had come up behind me to peek over my shoulder.

"Wait!" Baine cried, just as I started turning one of the pages.

I flipped back. "What?"

"That name there." Baine pointed, his eyes widening. *"William Azure."*

The name was just at the edge of the burn marks. I could barely read it. "Should that name mean something to us?" I asked.

Baine's gaze lifted to meet mine. "Sophia, that's Eleanor's father. *Your* grandfather."

My grandfather? I gasped and began sifting through the pages, searching for more information about my family line. My stomach sank the more I looked, because there were no answers to be found. The scorch marks were so dark and deep that I couldn't read any of the other names.

Nothing. Absolutely nothing.

"No... no, my family *has* to be here!" I flipped the pages again, but the edges crumbled beneath my fingers.

"Soph," Liam pressed. *"Pawee,* calm down."

"There has to be an answer here!" I cried. I flipped the page again, back and forth, but I couldn't read anything beneath the fire damage.

"An answer to *what?"* Liam asked.

I slumped in my chair and ran my fingers over my grandfather's name. "I just... I don't know. I thought there might be something to explain my heritage. Why I'm so powerful."

"I'll help you look," Imogen offered. She grabbed half the stack, which was less damaged than the rest, and returned to her seat at the table.

The room got really quiet again, but I felt a sinking feeling in my gut that we weren't going to find anything. I didn't know why I thought I'd find an answer in my lineage, because there wasn't one. Reading names wasn't going to help me understand the *Azaimperiai*. I wasn't sure there was an answer in the Anichi records at all... but we literally had nowhere else to go right now. We had to find *something*.

After another long, agonizing silence, Imogen gasped. She shot to her feet. "Ancestors, you guys! I found something!"

Just then, the door opened. Jake and Jonah stepped inside with bags of takeout. The scent of fried chicken hit my nose. Esis scrambled off the tabletop immediately and bounded over toward the food. Usually, I'd be hungry, too, but I didn't think about eating now.

"What'd you find?" I asked desperately.

"You found a clue?" Jonah asked. "Then I guess we're just in time."

Imogen blinked a few times, like she couldn't believe it.

What does it say? Luana asked.

Imogen took a deep breath. "I found Showana Harjo."

"*The* Showana Harjo?" Baine asked.

The whole room, including the Familiars, had gone totally silent. Imogen nodded. "Yes, and her entire lineage is here. I've traced it down to her closest living ancestors."

"Wait," Liam said, rocking Ava-Marie back and forth. "If we can get in contact with one of them, we might be able to *talk* to Showana and get more answers. We could get the last piece of the prophecy!"

"We can do that?" I balked. "I mean, outside of Ancestors' Day?"

"If Showana is one of her descendants' spirit guides, then yes," Liam said. "They can communicate with her for us."

That was a slim chance. But it was the only chance we had.

"Do we know any of her relatives?" I asked Imogen.

Imogen's eyebrows rose. "Yeah, but you're not going to believe it."

"Who is it, Miss Ahnild?" Baine asked.

Imogen drew a long breath. "Madame Wells."

"I can't believe we've had a direct line of communication to Showana this whole time and haven't used it!" I said to Liam as we walked toward the beach.

Everyone agreed we had to talk to Madame Wells, but Baine suggested it was best if Liam went, since he was the Toaqua chief and she was on the council. Imogen offered to watch Ava-Marie until we got back. Esis followed at my feet, and Julian flew overhead.

"I know," Liam said. "I wonder why she didn't tell us. I mean, I knew Madame Wells was half Anichi. She grew up here in *Hok'evale* before serving on my father's council. I just never thought she'd be related to Showana."

"Maybe she doesn't *know* she's related to Showana," I pointed out. "It's a long shot to assume Showana's her spirit guide."

"I don't know," Liam said thoughtfully. "Madame Wells has done so much in this war. She persuaded my father to side with the resistance. She knows something, and I intend to figure out what it is."

By the time Liam and I arrived at Madame Wells' house, the sun was starting to set. She lived on the beach in a house almost identical to Baine's. Liam knocked on the door, and I held my breath. We didn't even know if she was home. For all we knew, she was swimming in the ocean with her killer whale Familiar.

To my relief, the door swung open. "Chief," Madame Wells greeted kindly. "What a surprise. What can I do for you?"

Liam held his head high and spoke with a tone of authority. It really turned me on when he used his chief voice around me. "Madame Wells. May we have a minute?"

"Yes, of course. You and your wife are always welcome in my home." She opened the door wider, and we stepped inside. As I suspected, her house was laid out the same as Baine's, but it was a lot cleaner, and the furniture was nicer and set up at different angles. A plate of warm food sat on the table— salmon and rice. It looked like we'd interrupted her during dinner.

"Please, have a seat," she offered, gesturing to the couch.

Esis scurried onto the couch first and snuggled in the center. Liam and I took a seat on either side of him.

"Is there a problem, Chief?" Madame Wells asked as she sat in the recliner across from us.

"Yes and no," Liam answered. He laced his fingers together, like he wasn't sure how to approach the topic. "Madame Wells, were you aware that you're related to Showana Harjo, the *naderei*?"

Her eyebrows knitted together. "I am."

Liam gaped at her, like he didn't expect that answer. "Why didn't you tell us?"

"Because you won't like what she has to say," she said. "Or rather, what she won't say."

Liam's eyebrows shot up, though he kept a calm tone. "But the woman who made this prophecy is your ancestor. You may be able to contact her and learn the last piece of the prophecy— the Anichi piece."

Madame Wells sighed. "Nothing gets past the chief, does it? Yes, Showana Harjo is one of my spirit guides. I *can* contact her. But she will not share the last piece with you."

"Why not?" I asked, feeling hopelessly defeated. "She wants us to change this, doesn't she?"

"Of course she does," Madame Wells said. "But you do not know her like I do. I've already tried contacting her regarding the prophecy. Showana doesn't give absolute answers. She will *always* be a *naderei*, and *naderei* know there are always choices to be made. She doesn't like to interfere."

"You don't think she'll make an exception, just this once?" I asked.

Madame Wells sighed. "We can try. That much I can do for my chief. But know that any answers she may give you may arrive too soon in your journey. You may not be prepared to hear them."

"We need the Soul prophecy piece," Liam stated.

Madame Wells nodded lightly. "Very well."

She stood from her chair and went over to a chest of drawers, where she pulled out a small leather skin bag and matches. She returned to her seat and opened the bag. The scent of sage hit my nose. I knew it was the herb used in sacred rituals for contacting spirit guides.

"What is it exactly you want to know?" Madame Wells asked.

"We want to know what the Soul prophecy says," Liam told her. "And anything she can tell us about the *Azaimperiai*. We don't know how to work it."

"I can ask her that," she replied. "Anything else?"

Liam looked to me, and I hesitated. This was my one chance to ask Showana anything. I wanted all the answers we could.

"Ask her if I'm truly the chosen one," I added.

Liam squeezed my hand, while Madame Wells nodded.

"You may want to sit back and relax," Madame Wells suggested. "This may take some time."

Esis snuggled between Liam and me, like he was eager to watch the ritual— all he needed was a bag of popcorn.

Madame Wells emptied her bag of sage into a decorative glass bowl, then lit the leaves on fire. The relaxing scent filled her living room, but Liam's fingers tightened in mine. We both remained on edge.

Madame Wells closed her eyes and began muttering something under her breath in Hawkei. I'd learned many Hawkei words, but she spoke so fast I didn't catch any of them. On and on she went, until the sun dipped below the horizon and the room was cast in darkness. The clock on the wall ticked, but nobody moved.

Finally, Madame Wells stilled, and the Hawkei words died on her tongue. Her hands tightened on the armrests of her chair, and her eyes moved rapidly beneath her lids. I glanced to Liam for an explanation, but he was watching her intently.

Madame Wells' breath slowed, and it was then I needed no other confirmation. I knew she had reached her ancestors in the trance. This was similar to what had happened when I'd spoken to my spirit guides the night I got my spirit name.

Esis meeped and got to his feet. I glanced down at him, and he pressed his paws to my leg, looking up with deep interest. His gaze followed something I couldn't see. Liam shot a confused look down at him, obviously as curious as I was.

Can he see our ancestors? I signed to Liam.

Liam shrugged. *I don't know.*

We both turned back to Madame Wells, like we expected her to say something, but she didn't. Her eyes moved rapidly behind her lids, and I knew she was still in the trance. I just hoped Showana was giving her answers.

I held my breath until I thought my lungs might burst. Every so often, I'd catch myself and drag in a deep gulp of air, but I feared the sound of my breath might disturb her.

The longest silence I thought I'd ever endure stretched between us. I watched the sage burn down, until the last of the embers disappeared.

Madame Wells' eyes shot open, and she gasped, clutching her chest. Esis peeped and waved to thin air.

"Madame Wells!" Liam cried, shooting to his feet.

"I'm fine," she said breathlessly.

Liam hesitated, then returned to his seat.

My heart raced in anticipation of the news. "What did she say?"

Madame Wells took a few moments to catch her breath. "I'm afraid it's as I predicted. She does not wish to interfere."

"But she's a part of this!" Liam protested. "She made this prophecy. She interfered a long time ago. She can't abandon us now!"

"She will not abandon you," Madame Wells stated calmly. "She says the answers will come to you when you are most desperate."

"We *are* desperate," I pointed out. "We can't wait much longer. How much more desperate can we be?"

Madame Wells nodded in understanding. "The answers *will* come, Sophia. But there are things you must do first before you are ready to use the *Azaimperiai*."

"So, I *am* supposed to use it?" I asked, confused by Showana's crypticism. "You're *sure* I'm the chosen one?"

Madame Wells nodded. "Recall that the prophecy can be interpreted in many ways. It is what you make of it."

"Yes, she told me that before," I admitted.

"Then there's no need to question your interpretation, Sophia," Madame Wells reminded me. "The end is not here yet, and you must wait to use the *Azaimperiai* until the final moments."

"So... that's it?" I asked lamely. "It will work when we're in our darkest moments?"

Not very reassuring, when I wanted to use it now.

"I don't have all the answers," Madame Wells reminded me. "But Showana did want you to know one thing, Sophia."

"What is it?" I asked.

"All the answers you seek are close to your heart," Madame Wells said. "You must translate that which you *have* into that which you wish to *know*."

I bit my lower lip, feeling the frustration rise in my chest. "I don't know what that means."

"I wish I could be of more help," Madame Wells admitted. "But that is all she told me. I hope that in time, it all makes sense."

I swallowed down the lump in my throat. "I do, too."

I just hoped we figured out this mystery. *Before* the darkest times came.

Liam

FIVE

"Oh my gosh, Liam, look at your daughter!"

Imogen gushed as she held Ava-Marie up to me. I grinned. Imogen had put Ava into a big pink tutu skirt, with a sparkly pink shirt that had a unicorn on it. She wore matching ruffled unicorn socks and tiny slip-on shoes. Ava-Marie kicked happily and gurgled in Imogen's grasp.

It was the last night before I went back to work. Imogen had come over with a new outfit for Ava-Marie, and insisted she had to try it on. Sassy poked her nose at the skirt, appreciating Imogen's choice.

Sophia was making dinner. Her eyes lit up when she saw Ava-Marie all dolled up. Ezra and Stevie lounged on the couch. When Stevie saw Ava-Marie's outfit, she tilted her head curiously and got up to observe it.

"It's *almost* perfect." Stevie tapped her chin as Ava-Marie squirmed. "But I think something's missing... I got it."

Stevie took the pink hair bow out of her ponytail and clipped it into Ava-Marie's hair. It was almost as big as her head.

I couldn't take it anymore. I had to hold her. "Aren't you pretty?" I cooed as I lifted Ava-Marie out of Imogen's grasp. I had to maneuver my arm— the skirt was huge on her. "Yes, you're daddy's pretty girl."

Ava-Marie spit up. Imogen gasped and rushed to wipe away the drool before she dripped it on her new outfit.

"She *is* a daddy's girl," Sophia said as she pulled the lasagna out of the oven. "If I can't get her to stop crying, he can. There are times all she wants is Liam."

I nuzzled Ava-Marie close and kissed the top of her forehead. Yep. She was my girl.

The minute the food was ready, Ezra hopped out of his seat and helped himself to a heaping plate. Esis, who sat on the counter, crossed his arms and grumbled. Lately, it was like he and Ezra were in an eating competition, and Esis didn't like sharing food.

"Soph, you make the *best* Italian," my brother said in appreciation. Esis stuck out his tongue.

"I can see you appreciate it," Sophia laughed as Ezra took two huge slices.

Stevie giggled. "He eats like a bro."

"Because he *is* a bro," Imogen said. "You should've seen him at Orenda Academy. Total fuck boy."

"Yeah. I think my grocery bill has gone up since you've started coming over *every day*," I said flatly. Sophia gave me a warm bottle for Ava-Marie, and I started feeding her.

"I try to avoid being at home unless Drew isn't there to watch Maddie," Ezra said. "She knows I'm babysitting her."

"How's she doing?" I asked this question all the time, but I had a right to be worried. Maddie was far from being in a good place.

"She's in therapy now," Ezra said. "She started a few days ago."

I felt a bit of tension in my back loosen. "That's good. She's getting the help she needs."

Just then, the front door burst open. I started. Ava-Marie let out a cry before she went back to sucking on the bottle. Jonah stood in the doorway, eyes wide and mouth opened dramatically.

His gaze fell on Imogen, and a slick grin spread across his face. "You. Dirty. Ho!"

Jonah raced forward and hoisted Imogen up on his shoulders. She yelped and had to duck her head— she nearly hit the ceiling. Squeaks came stampeding in after Jonah and paraded around them both, swinging her head in a happy dance.

"Turn on the music! We have to celebrate!" Jonah cried. Imogen held on for dear life, while Sassy scrambled to get out of the way of Squeaks' hooves.

"Celebrate what?" Sophia asked, bewildered. Ezra and Stevie glanced at each other.

"Jonah, put me down!" Imogen demanded. She put a hand up to avoid smacking her head on the stone.

Jonah obliged. He slipped Imogen off his shoulders and swung an arm around her. "I am pleased to announce that Miss Ahnild is no longer our sweet, pure virgin. Welcome to the world of debauchery, my dear!"

Imogen made a *pshing* sound, but her tone was playful. "Wow, Jonah. You really couldn't wait to tell everyone when I finally got the D, could you?"

"You promised me *two years ago* I could tell everyone when it finally happened! I wasn't going to hold off a moment longer!" he burst.

Sophia squealed. "Imogen, is he serious? Did you and Cade—?"

"They *did*," Jonah gushed.

"Jonah," I scolded, and he fell silent.

Sassy tilted her head, and Imogen turned pink. Her voice came out in a whimper as she said, "Um... yes?"

Jonah gave a girly cry and flung his arms around Imogen. "I can't believe it! After all this time, you've finally consummated your love!"

"Wait a minute. How'd you find out...?" I said. Jonah's eyes flickered to Ezra.

Imogen's tone was blunt. "Couldn't keep a secret for more than a day, could you, Ez?"

"Don't look at me," he said, throwing his hands up. "I didn't say nothing."

"Why are you involved?" Stevie asked, giving a laugh.

"He came over to hang out and walked in on us at the end." Imogen facepalmed. "It was already over by that point, but he saw. I wish he would've knocked."

Knocking was not Ezra's strong suit. Maybe this would teach him to stop barging in everywhere.

"Hey, in my defense, I didn't see anything but Cade's ass, which was *not* something I ever wanted to see," Ezra objected. His look was introspective. "Though I gotta say, my buddy must be doing some glute workouts, because he is *toned*."

Imogen nodded. "Cade does have a nice ass."

"I bet you were groping that very fine ass just last night," Jonah teased.

Imogen tossed her hair over her shoulder. "As a matter of fact, I did. And I liked it."

"Ezra had nothing to do with it. I stopped by Cade's to drop something off for Jake, and I saw the condom in the trash." Jonah waggled his finger at Imogen. "You've been caught."

Imogen sighed. "I guess we have. It was nice to keep to ourselves for like... twenty-four hours."

"You've gotta be better than that with this group of whores," Stevie joked. Sophia nodded, because she totally knew.

"Ez, why are you always around when people lose their virginity?" I asked. He'd been in the house when Sophia and I had sex for the first time, too.

Ezra shrugged. "I'm a good luck charm."

"I bet you were the reason a lot of girls lost their V-card," Stevie said, crossing her arms and raising an eyebrow.

"I don't sleep with virgins, babe," Ezra countered. "You were the only exception."

Stevie softened, and Sophia said, "Aw. That's so sweet."

Sophia turned her attention toward Imogen. "So, how was it?"

I groaned. "Do we really need to hear this?"

Of course, they ignored me. "It was..." Imogen sighed blissfully. "It was absolutely wonderful."

"That good, huh?" Jonah batted his eyelashes.

"Well, it was a little awkward, at first. Neither of us had slept with anyone before, so we didn't know what to do," Imogen confessed. "But we figured it out, and I tell you, it was amazing."

"Congratulations, boo." Jonah planted a kiss on Imogen's cheek. "We're all very happy for you."

"Looks like you're the only one who hasn't banged his significant other, Jonah," Stevie teased. "That's an unexpected plot twist."

Jonah straightened up and sassily patted his bun. "When the time is right, our fucking will be legendary."

"That's a word for it," I grumbled, and everyone laughed.

The door flew open for the second time that night. A soaked figure stood in the doorway— it was Baine. It must've started raining. He dripped rainwater onto the floor as he stepped through. The dye that had turned his hair green seeped down his face.

"Does no one knock around here?" I snapped. *Seriously, people, boundaries.* The baby started fussing. I put the bottle down and put her over my shoulder to burp her.

"I have information," Baine said breathlessly.

"It'd better be pretty damn important," I said. I mean, Baine was my father-in-law, so he could stop by at any time, but this was my last night off, and it'd be nice to just chill out with my family and not think about the war for two seconds.

"It is." Baine took a deep breath and looked at Ezra. "By the way, your thunderbird and Julian seem to be having an argument. Dyami is making it storm."

I could hear Julian's loud whines all the way from here, accompanied by the crackle of thunder. I sighed, gesturing to my brother that I had the baby.

"I got it," Ezra said, and he left his dinner to head out into the rain.

Sophia got a towel from the bathroom. She handed it to Baine, and he wiped off his face. "Ah. Thank you, my dear."

He was Toaqua and could've just dried the water off of himself, but he seemed to be too preoccupied to worry about his clothes (or my fucking floor, for that matter).

Stevie sat at the table. "What's the big news?"

"Yeah, can't it wait?" I asked in irritation. "I'm coming in tomorrow."

"Chief Nahele is dead," Baine said abruptly.

His words caused everyone in the room to pause. The Familiars tilted their heads. I stopped bouncing Ava-Marie long enough for her to give a loud cry, which was the only sound.

"The chief of Nivita is dead?" Sophia asked. An expression of surprise crossed her face.

"Unfortunately," Baine replied. "Ancestors bless him."

"Who's replacing him?" I asked. Chief Nahele hadn't any sons or daughters, which is why he was still acting as Nivita chief. A chief's term only lasted until their firstborn child came of age and graduated from Orenda Academy.

"No one, as of yet. I think Oleander is taking over the Nivita tribe in his absence. Ancestors know the Nivita Elders don't dare oppose him," Baine stated.

Imogen bore a sad expression. "It must've been old age," she said. "He was an elderly chief."

Baine frowned. "Not exactly. He was caught in the crossfire between a member of the Air Council and his challenger."

"What? That's insane," Imogen gasped.

I was similarly shocked. I'd never known Nahele to get involved in the affairs of other Houses.

"Nahele was a peaceful individual. You all know he worked for harmony between the Houses, even during these dark times." Baine's voice was troubled. It dropped as he said, "There must've been more division among the Elders than we thought. He died trying to hold it altogether."

I nodded. During our trial, Chief Nahele had been one of the few voices of reason among the Elders.

"Do you have any details?" Imogen asked.

Baine sighed. "Well, he stepped in during a duel. Said that the Elders needed to get along and work together for the good of the Houses. He tried to stop it, and got too close."

"Who started the duel?" I asked.

"Elder Raviro," Baine said. "He's dead."

Jonah's fists tightened. I could hear his knuckles crack from here.

I shared his hatred. Elder Raviro was a child predator who molested his own son. His death was no great loss.

"Who killed him?" Sophia asked.

Baine's tone was flat. "His son, Renar."

My mouth dropped open, though I shouldn't have been surprised. I knew what Raviro had done to Renar. Looks like he'd finally gotten revenge.

Jonah's tone was angry— yet conflicted. He hated Renar, but he equally despised Elder Raviro. "Do you know how it happened?"

Baine shrugged. "Renar challenged his father to a duel, for a spot on the Elder Council. Renar's magic overpowered him."

Baine stared at the floor. "The rumors say Renar laughed while Alvarice ate his father alive. Though we have no confirmation."

My stomach churned. I didn't doubt the rumors. It sounded like something Renar would do.

"Wait? So Renar isn't getting punished for this?" Sophia asked in confusion.

"Duels are an old Hawkei tradition," I said. "If an opposer challenged an Elder to a duel, they couldn't say no. If the Elder killed their opponent, they kept their spot, but if the opponent won, they'd take the loser's place on the council. It's not very heavily practiced, since people don't want to take the risk of losing their life just to knock an Elder off the council, but every now and then it happens."

"So... Renar has taken his dad's place on the Air Council," Jonah replied with a scowl.

"Yes. Which doesn't bear well for us. He's another one of Oleander's little puppets. At least with Elder Raviro, he was looking out for his own selfish interests," Baine noted. "Renar will do whatever Oleander asks as long as his cockatrice gets a meal."

"The bastard likes watching," Jonah said in a low tone. "He gets a kick out of suffering."

Horror crept over my skin. I had no sympathy for Renar. What he'd been through as a child was horrible, but he'd become someone just as horrible as his father. He'd preyed on Jonah, and became a rapist. He'd gotten his vengeance on his father, but he had crimes of his own. He'd get his one day.

"What about the missing Familiars?" I asked Baine. "Have we gotten any farther on those?"

Baine shook his head. "Small developments, but nothing substantial. We can speak of it tomorrow, during the Toaqua Council meeting."

There was silence, until Sophia rushed forward. "Please, *pataa*, stay for dinner," Sophia said. "You look like you need to eat."

"No, no, I'm fine," Baine said wearily. "I must get back to my research."

"You've been researching the Anichi piece all day and night for us," Sophia said. She guided Baine into a chair and forced him to sit down. "Please stay."

Baine grimaced as he eyed the lasagna. "Oh, all right. I suppose I could stay for a small bite."

A small bite was apparently half the fucking dish. He must've been hungry, because he cleaned his plate. It wasn't a big deal. Sophia and I were used to making large meals, because it was rare that no one stopped by for dinner.

After everyone had left for home, we'd mopped up after Baine and put the baby down for the night. I sat on the couch with Sophia curled up on my lap. It was dark, the only light resonating from the fireplace. She played with my hair as she stared into the flames.

"This world is so strange," she said. "I've gotten everything I've ever wanted. It's like here, in our house, we can make this perfect little world where no one can touch us... then you step outside, and horrible things are going on out there. I wish we could lock ourselves inside and keep all the bad stuff out."

"It wouldn't be very fun. We'd miss out on all the gossip."

Sophia laughed lowly. "No, we wouldn't. Jonah would have to stop by with the latest issue every day."

Sophia's hands roamed over me. She'd been doing that since we were alone. She was fiddling with the button on my jeans.

"I know what you're doing." Didn't stop to resist, though, as her fingers trailed my waistband.

"I want you," she moaned. "It's been *so long*."

I frowned. "I don't want to hurt you."

"I've stopped bleeding. I'm past the six-week period," Sophia said. "Luana just checked me out this morning and said I'm good to go. It's safe, I promise."

"Is it killing you that bad to abstain for a month and a half?" I joked.

"I am literally dying," she pleaded. "We'll be safe. Please?"

I'd been so horny over the past few weeks my dick practically acted as a kickstand. Medically, Sophia was cleared, but I was still concerned. She had a hard labor, and I didn't want to set her recovery back.

"We're not going rough," I told her. "Nice and easy."

"I don't care. Just put it in me," she whimpered.

"Someone's being needy," I murmured as I trailed my lips over her neck. She moaned again. I kissed her, slow and sweet, and cupped her ass in my hands. She sat up, straddling my hips as she pressed her middle down against me, grinding feverishly.

It took all my self-reserve to lift her off by her hips. "Wait here."

I cautiously slipped into the bedroom. When I came back, Sophia had laid a blanket on the floor in front of the fireplace, scattering throw pillows around. She knelt beside the fireplace and gave a weird look to the foil packet in my hand. "What's that?"

"A condom," I told her. "We need it."

Sophia wrinkled her nose. "We've never used one before."

"Don't complain. You're not back on birth control, and we can't have another baby right now," I told her. "Take what you can get."

She rolled her eyes, but her smile was playful. "Fine. I'll tolerate it."

"I'm sure it's a terrible sacrifice." I sat beside her and put the condom aside. Sophia wasted no time jumping on top of me. She pushed me down and straddled my hips again, running her hands underneath my shirt to feel my abs.

Sophia ripped off her own shirt and tossed her bra free. My eyes went directly to her breasts. They were fuller and larger than before, and quite frankly, looked amazing. I reached up to touch them, but gently, because I knew she was breastfeeding and they had to be sore.

My hands dropped. One settled on her thigh, while the other dove inside her leggings. I slowly played around, feeling her outside while tentatively dipping a finger in and out. Sophia drove down, trying to get me to go deeper, but I drew back. I wanted to take things slow.

"You're always so careful," she complained as I rubbed the inside of her, and she moaned.

"It's you. Of course I'm careful," I whispered back. I'd brought a bottle of lube with me from the bedroom. I'd researched what to do the first time you had sex after having a baby, because I was kind of terrified I'd rip her back open or something, no matter how much she reassured me that wouldn't happen. I coated my fingers with it, and Sophia slipped out of her leggings and panties.

When she was naked on top of me, I started rubbing her again. She let out delirious moans as I massaged my fingers in and out.

"Shh," I hushed. "You're going to wake the baby."

Sophia quieted, but she bit her lip and closed her eyes, like it took all her self-control not to let any noise escape. I felt her clench around my fingers, and she had to lean forward to bite into my shoulder as I fingered her, taking control of her orgasm.

"That didn't take long," I murmured. "You really are needy."

She cocked an eyebrow as she caught her breath. "Like you aren't. You're so hard it's like I'm sitting on a rock."

"You gonna do something about it?" I asked, but she already was. She'd scooted backward and unzipped my jeans, yanking them down to my thighs. My pants weren't even off before she pulled my dick free. Sophia rubbed the tip of my head and watched me squirm, taking a few throaty gasps myself.

I didn't feel like fucking around with foreplay, because I wanted to be inside her *now*. I reached for the condom, but Sophia snatched it out of my hands before I could put it on and tore the package open. Before I had a word to say about it, she'd put the condom into her mouth, and ducked down. I gasped, and my hips rose off the floor as Sophia rolled the condom onto me using only her lips. She cradled my balls and held my shaft steady as her tongue laced forward, and I swear my eyes rolled in the back of my head.

I was still seeing stars when she drew back. My eyes narrowed. "Where'd you learn that?"

Sophia smiled. "Jonah taught Imogen and me. It was a whole class."

I hoped to the ancestors they hadn't been practicing on bananas or something, but I didn't give a shit, because two seconds later she'd climbed on top of me and sank down. Fuck, being inside her after a long break felt like the first time. She began rolling her hips in steady movements, before her pace quickened and she started slamming into me.

I was worried she'd be sore, but guess not, because she worked up to a frantic pace within a few minutes. My dick hardened even more, which I didn't think was possible, and she reached out for my hand, placing it on the back of her head.

"Pull my hair," Sophia gasped, and she sank lower, taking me in. This time, it was me who was at risk of waking the baby, because I let out a guttural moan.

Um, okay. Wish obliged. I lightly yanked, because I didn't want to hurt her, but she must've liked it because she groaned with pleasure. As I fisted my hands in her hair, Sophia picked up the pace, riding me like she never had before.

"Sophia, slow down," I said, but it was barely a protest. I wanted to be careful, and here she was acting like a fucking porn star. It was driving me wild.

Sophia obliged and began moving slower, but it was like she forgot what I said in an instant, as her movements became fast and furious once more.

Okay, enough of this. I grabbed her by the hips and swung her onto her back. My jeans were still on, but Sophia fumbled to push them lower as her hands grabbed at my ass. I entered her again, and her back arched off the floor. She squeezed, and I felt her nails scratch my skin.

"You like that?" I asked, taking slow, meaningful thrusts.

"Hey, Cade's not the only one with a nice butt," she breathed. She tried to push my ass down to get me to go deeper, but I resisted.

"I don't think so." I grabbed her wrists and slammed them down to the floor. "My turn to be in control."

I was able to last a lot longer with the condom. I took my time making love to her, giving slow and meaningful movements while I kissed her mouth and her shoulders. She pleaded for me to go faster, but I held back, and I didn't give my release until she came multiple times and her eyes looked like starlight.

"I always heard sex got worse after you had a kid," I joked. I'd lost my clothes somewhere in the process. We lay naked together under the blanket, enjoying the warmth of the firelight on our skin.

"We've always been the exception to everything," she replied.

She put her forehead against my chest and breathed in. "When can we have more babies?"

I gave a throaty chuckle. "We just had a newborn. You're going at full-speed here. Slow down."

"I know, but I'd like Ava-Marie to have brothers and sisters," Sophia objected. "It feels... nice planning for the future, even if it's a long way off."

I caught the hidden meaning she didn't say. *If I plan for the future, then we'll have to survive long enough to see it.*

But you couldn't put a Band-Aid on things you couldn't control. Bringing more kids into this fucked up world, even without a war going on, was a major decision.

"Wouldn't you like to finish college first?" I avoided mentioning the obvious— the war, the prophecy, all that— because sometimes it was good living in a fairy tale land instead of facing reality.

Sophia stared blankly ahead. "I'd love to go back to Orenda Academy. But I don't know if it'll ever happen."

I didn't know, either. The school would have to be rebuilt before classes began again. If they ever did. Unlike the *Azaimperiai*, growing our family was something Sophia felt she could control. Probably the only thing.

I kissed her hair. "We'll have more children after the war is over."

If it ever was.

"ANCESTORS, can someone *please* simplify for me what's been going on?"

It was late in the evening the next day, and the Water Council was having a meeting with the special ops team devoted to getting the missing Familiars back. Along with my Elders, Tabitha, Carter, Sam, Maddox, and James were here going over what we knew.

We knew fuck all, that's what we knew. We were no farther ahead with finding the Familiars than we had been months ago.

Lira was also on their strategy team, but she'd failed to show up. I wondered where she could be.

James leaned forward over the meeting table and gestured to the maps spread around. "We've had our spies search everywhere. They've covered every corner of the county, and haven't seen a damn thing."

"There's a lot of wilderness on the reservation. The Hawkei tribal lands span for miles," Ezra said. "It would be easy to hide them in a place too remote to find."

"That many Familiars?" Carter scoffed. "It doesn't make any sense."

"Maybe they're not in California. They could be hiding them somewhere else, in another magical location," Madame Wells suggested. "There's no shortage of supernatural communities to store them."

"Oleander would have to give someone a big pay day, and he can't afford that right now. Funds are short due to the war effort. He has to be keeping them somewhere close by," I said as I scanned the maps.

"Not to mention transporting many magical creatures of that size is bound to attract attention," Tabitha said. "The last thing Oleander wants is to deal with humans. He's keeping the Familiars on the reservation somewhere, I'm sure."

"Then *where?*" James slammed his fist on the table. One of the plants on the windowsill curled up and turned brown as a result of James' Nivita magic.

Carter put a hand on James' arm. "James, calm down. We'll find them."

James paused for a moment, then sat back. Wyatt scowled. He'd barely spoken this whole time, just played with his pencil. He looked like he'd all but given up.

"I promised you all we would get them back," I said. "A chief doesn't go back on the vows he made to his people."

"What are you gonna do, Liam?" Wyatt tossed his hands skyward. "Make them materialize out of thin air? There are no more leads!"

"We're just not looking hard enough," Tabitha objected. "We can do this."

Silence skittered around the table. Baine's head bobbed. He looked like he was struggling to keep himself awake.

I put my face in my hands. "Everyone out. Meeting's over. I need time to think."

Chairs scuffled backward. I heard footsteps as the door clicked shut.

We'd been going over this all day. Every minor clue our spies had managed to find was either irrelevant or coincidental.

Where the fuck had this monster taken them? You didn't just make Familiars disappear.

The room was silent, but I knew better. "I said *everyone*, Ez."

"I don't count." Ezra pulled a chair beside me and sat backward on it. "Whenever you say you need time alone, you really need someone to bounce ideas off of. So shoot. What are you thinking? It must be something crazy; otherwise, you'd have asked the council to stay here."

I let out a long breath. "He's hiding them somewhere supernatural."

Ezra's eyes widened. "You mean..."

"Yes. We would've found them by now if magic wasn't involved," I said.

"He's using some sort of ancestral land to cover his tracks. How many places on the reservation have magical power?"

Ezra put his hands on the top of the chair and leaned back. "Um... well, there's the Anichi temple, which is obviously ruled out. And the Elders enchant parts of the forest for the Elemental Cup every year, but the magic only lasts a couple of days."

"That can't be it." I stared at the maps. "There hasn't been an Elemental Cup since your year. Oleander postponed the tournament indefinitely until the war is over."

The door opened, and Stevie entered. She was carrying a cup of coffee and a takeout box from *The Falcon's Nest*, which she placed on the table in front of Ezra.

"Hey, babe," she said. "Thought you might need this. I figured it'd be a long day."

She looked between us. "Doesn't look like it's going well, though."

"Not really," I said. "We're more or less backed into a corner."

"Liam's worked out that Oleander has to be keeping the Familiars in a magical spot," Ezra said. "Though we aren't sure where."

"The reservation is big, but supernatural locations are rare. There can't be too many around," Stevie offered.

Ezra shrugged. "I don't know of many supernatural spots on the rez. Most of that shit is kept a secret from the tribe by the Elders anyway."

The answer clicked. It was just a theory— didn't know if I was right— but I sprang out of my chair.

Bad idea. The world immediately rushed to my feet, and the room spun. I tried to sit back down again, but instead, I slumped to the floor. I was only out for a second or so, enough time to black out from the time I fell to the time I hit the ground.

"Bro!" Ezra shouted. He slid beside me. The colors in the room merged together into shapes as I regained consciousness.

"Ha!" Stevie yelled. "I win!"

Dammit. I had really wanted to beat her on this one.

Ezra's gaze was hard. "You didn't eat today, did you?"

"Forgot," I told him. I didn't mean to. It was my first day back to work, and we'd had so much to cover. Though on a quick calculation of my senses, I was starving, and definitely dehydrated. I'd been so focused on my work I didn't notice.

I'd promised Sophia I'd take better care of myself. I was intent on keeping that vow, and had been doing good, but sometimes I slipped back into old habits of putting other people first instead of my health. Like today, for example.

Ezra was still going on about it. "*This* is what Perot was talking about. Do I need to nanny you?"

I wasn't getting a lecture from my little brother. My eyes flashed to Stevie. "Get my wallet," I slurred.

"What?" Ezra asked. "Why do you need that?"

I reached my hand down and fumbled in my pocket. I then drew a twenty out, holding it weakly out to Stevie. She snatched it up and slid the twenty into her waitress apron.

Ezra's mouth dropped open in confusion. She beamed. "We had a bet," Stevie sang. "First person to faint on the job has to give the other twenty dollars. I told Liam he'd collapse first, and I. Was. Right."

Ezra's words contorted with anger. "That's fucking sick," he spat. He helped me sit up and get back into my chair. He pushed the food Stevie had brought toward me before he rounded on her.

"Was this your idea?" he snapped. "Why can't you take your fucking disease *seriously*, Stevie? It's not funny!"

Stevie instantly went off like a cannon. "It's not *funny*? Well no shit, Ezra! It was all shits and giggles when I was puking in the bathroom at work earlier, I tell you!"

Ezra's face fell. "You were sick this morning and you didn't tell me?"

"I'm sick every morning," she shot back. "And you know what I do? I get up off the floor, I get dressed, and I carry on with my life, because that's what I have to do."

"Why don't you tell me this stuff?" he asked. "I'm your boyfriend, and it's like you try to hide it from me!"

"You have the biggest heart, Ezra. But sometimes, you want to keep me in a bubble, and I can't live life like that," she pleaded.

Ezra's nostrils flared. "Okay, so I want to keep my girlfriend alive. That makes me a real shitty guy, huh? I think you'd be taking this seriously, too. Instead, you're off making bets with my brother on who's going to faint first. That sure makes me feel great."

I wanted to sub in, but knew better. Couples handled this shit differently, and it was best to let them duke it out.

Stevie's look was hard. "Look, I get that it's kind of fucked up. And yeah, maybe a little morbid. But you don't get to tell us how to handle our disease, because you don't know how this feels. Being close to someone who has it is nothing like going through it yourself."

"I know that!" he yelled. "But don't you realize how twisted that is, to make a bet out of your health?"

"Honestly, making a game out of it is the only way not to lose our fucking minds," Stevie snapped back. "The only way to survive something like this is to turn it into a joke. *That's* how we deal."

Ezra made a pissed-off noise and turned his back on her. "Whatever. You guys do what you want. You're the two most important people in my life, and both of you are ill, and it's like neither of you care. I'm just done."

Guilt grew in my gut. When he'd slammed the door behind him, Stevie gave a cry of rage. "Ugh! Ancestors, he's so sensitive!" She kicked a chair angrily.

"Ezra? No, he's not sensitive at all," I said sarcastically.

"He doesn't get how I feel!" Stevie shouted. The next moment, she fell against the wall. She put a hand to her head, dazed.

"Careful," I said. "You're still in uniform, which counts. You'll have to give that twenty back."

Stevie slipped out a sly grin. "In your dreams."

I eyed the food. Ezra had stormed out, but I knew he was waiting outside. No matter how pissed he was, he wasn't going to walk out on me after I'd just passed out— which meant he'd erupt if he saw I hadn't eaten by the time he cooled off and came back. I flipped the lid of the box open. Hm. A chicken wrap— one of my favorites.

"Good thing he doesn't know about the death bet," I said as I took the first bite. "He'd flip a nut."

"He's just on edge." Stevie sank into the seat beside me with a sigh. "He can't understand that this is our way of coping. If we did everything we had to in order to remain at optimal health at all times, that's all we'd ever do with our lives."

"Right," I agreed. "And sometimes, what we do doesn't help that much anyway."

"He keeps comparing me to Teagan." She drummed her fingers on the table. "He thinks that my brother is healthier than I am, but CMSS affects him differently. We can do the same things, and I can end up in bed at the end of the week and he won't be just because his disease isn't as progressive as mine."

"He loves you," I told her. "He gets really protective of the people he cares about."

Stevie twirled a map. "I haven't gotten my period in a few months," she said. "It's freaking him out."

My eyes widened. "Do you think you might be pregnant?"

She shook her head. "No, I know I'm not. Perot confirmed that. This happens all the time. Used to happen before I met Ez. You know as well as I do that our bodies do weird shit at random times. Being a woman, it makes it even more complicated."

I got it. Sometimes, things were just off, and there wasn't much you could do except wait for the problem to correct itself.

"Thing is, now Ezra is worried there's something *else* wrong, and I've told him a million times I'm fine," she insisted. "It's just my body acting up, but he doesn't believe me. He's in paranoid mode. He's got this complex that everyone he cares about is going to get sick."

That made me feel awful, like it was my fault. I knew it wasn't, but I wanted to handle the casualties from my illness as much as I could. I tried to protect Sophia, Ezra, and everyone else I cared about from the blow back, but that wasn't always possible.

I knew in my heart my disease would hurt my daughter one day, and that sucked to think about. But what could I do? There was only so much in my control.

Stevie was right. The best way of handling it was to turn it into a joke.

"Anyway..." Stevie turned to me. "You figured out something, didn't you? That's why you stood up so fast."

"Yeah," I said. "Though it's just a theory. I figured we should talk about it with the others, back at my place."

We gave Ezra fifteen minutes to cool off before Stevie asked him to come back in. She gave him a hug when he entered. His eyes were red.

Fuck, had he been crying again? I didn't want him to get so upset over this. There was no use being miserable over something you couldn't change.

Ezra embraced her back, but his eyes remained open. He glanced at the empty takeout box before his shoulders relaxed.

Okay, me fainting today didn't need to happen. Yeah, I was sick, but I could've prevented that. I needed to be better. Not just for Sophia, but for my brother, too.

"I'm good to go. I feel better," I told him gently. "But I think I may have figured something out."

Ezra nodded. "Okay. So let's go."

We didn't talk about the argument. We all knew it was over.

We headed outside, where Julian was waiting with Dyami. The dragon breathed out a puff of smoke, which turned into a heart.

"Aw, buddy," I said, and I patted his scales. "I missed you, too."

Julian curled his tail. I climbed on his back, and Stevie hitched a ride with Ezra on the back of Dyami. We flew back to my house, where I heard salsa music blasting from inside.

Okay, Imogen and Jonah had moved out, but they were around almost as much as they had been before they left, so it wasn't like our routines had completely changed. They had pushed the furniture in the living room aside and were practicing their dance routines for the cabaret. Luana was with them, twirling in the middle of the room. Sierra fluttered above while Sassy and Squeaks performed identical movements. Esis sat on the coffee table and clapped, while Sophia watched in amusement.

"Where's Ava?" I yelled over the music to Sophia as I entered. The volume was intolerable for a baby.

"Your mother took her. She's on a play date with Jackson," she said.

Squeaks tripped. She leaned into Jonah while doing a crossover, which made him fall flat on his face. Imogen stumbled over him. Luana managed to leap over Sassy before she stepped on her tail. Esis put his paws over his mouth in shock.

"*Squeaky*," Jonah whined. "You've gotta get this routine down. The cabaret is only ten weeks away!"

"Oh, *only*?" I replied. Jonah gave me a look of disgust.

Imogen turned the music off, thank the ancestors. "We'll get it down, Jonah. Luana, you're really rocking that salsa. Thanks for helping us practice."

Luana grinned. *If I don't trip over Sassy, I'll be just fine.*

Now that the music was no longer blasting my ears off, I could hear outside. Someone was laughing hysterically. Several of us glanced out the window. Carter and James were walking by, probably on their way home from our meeting. Carter must've told a hilarious joke, because James was dying. Their two enormous reptiles, Carter's lindwyrm and James' dragon, walked side by side down the street.

"My gaydar is majorly going off with those two." Jonah thumbed at the window. "Has anyone else noticed them acting *very cozy* lately?"

"No way. They're just best friends. Buddies, like Ezra and Cade," Imogen said kindly.

Jonah's lips pursed. "Best friends, huh? Best friends in bed, maybe."

"Stop. Carter and James aren't into each other," I said, waving him off. "I need you to focus. We have bigger problems."

"Then Carter and James' love life? I would hope so," Jake replied as he swept inside. Sabor pushed the door open behind him in order to squeeze in. Squeaks eagerly cawed when she saw Sabor, and she went rushing to him. The two hippogriffs crooned as they nuzzled affectionately.

"My boo!" Jonah exclaimed. He flung his arms around Jake and made out with him in front of the whole room, for the Great Spirit and everyone to see.

Ugh, these two. They were bad. When they'd finally wretched apart, Jonah ran his fingers through Jake's hair and said, "You look tired. Long day, honey?"

Jake smiled. "It's a lot better, now that you're here."

Ick. As I was about to barf, someone emerged from my bathroom. Seriously, how many damn people saw fit to crash my home? This wasn't the local party house.

Except... this guy was someone who'd never stopped by before. Sam? What the hell was he doing here?

Sophia noticed my confused look and said, "Sam said he wanted to talk to you."

He'd been with me less than an hour ago. His complexion was pale—had he been gagging in my bathroom?

Luana looked on in interest. Sam locked eyes with her, and he turned completely red.

Yeah, okay, *talk to me*. More like swing by to talk to my friend, and he'd chickened out. "You got something to say?" I asked.

"Uh..." Sam's eyes darted to Luana, and he blushed harder. "Just, uh..."

Sam swallowed. He crossed the room to Luana and began signing. "Hi," he said as he signed. "I was wondering if... uh... you'd like to go on a date?"

I cringed. He *definitely* hadn't signed what he'd wanted to.

Luana's expression was confused. She signed back. *Okay?*

Sam's face brightened, like he couldn't believe she'd say yes. "Great! That's awesome," he gushed, still signing terribly. "Next Friday? I'll pick you up at eight?"

Luana sent a hesitant glance at Sophia before she signed, *Sure?*

Sam's face was ecstatic. Luana turned to me and signed like mad. *I'm gonna go.*

Couldn't blame her for her awkward departure. *See you later*, I signed back. Luana darted out of the house, leaving Sam beaming.

"It worked!" he exclaimed. "I can't believe it worked!"

"It didn't work quite as well as you thought, but points for trying," Imogen quipped. Sassy barked.

Sam's mouth fell open in horror. "What do you mean?"

"You asked her if she wanted to *cheese sandwich*," Sophia said. "Which doesn't make sense."

Sam groaned. "I wanted to ask her out on a *date!*"

"Yeah. Then right after that, you told her you would pick her up a tomato, not pick her up at eight," Jonah clarified. "She probably thinks you're a crazy person."

He scowled. "Okay, that sign language program I bought is useless."

"I'd say you were ripped off," I confirmed. "But why do you want to learn sign language, anyway?"

"Have you seen Luana?" Sam asked, and he gestured after the way she'd gone dramatically. "That woman is *smoking hot.*"

He slapped himself in the face. "And now I've made a total ass of myself. How can I tell her I like her if we can't communicate?"

"Body language, baby," Jonah purred. "It's all you need."

I threw a pillow at him, and it smacked him on the side of the head. Jake sent me a warning glare, but I ignored him.

Sophia faced Sam. "If you want, I can teach you sign language. That way, when you flirt with Luana, she won't think you're talking about food."

Sam's expression brightened hopefully. "You'd do that for me, Sophia? Really?"

"Of course," Sophia said. She leaned in. "And by the way, Luana already thinks you're cute. So you've got that going for you."

Sam swooned.

There was a knock on the door. Imogen opened it. Lira stood outside. Her hands were laced together, and she wore an ashamed expression.

"Lira?" I asked. "Where have you been? We didn't see you at the meeting."

She kept her gaze down. "That's what I wanted to talk to you about. May I come in?"

Imogen stepped aside. Lira softly closed the door behind herself and faced me. "You're my chief. I have to ask for your forgiveness."

"What are you talking about?" I asked.

Lira dropped her head. "You know there's a traitor in *Hok'evale*. Someone who turned the resistance in to the Task Force and brought them here during the battle over Christmas."

"Yes," I said. "Lira, if you've been hiding them—"

"It was me." Lira brought her eyes up to lock onto mine. "I'm the one who's been ferrying information to Oleander."

Shock echoed throughout the room. Jake reacted before I did. "It was *you?"* he thundered. His voice became harsh and condemning. "You're the one who revealed the resistance? Good Elementai died on your behalf!"

It was strange, seeing such a calm man like him completely lose his shit. Sabor gnashed his beak beside him, though Squeaks got in the way, to prevent him from charging.

"I'm aware," Lira said. "I know what I've done, and that lives have been lost for it."

"You do not know the gravity of your choices! You must be punished!" Jake said.

"She is Toaqua, Jake, and therefore mine to deal with," I told him sharply. "You have no authority at which to sentence her."

"She has committed a crime against the resistance! There must be justice!" Jake cried.

"Let her explain," Sophia said calmly. Jonah put a hand on Jake's shoulder, and he calmed down, though only slightly.

Sophia gestured for Lira to continue. Lira took a breath. "Before we left Orenda Academy, and after he took our Familiars, Oleander came to those of us who were still left at the school. He vowed to reunite any Elementai with their Familiar who'd be willing to spy on the Biyami. Naturally, all of us refused. I was tempted, but I didn't want to let my friends down. But the distance became too much to bear."

Her words cracked as she spoke. "I tried to adjust to *Hok'evale,* but it was impossible. I was desperate. I was dying for my chance to see my Familiar again... so I reached out to Oleander. I told him I would give him information if he let me see my Familiar, and Oleander agreed."

Lira's voice thickened with hatred. "But Oleander tricked me. He promised to let me see my Familiar, but when I got to the meeting point, she wasn't there. Oleander said he was keeping her in a special holding cell. I was to tell him everything I knew. At first, I said no, but he told his men to torture her. I could feel it, though I was miles away."

Lira wrapped her arms around her torso and shuddered. "I tried to hold off, but my girl was suffering so badly. So, I told him about the resistance. I told him where to find us. I thought that afterward, Oleander would reward me by giving her back."

A tear fell down her face, and Lira turned away from us. "But he didn't. And now she's dying. She's not going to last much longer. I know I'm going to die, too. So I have no reason to keep Oleander's secrets anymore."

"How could you do this, Lira?" Sam asked. His voice was only slightly held back from a snarl. "Do you realize how much I miss Zaria, yet I never turned us in!"

"I'm not as strong as you!" Lira shouted back. "My parents died in the riots. I have no one left but her."

Sam drew back. I noticed Jake's anger ebbing away. He understood how difficult the situation was. If Sabor was being tortured— if any of our Familiars were— we all might've done the same thing.

"I'm not trying to buy my freedom," Lira said. "I know what I did was wrong. But I know where the missing Familiars are."

"And you didn't tell us?" Sam snapped. "You've been on our special ops team for months!"

"I was afraid of the consequences that would be given to me by Liam. But I'm not afraid anymore," Lira replied. "Nothing scares you when you can feel death creeping across your skin."

"Tell us," Imogen said. "Where did he put them?"

Lira looked to Sophia. "You know the above-ground cave system, the one you and Liam wandered through during your Elemental Cup run?"

"Yes," Sophia said, and she grasped the Spirit Totem around her neck. Those caves were where we'd found it.

"The Familiars are there," Lira said confidently. "I'm sure of it."

"What?" Jonah blinked. "Why would they be there?"

"Because they need a place that has magic," I said. I thought we'd hit a dead end, but my theory had ended up being correct.

"But the Elders surveyed those caves after our tournament and didn't find anything," Sophia said. "They said the area wasn't magical."

"Because they were looking for healing magic," I said. "That doesn't mean the area doesn't have other supernatural qualities. Why would the ancestors ask Amelia to leave the Spirit Totem there if it wasn't special? It doesn't have to be anything specific. It could just be a place of ancestral power."

Lira nodded in confirmation. "Exactly. After your trial, Oleander went back to the caves and investigated. He discovered that it *was* a place of ancestral power. And he's been using that power to hide where the Familiars are. Keep them contained, and hide their cries from the rest of the world."

"Ancestral magic would be the only magic powerful to contain that many magical creatures of such a powerful class," Imogen mused.

I agreed. Holding creatures like dragons, wyverns, and other strong creatures hostage required a lot of magical energy. The Task Force had to draw that energy from somewhere.

"How do we know you're not lying, and luring us into a trap for Oleander?" Jake asked suspiciously.

Lira's gaze was cold. "Believe me or not, but I have nothing to lose. If my Familiar isn't freed, I'll be dead soon."

Lira's words carried a lot of weight. Jake was still unsure, but I believed her. Lira had that look in her eyes people got just before their magical creatures died. I'd seen it one too many times.

"I can't let this slide, Lira," I said. "There have to be consequences."

"Sentence me now. I waive my right to a trial," Lira said. "I want all your focus to be on saving those Familiars. And saving the life of my own, if there's still a chance."

I frowned. "I know you're my friend. And I appreciate that you came forward and told the truth. I know you were backed into a corner."

I sighed. "But I also know you ferried information to Oleander, and it nearly cost us everything. Winning that battle over Christmas was the only thing that kept the resistance alive. Treason against the tribe is a crime punishable by death, but I refuse to take your life. Therefore, I have no choice but to banish you from *Hok'evale*, Kinpago, and the rest of the Toaqua tribe. If your Familiar survives, and we bring her back, the two of you must leave tribal lands and never return."

"I don't care," Lira replied. "I don't want to be involved in this war any longer. I just want my Familiar back. I'll take banishment, if that's what's required."

"Then I will banish you," I said. "Once you help us find a way into those caves without getting caught."

Lira didn't flinch. "I have an idea. I know I'm asking for a lot, but you have to trust me on this."

"How can we trust you, after what you've done?" Jake asked.

Lira's reply was flat. "Because it's the only chance we've got."

sophia

SIX

"We're going in through the tunnels," Jake announced.

A huge group gathered around the long table in the military headquarters. We'd met here before, in the cave that connected to the back of Jake's house. Jake had wanted to keep the extraction teams small, but once news spread that we were heading in to get the Familiars, everyone wanted to help. Almost two weeks had passed since Lira's confession. I could tell that it was literally killing her to wait this long, but we'd needed more intel before we could make a move.

Jake was leading the Reject Team. I hated to leave Ava-Marie right now, but Jake insisted we needed my healing power, and I couldn't argue. Luana and I were our only hope of getting the larger Familiars out of the caves, since they needed our Spirit powers to move them.

"Our spies will be waiting for us at these three entrances." Jake stabbed a spot on the map Carter had drawn up based on intel Jake's team had gathered. It wasn't a complete map, but it was enough to guide us in and out of the cave system. "Once we're inside, we work quickly and efficiently."

"Are you sure you know what we're doing?" Imogen asked. She didn't like the fact that the map was unfinished.

I entwined my fingers with Liam's as my pulse quickened. I hoped this worked.

"We can't wait a moment longer," Jake said. "Our spies just learned that Oleander's getting in another shipment of noxite tomorrow. The war has depleted most of the tribe's funds, but he's managed to pull enough together to keep these Familiars sedated and chained up for at least another six months. We have to act before that shipment comes in. It's our only chance."

"I totally agree," Jonah said. He stood there with his arms crossed, looking very serious. He got that way whenever he and Jake talked about military stuff.

"Do we know how many Familiars are being held?" Tabitha asked.

She'd lost her Familiar before she'd been rescued from Kinpago. Drew, Wyatt, Maddox, and Sam were all in the same boat, and they'd be running in with their own team, along with Lira. Sam stood close by, shooting glances at Luana every two seconds. I could tell he really wanted to be on our team, but he wanted Zaria back more than he wanted to flirt with Luana. He'd be on the team that would get to the Familiars soonest.

"At least two hundred," Jake said with a frown.

The location of these Familiars was one of Oleander's best-kept secrets. Even Jake's spies had never heard whispers of it, until Lira's confession. For the last two weeks, they'd been working their way inside and funneling Jake information.

"We're lucky Oleander's low on noxite," Jake added. "According to intel, the smaller creatures are being locked in regular cages."

"Good thing!" Lindsey exclaimed. "If all those cages were made of noxite, our powers would be shit in there."

"Exactly," Jake agreed. "We can't wait around for Oleander to build the rest of those noxite cages. That said, noxite is *still* present within the caves. Larger and more powerful creatures are being sedated with it. That's why Sophia, Luana, and their Familiars are on my team."

Esis stood on the tabletop and drew himself up proudly.

Jake continued. "We'll be targeting the sedated creatures and using Anichi healing to get that noxite out of their system. Wyatt's team is going for the smaller cages."

Wyatt sent him a firm nod. I hadn't seen Wyatt look so confident in months. He'd been depressed since his Familiar went missing. To know that he'd see him again and brought his spirits back.

"As for the others, Amelia and Trace's team will take care of that," Jake said.

Amelia bounced on her toes. She looked eager to be heading a team. Finally, someone gave her permission to be the boss, and no one was going to complain about it.

"The others, as in...?" Bren trailed off. He'd be on Amelia's team, along with Lindsey, Miranda, and Cade.

"As in the ones that are locked up with noxite chains," Jake answered. "There aren't many. Like I said, Oleander's running low on supplies."

"How are we getting through the chains?" Cade asked. "It's impossible."

"Not impossible," Trace assured him. "Just difficult. Our powers won't work on the noxite—"

"Which is why we're going with brute force," Amelia finished for him proudly.

Lindsey cracked her knuckles. "Rough. Just how I like it."

Jonah smirked and glanced between Lindsey and Miranda. "I'll *bet* you do."

Liam rolled his eyes. "Can we focus, guys?"

Jonah cleared his throat and went back into military mode. Miranda and Lindsey were still snickering under their breath.

"We'll have back-up teams in the tunnels," Jake said, gesturing to his soldiers stationed around the room. I noticed they seemed split into two groups— Koigni on one side of the room, and Toaqua on the other. Though we were united here in *Hok'evale*, the Hawkei continued to stick to tradition, and Koigni and Toaqua were still polar opposites. "Should anything go wrong, we'll have enough people to get the Familiars out."

"Let's hope nothing goes wrong," Liam stated, but I could hear it in his tone— he wasn't counting on it.

I didn't think any of us were.

"We're all clear on our roles?" Jake asked, his eyes traveling around the room.

He was met with a collection of nods.

"Good," he said. "Then let's move out."

We left the military cave through Jake's apartment and started across the canyon toward the best cave entrance. When we exited Jake's home, I was shocked to see Doya standing outside the door. Instead of her usual velvet dress, she wore black cargo pants and a matching jacket. Her hair was tied into a bun at the base of her neck. She looked like a combat agent or something.

My heart lurched when I saw Ava-Marie wasn't with her. She was supposed to be babysitting her for the night.

"Where's Ava-Marie?" Liam demanded the second he saw her. Liam and I stopped, but Jake led everyone else ahead.

"Relax," Doya said. Naomi was at her side, and the fire lion narrowed her eyes at Liam. "I left her with your mother."

"Why?" I asked, worry seeping into my tone. Esis squirmed in my arms, obviously feeling the same way I did. "What's wrong?"

"Nothing is *wrong*," Doya insisted. "Except you didn't tell me the real reason you left her with me tonight."

"It wasn't really for the entire village to know about," Liam grumbled. "We don't need anyone leaking our plans to Oleander."

"Liam," I hissed. His eyes were dark as he eyed Doya. Their relationship was better than it'd ever been, but it was far from perfect. I knew Liam trusted Doya with our daughter, but I wasn't sure he entirely trusted her in this war.

Doya ignored Liam's harsh glare. "Elliot happened to mention something, and—"

"Fucking Baine." Liam sighed. "You two talk about everything, don't you?"

Doya cocked an eyebrow. She still looked scary every time she did that. "More than you think."

"That's not something you want to tell the Toaqua chief about one of his council members," Liam growled.

Doya huffed. "Can we stop this bickering for one night? I came to tell you I'm coming with you. I wish to help."

Liam opened his mouth like he was about to shoot something back at her, but he paused when he processed what she'd said. "You want to help us rescue the Familiars?"

Liam looked uncertain, as if questioning whether she had ulterior motives. To be honest, I wasn't sure at first, either. Doya had been a completely different person since she came to *Hok'evale*. Picturing her in battle made me uncomfortable, but if I wanted a relationship with my birth mother, I had to give her the benefit of the doubt. I had to give her the chance I'd want Ava-Marie to give me if I were in her position.

"Our team's full up," Liam said, making up excuses.

"Liam!" I protested. I turned to my mother and said, "Excuse us a moment."

I grabbed Liam by the arm and dragged him out of Doya's earshot. "We have to let her come."

"Why?" he demanded. "She could ruin the whole operation. She must have some ulterior motive."

"And so what if she does?" I asked. "If she wants to come along to kill Oleander, then let her. She'd be doing us all a favor."

Liam pressed his fingers to his eyes. "Look, I trust Doya with our daughter, but I still don't know her position in this war. I don't know how much we can trust her."

"Then trust *me*," I pressed.

I glanced back to Doya, and I noticed something in her eyes. She wore a subtle expression I knew all too well, as I shared it with her. Doya really did want to help us, and she had more than enough power to do it. She'd be an asset on our team.

"My mother wants to make up for what she's done in the past," I said. "That's why she spends all her time helping us with Ava. I believe she wants to change— or she never would've come to *Hok'evale* to reconnect with me. We have to give her a chance."

"On this, though?" Liam asked. "This is important, *pawee*."

"We need her," I said. "How come you trust her with Ava and not with this?"

Liam gaped at me, like he didn't know how to answer. "Ava's her granddaughter. She's proven herself with her."

"Let her prove herself with this, then," I argued. "Doya's the most powerful Koigni we know. She can help get those big Familiars out."

Liam glanced between Doya and me. Esis purred in my arms, as if taking my side.

"To be honest, Liam, I haven't been entirely certain of Doya since she returned, either," I told him. "But if she does have an ulterior motive, at least we'll get a chance to test that."

"Is that something you really want to risk?" he asked.

"I have no reason to believe she'd hurt any Familiars." A silent beat passed before I added, "You're the Toaqua chief. It's your call."

Liam drew a deep breath. Finally, he sighed and dropped his shoulders, then turned to Doya. "You and Naomi will stay close on our team."

Doya smiled, which looked strange when she wasn't holding her granddaughter. I still wasn't used to it. "Very well."

Doya started walking to follow behind the extraction teams, but Liam took her stance as offensive. He quickened his pace to step ahead of her, where he would lead the way as chief. My mother scowled. Though she'd been stripped of her title, she still had the pride and leadership of an Elder. But she was trying to play nice, so she didn't protest.

"I'm glad you're coming along," I whispered to her.

Doya smirked and whispered back, "I'm glad you know how to persuade him. Koigni women have a way with our Toaqua men, don't we?"

I chuckled, and Esis chittered. "Yeah, we do."

As we hurried to catch up with the group, I realized Liam and I weren't the only ones who'd been held back. Imogen had stopped in the middle of the path, shooting a pointed look at her younger brothers, Soren and Roland. Liam and I paused to watch their exchange.

"You two need to get it out of your heads that you're coming," Imogen said. "You'll get yourselves hurt."

"We've been training," Soren shot back.

Imogen placed a hand on her hip. "It doesn't matter how good you are throwing punches. Neither of you are bonded, and until you are, your magic won't stand a chance against the Task Force."

"Come on, Im," Roland groaned. "Give us a chance! You didn't let us break the kids out of the camps. Let us come on *one* mission."

"And let you get hurt?" Imogen cocked an eyebrow. "I don't think so."

"You don't think we're strong enough," Roland accused, crossing his arms.

Imogen pressed her fingers to the corners of her eyes. "It's not that. These kinds of missions are for bonded Elementai only."

Soren frowned. "You're just saying that. The second we bond, you'll come up with a new excuse."

Imogen sighed and tapped her foot. She pointed to a nearby tree that was barely as thick as my leg. "Uproot that tree, and you can come with me."

Her brothers gaped at her. "What?" Soren demanded.

"Uproot that tree!" she repeated. "Prove to me you have the power to tag along on this mission."

The boys looked shocked, but they each turned to the tree and tried to use their powers on it. Roland's powers were useless. Even as he knitted his brows in concentration, nothing about the tree changed.

"Let me try," Soren insisted. He aimed his hands at the tree, and the ground wiggled beneath it. Some of the leaves fell off as the tree gave heavy tremors, but he couldn't uproot it. Soren was close to bonding, and his powers were starting to awaken, but without a Familiar, he couldn't perform any impressive feats of magic.

"See?" Imogen said, like she'd proven her point. "You're not ready. Please understand that I'm trying to protect you. You're staying behind until you're bonded, and that's final."

The boys groaned, and their shoulders sagged. There was nothing they could do to convince her. "Fine, we'll stay," Soren grumbled.

"At least then you'll be safe," Imogen said. She turned and started toward the group again, and we fell into step beside her.

"Too bad your brothers aren't bonded," I told her. "We could use the extra men."

She sighed. "Yeah, but they're not good at following instructions. The second either of them bonds and comes along on one of these things, they're going to get themselves hurt."

"Well, let's hope we end this war before that happens," Liam said.

Imogen chewed her lip, looking a little unsure.

We caught up with the group, and Jake led the way through the tunnels. We climbed on the backs of the massive cave snakes as we'd done when we went to break the kids out of the child camps. I got a strange sense of *déjà vu* as I held on to the snake's scales and it slithered through the caves. This time was different, though, because Liam was right behind me, holding me close. Doya sat in front of me. Strands of red hair flew around her as the creature moved quickly.

My stomach sank as we departed *Hok'evale*. I knew I was doing the right thing going after the Familiars, but it broke my heart to leave Ava-Marie behind. Julian wasn't coming along either, because he couldn't fit into the caves. We didn't have an Air team this time, because we didn't want the Task Force spotting us from outside.

I took a deep breath and reminded myself my daughter was safe in *Hok'evale*. No matter what went down tonight, that was what mattered.

I steeled my nerves and focused my eyes forward. Those Familiars needed me. Whether I wanted it or not, I was a beacon of hope for this resistance, and I was prepared to do whatever my people needed. Right now, it meant rescuing those Familiars from Oleander's evil, slimy grasp.

The snakes slowed, and we dismounted in a wide tunnel. Jake led the teams through a smaller tunnel where the snakes couldn't fit. "We walk from here," he announced.

We all moved quickly, quietly, and efficiently. Liam stayed close to my side, and so did Doya. At the front of the group, Luana used her powers to light the path. Naomi's eyes darted the tunnels, keeping watch for any signs of danger.

The tunnels narrowed the further we walked. Soon, we came to a fork in the path. My heart leapt when I saw three Task Force members standing at the intersection. Each wore their dark uniform with a helmet on their heads. They carried noxite guns. Esis stood higher on my shoulder and shook a fist at them. Without thinking about it, I grabbed for Liam's hand and squeezed it tight.

"Relax," he said under his breath. "They're on our side."

He nodded forward. I followed his gaze to see Jake stepping toward the Task Force. One of the men lifted the visor on his helmet. I was surprised to see I knew him. It was Jones. He'd rented us the perytons to fly us to Orenda Academy my first day in Kinpago. He must've been one of Jake's spies that had infiltrated the Familiar holding cells.

Jake spoke lowly to Jones, so I couldn't hear what they were saying. After a few moments, Jake turned back to the group. He didn't say a word. Instead, he used hand signals to point the teams in different directions. Quietly, teams broke up as planned and followed the spies down various tunnels. Imogen and Cade exchanged a long, passionate kiss before saying goodbye. Cade left with Amelia, while Imogen came with us.

Luana's light dimmed as we followed behind Jones. Ahead, Jonah stayed close to Jake's side. Their Familiars followed the sentiment, their feathers brushing up against each other. Naomi crept along with slow, deliberate steps, and Sassy copied her to avoid making noise.

Soon, the sound of animal cries echoed through the cave. Birds squawked, their protests echoing down the tunnels. I heard the growl of feline Familiars and the howls of a wolf. Metal chains clinked together, and scratching could be heard from afar—like creatures were trying to dig their way out of their cages. My pulse quickened as my heart tore into pieces for the Familiars. Liam squeezed my hand tighter, until we saw a light ahead and the tunnel widened. The sounds of terrified Familiars was deafening.

Luana closed her fist, and the light in her hand dimmed. Beyond the opening to the cavern, we could see flames flickering off the cave walls, but I couldn't see anything else yet.

Jake put an index finger to his lips and whispered quietly. "There are Task Force members stationed at every other entrance to the cavern. We move as quietly as possible. If one of them spots us before we get those sedated Familiars healed, we're done for. Now let's get in there."

Our group shared a collective nod, and we started forward.

It was worse than I could ever imagine. Inside, the cavern was massive. The ceiling must have been at least thirty feet tall. There were so many tall cages I couldn't see to the other side. The cages were made of metal bars, like jail cells, and lined in rows that created aisles throughout the uneven cavern floor. Torches had been lit along the walls to light the space, but it was still dark and gloomy.

The cages closest to us housed large Familiars like griffins and pegasi. Dirt covered their beautiful white coats. They were crammed so tightly together that the creatures hardly had room to move. Inside a basilisk cage, the serpents were layered so thick we couldn't see the floor, and they slithered over one another. Food dishes were empty, and the cave was filled with the strong scent of urine and manure.

A manticore lay inside a nearby cage. He tried to lift his head and bare his fangs, but he was so sedated he didn't have the strength to roar. My stomach sank when my eyes landed upon a kelpie. She seemed like she'd been beautiful at one time, but now, the seaweed along the equine Familiar's back had shriveled up and was brown instead of green. Her head lay in the water dish in her cell, but there was nothing left except a few drops. She'd been left without enough water, and was dying for it.

"Let's go!" Jake hissed.

Liam and I hurried to the nearest cage, the one with the pegasi in it. Liam drew water from the air and wrapped it around the lock on the cage. He turned it to ice. The lock made a loud *cracking* noise, but with the sounds of angry Familiars shaking their chains and cages further down the row, it was barely audible.

Liam quickly melted the water, and the door swung open. I rushed inside and knelt beside the first pegasus. She was young, and her feathers were matted together. She'd been sedated and lay on the ground, barely able to lift her head.

I placed my hands on her back and took a deep breath. My magic channeled into the creature's body, and a strong metallic taste like copper filled my mouth. I pushed against the resistance of the noxite. Her metabolism sped up, processing the noxite quickly out of her system.

I knew it worked the moment she lifted her head. Her eyes seemed brighter, and she looked pleased by my help. I sensed something deeper within her— damage to her kidneys from the malnourishment. I wanted to fix that, too, but there were so many Familiars I had to heal. I couldn't overwork myself and risk not saving them all.

The pegasus stood, and I knew that had to be enough for now. Liam guided her out of the cell and led her down the tunnel we came through. The pegasus started running at the first sign of freedom. She'd soon meet up with the other teams who'd held back, as they would help guide the Familiars out of the caves.

I moved on to the next pegasus in line. In the adjacent cell, Doya had melted the lock with her Fire to get inside, and Esis was healing griffins. Jake and Jonah had used their Air power to manipulate the lock mechanism in another cage. Sierra was helping to heal the poor kelpie. Imogen had blasted a hole straight through the lock on a cell of a three-headed dog. The creature perked up when Luana placed her hands on him. It licked her with each of its three faces.

Down the line of cages, Jones used his Earth magic to open the cells of the other sedated animals. He waited eagerly with a peryton herd as we hurried to make it to all the creatures. I was working on healing a pack of wolves when Liam grabbed my arm and ducked.

"Get down," he hissed.

I immediately ducked as low as I could. My eyes darted around the cavern. I caught sight of two Task Force walking by at the end of the row. Jones' eyes met Liam's, and Liam gestured to the Task Force. Jones nodded firmly. The two Task Force turned down our row, but Jones lowered his visor and walked toward them. I held my breath, my heart pounding fiercely in my chest.

Jones spoke to the two men, though we couldn't hear what he was saying. I breathed a sigh of relief when the men turned away. Whatever Jones had said to them must have convinced them he'd already covered surveillance of this row.

"Let's hurry up," Liam said under his breath. "There will be more coming."

I worked quickly, but I could feel my magic waning the more creatures I healed. Esis and I were powerful together, but healing magic took a lot of energy, and we were both using it up quickly.

I swayed on my feet when I entered the peryton cage. A half-dozen peryton were packed in there so tightly, their wings were folded over one another.

"Quickly, please," Jones begged.

Liam steadied me as I knelt next to the peryton. I glanced to a nearby cage. Luana looked worse for wear than I did. Her face was pale, and she had her arm over Imogen's shoulders.

I placed my hands on the head of one of the deer, right between its broken antler. I had to push harder with my magic than I did with the pegasi, but slowly and surely, the creature's eyes opened, and he became alert. Others nudged their noses forward, and I placed my hands on two at once to heal them.

"Almost there, *pawee*," Liam encouraged.

The cavern had significantly quieted down now that we'd gotten a lot of the creatures out of their cages, but there were hundreds more still locked in. It wouldn't be long until the Task Force realized some had gone missing.

Just as I finished healing the last peryton, my fears were confirmed. A deafening squawk filled the cavern. It was so loud that the ground rumbled beneath our feet and rocks started to crumble above our heads. Esis squealed and ran into the peryton cage to hide in my lap. Squeaks and Sabor immediately perked up, and Sassy started barking. Naomi growled, and Doya instinctively formed a fireball in her hand.

I threw my hands over my ears and looked toward the source of the noise. A gigantic beast the size of a dragon flapped its wings and rose above the metal cages. I watched in awe as I noticed it was entirely covered in feathers in red and gold hues. It was a minokawa. I'd seen one in *Hok'evale* before, but they were rare in the Hawkei tribe. A noxite collar was attached around its neck, and the chains clanged against each other as the creature rose toward the ceiling. Amelia's team must've set him free, but he was too anxious to escape to go quietly.

A dozen Task Force men ran into the cavern from all different angles. They'd been guarding the tunnels and came to see what was making all the noise.

As soon as they saw the minokawa was free, they started barking orders at each other. They quickly called for backup, then aimed their noxite guns. Several darts landed in the minokawa's chest, while others were fired down the line of cells. I heard the shrill cry of Lindsey screaming, and my stomach plummeted to my toes. My friends had been caught.

The minokawa spiraled down from the ceiling, and we heard it crash in the distance. Metal groaned beneath its weight, and creatures cried as the huge bird crushed a handful of cages.

"Move!" Liam cried.

Task Force began flooding in from all angles, and we were quickly spotted. "There they are!" someone shouted, pointing at us. A man raised his weapon, but I realized with horror that it wasn't a noxite gun— it was a crossbow!

"Down!" Liam shouted. He grabbed me by the shoulders, and we ducked a second before an arrow whizzed through the bars of the cell and flew above our heads. I heard the pained cry of the peryton behind us as the arrow pierced its chest cavity. My pulse pounded in my ears when I turned to see the creature collapse. I rushed to place my hands over the wound, but

I was too late. The sound of a *hiss* came. I knew the arrow had punctured its lungs. The creature's eyes rolled back into its skull.

Esis hesitated beside me. His bottom lip quivered, and his big blue eyes watered as he looked up at me. I shook my head regrettably. There was nothing we could do.

"*Nooo!*" Jones wailed.

A huge blast of air swept by us a moment later. "Attack!" Jake shouted.

I noticed immediately that he didn't give orders to retreat. These Familiars were important. If they died, so did our people. We weren't just here to defend ourselves from the Task Force. We came to play offense— to get these creatures out no matter the cost. And I was intent on following those orders.

The blast of air continued onward, until it grew in intensity. When it hit the Task Force members, they were swept off their feet. Jake stood in the center of the aisle, his arms held at his sides as he manipulated the air. Jonah, Squeaks, and Sabor all went to join him. They aimed their furious magic at the Task Force. Wind swirled around the pair of them, and I could see they were about to attack again.

But before they could, one of the Task Force members whistled loudly. A huge hawk landed in front of our opponents. It wasn't as big as the minokawa or Dyami, but it was one hell of a beast— big enough to ride, at least. Jake and Jonah thrust their magic forward, but the hawk opened its wings. Their attack bounced off the creature, and the air blasted back in our direction. Liam, Esis, and I were thrown into the side of the cage we were in. I screamed as my shoulder slammed into one of the bars. Esis was small enough that he slipped right through and rolled on the ground in the next cage. The assholes were using their Familiars against us now!

Our entire team had been blasted back. Imogen and Luana had been tossed backward in their cage as well. Jonah and Jake had flown back nearly to the end of the aisle, along with their Familiars.

Doya had caught her shoulder on the corner of one of the cages. Her arm hung off her body at an odd angle, but she staggered to her feet and shoved her dislocated shoulder back into place.

"You want to play dirty?" she shouted at the Task Force. "Be my guest."

Doya thrust her palms outward, and streams of Fire erupted from her hands. Naomi transformed into a Fire beast, the flames consuming her entire body. She sprinted forward and jumped onto the hawk's chest, sinking her powerful jaws into the flesh where its wing met its back. The creature threw its head backward and screeched as Naomi ripped its wing from its body.

Doya's Fire caught several of the Task Force uniforms. Their legs went up in flames, and they screamed out in pain. Though the Koigni Task Force tried to put the fires out, Doya overpowered them, and the flames kept climbing up their bodies.

But she'd only gotten a portion of them. The ground rumbled beneath our feet from Nivita soldiers, and rocks started flying.

"We have to help her!" Liam barked. "Soph, how's your magic?"

Esis scurried back into my arms.

"A little weak, but I have some left," I admitted.

Liam grabbed my arm and dragged me to my feet. "Let's get rid of the Task Force. Jones, get the peryton to safety!"

Jones' eyes went wide at the sound of his name. He was still trying to recover from seeing one of the peryton die right in front of his eyes. Though this guy was a trustworthy spy, it was clear he wasn't cut out for war.

"Y-you've got it, Chief," he said, saluting Liam.

"Now let's go!" Liam cried.

We rushed out of the peryton holding cell and straight in front of the Task Force. I barely had a second to take everything in. Down the aisle, the tunnel we'd come through was crowded with Familiars eager to escape. Imogen, Luana, and their Familiars had rushed down there to help the creatures through, but the tunnel was small. It would take time.

Jake and Jonah had been distracted by a group of Task Force that had flown over the cages on the backs of their hippogriff Familiars. The hippogriffs fought one another, and feathers flew everywhere. I saw the flicker of Jonah's lightning in his hands, but he hesitated attacking, as he didn't want to hurt Squeaks or Sabor.

The bulk of the Task Force were fighting against Doya, but she dodged their attacks or used massive fireballs to counterattack. The fight had broken out only moments ago, and already there was blood everywhere— mostly from the hawk Naomi was ripping to shreds.

Liam and I rushed to Doya's side. The three of us moved forward as a unit, advancing on the Task Force. Liam gathered water from the air, and from what was left in the Familiar water dishes. He formed it into long whips and slashed them at the Task Force members. By the angry look on his face, I wouldn't have put it past him to stop their hearts, but he wasn't close enough.

They retaliated with water balls of their own. With each one they threw, I laser-focused a force field toward it. The water balls erupted against my force fields and melted onto the cave floor. Liam was close enough to manipulate the water and add it to his whips. Not a single drop touched us.

"Jones!" Liam shouted. "Get those creatures out of here! We've got you covered!"

I expected Jones to head off behind us, where the other Familiars had gone, but he must've noticed the tunnel was congested and decided to go a different way. Jones hopped on the back of one of the peryton and gave an order. They flew out of the cell together and flapped their wings toward the ceiling of the cave.

"Jones, no—!" I started to say, but it was already too late.

Crossbow triggers sounded, and the peryton let out a collective cry. Jones screamed as arrows stuck into his chest. His head lolled on his shoulders... then everything gave out. His body slumped off the peryton and spiraled downward until—

Thwack!

Jones' body landed on the ground between us and the Task Force. Five arrows stuck out of his chest, and blood seeped down his Task Force uniform, pooling into the rocks beneath him.

His neck twisted oddly toward me. I'd seen that look in his eyes too many times; they'd gone completely lifeless.

The peryton flew off, crying for Jones but knowing they'd die if they stuck around. Esis went to run toward Jones, but I grabbed him and dragged him backward. "Esis, stay!"

Liam lashed out with another water whip, and Doya increased the intensity of her Fire. Esis screeched, and to my surprise, Anichi light burst out of his tiny little palms. He aimed it at the Task Force members to blind them, and several staggered backward at the assault.

Naomi landed a killing blow to the hawk's throat, and the creature slumped to the ground in a pool of its own blood. Its feathers had caught Naomi's Fire, and the creature began to burn.

"No!" one of the Task Force screamed. He dropped to his knees and cradled the hawk's head in his lap. It was obvious it'd been his Familiar. "What are you waiting for!?" he growled at his men. "Get them!"

A few men raised their crossbows. I noticed at least half the soldiers had them. It must've been Oleander's weapon of choice after noxite guns, now that they were running low on supply. One of the men aimed an arrow straight at Esis' heart. I guess he thought going for my Familiar would be an easy way to take me out.

Big mistake.

At that moment, I fucking lost it. A passionate feeling akin to rage ignited inside of me, but it wasn't anger. It didn't spark my Fire like I was so used to. It wasn't aimed at the Task Force, and I wasn't out for revenge. Rather, a deep-seated love for Esis swept through me with so much force it nearly knocked me off my feet. All I wanted to do was protect him.

My Spirit magic responded to the call for protection, and power surged through me like never before. My fatigue from earlier was completely forgotten. I threw up a force field around Esis the second the man pulled the trigger, but the force field expanded further than I expected, encasing Liam, Doya, and me inside it as well. The arrow connected with my force field and shattered to pieces. Splinters flew off in all directions. I couldn't see the men's eyes beneath their visors, but they stiffened in surprise. No one had expected an Anichi bitch to step in.

Nobody tried to kill my Familiar and got away with it.

Anichi magic began to glow out of my skin, light pouring out of every pore in my body. Even Liam halted in surprise as he took me in. But I wasn't focused on him. All I could think about was *protection*. The Task Force were a threat to the people I loved, and I had to eliminate that threat.

I stepped forward, my force field expanding around me. It shimmered slightly, but the Task Force couldn't see it. All they knew was I was lighting up like a Christmas tree, and it was totally unnatural.

"Fire!" one of the Task Force members shouted. Noxite darts and crossbow arrows shot toward me, but they fell flat when they hit my force field. Some of the men hesitated as I continued walking, and they started backing up.

"You want to fuck with my Familiar?" I growled. "Burn in *Aiya Nocshun!*"

My Spirit magic exploded out of me. My force field expanded like a bomb going off, throwing the Task Force backward. Cages upended and crashed down into heaps, crumpling like tissue paper.

I stalked forward until my magic was within reach of the man who'd tried to kill Esis. My own force field was still up to protect me, but I formed another one around the Task Force member. He freaked out and shot another arrow at me, but it was useless. It shattered like the others.

I tightened my fingers, controlling the force field and ordering it to shrink around him. He let out a shrill cry as it started to squeeze him tightly— until it was so tight that I'd crushed all the air from his lungs. The man's back arched, and he went completely rigid under my control. The other Task Force members backed away in utter horror as the invisible force crushed him so hard his helmet cracked. I squeezed harder, until I heard the sound of bones breaking.

I couldn't see his eyes beneath his visor. Perhaps that made killing him easier. But I did see the slacked-jaw look he gave, and I saw his veins engorge beneath his skin. The blood vessels exploded, filling his skin with a purple hue.

As my Spirit magic encompassed him, I could feel something within him the same way I healed. I couldn't explain it, but it was like I could *feel* his spirit. It was bitter and cold— tainted by Oleander's rule. I wasn't proud of taking his life, but I knew it had to be done to save the ones I loved.

Suddenly, the spirit I felt within him vanished. It was there one second and gone the next. I knew then I'd actually done it— I'd killed him.

I dropped my force field around the man, and his body slumped to the ground. Three Task Force members remained. The others had either burned to death at Doya's hand, or had been slashed bloody by Liam's Water power.

One Task Force member stared down at the other man's body, then looked up at me. He must've been scared shitless, because he didn't even try to shoot noxite my way. Instead, he dropped his gun and fled toward the nearest tunnel. The others quickly followed.

I let them go, then dropped my force field. It took a few seconds for the fatigue to hit me, and when it did, Liam was there to catch me.

"Holy shit, Sophia," he breathed as he steadied me. "That was—"

"Impressive," Doya said as she approached.

Liam's eyes were wide, like he couldn't believe what he'd seen. Honestly, he looked a little scared. Doya, on the other hand, dropped her chin slightly, like she saw me as an equal.

Esis chittered proudly and climbed up my pant leg to stand on my shoulder. He clapped his paws together, as if celebrating my newfound power. Then he tapped me on the cheek, and when I looked, he flashed Anichi light in my eyes.

"Hey!" I protested, shielding my eyes. "Be proud of your light, Esis, but don't shine it at me."

Liam let me go, and I found my balance again. Naomi returned to Doya's side back in her regular form.

"Are you okay, *pawee*?" Liam asked breathlessly.

I drew myself up. The fatigue was already starting to fade, as if my magic was being replenished quickly. "Yes, I'll be fine."

"But what you did there..." Liam trailed off. I didn't think he knew what to say. I'd surprised him.

"She did incredible," Doya said. I never thought I'd hear her say that, considering my first day in her class I couldn't even light a candle. I didn't like that it took killing someone to make my mother proud, but it felt good to get a compliment from her.

But the high was short-lived. Across the cavern, we could hear the roars of various creatures. Cages rattled as others tried to break out. Our friends were still trying to fight off the Task Force.

"Don't congratulate me just yet," I replied. "We have a lot more Familiars to save."

"Then let's go," Doya said firmly.

I glanced around for our team, but they'd been distracted by their own fights and had moved on. I didn't see them anywhere and prayed they were all right. We hurried to the next aisle, where our back-up teams were rushing back and forth to unlock the cages. Almost all the creatures there had been released. Above us, I caught sight of Lindsey and Miranda escaping on the back of a chimera.

We continued on, until I caught sight of the minokawa at the center of the cavern. It lay atop a heap of twisted cages. The noxite darts it'd been shot with wasn't enough to knock out the huge creature, but they'd been enough to sedate it so it couldn't fly.

"This way!" I shouted to Liam and Doya over the roar of battle echoing throughout the cavern.

They ran behind me as I rushed over to the bird. "Esis, we're going to heal it!" I told him. "This bird is getting out of here today."

Esis nodded firmly. The creature startled when we approached. It was so big that when it moved, I jumped backward. For a second, I thought its talons might get me. Then its eyes connected with mine, and they softened.

"Relax, big guy," I told him. "I'm here to help."

I placed my hands over massive feathers and channeled my magic into the bird. Esis did the same. The metallic taste of noxite filled my mouth again, but with as many creatures as I healed earlier, I was practically a pro at this now. It was difficult to heal with the noxite collar around the creature's neck, but not impossible if I channeled to other areas of its body. The metallic taste started to wane. I almost thought I was done, until my magic slammed into massive resistance. Pain shot out through my arm, and I realized in horror that one of its wings was hurt.

"What is it?" Doya demanded when I gasped.

"It's hurt," I said. I continued to explore its body for diagnosis. "Impaled, I think. It's not going to fly without healing."

The creature lifted its wing, as if to explain. A huge, bloody hole ran straight through the center of its wing. One of the cage rods must've snapped and impaled the creature when it fell.

"Hurry up," Liam said. "I don't think we have much—"

Just then, a herd of alicorns swooped down from above. They'd been flying so high toward the ceiling I didn't see them at first. Task Force members jumped off their backs. A sharp breath passed my lips. I didn't have time!

I raised my hands to fight back, but Liam stopped me. "Heal, Sophia! We'll fight them off."

Fire ignited in Doya's hands, shooting higher than flames I'd ever made before. Naomi immediately shifted into a Fire lion, and Liam advanced forward. He twisted his hands, and Task Force members started to fall at the drop of a hat. He'd gotten so good at killing people with his magic that all it took was appropriate proximity.

It wasn't fast enough, though. Other Task Force retaliated. A Yapluma man twisted his fingers, and Liam gasped for breath. He'd sucked the air straight out of his lungs!

Doya realized it before I did. Without conjuring a single fireball, she directed her magic through the elements around us and lit the man's uniform on fire from a distance. He screamed under her attack. It all happened so fast that I didn't have a second to react. The next moment, the two were on their feet, fighting back.

"I'm impressed," Liam said, still gasping to catch his breath.

"What?" she asked as she threw a fireball at some guy's head. "You didn't think I had it in me to save a Toaqua?"

Liam shrugged as he sucked water from a pool of blood on the ground. But it wasn't just water— the blood cells came with it, and Liam held a blood-red water ball in his hand. He instinctively threw it at a Task Force member. "I didn't realize you'd gone soft."

"Pft," Doya breathed. "You're my daughter's husband and chief to the man I love. Don't fool yourself into thinking I wouldn't protect you."

Liam and Doya worked quickly and together seamlessly. I didn't know how they did it with all the differences they'd faced in the past. But they sure as hell knew how to work together in combat.

Esis chirped, and I turned back to the minokawa. We worked double time to heal the creature. I threw a frantic glance back at Liam and Doya to see another team had come in, and they were each fighting their own battles. Doya was waging war against three Koigni men, while Liam was fighting off a huge three-headed serpent.

I pinched my eyes shut and focused on healing the minokawa. In under a minute, the hole in its wing was completely healed up, and feathers had started to grow back. The creature stood and shook its feathers, then bowed its head gracefully at us. I didn't need the translation to know it was offering us service, if we wanted it. He was willing to stay to see this thing through.

I reached up for the feathers on the back of its neck, then pulled myself onto its back. Esis didn't follow at first. "Come on, Esis!" I called down to him. "We have to break these cages open!"

Esis hesitated, looking out toward the battle. I followed his gaze, and my guts sank. Bodies littered the floor— both Hawkei and Familiars. Flames blazed in the crowd. Doya was finishing off one last Task Force member, but I didn't see Liam anywhere.

Doya formed her flames into the shape of a phoenix, then sent the fiery bird diving toward the Task Force member. His body lit up in flames.

"Doya!" I screamed down at her. She didn't hear me at first over all the screams. Or she wasn't listening.

I had to try something else. "*Mother!*"

Her gaze snapped in my direction.

"Where's Liam!?" I screeched. He'd been right here seconds before!

She glanced around, startled. "I don't know. I lost him."

Shit. He better be okay, or there'd be hell to pay.

"Let's go!" I called down to her. "We have work to do."

Doya ran over and gracefully jumped onto the back of the minokawa. Naomi followed shortly after.

The minokawa turned to take flight, and I noticed something nearby. "Wait!" I called out to the creature, and it halted in its tracks.

Down the aisle, the resistance was supposed to be breaking creatures out of their cages. Instead, half a dozen Toaqua and Koigni resistance members were engaged in a scuffle. They weren't trying to kill each other, like with the Task Force, but they sure as hell weren't getting along.

"You're Toaqua scum, you are!" a girl shouted to another.

"Koigni bitch!" she snarled back.

Fists started flying. Ancestors, did they have to do this *now*? I kicked my heels against the minokawa's side, and he started forward. It wasn't until the creature's shadow crossed over them that they noticed us.

"Hey!" I snapped from above them. All eyes turned up to me in shock. "We're here to fight the Task Force, not turn against our own. Like it or not, we are one people now, united against Oleander and what he's doing here. You must set your differences aside and realize that we all share one common goal. Those creatures in cages are what is most important!"

A couple of the Toaqua hesitated, like they weren't willing to put their pride aside and listen to a Koigni. My anger flared. I was about done with this shit. They needed to get it together *now*.

"If your Toaqua chief can fuck a Koigni, you can work together to pick a few locks," I growled. "Turn your rage to the cages, and get those Familiars to safety!"

They all seemed flustered by my comment, but they turned to nearby cages and started using their powers to break them open. I glanced back at Doya, expecting her to have given them her *look* that had the power to ignite fear in anyone, but she wasn't giving it. She was looking at me with pride.

"Very good, Sophia," Doya praised, sounding impressed. "You sound a lot like me when you're ordering people around."

I snorted. "Yeah, well I didn't get it from my *pataa*."

Doya chuckled, but it didn't last long. She quickly got serious again. "What's your plan, Sophia?"

I held tight to the minokawa's feathers and scanned the cavern in determination. Liam had to be out there somewhere. "We're going to find my husband."

Liam

SEVEN

I'd lost my wife in the chaos, and everyone else. It was fucking madness in here.

The tunnels were crowded with Familiars. Animals were stampeding everywhere. The ones that could fly were pushed against the ceiling, while Task Force swarmed into the caves.

I had used most of the water in my possession to kill the three-headed serpent, but I still had a water ball left. I tossed it into the helmets of Task Force members I couldn't reach, calling the water back so I could use it over and over. Anyone who was close enough to me to stop their heart, I killed.

I didn't want to take lives, but at this point, I had no choice. Wounding the enemy only increased the chances the rest of my team didn't make it out of here. They couldn't fight back or interfere if they were dead.

I heard a yell. Jonah was pressed up against a corner, surrounded by five Task Force members. He whipped out his wind at them, but the Task Force brought up Earth shields to block it. They were all Nivita. Squeaks clacked her beak in a warning to stay back.

I ran up from behind. I sent my water ball whizzing out, freezing it to ice. It went sailing in an arc, connecting with Task Force members and crushing their helmets inward. The water ball ricocheted around the room, until all were out of commission. They sank to the ground, and I reached out and pulled Jonah out from the circle. Squeaks squawked in relief.

"I lost Jake!" Jonah's eyes were panicky as he floundered to stay on his feet. It was so loud in here, I barely heard him over the noise.

"We'll find him, Jonah! Jake's a general. He knows how to survive," I told him. My eyes scanned the room. It should've been easy finding someone as big as Jake in all this mess, but I didn't see him. There were simply too many bodies.

"I can't use my powers in this cave. We're too close quarters," Jonah complained. "If I start shooting off Storm Lord powers, I'll kill us all."

"Then let's get out in the open." I turned in place, looking for more allies. "Imogen!"

Imogen was still trying to help the creatures escape, but she was going under. Sassy perched on her shoulder, trying to maintain her balance. A peryton knocked her down. She screamed as Familiars began trampling over her in a mad dash. Sassy let out a cry of pain.

"Im!" Jonah sent a shock wave of Air through the cave. It caused several Familiars to stumble, and others to lose their balance. A pegasus nearly fell over on her, but Jonah used his Air magic to grab Imogen and yank her and Sassy back to us. He lifted her to her feet, and her head lolled in a daze. Squeaks nudged Sassy in worry. The fox rose with Squeaks' help.

"You okay, Im?" I asked. She was covered in cuts and bruises. Luana had been with her the last time I saw, but she wasn't anymore. I had no idea where she'd run off to.

A gash above her eye bled, but Imogen lifted her gaze. "I'm fine. Where's Sophia?"

"I lost her. I think she took off with her mother." Seriously having a mini-freakout right now.

"If she's with Doya, she's alive," Jonah said. "Let's get the rest of these Familiars out of these caves."

"How?" Imogen yelled. "There's not enough space for—"

An explosion boomed throughout the cavern. Jonah knocked Imogen to the floor and crawled over her protectively, while I fell on my face from the blast. Squeaks and Sassy were tossed into the wall. The water I'd had splattered everywhere. I covered my head. Debris littered down, and I saw Familiars and Task Force go flying with the burst of the explosion. My ears painfully rang with the sound.

I lifted my head. As the smoke cleared, I saw bodies— both Elementai and animal. Blood leaked into the stone. Some creatures were ripped in half. Limbs littered the area.

A large hole had been blown in one of the cave walls. There stood Jaymin Riske, two of her Nivita demolitionists beside her. She stood victoriously as Familiars rushed through to escape.

I staggered to my feet. Jonah let Imogen up and helped her stand. They rushed to their creatures. Squeaks was okay, but Sassy looked exhausted. Familiars flooded through the exit Riske had created. With hatred, Jaymin Riske began bringing down parts of the ceiling. They crashed into Task Force members, smashing them flat, and winged Familiars flew out of the cavern.

I couldn't hear Jonah's words. He signed to me instead. *Jake didn't approve of her being here!*

She'd found out regardless. I ran toward Jaymin, until I was standing feet away from her. "This wasn't part of the plan!" I screamed. We had no one waiting for those Familiars on the other side through the holes she'd created, to lead them back to *Hok'evale*. They'd be lost and confused.

Jaymin said nothing, just smirked at me and ran off. She viciously attacked the Task Force members with a vengeance, smashing boulders together in order to crush them.

Whatever, fuck her. I had no time to deal with her nonsense. We'd created a plan with Jake, and we were going to stick to it.

"Sophia!" I cried. I didn't hear my own shout. The cave was starting to clear out now. Most of the Familiars had fled through the various exits, and the Task Force was either mostly dead or fighting off Jaymin and her cronies.

Imogen shouted something, but neither of us could hear her. She signed quickly. *Sophia's not in here. She might've moved on.*

I nodded. There were two parts to the cave system. We were assigned to the first, where most of the creatures were, but another part held dragons and other large creatures. Sophia and Doya could've moved on to the second. *Let's go*, I signed.

We scrambled over bodies. I slipped on a puddle of blood, but Jonah grabbed my arm to keep me steady. Squeaks led the way to clear a path, and blood smeared on her feathers. The hippogriff almost looked like she was *enjoying* this. Her species had a weird way of appreciating violence.

As we came to a narrow tunnel that led to the second part of the caves' system, we found Luana. She was kneeling next to a tiger-like creature that had four tails and a horn on its head. The creature gasped quickly while Sierra fluttered above its head. Luana tried healing it, her glowing hands encompassing the creature's body, but it didn't work. The creature gave a shuddering breath and went limp.

Luana's eyebrows knitted together, and her face dropped. She clambered slowly to her feet. Sierra landed on her shoulder and glowed white, giving her Elementai some of her remaining healing energy.

Luana's eyes widened as she noticed us. *You guys okay?*

We lost our hearing from the explosion, I signed. *We were right next to it.*

Luana didn't waste any time. She put her hands over my ears, and I felt my hearing return in its fullest. She healed Jonah, Imogen, and Squeaks before turning to Sassy, who was the worst for wear. As Luana's healing magic flooded through her, Sassy recovered, and she gave a few yips in thanks. Luana's eyelids fluttered.

I'm running out of healing energy, Luana signed. *I don't have much left in me.*

"Then let's get the rest of those creatures and get out," I replied, signing as I spoke.

We slunk along the wall. I expected the Task Force to have set up a blockade, but we didn't come across any.

The hall opened to reveal a cavern larger than the first. The roars of dragons and other monstrous creatures shook the walls. There was the sound of women shouting up ahead. We came to a halt as we witnessed Doya and Sophia totally making the Task Force their bitch.

Doya had whipped up a firestorm. She was directing a whirlwind of fire toward anyone who dared to get too close. Naomi ran within the whirlwind as a Fire lion, leading the charge. As Doya spun her hands, Naomi pounced, and Doya grew the firestorm so large that a whole line of Task Force recruits was wiped out, burned to ash.

Damn, Doya was such a fucking badass. Having her on our side was definitely an asset.

Sophia tossed fireballs at the Task Force members who had managed to writhe out of Doya's grasp. A band of Task Force tried to escape the cave, but Sophia conjured up the Fire dragon she'd created on the beach, and sent it after the brigade. The Fire dragon swallowed up the entire brigade, engulfing them in flame. I could see nothing but shadows within the tremendous flames as the bodies burned.

Yep. That was my wife.

Esis sat on her shoulder. He shook his tail, and as he did so, a dome of light burst from his paws. It expanded, colliding with the bodies of the Task Force and sending them flying. Several Task Force hit the walls of the cave *hard*, their bodies sliding down and going still.

Other resistance teams were in here, but they'd left the fighting of the Task Force up to Doya and Sophia, who were more than capable, while they tried to get the other creatures out. I passed Amelia and Trace on my way to Sophia. Both of them knelt beside a cell.

"There you guys are! How are you getting them out?" Jonah breathed.

Amelia held up a pair of bolt cutters. "Hey, where magic doesn't do the trick, tools will."

"Where's the rest of your team?" I asked.

"Lindsey, Bren and Miranda are escorting the Familiars back through the caves," Trace said in a rush. "Cade ran off with Jake somewhere."

This was a crazy situation. We were breaking ranks all over the place. I'd planned to help Sophia take out the rest of the Task Force, but she didn't need my assistance. There were only a few Task Force members left. Sophia didn't even need to raise her hands— all she did was *look* at them, and they burst into flames, bodies collapsing onto the stone floor.

"Well, hey there, Mrs. Badass!" Jonah called out. She glanced our way and came running.

"Thank the ancestors." Sophia embraced me and ran a hand through my hair. "Where have you all been?"

Esis kissed my cheek. I shrugged and said, "Pretty much everywhere, but that's not important. Where are we at?"

"We don't have a lot of time before the Task Force comes back with reinforcements," Sophia rushed to say. "We have to get the rest of these creatures out."

"Have you seen Jake?" Jonah asked.

"Or Cade?" Imogen added.

Sophia shook her head. "No, but the faster we work, the faster we can find them."

"Let's move," I said. "Jonah, Im, help Amelia and Trace with the cells on the left. Sophia, Luana and I will work on the cells on the right."

"I'll block the Task Force and buy you time," Doya said, storming toward the tunnel opposite the one we'd come down. "They aren't getting past me."

Naomi growled in agreement as she charged after Doya. Sophia and I turned to the closest cell. These cells were different from the rest. Instead of bars, large iron doors, big enough to fit a dragon through, were built into alcoves of the cave walls. I could hear the dragons inside, roaring to get out. The sound of chains clanking could be heard as the dragons scraped their claws against the stone.

The doors were locked by a large sliding bolt. I could feel the noxite emitting from the doors. I tried to yank on the bolt, but it wouldn't move.

There was some kind of locking mechanism holding it in place. Sophia conjured a fireball, but I grabbed her arm.

"Our magic isn't going to work on these," I said. "We need another plan."

Squeaks came stampeding out of nowhere. She rose up on her front legs and kicked the bolt that held the door open, over and over.

Eventually, the bolt broke off. Squeaks ran to the next cell, pounding her hooves on another. Sassy changed into a kitsune and wrapped her vines around another bolt, using her strength to rip it off.

"Here!" Amelia tossed me a set of bolt cutters. I caught it, and Sophia and Luana squeezed their way through the heavy iron door. I tried to push it open, but even with three people, it was an impossible task. These doors were meant to stay shut permanently.

It was pitch black inside. Sophia, Luana and Esis shone light from their hands so we could see.

As the cave lit up, revulsion crawled over my skin. The cell was filthy, a dirty water bowl in the corner with matted straw scattered throughout. There was nothing but a small slot in the cave wall to shove food through.

The dragon in the cell was held by a noxite collar and chains around its ankles. The collar and chains were padlocked to the wall. The dragon had scale rot, and several sores on its side were festering with infection. He slept, sedated from the noxite.

I had to take a few breaths to stay calm. I *hated* seeing animals being kept in this way. Our Familiars deserved more than this. It was hard to witness.

Luana, Sierra, Sophia and Esis began healing the creature. Luana tended to the sores and scale rot, while Sophia and Esis worked on getting the noxite out of his system. I used the bolt cutters to cut through the noxite chains binding the dragon's legs, destroying the iron collar around his neck.

The dragon started. Esis jumped out of the way as its fangs snapped, and I pushed Sophia down so she wouldn't get bitten in half. I laid a calm hand on its neck.

"Easy, bud," I told him. "We're here to help."

The dragon calmed, though smoke furled from his nostrils. He noticed we'd freed him from his chains, though his eyelids still lolled from the sedation.

I'm out, Luana signed, almost in devastation. Tears sparked in her eyes. Sierra tried to emit a beam of light, but her wings flickered like a flashlight.

"I'm done, too," Sophia said. "If I heal anymore, you'll have to carry me out of here. I need time to recover."

Their magic had done enough to get the dragon conscious. But we couldn't get that door open wide enough for the dragon to fit through. It would have to come down completely.

I put a hand on the Familiar's side. "You're free now. I know you're tired, but we're gonna need your help to get out of here, buddy. The lock's broken. We just need a little push."

The dragon shook its head. It gave a small moan before it backed up, preparing to charge. I yanked the girls out of the way just as the dragon lowered its horns and ran forward. It slammed its horns into the door, and it fell forward with a crash. The dragon stumbled out of it, and we followed.

The dragon shouted with ecstasy once it was free. It spread its wings and groaned, wincing due to the pain. The cell wasn't big enough for him to stretch his wings, so this was probably the first time he'd opened them in months.

"Let's move onto the next cell," Sophia said, and we slipped into another, one that Squeaks had already broken the lock on.

Most of the creatures weren't heavily sedated. The Task Force really had been running out of noxite to keep them drugged. They were tired, but they could walk. Some could even fight. I thanked the ancestors they could, because we didn't have a backup plan to carry such big creatures out of here.

It wasn't all happy endings. A sea serpent we'd found in a cell was dead. It couldn't survive long outside of water, and there was no saving it. A lot of the Water creatures were like that. Being Toaqua, it broke my heart to see them like that, but there was nothing we could do. We had to save the ones we knew could make it.

A well-known cooing caught my attention at the other end of the cave. That had to be Eirakari. The lock to her cell had been broken, but the door was twisted. It had jumped off its track, and therefore, was impossible to slide.

Somebody was trying. Drew yanked at the door, angrily trying to get Eirakari out. I reached forward to help him pull the door aside, bending the iron back. I felt the noxite draining my powers the moment I touched the door, but Drew wasn't giving up, so neither was I. Together, Drew and I were able to force our way in. Eirakari was waiting inside, but she wasn't the only one. Drew's Familiar, Ace, was also there. He barked happily and spun in circles the moment he saw Drew.

"Ace!" Drew flung his arms around his German Shepherd. Ace licked Drew's face in joy.

Eirakari huddled in the corner of her cell, frightened of the noise outside. I scratched her behind the horns. "How are you doing, Eira? Ready to see Maddie?"

Eira let out a low moan. I used the bolt cutters to free her from her chains, before I released Ace. Eira wrapped her wings around me in a hug, while Ace jumped up and down.

"How do we get them out of here?" Drew asked. "That door's not moving, and Eira's not big enough to charge it down."

Drew's question was answered when the head of a dragon burst through the iron door. It was the same male we'd freed on our first try. The dragon bellowed for Eirakari to follow, and the dragoness romped through it.

Eirakari was the last dragon we had to free. All the cells were busted. My mouth fell open when I saw someone I knew step out of the doorway Luana and Sophia were prying back.

"Hudson?" I asked in shock. He was the Koigni guy who'd been Defortai and reassigned to Biyami after he'd bonded with a giant snail. He looked pretty rough. He was filthy, and I could see the outline of bones that jutted out of his clothes due to starvation. He had this crazy look in his eyes that was somewhat off-putting. "What are you doing here?"

"I've been in here for a couple of weeks," Hudson admitted, and a blush rose to his cheeks. "I, uh... tried to sneak in to break Gooby out, and got stuck in his cell. The Task Force thought it'd be funny to keep me here."

I facepalmed. Only Hudson.

"Why would they keep Gooby in here, though?" Imogen questioned. "I mean, he's small, isn't he?"

There was the creaking of iron busting apart. Sophia and Luana ran out of the way. Squeaks' beak dropped, and Sassy craned her head backward. Many of the dragons in the cave swiveled their heads to watch as a massive Familiar slid free.

Gooby had a growth spurt. A *major* growth spurt. The giant snail was now twenty feet tall, and just as long. His feelers reached out, scanning the cave walls. Hudson climbed onto his Familiar's neck and sat just before the shell, giving a major grin.

"You haven't seen him in a while, but he's grown a bit." Hudson patted the snail's shell. "I think it's time we showed the Task Force what he's made out of."

"*Ancestor's cock!*" A wail came from across the cavern, along with a lion's roar.

That was Doya for sure. She'd been overwhelmed. She ran into the cavern, blasting fireballs off behind her. They took down three soldiers at a time, but the reinforcements had arrived. Three brigades of Task Force members flooded into the tunnel, outnumbering us. They weren't carrying noxite guns, which meant their elements were shoot-to-kill.

A Task Force general at the start of the brigade screeched to a halt when he saw Drew. I couldn't see his expression behind his helmet, but by his tone, I knew he was smiling.

"Back for more, boy?" he asked. "You must've liked it when I broke your legs."

"You can go to hell," Drew seethed. Ace bared his teeth and growled lowly.

The general emitted a low laugh. "Torturing you was the highlight of my job. I got pleasure from taking off your fingernails one by one. Now that you're all healed up, I can't wait to start all over again."

Drew gave a rageful cry. He shot out a jet of fire from his fist, but the Task Force general jumped out of the way.

It gave Ace just enough time to fire up.

Before our very eyes, Ace began changing. His fur became fire, and his eyes shone red with all the fury of hell. Flames roared off of him so large, I could feel the heat from here. Drew's eyes widened in shock as he watched his Familiar morph.

His Familiar wasn't a dog at all. Ace was a hellhound.

Ace bounded forward. The footprints he made singed the stone and made it turn black. Ace pounced. He dove his fangs into the general's jugular, and the general screamed in agony. The hellhound's flames lit up the Task Force member's uniform and licked at the helmet, melting it around his face. The screams died out.

In seconds, skin and muscle turned to ash, and all that was left of the Task Force general was bones, his singed skeleton giving off a gross smell that permeated the whole cave.

Drew stroked Ace's head, his fingers fanning over the flames. "Good boy." Ace barked and licked his hand.

One down, dozens more to go. The dragons that had been captured turned and faced the Task Force brigades, preparing to die fighting rather than be captured again.

Hudson's teeth were bared. He pointed to the Task Force. "Okay, Gooby. Let's bring it on."

Gooby lunged out. The snail opened his mouth. I, along with several other people, gasped aloud as Gooby enveloped three Task Force members into his giant mouth. There was a horrible crunching sound, and then silence as the snail swallowed the soldiers in one bite.

Holy shit. I was never making fun of Hudson ever again.

The Task Force freaked as Gooby moved in. The cops shot their elements at Hudson and the snail, but the spells merely bounced off his shell, sending elements ricocheting in every direction. Gooby continued to scarf up Task Force like they were his last meal. I watched with revulsion, while Sophia cringed and the rest of them observed with disgusted faces.

Hudson was laughing like a fucking madman as his Familiar devoured the Task Force alive. He was getting a kick out of this.

It was terrifying that a creature who had basically been a big joke at the start of the year had become a man-eating monster. Hudson and his Familiar had been the laughingstock of the school only a few months ago, but nobody was laughing now. The Task Force that tried to run got stuck in the snail's thick mucus trails. It caught them like goo, trapping them so they couldn't escape. Gooby slid over them, and the soldiers were sucked into the snail's waiting mouth.

Doya watched in appreciation, tapping her chin. "Hm. Perhaps I under-estimated him."

The Task Force created a traffic jam as they dove out of Gooby's way in an attempt to escape. The snail reared back. When he opened his mouth, flames erupted, engulfing the Task Force in one breath.

No fucking way. He was breathing *fire*!

"Run!" I grabbed Sophia's wrist and pulled her along behind me. Hudson wasn't careful about where his Familiar was shooting fire. It was going everywhere. The guy was a loose cannon.

The dragons had begun a stampede in the chaos. Eirakari pressed close to the wall so she wouldn't get crushed. I looked for an exit, but the Task Force's fight with Hudson had blocked off the main cavern, and the one we'd come through earlier was too small to fit dragons through.

"Imogen! We need a way out!" I called.

Imogen took a few deep breaths. She looked upward and threw her arms above her head. She gritted her teeth as she concentrated. Above us, cracks appeared in the rock. Plants grew through them, making the rock overhead unstable. Her vines weaved throughout the cave ceiling, forcing the rocks apart. Sassy helped, her vines reaching up to the ceiling to pull rocks away from the hole she was creating.

When the hole was big enough for the first dragon to fly through, Eirakari left. She flew upward, crawling her way through the opening. More dragons followed as the hole became bigger and bigger. Imogen collapsed to her knees in exhaustion, and the last dragon slipped through.

"Good job, Im," Jonah said. He lifted her into his arms, carrying her closely to his chest. "You're just as strong as the rest of us."

Imogen's head collapsed against Jonah's shoulder. Sassy had passed out. Squeaks hefted her onto her back and flew out the hole. The resistance members that were Yapluma began flying people out.

"Hudson, come on!" Sophia screamed.

Hudson wasn't listening. His maniacal laughter rang throughout the caves as Gooby continued his carnage.

Okay, it was official. Kid was nuts. He was on his own.

"He can take care of himself! Let's go!" I cried.

Jonah didn't wait for Sophia to argue. He used his Air powers to fly us upward, out through the escape Imogen had created. The dragons, and the rest of the resistance, were waiting in the forest beside the cave system. We landed beside them. Jonah didn't put Imogen down, though Trace rushed over.

"Is she going to be okay?" Trace worried as he observed Imogen's features.

"She just needs a minute," Jonah said. "I've got her."

Sam had reappeared. He was riding Zaria, who had a saddlebag flung over her back. I was glad to see the two of them had been reunited. The black alicorn's fur glimmered dark blue as she tossed her head.

"We've got all the Familiars out," Sam breathed. "Now it's just a matter of holding off the Task Force until we get them back to *Hok'evale*."

"Did you find Lira's Familiar?" I asked.

He nodded and opened the saddlebag. Lira's Familiar, a small blue ferret, was resting inside. I hoped she lasted long enough to get her back to Lira.

"Where are the others?" Sam should've had a whole team with him.

He frowned. "Tabitha took Lira back. She collapsed before we got to the caves. Wyatt managed to free Tuskin and Tabitha's Familiar, so they made it out."

"What about Maddox?" I insisted.

Sam dropped his head. "His Familiar died while trying to escape. Maddox didn't make it."

A pit grew in my stomach. I didn't ask for details. I didn't need to know— the only thing that mattered was Maddox... just like Jones... was gone.

"Everyone follow me!" I shouted. "We have to get to the vantage point."

Our team walked through the forest, while the dragons flew overhead. About a half a mile away, Julian was waiting in a clearing to lead the rest of the dragons to safety. Julian saw me coming and roared a greeting, pushing his head into me affectionately. I almost fell over.

"I'm okay, Jules. Any Task Force around?" I asked.

Julian huffed and shook his head. It wouldn't stay that way for long.

Jake and Cade were both in the clearing. Jonah put Imogen down, and she fell against Cade. He held her close while Jonah embraced Jake.

"I thought I lost you," Jonah said in a thick voice.

Jake gave a humored noise, though it sounded... off. "Never."

Sabor helped Squeaks put Sassy down. Arabelle curled against her, purring.

Imogen put a hand to her temple. Sassy came to and padded to her Elementai's side. "I'm okay. I can walk," Imogen forced out. "Though I don't think I could grow a plant to save my life."

"Magic's not needed. We're almost home free," I said. "We just have to get back."

Jake didn't respond. Jonah squeezed Jake's hand. "Babe, something's on your mind. I can tell."

Jake's eye slightly twitched. "I've received intel that Oleander's Familiar is somewhere within the area."

"Skylis?" Jonah asked.

"No," Jake said. "His real Familiar, the one he's bonded to, not the one he's got under mind control. We think the creature is nearby."

"What? You mean, the caves?" Imogen squeaked.

"The Task Force Headquarters. It's to the south, within a mile of here." Jake scowled. "But we don't know what building, and it's too uncertain to risk a team going in to search."

"Fuck that," I started. "If there's a chance we can kill Oleander, we're taking it." We were supposed to go back with Julian and the others, but this was too good an opportunity to waste.

"Where'd you get the intel from?" Sophia asked.

Jake scowled. "Jaymin Riske."

Jonah's jaw dropped. "Babe, you can't be *seriously* considering listening to her."

"Jaymin wants to win this war as badly as we do," Jake said. "And though I don't trust her, she wouldn't lie about something like this. She despises Oleander with a passion."

"Yeah, and she wants him gone, so she can seek power for herself," Imogen grumbled.

Sophia chewed her lip as she worked things over. "Jaymin Riske or not, we have to believe her. There might be a chance to stop this war for good."

Jake shook his head. "No. It's been decided. We only have a shred of information. That's not enough intelligence to act upon."

Sophia came forward. "I'll do it. We're not walking out on this."

"You're the chosen one, Sophia. We can't risk losing you," Jake argued.

"I'm the one who's prophesied to bring an end to this war. I have a chance to end it now," Sophia said firmly. "You have no choice but to let me go."

Jake couldn't argue. His mouth became thin as he said, "Fine. But you're not going alone."

"Of course she's not. I'm going with her," I stated.

"And me," Imogen offered weakly, though she wavered on her feet.

"I'll come along too, as always," Jonah added.

Jake's eyes looked sad. "Why is it whenever I have you, you always slip back out of my grasp?"

"I'm high maintenance, baby," Jonah purred. "You knew that when you met me."

"You're bringing me," Doya said. "No exceptions."

"No, Mother," Sophia said. "Most of these creatures are too weak to fight. They'll need you if they're spotted by the Task Force."

Madame Doya's lip twitched. "I will not leave you alone in a time like this."

"I'm Eleanor Doya's daughter. I'll be fine," Sophia insisted. "And I don't like leaving Ava-Marie alone for so long. If something happens to Liam and me, I want someone back in *Hok'evale* who can help protect her."

Madame Doya hesitated. "Very well. I suppose you're right."

"Same goes for you, Cade." Imogen sighed. "We need strong Elementai to get those dragons back."

"You're tired, Imogen. I won't leave your side," he protested.

"She's got the Storm Lord," Jonah said. "I'll die before they lay a finger on her."

"You can't go out there. You're exhausted," Cade argued.

A twinge of guilt ran through me. I knew Imogen should head back to *Hok'evale,* but we needed her brains if we were going to figure out where Oleander's Familiar was, and quickly.

"Cade, I need you at my side," Jake said. "I know it's difficult leaving her, but understand I am in your same position."

A muscle worked in Cade's jaw as he looked between Jake and Jonah, then back to Imogen. He was trying to decide between his loyalty to the resistance and his need to protect Imogen.

Imogen's eyes were pleading. Finally, he said, "Fine. But if you guys aren't back in a few hours, I'm coming to look for you."

"As am I," Doya added sternly.

"Go." I glanced behind us. "Before the Task Force catches up."

Reluctantly, Jake climbed onto Sabor. Cade swung onto Arabelle, while Doya and Naomi lifted themselves onto the male dragon we'd freed. Amelia and Trace took a singular dragon, while Drew and Ace hopped onto Julian.

Luana swung herself on behind Sam. She wrapped his arms around his waist, and he blushed. Zaria gave a playful nicker.

Julian headbutted me. I gave him a pat. "See you soon, Jules."

He growled and lifted his wings. The dragons followed him as Julian took to the air. Soon, their wings blocked out the skies as they soared toward home.

The surrounding forest was quiet. Jonah sighed, almost in relaxation. "Isn't this *nice?* We've finally got the *original* gang to go back in the field, no distractions included."

"Focus, guys," I said. "We're on a time limit."

"Agreed," Sophia said nervously. "The Task Force is bound to show up any moment. We should move."

"I can't walk another step, honestly," Imogen said. "I need help."

"Up you go." Jonah lifted Imogen onto Squeaks' back. She and Sassy rode while the rest of us walked through the woods. We wandered around the cave system, instead of through it, as we knew the remaining Task Force was searching inside.

"The Task Force headquarters will be crawling with cops," Jonah said.

"Yes, but most of them won't be there. They're in the caves trying to find us, or elsewhere in Kinpago," Imogen pointed out. "If we hurry, we might be able to get in and out."

Jonah's tone was anxious as we walked. "Guys... what if Oleander's Familiar is something really terrifying?"

"That doesn't make sense. He wouldn't have captured Skylis if it was," I argued. "It might be dangerous, but it can't be anything special. Otherwise, he'd be parading it around."

"I don't get how Skylis is controlled by Oleander, anyway," Sophia said. "I know it's the collar, but a creature that powerful has to be enslaved by strong magic."

"When I was looking through his files at Tribal Headquarters, the collar instructions said it was a mind-control device," I commented. "Don't know where he'd get it."

"Mind-control is a vampire gift," Imogen stated. "That collar was probably made by Midnighters."

Jonah blanched. "Oleander has *vampires* working for him now?"

"Vampires don't work for anyone," Imogen said. "They get paid, and a device like that needs to be recharged. If Oleander is running out of funds, he won't have the cash to pay the Midnighters, and eventually the magic on that collar will run out. Skylis will hopefully turn on him then."

"That'd be the fucking day," I muttered. But I wasn't counting on it.

The Task Force headquarters came into view as we left the forest. The military base was set up in a square, barbed wire fencing circling the perimeter. Our vantage point was on a cliff side overlooking the base. The camp had a few Task Force walking around it, but it seemed vacant except for one building.

"There," Imogen said. She pointed to a small cabin on the military base. Several guards were stationed around it. "I'll bet anything that's where Oleander keeps his Familiar. Why else would it be so heavily guarded, when the rest of the buildings are vacant?"

"We need a distraction," Sophia whispered.

"Leave it to me," Jonah replied. He slipped into the trees. As we waited, we watched over the Task Force base. Sophia tilted her head as she observed a soldier wheel a motorbike past one of the mess halls. He placed it up against a wall and left it there.

"Liam, it's your bike," Sophia hushed. My eyes widened in realization as I recognized it. Holy shit, that *was* my bike. They must've found it after the battle of Orenda Academy, the bastards.

Imogen gave me a sympathetic look. "I'm sorry, Liam, but we can't retrieve it. It's too risky."

"I know." Still disappointing, though. That bike was one of the few things I had left of my dad, and it was in the Task Force's hands.

A lightning bolt crackled down from above. It struck one of the barracks, lighting it ablaze. There were shouts. The guards protecting the cabin left their posts and ran toward the hall, to help put the fire out.

"That was Jonah. Let's go," Imogen said. We slid down the embankment and to the barbed wire fencing. Sophia's fingers burned red, and she ran them along the fencing. The fence cut in half down the trail she'd created, leaving a hole big enough for us to slip through.

"Sorry, Squeaks, you gotta stay outside," Imogen said as she slid off. "Sassy, you should stay with her."

Sassy gave a lonesome call as Imogen slipped through the fence. Esis was the only Familiar that came with us.

Jonah reappeared. He squeezed himself through the hole. "That should keep them busy for a while."

"Not too long," I said. "Let's move."

We crouched down as we ran toward the cabin. There were guards around the back entrance. They turned their guns on us as they saw us coming, but I stopped their hearts, and they dropped to the ground.

I barely flinched when I took a life now. It was almost like second nature— I did it without thinking, like breathing.

It was something to worry about.

Jonah dragged the bodies to a nearby alleyway while we fiddled with the back door. The back entrance was locked, but I took some water from the air and froze the lock inside. The door burst, and we headed in.

This was some kind of headquarters for Oleander. His stuff was all over it. Tribal files, paperwork, and office supplies littered the desk inside.

On top of a cabinet was a small creature. The creature was a tiny rodent, a squirrel-mongoose hybrid called a raiju. It had soft brown fur and large black eyes that sparkled as they widened, with tiny paws and a fluffy tail.

Honestly, it looked a lot like Esis.

The raiju noticed us. It squeaked and jumped off the cabinet, running forward. It climbed onto the desk beside us and swished its tail, happy to see us. I bet the creature had been kept locked up in this office for who knew how long.

All of us paused. None of us said anything. We didn't expect Oleander's Familiar to be so small.

"Are you sure it's Oleander's?" Jonah asked. At Oleander's name, the raiju's ears perked up. It stood on its hind legs, sniffing the air. It was pretty much confirmation.

I started forward. "Let's get this over with."

I went to snatch the raiju, but it jumped backward, alarmed. Its little chest panted as he took me in. The raiju began quivering, and I reached out again. Esis gave a trill and sailed off Sophia's shoulder. He planted himself in front of the raiju and spread his arms, giving loud squeaks.

"Esis doesn't want us to kill it," Sophia marveled. The raiju cowered behind Esis, who stood his ground.

"Are you kidding me? This is the Familiar of the most evil fucking man alive!" I burst. "We have no choice. Ouch!"

Esis had bitten my hand when I'd tried to grab the raiju again. That hurt, the little bastard.

"Maybe we should listen to him," Sophia mused. "You said yourself Esis has good instincts."

"Esis doesn't understand," I shot back at her. "This has to be done."

Jonah seemed torn. "Does it, though?"

"Come *on*, guys! We shouldn't be sitting here arguing about killing Oleander because this thing is cute!" I snapped.

The raiju lay against the desk and shook. It looked really pathetic, but I refused to let it tug at my heartstrings. This was war. Some terrible shit had to be done.

"It can't even defend itself," Jonah said quietly.

Esis made loud squeaks and shook his arms, pointing at Sophia, and then at me. Sophia tilted her head. She didn't get what he was trying to say, and neither did I.

Imogen put a hand to her chin. "We could take it back to the resistance. Use it as a bargaining chip."

"What's the point of that? We kill it now, the war is over!" I hissed.

"There's no guarantee that if we kill Oleander, the war is done," Jonah argued. "The other Elders still want to wipe us out."

"But it'll be a heavy blow," I insisted. "We'll have the advantage."

"Jonah might be right," Imogen said slowly. "Taking it prisoner and using it as a hostage might be the better move."

"Regardless, Oleander needs to die," I said. "And if we kill him, his creature dies, too. So sparing it is irrelevant."

"We need to be smart about this and strategize," Imogen argued. "Using this creature as bait might be a way to get Oleander to agree to a truce. That way, no one else has to die, in battle or otherwise. If we kill this creature now, Oleander will die but the war might continue."

I gave a skeptical noise. "If you think Oleander is going to agree to a stalemate, you're delusional. That man wants us eradicated."

"For his Familiar he might," Jonah spoke up. "That's a bond that goes deeper than anything, and he knows his life is on the line if we have his creature. It doesn't always have to end in violence."

"Jonah, your stupid morals aren't going to help us!" I shouted back, and Jonah cringed.

"Don't be like that! You *always* want to go with the hard call!" Imogen protested.

"Yeah, because I'm a chief," I shot at her. "That's my job, to make the hard choices no one else wants to."

"I'll do it," Sophia volunteered, and our argument broke. "I'm the chosen one. This is my decision."

Esis' face fell. She picked him up and moved him aside, before she faced the raiju. Her face softened. "I'm sorry, little guy."

The raiju whimpered as Sophia raised a fireball. She took aim.

It was then an explosion rocked the ground beneath us. We staggered. It wasn't close enough to harm us, but the windows in the cabin shattered. Someone was setting off bombs in the camp.

The raiju bolted. It ran throughout the cabin, bouncing off furniture.

"Grab it!" I cried. Sophia shot fireballs after the creature. I flung water balls, while Jonah whipped out his Air.

All of us missed. The raiju jumped onto a chair, then slipped out the broken window. It ran, vanishing out of our sight.

"Fucking *dammit!*" I roared. I kicked the desk, and it skittered to the side. We had it in our grasp, and a moment of indecision had ruined our chances.

"What the hell was that?" Jonah gasped. We could smell smoke coming in from the barracks nearby.

"Let's not stick around long enough to find out. Come on!" Imogen shouted.

We ran out of the cabin. My eyes searched the area for the raiju, but I didn't see it anywhere. The creature was long gone.

The Task Force base was in chaos. Several buildings had exploded, and fire was overtaking the campus. Task Force soldiers ran everywhere, trying to control the flames. We pressed against the cabin to avoid being spotted. My eyes were glued to the hole in the fence, but we couldn't slip through it without being seen.

"In here." Sophia ran toward the nearest building, and we followed. It was a nearby barrack, void of Task Force. The recruits were out battling the fires.

But the barracks weren't completely empty. Two blond-haired boys, ages twelve and seventeen, were setting up *fucking explosives* around the barracks. Sophia gasped as she recognized who they were.

Imogen's eyes popped out of her head at the sight of her brothers. "Are you *kidding* me?! What are you two doing here?"

"Jaymin said we could help!" Soren yelled. He didn't stop to confront Imogen, just kept setting up explosives like nothing was wrong. He was the oldest of the two brothers, but even though he was almost of age, he didn't belong here. The kid had no idea what he was getting into.

"I told you to stay home! You're not ready!" Imogen seethed.

"Stop telling us we're too young!" Roland burst. "We can do this!"

My insides boiled with rage. It was like Jaymin Riske to use child soldiers to further her cause. The bitch knew no bounds.

"We've already placed explosives all over the barracks," Soren shot back. "All we have to do is set them off like the rest."

"You need to get out of here, before the place goes up in smoke!" Imogen cried.

"We can do this!" Roland said. "We're capable, we—"

Boom!

Fire billowed around us. Sophia instinctively formed a shield, but though she tried, her magic didn't reach the boys in time.

Imogen's scream shattered the air. The barracks crumbled inward. A beam fell, smashing against Sophia's shield. It broke, and the four of us were forced apart, Imogen and Jonah on one side and Sophia and I on another. I pushed Sophia out of the way of a heavy block of concrete and crawled over her body, protecting her from the blast.

The explosion took seconds, but it felt like an eternity. When the building finally stopped crumbling, I looked up. Part of the ceiling was still intact, but most of it was rubble around us, blocking our way from reaching the rest of our team.

Esis gave a scared chitter. He'd clung to Sophia during the blast, and was alive, but scared.

My ears didn't ring. Sophia's shield had protected our hearing from the blast. I was still collecting my bearings as the smoke cleared, putting the pieces together.

Jaymin's team had set off another explosive device with the boys still inside.

The boys were already dead. I knew that. We'd all seen it.

Poor Roland had been blown to pieces.

Soren's voice came out choked and gasping. "I'm... sorry, Imogen."

Through a gap in the destruction, I saw Imogen clutching Soren. His chest had been split open. His blood soaked her clothes as she whispered, "You're gonna make it, you're gonna make it."

Esis slipped out of Sophia's grasp. He writhed through the small opening in the rubble, to Soren's side. By the time he reached them, Soren had already drawn his last breath. Imogen was wailing in grief.

"Esis, it won't help," Sophia choked out. Esis either didn't hear, or didn't listen. I watched through a tiny gap as Esis put his paws on Soren's chest, his blue eyes narrowing in concentration.

Nothing happened. Esis' little mouth dropped open. He tried again, but though his paws glowed white, Soren didn't stir.

Esis stepped back and gasped, almost in shock. Little guy didn't understand what death was. He didn't know it was permanent. I'd seen him try to heal people who'd died before.

As his ears drooped, he drew his paw away, and the glowing faded. His lip trembled as his blue eyes dripped tears.

"Liam! Sophia!" Jonah was viciously trying to clear the rubble to get to us. As he moved concrete and bricks, I heard the creaking of the ceiling overhead.

"Jonah, stop!" I cried. "If you keep moving shit around, the whole building might topple in!"

Jonah stopped. I could still hear the sound of his ragged breathing, on the edge of panic.

"What do I do?" Jonah asked.

"Get yourselves out! Sophia and I will find another way!"

"I won't leave them," Imogen sobbed. I knew she was still holding Soren's body close.

"You have to, Im!" I listened to Jonah forcibly dragging her away. Another beam came down. I yanked Sophia aside before she could be crushed by it.

"Esis, come on!" Sophia called. Esis wiggled his way to us. He jumped into Sophia's arms and clung to her shirt.

"Come on, Soph. Let's try to dig our way out." I began moving things aside carefully, though my arms didn't seem to work right. They ached, and every movement made my back surge with pain.

I was so tired. I wanted to give up. The only instinct that kept driving me on was an urge to preserve Sophia's life at all costs, and a promise to myself I wouldn't leave my daughter fatherless.

Sophia and I finally pulled ourselves out of the wreckage. She helped me to stand. We searched for Imogen and Jonah, but didn't see them anywhere.

The whole base was going up in flames from the explosions. Sophia turned on the spot. Task Force were coming in from all surroundings, summoned back here to handle the situation. There was no way out. Any second, we'd be caught.

I spotted the bike. It was a short distance away. I grabbed Sophia's hand and broke into a run. We were feet away from it when I felt someone grab me by the collar and yank me down.

"Liam!" Sophia screamed, and Esis cried out.

A Task Force member had grabbed me around the neck and forced me down. He tried to climb on top of me, but I threw him off. I didn't have time to scramble to my feet before he yanked me to the earth again, trying to detain me.

"Start the bike!" I cried. I turned over on my back. The Task Force member had lost his helmet and was bleeding from a cut on the face. His teeth were clenched in rage.

"You kids have caused enough trouble," he growled. "I'm ending it all."

I heard the engine fire up. The Task Force member put me in a choke hold. I began seeing stars as he deprived me of oxygen.

I heard Sophia cry out my name again, and it gave me the last boost of energy I needed. I forced the soldier off of me. He grabbed my ankle, in a last-ditch attempt to contain me. He was strong, and I was exhausted. If he got over me again, no way would I get back up.

"I'll make it painless, kid," he grunted. "Stop resisting!"

"Eat... a bag... of dicks!" I kicked the Task Force member in the face as hard as I could. I heard a crunching sound as my foot connected. He cried out and fell to the side. I got up and ran, slinging a leg over the bike. My hands curled around the handlebars.

"Hold on to me," I said breathlessly. Sophia wrapped her arms around my middle, and I felt Esis' claws latch onto my jacket.

I revved the bike and shot forward. The bike kicked from zero to sixty in a matter of seconds. I rode the bike through the headquarters while explosions were going off behind us. I could literally feel the heat as it emitted from buildings, fire blazing out from the structures in monstrous infernos.

Sophia calmed the flames so we could drive through. Task Force members jumped out of the way to avoid being run over as I headed for the main exit.

A battalion of Task Force stood in front of the main gate. They raised their hands, elements brewing in their palms as we grew close. They began firing them off, but I weaved the bike so their shots wouldn't connect.

The battalion wasn't going to move. If I tried to drive through them, I'd crash the bike, and we'd be done for. But the main gate was our only way out. If I drove back, the explosions would kill us both.

Sophia's hold tightened on me— she didn't think we'd make it. Fuck all if I wasn't going to try.

My eyes landed on a ramp near the main gate. It was meant for loading supplies, but we could use it as a jump.

Most people wouldn't have the balls to try something like that, but I was a crazy motherfucker, and I was going to do it. I pushed the bike to its limit until the engine was whining in protest. We took the ramp. Sophia squeezed me, crushing the air from my lungs as we sailed over the Task Force. The jump was ten feet long. I heard Esis give a high-pitched scream behind me as the ground drew near.

It was a rough landing. The bike skittered to the side, but I saved it at the last second. The Task Force was too dumbfounded to shoot after us as I drove the bike back onto the main road, toward the beach.

We could ride the ocean all the way to *Hok'evale*. Ancestors, I hoped this thing had enough gas. Sophia's hold had lightened on me, but I could feel her ragged breathing against my back.

When we got to the beach, I slowed the bike to a stop and looked back to Sophia. "Everyone all right?"

Esis' fur was poofy all around him. He made a grumbling noise.

Sophia swept her hair back. "I'm fine. I can't believe we made it out of there. Do you think Jonah and Imogen...?"

She drifted off, unable to ask the question.

"We'll find out when we get back to *Hok'evale*." Not much more I could say.

I drove the bike onto the waves. I had enough magical energy to suspend the bike on the ocean's surface, but it was all I could do at the moment. Water rushed out in two equal arcs on the sides of the wheel as I pushed the bike to go as fast as it could.

The engine sputtered and died just as we drove the bike onto *Hok'evale's* beach. Sophia clambered off. I pushed the bike to my mom's house, where I rested it against the porch.

We were supposed to regroup in the town square once the mission was over. Sophia and I rushed back into the village, where hundreds of Familiars were being reunited with their Elementai. Relief flooded through me when I spotted Jonah, though I felt sick when I realized Imogen wasn't with him. Squeaks was at his side, though her head was hung low.

Jonah's shoulders dropped when he saw us. "You guys are safe. Thank the ancestors."

"Where's Im?" Sophia asked.

His face fell. "She and Sassy are with her family. She had to tell them the news."

So she was okay... on the outside. Inside, she was torn apart. Two of her brothers had died right before her eyes, so soon after she'd gotten Trace back.

Thinking of losing Ez like that...

My throat got tight, and I pushed the thought out of my head. I couldn't bear to consider it.

Sophia frowned. "Do you think that she'll relapse?"

"I don't see how she could," Jonah said with a sigh. "There's no nightshade available."

"That doesn't mean there aren't other drugs, and she's at a vulnerable point in her recovery," Sophia pointed out.

"We'll be there for her," I offered. "We'll do our best to make sure she doesn't slip back."

I looked at Jonah. "How'd you guys make it out, anyway?"

"Doya and Cade came back for us," Jonah said. "Doya about wrung my neck when she realized Sophia wasn't with us. You should go see her."

Sophia stroked her Familiar. "Come on, Esis."

As Sophia vanished into the crowd, Jonah dropped his voice. "I didn't tell Imogen yet, because I think she'll lose her mind if she finds out. Jake told me that Jaymin Riske... she got away."

"What?" I snarled. "How did that happen?"

"I don't know. She vanished after the explosions. The resistance sent people to chase after her, but Jake doesn't think they're gonna find her." Jonah stared at the ground. "She's gonna get away with it."

I hoped Jaymin had been taken out by one of her own bombs, and we had yet to recover the body, but I wasn't that optimistic.

Sometimes, fate could be so cruel. Imogen's brothers were dead. Jaymin Riske was responsible for their deaths.

And she was nowhere to be found.

sophia

EIGHT

A week had passed since we'd saved the Familiars. For the most part, *Hok'evale* had changed for the better. People had been reunited with their Familiars, and all seemed fine... for now. But things weren't okay for everyone, and it was as if Ava-Marie knew it. Her cries cut through the stillness of the morning, tearing my heart apart.

"It's going to be okay," I whispered, though it sounded like a lie.

I cradled Ava-Marie in my arms, rocking her back and forth on a chair in the living room. It was early morning, and the sun hadn't even risen yet. Liam was still asleep in the bedroom, and I was doing all I could to calm my wailing child.

"Ava, please. Daddy needs to sleep. He has important work to do this morning. It's going to be all right. Mommy's here," I promised. I'd never let anything hurt her.

I couldn't say the same for my friends. Imogen had been devastated by the death of her brothers. This was different from when she grieved for Trace and Cade. She'd seen her younger brothers die with her own eyes— held their bodies in her arms. There was no chance they were coming back. Ever.

Imogen wasn't the only one struggling. Liam had been working long days, dealing with the aftermath of the fight— from conducting funerals as chief, to working with Jake and Jonah on military strategy. We were preparing for the Elders to retaliate at any time. It wasn't like our location was a secret anymore, not after the battle that ensued on Christmas Eve.

But Luana hadn't reported any suspicious activity surrounding her shield. The Elders had lost a lot of Task Force members recently, and they were running low on supplies. Not to mention their headquarters had just been demolished. Their numbers still far exceeded ours, but they needed time to recover, too. We'd be ready for them when they did.

My training involved daily lessons with Luana, learning how to help her shield the valley. It was different from any other magic I'd used before, because it was cast at a distance. It was harder to control magic I couldn't see with my own two eyes.

Ava-Marie wailed again, and I pulled her closer to my chest.

"Earth, Water, Fire, and Air..." I began to sing the ancestor's song. *"Gifted to us by the breath of a prayer."*

Ava-Marie began to settle. I continued singing and rocking her until she drifted off. I was so exhausted and wanted to return to bed, but I worried about waking her, so I didn't move.

Soon, I heard stirring from the bedroom. Esis walked into the living room, rubbing his eyes. I could hear Liam starting to get out of bed.

"Hey, buddy," I whispered softly as Esis jumped onto the arm of my chair. "How'd you sleep?"

Esis responded by yawning widely. In other words, Ava-Marie had kept him up, too. I scratched him behind the ears, and he leaned into me, purring. He rested his head on my shoulder and stared down at Ava-Marie.

"The sleep deprivation is worth it, though, isn't it?" I asked him. "Family is so important. She's perfect."

Esis chittered in agreement.

"Hey, *pawee*," Liam said in a tired voice as he left the bedroom. The sunlight had just started to fill the living room.

"Good morning," I said quietly, so I wouldn't wake Ava-Marie.

Liam leaned down and kissed me on the lips. "How is she?"

He gazed down at his daughter in admiration.

"Sleeping, for now," I said. "How'd it go last night?"

Liam hadn't made it back from work until after I'd gone to bed.

He sighed. "Cade and I had a chat about Imogen."

My eyebrows shot up. "How's she doing?"

I hadn't seen her yesterday, as she was tied up with the military strategy team like the rest of my friends. Even Doya had joined the team, as Jake had promoted her after she proved herself useful in freeing the Familiars.

Liam frowned. "Not well. Carter's pulling her from the strategy team for a while, until she gets back on track."

I shifted uncomfortably in my chair. "What do you mean?"

Liam sat on the couch and raked his fingers through his hair. "She's dead-set on revenge against Jaymin. Every suggestion she makes ties into tracking Jaymin down. It's distracting the team from the real issues."

"Jaymin *is* a real issue," I pointed out. "But I get what you're saying. We have bigger problems to deal with."

Liam drew another deep breath. "Thing is, Im knows she's going down a dark road again. She agreed with Carter that she needed to take a step back. Cade's afraid she's going to start using again."

"She won't," I stated confidently, but I wasn't sure. I'd never been addicted to nightshade. I didn't really know what it was like.

"She's taking precautionary measures this time," Liam said. "Along with a leave from work, she's doubling her therapy sessions. I think you should visit her today."

"I will," I promised.

"Thanks, *pawee*." Liam stood and placed a kiss on my forehead. "Make sure to send her my love... and maybe some cupcakes. Cupcakes make everything better."

I crinkled my nose at him. "Unless you scrape the frosting off before you eat them."

He rolled his eyes. "I thought we agreed you'd stop picking on me for that."

"Not that one," I teased. "You'll never live that one down."

Liam shook his head. "I love you, Soph."

I smiled. "I love you, too."

It wasn't long before Liam left for work. I fed Ava-Marie and was just changing her into a cute outfit with unicorns on it when Luana arrived for our lesson.

Change of plans, I told her. *We're going to visit Imogen today.*

Is she okay? Luana asked.

She needs us, I signed.

Luana helped me bundle Ava-Marie up, and we left the house with our Familiars. We hit up *The Falcon's Nest* for takeout, then stopped by *Jaguar Confections* to pick up some cupcakes. Each was powdered with a fine edible glitter that was enchanted by the Arcanea sorceress who ran the shop. The glitter changed colors in a mesmerizing display.

When we arrived at Cade and Imogen's apartment, Imogen was alone. She answered the door. Her eyes were bloodshot, and she clutched a clump of used tissues in her fist. She wore an untied bathrobe over her pajamas.

I'd become attuned to her bloodshot eyes ever since we found out she was doing drugs, and I had a moment of panic. But I quickly realized it was because she'd been crying, not because she was high.

"What are you doing here?" Imogen asked, signing as she spoke. Sassy yipped in excitement when she saw Esis in the doorway.

"We came to bring you breakfast," I stated simply. I placed the takeout bag in her hand and stepped inside without asking for an invitation.

"Um... that was nice," Imogen said, sounding unsure about the gesture.

Luana followed behind me. Sassy barked as Esis rushed over to her, and Sierra fluttered onto her head. The three started chasing each other around the apartment.

Cade's apartment looked different from the last time I'd seen it. I hadn't been over here much, since we had more room at our place. The ping-pong table was moved over to the edge of the room, and there was a lot more color. A tapestry with floral designs all over it was hung on the wall, and there were matching throw pillows on the couch. A beautiful flower arrangement sat on the kitchen counter, but it was slightly wilted, as if reflecting Imogen's grief.

I walked over to the couch and dropped my diaper bag, then pulled Ava-Marie out of the cradleboard I'd been carrying her in. I laid a blanket on the ground and set her on top of it. "Tummy time!" I announced. She stared up at me with wide eyes.

Imogen and Luana both sat. Imogen reached into the bag we'd brought and handed out breakfast sandwiches.

Thank you, Luana signed when she took hers.

"How are you doing, Im?" I asked, settling into the couch beside Luana.

Imogen unwrapped her sandwich and took a bite. She went silent for a few moments, but didn't seem like she was enjoying the food. It seemed like an excuse to mull over her answer.

Finally, she swallowed and set her breakfast aside on the end table. She signed while she spoke. "Not well, as you can imagine. I know the funeral was supposed to help me cope, but..."

"I get it, Im," I said sadly. "I went through the same thing with my grandparents."

I didn't say it out loud, but we all knew what I meant. Seeing someone die in front of you made it a hundred times harder to keep going.

"I'm not asking you to move on," I promised. "I don't think you ever really can. But please know we are here for you."

Imogen took a deep breath and wiped her nose with a tissue. "This isn't like last time. I don't want to hide from you guys. I don't want to do this alone. I want your help."

That's good! Luana signed.

Imogen frowned. "I just don't know how you *can* help."

There's a ritual we can try, Luana offered. *It's a blessing on the spirit.*

Imogen hesitated. "I— I don't think I'm ready to let my brothers go."

Of course not, Luana replied. *I'd never ask you to do that. But this might help you say goodbye.*

Imogen wiped at her eyes. "O-okay. I can try."

We finished our breakfast, but Imogen barely took a glance at the enchanted cupcakes. I left them on the counter for her to snack on later.

For the ritual, we'll need something to represent your brothers, Luana told Imogen. *Something you're willing to give up.*

Imogen pressed her finger to her chin, thinking. After a few moments, something sparked in her eyes. "I think I have something."

Imogen went into the kitchen and stood on her toes to reach high into one of the cupboards. She pulled down a mug that was shaped to look like a fox. Imogen teared up as she cradled it in her hands. "Soren and Roland brought this to me in rehab. It was a get-well gift."

My heart fell for her. "Im... are you sure you want to use that for the ritual?"

She sniffled, then nodded. "Yes. It's the one thing I have from both of them."

That will work perfectly, Luana told her.

Luana explained the ritual would have to take place outside, but she didn't tell us how it worked. Imogen didn't ask, just went to the bedroom to get dressed. I bundled up Ava-Marie again, and we left the apartment with our Familiars.

We walked up a path carved in the edge of the canyon and entered the forest surrounding *Hok'evale*. The village was long behind us when we finally stopped. The trees were thick, but the foliage was dull, as it was only the end of February. Above us, the clouds blocked out the sunlight.

This spot is perfect, Luana signed when we entered a small clearing. She lowered herself to her knees, and Sierra fluttered onto the branch of a black walnut tree nearby. Esis jumped off my shoulder and scurried up the tree to sit next to her. Sassy stopped alongside Imogen.

"How does the ritual work?" Imogen asked, kneeling beside Luana.

I removed Ava-Marie from the cradleboard and sat at the base of a tree to watch. My daughter slept soundlessly.

Luana gestured around the forest. It was really quiet, and though it was chilly out, it was peaceful. *The ritual requires a combination of Nivita and Anichi magic. It is a simple prayer, but if you open your heart to the ancestors, they will hear you. Choose a seed.*

Imogen glanced around the forest floor and picked up a walnut from next to her. Sassy sniffed it, then nodded in approval.

"I choose this one," Imogen said, holding it out to Luana.

Luana smiled sweetly. *I need you to dig a hole.*

Imogen placed the walnut into the mug to free up one of her hands, and she waved her palm over the ground. Her magic brushed dirt away, until there was a small but deep hole between the two of them.

Luana signed, *New life comes from death. Where one thing falls, another may grow, something beautiful and wondrous to honor what was lost. But you must be ready to allow your love for your brothers to change into something else— to transform into something that will benefit the world. But you must choose to allow your pain to grow into something beautiful, instead of something that will harm others.*

Imogen blinked at her. The forest was quiet.

Let us pray, Luana signed. She reached out her hands, and Imogen joined her hands with hers. Together, they cradled the mug and walnut in their hands.

For several long moments, there was nothing but silence as I observed. Then Imogen bowed her head and began to pray. "Dear ancestors, I pray for the strength to make it through this difficult time. My brothers are gone far too soon, and all I wanted to do was protect them."

As she spoke, tears beaded in her eyes. Luana's hands glowed a brilliant white, but Imogen didn't seem to notice as she squeezed her eyes shut tightly. My chest tightened as I watched.

"I am not the only one who's hurting," Imogen admitted to the ancestors. "I wish the best for all of *Hok'evale*. I pray that my brothers are taken care of in the Ancestral Lands. I pray that my parents are able to recover from their deaths. I pray for those who have lost anyone in this war on both sides, that we may see them again. I pray I will forge ahead in my recovery, and remain clean even while I am suffering. I pray for the strength to help the resistance win this war, for the guidance for each of us to do that which you desire of us. I pray that whatever happens, my brothers' deaths won't be in vain, and that something good might come out of this terrible war."

Imogen blinked her eyes open just in time to see Luana's Anichi magic swirl into wisps, encompassing the mug and the seed inside. Luana's eyebrows knitted together tightly in concentration. Her light seeped into the object, filling it as if infusing her magic inside.

"*Akotee et veni*," Imogen whispered.

Together, Imogen and Luana lowered the mug into the hole. Tears began to stream down Imogen's face, dripping into the soil. She didn't use her magic to cover the hole, but instead, filled it with her hands, burying the Spirit-infused mug with the seed inside. She smoothed her hands over the ground, as if the hole had never been there in the first place.

Luana reached out and rubbed Imogen's shoulder, then signed, *It's time to let go.*

Imogen nodded in understanding, as if she knew exactly what to do without instruction. Imogen let one last tear fall into the dirt, then got to her knees and backed up. Sassy quickly backpedaled a few steps to follow, and Luana came to stand by me.

Imogen closed her eyes and lifted her face toward the sky. At that moment, it was like she could control all the elements at once. Sunlight broke through the clouds and poured down through the canopy to touch her face. The wind blew, but it wasn't as cold as before. It was warm and pleasant— like a blessing from the ancestors.

As the wind picked up and the sun shined brighter, Imogen's power grew. A sapling poked up through the dirt where they'd planted the seed. At a record pace, the sapling sprouted and grew faster than I'd ever seen Imogen revive a plant before. Within seconds, it was as tall as Imogen, sprouting branches and leaves that glowed with the Spirit magic Luana had infused into the seed.

I scrambled to my feet, holding tightly to Ava-Marie as I watched in awe. The tree continued to grow, expanding out through the clearing and higher than our heads. Esis' jaw dropped from the branch he sat on, and Sierra fluttered her wings in excitement.

Branches continued to grow, and green leaves sprouted in a vibrant display. The tree trunk expanded until it was the thickest tree in the woods, and taller than any other trees around us. I'd gone speechless as I stared up at the towering branches.

Imogen took a deep breath, then let it out in a huge sigh of relief. When she opened her eyes, peace washed over her features. The glowing of the tree dimmed, and the wind died down, until the forest returned to normal. It was as if the tree had been there all along.

"Im..." I said breathlessly. "That was beautiful."

She wiped the remaining tears from her face. "It felt... amazing."

Sassy barked happily and jumped up and down from Imogen's feet. Sierra fluttered around the tree, observing it from every angle, and Esis clapped from his branch. He let out a bright cheer, and the sound of his voice echoed back to us—

My gaze snapped upward. For a second, I *thought* it was an echo, but it was too localized for that. I saw a blip of white in a nearby tree, but the creature was gone before I could make sense of what it was.

Did I just see...? Luana didn't finish signing. She was too shocked by the creature.

I saw it, too, I signed back. I looked to Esis, as if he could explain what we'd just seen. He jumped down from his branch and stood on his hind legs. His eyes went wide, and he sniffed the air.

"What?" Imogen asked. "What is it?"

"I think—" I started to say, but I was cut off when Esis started scampering in the direction the creature went. There was no warning— he just started running.

"Esis!" I screamed. It woke Ava-Marie, and she started crying. I ran after Esis, but I couldn't keep up with the baby in my arms.

Sassy was quicker than I. She rushed on ahead, barking to get Esis' attention. But he didn't seem to care. He sprinted forward, like nothing else in the world mattered to him but catching up with that animal.

"Sassy, slow down!" Imogen called. Imogen ran after her and surpassed me, and Luana followed close behind.

"Esis, you'll get lost!" I yelled. I could hear his upbeat chitters far ahead in the forest, but I couldn't see him or Sassy from here.

Eventually, Imogen came to a halt. Sassy was digging in the dirt, her nose shoved into a deep hole. Luana stopped beside me, trying to catch her breath.

"Where'd he go?" I gasped. Ava-Marie had stopped crying, thank the ancestors, but she wiggled in my arms.

"Down there!" Imogen pointed at the hole. It was big enough for Esis, but Sassy didn't fit. She stuck her head inside, her butt pointed up into the air. Frustrated, she yanked her head out of the hole and started sniffing the ground. Sierra fluttered ahead to follow Sassy.

"Wait. Where's she going?" I asked.

"I think she caught his scent," Imogen said.

Sassy's steps slowed to a careful crawl, but we followed behind. The terrain was uneven. I was getting more and more uncomfortable by the second carrying my daughter through the woods.

"Esis!" I shouted. We couldn't be out here forever with a newborn. She needed to eat soon.

Just then, Sassy let out an excited bark. She led us down a steep hill, until we spotted a cave opening tucked deep into the rock. It was hidden between two large boulders, and we could've easily missed it, but it was large enough for us to fit through. Sassy went through first, and Sierra followed. I glanced between Imogen and Luana.

Do you know this place? I asked Luana.

She glanced to the cave opening without an ounce of recognition in her eyes. *I've never been here. But I trust our Familiars.*

"Me, too," Imogen added.

The crevice leading inside the cave was dark and ominous. I questioned if Sassy actually knew what she was doing, but I agreed with them. We could trust our Familiars, and they obviously knew something we didn't.

"Okay," I agreed. "Let's go."

Imogen led the way, and the three of us entered through the opening in the rock. Ava-Marie's eyes scanned the cave ceiling as we walked. The crevice opened to a wide tunnel. Ahead, Sassy barked, and we could see Sierra lighting the way with her magic.

"Come on." Imogen gestured us forward. "I feel a cavern up ahead."

The tunnel was long, but it was less than a minute before we saw sunlight up ahead. The tunnel widened, giving way to a large cavern— and I wasn't prepared for what we saw next.

Hundreds of rodent-like creatures filled the cave. They were the size of squirrels, with fat bellies and big tails. Their noses were small, and their eyes huge. Each had long fox-like ears, and some had curved horns on their heads.

Kurbles!

"Ancestors," I breathed, unable to believe what I was seeing. My heart pitter-pattered at the sight. "We found them!"

The cavern spanned wide and stretched forty feet above our heads. There was a huge hole at the top of the cave, shaded by overhanging trees. A waterfall trickled into the cave, and green vines hung along the walls. Sunlight poured through the opening, glistening off the water. A huge tree grew up from the center of the cavern, poking out the hole at the top of the cave. A rainbow reflected off the waterfall's stream. Along the edge of the cave were various holes, like cubbies, just big enough for one kurble family to fit into each.

Kurbles of all ages hung from branches or swung from vines, using them to leap into their cubby holes. Others bathed in the trickling stream, or shot spouts of water out of their mouths at each other. Huge piles of shiny rocks had been placed all throughout the cavern. Kurbles stood on top of them, as if guarding their stash. Gleeful chittering filled the entire cave. For a moment, all we could do was stop and stare.

The kurbles were all different colors, and some had marbling in their fur, stripes, or spots. Others were brown with various shimmering undertones. Female kurbles had pouches, I realized. Several hopped around with big-eared joeys peeking out of their pouches.

They were marsupials! I couldn't believe I'd never thought of that before. I'd always figured Esis to be some kind of rodent.

Most of the kurbles were crowded toward the far end of the cavern. I didn't see why, until they hoisted one of the kurbles upward and started cheering loudly. The kurble on top shot his fists into the air and squealed happily. It was then that I realized it was *Esis!*

"Esis!" I cried, stepping further into the cave.

I didn't realize what I was doing until I did it. Hundreds of eyes turned toward me. They were all different colors— sapphire, emerald, and ruby. Instantly, the entire cave went silent as the kurbles were alerted of our presence. Not a single one moved as they took us in. My breath halted in my chest. I worried that I'd frightened them, when the truth was I'd just been scared for my Familiar.

Esis was the only one that didn't seem to be holding his breath. He hopped down from the other kurbles' shoulders and scurried toward me, then turned back to his friends. He stretched tall and spread his arms out wide, then turned his nose to the ceiling and let out a high-pitched tune.

The kurbles. Went. Wild.

Hundreds of them echoed Esis' tune, filling the cavern and the forest with their glorious song of homecoming. I let out a sigh of relief. They were *celebrating.*

All at once, kurbles started rushing toward us from all angles. Five of them scurried up my pant leg and fought to sit on my shoulders. Two of them made it to my head while I laughed incredulously. They couldn't fit. One of them tumbled off, but the kurbles at my feet caught him.

Imogen and Luana were in a similar situation, practically being tackled by kurble kisses. Imogen held her arms out wide, and eight kurbles perched on her outstretched arms. Luana laughed gleefully as she knelt down to pet each of them in turn. They scampered onto her back and started playing with her white hair.

Sassy rolled around in the dirt, yipping happily as kurbles licked her face. Sierra glowed. A group of kurbles had stopped to stare at her, mesmerized as she landed on one of their noses.

The kurbles on my back snuggled in close and looked over my shoulder to eye Ava-Marie. She stared up at them in absolute wonder.

"Esis, this is amazing!" I cried.

I looked down to him, only to realize he was gone. I glanced around the cavern and spotted him near the stream. He was on all fours with his head bent down, aiming his horns at a black kurble that was bigger than he was. The black kurble mirrored his posture, and my heart leapt.

"Esis, no!" I started, but it was already too late.

The kurbles charged for each other, and their skulls connected. Neither gave up, though. They kept pushing against each other, locked in a testosterone-fueled battle. Esis curled up his little nose, and an Anichi glow began to illuminate his horns.

Blast!

Esis' Anichi magic exploded into a shield, blasting the black kurble backward. The kurble somersaulted, coming to a halt at the base of one of the rock piles.

"Esis!" I scolded, but he just looked at me with a cheeky grin on his face.

The black kurble stood and dusted off his fur, like he wasn't bothered at all. He scurried over to Esis and held out his paw. The two clapped them together, like a hand shake, and I realized they hadn't been fighting— they'd been sparring. It had to be something male kurbles did.

Another kurble came up to Esis then. I guessed it to be a female, because it was slightly larger than Esis but didn't have any horns. She was all white, except for a tuft of blue fur in the center of her forehead to match her eyes. She tapped Esis on the shoulder, and he turned.

When he saw her, Esis threw his arms up and cried out in exhilaration. He threw his arms around her, and the two locked into a tight embrace. I observed curiously, but it didn't hit me until Esis drew away with tears in his eyes.

Esis knew her.

"Esis?" I asked, stepping forward cautiously, so I wouldn't step on any tails or paws.

He looked up to me brightly and clapped the female kurble on the shoulder.

I knelt down beside them. "Esis, is this your mother?"

He beamed and nodded eagerly, and my heart warmed. We'd found Esis' family!

"Ancestors," I breathed. "This is where you came from."

He chittered proudly, and I took that to mean *yes*.

I couldn't believe it. This was Esis' home— and he'd left it and journeyed miles to find me in Kinpago, so we could bond. He'd left his family so he could find *me*.

Love for my little guy spread so far throughout my core that it almost made my heart shatter. Esis had been apart from his family so he could be my Familiar, but now, they were reunited. I was so happy that he'd finally found his home again— and that we'd solved the mystery of where he'd come from.

"This is fantastic!" Imogen squealed. One kurble was trying to lick inside her ear, while another was pulling her necklace off. A striped kurble with ruby eyes got hold of the bow she wore and ripped the rhinestone off of it, then scurried over to one of the rock piles to add it to his rock collection.

"It's amazing," I agreed. I couldn't find any other words. I'd never seen anything like it.

I turned back to Esis to see another kurble had come up to him. She was smaller than his mother, with brown fur and green eyes. She fluttered her eyelashes at him and chittered.

Esis looked totally star-struck. He reached an elbow out, like he was going to lean up against a nearby rock, but he kept his eyes on the female kurble and missed the rock entirely. He went reeling backward, head over heels into the stream.

Luana bust a gut laughing, and I couldn't stop either. Esis grumbled as he crawled out of the stream and shook his fur out.

"Wow, Esis," I teased. "You have a *strong* game."

He narrowed his eyes at me and flipped me off.

He gets that from you and Liam, Luana signed, still laughing.

Liam, for sure, I teased back.

Watching Esis interact with his own kind was incredible. They chased each other around, and he bounded through the cavern brightly, like I'd never seen him before. He even seemed to climb the tree and swing from the vines with much more agility and ease.

The kurbles were the most friendly creatures I'd ever met, and they kept swooning over Ava-Marie and touching her head, like she was a precious gem. When I nursed her, they just sat there, staring at me like breastfeeding was some sort of spectacle. It was sort of creepy at first, until I realized they'd never seen it before and were just curious.

Luana sat on the ground. The kurbles gathered in *layers* around her, so much that she was practically drowning in them. Imogen helped a group of kurbles sort their rocks, and Sassy splashed with them in the water.

It was pure bliss.

But eventually, Ava-Marie couldn't take it anymore. Esis noticed her getting fussy and started waving goodbye to the other kurbles. He looked up at me with hope in his eyes, as if asking if we could come back again.

"You'll see them again, buddy," I said, patting him on the head. "I promise."

He beamed. The kurbles sang a delightful tune as we left the cave.

I was still riding the high of the kurble cavern when we returned to town. Imogen and Luana were raving about the experience beside me. I was still trying to process it all.

"Let's go tell the others," I burst in excitement. "We finally found out where Esis came from."

It was strange that a day that started out so melancholy by mourning Imogen's brothers had turned so bright by reuniting Esis with his family. And that's when I realized that the kurbles were a sign of hope.

No matter how tough this war proved to be, we could always find love and wonder in our lives.

Liam

NINE

Since the battle over Christmas, I'd moved on from training students to training soldiers. Everyone who was of age and who we could spare was preparing for another inevitable fight with the Elders.

My Anichi students had made excellent progress since they'd helped restore the shield around the town. Many of them were able to do other forms of minor Anichi magic, like make light, though they still needed to gather power from crystals and the earth to access their powers.

I just wished we could break the block on their magic, so they could bond with Familiars and use their powers for themselves, instead of relying on harnessing magic from other sources.

Today, we were in the clearing that was used for education inside *Hok'evale*, blasting targets. Linus and Zoey were two of my former students who'd been assigned to the soldier group I was training. They'd recently turned eighteen, and had signed up for the resistance army. They were getting ready for their first battle, whenever that was to come. Linus was Anichi, unbonded, and Zoey was a Koigni girl with a enfield Familiar, a fox-wolf hybrid.

Linus was one of the people who'd gotten the shield back up during the crisis. He held a crystal tightly in his hand, and absorbed its energy as he sent larger and larger blasts of white orbs toward the targets we'd set up at the end of the clearing. One of the orbs was six feet across, and it knocked over the target as it went sailing by.

"Careful," I said as Linus wavered backward. "You're playing with fire by using too much energy at once. Keep doing that and you'll hurt yourself."

Julian growled in agreement. He beat his wings behind me, and Linus gave him a surly look.

"Is that even possible?" Linus asked. His tone was skeptical. Several people looked our way, and I sighed. Linus liked to backtalk. He was a good student, but he still assumed he knew it all.

I gestured for the class to come inward. "Gather round. This is important."

The young soldiers circled around me. I opened my palm and took water from the air, growing it into a small orb. "We've already discussed before how magic is energy. Elementai take energy from their Familiars. Anichi currently access their powers by harnessing what is in the earth around them, or in crystals."

I grew the water ball so that it was a foot across. "Some Elementai naturally have more magical potential than others. They're able to access, store, and harness more energy than other elementals can. An Elementai's abilities can be increased steadily over time, like working a muscle, but if too much magic is expended at the same time, there can be consequences."

"Like what?" Linus asked as he watched the ball spin in my hand.

"Magic can be replenished. It's like any other form of bodily energy. When we eat and sleep, we restore energy to our bodies. Magic can also recharge, depending on how often we give it rest. But like food and sleep, if we don't give our magic enough time to refill, we die. If we become sleep-deprived, we go mad. If we don't eat, we starve." I closed my fingers, and the water ball vanished. "Our magic has limits. Any supernatural that goes past that limit puts themselves at risk."

"I thought you said the connection between an Elementai and a Familiar provided an endless source of life-energy," Zoey said.

"In a way, but that life-energy isn't meant to be used up in one go," I explained. "Pushing yourself past the boundaries of your own magic results in your body being forced to find that energy elsewhere. If you go slightly over the limits, you'll faint. If you push farther than that, your magic will suck energy from your organs and tissues, potentially leaving you with life-long health issues. Beyond even that, if you perform magic that's far beyond your reach, all of the energy will be depleted from you at once to perform the spell, and you will die. Imagine running a marathon for days on end, not stopping to eat or rest until you collapse from heart failure. It's more or less the same thing."

I shifted. "Once that happens, your body dissolves. You become your element as you die. Koigni turn to ash. Yapluma fade into the wind, Nivita become the earth, and Toaqua are reduced to puddles of water. I assume Anichi would turn into spirit ether, though I can't say for certain."

"Can't you just stop it if you sense you're going too far?" Linus said.

"It's like pulling the trigger," I said. "Once it's done, you can't reverse it. That's why it's important to know your limits before you head into battle, and to rest your powers after performing impressive feats of magic."

"You did it," Zoey pointed out. "When you took magic away from Elder Poole and Elder Malison during the battle. Something like that should've killed you, and you survived."

"I got very lucky. I was only able to do so for a few seconds, and I didn't hold on to it for long," I stated. "If not for Julian, I would've died."

Julian groaned, and I patted him on the cheek. "I think that's enough for today. We've been practicing drills all morning. Rest your magic, and we'll pick back up tomorrow."

The soldiers dispersed. Linus muttered something under his breath and eyed the targets. I knew he was gonna come back later and keep firing at targets.

If the kid kept this up, he'd knock himself on his ass, but whatever. Some people didn't learn unless it was the hard way.

"Liam? Can I have a moment?" Taylor came up to my side. She was one of the soldiers I was training. She held her red armadillo close as she walked up to me.

Taylor had been the first person we'd helped to escape Orenda Academy after her brother, Levi, had been burned to death by Haley's magic. She hadn't always been the nicest, but since she'd been here in *Hok'evale*, she'd been a great asset to some of our special ops teams.

"What's going on?" By her tone, it didn't sound like good news.

Taylor took a breath. "I wanted to talk to you about Lira."

Surprise stirred within me. Lira was Toaqua, and Taylor was Koigni. I'd seen them talking a few times, but hardly ever saw them together. Why did Taylor want to know about her?

"Lira left," I told her. "She and her Familiar headed out days ago."

After we'd rescued the Familiars, Lira had been allowed to stay long enough for her creature to heal before she'd been banished. She took her Familiar and left, though she didn't say where to. I felt bad that she had to leave, but Lira didn't show any reservations about it. I think she was tired of Hawkei society as a whole and was ready to start over somewhere else.

"I know," Taylor said. "I was going to go with her. I stayed behind because I thought I should help the war effort, until I realized…"

Taylor drifted off. She didn't need to finish her sentence. I could tell what she wanted to say.

"I didn't know you two were that close," I said.

"We kept it pretty quiet," Taylor said softly. "We broke up when Lira confessed where the Familiars were. I was mad at her for keeping it from me. But now I've come to realize that was the wrong decision."

"And now you want to go after her."

"My aunt says I need to follow my heart," Taylor started. "And Lira took it with her. I don't know if she'll have me, but I have to try."

"I think Lira will be very glad for the company," I said. "She didn't have anyone left."

"I know," Taylor said sadly. "Besides my aunt, I don't have any family left, either. It's one of the things we bonded over."

Taylor looked away. "I thought that we might be able to create a new family together."

"Do you even know where she went?"

"The west coast of Florida. Her family left her a house down there. They used to take vacations to Orlando every summer," Taylor said. "If I leave now, I can catch her. That is… if you guys don't need me here."

We *did* need Taylor. We needed every living body who could contribute to the war effort against the Elders.

But if I was separated from Sophia, nothing could keep me from her. Not even a damn war. And I could tell just by hearing Taylor's voice whatever she and Lira had shared was real.

Some people would call her a deserter. Not me. I knew that this war would lead everyone on different paths.

"Go after her," I told Taylor. "You can save yourself from whatever happens. And I thank you for telling me and not just ditching."

"I didn't think I could leave without telling at least one person," Taylor said. "You all deserve an explanation."

"You don't need to explain," I said. "Anyone who doesn't get it hasn't been there."

Taylor smiled. "Thanks, Liam. I wish you all luck."

The curls on her back bounced as she ran away. I didn't think I'd ever see her again— in fact, I hoped not to.

The more people that were far away from here, the fewer casualties there'd be when shit hit the fan.

"Bro!" Jonah came hurtling in from out of nowhere. He was panting. He leaned over his knees and breathed hard when he got to me. Squeaks wasn't with him.

"Fucking ancestors, what's going on *now*?" I complained. Couldn't get one day of peace around here.

"Uh, your wife is going nutty in the square, that's what," Jonah shot at me while trying to catch his breath. "I tried to stop her, but she went full-on psycho."

"What? Why?" I asked.

"Mia's... here..." Jonah gasped.

I gaped. "My ex?"

"No, some random ass bitch. Yes, your ex!" Jonah shouted.

Mia had come to *Hok'evale*? That was bad news. "How'd she get through Luana's shield?"

"She asked for sanctuary. The guards let her in," Jonah said. "*Hok'evale* law states they can't turn away anyone asking for shelter, permitted they're not an enemy, and she wasn't on any of the watch lists."

Whether Mia was an enemy or not was still to be seen. "Did she bring the Task Force with her?"

"Nah, man. It's just her," Jonah said. "And I suggest you get to her before Sophia turns her into a shish kabob."

"Jules." I yanked myself onto Julian's back. The dragon crouched down and sprang forward, launching himself into the sky.

Julian tilted in midair. I pressed myself to his scales and clung on tight as he flew toward the center of town.

People were holed up in their houses and hiding behind walls as fireballs soared throughout the square. In the middle of it, I spotted Mia. She danced around the fireballs and jumped from spot to spot, screaming in fear. She had a large coat wrapped around her form, the edges singed with flame.

There were wild yells coming from the square that weren't Mia. Sophia was chasing her around like a fucking maniac. She flung fireball after fireball, nearly missing each time while Mia cried out for her to stop. I didn't see Esis anywhere.

Julian landed. I jumped off his back and sprinted forward, hoping I'd stop this before it was too late.

Mia tripped and fell on her knees a few feet in front of Sophia. Sophia raised a tremendous fireball to deliver a killing blow.

"Sophia, stop!" I shouted. I grabbed her and held her back. I almost got a fireball to the face, but Sophia held back when she saw it was me.

"Let me have her!" Sophia raged. "She's mine!" In front of us, Mia cowered, quivering and shaking.

"Soph, where's the baby?" I asked when I noticed Ava-Marie was missing.

"With Luana," Sophia growled. "I needed my chance to get a shot at this bitch. I ran out of the house when I heard she was in town."

Tears streamed down Mia's face. She wasn't wearing any makeup. Her long hair had been cut short around her ears in a jagged fashion, and her nails were broken. Her clothes were ragged and torn, like she'd been living in the woods for weeks. I'd never seen her look so poorly. "I came alone. Just give me a few moments to speak."

"You don't deserve last words!" Sophia yelled. "You almost got my husband killed!"

Mia's lip trembled, and she didn't say anything more. She dropped her coat and revealed a small bundle in her arms.

My heart caught. It was a little boy, only a month or so older than Ava-Marie. He had Micah's features, but Mia's eyes. He squirmed in the blanket, and Sophia's eyes widened. Julian gave a surprised growl.

The whimpers of a dog could be heard nearby. A canine Familiar with a gem on its forehead limped out from behind a building, holding a hurt paw. It was Mia's Familiar, Taryn.

"We've left the Elders. Micah is looking for me," Mia begged. "We need sanctuary."

"Why should we give you sanctuary? You're a traitor," Sophia snarled, though her eyes lingered on the infant. Her mothering instincts were warring with her to calm down.

Mia gave a sob. "If you won't accept me, take my son." Mia lifted the baby up to us. "Kill me, and spare him. I don't care what happens, as long as my child lives."

Taryn gave a whine, and Sophia's eye twitched. She looked like she wanted to reach out and snatch the baby out of Mia's arms, before I stepped forward. I put a hand on Mia's arm and helped her to her feet.

"Why are you here, Mia?" I asked. "This better not be some sort of trick."

"It's probably a trap. I bet her husband is setting us up," Sophia said.

Mia hiccupped. "N-no. Micah and I aren't married. We didn't go through with the marriage. We postponed the wedding because of the war."

She took a quivering breath. "I tried to stay with him, but Micah shook the baby. I knew if I didn't leave him, Mattias would die."

Sophia stared coldly. "That's a pretty story, but I'm not sure I believe it."

"You don't have to believe anything. I came here to save my son," Mia shot at her. "Execute me if you'd like, but my son is an innocent."

The baby wiggled in her arms. Mia noticed me staring at her jagged haircut. "I had to cut it." Mia touched the uneven ends. "So he couldn't grab it and force me to remain."

Sophia crossed her arms. She was going to say something else, but was cut off by the sound of footsteps. Wyatt skidded on scene. He stood in front of us, blocking Sophia's path to Mia.

"You can't do this," he burst. "It's wrong."

"Wyatt, get out of the way," Sophia hissed.

"I'll vouch for her," Wyatt offered. "Anything she does while she's here, I'll take responsibility for."

Mia's eyes widened, like she couldn't believe that Wyatt would offer to do such a thing.

Sophia scoffed and rolled her eyes. "Please."

Fuck if she wasn't acting like Doya right now. I took Sophia by the shoulders and pulled her aside, far enough away so no one could hear us speak. "*Pawee, Hok'evale* has rules. Chief Cauac wouldn't appreciate you turning the square into an execution ring. You aren't judge and jury here."

"You are!" Sophia burst. "Mia is Toaqua, so you have precedence over her fate!"

"I'm not gonna kill her, if that's what you're asking," I said flatly. Mia had betrayed all of us— most of all, me, but though she might deserve death, I wasn't going to be the one to hand it out. All of us had been in a tough spot when we'd left Orenda Academy. I understood her choice, even though I couldn't forgive her for it.

"You can't keep her around! She's a liability. She could be ferrying information to the Elders," Sophia said.

"Her son's more important than all of that. She was devoted to Micah. She wouldn't have left him if she didn't want to protect her child," I said. "She's going to do whatever it takes to keep him safe."

"How can we trust her? This might be some sort of trick," Sophia accused.

"We can't trust her. But she needs our help."

"So? We don't have any obligation to her. She had a hand in your execution," Sophia snarled.

I stared at her. "Sophia, if you're okay with abandoning a single mother and an infant to the streets, you're not the woman I married."

"Then we take the baby, and kill her." Sophia shrugged. "Problem solved."

"Ancestors, has Doya gotten to you?" I hissed. "Do you want that baby to grow up without his mother? His father's already an asshole."

Sophia flinched. She cast a look back at Mia, and though it was full of disgust, I could see her breaking. As much as she despised Mia, she couldn't take her away from her son. Sophia cared about kids too much, even kids that weren't her own, and that would always be her biggest weakness.

"So we can't cast her out, and you won't throw her in jail," Sophia seethed. "What do we do with her?"

"We offer her sanctuary. But at a price. She has to live with Wyatt, so he can watch her."

"Wyatt has some stupid crush on her! He's not infallible," Sophia protested.

"No, but he can keep an eye on her," I pointed out. "And ferry that information back to me."

Sophia let out a breath. "He's in love with her. That's not going to work."

"Yes, he loves her. But he's not dumb. He's loyal to me, and he knows the war effort is more important than his personal feelings."

Sophia ran a furious hand through her hair. "How dumb can you be to put your faith in Mia a third time?"

"I'm not. Which is why I'll be putting surveillance on her, beyond what Wyatt can offer, until I'm sure she's here for the right reasons."

Sophia gave a pout. "This is a lot of work to maintain one traitor."

"Soph, we gave Doya a chance," I reminded her gently. "Mia deserves the same treatment."

That got to her. Sophia's shoulders slumped, and she muttered, "If not for that baby, I'd be frying her."

"Believe me, I know." We turned back to Wyatt and Mia. Wyatt had his arm around her, and Mia was still sniffling. The baby gurgled in her arms, while Taryn kept low.

"Okay, here's the deal," I stated. "Mia, we can give you sanctuary, but you have to live with Wyatt. Wyatt, since you're keen to take responsibility, anything she does, you'll be held accountable for. Which means taking the sentence if she commits a crime against the resistance."

"Deal," Wyatt said. He didn't even hesitate.

"Thank you, Liam," Mia said. She began crying tears of relief.

They hardly moved me. Her kid was the only thing that had saved her ass today. "Do you have any information you can offer to the resistance in exchange for your safety?" I asked Mia.

She shook her head. "Micah kept me out of everything. I think he knew I was going to run."

"Of course," Sophia muttered.

Wyatt shot her a glare. "Come on, Mia. Let's get you settled into your new home."

Mia's sniffles could be heard as Wyatt guided her out of the square. I sighed. With Sophia and Mia in the same vicinity, I wasn't sure this village was big enough for the two of them.

"Take it easy, sweetheart. Mind your head."

Ava-Marie flailed as I placed her into the bath sling in the sink. She let out a happy high note as she touched the warm water. Soap bubbles went everywhere. They fluttered into the air, and Ava-Marie watched them rise, giving a wide grin.

She could smile now. My stomach flip-flopped every time I watched her do it. I couldn't help a smile from spreading over my face whenever she grinned back.

Ava-Marie kicked her feet and smiled wider. She loved baths. She liked playing with the water. She smacked her hands down and made a loud noise, sending droplets everywhere.

"You're Toaqua, aren't you?" I cooed. "Yes, you are."

I knew Elementai inherited the powers of their same sex parent, and Ava-Marie would be Koigni. But hey, she had two generations of Toaqua in her bloodline, so fingers crossed.

I put a few bubbles on her nose. She wrinkled her nose and sneezed. The movement surprised her, and her eyes grew wide.

"Was that scary?" I gasped. "Don't worry. Watch."

I moved my fingers, and Ava-Marie's eyes sparkled as she watched water rise out of the sink, forming into tiny creatures like dragons and unicorns. Ava-Marie gurgled and reached out her hands. The water animals skimmed over her fingertips. I made them dance and run up her arms. She squealed with joy.

My insides stuttered. I didn't know if there'd be a time when I got tired of observing her. She was so little, but she had such a big personality.

I bathed her while she played with the water animals. I heard the clicking sound of little nails. Esis skittered onto the counter, tilting his head at Ava-Marie.

He put a paw in to test the water. "Esis, don't you—"

Too late. Esis slid into the sink. The water splashed upward and hit Ava-Marie in the face. The water animals dropped. Ava-Marie took a deep breath and started wailing.

"You bastard," I told Esis with a sigh. He shrugged at me.

At Ava-Marie's whines, Esis swam over to her and patted her on the head. Her whimpers stopped, though her lip stuck out with a tremble.

"It's okay, honey. It's just a little water." I poured the water over her back, and she calmed down. Meanwhile, Esis inched closer to her. He took the bubbles and made a beard around his chin before giving himself a hat. Ava-Marie smiled again.

Esis was one of her favorite Familiars. Ava-Marie ran her fingers up and down Esis' wet fur while I finished her bath. Esis scrubbed himself like he was in the shower. His tail flicked soapy water into my eye. I swore loudly and tried not to kill him.

When Ava-Marie was done with her bath, I wrapped her in a fluffy pink baby towel, with a hood that looked like a unicorn. I swear, everything people bought my daughter was pink and unicorn related. It'd become some kind of theme.

Esis held his arms up for me to pick him up, too, but I scowled at him. "Get your own towel, asshole."

Esis slumped in the water and blew bubbles in disappointment. The door opened, and Jonah and Squeaks squeezed through.

"Isn't it my favorite girl!" Jonah cried upon seeing Ava-Marie. "Don't you look so adorable in that pink wrap Auntie Jonah got you!"

Ava-Marie squealed. For some reason, she thought Jonah was hilarious. She grinned and made loud sounds whenever he walked into the room. Squeaks nuzzled the blanket, and Ava-Marie stroked her soft head feathers.

"I must be funny, huh, Ava?" Jonah sang. "You think Auntie Jonah's funny."

"Funny looking, maybe."

Jonah stuck out a hip. "You mind your mouth."

Jonah turned on the TV, looking for a soccer game. There was some big sports thing on tonight, and everyone was coming over to watch. I opened the bedroom door, and a group of kurbles came scampering out of it. Since Sophia had found the kurble group, Esis had brought over a lot of friends. My house was constantly packed with the little buggers now.

The flood of kurbles jumped onto Squeaks' back, while some of them ran to the sink to take baths. Others rummaged through the cupboards for food. It was annoying, but I didn't bark at them. Sophia liked them hanging around, and if she was happy, I was happy.

A female kurble with brown fur and green eyes ran along the windowsill. Esis clambered out of the sink and shook the water out of his fur. He slicked his hair back and strode up to her, puffing out his chest. She preened, and Esis began singing this awful song that sounded more like noise than music.

Esis' girlfriend never left. She was more or less a permanent fixture in the house. Sophia had named her Buttercup.

I closed the door behind myself and set Ava-Marie on the changing table. I used my powers to dry her off and put on her diaper, then went through her clothes. I held up a onesie and a pair of leggings. I got the onesie on easily enough, but that's not what I was worried about.

"You wanna try this again?" I asked. I tried to slip on the leggings, but Ava-Marie flailed her legs and screamed.

I sighed. Stevie, Imogen and Jonah had done their damage and ruined pants for Ava-Marie. She hated to have them on. I think she wanted her legs free. As such, she made it clear she liked the skirts and dresses she'd been gifted. I gave up and put her into a skirt that looked like a bunch of multicolored ribbons with rainbow socks. I knew she'd get the socks off one way or another, but I'd be damned if I let her get cold. It was getting warmer now, so we didn't need to bundle her up as much, but it still wasn't pleasant to deal with a baby who screamed whenever we tried to slip her into leggings.

"You're a little drama queen," I told her. Ava-Marie cooed in what sounded like agreement.

I emerged from the bedroom. By this time, Jonah was sprawled on the couch, Squeaks lying on the rug with the kurbles all around her. Their wide eyes were planted on the screen, while Esis and his girlfriend held hands on the armchair.

Sophia, Luana and Imogen walked through the door, carrying groceries for tonight's pre-game meal. The kurbles raced up and started going through grocery bags. Sophia smiled as she saw me carrying Ava-Marie.

"How was she?" Sophia said.

"Like a little angel. Hardly fussed," I said.

"Why can't you be like that for Mommy?" Sophia teased. She nuzzled her nose to Ava's, and the baby cooed.

Sophia's mood had drastically improved since yesterday. Mia had meekly agreed to all her demands. I asked Sophia what "rules" she'd imposed on Mia, and all she'd responded with was, *making sure she knows to stay the fuck away from us.*

Imogen had a sly look on her face. Sassy nosed through the bags as Imogen pulled out a clear glass jar. Luana giggled.

"What's that for?" I asked. Sophia took the baby from me.

"It's a swear jar," Sophia said confidently as she bounced Ava-Marie on her hip. "Dollar per word."

"We came up with it on the way to the store." Imogen laughed.

"Are you fucking kidding me?"

"Liam! I don't want our daughter's first word to be *fuck!*" Sophia said. "This is the only way you'll curb the habit."

I took out my wallet, shoved a twenty in the jar, and said, "There. For the rest of today's fucking fucks."

"You only have eighteen left now," Jonah said.

"Come on, guys! This is stupid," I whined.

Sophia sighed. "Liam, I'm tired of your shit."

"Ha!" I pointed at the jar. "That's a swear word!"

Sophia scowled and put a dollar bill in the jar. I had a feeling that swear jar was going to pay for Ava-Marie's wedding by the time she was six-months old.

Ezra entered, and Jonah raised his head. "Hey, man," Jonah said. "Ready to watch the game?"

Ezra paused. He mulled his words over before he said, "Maddie said she wants to talk to us."

Jonah lowered the volume. All of us turned Ezra's way.

"What about?" Sophia asked.

"I don't know." Ezra's face was puzzled. "She said it was important."

"Right now? Well, okay. Who'd she want to speak to?" I asked.

"All of us," Ezra said. "She said it wouldn't take long."

Jonah turned off the TV and got up. "Well, let's talk to her, then."

Nobody objected. Maddie rarely spoke. If she wanted to speak with all of us at once, it had to be about something that couldn't wait.

Sophia wrapped Ava-Marie in a large baby blanket and handed her off to me. We followed Ezra out of the house and through town, until he led us to a pathway that wandered into the forest. We came to a pool, where a group of hippocampi were swimming and playing. Kelpies lounged on the rocky shore near the pool, watching as the hippocampi jumped out of the water to do flips and tricks. One hippocampus with zebra scales whinnied and splashed its mermaid tail at a kelpie, who shook its seaweed mane and snorted out salt water.

Maddie and Drew were in the clearing, feeding the creatures. Maddie carried a basket of seaweed that she hand fed the hippocampi with, while Drew tossed them grain. Eirakari laid nearby, curled around Ace. The hellhound barked a hello, and Maddie turned to greet us.

"Hey, Mads," I said. "What's up?"

Maddie smiled— actually smiled, for the first time in forever. She'd gotten some color back into her cheeks and had gained weight. She looked a lot better than she had a few weeks ago.

"Hey," she said. "Glad you all could come. Have a seat."

She gestured to the multi-colored rocks clustered around the pond. I sat down. A hippocampus rose out of the water and touched her nose to Ava-Marie's chest. Ava's eyes grew wide, and her fingertips lightly touched the creature.

Sassy perched on top of Squeaks, and Sierra on top of Sassy. Dyami was nestled close by in the trees. Ezra, Jonah, Luana and Sophia all took seats next to mine, while Drew and Maddie shared a seat across from us.

It was peaceful at the pool. Maybe that was the reason why Maddie had chosen this place to break whatever news she had to offer.

Maddie took a breath, and her smile faltered. "I'm doing better, thanks to the support of all of you. I'm finally getting a handle on my emotions, and for the first time in a long time, I think I have control of my life again."

"That's great," Imogen said. I sensed my sister wasn't done.

"But," Maddie started, "to keep getting better, my therapist said I needed to let you guys know some things. So I could move past it."

Drew put a hand on her knee. She entwined her fingers with his and said, "I think it's time I tell you guys what Oleander did to me at Orenda Academy."

Blackness curled up and settled amongst my insides. I didn't want to know what had happened to her— it made me feel nauseous just thinking about it.

Yet this wasn't about me. It was about Maddie. So I had to get a grip and be strong enough to shoulder whatever she was about to tell me.

"Mads, you don't have to do that," Sophia said. But Maddie shook her head.

"It's important. You need to know." Maddie squeezed Drew's hand again. "But I'm only going to talk about this once, and never again. So pay attention, because I never want to relive what I went through after today."

"We're listening, sis," Ezra encouraged. "Go ahead."

Maddie's face became ashen. "The truth is, they tortured Drew while we were in Oleander's custody. But they tortured me, too, just in a different way."

Maddie stared at the water, like it was easier to talk about it while looking at the hippocampi instead of at us. "Have you guys heard of a place called Darke Island?"

"No," I said. All of us wore blank faces— except for Imogen.

"Darke Island?" Imogen repeated. "That's a place of exile for supernaturals."

I was surprised. I didn't know such a thing existed. I guess if I wracked my brain hard enough, it sounded familiar, but it wasn't something I typically thought about.

"Exactly." Maddie nodded. "There's a prison there; Darke Institute for Supernatural Offenders. It's where they send the worst of the worst."

"What does that have to do with—?" Jonah said, but Squeaks made a noise to shush him.

Maddie swallowed. "There are rumors. At the Institute, they perform experiments on the prisoners. Stuff that's highly illegal, stuff you couldn't get away with unless you were experimenting on people that no one would notice missing."

"What kind of experiments?" Imogen asked.

Drew began rubbing Maddie's back. Her voice shook a little as she said, "Experiments to take away a person's magic. And Oleander performed them on me."

Several people gasped. My jaw dropped open.

Imogen managed to stutter out, "But that's impossible."

"I don't know if it's possible or not," Maddie said. "It's unclear if a person can take away another supernatural's magic. But Oleander damn sure tried."

How sickening to consider. If someone took my magic away from me permanently, and then used it to make themselves stronger, I think I'd lose my mind. Next to losing my Familiar, I didn't think anything could be so painful.

Maddie's hands became fists. "He wanted to see if he could harness my powers for himself. He was jealous of me. He wanted to be a prophet, and foretell the future. He heard the Institute was trying to transfer magic from one person to another, and thought that he might succeed with my *naderei* powers. That way, he could foresee how to win the war."

Maddie let out a cruel laugh. "He wasn't successful, anyway. Everything he tried failed. He didn't even come close."

"What did he do to you?" Sophia whispered.

Maddie's eye twitched. "He weakened me first by withholding food and water. He forced me to stay awake and deprived me of sleep. When I was almost certain I'd gone crazy, he took me to this chamber... fastened me down with these leather cuffs on this cold, metal table, so I couldn't move."

Bile rose in my throat. Damn Oleander. Damn him to hell for everything he did.

"He put these... crystals by my head." Maddie shivered. "I'd never seen them before. They were blood red, and jagged— some sort of black liquid ran within the crevices, like smoke. I didn't know what they were. But my magic could tell there was something in them that was pure evil. I didn't think they came from nature... they came from something... awful."

Maddie's eyes became distant. "When he commanded the crystals to take my power, there was so much pain. It felt like my veins were on fire, like my head was going to erupt. Every part of me felt like I was getting torn to shreds. Visions raced through my head. I saw so many things, visions of the future. But I couldn't hold on to them because my body was in agony."

Maddie's breaths became ragged. "Then the crystals would explode. They'd shatter into a million pieces, scattering everywhere, and the pain would stop. Oleander would get so furious. He'd demand me to tell him what I saw. I was usually too delirious to tell him. If I remembered, I'd make something up. Then he'd put two new crystals beside my temples, and we'd do it all over again."

Drew's face was hard. By the darkness in his eyes, he was thinking of all the terrible things he could do to make Oleander suffer. Nearby, Ace gave a deadly growl.

"He did this day after day." Maddie put a hand over her mouth. "It never stopped, not for weeks. I thought about taking my own life to end it, but I just couldn't. I knew if I died, Drew would, too. I didn't want to give up hope. I put everything I had into believing I'd get out, and I did."

Maddie straightened up. "But eventually, the torture slowed. I think he was running out of crystals to try on me. I knew they had to come from

Darke Island— where else would you get such wicked things? But whoever his contact was there had stopped sending them. Oleander hadn't taken me down to his chamber for two weeks by the time I escaped Orenda Academy. But by then, the crystals had already done their damage. I have visions nearly every day now."

Imogen shifted uncomfortably. "Maddie... do you think the crystals act as a trigger for your powers?"

"I'm not sure. I think Oleander was trying to rely on them as some kind of conduit, to transfer my magic into him, like transference," Maddie explained. "These crystals would allow him to do that, but my powers always broke the crystals before he had a chance to try."

"Do you know what they are, Im?" Jonah asked hopefully. All of us looked at her.

Imogen frowned. "I'm sorry, no. These crystals... if that's what they are... are strange to me. I've never heard of such a thing that can take away a supernatural's powers. Noxite can do that, but only for a short time, and it certainly can't transfer them to someone else."

Dead end, then. That was never a good sign for us.

Maddie stood. "I won't say any more about it. I've told you guys everything you need to know. I don't think Oleander can get his hands on any more of those crystals, but if he can, you'd better be ready for it."

I stood. I shifted the baby into one arm as I wrapped the other around Maddie. "Thanks for telling us, Mads. I know it couldn't have been easy."

"It wasn't," she muffled into my shoulder. "But I do feel better now. And I can finally have a chance to heal."

Ava-Marie squirmed against us, and my stomach dropped. There were no limits Oleander would stop at to achieve his ruthless goals. The worst thing about it was, there was magic in this world we still didn't understand.

Magic Oleander could use against us to win.

sophia

TEN

Maddie's confession was a knife to the gut. I couldn't imagine what Oleander had put her through. It had to be torture to tell us the story, but she was doing much better than she had in months. She even agreed to come over for dinner the following week.

Ace belched from under the table, letting out a plume of flame. Esis slumped in his chair. He patted his full belly and copied Ace. Ava-Marie startled in her bouncer.

"Ace!" Drew scolded. "You're setting a bad example."

Buttercup jumped onto the table and grabbed Liam's cup of milk. She downed it in just a few gulps, before Liam could grab the glass from her.

"You little gremlin!" Liam growled.

Buttercup dropped her head and fluttered her eyelashes at him. Then she let out a huge belch and scurried off into the next room. Esis' eyes brightened, and he raced off behind her.

Maddie snickered. It was good to hear her laugh. "*I think they're cute.*"

Liam frowned and held up his empty glass, like it proved something. "They're not so cute when they raid your food every chance they get."

It was true. The kurbles who'd been hanging around had cleaned out our fridge in two days. Our food bill this week would've been double our usual amount if Liam's mom wasn't helping. She offered to donate food each week to feed the little critters, and was working on weaving baby blankets for each of them.

"Oh, but *look* at them," I said, gesturing to the kurbles in the living room.

Esis tackled Buttercup and the two of them went rolling across the floor. Buttercup righted herself first and leapt on top of him, pinning him to the ground. Esis responded by nipping at her ear, then flipped her over and sat on her belly.

"You think those mating rituals are *cute?*" Liam balked. "Esis is growing up too fast!"

"Those aren't *mating rituals,*" I said. "They're just playing."

Buttercup started licking Esis' nose, and my Familiar didn't protest. Maybe there *was* something to Liam's *mating ritual* claim.

"Either way, I love them," Maddie said. "And so does Ava."

Esis and Buttercup had stopped wrestling each other and were tickling Ava-Marie's toes now. She smiled brightly and kicked her skirt.

"See, Liam? We *have* to keep them," I begged.

He rolled his eyes. "As long as there's food in the cupboard when I get home."

"There was enough to make this pasta," I pointed out.

"Which was *amazing,* by the way," Maddie praised. "You could give Mom a run for her money."

"Really?" I asked. The compliment meant a lot.

Drew finished off his milk and wiped his lips with his napkin. "Totally. That was fantastic, Sophia."

"Then we'll have to invite you over more often." I stood and started cleaning up our plates. Liam helped me wash dishes, while Maddie went to hold Ava and Drew played with Buttercup.

A knock came at the door, and I answered it. Baine stood there, his hair in disarray. It was no longer green, but a bright bleach blonde. He noticed me staring and quickly flattened the strands.

"What is it, *pataa?*" I asked. Eirakari was curled up not far from Julian, and she kept throwing glances at Baine's hair.

"It's about the *Azaimperiai.*" He held up the tomahawk. Since I'd failed to get it to work, it'd been in his possession, as we hoped it would help him with his research.

Liam came up behind me. "Come in."

Maddie and Drew noticed Baine's hair immediately, and they both went silent.

"What is it?" Baine asked innocently.

"Um... Professor?" Drew started timidly. "Did an Anichi creature crap in your hair?"

Baine cleared his throat. "Ah, not really my color, is it? Had to bleach the green out."

"You could just cut it," Liam suggested.

"I suppose I could," he said. "Though I have to say, Eleanor seems to like it like this. I might keep it for a while."

"Ancestors," Liam mumbled under his breath.

"What is it you found, *pataa*?" I asked quickly. I gestured to the living room, and we all took a seat. Maddie played with Ava on the floor, and Buttercup snuggled in Drew's lap.

Baine took a deep breath. "I haven't found much, I'm afraid. That is why I've come. I fear I may need to return to the temple to conduct more research."

I gaped at him. He couldn't go back. The temple was a death trap!

"What is it you expect to find there?" I asked.

"See these runes?" Baine pointed to the symbols along the side of the *Azaimperiai*. "I've gone through every text I own, and I'm unable to translate them. I thought perhaps there's a translation in the temple somewhere."

"But there's nothing left of the room you found it in!" I protested. I didn't want *anyone* going back to that temple. Both he and Liam had nearly died the last time they'd been there.

"Can I see?" Liam asked, holding out his hand.

Baine handed him the tomahawk. "I realize that, Sophia, but there has to be *something*. This wouldn't be part of the prophecy if we weren't able to use it."

Liam's brow furrowed as he looked over the runes. "These have to be instructions. But you're right. I haven't seen these symbols before, either. They *look* Hawkei, but I don't recognize any of them."

"Let me see," Maddie suggested. She looked over the symbols, but her expression mirrored her brother's. "I don't get it, either. It's nothing Dad ever taught us."

"How fluent are you two in Hawkei runes?" I asked as Maddie handed the tomahawk over to Drew.

"Pretty fluent," Liam said. "I was taught the runes for my chief training, but the others weren't. Dad kept scrolls in his office, and now and then, Maddie would sneak them out, and we'd translate them. It was like a game to us."

"Exactly," she said. "A puzzle. All of us— Liam, Ezra, and I— got really good at it."

"So it's something that wasn't in the scrolls," I theorized.

"I don't know." Liam hesitated. "I've never run across Hawkei symbols I couldn't translate."

"I think I understand this," Drew said.

All eyes turned to him, and his spine straightened. He cleared his throat.

"Not the runes," he quickly explained. "But I think I know why you can't read them."

"Well...?" Liam prodded, eyebrows raised.

Drew twisted the tomahawk around in his hands. "Your father's scrolls, the ones you learned to read on... those were Toaqua scrolls, right?"

"Yes," Maddie answered.

"So, you only know Toaqua symbols," Drew stated.

A crease appeared between Liam's eyebrows. "What do you mean, *Toaqua symbols*? All Houses use the same Hawkei language."

Drew shook his head. "Or so you believe. When I was a kid, I found a Koigni scroll in my grandmother's attic. It belonged to a very distant relative who served on the Koigni Council ages ago."

"What's your point?" Liam asked.

Drew cleared his throat and hurried to say, "Well, I did some translating of my own as a kid, and the Koigni scrolls contained some... secret symbols."

Maddie tilted her head at him. "You're saying Koigni created a secret language to hide messages?"

"Exactly," Drew said.

"So, can you translate this?" Baine asked.

Drew shook his head and handed the *Azaimperiai* back to Baine. "Sorry, but these symbols aren't Koigni."

"Then what are they? They're—" Liam cut off as he realized the answer.

"Anichi," I finished for him. "Anichi must have developed their own language, a derivative of Hawkei, like the Koigni did."

Baine looked flustered. "Well, I-I don't know how to translate Anichi symbols."

A smirk fell across my face. "Then it's a good thing we know someone who does."

My heart beat frantically as Liam, Baine, and I left the house. Maddie and Drew offered to stay behind to watch Ava-Marie as we went to find answers. Part of me was scared about them. Another part of me was excited we were moments away from knowing how to use the *Azaimperiai*—moments away from an answer to winning this war.

The Cauac house featured traditional Anichi architecture, but it was bigger than many of the other huts in town. It was made of tall sticks with thatched roofing, but had modern touches like a porch light and ornate glass windows.

Esis scurried ahead of us and knocked on Chief Cauac's door before the rest of us had reached it. His fists were so tiny he barely made a noise. We stepped up to the door, and I knocked loudly.

A few moments later, Chief Cauac answered. I could see Luana behind him on the couch, weaving a colorful blanket. She stiffened when she saw us in the doorway. Though their house had a traditional Anichi appearance, the inside looked modern, with hardwood floors, a TV on the wall, and overhead lighting.

"Sophia," Chief Cauac said brightly. "How may I help you?"

I held the tomahawk out to him. "It's the *Azaimperiai*, Chief. We were wondering if you could translate the runes."

He took the tomahawk gently from my hands and eyed it, like it was a precious piece of gold. "These are Hawkei symbols."

"We believe they may be secret Anichi symbols," Baine said. "Do you happen to know what they say?"

Chief Cauac gestured us inside. "I'm a bit rusty, but I may be able to help. Come in."

The three of us stepped inside. Luana set down her project and moved over on the couch. Esis immediately bounced on the back of the couch and started chasing Sierra around. She fluttered her wings at him and raced around the room, as if daring him to catch her. Chief Cauac's companion, a large white jaguar with blue stripes, sat curled by the fire, looking content.

Everything okay? Luana asked.

I briefly explained to her what was going on.

Pataa can help. I'm sure of it, she signed confidently.

We all went quiet as Chief Cauac inspected the symbols. He ran his fingers along the indents delicately. The crease between his eyebrows deepened the longer he stared. I shifted uncomfortably in my seat.

"Any clues as to what it says?" Liam asked.

Chief Cauac narrowed his eyes at the runes, like it'd help him read it better. "You're sure this is the *Azaimperiai*?"

Baine nodded firmly. "Certain."

Chief Cauac knitted his brow.

"We haven't been able to use it, though," I stated. My stomach sank the longer he stared at it. "We thought the runes might be instructions."

Chief Cauac took a deep breath, then dropped his shoulders. "I'm afraid not."

Baine looked positively puzzled. "Then what do they say?"

Chief Cauac handed the tomahawk back to Baine. "The closest translation would be, *The Spirit of Anichi thrives.*"

Liam and I exchanged a glance, but it was me who spoke. "W-what does that mean?"

"It was a saying the Anichi used in the last war," Chief Cauac explained. "It was a sort of motto— meant to bring them hope when we were being slaughtered. It meant no matter what happened to us, Anichi would live on."

"Well, it has to be some sort of clue," Liam insisted.

"I'm not sure it is." Chief Cauac sighed. "I'm afraid these runes are nothing more than decoration."

"So... we're stuck at another dead end?" I asked.

Chief Cauac looked uncertain, but sad. "I'm very sorry. I would like us to figure this out as much as anyone, but much of our knowledge on these matters has been lost."

"I will continue my research," Baine promised. "We'll figure this out—"

He was cut off by the sound of Esis' squeal. Sierra fluttered above my head, and Esis screamed as he jumped onto the couch to chase after her. He leapt onto the back of my neck and used it to kick himself upward in an attempt to catch the luna moth. His tiny little claws dug into me and caught on the Spirit Totem string around my neck. As he went soaring off of me, he pulled the string with him, nearly choking me with it.

"Ow, Esis!" I cried.

He rolled onto the ground behind the couch and shook his head. I rubbed the back of my neck where he'd scratched it and pulled the Spirit Totem from under my shirt to readjust it. When I pulled my fingers away from my stinging neck, I saw a light line of blood.

Let me help, Luana offered.

She placed a hand over the scratched on my neck and quickly healed me. As I started to put the Spirit Totem back under my shirt, she grabbed my wrist to stop me.

What? I asked, shooting her a quizzical expression.

Luana eyed the Spirit Totem carefully. *Those runes... they look the same as the ones on the* Azaimperiai.

I looked down to the Spirit Totem and realized she was right. I always took them to be decorative, but it wouldn't hurt to find out what they said.

"What'd she say?" Baine asked, unable to follow along with her quick signing.

I pulled the Spirit Totem over my head. Esis had perched on the couch again and was gently stroking the area where he'd scratched me.

"Luana pointed out these runes look the same as the ones on the tomahawk," I translated. "Chief, could you tell us what they say?"

"I can try." Cauac reached out to take the Spirit Totem from my hands. Beside me, Liam and Baine held their breath.

The runes were much smaller on the Spirit Totem. Chief Cauac had to grab a pair of reading glasses to see them. We waited several minutes in silence as he twisted the totem around in his fingers.

"What do you think it says?" Liam asked me quietly.

I shook my head. "No idea. But it's from the ancestors, which means it's probably important."

I found myself holding my breath. Even Esis was as still as could be behind me.

Finally, Chief Cauac spoke. "My translation isn't perfect, but it seems to say..."

He hesitated, as if searching for the right words. Liam was practically sitting on the edge of his seat by now.

Chief Cauac cleared his throat. "The best I can tell, it says, *Should the child of fire...*"

He trailed off. "No, that's not right. *Should the Koigni child accept her fate, an innocent soul must be...*" He contemplated the translation of the next rune. "*Must be freely given. The tribe will be reborn with the chosen one's greatest sacrifice.*"

I gasped. I'd gone completely speechless.

Chief Cauac repeated the translation, sounding confident in it this time. "*Should the Koigni child accept her fate, an innocent soul must be freely given. The tribe will be reborn with the chosen one's greatest sacrifice.*"

Liam's eyes went wide. "Does that sound like...?"

"Like the final prophecy piece?" I finished for him. "Absolutely."

"Wait," Baine said, slow on the uptake. "You think *this* is the prophecy Showana gave to Anichi?"

"It fits, doesn't it?" I pointed out, feeling hope surge through my chest.

We may not be closer to using the *Azaimperiai*, but we were closer to ending this war. "It makes perfect sense!" I cried, shooting to my feet.

Luana nodded in agreement as I signed for her.

"Anichi had lost their piece," I said. "The ancestors sent the Spirit Totem to me, not just because they chose me as a Spirit Warrior, but because they knew I needed this message— *we* needed it."

I ran the Anichi piece back over in my mind. There was a deep message there— something the ancestors wanted me to hear. I wasn't sure what it was yet, since I'd known for almost two years I'd have to give my life for the tribe. Showana had told me so when I contacted her in the temple on Ancestors' Day. She'd said I'd have to give up the very life I cherished. This prophecy reiterated that— I'd save the tribe through my greatest sacrifice.

So where was the message Showana wanted me to hear?

My breath stalled in my chest when it hit me. Never before had Showana put it in those words. An *innocent soul* must be given.

Problem was, I wasn't innocent.

But I knew who was.

❦

"WHAT'S WRONG, *PAWEE*?" Liam asked as we got ready for bed that night.

He whispered quietly, as Ava-Marie was already asleep in her crib. I folded a receiving blanket and couldn't meet his gaze. The wording of the prophecy had been eating away at me since we'd returned home. I wanted to convince myself I was interpreting the prophecy wrong, but I couldn't come up with an alternative explanation.

My gaze drifted over to Ava-Marie, where she lay silently in her crib. She was so precious. So beautiful. I knew exactly what the ancestors wanted.

The prophecy spoke of an innocent soul, and she was the only innocent soul I knew. Giving up Ava-Marie would be a far greater sacrifice than giving my own life. I'd give myself up for her a million times over and it would never be enough to fulfill this prophecy. I couldn't bear the thought that my suspicions might be true.

Just considering it made my lungs seize up. I thought I might puke.

Liam came up behind me and ran a finger over my skin beneath the strap of my nightgown. He pressed his warm lips to the back of my neck. "You're awfully quiet."

I set the receiving blanket aside and turned to him. "It's nothing," I lied.

I quickly corrected myself, knowing I couldn't hide my feelings from him anymore. We'd moved past that long ago.

I sighed. "Truth is, I'm worried about what the Spirit prophecy says."

I didn't voice my real concerns. If he knew what I was thinking, he'd lose his shit.

Liam took my face in his hands and pressed his lips to mine. My heart lifted, and he held the kiss for a long time. When he finally pulled away, he'd gone breathless.

"It scares me, too," he admitted. "I know what I signed up for when I fell in love with the chosen one, but I don't want to lose you, Soph."

I sniffled. I opened my mouth to say something— to tell him the ancestors had no intention of taking me from him— but I couldn't manage to choke the words out. How could I say something like this out loud? I was still trying to give myself permission to explore the possibility. It didn't seem real.

"I don't want to lose any of you," I whispered. That was all I got out before I choked up again. Tears began to well in my eyes.

"*Pawee.*" Liam lifted my chin to get me to look into his eyes. "We'll figure something out. I promise. Prophecies always have loopholes, right?"

Not this one, I tried to say, but I couldn't. I coughed, and Ava-Marie stirred in her crib.

I took Liam's hand. "Let's talk about this in another room."

Liam followed me across the hall into Imogen's old room. All her belongings had been removed, but the furniture and bedding was still there. Liam and I sat on the bed.

"Look, Liam," I started. "The thing is—"

He squeezed my hand, cutting me off. "I get it, Soph. You're scared. There's not a day goes by that I'm not terrified, too."

"This is different," I said.

"I know." His voice cracked. When I looked him in the eyes, tears beaded on his lower lid. "And I'm not ready for the ancestors to take you from me. I never will be."

"Liam, I—"

Liam cut me off by swooping in for a kiss. He reached his hand up to cradle the back of my neck. It was so warm and comfortable in his arms. It was like in that moment, nothing could hurt us. Not this war, not this prophecy— *nothing*.

And I liked it like that. But we had to talk about this.

"Liam—" I said, but he silenced me with another kiss.

His hand traveled down my back, then cupped my ass as he dragged me on top of him. "Shh, *pawee*. I don't want to talk about it right now. I just want this moment with you."

I couldn't argue. How could I drop this bomb on him right now, when we could share this beautiful moment together instead?

I relaxed into Liam's embrace, and he moaned as I straddled him. He started kissing me more passionately, but his hands were gentle on my back. This wasn't the raw sex we often enjoyed. This was tender, like we could both feel wounds opening within our hearts and were trying our damndest to take gentle care with them.

I lifted my hands to Liam's hair and started massaging my fingers through the strands. I could feel his erection forming, as there was nothing between us but a few thin layers of fabric. His fingers inched up my nightgown, until I lifted my arms above my head and he stripped it off. We started kissing again, and his hands came up to cup my breasts. They were tender, but he was gentle with them, and my heart hammered at the feeling of his hands on my skin.

"I love you, Liam," I whispered, before kissing him again with passion that made my whole body start to glow— literally.

"I love you, too." Liam grabbed my waist with one hand and cradled my back with the other and lowered me onto the bed.

His shadow danced across the ceiling as he loomed over my glowing form. Tingles danced up and down my body, as I got a thrill from watching it. His hands trailed from my breasts, all the way down my body and back up. He stopped at my panties, then shot me a hot smirk. He ducked down and stripped the panties off with his teeth, then teased me by running his tongue over the sensitive area between my legs.

I moaned and reached for him, begging him to come closer. His lips met mine again, and my hands roamed over him. I wanted him. I wanted him *now*. I stripped off his t-shirt, then practically ripped his pajama pants and boxers off of him.

He chuckled lightly. "*Somebody's* eager."

"Shh," I told him. "No talking."

After that, he went quiet. We didn't need to talk. We'd gotten into a rhythm with our bodies that we could *feel* the emotions flowing through each other. I could tell Liam was in a vulnerable place right now. He was just as bothered by the prophecy piece as I was, though for different reasons. He needed this comfort right now, and so did I.

When we were together like this, it was easy to believe everything was going to be okay, no matter the outcome. When the moment ended, the fear would creep back in and I wouldn't believe it anymore.

But that didn't matter right now. Right now, that fear was forgotten as all I felt was love flooding through me.

Liam positioned himself above me, and I wrapped my legs eagerly around his middle. I was ready for him, and he slid inside of me with ease. My back arched, and I let out soft moans as he moved inside of me.

Liam was making enough noise for the both of us that he didn't notice when the night stand beside us creaked. I looked over to see it scooting along the floor. My first instinct was the room was haunted, until I noticed a light shimmer in the air next to the bed.

It was a force field. *My* force field!

Without realizing it, I had conjured a force field to protect us. It was moving outward and pushing the furniture with it. I consciously pushed the force field outward, encompassing the other furniture in the room inside. But it didn't stop there. As Liam's love flooded into me, I expanded my force field with ease. It was easy to do, because Spirit magic was born out of comfort, love, and security.

I only told my force field to stop when it was large enough to protect the entire house and Julian sleeping outside. Liam hadn't even noticed.

I drew him closer, locking my legs around his middle and wrapping my arms tightly around him. He gasped for breath, and I let up slightly, but only enough for him to breathe. I wanted my family close at all times. I cherished the love we shared. I wanted more of this— of *us*. It was like he could never get close enough to satisfy me.

Tears began to fall down my cheeks, but I remained quiet. I hoped Liam wouldn't notice, but a tear ran down my cheek and onto his skin.

He drew away and looked down at me. "*Pawee*, what's wrong?"

I shook my head. Men always thought tears meant something was wrong. "Right now? Nothing. I'm just so in love with you."

"I know, Soph. I love you, too."

As if he meant to prove it, Liam wrapped his arms tighter around me and moved inside of me quicker and harder. I moaned in pleasure as a wonderful, freeing sensation built up inside of me. All the tension eased from my body, and together, Liam and I rode the wave of climax. It was a beautiful high that I wanted to experience with him over and over again.

And we did. *Twice.*

Long after we had reached our physical limits— and continued to push them— we fell onto the mattress beside each other, panting. I stared up at the ceiling, feeling so in love.

Behind my force field in our little slice of heaven, nothing could hurt our family. Not tonight, at least.

I just wished I could protect us forever. But in my heart, I knew I couldn't. I could pretend for the rest of tonight, but tomorrow, I'd have to tell Liam what I knew was the truth.

I had a choice to make. The prophecy demanded I give up an innocent soul, and make the greatest sacrifice a mother could.

There was no turning back. To save the lives of thousands, to save the tribe... Ava-Marie would have to die. Yet how could I seriously consider sacrificing the child I loved? The thought was so unbearable, it felt like my insides were being ripped out piece by piece through a hole in my chest.

When I thought of giving up Ava-Marie, my immediate response was to damn the tribe to hell. She was a baby— she had no part in this. She'd done nothing, and the Hawkei were guilty.

Yet there were other innocent Hawkei children... families who'd never harmed anyone. Could I sacrifice all the other infants in the tribe, all the other children who could have a future, just so my daughter could live?

Yes, I thought immediately, but the answer was as unbearable as the alternative.

I didn't feel there was a right choice I could make. Little ones had to die. Either my own child... or thousands of others.

If only I could lay my life down for my daughter's, like I had once before. I was willing and able. I would gladly die so she could live— but the ancestors didn't want me. They asked for *her*.

The choice was in my hands. Ava-Marie, or the tribe?

I couldn't save them both. But I knew. Losing either...

It would ruin me.

Liam

ELEVEN

I got home early from work, around five on a Tuesday. Sophia was bustling around the kitchen, putting things into a wicker basket as if trying to distract herself. Ava-Marie lay in a playpen, playing with the artifacts Baine had given her.

Baine clearly didn't know what to buy infants, so he'd given Ava-Marie a bunch of old things he'd found on his adventures over the years. She was fascinated by them, her eyes glimmering as she played with a sewn cloth doll, a round leather ball, and a set of wooden blocks at least a hundred years old.

Whenever Baine visited, Ava-Marie reached for him, as if eager to see what ancient toy he'd brought her next. Esis and Buttercup perched on the playpen's edges, looking down and watching in observation.

"What's all this?" I asked Sophia. I reached down to stroke Ava-Marie's back. She glanced up at me once before grabbing the cloth doll and tossing it at Esis. It hit him, and he went flying off the playpen with a trill.

"Ava, that wasn't nice," I scolded. Ava-Marie made her famous annoyed face and grabbed at the ball. Esis rubbed his head and tossed the doll back in the pen with a grumble.

"I thought we could have a picnic." Sophia's voice was cheerily fake, full of false light. I caught onto it immediately. She hadn't been the same since we discovered the Anichi piece of the prophecy yesterday. I had yet to figure out what was going on with her.

"It's a little cold, isn't it?" It wasn't that warm out, only fifty degrees or so.

"Vanessa and Bren invited all of us. They're warming a clearing to make it comfortable," Sophia explained. "I thought it'd be good to get out of the house."

We hadn't seen Vanessa and Bren in a while. It'd be nice to visit, and I was kind of sick of being cooped up all winter.

Sophia wouldn't meet my eyes. I caught her as she walked by and rubbed her shoulders, forcing her to face me. "Something's on your mind."

Her eyes screamed yes, but she forced out, "Later. Let's just enjoy the moment. We'll talk about it tonight."

Sophia avoided stuff when there was no way to fix what was coming. Whatever she had to talk about was dire. But she wasn't ready to face it yet, and needed a break, so I said, "Okay. Tonight."

Bren and Vanessa had elevated the temperature in order to enjoy the day. We dismounted Julian and met them in a clearing outside the village, which was almost more like a park. It was seventy degrees in the small area, and the air smelled clean. Bren was grilling, while Vanessa sat on a quilted blanket beneath a tree. She was shuffling large, square cards, while her son Xavier played with Aisha's tail. The dragon was playing with Kingston. The manticore perched in a tree, shaking branches. Julian squeezed through the trees, his tongue lolling out of his mouth as he gazed at Aisha.

They weren't the only ones in the clearing. Jonah and Jake were playing badminton, while Imogen and Cade watched. Arabelle and Sassy had curled up against each other, their heads bouncing from left to right as they watched Jake and Jonah smack the birdie back and forth.

The woods around *Hok'evale* were filled with previously-thought extinct magical creatures, flocking to Bren and Vanessa's warmth. Into the clearing walked a creature with a long neck and a small, dished face, black eyes glinting like coal. It had antennae twisting out of its head, and talons like those of birds on its feet. Its body was a mixture of white and blue feathers with pale fur. Two butterfly wings rose out of its back and shone in the sun, reflecting colors into the grass.

"It's a windfarer," Vanessa explained when she noticed my confused look. "Fae creatures. They're unusually rare in these parts."

Fae creatures were part of Arcanean lore and came from Malovia. It was exceptionally unique to see one outside of Europe. Someone must've brought it here. Behind it, more animals followed. A tiger with black and teal zebra stripes, a white mane and black horns prowled next to a golden lynx with four-pronged antlers that were growing green leaves. Rabbits with wings of hawks and tails like oxen perched in the branches, twittering like birds.

Ava-Marie's eyes locked on to each creature as it came into the light, and she kicked her feet against Sophia's side. Our Familiars observed the wild creatures calmly and made no move to attack. The windfarer lay down by Julian's side, and the rest followed suit. Julian, who had been trying to catch Aisha's eye, preened, not impressed.

If our Familiars were comfortable, it was fine to relax. These creatures, though wild, wouldn't hurt us.

Squeaks was lying next to Vanessa. Sabor stood over her. Sophia knelt and propped Ava-Marie up against Squeaks' stomach. The hippogriff swung her head around and rustled Ava-Marie's hair, brushing it backwards with a warm gust of breath. Ava-Marie stroked her fingers against Squeaks' beak, and the bird cooed.

"Squeaks, come and play," Jonah said. He gestured to her, but she shook her head, and he huffed.

"What's up with her?" I asked.

"Squeaks has no energy lately," Jonah complained. "And she eats like a horse. I don't know why."

"Doesn't she *always* eat like a horse?" I questioned.

Jake tilted his head at Squeaks, before he said, "Let her be. She'll recover her strength in time."

Sophia sat down next to Ava-Marie and crossed her legs, while I took a seat on the picnic bench nearby. "What are you playing with, Vanessa?"

"Oracle cards," Vanessa said brightly. "I like to mess around with them."

"Ooh!" Imogen heard us, and her eyes brightened. "I want to play!"

I cringed. "Elementai don't take well to oracle cards. Why are you using them?"

Imogen rolled her eyes. "Relax, Liam. It's just for fun."

"Come join in." Vanessa waved her over, and Imogen joined the circle. Jonah curiously stood nearby as the oracle cards were shuffled.

The oracle cards themselves were green, the undersides decorated with beautiful drawings of women, nature, and ethereal creatures. Vanessa fanned the cards out on the blanket and said, "Okay, Imogen. You draw first."

Imogen picked a card and showed it to Vanessa. A woman with a dress made of leaves was petting a dragon that was nestled in her lap. Vanessa looked at it, then smiled. "That's the card of Rebirth. You are currently in the process of moving past your trauma and breaking through limiting cycles. If you look to the earth, she will heal you."

"That's a good reading," Imogen said.

I approved. Imogen had been through a lot lately. It was good the cards deemed she was getting past it, though secretly I didn't believe in this nonsense.

"Ooh, do me," Jonah gushed. "What's my fate?"

"Hold on, silly." Vanessa laughed, then she shuffled the deck again. She fanned them toward Jonah, and he yanked out a card so hard it caused the rest of them to fall to the blanket in a heap.

As Vanessa scrambled to reorganize them, Jonah squeaked, "What's this mean? It looks sexy."

On the card, a naked woman with a halo of light around her head held her stomach. Above her hands, a flame burst out of her chest.

Vanessa narrowed her eyes. "That's the Center card. You have a choice to make soon, to follow your heart or the mistakes of your past. The closer you come to making a decision, the more conflict there will be. Choose wisely."

Jonah handed Vanessa back the card, giving a sheepish glance at Jake. Vanessa shuffled the cards and said, "Okay, Liam. Your turn."

"Uh, fuck no," I started. "I'm not playing this shit." Last time we'd had a reading, I'd drawn the Death card. This wasn't my thing.

"Too late, already pulling a card for you." Vanessa held up a card of a woman looking over her shoulder, holding a flower in her hand as birds flew by. "I've never pulled this before. This is the card of Rebellion. This is a reminder that you need to rest and nurture yourself; otherwise, you risk ruining everything you've worked for. See, Liam, even my oracle cards think you work too hard."

I scowled. "I do not."

Vanessa rolled her eyes. "Whatever you say." She shuffled the cards again, then fanned them out before Sophia. "Okay, Sophia, your turn."

Sophia hesitated, as if she was scared to draw a card. But eventually, she reached out and took one.

Vanessa frowned slightly when she saw it. Upon it was the anguished face of a woman, her hair twisted with dying flowers. She looked to be angry, or in pain. "This is my least favorite card. Abrasion."

"What does it mean?" Sophia asked.

"You have to pull back on your emotions and let the truth reveal itself, even if it's painful," Vanessa said. "You must let go of your feelings to let the next step be as painless as possible, though it's going to be difficult regardless. The only way to avoid it is to approach it with understanding instead of anger."

Sophia paled, as if the card's meaning had confirmed whatever was on her mind. I scoffed. "Don't worry, Soph. They're just stupid cards."

She didn't answer me. We had to stop doing these fucking readings. They never went well for her.

"This is like when we got our tarot card readings from Hattie. Remember?" Jonah asked.

"Yeah," Imogen said slowly. "When I pulled my tarot card, I got the Seven of Cups, which signified illusion. I was under the illusion Trace was dead, which he wasn't. I also got the Star, which meant I would go through many challenges, but it would be worth it in the end. I would embark on a spiritual journey and come out stronger."

Imogen beamed. "I totally think Hattie was talking about my recovery. And she was right. I do feel surrounded by peace."

"And I got the Ten of Cups. Which meant walking away from my family, and making another one," Jonah said. He smiled again as he looked back at Jake. "I think that's definitely in my future."

"Liam, you got the King of Swords, which is a card of authority and leadership. It predicted you being chief!" Imogen said.

"Yeah," I said. "I'm *sure* it's not just coincidence."

Imogen narrowed her eyes at my sarcasm. "Seriously? How can you deny that? It's like, too perfect to be wrong."

"Maybe tarot and oracle cards are just so broad, they can come true no matter what happens," I said.

Imogen let out a puff of breath. "You're no fun."

Jonah tapped his chin. "Whatever you think, it seems like each of our readings have come true."

"Yes, except—" Imogen broke off. She glanced at Sophia, then looked away.

I scowled. During our tarot reading, Sophia had drawn the Three of Swords— the card of heartbreak. Hattie had said Sophia would make a great sacrifice, and lose the life she cherished because of it.

Sophia shrugged. "It's fine. It's just a game."

Her voice didn't convince me. Sophia believed her readings were real.

Vanessa shifted. She put the oracle cards away in her bag and said, "Um... I'm going to help Bren. Dinner's almost ready."

Vanessa walked away. I noticed Julian was blowing smoke hearts in Aisha's direction. Aisha's tongue flickered out to touch them, and her eyes fluttered. Nearby, Esis handed out a flower crown to Buttercup. She adorned it, and Esis puffed out his chest proudly.

I hurried to change the subject. I didn't want to talk about those stupid cards any longer. Elementai shouldn't be messing with them in the first place. "By the way, we should tell you guys that Sophia and I found the Anichi piece," I said to Imogen and Jonah. "Chief Cauac was able to interpret the symbols on Sophia's Spirit Totem and tell us what it meant."

"What?!" Jonah floundered, and he sat beside me.

"Tell us everything," Imogen said firmly.

I looked to Sophia. She put a hand on Ava-Marie. She paused, before she recited, "*Should the Koigni child accept her fate, an innocent soul must be freely given. The tribe will be reborn with the chosen one's greatest sacrifice.*"

The only sound that could be heard for long moments was that of the Familiars playing. Imogen was the first to take a breath. "Prophecies can be interpreted, right? Maybe this means you won't die— you'll just have to give something up."

"That's what I'm worried about," Sophia said.

Jonah looked confused, but Imogen's eyes cleared. She gasped. I didn't understand her reaction.

"We're not losing you, *pawee*," I snapped. "I don't care what the prophecy says; I can't let you give yourself up."

"We knew from the beginning that might be the case," Sophia argued. She sounded very tired. "This is nothing we weren't sure of."

"But... if the prophecy's true, Sophia... that means you will die," Jonah objected.

A thin line of tears dotted Sophia's eyelids. "If we're *lucky*, it'll be me."

"What the fuck do you mean?" I didn't like the sound of that at all.

Imogen reached out and squeezed Sophia's hand. Sophia had tears in her eyes as she watched Ava-Marie play with Squeaks' feathers.

Jonah's expression darkened. He turned sharply and headed over to Jake, nearly in a run.

I was left baffled. Looked like I was the only one who was slow on the uptake of the prophecy's true meaning. Imogen gave Sophia a look, and my wife stood. She reached out her hand for mine. "Take a walk with me?"

"Sure." I let her pull me into the forest.

Imogen stayed behind to watch Ava-Marie as we left the clearing. The temperature dropped, leaving the area cold again. There were no magical creatures out here that we could see. They were all hiding in their dens away from the chill, which seemed to permeate not just the outside world, but every pore of my being. This conversation wasn't going to be good.

We walked for almost a quarter of a mile in silence. I was wondering when Sophia would break the damn ice. My breathing became more labored than usual, and Sophia glanced up. "You okay?"

"I'm having trouble keeping up," I admitted.

Vanessa hadn't been lying when she said I worked too much. I was addicted to my job. And it was quickly becoming a problem. Every morning, I woke up exhausted now.

"I'm sorry." Sophia frowned. "I wouldn't have made you walk this far, but I don't want to be overheard."

"Why not?" I stopped. She let go of my hand and faced me on the path.

Sophia's face twisted. "Because I know how you're going to react."

"React about what?" She was scaring me.

"Liam, come on." Sophia's shoulders sagged. "The prophecy says an innocent life must be freely given. What do you think that means?"

A sickening dread coursed outward, causing my veins to freeze. The reason why I hadn't realized it came slamming into me— because I refused to consider it a possibility. My brain didn't even want to think about it.

"We're not giving up Ava." My voice sounded so hollow. This couldn't have been what the prophecy meant, could it?

"Showana didn't want to talk to us when Madame Wells summoned her. Why wouldn't she, unless she didn't want to tell us we had to sacrifice our child to save the tribe?" Sophia pleaded.

"Fuck the tribe!" I shouted. "I'm not sacrificing our daughter!"

"You act like I want to!" Sophia shuddered. She rubbed her hands with her face before she turned away, slamming a fist against a tree.

"It sounds like you've made a decision." Our own *child?* How could Sophia consider this?

"It's not like that." Sophia took deep breaths, as if she was in terrible pain. "I love our daughter more than anything— more than my own life, more than even *you*, Liam. And I hate what the ancestors are asking me to do. It's killing me. This is the hardest decision I could ever make."

"I don't even know how you can consider it. This is our baby." Ancestors, I was going to vomit. My whole body shook. Thinking of Ava-Marie, still and cold— it practically dropped me to my knees.

"You know I want Ava!" Sophia said. "But I can't stop thinking about all those other kids. If we lose the war, the Hawkei are gone forever. We aren't the only people who are parents, Liam. Thousands of babies will die. Is that worth the life of one child, even if it's our own?"

"Of course it is."

But still... that got me. All those poor babies, dead from the war... I could barely stomach it. I'd still pick Ava-Marie, even if it made me a monster for doing so, but the weight of making that decision was suffocating.

"Think about Jackson. He's only two," Sophia stammered. "What about him? What about Katie and Christian? What about the rest of Imogen's siblings, the brothers she has left? What about Vanessa's son, or Mia's? Can we damn them all to save our daughter?"

My knees shook. Protecting Ava-Marie was my number one priority, and she was the one I loved the most... but yet, not the only one I loved. When she was born, I kept thinking she was worth sacrificing the whole world for. Could I really live up to that promise?

"Prophecies can be changed," I said. "We can stop this. The prophecy never said she needs to die."

"I know. But the wording seems clear. I don't think there's a loophole on this one."

"There has to be, Soph! For ancestors' sake."

"This is more than the prophecy. I keep going back to that night." Sophia wrapped her arms around herself and squeezed tightly. "Her birth... it was so strange. So many odd things about it. What if Ava-Marie wasn't supposed to survive?"

"That's bullshit," I spat. "How can you think like that?"

"Listen to what I'm saying," Sophia pleaded. "Ava *wouldn't* have survived if Luana hadn't interceded. Without her magic, she'd be gone. I thank the ancestors every day that she's here, but what if it's not meant to be? What if my sacrifice had been meant to take place *that night*?"

I gave a sarcastic noise. "I'm not leaving my child's life up to something as manipulative as fate."

"Your mother and I have discussed this over and over since it happened," Sophia said. She could hardly breathe as she burst into tears. She was crying harder than I'd ever seen her. "And we both agree. She's never had an infant survive that dangerous of a birth, but Ava-Marie pulled through. I know in my heart Ava was *supposed* to die that night. And now that she's still alive, maybe the ancestors are asking me to give her back."

"The ancestors can go fuck themselves." I shoved my hands roughly into my pockets. Cold dread was climbing over every inch of my body, and I despised it. I thought I'd moved past all this, but no matter what I did, it was like the dark side of me wouldn't let go.

I couldn't lose my child. I'd go insane. And I'd fight the ancestors, the Great Spirit, and whatever other miserable bastard tried to take her from me.

Sophia shivered. "I can't stop thinking about it. And I won't do it, not of my own volition, but what if I don't have a choice?"

"You always have a choice, Soph. Showana Harjo made that clear. She gave you an out and said that your decisions would shape the fate of the tribe. Other Koigni children would rise to take your place."

"But can I back out this far in? We're in the middle of a war. This isn't going to end well for anyone, and Maddie said us winning would be worse than us losing," Sophia insisted. "I think the time for me to run away from my destiny is long past. There's no turning back."

The tears ran down her face and met her trembling lips. "I don't have any control over this. I worry the ancestors are going to take Ava-Marie away from me no matter what I choose."

"Soph." I took her in my arms. A cold wind blew by, and I braced us against it. Sophia quivered against me and thought.

When I was a boy, I thought my father could defend us from anything. He always protected the family, and sheltered us from whatever storm came along. I aspired to be just like him, to protect Sophia and Ava-Marie from the shadows that festered in the dark.

I didn't think I could shelter my family from this, though. This felt too big.

I was the head of the family. It was my job to lay my life down for those I loved, but fuck all if the ancestors wanted me. They demanded my child.

I refused to give her up. And if they wouldn't take me in her place, I'd fight. I'd fight until everybody else was dead, if I had to.

"Don't you see? It's unavoidable. My tarot reading was the Three of Swords. The card of heartbreak. What does that sound like to you?" Sophia sobbed. "The rest of you had your readings come true, but mine is yet to be. Hattie was a witch. Her reading was influenced by her magic, which makes it unavoidable. What worse heartbreak could there be than to sacrifice—"

"Those cards are fucked. It's not real," I choked out.

"And yet it keeps coming up. It's undeniable. I pulled the card of emotional pain, unless I can let go." Sophia swallowed. "But I can't let go of my daughter. If she dies, I'll die with her."

No doubt I'd soon follow. My heart would give out.

"There has to be a way to save both Ava and the tribe. You hear me?" I squeezed her shoulders.

Sophia stared outward into the abyss. Her gaze was more afraid than it'd ever been. Sophia was always brave, but how could you be brave when the ancestors asked you to make a sacrifice like this?

"Maddie's biggest lesson is prophecies aren't set in stone. It might not turn out like we feared," I said softly. I lifted Sophia's chin. "You've gotta have faith."

Her voice trembled. "I don't see how we're going to make it out of this one."

I gave a low laugh, but it was more or less just to calm her down. "We find a way to make a miracle."

She stepped away from me and ran a hand through her hair. "So what do we do now? I know we have to get the *Azaimperiai* to work, but other than that, I'm not sure there's a way forward."

It was like my heart stopped when I considered the possibilities. "Prophecies have loopholes. I know you don't think this one does, but why wouldn't it? What if the sacrifice isn't killing Ava-Marie, but giving her to the other side?"

"That's worse than death. I'd sooner send her to the Ancestral Lands than let Oleander touch her!" Sophia snapped. "Do you want her to end up like Maddie?"

"Then there's only one other alternative."

Sophia stared at me. The wind whistled through the trees, and she said, "You can't be asking me to do that."

"Yes, I'm asking. For fuck's sake, I have to do it, too!" I said. "This is the only way to save her life."

Sophia turned away from me, but I grabbed her shoulders and forced her to face me again. "Listen to me. We send Ava away. We give her to someone else to raise, and they'll make sure she's safe. If she's far away from *Hok'evale*, far away from Kinpago, the prophecy can't touch her. And you'll fulfill it by making your sacrifice. Then you can save the tribe."

The tears were still pouring from Sophia's eyes. "She'll never know who we are. If I give her up, I'll never see her again."

"If you don't, she'll die." My voice was as hollow as the night I'd tried to take my own life. The only reason I wasn't crying was because I didn't think I had anything left in me. The reality of what I had to do was still so overbearing, so finite. It was like the world was coming to an end, and I couldn't comprehend it.

"But she needs me," Sophia whimpered. "I'm her mother."

I was going against instinct, here. Sophia's job as a new mother, in the first months of her child's life, was to do everything to protect that child and keep it close. I was asking her to let go of that. Not to mention my own feelings were screaming at me not to let my daughter go.

Yet I cared about Ava-Marie more than I cared about myself. Whatever happened to me, whatever I felt, it didn't matter. She had to come first.

"Doya made that sacrifice for you. You wouldn't be here if she hadn't let you go. You have to make the same decision," I pleaded. My voice trembled. I hated the whole fucking world right now. Every time Sophia and I caught a break, it was like the universe knocked us down again. Why was it asking us to do the most impossible thing, when we'd had so little time with our girl?

At the reminder of her mother's sacrifice, Sophia gave an emotional sound. Her lip trembled. She wiped away at her face. "Okay. So we send her away. I'll make the sacrifice to save the tribe, but only for her. And not until it gets so awful, we have no other choice."

Soothing relief and horrible, agonizing pain shot through me all at once. Sophia wanted to buy us some time, and it was a treasure, but things were going to get awful, fast. This war was quickly coming to a head, and I wanted Ava-Marie long gone before that happened. That gave us so little time before we had to let her go.

My voice choked up as I said, "Who do we ask? Jonah and Imogen are the obvious choices."

Sophia shook her head. "We need them to help us fight. We can't break up the team now."

"What about your adoptive parents? Robert and Susan?"

She frowned. "It feels unfair to ask them. They took me in as a baby, and it wouldn't be right to ask them to do it again. Plus, they have their foster kids. There aren't enough homes to foster those kids as it is, and it isn't fair to put them on the street just to give our daughter a home."

"Then who?"

Sophia pondered for a moment. "Vanessa and Bren," she said. "They have an infant. They'll know how to take care of Ava, and they're good parents."

I trusted both of them. And neither of them were as involved in this war as the rest of my friends. They were a good choice. "All right. Let's ask them now."

I put my arm around Sophia's shoulders as we walked back to the clearing. She was still sobbing. I squeezed her shoulder. "I'm sorry, Soph."

Sophia gasped, and the sound cut clear through me. I was Ava's father— it was my loss, too. But I felt like I had to say something to stop my wife's heart from breaking. I didn't think my own was salvageable.

When we returned to the clearing, Vanessa, Bren, Jake and Cade were eating. But Jonah and Imogen had waited for us. They stood by the entrance to the forest path, their expressions wary.

"I'm so sorry, you guys." Imogen shifted Ava-Marie on her hip, then passed her over to Sophia. Sophia nestled her tight. Esis, who'd seen us returning, ran over and sat at Sophia's feet, peering upward at her with a loyal expression.

"Prophecies are weird," I rushed to say, but they sounded like empty words. "Maybe it's not what we think."

Imogen looked down. Jonah moved from one foot to the other as he asked quietly, "What are you gonna do?"

"We have to send Ava away," I said. "We don't have a choice."

Imogen gasped. Jonah looked near tears as he said, "Bro..."

"We have to save her life. It's our only shot," I added.

Sophia didn't say anything. Her eyes were watching Ava.

"Who were you gonna ask?" Jonah asked.

"Vanessa and Bren," I started. "Could you guys give us some space?"

Imogen and Jonah drew away. Both of them got the attention of their significant others, and we approached Vanessa and Bren. Vanessa was bouncing Xavier on her hip, while Bren cleaned up from dinner. Sophia and I hadn't eaten, but neither of us desired anything resembling food. It'd taste like sand in our mouths.

Vanessa noticed Sophia's red-rimmed eyes, and her face fell. "Sophia, what's wrong? Why are you crying?"

Sophia sniffed. Bren came over with a concerned expression.

"We found the Anichi piece of the prophecy," I explained. "It says that Sophia has to give up an innocent life in order to prevent the Hawkei from going extinct— someone she loves. We... we think it means Ava."

Vanessa's mouth dropped open. Bren shook his head in disbelief. "Nah. The ancestors aren't asking that Ava-Marie *dies*, are they?"

"We're trying to avoid that." I spoke softly. "We figure... if Ava's not around, she can't get hurt. And if Sophia gives her away, she's making her sacrifice to save the tribe."

Vanessa shifted Xavier. "Are you asking us to take her in?"

"Well..." My voice drifted off. Sophia nodded, and I forced out, "Yes. We need someone to adopt her, and get her out of here."

Ancestors, this felt horrible. It felt like I was pawning off my kid. Or selling her, or something. Every awful thing Doya had ever done seemed excusable, in this light.

Bren waved his hand. "Say no more, Liam. We'll take her."

My heart dropped. I was keenly aware of Ava-Marie kicking at my arm as I said, "But you'll be adopting a child, and leaving *Hok'evale,* probably the state. I know it's a lot to ask—"

"It's nothing to ask," Bren said. "Of course we'll take her in."

"You don't need time to discuss it? This is a big decision," I said.

"We don't have to. We've been thinking about leaving anyway, for Xavier's sake," Vanessa said. "This makes our decision easy. You guys are our friends, and your daughter needs our help. We'll raise her like she was our own. We promise."

Bren nodded, and my small hopes fell flat. Part of me had been hoping they'd say no... but that was selfish of me.

"Just... give us more time with her," I said. "We don't want to let her go until we have to."

Vanessa nodded. "We'll be ready to leave when that happens, Liam. Take all the time you need."

My throat got so tight that I couldn't say anything more. My eyes burned, and I forced myself to turn away from them.

My final words carried a heavy weight. They implied Sophia and I needed to enjoy our time with Ava-Marie as much as we could.

Before she was gone out of our lives— forever.

TWELVE

The next two weeks passed in the blink of an eye. I never let Ava-Marie out of my sight. I didn't know it was possible to grieve for someone before you'd lost them, but I did. Since the day we heard the wording of the Spirit prophecy piece, a weight like a brick had settled in my gut, and no amount of kisses or hugs seemed to lift it. I couldn't bear to give up my daughter, but more than anything, I wanted her to be safe.

But I couldn't give her up yet. She needed me.

I woke one morning to the weight of Ava-Marie on my chest. I lay in the recliner in the living room, and Ava-Marie was curled soundlessly against me. An afghan was draped over my legs. It hadn't been there last night, and I knew Liam had put it there to keep us warm.

Sunlight spilled in through the window. I realized that I'd slept in a lot longer than normal. I wondered why Liam didn't wake me before he left for work. I glanced around for Esis and Buttercup, but they were nowhere to be seen. They were probably off making kurble babies. Honestly, I wouldn't be surprised.

Ava-Marie stirred, and I stroked her hair. I couldn't take my eyes off her. She grabbed tightly to my shirt and started to cry. I consoled her by pushing the fabric of my shirt aside and breastfeeding her.

After Ava-Marie was fed and changed, I sat down again to cuddle her, only to notice how silent the house was. It was unusual, since there was usually *someone* over, or kurbles running around making noises.

I furrowed my brow as I stood and peeked into the hallway. "Esis?"

There was no response.

"Esis, you here?" I was starting to get worried.

I cradled Ava-Marie in my arms and opened the door to Jonah's old room, but there were no kurbles inside. I checked Imogen's empty room, then the bathroom, before opening the door to my room.

I gasped when I saw a form lying there on the bed. Liam was sleeping with his back to the door and a pillow over his head. Esis and Buttercup were curled up near his stomach, cuddling him. Ava-Marie made a noise, and Liam stirred.

"Liam, what are you doing here?" I asked. "I thought you were at work."

He groaned and rolled over. His features were ashen, and he blinked a few times, like the sunlight hurt his eyes. He winced as he tried to shift on the bed. His voice came out strained. "I'm not going to work. Not today."

"Ancestors!" I rushed to his side and pressed my hand to his forehead. It was boiling, but I didn't know if that was because he was running a fever or because he'd been sleeping under the pillow. "What's going on?"

Liam cleared his throat and winced again. "Flare-up."

"Let me heal you," I demanded. I didn't wait for his answer. I began channeling my magic into him. A bit of color returned to his face, but it was barely noticeable. My powers had hardly worked.

Liam pushed my hand away. "It's fine, *pawee*. I'll be fine."

"You will *not* be fine. Liam, you promised to be honest with me about how you felt."

He sighed deeply and finally met my gaze. "You're right, *pawee*. I'm sorry."

I sat on the side of the bed and pushed the hair from his eyes. Ava-Marie stared down at her father, and Esis and Buttercup both stirred to look at him.

"So, how *are* you feeling?" I asked. I'd felt it when I was healing him, but I wanted to hear him say it out loud.

"Awful," he admitted, though he barely sounded like himself. He spoke slowly, like he was confused about which words to use. "My muscles are so tight I can hardly move."

Tears brimmed his eyes, like he was ready to cry from the pain. When he got like this, it was hard for him to even talk. Putting sentences together to form conversation was a monumental task.

"Let me make you breakfast," I suggested.

"No, *pawee*," Liam quickly declined. "I won't be able to keep it down anyway."

"Can I make you some tea?" I asked.

He shook his head. "I just need time."

"Well, I can't sit around and do nothing," I protested. "I want to help."

He drew a heavy breath, but it seemed labored. "Can you open the window?"

"Yeah, I can do that." I stood and opened the window, since it was the only thing that made me feel like I was useful.

Liam shifted on the bed again, like he couldn't get in a comfortable position. It was clear sleep was going to be nearly impossible for him today. I worried that would slow his healing.

"Let me try healing you again," I offered. "Esis can help."

Esis' ears perked up at the sound of his name, and he stood alert, like he was ready to help.

Liam shrugged. "You can try, but—"

"No buts," I insisted. "We're going to make you better."

I set Ava-Marie in her crib. She fussed a little, but when I handed her a rattle, she quieted down. I sat next to Liam again and placed a hand on his chest. His breathing was labored, and his face had paled again. Esis stood near his head and placed a palm between his eyebrows. Buttercup seemed to realize what was going on and came over to curl in my lap. I held her and worked on drawing energy from her and Esis at the same time.

Warm, calm energy flowed through me, and my hand glowed. Liam's systems pushed back, resisting my magic. Today, his illness tasted like ash in my mouth. His lungs were struggling to gather air, and every muscle in his body seemed tense and knotted. I pushed past the barriers, and my magic filled his body, but it only did so much. When I pulled away, Liam was breathing easier, but I could tell by the look on his face he was still in a lot of pain.

"Thanks, *pawee*," he whispered without opening his eyes.

"Any better?" I asked nervously.

"Kind of," he said. Ava started crying, and he added, "Don't worry about me. Take care of our little girl."

I frowned as I stood and went to Ava-Marie's crib. I thought Liam was downplaying how he really felt, but I'd done all I could. I felt hopeless. There was only one more thing I could do.

"Come on Esis, Buttercup," I said at the door. "Let's give Liam some space to sleep this off. I love you, Liam."

"Love you, too, *pawee*," he replied, though it sounded like he didn't really know what he was saying. He was totally out of it.

The kurbles bounded out of the room beside each other, and I shut the door behind them. I set Ava-Marie in her bouncer and went to the kitchen to grab a notepad. I scribbled out a note to Professor Perot, then went outside to where Julian was curled up by the door. He had a sad look on his face.

"Liam's not well today," I told him, though he looked like he already knew. "Can you deliver this letter to Perot?"

I held out the envelope, and Julian became alert. He stood and took the letter in his talons, then gave me a firm nod, like he understood. Within moments, Julian had taken off to the skies.

I went back inside, nerves knotting in my belly. I tried to keep busy by playing with Ava-Marie, but I couldn't really focus until I heard the sound of wings beating outside. Julian had returned, along with a note from Perot stating that he'd written a prescription for Liam and sent it to the pharmacy, but that I'd have to pick it up myself.

"Looks like we're going for a walk, Ava," I told her as I slid her into the cradleboard. "Esis, Buttercup, you want to come along?"

Esis nodded eagerly, and Buttercup started chasing her tail in excitement.

The walk to the pharmacy wasn't far, and though the clouds were thick overhead, the temperature was warm. Ava-Marie kept making the cutest noises, and her eyes darted everywhere as she took in the world. I was going to miss her curious soul.

Stop! I told myself. I'd promised I wouldn't look into the future. If I kept worrying about it, I'd forget to enjoy the time we had left. I vowed to live in the present moment with my precious little girl as long as I possibly could.

Right now, however, I didn't have time to stop at the stream or show Ava-Marie the pretty colored fabrics at the market. I couldn't spare a walk along the edge of the canyon in search of shiny rocks for Esis and Buttercup's collection. I was in a rush to get Liam his medicine, so he could make it through the day.

We arrived at the pharmacy, and I turned the corner next to an aisle of candies Esis was eyeing eagerly. When I saw who was standing in front of the counter, I took a startled step back. She had a canine Familiar at her side and carried a little boy in a sling across her front.

Mia.

She looked better than the last time I saw her, though she didn't look quite how I remembered her. Her short hair was tied back, but she didn't wear any makeup, and for once her boobs weren't spilling out of her shirt. For the first time, she looked down-to-earth.

I was surprised when I caught the thought going through my head. Never would I have described Mia as *down-to-earth*. Wyatt must've really been helping her. The arrogance she once wore in her features had been washed away. I could almost believe that everything she'd been through— becoming a mother, leaving Micah, and coming to *Hok'evale*— had humbled her. Was I being fair to hold on to this grudge for what she'd done to Liam?

Yes and no, my instinct said.

I stepped closer to the pharmacy counter to wait my turn. Esis and Buttercup ran around my feet, playing a game of tag. I overheard the pharmacist giving Mia a prescription for oral thrush. I knew it was common in babies, but I was glad Ava-Marie hadn't gotten it.

Mia thanked the pharmacist and stepped away from the counter. I held my breath, hoping by some miracle that she'd walk off without spotting me, but I wasn't so lucky. Mia nearly ran into me, and her son started to cry.

Her eyes went wide in shock as she stopped in her tracks. She backed away— like she was *scared* of me. After the way I treated her the last time we met, I couldn't blame her.

I would've liked to give her another piece of my mind. After everything she'd done, she deserved whatever karma she got.

But looking at her now, how she seemed like a totally different person, I wondered if she'd already gotten that karma. I supposed that was for the ancestors to judge, not me. At least she'd left Liam and my family alone since she'd come to *Hok'evale*. That much I could give her credit for.

Mia turned down her gaze. It was strange how immediate her reaction was, like she didn't contemplate it at all. Micah had really done a number on her. She was scared, timid. It wasn't until that moment that I realized how bad it was— that she was a victim as much as my enemy. How could I preach peace and unity of the Hawkei when I'd treated Mia so horrendously?

Mia went to take a step around me, but I stopped her. "Mia, wait."

She stopped dead, like she was used to doing what she was told. Fucking Micah.

Her Familiar, Taryn, growled. Esis and Buttercup had stopped chasing each other and looked on high alert, like they'd defend me if Taryn pounced.

"I was just leaving," Mia said in a small voice.

"This won't take long," I assured her.

She stopped to listen, though it didn't look like she wanted to.

"I just wanted to say... I'm sorry." The words felt like thorns on my tongue, but I meant them.

"You... you are?" she asked. Taryn's growls ceased from beside her.

"I overreacted when you came to *Hok'evale*." It was hard to admit, but I had to say it out loud— for both of our sakes. "I know you want a better life for Mattias."

Her son stirred in her arms. Mia blinked a few times, like she couldn't wrap her head around my apology. "That means a lot."

"I can't forget what you did to Liam," I stated, to be clear. "But... I want you to know that you're welcome in *Hok'evale*. I won't do anything to harm your life here."

A smile touched the corners of Mia's lips. I didn't think I'd ever seen her smile before. It was strange. "Thank you, Sophia. I know I can't take back what I did to Liam, but I am sorry. Honestly. I hope that one day you can finally forgive me."

"I do," I said. The words came out of my mouth so fast I didn't even realize I'd said them. Were they true? Did I really *forgive* Mia? I'd never forget it, and I couldn't ever trust her fully, but I *could* forgive her. I could let it go. And that was one of the most freeing feelings in the world. "I forgive you, Mia."

She breathed a sigh of relief, like she'd been carrying a fifty-pound weight on her shoulders and my words had lifted it. "Wow, Sophia. I don't know what to say. Maybe... maybe now I can actually make *Hok'evale* my home. For me and Mattias."

I gazed down at her little boy. He was a few months older than Ava-Marie, but he reminded me of her a little. They had the same Toaqua genes, and looked like they could be related.

"I hope so," I said, though all this was difficult to admit to her face.

"Good luck, Sophia," Mia added. "With whatever path the ancestors choose for you."

Then Mia turned and left the store.

It was strange to hear such words from one of my enemies, but then again, that made the well wishes worth even more. Mia wasn't just saying that to turn around and stab me in the back later. We were headed our separate ways, and by some miracle, we wished each other well despite our deep-seated hatred for one another. I'd never experienced such a strange phenomenon.

I was still reeling from shock when I returned home. Julian was standing outside the door, shaking his head wildly like he was trying to tell me something.

My guts sank immediately. "What is it, boy?"

Esis and Buttercup caught on quicker than I had and went running for the door. I quickly followed behind. I dropped the pharmacy bag on the counter on my way through the kitchen, then rushed behind Esis down the hall. I gasped when I saw Liam lying in the doorway to our bedroom.

"Liam!" I cried.

Esis was already at his side, trying to work his healing magic. At the sound of my voice, Liam lifted his head. He looked at me, but his eyes didn't focus. I took his head and cradled it in my lap. Ava stirred from where she was tied to my back.

"Just fainted on my way back from the bathroom," Liam struggled to get out. He tried to get to his feet, but I could tell he needed help. He was heavy as I supported him the few feet to the bed. He crashed down onto it, like he was going to pass out again if he took another step. "Thanks."

"Don't move," I told him quickly, though I didn't know why. He wouldn't move if I lit his ass on fire. "I'll be right back."

I hurried back to the kitchen and grabbed the pills Perot had prescribed him, then filled a glass with water at the sink. I returned to the bedroom, where Esis and Buttercup were helping Liam under the covers. Buttercup pulled the sheets to his chin, then licked his forehead. It seemed like a kind gesture, like something a mother kurble would do to her child. But Liam's long hair got tangled in her mouth, and she practically choked on it as she coughed it out.

"Take these," I demanded, handing him two pills and the water.

Liam placed them in his mouth, but he looked like he was going to gag. After a few tries, it finally went down. I suspected he used his magic to force the water down his throat with the way he gagged. *Ouch.*

"What's that?" Liam asked, looking down to the paper in my hands. I'd accidentally grabbed Perot's letter with the pharmacy bag.

"It's a note from Perot," I told him. "Along with the pills, he's prescribed you a new work schedule."

Liam groaned. "*Pawee*, I've already cut back. I want to spend as much time with Ava-Marie as possible."

"Well, you haven't cut back enough," I snapped. "Even Perot thinks so."

"Let me see." Liam held out his hand, and I passed him the letter. His eyes roamed over the schedule, but he looked like he was having a hard time reading it. "*Pawee*, I can't take every Wednesday off."

"Yes, you can," I insisted. "You need a break in the middle of the week."

"People are depending on me," he argued.

"You're chief!" I cried. "You set your own hours. And you can't help people if you're too ill to work."

Liam frowned, but he knew I was right. He glanced at Ava-Marie, as if he was doing this for her— because he knew his time with her was running short. "Okay. I'll stick to Perot's schedule."

"Good," I told him, though I wasn't sure if he was just saying that because he didn't have the energy to disagree right now. We'd see once he was well enough to go out again. "Is there anything else I can do for you?"

"Keep me company while I wait it out?" he suggested.

I wanted to do just that. I thought it'd be easy, but it was harder than I could've ever imagined. After only a few minutes, Ava-Marie started throwing a fit, and I had to leave the room to calm her down because her cries were making Liam's migraine worse. After forty-five minutes, I'd changed her, fed her, and by some miracle managed to calm her down— until I felt something leaking out of her diaper.

I crinkled my nose as I held her a foot away from me. "I see why you were upset."

Ava-Marie started wailing again as I took her to the sink to give her a bath. After I dried her off and dressed her, I turned around to see that Esis and Buttercup had snuck into the fridge and spilled an entire gallon of chocolate milk on the floor.

Frustrated, I set Ava-Marie in her bouncer and went to mop it up. Esis and Buttercup scurried away and didn't even offer to help. The little monsters knew they were in trouble. My frustration surged when I saw that at least a third of the gallon had seeped underneath the refrigerator. Normally, I'd ask Liam to use his powers to help clean it up, but I didn't want to bother him right now, and I didn't think he could perform that kind of magic today anyway. I moved the fridge by myself to clean underneath it, only to find a huge stash of moldy bread behind it.

"Ugh, Esis!" I complained loudly. The kurbles had been hoarding food behind the refrigerator!

Esis and Buttercup snickered from one of the guest rooms. Huffing, I pulled a pail out from under the sink and filled it with bleach water to clean up the mold. In the middle of cleaning, Ava-Marie started to wail again, but

I couldn't hold her when I had bleach all over my hands. I had to finish cleaning before I could console her, and by then, I could hear Liam groaning in pain from the other room.

"Sophia?" Liam called.

My frustration grew, because there didn't seem to be anything I could do to console Ava. "I'm trying," I called back to him.

"*Pawee?*" he called again, like he hadn't heard me.

I didn't want to bring Ava-Marie into the room wailing like this, but Liam wouldn't stop calling my name. I went to see what was the matter.

"Can you turn the humidifier on for me?" he asked. "I can't breathe."

I did my best to help him while Ava continued to wail in my arms. But when I plugged in the humidifier, it wouldn't turn on.

"It's not working," I complained.

Liam didn't respond. He just lay there helplessly, trying to take in air.

Ava-Marie went silent. Projectile vomit shot out of her mouth and leaked down my shirt. "Ancestor's cock!" I cried.

Esis chuckled at my use of words, but to me, it was the furthest thing from funny. This day could suck it.

"Forget about it," Liam insisted. "Go clean up."

I wanted to help him out, but the stench of vomit was too much. I couldn't help it when heat rose to my face. I was on the verge of tears, but I tried to hold it in. I couldn't take it anymore. Ava started crying louder, and I realized my skin had heated so much that I was making her uncomfortable. I hurried out of the room, but I stopped in my tracks in the hall.

Doya stood in the living room, a hand on her hip. Naomi prowled at her side. She cocked a curious eyebrow. "Ancestor's cock?"

"I'm not the one who came up with it," I snapped. I wasn't in the mood for her attitude. "You're the one who invented the phrase."

"To hear you say it only reminds me how much of my daughter you truly are," she said.

I pushed a strand of hair out of my eyes, but I hadn't realized vomit had trickled down Ava's cheek onto my fingers. I ended up running puke through my hair. Ugh.

"What are you doing here?" I asked in a softer tone.

"I knocked, but you didn't answer," she said. "Professor Perot told me Liam was sick. I thought I could help."

Ava-Marie continued to wail, and I couldn't hold it back any longer. I totally broke down and started crying in front of my mother. "Yes, please."

Doya held her arms out and stepped toward me. "Let me clean Ava up. You go take a shower."

I sniffled as I handed my daughter over. I didn't want to let her go, but I couldn't spend the day covered in puke, either.

Ava quieted as soon as she was in Doya's arms. For a woman who never raised a child, she had a way with babies. My mother rocked her back and forth and sang a traditional Hawkei lullaby to her. I'd never known before how lovely she sang.

My heart broke as I left the room. I rushed through my shower and threw on a baggy t-shirt and jeans after I'd finished. When I returned to the living room, Ava-Marie had fallen asleep in her swing, and Naomi was curled next to the fireplace. Doya rifled through a duffel bag she'd brought along.

"What's that?" I asked. For a second, I thought she was going to offer to stay overnight to help with Ava-Marie. It was selfish of me, but I didn't want that. I wanted all the time I could have with my little girl— *alone.*

Doya looked up at me. "I admit, I'd planned to visit before I heard Liam was sick. I had an ulterior motive."

I sighed and sat on the couch opposite her. "Don't you always?" I teased, though it left the air feeling a little stale.

Doya shifted in her seat, like she was uncomfortable with the accusation, but the discomfort flashed off her face in a moment. She held her chin high and wore that regal look she'd perfected. "I wanted to give you this, Sophia."

Doya reached into the duffel bag, and I gasped when I saw what was inside. She held up a white dress stitched with red, orange, and yellow beads. No, not a dress— *regalia.* It was obviously old, as the corners had yellowed with age. Most of the beads had fallen off, but I could still make out the pattern they were supposed to make. It was flames, made to blend together with various shades of white beads swirled to create Anichi symbols.

"Ancestors," I breathed. "It's beautiful."

"It was my father's," she told me. "After my father died, I wasn't left with much family on my Anichi side, but he did have a cousin who kept his regalia. That cousin returned it to me."

She set the regalia in her lap and gazed down at it, running her fingers over the surviving beads. "I thought since you didn't have your own, we could modify it to fit you."

I stood, still taking in the beauty of the regalia. The bead work was incredible, and the symbolism undeniable. Doya's father— my grandpa— had chosen the pattern to signify the love and compassion between himself and my grandmother, Viola. As I looked it over, I *felt* myself, like the regalia symbolized my own personality and magic— two warring sides, my compassionate heart and my raging passion.

"I'd love that, Mother," I said, without realizing what I'd said.

Doya's features softened. She looked down to the regalia. A curtain of red hair concealed her face, like she didn't want me to see how she truly felt. I was starting to think Doya had more of that compassionate, caring Anichi side in her than I ever knew. She just didn't know how to show it.

The moment passed quickly, and Doya cleared her throat. She reached back into the duffel bag and pulled out a plastic container. It was split into several sections, each housing a different color of bead.

"I'm glad to hear that, Sophia," she said. "I brought along beads to repair it, if you'd like to learn."

"Absolutely," I answered eagerly.

Doya helped me into the regalia, and she took measurements to make adjustments to the fabric when she got home. I was surprised to see it fit me quite well, as it wasn't meant to be skin-tight. We needed to bring in the area around my waist and cut a few inches off the bottom, but Doya assured me she could do it without harming the bead work.

If someone had told me a year ago Madame Doya could sew, I wouldn't have believed them. I'd have thought her only hobby was tormenting her students. As it turned out, Doya was a *master* seamstress. She pulled out a few scrap pieces of fabric and began showing me how to work the beads, so I could practice before I started on my regalia. She worked quickly and efficiently. I was surprised to see how fast an image was taking shape. She was using various colors of blue beads, creating a small image of ocean waves. It was an interesting choice of artwork for a Koigni woman.

Mine, on the other hand, looked frumpy. It'd be a miracle if I managed to create a recognizable image at all.

"I don't know why this is so hard," I complained. "I can be artsy. I have my photography, after all."

"Bead work requires patience," Doya said calmly. Never before had she given instructions in such a peaceful way. In fact, I was surprised she had the word *patience* in her vocabulary at all. I think being in *Hok'evale* had brought out the Anichi in her. "It's not like photography."

I frowned. "Photography can be hard. You have to consider the lighting and the angle. It's a lot of work to come up with the perfect shot."

"I didn't mean it harshly, Sophia," she said as she wove more beads into her fabric. "I just meant it will take you time and practice to learn bead work."

I slowed down and tried again. As we worked, the room went silent. I dared to break it by asking, "What was your father like? Can you tell me about him?"

Doya drew a deep breath, but she didn't look at me. She kept her eyes on the needle she was working through the fabric. "My father died when I was very young— it was a heart condition he'd lived with all his life. I'm afraid I don't remember him well. What I do remember of him is that he was the kindest man I've ever met."

She stopped sewing and got a faraway look in her eyes as she thought about him. "William Azure was the kind of man who would drop anything for someone else. My mother told me stories about how he would pay for other people's groceries or visit hospital patients. He wasn't the kind of man to preach his good deeds. He had no interest in politics, but he made sure that the world was a better place with him in it."

I thought I saw tears bead in her eyes, but she shook her head, and they were gone a moment later.

"I wish I had the chance to get to know him," I said.

She swallowed. "Me, too. He died too young."

"Is there anything you *do* remember?" I asked.

She shook her head. "Not many specifics. I can remember small things, like my father pushing me on the swings, or taking me to the beach to view the hippocampi dances."

"That sounds like fun," I remarked. "I've never seen them."

Doya began working the needle into the fabric again. "No, you wouldn't have. Most Koigni don't care, as it's considered a Toaqua tradition. I suppose that should've been my first clue my father wasn't Koigni."

I tilted my head. "Did he ever show you his power?"

"No, and I suppose he couldn't have, anyway," she said. "Like all Anichi here, he was unbonded. He didn't have magic."

My heart dropped. "That must've been hard for him, to live in this society without bonding, without power."

"He had my mother," Doya pointed out. "I think to him, she was the one he bonded with."

"What was she like?" I asked. I'd met her before, but briefly. She was my ancestor, and had appeared to me on several occasions, but all I knew about Viola was she had a firebird Familiar.

"A lot like me, I suppose," Doya said. "But... kinder."

She spoke the word slowly, like saying it aloud was painful. The fact she admitted her unkindness in any capacity, however, was a step forward for her.

"My mother was my best friend, before she died of cancer," Doya continued. "She served on the council as I did, and taught me everything I know about leadership. I suppose... I suppose there are some lessons I could've listened closer to."

It always shocked me when Doya offered an apology. She didn't come out and say *I'm sorry*, but it was there.

I heard the sound of the bedroom door opening, and Liam crossed the hall to the bathroom. Esis and Buttercup followed, like they might be able to catch him if he collapsed.

Doya and I both went quiet. Tears rose to my eyes as I heard gagging sounds. I went to the bathroom and knocked on the door. "Liam, do you need help?"

"I'm okay," Liam forced out. The noises coming from him were so violent. I went to the kitchen and poured a glass of water. I opened the bathroom door and slipped it through, putting it on the counter. He muttered a quick *thank you* before he gagged again.

I entered the bathroom, where Liam was on his knees. He looked exhausted and pale, but better than he had before I'd given him his meds. I hoped he hadn't tossed them up.

"We have to do something to get your pain down," I said. I put my hands on my hips. "If this gets any worse, we have to go in."

Liam scowled. He'd do anything to avoid going to the hospital. "A bath might work," he said. "But I need help."

"You don't even have to ask," I said. Doya had Ava handled. I could help with this.

I filled the tub with water as hot as he could tolerate, got some clothes from the bedroom, and helped him in. He shuddered as I moved the washcloth over his back, like even my touch was agonizing to bear.

He couldn't even bathe himself when he was like this. It was tough seeing such a strong person be reduced to a trembling mess, especially someone you loved so much. It was strange, thinking this was the same man that had performed incredible magic during a battle months ago, unable to even take care of himself properly.

But that's how illness worked. I never knew how he was going to be on any given day. And it was hardly ever predictable. It was only because he trusted me with everything that he was willing to be this vulnerable. A slight positive in all this mess.

"Are you going to be okay in here?" I asked as I finished washing his hair.

"I just need time to rest," he said. "Let me soak for a bit."

I stood reluctantly. I didn't want to leave him, but it would make him feel worse if I sat in here and hovered, so I returned to working on my regalia. As I sat down and took the beads in hand, Doya gave me the look she always did when something was on her mind.

"Yes?" I asked, not wanting to mince words.

Doya took in a long, drawn-out sigh. "Sophia... I hate to speak of the obvious, but my own father died young. It is something I never got over, and I don't wish for Ava-Marie to experience—"

"Don't." Tears rose to my eyes when she spoke of it. "He's just having a bad day."

"I'm only saying you need to be prepared," Doya said. "I was never a great advocate of marriage for women— too many restrictions. Many great women have been ruined by their husbands. I would've preferred you'd stay single, but here we are."

"Like you wouldn't marry my *pataa*," I teased.

Doya let out a huff. "I would marry your father, if he asked," she admitted. "But only because I am certain he cannot control me."

No surprise there. Doya totally wore the pants in my parents' relationship.

"Liam takes care of us. He loves me."

"But he cannot hold out forever if the ancestors call him home," Doya said, and her voice became gentle. She put her hand lightly on mine. It was an odd gesture, something I wasn't used to. "I want you to be aware you might not grow old together."

"I believe anything is possible," I said firmly. "We've always beaten the odds before."

Doya gave me a fond look, like my refusal to back down was admirable. "I only want you to be ready. If you're made a widow, you must be prepared to raise your child on your own."

Doya sat back against her chair. "I know you can do it. But I am also concerned for your happiness, and I don't wish for you to be lonely."

Little did Doya know, her fears about my child being fatherless were unfounded. I was giving Ava-Marie up. In a few months, maybe even weeks, I'd have to sacrifice her to save the tribe, and never see my daughter again.

I wanted to talk to Doya. I wanted to ask for her advice, ask her how she possibly managed to give me up and survive it. Because the thought of someone tearing Ava-Marie from my arms was enough to make me wish to die. I didn't know how Doya was still here, how she had made it through.

But I couldn't. Not yet. I wouldn't admit to myself that I had to let my baby go. When the time was right... I'd ask. Not today, because this conversation alone was already breaking my heart. I couldn't handle another blow.

"You're acting like we're already planning my husband's funeral," I hissed.

"It's better to have this conversation now rather than later," Doya said. "Women must be strong in this world. We're the ones who hold it together when men are tearing it apart, and we mend the broken pieces when the men come home from war. If we do not stand tall, everything collapses."

I blinked back the tears. "Well, I'm not giving up. Perot's treatments are getting better every day."

"I can only give you a piece of advice from your grandmother," Doya said. "She loved my father up until the bitter end. She was grateful for the years she got with him. She always said the real tragedy would be to never know him at all, and the miracle was getting the small moment she had with him. So enjoy your time, but be ready."

Doya stroked my hair. I didn't answer. I was about to lose Ava-Marie. I couldn't bear the thought of losing my husband, too. Was my entire family going to be ripped away from me, leaving me alone?

I heard the bathroom door open. Liam had dressed himself— that was a good sign. He couldn't do that without me unless he was recovering. The bath must've worked.

Liam rubbed his eyes as he entered the living room. "Everything good in here?"

"Yeah—" I started to say, but I was cut off by the sound of Ava-Marie stirring. She woke and started to cry. I set my beads aside and hurried over to her. "Shh, sweetheart. Don't cry."

I unbuckled her from her swing and picked her up, patting her gently to calm her down. She started to wail, and I shifted her in my arms. Rocking her didn't seem to help. I felt hopeless.

"I don't know what she wants," I admitted. I felt like the worst mother in the world. This was a shitty day.

"I know that cry," Liam said quickly. "She's hungry."

I scrunched up my face. "How can you tell?"

Liam shrugged, but he'd already started making his way across the room to the kitchen. "It's in her tone. She wants milk. Let me make her a bottle."

Doya's jaw dropped as Liam struggled over to the fridge and started warming up milk for Ava-Marie. It was like she couldn't believe he was walking at all when he looked like shit. Sometimes I couldn't believe it either, but I'd seen Liam perform such impossible feats I wasn't surprised anymore.

I carried Ava-Marie over to the kitchen. "Liam, don't worry about it. I can feed her."

Liam looked exhausted, but he gave me this look like he wasn't messing around. "Let me help, *pawee*. I've been totally useless today. Just give me this one thing, okay?"

I could see the sadness in his eyes. It tore him to pieces when he couldn't do anything to help. "Okay. Just this one thing."

Liam sat on the couch to feed Ava-Marie, while Doya and I worked on cleaning up our project. Esis and Buttercup sat at his feet.

"Liam's a good man," Doya said lowly, so Liam couldn't hear. She couldn't take her eyes off him as he rocked Ava-Marie back and forth. His eyes drooped, like he was ready to fall asleep, but he remained alert to his daughter in his arms.

"Yeah," I agreed. "He is."

"I'll bring the regalia back after it's resized," she offered. "Then we can get to work on the bead art."

I nodded. "I look forward to it."

After Doya and Naomi left, I sat on the couch with Liam and wrapped an arm over his shoulder. He leaned into me and rested Ava-Marie half on my lap, half on his. I breathed deeply, taking in the beautiful moment with my family.

"How long was Doya here?" he asked.

"Maybe two hours," I answered.

"How'd it go?"

"Good, actually," I said, like I was surprised. I shouldn't be surprised by anything anymore. "She brought me her father's regalia and started teaching me how to repair the bead work."

"That's good," Liam said weakly, staring down at Ava-Marie. I ran my fingers lightly through her hair.

After a beat, the silence was cut by the sound of a knock at the door.

Liam and I exchanged a glance, as if asking the other if we were expecting company.

"Did your mom forget something?" he questioned.

I glanced out the window to see Eirakari outside next to Julian. I smacked my forehead. "Dinner! It's our night with Maddie and Drew. I forgot to tell them you were sick."

Liam shrugged. "They can still hang out."

"But I didn't make anything," I groaned as I stood to answer the door.

I was already formulating a speech in my head about how sorry I was that we forgot about dinner. When I opened the door, I saw Maddie and Drew weren't the only ones there. Lindsey and Miranda had tagged along, as well as their Familiars.

"Hope you don't mind that we brought some guests along," Maddie said chipperly.

I opened my mouth to say it was fine, but my words halted on my tongue. Maddie's eyes rolled back into her skull, and her knees buckled beneath her.

"Maddie!" Drew cried, catching her before she fell backward down the stairs.

Maddie started to seize— like she had the last time she had a vision. It terrified me to the very core, but I pushed the terror aside and jumped into action.

"Get her inside!" I cried.

There wasn't much room on the landing, and Drew was a scrawny guy. He couldn't hold her up very long, and I didn't want her to fall. I looped one of her arms over my shoulder and helped Drew move her the few feet inside.

"Ancestors!" Lindsey freaked as she helped Maddie inside.

Eirakari let out a worried cry and stuck her head inside the door as Maddie continued to seize. Liam noticed something was wrong immediately and shot to his feet, but he moved so fast his body couldn't handle it.

I saw what was about to happen a split-second before it did. Liam's eyes glossed over. I made the instinctive choice to abandon Maddie with Drew and rush over to Liam. I caught Ava-Marie before she could drop out of his arms. Liam slumped onto the couch.

Great. I had one seizing Toaqua on my kitchen floor and her unconscious brother on my couch. It sounded like some sort of party, but it was anything but. My heart raced, yet there was nothing my healing powers could do for either of them.

It seemed like a lifetime passed before they both came to, but it was only a few seconds.

"You okay?" Drew asked Maddie. Ace came up to lick her face, and Eirakari gave a gleeful meep. Esis and Buttercup both looked relieved.

"Maddie, oh my gosh!" Miranda squeaked.

"I'm fine," Maddie said, like it was no big deal, though her face was pale.

The three of them crowded around her and helped her to her feet. Liam shook his head and took in the room. He noticed Ava in my arms, and I saw the moment recognition hit him.

"Fuck," he groaned. "I passed out while holding *Ava?*"

I nodded sheepishly. I wish I could've said that didn't worry me, but it did. I didn't want him to hold her when he was ill like this anymore. Liam took a moment to process it, then looked over Maddie with a worried expression on his face.

Maddie shrugged Lindsey and Miranda off and dusted off her jeans. "Sorry I passed out on your kitchen floor, Sophia."

I eyed her curiously as she acted nonchalant. Had she been having *that* many visions that it didn't bother her anymore? "It's been that kind of a day. Are you okay?"

Maddie didn't quite meet my gaze. "Fine. It happens all the time. It's over, and I'm better now."

"I don't believe you," Liam asserted. He didn't stand, because he still felt like shit, but he crossed his arms in an authoritative way.

Maddie sighed. "You *always* think something's wrong, Liam."

He cocked an eyebrow. "If everything were hunky-dory, you wouldn't be having visions. I know you Mads, and your *everything-is-fine* act is shit. What's going on?"

Drew shot Maddie a look, like they both knew something and didn't want to tell us. Lindsey and Miranda shared a similar look. I was really confused by it.

Maddie sighed. She came over to sit by us before she answered. Drew and Ace followed, while Eirakari ducked her head back outside. The door swung shut behind her. Lindsey and Miranda squeezed together on the recliner, cuddling close.

Maddie drew a long breath. "I've been having visions of the future."

"No shit," Liam said flatly.

Maddie dropped her gaze and twisted her hands around in her lap.

"The thing is, I've been hiding from you just how much I've seen— how much I *see* daily."

"What is it?" I asked, leaning in.

Maddie eyed me up and down, and her features softened when her gaze landed on Ava-Marie. "I can't tell you."

"You always say that," Liam huffed.

"And I mean it!" she shot back. "I don't know what it means yet. Lindsey and Miranda are helping me decipher it, but—"

"Lindsey and Miranda?" Liam growled, shooting a look their way. Lindsey held up her hands, like she was innocent. "You'll tell *them*, but you won't tell your own brother?"

"I don't know how!" Maddie burst.

"She's right," Drew said. He wrapped an arm around Maddie's shoulder and took her hand in his. "It's... it's hard to explain."

He shot her a look, like he didn't even know where to begin.

"We didn't mean to find out," Miranda added quickly.

"So, what, you just overheard?" Liam accused.

"Basically." Lindsey rushed to defend her girlfriend. "We were... well, we were fooling around someplace we probably shouldn't have, and heard Maddie tell Drew."

"Tell him what?" I questioned.

Maddie groaned. "It doesn't make any sense."

"The least you can do is tell us what you told them!" Liam demanded, gesturing to Lindsey and Miranda. "This is unfair."

"Says the guy who hides *everything* from *everyone*," Lindsey challenged. "How long did it take you guys to tell us about the prophecy pieces?"

Lindsey wasn't being harsh, just pointing out the situation.

Liam huffed but avoided answering. "What is it you know?"

"That's not for us to tell," Lindsey shot back. "Consider for a moment that your sister is doing her best. And don't try to drag us into it. We want to help, but we're not stepping into the middle of your family drama."

The room went quiet for a moment. Liam was such an alpha— a reluctant one, but an alpha nonetheless— that he didn't really know how to take Lindsey. She was a Koigni chick through and through.

"Can you at least give us a clue?" I asked, breaking the awkward silence.

Maddie frowned. "Not yet."

She was quick to add, "And it's not because I'm hiding anything or don't want to tell you. It's because I literally don't know what it means yet. I need time to figure out the clues. Once I understand it, believe me, I *will* tell you."

Liam only looked half convinced. "I hope that's true, Maddie. You'll be wise not to keep your chief in the dark."

She nodded in agreement. "I don't intend to."

But there was something dark in her eyes. I didn't think she was lying to us, but I didn't think she was telling us the whole truth— whether she knew it or not. Maddie suspected something.

I sensed whatever it was may just break us in a way we'd never recover from.

Liam

THIRTEEN

"Look, I'm a walrus!" Jonah put two chopsticks under his lips and flapped his hands like they were flippers. Squeaks bent her beak down and picked up a pair, trying to imitate him. Imogen laughed, but Sophia barely smiled.

Sophia had ordered Chinese. Not my favorite, but she didn't want to cook, and asking her to do anything when this impending doom was swarming around us felt cruel. Jonah and Imogen had come over and were doing their best to cheer us up, I could tell, but neither of us felt particularly happy.

Not Ava-Marie. She giggled in her high chair as she watched Jonah make faces. She could laugh now— one of my favorite sounds— and it was the loudest laugh I ever heard, starting with a squeal and ending in a fit of giggles.

"You're all a bunch of fucking weirdos," I muttered, but I still smiled. Jonah could be as stupid as he wanted, as long as it made my daughter laugh.

I shifted uncomfortably. My recent flare-up had been one of the worst. I was only working four days a week now, as per Perot's orders, but I didn't mind. It gave me more time to spend with Ava. I could get around now, but I was still recovering.

Sassy darted around the floor, looking for rice anyone might've dropped. Esis had two chopsticks and was feeding Buttercup dumplings. The kurbles crooned, and Buttercup fondled her front like she had breasts. Esis thumped his tail.

I rolled my eyes. Okay, we *really* needed to get out of the house.

"Let's go for a walk." I stood and began cleaning up. Sophia helped me, while Imogen put her food away and Jonah shoveled the rest down.

We didn't take the cradleboard. Sophia wanted to hold Ava-Marie. We walked down the streets of *Hok'evale*, taking in the spring air. It was a sunny April day, streets wet from the rainstorms last night. The kurbles rode on Squeaks' back, and Sassy splashed in puddles ahead.

Julian roamed behind us and bumped his head against me. I rubbed the area between his horns, and his tongue lolled. "Where've you been, bud?" I asked. "You haven't been around."

"I'd say he's been sneaking out to see Aisha," Imogen teased, and she wiggled her eyebrows. "I've seen them flying over the beach a few times this week."

Julian groaned. "Oh, really?" I asked. "Jules, do you have a little crush on Aisha?"

Julian made growling noises, as if to say it was more than a crush. Jonah threw an arm against Julian and said, "He's been getting freaky with the dragon ladies, if you know what I mean."

Julian whipped his tail around and smacked Jonah face-first into the dirt. Squeaks chirped out a low warning.

Jonah got up and wiped his face of mud. "Ugh. Remind me to never tease a dragon. He's got a worse temper than you."

"That's my boy," I said, and I gave Julian's side a pat. He grumbled.

We passed a shop we'd been by several times before— *Forgotten Earth*. I glanced at the front window by chance and stopped dead when I saw a familiar face.

"Guys, it's Professor Amber," I said in awe. She was inside the shop, putting things on the shelves with a pleasant smile on her face. She looked the same as she always did, her wiry red hair wrapped in a scarf, beads and shawls draping off her tiny form.

"Let's go say hi!" Imogen said.

We left the Familiars outside and entered the store. Immediately, we were hit with a heavy waft of incense. Tarot and oracle cards, along with books on magic, were stacked in neat rows on bookshelves beneath banners that hung from the ceiling. Statues of idols, relics and angels lined one side of the room, next to a massive rack of crystals that held every stone imaginable. Candles and incense holders were placed beside jewelry that represented totems of animal. There were statues of Scandinavian deities and pagan goddesses, like the ones worshiped by the Arcanea and the Miriamic Coven.

It was a metaphysical store. Trust Professor Amber to run such a shop. Her orangutan Familiar sat on a pillow in the corner and played some weird stringed instrument.

Professor Amber turned around when she saw us. She smiled brightly. "Liam! My child!" She spread her arms wide and wrapped me in a bony hug, pressing her lips to my cheek. "How *wonderful* to see you in my humble domain!"

"I'm happy to see you, too," I said. I didn't object to the kiss. That was Professor Amber.

"I've heard you were around, but the ancestors didn't see fit for our life paths to cross until this moment in universal time," Amber swooned.

Her eyes lit up when she saw Ava-Marie. "And who's this little angel? Is she your daughter, Liam?"

"Yes, she's mine," I said proudly. "This is Ava-Marie."

Professor Amber made a tittering sound and patted Ava's cheeks. "She is just darling! Oh!"

Amber staggered back dramatically. Imogen and Jonah's eyes widened, and Amber proclaimed, "I sense great *power* in her! Yes, I do indeed! She will have a great destiny, a fate set by the gods! You are very lucky to call this child your own."

"She's special for sure," I said. Sophia's eyes narrowed. She opened her mouth to say something, but I nudged her.

"Don't take it offensively. It's just Professor Amber," I said under my breath.

"I don't like predictions about Ava." Sophia scowled. She'd had enough of prophecies in her own life and was more or less determined Ava-Marie wouldn't be held by one— even if it was just something a silly hippie had said.

"She's a crazy old lady," I told Sophia. "It doesn't mean anything. Let her have her fun."

Sophia let it go. Imogen moved around the shop, her fingers brushing the crystals. "This store is amazing, Professor. I didn't know you had such an interest in metaphysicality."

"It was a dream of mine, to open a shop like this," Professor Amber said in a dreamy voice. "The Elders would've never permitted it, but here, I can do whatever I like."

I heard a cracking sound. Jonah had broken something. He winced and mouthed *sorry* to me. He'd been playing with one of the glass idols, and it'd fallen and shattered on the floor. I glared at him, and he moved to kick the shards under a nearby counter.

Professor Amber hadn't noticed. She unrolled a long poster that was made of thin strips of wood, bound together with string. The poster was blue, with white stars painted throughout the design. The stars came together to form creatures; a thunderbird, a sea serpent, an owl, a unicorn, a dragon, and a phoenix. There was one more that was hard to make out, depicted as many creatures layered upon one another— a changeling of sorts. Each of the animals was placed in a circle around a glowing Hawkei symbol that stood for the Great Spirit.

"This is my latest addition to the shop," Amber said. "Come and see!"

"Ooh," Imogen gushed. "It's a poster of the Hawkei zodiac."

"The what?" Sophia asked. She leaned in closer to look at the poster, and I finally got a chance to snag Ava-Marie from her. She hardly let me hold the baby these days, so I stole her whenever I could.

"Many cultures have zodiacs. The Hawkei had theirs even before we got our Familiars," I told her. "It's a seven-year cycle, with each year representing a different animal."

Sophia studied the poster, then finally pointed to the changeling. "What's that?"

"That's a *mutabeecha*," Imogen replied with bright eyes.

Sophia furrowed her brow. "A what?"

"*Mutabeecha*," Imogen repeated. "I learned about them in my cryptozoology class. They're creatures of lore, known to exist only in the spiritual realm as companions to the Great Spirit. The creature aligns with the Year of the Great Spirit."

Sophia leaned closer. "What *is* it, though? I can't make sense of its form."

"That's because the form changes," Imogen explained. "*Mutabeecha* is a Hawkei word that roughly translates to *form changer*."

"Like a shapeshifter?" Jonah asked.

Imogen nodded. "Exactly. Each *mutabeecha* takes on a single form for each of the five elements and can shift between them."

"What are their five forms?" Jonah asked. "Perhaps a hippogriff for Yapluma?"

"It depends on the *mutabeecha*," Imogen said. "Each only has five forms, but whichever form it takes in each element can be different from others."

Sophia skimmed her fingertips over the dragon design. "The prophecy says I was born in the Year of the Dragon. Isn't that the Koigni House symbol?"

"Yes. I was born in the Year of the Sea Serpent, which is my House symbol," I told her.

"Thunderbirds are for Yapluma, and I think the symbol for Nivita is... uh..." Jonah stammered.

"It's the unicorn, dummy," Imogen said flatly.

Jonah scoffed. "I knew *that*."

"May I ask which day you were born on?" Amber asked curiously.

"June twenty-first, same as Liam," Sophia replied.

Professor Amber gasped and flailed her hands. "No wonder you are so powerful! Your House has truly been waiting for someone like you!"

"What do you mean?" Sophia raised an eyebrow.

"The Summer Solstice is a particular day of power for those in Koigni House," Amber gushed. "Fire children born on that day, during the Year of the Dragon, are *exceptional* fire elementals. All Koigni can harness the power of the sun, but only those born on the Summer Solstice in the Year of the Dragon can use it in incredible ways."

"Does this explain why Sophia is so overly powerful?" Jonah questioned, stroking his beard.

"Perhaps. Children born on Solstice days are always talented Elementai, but those who are also born in their corresponding *year* on any given Solstice are extraordinary Elementai," Amber said.

Sophia drummed her fingers against the counter. "My daughter was born in December. What's Ava-Marie's sign?" she asked.

"Last year was the year of the Phoenix," Amber said. "It is a sign of Fire, but also, a sign of *change* above all. It's the Anichi House symbol."

"How can that be? The phoenix is a Fire animal," Sophia said.

"Not always," Imogen spoke up. "They're rare, but phoenixes can come in all varieties, like dragons do. There can be ice phoenixes, and earth phoenixes, and the like. The thing that categorizes them as a species is their ability to reincarnate after death."

"Chieftess Annette's phoenix didn't reincarnate when Anwara killed him," Sophia pointed out.

"Because it was killed by another phoenix," Imogen responded.

"Phoenixes don't die unless their Elementai does or if they're killed by one of their own kind. You can't destroy them any other way."

Amber nodded. "Those born in the Year of the Phoenix are known to bring about great transformations in the world, reshaping it for better or for worse."

"What solstices correspond with the Houses?" Sophia asked.

"The Spring Equinox is for Earth, the Summer Solstice for Fire, the Fall Equinox for Air and the Winter Solstice for Water," Amber listed. "The Anichi House doesn't have a Solstice, preferring to make their day of power the turn of the New Year."

Professor Amber poked Ava-Marie on the nose. "What day was this little sweetheart born?"

"Christmas," I said. "Does that have any influence?"

Amber let out a giddy note. "And so close to the Toaqua Solstice, too, *and* the New Year of Anichi! Your daughter has the best of both worlds. She'll be blessed by the zodiac on *three* sides. That is incredibly rare. I don't know of an interhouse Hawkei child that's ever been in such a position."

Sophia squirmed. Imogen rushed to say something. "You said... Koigni children born in the Year of the Dragon that are also born on a solstice can harness the power of the sun?"

"Oh, yes." Amber nodded. "Just like Liam can draw his life energy from the moon. He was born on a solstice in the Year of the Sea Serpent. Why do you think he's still here?"

There was a long beat of silence, and Amber's Familiar stopped playing the instrument. My mouth gaped open.

"Hold on," I said. "You're saying... I'm able to survive without a Familiar, because my life energy is attached to something that's not a magical creature?"

"Well of course, Liam," Amber said airily. "How do you think you've survived without Nashoma all these years? You're pulling your magic from the *moon*, not from your Familiar. Otherwise, you'd be dead by now."

"But if that's the case, shouldn't everyone outlive their Familiar?" Jonah asked.

"No, my dear. All Toaqua can pull magic from the moon, to a point, but only those born on solstices during the Year of the Sea Serpent have the ability to live off a power that is not from their Familiar. Liam was very lucky to have his birthday fall on such a special day; otherwise, he would not be here."

I sputtered in outrage. "Why didn't you tell me this *years* ago?"

Amber shrugged simply. "I didn't know your birthday until now. Mystery solved."

Ancestors, I was so frustrated with Professor Amber. No wonder nobody knew why I hadn't survived— this was fringe stuff. I wasn't even sure if I could believe her.

But Imogen brightened and said, "That makes sense! Liam, you're so powerful because your magic is powered by the moon. And Sophia's is powered by the sun!"

"Precisely," Amber stated, as if that was the end of it. She held out a tray of cookies and said, "Anyone like to try? Baked with the finest cannabis, homegrown at my own cottage."

Imogen shook her head. "No, thank you. I'm in recovery."

"Cannabis is not a drug, my dear, it is a *medicine*," Amber said. "But I appreciate your honesty."

Jonah dived in. "I'll have some!"

Sophia put her hand on the poster. "May we take this? We'll pay for it."

"No need, my child. It is yours. Consider it a gift," Amber said kindly. Sophia rolled it up, and tucked the poster under her arm.

After Jonah had eaten some weed cookies and Imogen had ordered a full week's paycheck worth of items to be delivered to her apartment, we left the store. Ava-Marie kicked against me as I loudly complained, "This is insane! Amber had all this knowledge, and she didn't tell us anything? I would've liked to know why I didn't fucking die three years ago, you know."

"Hold on. We don't know if this is real," Sophia objected. "Amber could just be spouting nonsense. We know she believes in some crazy things."

"But Professor Lopez said the same thing during Hawkei Legends, remember? He said Koigni can pull from the sun, and Toaqua the moon," I said. "We just didn't look that far into it. At the time, we considered it a story."

"We should... do some research," Jonah said in a mystified voice, struggling to string two words together. He was so fucking high right now.

"We need an *astromancer*. An enchantress will be able to tell us what all this astrology stuff means," Imogen said. "Let's find Lani. She's half astromancer. She can help."

The Falcon's Nest was packed when we got there. We managed to find a table near the back, and Lani rushed over with her wombat Familiar.

"What can I get you guys?" she asked, holding up a notepad.

"Like, the biggest burger you have," Jonah said. "And a pepperoni pizza on top of it. Extra cheese." Squeaks licked her beak, while the kurbles clapped in appreciation.

"You just ate!" Imogen exclaimed.

"So? I'm starving." Jonah rubbed his stomach. I rolled my eyes. Now was not the time to get the munchies. The guy was a bottomless pit.

"Actually, we were hoping you could help us," Sophia said, and she unrolled the poster.

Lani's eyes spread wide when she saw it. Her expression glowed when she saw the Hawkei zodiac spread out in front of her.

I caught her gaze and knew it well. Longing. Lani had really wanted to be an astromancer. She'd been kicked out of her society when she was young, but it was clear she still had a passion for star magic that her Elementai side couldn't satisfy.

Lani glanced back to the kitchen, then said, "I have a little time. What do you need?"

Imogen told Lani what Amber had told us. Instead of being shocked, Lani nodded in understanding, like the knowledge we'd gained was feasible. "I think your professor is right," she began. "I didn't get a chance to learn much about astromancy, but I did learn the basics. The days we are born on have significance to our powers as supernaturals. The transition of the year and the time of one's birth can have major effects on whether someone is born a talented supernatural, or average."

"I don't understand how it works, though," Sophia said. "Aren't these charts just random events?"

"Not at all. Zodiacs are powerful forms of magic," Lani said. "The movements of the stars and planets have a heavy influence on all magical beings. From what I can tell you, Professor Amber's theory is correct. I don't see any other way Liam could be alive, unless his magic is sustained by the moon. He shouldn't be able to cast at all, without a Familiar alive. That means he must be pulling from a different source, and the only thing that can sustain Water magic is the moon herself."

"So how do we channel energy from astral bodies?" Sophia asked in interest.

"I'm not quite sure," Lani admitted. "That's not something I studied when I had the chance to. But take Starbeasts, for example— Familiars made from the stars. They can influence planetary bodies, so why couldn't you pull from them?"

I'd studied Starbeasts a long time ago in my Hawkei Legends class, and knew they were powerful. What Amber said had to be true.

There was a call from the kitchen, and Lani turned her head. "I have to go. I'm sorry, I've told you everything I know, but if you need more help you can always pick my brain."

Lani darted off. Ava-Marie gave a loud yell. I bounced her in my lap, and Sophia said, "We should try out this theory. I want to see if my powers are greater under the sun, and yours under the moon."

"We'd better get a move on, then," I said. "We only have a few hours until sunset."

Jonah insisted on waiting around until he'd eaten his burger. Squeaks devoured the pizza with the help of Sassy and the kurbles. We headed to the beach, as that was our usual spot to practice magic. But when we got there, we saw it was crowded with people enjoying one of the first warm days we had.

"Now where do we go?" Imogen asked.

"There's a cliff side not too far from here. It's usually deserted," I said. "But we should drop off Ava-Marie first."

Sophia's eyes narrowed. "No. She stays with us."

"Soph, we're throwing magic around. It's better if she's with my mom," I stated tiredly.

Sophia's form remained rigid, even as we entered my mother's home. When we walked inside the living room, Maddie and Drew were messing around with some role-playing card game.

"Hey," Maddie said. She put down the cards and turned toward us. "What's up?"

"Would you mind watching Ava for a while?" I asked. "We won't be gone long, just a few hours."

Maddie smiled. "I always love spending time with my favorite niece. Sure."

I went to hand Ava-Marie off, but Maddie held up a finger to me. A blank look crossed her face, and Drew noticed. He took a pillow off the couch and threw it onto the floor.

Maddie took a deep breath, then sank to her knees on the pillow. Her eyes moved behind her lids as she breathed evenly, face knitted in concentration. It almost looked like she was meditating.

After a few seconds, her eyes opened. Drew handed her a leather journal and a pen. Maddie scribbled something into the journal quickly before snapping it shut.

"Visions again?" I asked, raising an eyebrow.

"Yes. Just a snippet of something," she replied. "Nothing too dramatic."

"You seemed very calm this time," Sophia commented.

"The reason I get sick when I have visions is because I fight them," Maddie said. "If I allow them to come, it doesn't affect me and the seizures stop. I just have to take deep breaths and allow the ancestors to show me what they want me to see."

"That's a big change," I said.

Maddie shrugged. "I've decided to stop fighting my destiny. I'm a *naderei*. I've tried, but I can't change it. I might as well accept it and use my powers for good."

"That's a good mindset to have," Imogen offered.

"Hey, it's better than fainting every other day," Maddie said. She reached out for Ava-Marie again, and I handed her over— though somewhat reluctantly.

Maddie saw my expression and rolled her eyes. "Mom's *home*, Liam. She can help if the visions get too bad."

I relaxed. I trusted Maddie, but who knew if she'd be able to watch Ava properly, and though Drew was a sweet guy, he looked like he knew shit all about babies. "We won't be long."

It was a difficult climb up the cliff side, so Julian flew Sophia and I up, while Imogen and Jonah rode on Squeaks' back.

The cliff side was spacious and beautiful. It was technically outside the boundaries of *Hok'evale*, and outside the town's shield, but we'd be safe up here. There was a cropping of trees to our back, where a river wound out of them. A waterfall ran off the side of the cliff and into the continuation of the river far below. The cliff side was blooming with spring flowers that the kurbles began weaving into crowns. Squeaks lay on her back and rolled in them, while Sassy darted to smell the scent of the flowers. Sophia raised her hands to create a shield around us to keep us safe, just in case.

We weren't the only ones up here, though. Amelia and Trace were sitting on the edge of the cliff, dangling their legs off as they observed the ocean.

"Ancestors! Can't we get some privacy around here? It took us *hours* to find this place," Amelia whined.

"Lighten up, Am," Sophia told her. "We're just here to do some training."

Amelia rolled her eyes. "Well, there goes our date." She got up and helped Trace to his feet. "What are you up to?"

"We heard that Elementai born on Solstices during their House zodiac year can survive on other magical sources than their Familiars. Koigni can pull magic from the sun and Toaqua from the moon," Sophia said. "Liam and I were both born on the Summer Solstice during our House years, so we want to try it out. We think it's the reason Liam's still alive."

Amelia raised an eyebrow. "Interesting. I'd love to see it in action."

I nodded to Trace. "How you doing?"

"Fine, thanks," Trace said. It was a pleasant response, but his expression was dull. Trace had taken Soren and Roland's deaths harder than Imogen. I hadn't seen him around much since we'd rescued the Familiars. His eyes had been bright before, but now they looked a little broken.

"Where are your Familiars? I don't see Kiwi," Sophia commented.

"We left them at the house. They wanted to nap, and we wanted alone time, honestly." Amelia shrugged.

I looked upward. "We're losing daylight," I said. "Sophia, you should go first."

Sophia sat on the ground and crossed her legs. She turned her palms upward, as if absorbing the light of the sun. She closed her eyes and concentrated. Esis left Buttercup and scrambled onto Sophia's lap, looking up at her with interest.

"What do you feel?" Imogen asked.

A crease ran between her eyes. "I'm not sure," Sophia said. "I can definitely feel the sun's power moving through me. It's like drawing from Esis, but different. I can take more magic from it if I focus."

"Well, let's see it," Jonah said. "Do something."

I waved at Jonah, to get him to shut up. But Sophia opened her eyes and looked up. A column of fire erupted from her palm, shooting twenty feet into the air. She sustained the flame and twisted it into a heart design, then molded it so it took the shape of a Fire unicorn. The Fire unicorn ran throughout the sky, galloping overhead and leaving embers behind where its hooves touched.

"Impressive," I said as the unicorn fizzled out. "Where'd you get that idea?"

Sophia shrugged. "I just thought of Ava."

Our child was all that was on her mind lately. Sophia waved her hands. Strands of fire streamed from her fingers and weaved together, creating a pattern. She sent the fire strands toward a pile of boulders that were collected near the waterfall. As her Fire touched them, the rocks sizzled and melted into a puddle of molten liquid. Imogen gasped in awe, and Trace's eyes widened.

"Holy shit!" Amelia screeched. "I've never seen a Koigni *melt shit* before!"

The rocks had been turned to lava in seconds by her power. As Sophia drew her heat away, the lava hardened. Sophia turned her powers on more boulders in the area, and they became goo at her touch, dissolving away into nothing but fluid rock. The cliff side got so hot during Sophia's casting, we all had to back off a few feet to avoid the heat.

"Well done, *pawee*," I praised. "Very impressive."

"It's more than impressive," Imogen said. "Sophia's doing something not even Koigni Elders could do. She's literally taking the powers of the sun to make her magic so intense, it's beyond anything the Hawkei have ever known."

As the sun began to set behind her, Sophia's powers dwindled. Her magic was still incredible, but not as revolutionary as what she could do before.

The moon shone overhead, and Sophia swept her hair back. "I'm tired, Liam. Your turn."

I hadn't noticed it before, but now that I was aware of it, I was stronger when the moon was overhead. I felt better, too. It was like my body naturally absorbed the moon's light and turned it into energy for me. It was so slight, yet I could feel a cold chill pumping through my veins like ice.

"Bet you can't move that waterfall," Jonah challenged.

I made a scoffing sound. I liked a challenge. I stopped the flow of the river with one hand and froze the waterfall with the other. The river pressed up against the invisible block I'd made as I moved the contents of the frozen waterfall to the ocean a mile off. The ice hovered through the air until I collapsed it into the ocean. Waves went crashing upward in a spectacular display.

"Liam, don't wear yourself out," Sophia warned, sounding anxious.

"This is easy for me," I said. And it was. I would've struggled in the daytime, but with the help of the moon, I was doing this no problem. I'd fallen to my knees when moving a river during the riots almost two years ago, but I'd grown stronger since then. I let the river flow once more, and it crashed back down into the riverbed, flowing over the edge of the cliff.

"Can you really manipulate water from so far away?" Imogen asked in disbelief. Her eyes had seen it, but she struggled to admit it was reality.

"Why not?" I concentrated on the ocean. Even from here, we could see the waves swell as they crashed against the shoreline. I could feel the strength of the ocean surging through me, and it was powerful. I could stir the sea, even from a great distance.

I was concentrating so hard, I didn't notice footsteps behind me. Everything changed in an instant. Before we had a warning, Sophia let out a cry of pain and sank to her knees. Esis jumped off her shoulder and yelped. Three noxite darts had been shot into her back.

I was shoved to the ground before I could rush to my wife. My hands were yanked behind my back roughly, and I cried out. I felt my magic draining as noxite cuffs were slapped on my wrists before I had a chance to summon my powers.

I lifted my head. Ahead of me, everyone was on the ground— Amelia, Trace, Jonah, and Imogen. All of them had been shot with noxite. Amelia and Jonah were both unconscious, completely knocked out. Trace stirred, but he was only able to get on his hands and knees. I saw dozens of Task Force boots march around us as orders echoed from one end of the cliff side to the other.

The fucking cowards had snuck up on us from the back. They'd been waiting for someone to cross the protective veil, and we'd been stupid enough to do it, thinking we were too close to the town limits to be in any real danger. I figured the cliff was too tough to climb— a bad mistake. Sophia had put up a shield, but she'd used up so much energy messing around with her new magic that the force-field had failed... and we hadn't noticed until it was too late.

Now that we were down, the Task Force was working on subduing our Familiars. Squeaks gave a scream and rose up on her back legs, pawing at the Task Force. Ropes had been lassoed around her neck, wings and ankles. The Task Force yanked her downward, forcing her to the ground. Buttercup scampered off into the woods, diving into the sanctuary of the trees.

Esis did not follow. His hair raised as he displayed his teeth, hissing at the Task Force members as they approached Sophia. Esis laid a paw on Sophia's head, and she came round, but she still looked so weak.

The fuckers had forced an iron muzzle on Julian. He'd tried to breathe fire, but they'd got it over his mouth before he knew what was happening.

There were so many of them. Not even a dragon could fend them all off, not when the rest of us were down. Julian pulled free of the Task Force, but the muzzle was still on his face. He swung his head viciously, giving roars of rage.

"Julian, get help!" I cried as the Task Force approached him with chains. If they tied him down, we had no hope. The soldier that had cuffed me yanked me to my feet and held me tight. His grip was so firm on my arm it was cutting off circulation.

Julian's eyes watered. He moaned and shook his head, not wanting to leave me.

"*Go!*" I yelled, and Julian staggered backward. The closest person to him was Trace. Julian flung Trace onto his back before he took off into the sky as the Task Force shot their elements at them. All of them missed, and Julian flew back toward *Hok'evale* at full speed.

"Leave the dragon!" the captain growled. "We're here for the chosen one!"

I heard a yelp. A Task Force member had grabbed Sassy by the scruff. The fox bit the hand of the Task Force member trying to shove her in a bag. She pulled herself free and rushed to Imogen, nosing her awake as Esis channeled his healing magic into her. He was so small the Task Force didn't notice him.

Imogen groggily stood. She staggered to Sophia, whose head lolled. Neither of them were capable of fighting. Imogen helped her to stand. The two girls leaned against each other as they backed away to the edge of the waterfall. The Task Force approached, surrounding them from all sides.

"There's nowhere to go," the captain barked. "Surrender now, and we won't hurt you."

That was a fucking lie. We were dead if these bastards brought us to Oleander. We had to escape somehow, and yet, there was no way out.

Imogen looked pleadingly at me, and I got her meaning. I gave a quick nod. Imogen grabbed on to Sophia's shoulder and pulled her over the cliff side, over the waterfall. Sassy took Esis in her mouth and jumped after them.

I smashed my elbow into the throat of the soldier holding me. He gagged and let me go. I ran forward and launched myself off the edge of the cliff, sailing downward.

I heard the screams of the girls below me, and fought off the panic that was building in my chest. I couldn't cast when I was in noxite cuffs. I needed to get a hand free, and I had seconds to do it, before we smashed against the rocks and died.

That left only one option. I didn't leave time to think about it. I broke my thumb. Blinding pain shot through my hand, but it was only for a moment. The adrenaline pumping through me made the agony vanish as the bottom of the waterfall drew near. With my right-hand free of the cuffs, I raised it, and a wave rose up to catch us before we smashed on the rocks below.

My magic was sloppy. I hadn't had time to complete the spell. Once the wave caught us, it wavered, crashing us back into the river. The river rushed by violently, careening us head over heels. I caught a glimpse of the girls up ahead, but only seconds before I was pushed under. My skin was sliced open on jagged rocks lining the riverbed, and blood seeped into the water.

I forced the river to slow us down. The river split in two directions, one toward the ocean and another into a small pool. My powers pushed us into the pool, and all became still and quiet.

Imogen clambered on shore. She crawled on her hands and knees, coughing up water. Sassy swam out of the pool with Esis in her mouth. She placed him on land and licked at his fur. The kurble came around, blinking his eyes in a daze.

I was panicking. I didn't see Sophia. My powers couldn't feel her anywhere nearby.

"Soph!" I cried. "*Sophie!*"

"Liam!" Imogen shouted, and she pointed to a spot below. I saw a murky shape twelve feet down. I held my breath and dived.

As I swam close, I saw Sophia had passed out. Her features showed no resonance of life. I grabbed her, and my magic shot us upward. I carried her onshore and placed her on the ground.

There was water in her lungs. I could feel it sloshing around.

"Come on, *pawee*, stay with me." I moved my hand over her face and commanded the water in her lungs to come out.

Sophia shot upward, and her eyes opened. She leaned over as she vomited up the water. Relief ran through me, and I almost cried. Sophia's body shivered as Esis laid his paw on her head once more, to heal her.

"You're all right, *pawee*," I sobbed, rubbing her back as she coughed up water. "You're all right."

Sophia eventually got her breath back. She sat up and leaned against me, trying to take in air while dazed.

Our one blessing had been leaving Ava-Marie behind. What would've happened if she had been with us? I shuddered to think of it.

Esis reached out. He healed my broken thumb, and the thudding pain went away, though it was replaced by a much worse feeling.

Imogen was quivering. "*Jonah,*" she whimpered.

Terror flooded me as I realized what had happened. We'd left Jonah,

Squeaks, and Amelia behind. Who knew what the Task Force was doing to them, or where they'd taken them?

"We'll get them back," I promised the girls in a shaking voice, forcing myself to believe that wasn't a lie. We weren't going to leave Jonah and Amelia to their deaths.

No matter what, we'd bring them home.

FOURTEEN

I was fuming when we burst through the doors to Jake's house without knocking. The Task Force had taken my sister and one of my best friends. I was ready to burn all of Kinpago to the ground to find them. We were still dripping wet, as Liam hadn't bothered to draw the water out of our clothes yet. I left a trail of water behind me as I stomped through the house.

"Jake?" I called.

No answer came.

"He better be here," I grumbled. "I'm not waiting around."

"Sophia, calm down," Liam insisted, though I could hear the terror in his tone. He was one to talk. "We have to be rational."

"Rational my ass!" I whirled around in the middle of the living room.

Imogen's lips trembled, and her eyes glossed over. Sassy shook at her feet, and Esis scurried in nervous circles. I didn't think Imogen had processed that Jonah had been taken. She'd already had so much ripped away from her. I wouldn't let Jonah and Amelia go down with the others.

"There's nothing rational about what just happened!" I seethed. My voice cracked, and my chest compressed as if bricks were piling up on my lungs. "It was my fault. I let the force field down, and now we're paying for it. Forgive me if I want to do something to fix this."

Liam grabbed me by the shoulders and shook me a little. He winced, as if my skin was burning him. He drew back, but the sharp breath he took helped snap me back to attention. I listened carefully to what he had to say.

"We *will* get them back, Soph," Liam promised. "But we *have* to be strategic if we have any chance of that. Imagine if we went into the child camps guns blazing and no plan! Or if we did the same to rescue the Familiars. The Task Force would've fried our asses. We don't even know where they've taken them."

"The academy, obviously!" I'd bet my magic they were there.

"Not obviously," Liam replied. "We've already broken people out of there once. Oleander's smart enough to move the prisoners someplace else, somewhere secret. We need a plan before we're captured in our attempts to save them!"

My shallow breaths grew deeper as I took in his words. He was right. If we stormed Kinpago without a plan, we'd never find them. We had to treat this like any other military operation, despite the personal ties.

"Okay," I caved, holding back my anger. I'd save it for the Task Force. "I'll do whatever you tell me, Liam. You're my chief."

Liam nodded firmly and opened his mouth to say something else, but he was interrupted by the sound of a door slamming at the back of the house. Heavy footsteps sounded, and we all looked up to see Jake and Sabor emerge from the hall that led to the military headquarters. Jake's features were tight. His face fell when he took in our soaking wet forms dripping water all over his floor.

"What's happened?" he demanded.

"It's Jonah—" Imogen started to explain, but her voice broke.

Jake's features clouded, like he'd just been hit in the side of the head by a frying pan. "*What?*"

Liam rushed to explain. "It's the Task Force."

"Here?" Jake raged. "In *Hok'evale?* How'd they get past Luana's shield?"

"They didn't," Liam clarified. "We were outside the veil when—"

"You were *outside!?*" Jake's hands curled into fists. "Why would you—? Forget that. What happened to Jonah?"

Liam's gaze dropped. "The Task Force attacked. They took Jonah, Squeaks, and Amelia."

For a moment, I couldn't read Jake's expression. His features had gone totally blank as he took in the news. Usually, he remained calm and cool in these types of situations. It was part of his job— to look at things logically to come up with the best plan of attack.

But there was nothing logical about losing the man you loved to the enemy.

A fire ignited in Jake's eyes, and his features contorted into fury. "FUCK!" he screamed.

Jake's hands fisted at his sides, and a muscle popped in his jaw. He glanced around for something to take his anger out on, and his eyes landed on a vase on the end table. He grabbed it and threw it against one of the floor-to-ceiling windows, cracking the glass. The vase shattered, sending bits of broken ceramic spinning across the floor.

Sabor was equally enraged at the news. He reared up on his hind legs. When he came back down, his front hoof went straight through the glass end table. I didn't think he'd meant to do it, but shards of glass went every-where. Imogen and I flinched into each other.

"Whoa, Jake!" Liam said, holding his hands up.

Jake paced back and forth. The air in the room swirled around him in a whirlwind. "How can you act so calm!?"

"I'm *not* calm!" Liam burst. "I'm furious! Jonah's my best friend. Amelia is my sister-in-law. I'm trying to keep a goddamn level head, because no one else is right now! The longer we spend freaking out, the less time we have to come up with a plan of attack. My goal right now is to get them to safety."

Jake stopped pacing and ran a hand down his face and into his beard. When he did that, it was a moment of defeat, and I *felt* it. The Task Force had us where they wanted us. If they caught Jake and I in the wrong mood — our commander and the chosen one— the resistance was done for.

It was no mistake they'd gotten away with Amelia and Jonah. They were the target.

Jake's tone softened, though the fury never left his eyes. "I think I know where they've been taken."

Imogen gaped. "You don't think they'd hold them at the academy?"

"No." Jake took a deep breath and glanced to Sabor, whose eyes were still distant with the news. "We recently received intel that the Task Force has run out of room to hold prisoners at Orenda Academy. Instead, they've converted..."

It looked like it was too hard for him to say. "They've converted the *Hozho* into a prison ship."

"*What?*" Imogen, Liam, and I all squeaked out in unison.

Jake pressed his fingers to his eyes. "We've had Yapluma searching for it, and we're close to finding it. We know it's in the area, but Oleander isn't playing by the rules. He's using massive Yapluma power to cover it up."

"Jonah's the strongest Yapluma there is," Imogen pointed out. "He'll counteract their magic."

"Not if he still has noxite in his system," I said. "That can knock out even the Storm Lord."

"Come." Jake cocked his head toward the headquarters. "I want you to see something."

Jake led us down the hall to the back door. It opened to the cave system, and we filed down the stairs into the headquarters. Jake's strategy team was there, including my adoptive parents, Carter, and James. They were all hunched over a map and barely noticed we'd entered.

"We have a situation," Jake announced.

My parents looked up. Their faces paled at the sight of my dripping form. Liam noticed, and he instantly dried us off. Esis shook out his fur, looking happy to be dry again.

Dad stood, and Mom got to her feet beside him. She held on to him, sensing the worst. I didn't know how to tell them.

"What's happened?" Dad demanded.

Liam was the one to step forward. "There's no easy way to say this, Mr. Henley. The Task Force has taken Amelia."

Mom stumbled to the side, and Dad gasped as he caught her. "What? H-how did this happen?"

At the same time, Mom asked, "Where have they taken her?"

Jake answered my mother's question first. He stepped forward and stabbed a finger at the map on the table. "The *Hozho*. It has to be. That's the only place they have left for prisoners."

"We're coming with this time," Dad insisted.

I glanced to them and their Familiars. My parents weren't in the best of shape, and I'd never seen either of them or their Familiars perform spectacular feats of magic. They'd barely survived the last battle over Christmas, and that was with Amelia's help. I worried they'd get hurt if they came along.

"No," I stated firmly. "It's too dangerous."

"This is our daughter," Mom reminded me. "Your *sister*. We're helping."

Jake studied the map closely. "You can help by locating the *Hozho*."

Carter ran his fingers through his hair. "We've been trying. There doesn't seem to be a pattern."

Imogen came up beside Jake and practically shoved Carter aside to get a good look. I peeked at the map to see it was outlined with locations where the resistance had spotted the *Hozho*. They were trying to predict where to find it next.

Imogen narrowed her eyes at the map. "It's because your data's incomplete. There's a pattern if you look for the missing data points. Let me see this." She grabbed the map and stole it away from the others to look closely at it.

Meanwhile, Jake turned to Liam. "What are your thoughts, Chief?"

The tone Jake used was unusual. He wasn't just asking Liam's opinion — he was handing the decisions over to him. It was like he knew he wouldn't be able to handle making the right choices at a time like this, and he trusted that Liam would.

Liam jumped into chief mode immediately. "We need to keep our extraction teams small. The *Hozho* is big, yes, but we're going to need the element of surprise. We can't go in like we did with the camps or the Familiars. There won't be anywhere to run once we're on that ship. We can't let them know we're there until we have Jonah and Amelia, and are able to get them out."

Jake nodded firmly. "Agreed. Small teams of the most powerful Elementai we've got."

"Who, exactly?" I asked. Liam and I were in for sure. But we couldn't risk screwing this up by choosing the wrong team.

Jake didn't get a chance to answer before a door above our heads flung open, slamming into the cave walls.

"We're coming!" Trace said desperately.

He hurried into the room, and Luana rushed in behind him. She was followed by another guy I'd only met a few times. It was Trevor, Amelia's roommate from Kinpago. His blue feline Familiar was at his side. Kiwi rode on its head, grasping onto its fluffy mane.

"Kiwi says Amelia's in trouble," Trevor stated breathlessly.

What's going on? Luana demanded. *Julian's having a cow!*

"Amelia and Jonah have been captured," Jake replied hastily.

Luana's eyes widened. Sierra's wings drooped from where she sat on her shoulder.

"Problem is, it might take a while to find them," Jake admitted.

"No, it won't," Imogen said.

Carter's mouth dropped. He looked like he was about to shit himself that Imogen figured it out so quickly.

"You know where the *Hozho* will show up next?" I balked.

Imogen slammed the map back down on the table. She pointed to a spot on the map. "They'll be here tonight."

"How do you know?" James gaped.

Imogen shrugged. "I had a thing for math and puzzles growing up."

Jake cocked an eyebrow. "You're sure there's a pattern?"

"Positive," Imogen stated. "They're working in a zig-zag, trying to throw us off, but there *is* a pattern. They have to fly in the same position around the area to keep adding prisoners. The ship can't fly too far away from Kinpago. I'm sure this is where we'll find them."

"Good work, Im," Liam praised.

"Which only leaves one question," I added, crossing my arms. "How are we getting on the ship?"

FLYING to the ship didn't prove to be an issue. It was *finding* it that was a bitch. The clouds were thick as ever, as if one hell of a storm was rolling in, and we couldn't see for shit. I figured we had the Elders to thank for that, or whoever was controlling the weather to conceal the *Hozho*. They were smart about it, too, creating cloud cover for miles, so we couldn't use it to predict the location of the *Hozho*. But I trusted Imogen, and I knew she wouldn't fail us.

Jake flew through the sky, using his Air powers to levitate himself. He cleared a path in the clouds so that we could see, but it was so dark all I saw was blackness ahead. I couldn't use my Anichi light, as we didn't want to alert the Task Force of our arrival. Thank the ancestors Julian had excellent eyesight and could see where he was going.

Liam's arms tightened around me. I sat on Julian's back, clinging tight to one of his spines. Esis rode on Julian's head, stabilizing himself with one of Julian's horns.

Trevor sat behind Liam, looking terrified to be on the back of a dragon. I didn't know Trevor well, nor what he was capable of, but he was Amelia's friend, and he wouldn't back down when insisting he come along to rescue her.

Luana, Imogen, and Trace sat on Sabor's back. The weight was almost too much for the hippogriff, but he was one hell of a determined Familiar. He managed to keep up with Julian by sheer determination. Imogen clutched a bag at her side, which held leaves and pebbles she planned to use as weapons. Sierra rode on Sabor's feathers. Sassy was having fun riding the wave of Jake's magic. She moved her legs like she was running in mid-air. Kiwi flew along beside her and kept throwing her dark glances. We didn't have room for Trace or Trevor's Familiars, so they'd had to stay behind.

"Keep your eyes peeled!" Imogen shouted over the roar of the cold wind. "We should be arriving any moment—"

She cut off as a terrifying *thud* sounded through the sky. I hadn't processed what had happened before Julian swooped downward, narrowly missing the rudder of the boat. Kiwi spiraled twenty feet before catching himself with his wings. The dumb bird had slammed straight into the side of the cruise ship. How he was my sister's Familiar, I'd never know.

I winced, and Kiwi fell into flight beside us again. My heart raced, but it slowed as Julian spread his wings and our flight evened out. Julian glided through the thick clouds, never making a sound with the beat of his wings. Jake gave a signal, and the Familiars doubled back silently.

We stayed beneath the ship, where the crew wouldn't see us. Julian landed on the hull of the ship, his claws digging in tightly to the metal. I held on with all my might, as we were almost upside down, thousands of feet above the ground. Sabor dropped off the others on the lower deck, then came back for us, as it wouldn't be possible for Julian to drop us off without being seen. We jumped onto Sabor's back— which was frightening with being up so high, but Jake helped with his magic. Liam gave Julian a firm nod. He'd wait for us here, until we made our escape.

Sabor flew us up to the lower deck and landed beside our friends. Imogen, Luana, Jake, and Trace were already crouched down behind a lifeboat. There were no Task Force around, but we stuck to the shadows, in case anyone spotted us through the windows.

"I'll bet anything they're holding them under the deck, in the economy class rooms," Liam whispered. "The first-class living quarters will be reserved for the crew. We move quickly and efficiently, and we take out any Task Force we see as quietly as possible. The last thing we want to do is attract attention."

Imogen saluted him. "Got it, Chief."

"I can try to make us all invisible," I offered. "We have a better chance of going undetected."

"Do you think you can?" Liam asked.

I shrugged. "I might as well try."

I reached my magic out to feel for surrounding light. It was dim, but there was enough light coming from the ship that I could make out everyone's shadows. I directed the light around us, and it wrapped like a warm cocoon over my skin. I was watching Imogen. One moment she was there, and the next she was gone. For a second, I felt pride swell in my chest. Then she moved, and she instantly became visible.

"It's not working," Imogen pointed out.

"I can't track your movements," I said in frustration. I could turn myself invisible, but it looked like I struggled to do that with anyone else.

"We don't have time for training," Jake pointed out. "It was a good idea, but one we'll have to abandon."

Liam quickly reminded everyone of the plan. "Sophia, Imogen, Trevor, and I will take the bow of the ship. Luana, Jake, and Trace will take the stern." He shot a glance to Amelia's Familiar and added, "Kiwi's with you. We all know the signals. Let's make sure none of us get hurt tonight, okay?"

We all nodded. I didn't think any of us could handle losing someone again.

Liam glanced up and down the deck, then shot a glance to the windows above us. "We're clear. Let's go."

There were a few lights on the ship, but it was so foggy it was easy to cross the deck undetected. We slipped into a stairwell and split up at the bottom. The hall was narrow, and there were so many endless doorways, it was hard to tell where to begin.

Down the hall, Jake was using his Air powers to feel inside the rooms. "Nothing here. Let's keep going," he hissed.

Liam worked in a similar fashion, though he used his water magic to feel for heartbeats. We must've passed by a hundred rooms, and Liam had determined each of them empty.

As we reached a crossroads, Liam flung his arm out. We stopped in our tracks and pressed ourselves up against the wall. He quickly signed, *Someone's coming.*

Nobody made a sound. Liam's gaze became calculating, like he was trying to determine the approaching enemy's distance.

The man's footsteps neared, and Liam attacked. He leapt forward and grabbed a Task Force member around the throat, then shoved him up against the wall. He quickly formed a water ball in his hand and held it up threateningly.

"Where are the prisoners that were brought in today?" Liam hissed.

The Task Force member didn't seem bothered by Liam's threat, because he retaliated by shoving his hands into Liam's chest. Air magic blasted through his palms, sending Liam straight into the opposite wall.

"Like hell I'd tell you," the man snarled.

I reacted immediately, shooting a ball of Anichi light at the man. He stumbled back, but I hadn't focused the magic enough to do any real damage.

I was about to fry his ass when Liam lifted his hands. One pointed at the man, while the other urged me to stay back.

The man went still as Liam's magic pulsed through him. His fists tightened, and he groaned in pain. I couldn't see his face beneath his visor, but I imagined him gritting his teeth. For a moment, I thought Liam was going to stop his heart, but he took a different approach instead.

"Tell me where to find them," Liam growled. "This is your only chance."

The man sputtered. "Your friends *deserve* to die!"

Liam gaped, like he couldn't believe the man dared to make such a bold statement. He quickly composed himself and spat, "For what crimes?"

The man groaned again. Whatever Liam was doing to him made it difficult to speak. "You've torn the Hawkei apart. You have disgraced the Great Spirit. You and your friends shall perish in *Aiya Nocshun*."

Liam's eyes flashed. He was incredibly sensitive when it came to *Aiya Nocshun*, as he once feared he may end up there himself. I could only imagine the dark images going through his head, reminders of the horrible nightmares he'd had of that place.

"Only the Great Spirit can judge us," Liam said. "Let's see how he judges *you*."

I didn't expect what came next. Liam twisted his fingers. Water began to pour beneath the man's helmet, soaking into his uniform. My jaw dropped as I witnessed a new level of magic I'd never seen Liam use before. He was sucking the water straight out of the man's body— from his blood, from his organs... straight from his cells.

It was horrifying to watch. But another part of me felt protected by Liam— like nothing could touch any of us with such a powerful Elementai on our side.

Liam's lips curled into an angry sneer as water continued to pour out of the man's body like a faucet. Finally, the stream of water slowed, and Liam dropped his hands. The man dropped to the ground— dead. When he landed, his Task Force helmet rolled off his shoulders, and we caught the horrifying view of his face. His skull had sunken in, and his skin clung tight to his form. He looked like he'd been dead for a thousand years— like a mummy.

Liam shuddered as he looked down at the man. I could see the regret in his eyes, but we knew this was a war. We couldn't hesitate and risk the enemy getting the upper-hand. He'd done what he had to do.

"Come on." Liam cocked his head.

I followed behind him, trying not to dwell too long on what we'd just seen. Esis and Sassy stepped around the man's body nervously, while Imogen tip-toed around it, so she wouldn't step on him. Trevor stared down at the man and gagged.

Imogen grabbed him by the arm. "You have to keep up."

Trevor hesitated, then went to follow. "I've just never seen—"

Trevor was cut off by the sound of huffing coming from down the hall. We all turned. My guts sank when I saw a fucking *rhino* standing there! It was so wide its shoulders touched each side of the hall. Its leathery skin was pitch black, and a shiny gold horn sat on the end of its nose. The tip glistened, as if in warning.

Shit! We had one hell of an upper-hand with the Task Force, but fighting off magical creatures was another thing.

The rhino dipped its head, aiming its horn at us. He scuffed his foot on the floor and huffed again. My heart pounded as I realized we'd just killed its Elementai— and it was out for revenge.

"Run!" Liam cried.

The rhino began to charge, and we all whirled around to race after Liam. Esis let out a high-pitched squeal as he scurried down the hall. Sassy turned into a kitsune, but she was running so fast she didn't have a chance to turn and face the rhino. I didn't know if it'd do any good. Who knew what kind of magical abilities this creature had?

"Im!" I cried as we sprinted down the hallway. If anyone knew anything about this creature, it'd be her. "Any weaknesses?"

"Not off the top of my head!" she squealed.

I started trying doors as we passed by them, but each one was locked, and it was slowing us down. The rhino was catching up to us fast. As I tried another one, I dared a glance back to see how close he'd come. My stomach jumped to my throat as I saw he was only a few yards away from me.

"In here!" Liam shouted. He'd gathered water out of the air and used it to break a lock on the door across from me. He grabbed me by the back of the shirt and yanked me inside. Imogen, Trevor, Esis, and Sassy all fell into the room behind us, and we landed on the ground in a heap. I threw up a force field as fast as I could, which sent the door slamming into the wall.

For a split-second, I thought we were safe, until the rhino slammed his shoulder up against the door, and the whole room shook violently.

"He's going to get through!" Trevor cried as he rolled off Imogen.

"No, he's not," I promised. I concentrated on strengthening my force field, and pushed it out to press against the walls of the dark room we were in.

Esis shook from beside me and held his palms up. Little beams of light streaked out of them, lighting the room. It was tiny, with nothing more than a bed, a dresser, and an end table. It was definitely one of the cheapest guest rooms on board.

The rhino slammed into the door again. I felt the walls shudder against my force field, but they didn't give way. Again and again the rhino tried to get through. I could hear the murderous intent in its battle cry. But it was to no avail.

Finally, the shaking ceased. A loud *thud* came from outside the door, and I realized that it was the rhino falling. My heart rate began to slow.

"What happened?" I asked, looking to Liam.

He furrowed his brow. "I think he died. His minutes were numbered the second I killed his Elementai."

Trevor breathed a sigh of relief. "So, we're safe?"

"Not yet," Imogen replied, still trying to catch her breath. "Someone must've heard the commotion."

"Agreed," I stated. "We have to move on, before someone finds us."

Imogen went for the door. "Let's go."

"Wait!" Liam grabbed her by the wrist. He pressed his index finger to his lips, and everyone went quiet. "I hear something."

I listened closely, and I realized I heard something, too. It was the sound of a voice, though I couldn't tell what it was saying. At first, I thought it was someone screaming down the hall— someone coming after us. But the closer I listened, the more I started to make out the words.

"Help me!" a woman's voice wailed. "Somebody help me!"

My stomach dropped out of my abdomen. "That's Amelia!"

Liam realized it at the same time. "It sounds like it's coming from below us."

I raised my hand, and fire glowed in my palm. "I'll blast a hole in the floor."

"No." Liam stopped me. "We don't know what's below us or what we'd fall onto— or if we'd hurt Amelia."

"There's gotta be another stairwell nearby," Imogen said.

"Then let's go." Trevor was in a rush to get to her. I knew he and Amelia were really close friends. He cared deeply about her.

We opened the door. Though the rhino's body was blocking the way, we crawled over him and continued down the hall.

Just as Sassy slid down the dead rhino's neck to follow us, I heard the sound of angered shouts down the hall.

"The Task Force is coming," I hissed.

Several Task Force members came flooding in from nearby hallways. They took one look at the shriveled man on the ground and his dead Familiar and aimed their noxite guns at us.

We all reacted at once. Liam and Trevor shot water balls, while Imogen aimed leaves at the Task Force. They went spinning like throwing stars and gained so much momentum they sliced a few men's uniforms, causing blood to start rushing out of the wounds.

I gathered magic in my palms, and a huge fireball at least three feet wide spun down the hall. Before my magic reached them, I heard the click of noxite guns.

Esis reacted the fastest. He jumped on top of the rhino and threw his paws up.

"Esis!" I cried, but a moment later, I realized I had no reason to fear.

A force field ballooned out of Esis' hands, The noxite darts slammed into it, crumpling like soda cans before falling to the ground.

It all happened in a split-second. My Fire magic reached the men, and it knocked them on their asses, completely taking them off.

I blinked a few times. "Esis, you made a shield! Good job, buddy."

"Yeah, great," Liam grumbled. "We don't have time to stand around congratulating each other."

Esis ignored Liam and cheered for himself. He jumped off the rhino and into my arms. I caught him, and we hurried away from the Task Force.

We turned down another hall and came to a stairwell. From up above, I heard the sound of footsteps as more Task Force members rushed below deck. We slipped down another level before they heard us. Liam gestured for us to duck into the shadows. I held my breath as the sound of Task Force footsteps faded above our heads.

"They're gone," I whispered. "Let's go find Amelia."

My heart pounded as we emerged from the stairwell. I tiptoed quietly, listening intently to the sound of my sister's cries. I didn't hear them anymore.

Imogen pointed. "We heard her down that way."

We slunk quietly down the hall, but there didn't appear to be any Task Force on this level. I waited to hear Amelia's voice again, but we turned another hall and I still heard nothing.

Then it came— the heart-shattering sound of my sister's tortured cries. I stopped dead, trying to gauge if what I'd just heard was real or a figment of my imagination. The screams continued.

"Fuck," Liam growled under his breath.

Sassy ran on ahead, her nine tails quaking in anger and her vines whipping around her. Trevor was close at her heels. He gathered as much water as he could from the air, creating two giant water balls in his hands.

The rest of us ran behind them, following the sound of Amelia's voice. Liam was slowing down. We'd been running our asses all over this ship, and it wasn't doing his flare-up any good. He doubled over and caught himself on the wall, gagging.

"Liam!" I gasped.

"Forget about me," he urged. "Go get Amelia."

I hesitated. I needed to get to Amelia stat, but I couldn't leave Liam here for the Task Force.

Then Amelia cried out again, and I knew I had to go on ahead. I couldn't bear to think of what she was going through in that moment, with those harrowing cries echoing down the hall. I had to end whatever they were doing to her— now.

"I'll take care of myself," Liam insisted. "Go."

"Here." I shoved Esis into his arms. "Take Esis. I'll be right back."

I abandoned my husband and Familiar to go find my sister. Ahead, Sassy and Trevor turned the corner, with Imogen close behind. Maniacal laughter rang down the hall. It was a woman's, but it wasn't Amelia.

"You think someone's coming to save you?" the woman sneered. "Think again!"

I rounded the corner and stopped dead in my tracks when I saw Amelia through an open doorway. Trevor and Imogen had paused momentarily to take in the scene as well.

Amelia sat in one of the guest rooms, but it wasn't like the one above us. The window was nothing more than a small round hole that even Esis would have trouble fitting through. All the furniture had been removed, except for a metal chair that she sat tied to with noxite cuffs. Her face was bruised and swollen, and blood was matted in her hair. Cuts ran up and down her arms, as if someone had been using her skin as a chopping board. The ends of her hair had been singed, and her fingertips were red and blistered.

"You want to get out of here?" a woman taunted. "You better start begging the ancestors for mercy."

The woman leaned over Amelia, her waterfall of brunette hair concealing her features. She wore all black, like the other Task Force, but didn't have her helmet on. She held up a dagger threateningly, then ran the tip of it across Amelia's chin. She didn't break skin, but it was a horrifying sight. For a moment, I couldn't even process it as *real*.

Trevor stepped forward into the open doorway. "*You* should be the one begging for mercy."

Relief flooded Amelia's features when she saw him. Trevor raised his hands to throw his water balls at the evil woman. She stood up straight and tossed her hair over her shoulder, and that's when I realized with sinking clarity I recognized her.

It was Jill Larsen, the Koigni bitch who'd been in my Hawkei Careers class. She'd gone to work on the *Hozho* when she graduated and had turned Amelia in as a spy. Now she was getting her kicks by physically torturing my sister!

I barely had a second to process it before Trevor's water balls were whizzing out of his hands. They slammed straight into Jill's face, and her head snapped backward. It was barely enough to get her to stumble to the side. She wiped her nose, and blood dripped onto her finger.

Her features darkened. "Oh, asshole. You're gonna pay for that one."

Fire ignited in her palms, but a fireball formed in mine just as quickly. "You really want to try that, Jill?" I threatened.

She looked me up and down and scoffed. "What are *you* going to do about it?"

Imogen controlled the pebbles in her bag, and several rose up into the air. In front of her, Sassy's vines snapped. "You really want to test that when it's three against one?"

Jill threw her head back and laughed. "Underclassmen never learn, do they? I don't have to face any of you."

I didn't know what she meant, until she snapped her fingers and a creature jumped out of the shadows. I reared backward, unable to even describe what it was. All I saw was a flaming ball of fire at least five feet across, hovering in the air. It wasn't something Jill had conjured up. It had eyes, a mouth, a nose and fur beneath the flames, but it was completely round, like a giant, living fireball.

I could feel its Fire coming off of it in waves. My guts twisted as I realized this was Jill's Familiar. I'd never known what she was bonded to before, and whatever it was, I'd never encountered one in my life.

"Get them, Bernardo!" she commanded her Familiar.

Bernardo? What a lame-ass name.

The creature lunged at us, and we all jumped backward through the doorway. For what he lacked in name, he made up for in terrifying power. I threw the fireballs in my hand at the creature, but it did nothing to hurt it. Imogen shot her pebbles toward it as she rushed to back away, but the creature seemed to be *made* of Fire to some extent. The pebbles went straight through it. Fire crackled in the air, and a roar erupted out of the creature, sending scorching heat waves over us. Sassy snapped out her vines, but she jumped back as Bernardo's Fire singed them.

The creature swooped through the doorway, manipulating its fiery form to fit through. Imogen and Trevor went one way, while I went the other. The creature had separated us, but I took that as an advantage. It meant we had him surrounded. Bernardo turned toward Imogen and Trevor and began advancing on them.

"What the hell is that!?" Trevor cried.

"No clue," Imogen squealed.

That was a first. If Imogen didn't know what this thing was, we were screwed.

I got an idea. I hoped to hell it worked. "Hold on, guys," I called to them. "I've got this."

I reached out with my magic and began to siphon Fire from the creature. It was intrafusion, as Liam had taught me how to do. A massive fireball began to form between my hands, but no matter how much magic I stole, the creature's flames didn't die down.

Fuck, Jill's Familiar was *strong*.

Amelia's cries rang out through the hall again. I pulled harder on Bernardo's magic, until the fireball in my own hands was too big to control. I let it go, flinging it down the hall toward the creature. It collided with him, but I was totally shocked when he didn't even stumble. All the Fire did was sink into his form, like he'd *absorbed* it— like they'd become *one*.

Good luck fighting Fire with Fire. That wasn't fucking happening.

Bernardo shot fireballs down the hall toward Imogen and Trevor. They ducked out of the way, but the fireballs came so quickly I feared one of them might catch my friends. I turned to other methods and created a force field. I pushed it outward, to encompass Jill's Familiar. Its fireballs impacted with the side of my force field, but I had to push further if I wanted to immobilize him.

I had a theory, but only moments to test it. Pushing my Anichi magic outward, I separated the force field from myself. It encompassed the creature. I intended to squeeze it to death, like I had the Task Force member in the caves. I wanted to cut off its oxygen, to kill the flames.

But the harder I squeezed, the more enraged the creature became. It hissed, and its Fire turned from a blazing red to a sweltering blue. His Fire pushed against my shield, and I began to sweat profusely.

He was burning my shield! I didn't know how much longer I could hold it up. Red-hot pain started to sear my insides as his magic fought against my own. I tried to use my Fire to calm it, but my magic warred inside of me. I couldn't use both Koigni and Anichi powers at once— not if I wanted any control.

"Gah!" I screamed out in pain.

From inside Amelia's prison cell, Jill laughed gleefully. "Ancestors," she scoffed to Amelia. "Do they really call your sister the *chosen one?* This will be fun to watch. Excuse me while I go enjoy the show."

Jill stepped out into the hall. I'd advanced on her Familiar, so she came in behind me. She laughed, as if pleased to see me shaking in my boots.

I whirled on her, still keeping my shield secured tightly around her Familiar. "Fuck you, Jill! Fuck you and all you've done to my sister."

She crossed her arms and leaned against the doorway, like this was nothing more than slightly amusing to her. "What do you think of Bernardo? He's very strong, don't you think?"

I winced as another wave of heat washed over me. Bernardo writhed in the magical cage I'd built for him. I willed to call upon the powers of the sun, but it had long dipped beneath the horizon. The sun's magic wouldn't save me now.

It was clear to me then there was no way I could kill this creature— whatever he was. The only thing I could do was go for Jill. If I killed her, Bernardo would die.

"Imogen, Trevor, run!" I commanded.

"No, Sophia!" Imogen cried. "We're not leaving you."

"Trust me!" I replied.

Jill chuckled. "How noble. Sacrificing yourself for your friends? Go ahead. Oleander will reward me with riches when *my* Familiar kills the chosen one."

I scoffed. "What riches? He can't even afford the war he's fighting."

Her features faltered for a moment, but her lips curled back into a sneer. Apparently, Oleander had been hiding a few secrets from his Task Force.

"You think you're stronger than the chosen one?" I challenged. "*Prove it!*"

I let go of my hold on Bernardo and whirled on Jill. A fireball erupted from my palm before I thought about it. It whizzed toward her head, but she countered my attack with a fireball of her own. It connected with mine, and the two went flying off in opposite directions.

Before I could react, she'd already formed another fireball in her palms and shot it my way. It morphed into the shape of a dragon, growing to fierce proportions that filled the hall. The Fire dragon reared its head and lunged for me, its jaws chomping in my direction.

I didn't think. I just reacted.

My hands shot up, and as the dragon was about to clamp its flaming teeth over my head, I reached for its neck. It was made of Fire, so my fingers didn't touch anything solid. But it didn't hurt, either. It should have. Jill was acting in defense. But as my fingers swiped through its neck, its head was severed. Its body continued to rage in flame, but its head fizzled away to nothing.

Somehow, I had taken control of Jill's magic. I had made her Fire my own and taken the head of the Fire dragon.

Jill's features contorted in rage. Surely she'd never seen someone do *that* before. But she only took a second to consider what had happened. Moments later, a head was growing out of the Fire dragon's neck. It split into three parts, making it a three-headed monster that looked intent on eating me alive. She lifted her arms to command her magic to attack, but I raised my arms at the same time. I conjured a force field, cocooning myself inside of it. The three heads of her fire-dragon came at me, but they slammed into the side of my shield. Their heads flickered, then returned to their distinct dragon shape.

Jill's eyebrows knitted in confusion. She sent their jaws snapping at me again, but they didn't reach me. "What the hell?"

"What?" I shrugged, pleased I'd caught her so off guard. "No one told you the chosen one was Anichi?"

I advanced on her, and as I did so, I expanded my force field, encompassing her fire-dragon inside. Once it was inside my shield, I gained complete control of it, and the flames fizzled out at my feet.

Jill took a few steps back down the hall, looking terrified of me. "The Anichi died out!"

I chuckled. "That's what Oleander wants you to think."

"Oleander wouldn't lie to me," she said, her breath wavering. "You're the liar!"

"Am I?" I challenged. "Well, enjoy this bit of honesty. You will *never* touch my sister again."

I lunged at her, and my fingers clamped around her throat. She called upon her Fire to burn me, but I sucked the motherfucking heat straight off her body. I didn't know how— I shouldn't have been able to. It should've burned me. But I didn't feel a thing.

In the Hawkei tribe, we had a tradition. Should a traitor be sentenced to death, they were to be killed by the element opposite them. Jill was Koigni, which meant she'd be executed by water. I didn't have Water power, but I felt an execution was in store. No way was she going out by her own element.

Wrapping my fingers tighter around her throat, I called upon my Anichi powers. Amelia's whimper sounded down the hall, and the urge to *protect* washed through me. Amelia was my first friend, my lucky charm, and my rock when I needed her most. She was there for me during my naming ceremony. She was the one who'd sent me the Spirit Totem. She kept me safe from the Elders' grasp on more occasions than one. Though she wasn't blood, she was my sister— she was my *tribe*.

I loved and protected my tribe.

Healing magic washed through me, but I didn't channel it outward toward Jill. I reversed it, shutting her systems down from the inside out. She was healthy, and my magic tasted sweet as it swept through her. But as I shut down her immune system, as I stole the health right out of her cells, my magic turned bitter on my tongue. I felt her heartbeat slow and her kidneys struggle. Her lungs swelled, and she gasped for air.

"Don't," she squeaked out.

I didn't justify her pleads for mercy with a response. She'd tortured my sister, and her fate was in the Great Spirit's hands now.

Blood vessels erupted in Jill's eyes, and dark spider-veins cobwebbed across her face. Her bloodshot eyes rolled back into her skull. One by one, each of her systems failed, until her heart completely gave up.

I didn't stop until I saw the life drain out of her eyes.

With satisfaction, I dropped her, and her lifeless body slumped to the floor. I stepped back, breathing heavily. I could hardly process what I'd done. I'd *murdered* Jill. I'd made her look into my eyes as I literally sucked the life straight out of her.

But it wasn't in cold blood. Jill wasn't just in bed with the enemy— she *was* the enemy. And she deserved every bit of wrath I'd brought down upon her.

I had mere moments to take in what I'd done. Then I heard Imogen's fearful cry down the hall, and I whirled toward the sound. Bernardo was bigger than ever. His flames had grown so large that his form went from floor to ceiling, wall-to-wall. I couldn't even describe him as a fireball anymore. He was more or less just a mass of raging flames.

The creature must have felt his Elementai die, but he was in too much agony to realize who was responsible, because instead of turning on me, he went straight toward Imogen and Trevor. The creature raged forward, charging toward them.

"Look out!" Trevor cried, shoving Imogen aside.

Imogen yelped as she was hurled into the next hallway. Sassy barked and followed, but Trevor wasn't fast enough. Bernardo slammed straight into him, lighting his entire form ablaze. The flames seemed to erupt, as if Bernardo himself had disintegrated upon impact— but not before claiming his final victim.

Trevor's pained cries echoed down the hall. I thrust out my Koigni magic in his direction to try to kill the flames, but I was too late. Before I could reduce the flames at all, Trevor's screams halted. Flames consumed the hallway, lighting up the walls. Trevor became nothing more than a charred figure of what he'd once been, his flesh eaten away by magical forces none of us could stop. The horrifying stench of burnt human flesh filled the hall, and Trevor's body dropped to the ground.

"What the *fuck!?*" Liam cried.

I saw the water before I saw my husband. A huge ball of water gathered in the air above the flames. It dropped, and Trevor's body sizzled as the fire was put out.

I took a cautious step forward, as if expecting the flames to ignite once more, but they didn't. A lump rose in my throat. Holding back the tears felt like swallowing a brick. I wanted to mourn for Trevor, but I didn't have the luxury of grieving right now. I had to remain alert.

Liam, Imogen, Esis, and Sassy emerged from the adjacent hall. Imogen's hand shot over her mouth, and Sassy sniffed Trevor's blackened form. Esis' bottom lip quivered.

"Trevor," Liam said breathlessly. It sounded like an apology.

"I couldn't control the flames quick enough," I said, biting my lower lip. Part of me felt like his death was my fault. I would always live to regret that.

"You couldn't have, Sophia," Imogen said, stepping around Trevor. "That creature... whatever it was... was too strong."

I furrowed my brow. "Where did it go?"

Sassy padded to a ball of orange fur on the floor I hadn't seen before. She nudged it with her nose and rolled it over. That was when I noticed the face on it. Its eyes were closed, and it'd gone totally limp. The little orange puffball had been *Bernardo*. He was some kind of little Koigni pom pom that grew to massive proportions when lit aflame.

"Whoa," Imogen breathed. "I can't believe *that's* what we were fighting."

"Forget that," I said quickly. "Let's get Amelia out of here."

I whirled toward the room Amelia was in. Her eyes were closed, and her head had lolled to the side. I knelt at her side and took her face in my hands.

"Amelia? Am?" I slapped her lightly, to get her to wake.

Her eyes fluttered open. Tears spilled out of her eyes and dripped down her dirty cheeks. When she spoke, it sounded strained. That's when I noticed bruises around her neck, as if Jill had tried to strangle her.

"Sophia? Did... did Jill hurt you?" She could hardly keep her eyes open.

"No," I assured her quickly. I tried to heal her, but my magic resisted.

"Leave, before she comes back," she strained.

"She's taken care of," I promised. I cocked my head at Imogen. "The cuffs are giving me trouble."

Imogen dug into her bag and pulled out a spare bit of wire she'd brought along. She knelt behind Amelia and picked the locks on the cuffs. When she was free, Amelia slumped forward into my arms.

"Am, you've gotta sit up," I insisted. "I'm going to heal you."

She tried, but it was really hard for her. Liam helped her stay upright, while I took her face in my hands and channeled my healing magic into her. Esis came to my side to help. A dull pain radiated up and down my arms as I healed the cuts along her skin. As my magic explored her injuries, I found many areas of resistance I hadn't seen from the surface. The bottoms of her feet were burned thanks to Jill, and there were bruises all throughout her abdomen. One of her ribs had been cracked. I didn't know what had Jill so enraged to do this sort of thing to Amelia, but one thing was for certain. I'd made no mistake killing that bitch.

Once I'd healed all Amelia's injuries, I worked on getting the noxite out of her system. After a few minutes, Amelia was finally able to lift her own head. She looked much better, though she was still covered in dry blood and beyond tired.

"Let's get her off the ship," I said quickly.

Amelia winced. "They have Jonah."

"Do you know where?" Liam asked.

She shook her head. "No. He tried to fight back, and they moved him to another part of the ship. He's in worse shape than I am."

My stomach sank. "Jake's going after him. He's probably rescued by now."

I hope.

"Either way, we have to get you off the ship," I said. "We'll go looking for Jonah once you're safe."

Amelia nodded. "The sooner the better."

I helped her stand, and though she winced, she was able to walk on her own two feet.

"This way." Liam cocked his head.

I led Amelia out of the room, but Liam was careful to block her view of what was in the other direction. After what she'd been through today, we didn't need to add Trevor's charred remains to her list of nightmares.

Liam led the way, and Imogen and Sassy brought up the rear. Esis sat on Amelia's shoulder, working in more healing magic, though I didn't know how much more would help. What Amelia needed was rest.

We snuck upstairs, past the Task Force who were still searching the halls for us, and ducked into one of the guest rooms. Liam went to the window and opened it. He whistled into the night, calling for Sabor.

The hippogriff flew up to our window a few moments later. He hovered there, awaiting a rider.

"Amelia, you're going to ride with Sabor," Liam said. "He'll keep you safe until the rest of us get off the ship."

Amelia nodded and hurried over to the window, like she couldn't wait to get off the *Hozho*. As she straddled the window, she turned back and said, "Thank you guys for saving me. The ancestors were right to choose you."

She turned to face me directly. "Stay safe, Sophia. I want my sister to come home in one piece."

"I will," I promised.

"Hurry," Liam urged. "We still have to find Jonah, and the Task Force are everywhere now."

Amelia didn't bother with a goodbye. I didn't think any of us wanted to say that. There'd been too many times lately when that *goodbye* was the last one we had. I wouldn't let it be that way for us.

Amelia hopped on Sabor's back, and he flew off into the clouds. Liam waited a few moments to make sure they were safe before turning back to us. "How is everyone?"

Imogen took a deep breath. "Apart from the nightmares I'm going to have, peachy."

"As long as we've got our strength," Liam said. The nightmares were nothing new for any of us.

"I'm good," I told him. Though I'd exhausted a lot of my energy earlier, I could keep fighting.

Sassy whipped out her vines to show she was still on board, and Esis gave a salute.

"Let's go." Liam led the way out of the room again.

We slunk through the shadows toward the stern of the ship. We hadn't heard anything from the other team toward the bow, so we had to assume they'd found something in the other direction. Several times, we heard Task Force coming and had to duck into different rooms to avoid getting caught. Luckily, we weren't spotted.

We ended up on the main deck, but this ship was huge. Getting to the other end was like going through an endless maze.

"Do you think they already got Jonah out—?" Imogen started to ask, but she was cut off by the sound of a huge *crash*. The whole ship shook. Esis held tighter to my shoulder. The three of us each braced ourselves against the wall. From a distance, we could hear screaming.

"Not today, you motherfucker!" Jake yelled.

Liam frowned. "I'm guessing that's a no. But at least we found them."

We followed the sounds of shouts and came to the main lobby. The huge crystal chandelier that once hung in the center of the room had crashed to the ground, and glass littered the floor. That must've been the noise that had shaken the boat. Three Task Force members and a chimera lay dead beneath it.

All around us, magic whizzed through the air. Jake, Luana, and Trace were being backed into the ballroom by advancing Task Force members and their Familiars. There had to be at least three dozen of them. We were easily outnumbered.

"Surrender!" one of the Task Force shouted.

"Never!" Jake spat.

The Task Force didn't bother giving second chances. These men didn't have noxite guns, but they ordered their Familiars to attack. A basilisk, a three-headed canine, an alicorn and a bull charged. Jake thrust his Air magic outward, and though it knocked the canine aside, the alicorn charged straight through it like it was nothing.

Luana threw up a shield, and the bull rammed straight into it. Liam, Imogen, and I reacted quickly, jumping into the fight without question. Liam used cloud vapor to create long strands of water he whipped at the Task Force. Imogen hurtled her pebbles through the air, and a dozen embedded deep into one of the Task Force's abdomen. A woman let out a pained groan, then fell to her knees and onto the floor.

I thrust Anichi orbs toward the enemy. I hit two Task Force at once, but they quickly retaliated.

A gust of Air swept me off my feet. Esis got caught up in the whirlwind and screamed as he spiraled upward toward the ceiling and was flung across the room. Though I threw up my shield, the Air continued to blast into it, pushing me back. I clawed at the wooden dance floor as I was swept toward the other side of the ballroom, but it was to no avail. I rolled a few times before slamming into the wall, gasping for breath. Esis swayed beside me as he too came to a stop.

My eyes scanned the ballroom, but it was hard to see anything past the elements raging everywhere. Fog seeped into the room from Toaqua controlling the water particles in the air, and the carpet lit aflame from Koigni attackers. Yapluma powers swirled the other elements, making them worse. A Nivita Task Force member had used her magic to rip plants from their pots and was fighting against Imogen. Sassy whipped out her vines to block the blows.

My eyes landed on a Task Force member with his gaze set on me. His fingers twisted as Air continued to assault me, blowing my hair in all directions and making it hard to breathe. I shot a fireball at him, but all it did was fly back in my direction. Throwing my shield back up, I blocked the wind to give myself enough time to grow an Anichi orb in my hand. I drew my arm back and flung it upward. It ricocheted off the ceiling at the perfect angle and hit the guy in the head. He crumpled to the ground, and I was free of his Yapluma assault.

No sooner had I leapt to my feet than a lizard the size of my hand fell from the ceiling and landed directly on my face. I yelped and grabbed for it, but a burning hot pain seared my skin. It was a *Fire lizard*, and it was hell-bent on attacking me. I yanked harder, but it gripped onto my face so tightly I couldn't get it off.

Esis jumped onto my chest and chomped down on the lizard's tail. It squealed and dropped to the floor. A trail of blood followed it as it scurried away. My face ached from the burn, but adrenaline pulsed through my system so quickly I barely felt it.

The surrounding battle continued in full-force. Trace and Imogen were overpowering a group of Nivita Task Force and turning their plants against them. Tree branches grew to massive proportions and whipped around to knock out five Task Force in once swing. Imogen used her magic to draw more trees out of their pots. They walked on their roots and snuck behind Task Force members to smack them *hard*.

Sassy rolled on the ground, tackling a striped feline Familiar, while Kiwi dove at an alicorn, using his talons to tear the flesh around its eyes. The basilisk had attacked Luana from behind and wrapped its body around her legs. Her feet swept out from under her, and the serpent dragged her back, distracting her from using her shield to protect our people. Sierra glowed a blinding white and fluttered her wings in the basilisk's face to distract him. When that didn't work, she shot a force field outward. It assaulted the basilisk's nose, and blood sprayed everywhere. One of its fangs cracked in half and clattered to the floor.

Not far from Luana, Jake was fighting three Yapluma at once. He blocked each blow of their magic, but he was struggling to keep up.

One of them got cocky and came too close. Jake abandoned his magic to go hand-to-hand. He grabbed the Task Force by the uniform and screamed in rage as he launched him through a nearby stained-glass window. The window shattered, sending colored pieces of glass all over the deck outside. Jake jumped through the window to finish the job.

Liam was using his magic to stop the hearts of people who got too close, but they retaliated with their powers so quickly that blocking their attacks took most of his energy. I could see he was getting fatigued. The color had drained from his face, and he stumbled away from advancing Task Force weakly. A fireball hit the floor beneath him, and he jumped out of the way, stumbling backward into the stage. String instruments and falling music stands clattered together, filling the ballroom with a deafening echo. Liam's fingers curled around a violin, and he hurled it toward a Task Force member. It hit them in the face, and the violin shattered to pieces.

Task Force kept coming at him from all angles. I threw up a force field around him from a distance, and it gave him reprieve from the attacks.

But I didn't have long to focus on him. A terrifying creature was headed my way, charging. It was at least as big as I was, but walked on eight legs. It had the hard shell of a scorpion, and a matching curled tail with a stinger on the end. Its face, however, was more like a spider, with hundreds of tiny eyes and huge pinchers. Its shell was dark black. I could see the red of magma-like magic swirling in a layer beneath it. If this freaking thing got me in its jaws, I'd lose a limb.

I shot an Anichi orb at it, but that only slowed it down half a step. Esis growled and lowered his horns, like he was about to attack.

"Esis, no!" I demanded.

I threw a fireball at it instead, and it landed square in its face. The creature reared back and let out a high-pitched scream. The ground shook as it landed on its feet again. For a second, I thought I had the upper hand. Then it shot an evil glare at me from each of its hundred eyes. It opened its pinchers, revealing the deep, dark hole of its mouth. I conjured up another fireball, but it was too late.

Fire erupted out of the scorpion-spider's mouth with forceful magic I'd never seen before. A deafening *boom* sounded, and a shock wave rippled through the air as the creature's magic exploded throughout the room.

Everything happened so fast. Instinctively, I threw up a shield around Imogen, Liam, and Trace, since they were closest to me.

But I'd missed shielding myself.

Everything happened in slow motion. The room shuddered as the explosion rocked the ship. The wall beside me blasted into nothing, and the shock wave sent Esis and me reeling through the air. I landed at least twenty feet away from where I'd been standing a moment ago. Every inch of my body ached. Above us, the ceiling gave way, and building material rained down on us. Dust billowed into the air, and I couldn't see anything.

At first, I didn't know what had happened. I was so stunned that all I could do was gasp for breath. It hadn't even occurred to me that there'd *been* an explosion. My ears rang a high pitch, but I couldn't hear anything else. My head swam in confusion, and my vision blurred.

Then there was the pain— a searing pain beyond anything I'd ever felt before. It pierced straight through my stomach. When I tried to move, the pain intensified. I felt pinned in place by something I couldn't see or understand. I tried to investigate, but I'd gone so light-headed that I could hardly keep my eyes open, let alone move my body.

As the dust began to settle, I started to really process the pain. It was like a fireball had embedded itself in my stomach. It was so intense that when I tried to scream, nothing came out; I was in too much shock.

Screams filled the ballroom. My head lolled to the side, and I caught sight of Liam standing near the stage. He looked shell shocked by what had happened, and he pressed a palm to his ear, like the explosion had damaged an eardrum. Other than that, he seemed relatively unharmed. My shield had protected him.

Liam's gaze swept over the room, and his eyes landed on me. I'd never seen his features fall so fast. Utter heartbreak entered his eyes— like the ancestors themselves had swept away every ounce of hope he held with him. I wanted to signal back to him, but I couldn't move. Even my eyes wouldn't focus.

I thought I saw his lips move— to shout my name— but I heard nothing over the ringing in my ears. My vision blurred again. All I saw was Liam's silhouette rushing my way. Then came six other figures. Task Force members had rushed in to block his path, and they started attacking.

My breaths came in shallow heaves. I wanted to help him, to fight back, but my head hadn't cleared yet. I didn't know how long it would take. When I tried to move again, an ungodly pain rippled up my abdomen. I slipped in and out of unconsciousness, fighting against it with every ounce of fight I had in me. I had to get up. I had to help my friends!

I scanned the room. Imogen, Trace, and Luana were racing out of the ballroom with their Familiars in search of safe cover. Tears streamed down Imogen's cheeks, and I thought I saw her lips move to call my name. Sassy dragged her back, as if trying to convince her there was no saving me. It must've looked like I was already gone. I couldn't control the lifeless stare in my eyes, nor the stillness of my body as shock settled in.

Jake was nowhere in sight— probably still fighting Task Force on the deck. Liam was on the other side of the ballroom. The Task Force had pushed him back toward the doors that led onto the deck. Rage like I'd never seen before marred his features as he fought back against Elementai and Familiars alike.

I tried one last time to push myself to my feet, but that pain returned, burning my insides. I finally regained control of my body and looked down to see—

A rod. A rod from the collapsed ceiling had speared straight through my abdomen and out my back. It pinned me down, draining the life from me. Blood poured out of my stomach, staining my shirt and pooling into the rubble beneath me.

I should've been freaking out beyond belief. I shouldn't have been able to breathe at the sight of a freaking *rod* through my stomach. But all I could think was I had to get the motherfucking thing out of me, so I could fry the

Task Force and save my friends. I didn't have the luxury of freaking out right now.

I grabbed the rod in my hands and yanked. It was agonizing beyond belief. No pain came close— not even the night I gave birth to Ava and nearly died. The more I pulled, the more it felt like the rod was tearing through my insides, literally ripping my guts out. I writhed in the rubble, and though I screamed at the top of my lungs, I barely heard it past the ringing in my ears.

The rod broke free of my flesh, and I tossed it aside. Beside me, the rubble shifted, until Esis popped his head out and scurried out of his hole. He barely looked white anymore, with dust covering his entire form. His blue eyes connected with mine. He took one look at the blood, and his eyes went wide in horror.

I gritted my teeth as I pressed my hands to the gaping wound. "Esis, help!"

Esis was at my side in an instant. He pressed his paws to my wound, and I gasped as another wave of pain rippled up and down my body. I wasn't about to bleed out here like this. I had to protect my friends!

With stone-cold resolve to protect, the healing magic came easily. My hands glowed white, and mine and Esis' healing magic poured into me. Slowly but surely, the pain began to melt away, and the bleeding slowed. My skin started to knit itself together, and my organs repaired themselves from the inside out.

When I finally felt like I could move again, I looked toward where I'd last seen Liam. He was out of the ballroom now and on the deck, but I could see him clearly through the doors. He'd gathered so much water out of the clouds that a water ball the size of a swimming pool hovered above his head. There weren't very many Task Force left— as he'd taken care of them— but those who were continued to attack. Liam dodged a fireball, then turned his raging anger toward the Task Force. He thrust his swimming-pool-sized weapon at the Task Force, and the water engulfed them. They went sweeping across the ballroom. Water splashed everywhere, covering the entire floor until it came to wash against the rubble pile I was in like a crashing wave. Water splashed upward into my face.

It all happened so fast. I scrambled to my feet to go help him, but I barely got upright before the bull I'd seen earlier charged from out of nowhere. He came from the side, so Liam didn't see him. By the time Liam caught sight of him, it was too late.

The bull's head connected with Liam's hips, and the creature reared upward. Liam had nothing to hold on to as he went flying backward—

And over the side of the ship.

It was as if someone had taken a sledge hammer straight to my chest. Hell, they might as well have assaulted me with a hundred sledge hammers from every angle. One second my husband was there.

The next, he was gone.

I thrust out a force field in front of the bull, but Liam was already gone. His body had vanished beneath the deck of the ship— falling to his death.

"*No!*" I screeched, heartbreak shattering my tone.

My husband... gone? It couldn't be true.

But it was.

Liam had been launched over the side of the ship so quickly that no one could react. He wasn't Yapluma. He couldn't save himself. And there was nothing I could do, either.

I didn't think I could feel pain worse than being speared with a rod all the way through, but I was wrong. Watching my husband fall to his death was the worst pain I could ever imagine. My lungs ceased to work, and I gasped for breath. Tears flooded my eyes and fell like a waterfall down my cheeks.

I wanted to tell myself I was imagining things— that I was wrong about what I'd seen, but I'd already seen so many forms of death in this war. It was no longer something I could write off as imagination.

"*Liam!*" I wailed. It was a grave wail that echoed across the whole ship. At my feet, Esis cried out mournfully.

The ground rumbled beneath me. At first, I thought it was my own legs shaking. Then I looked upward, and I saw the ceiling quaking at the vibrations of the ship. I realized with horror that a second cave-in was imminent. I grabbed Esis and raced out of the way.

A deafening sound filled the ballroom as what remained of the ceiling crumbled downward. I sprinted as fast as I could— but I wasn't fast enough. A piece of rubble fell from the ceiling and knocked me in the head.

Throbbing pain radiated across my skull as I collapsed to the ground. My vision came in and out of focus, just enough that I witnessed a shadow cross over me. *Task Force,* I thought at first. I wanted to lift my hands to fight back, but I couldn't seem to find them. Then I saw that the shadow had eight legs, and it hit me with horror that it was the scorpion-spider, come to finish the job.

Its jaws opened, and before I could even think of fighting back, the pinchers clamped around my leg. Searing hot pain shot up my calf as the creature used its Fire power on me. I wanted to blast the sucker backward, to kick it in the face— anything. But the blow to my head had been my undoing. I couldn't stay conscious enough to do anything. Horror twisted in my belly, and I was certain this was the end as darkness enveloped me.

I didn't care. I wanted to die now. Liam was gone. My beloved husband was dead. I might as well die with him. The Task Force had broken me and taken everything from me. I didn't want to go on.

This was the moment Showana had predicted. The day of my death. At least if I was dead, I'd make my sacrifice, and the prophecy would be fulfilled. Then the tribe would be saved, and Ava-Marie would be safe.

And I could join Liam in the Ancestral Lands, forever.

My only regret would be that I didn't have enough time with Ava-Marie. Tears streamed down my cheeks as I thought of leaving her behind. With all my strength, I lifted my hands to clutch the Spirit Totem around my neck.

Ancestors, I prayed. *Bless my daughter. Do not let her grow up in a world ravaged by war.*

I saw the light— the one leading to the Ancestral Lands. It was blinding but beautiful. I wanted to go toward it. But the pain continued, and I couldn't move.

A shadow passed in front of the light, though I couldn't make it out. The creature was big and walked on four legs. It seemed to be running on air, and it looked as if gorgeous white magic flowed out from behind it. I had to be imagining it.

The creature gave a deep growl and lunged. My heart lurched. I thought it was coming for me— that it was here to bring an end to my life. I welcomed it, if it meant Ava would be safe from this war, that my sacrifice was worth something.

But the creature never touched me. It slammed straight into the scorpion-spider, and the burning pain in my leg eased as the spider was thrown off of me. All I could make out were shadows. The scorpion-spider rolled across the floor, then jumped to its feet. It shot fireballs out of its mouth to attack, but they seemed to drift straight through the animal.

The newcomer planted his paws on the ground to face my attacker. He wasted no time retaliating. A bright white light erupted from his chest. The scorpion-spider went reeling through the air, flipping over and over. It landed hard on the other side of the ballroom, all eight legs sticking straight into the air. It gave a final twitch, and I knew it was dead.

And so was I... I couldn't fight any longer, and I succumbed to the darkness.

I lingered in the darkness for what felt like ages. Waiting for the end.

Sophia! a deep voice boomed, stirring me. *Get up. You have work to do.*

I didn't know how much time had passed. My eyes blinked open. I felt the coldness of the wooden dance floor beneath my cheek. All I saw was dark black fur.

For a second, I thought it was Esis covered in soot. What other creature would approach me so boldly without hurting me?

But as my gaze traveled up the creature's leg, I realized it was a hell of a lot bigger than Esis. I looked upward to see a black wolf staring down at me. He was huge, nearly the size of a horse, and he held his head up regally. He looked healthy and unharmed, like he'd only shown up to the battle instead of fighting in it. It was the creature who'd fought off the scorpion-spider.

Sophia, you must awaken, the deep voice said. The wolf dropped his head toward me in a kind gesture. I realized it was *him*. He was the one speaking to me. How could that be?

"W-what?" I asked, still trying to get my bearings.

I pushed myself upward and glanced around the room. For a moment, I forgot where I was. Dust was still settling around the ballroom, though I didn't see another living soul in sight. Rubble was piled up all around me. I realized that the final cave-in had blocked me from the doors to the ship deck.

Esis had been knocked out and pinned under a plank beside me. I tossed it aside and cradled him in my arms. He stirred, but he hadn't completely come to.

I looked back to the black wolf. Something about him seemed incredibly familiar, but I couldn't put my finger on it. I had the strangest inexplicable feeling that we shared a deep connection— that we even cared for each other. I reached out a hand to touch him, as if laying a hand on his fur might stir my memory. But my fingers met nothing but air. My hand went straight through him, like he was a ghost. I knew then who he was.

"Nashoma?" I asked breathlessly.

He nodded firmly. *It is I.*

My stomach dropped. Nashoma being here was confirmation of my husband's passing. Why else would he arrive, if not to escort Liam to the Ancestral Lands?

But that didn't explain why he'd come to me.

"What are you doing here? How?" I gaped. This was beyond anything I even knew was possible.

I am here to defend you, Sophia, he said. *Your soul is entwined with Liam's, and I must protect the pieces of soul he has left.*

"But Liam... he..." I choked on the words. I couldn't say out loud he was dead. Instead, I forced out, "Pieces of his soul?"

When Liam lost me, he entwined his soul with others to survive. You, Ava-Marie, and Julian all share a part of him. His family means more to him than anything. Therefore, I serve as your guardians, in this life and the next.

"Julian?" I croaked out. "But he's not his Familiar. You are."

Nashoma nodded in agreement. *And yet Julian and Liam share a strong bond— a bond that I am pleased to honor and support. Julian is a magnificent companion. As are you, Sophia. I protect and defend you all with my spirit.*

Tears welled in my eyes. "But Liam... he fell over the side of the ship. He's gone, Nashoma. No Toaqua could survive that."

Nashoma held his head high. *You underestimate your mate, Sophia. Come— we must find him.*

Liam

FIFTEEN

I could only think in fragments.

Sheer agony.

Utter devastation.

I didn't care that I was falling. I wanted to die. I'd seen my wife be speared through, a pipe ripped through her body while her organs streamed blood.

I knew she couldn't live through that. There was just no way. She was already gone.

I didn't want to live. It was a good thing the Task Force had tossed me over the side. I was ready for it to end. I fell through the clouds, past the *Hozho's* underbelly, and hurtled through the heavens on my way to complete hell.

Then, against my will, I felt a force lift me upward. I cried out in rage and tried to fight it, but to no avail. The Air magic carried me up and deposited me on the lower deck. I fell onto my hands and knees as Jake stepped aside. Imogen, Trace and Luana gathered around me in a huddle.

Jake was leaning over the railing, breathing heavily. His body shook. Tears streamed down Imogen and Luana's faces— they'd seen what had happened.

"Why didn't you let me die?" My voice shook darkly. "I wanted to die."

"We're not losing anyone else on this mission," Jake spat. He turned his back on me, tone intense. His hands gripped the railing so tightly they turned white.

"It doesn't matter. We've lost Sophia." I completely broke. "There's no point in anything anymore. Leave me. Let the Task Force find me. There's nothing more they can do to me now."

As much as I was grieving, I was also desperate. I hadn't seen Sophia's body. There might be a way she could be alive yet. We had Luana. We could heal her.

I leapt to my feet. Someone called my name, but I didn't answer. I ran up the stairs to return to the main ballroom. Footsteps were behind me. I skidded to a stop when I saw that the area had been reduced to little more than a pile of rubble.

My gut clenched, and fear overtook me so powerfully it rocked the foundation of my life. "*Sophia!*" I cried out.

No one answered.

She was buried under the rubble. I began clawing at the wood and metal, getting splinters and breaking skin. Blood began to run down my hands, trickling past my wrists and arms as I desperately searched for my wife, trying to dig her out.

I saw her nowhere. I pleaded with the ancestors that Esis was somewhere nearby, but I didn't see him, either. Both of them were buried somewhere, and I refused to let this be my wife's final resting place.

The others gathered at the edge and watched me fling aside concrete. No one went to intercede, though I could hear Imogen crying.

"Liam, the Task Force must've taken her body," Jake said, though his voice cracked. "It's over."

"It's not over. She *has* to be here," I sobbed. Though I'd gone through so much of the debris, there was still no sign of her.

I feared Jake was right. They'd taken Sophia's remains as a trophy for Oleander.

The thought of him using her body like that, parading it in the streets as a sign that they'd won... *ancestors, end me now.*

"We only have a limited amount of time. Sophia's gone. She couldn't have survived that collapse. Jonah might still have a chance," Jake growled.

"I'm not leaving her!"

"Liam! Stop!" Imogen darted forward and shook me. "Sophia might be gone, but you're all Ava-Marie has left. If you stay here, the Task Force will find you. You'll die, and leave her an orphan. You can't do that to that little girl!"

My insides churned. I'd forgotten about my daughter in the midst of my pain. Ava was now motherless. I was all Ava had left in the world. I was a father. She needed me.

"Sophia wouldn't want you to be like this. She'd want you to keep going," Imogen insisted. Imogen wiped at her face frantically. "We came here to rescue Jonah. If we don't, Sophia's sacrifice will be in vain. I don't want to go on without her either, but we *have* to. We have no choice."

Imogen's reason broke through my endless grief. I wouldn't leave Jonah and Squeaks to their deaths. If Sophia had died today in an attempt to save them, I refused to allow her death to be meaningless. I'd rescue them, and kill any Task Force member that got in my way.

Luana helped me to shakily stand. "Where are they?" I didn't care what was between Jonah and I. I'd bring this ship out of the sky if I had to.

"We don't know. We've searched everywhere," Jake stuttered. He was on the verge of losing it. Inwardly, I knew he was terrified of experiencing what had just happened to me.

I'd cut my own throat before that happened. Jonah's life had been hell. He deserved happiness, a chance to know what a true family was like, and he had that chance with Jake. I wasn't letting my friend lose everything.

"We should go to the steering hub," Trace suggested. "They'll have maps up there of the entire ship. I'm certain they'll have prisoner records."

"Fuck it. Let's go." I led the way around the deck. Dreadful pain was pumping through my muscles, but I didn't allow it to faze me. Nothing could hurt worse than the grief of losing my Sophia. My body was a fucking afterthought.

The steering hub was at the top of the ship. We had several flights to climb before we made it there. I stopped at the end of the first one, breathing hard. I had no energy left, and hardly any will to fight on. I had a dark thought we'd never get off this ship.

"We should fly up," Imogen whispered to Jake.

"It'll expose us," he argued.

"But we'll get there faster," Imogen pointed out.

Jake sighed. He took a look at me and raised his hands. "Hold on."

I felt Jake's Air magic wrap around us, levitating us upward. We passed floor after floor. I kept a water ball formed in my hands, expecting the Task Force to spot us at any second.

And I wanted them to. I wanted to find them, make them pay for taking Sophia away from me. I wanted them to suffer like I had suffered.

But despite my pleading with the ancestors for revenge, we didn't see anyone. We made it to the platform at the top of the ship, where the steering hub was located. The door was locked, but Sassy used her vines to rip off the door handle, and we forced our way in.

My eyes widened when I entered the room as we met a familiar face. "Professor Cheveyo?"

It was him. His two braids hung down his back as he messed with buttons on the ship's control panel.

His Appaloosa stallion nickered a soft greeting to us as we entered. Cheveyo turned. His expression was one of relief as he took in the sight of us.

"My chief," Cheveyo said. He clapped a hand on his chest and bowed lowly to me.

"Cheveyo, where have you been? We haven't received intelligence from you in weeks," Jake snapped.

"Yeah, and why are you controlling the ship?" Imogen asked curiously.

"I was once a captain in the Navy. Oleander hired me to steer the *Hozho*. I took the job to ferry information," Cheveyo said to Imogen, before he turned to Jake. "I apologize being unable to contact you. They've caught on to me. My Familiar and I haven't been allowed to leave this hub in days. But what in ancestors' name are you doing here?"

"We've come to rescue Jonah Chanee. Do you have a record of where he might be?" Jake said, getting right down to business. "He's someone the Task Force would want to keep contained."

"The Storm Lord. I remember," Cheveyo said. "They're containing the most powerful prisoners in the boiler room. It's certainly where they're keeping him."

"Do you know how to get there?" Jake wasted no time, his voice ringing with urgency.

Cheveyo nodded. "I would have to guide you. The Task Force is stationed all over this ship, and if you want to avoid them, you'll have to follow my lead."

"What about the ship?" Imogen asked.

"The ship will steer herself, for the time being," Cheveyo began. "Give me a moment to set the right parameters."

Cheveyo turned back to the control board. As he worked, the grief of losing Sophia overwhelmed me, making it feel like I was suffocating.

I had to talk. I had to do something; otherwise, I was going to snap in two. "Why does the Task Force hate us so much?" I asked hoarsely. "Why do they keep fighting for Oleander in a war that doesn't benefit anyone, just causes destruction?"

"The rebellion, including you and your wife, have been the victim of propaganda by Oleander," Cheveyo said as he worked, keeping his eyes on the board. "He's been spreading lies about all of you."

"Like?" My tone was full of rage. How dare that bastard slander my wife's name. One of these days, he'd be mine, and I'd rip him limb from limb.

"It was easy to convince the Defortai you're going up against the will of the Great Spirit. That both of you seek to take over the tribe and gain all the power for yourselves. Oleander's spun a web of lies that the two of you wish to change everything about the Hawkei way of life. He's telling the story that anyone who isn't mixed House will be executed, if the rebellion wins the war. He's done a very good job of separating the tribe into a mentality of *it's us or them*."

"What a load of bullshit. How can anyone believe that? There aren't even enough mixed House children to sustain the tribe," I spat.

"Desperate people will believe anything, especially in times of war. Many are happy to follow Oleander because they believe his destruction won't happen to them. That as long as Oleander doesn't touch their families, they are safe." Cheveyo shook his head. "They don't realize all of us are in danger. When Oleander is done with his current enemies, he'll come for the rest, and there will be no one left to speak up then. Pandering to him will only keep one alive for so long."

"Well, I guess his propaganda worked, because the brainwashed Task Force had no trouble *murdering* my best friend," Imogen said hatefully, and I died inside.

Cheveyo paused. "The chosen one is dead?"

My throat tightened, and I nodded. Imogen, Luana and Jake all dropped their gazes. Cheveyo stopped what he was doing to bow to me once more. "I give you my deepest sympathies, chief, and share in your sorrows. We'll fight to the bitter end to make sure her sacrifice wasn't in vain."

Cheveyo straightened. "That should buy us some time. Come. We must hurry."

Cheveyo ran out the door, and the rest of us followed. His Familiar's hooves clopped on the stairs as we wandered downward, away from the steering hub and onto the main deck.

Elements whizzed over our heads. All of us ducked, and I pushed Luana out of the way. A horde of Task Force had their hands raised, elements firing. There were six or so, magic flashing against the darkness of their helmets.

"We knew you were a backstabber, Cheveyo. Betraying your own race!" a Task Force member cried. "Oleander will reward all of us when we bring your body—"

I didn't give them time to taunt Cheveyo— didn't even give them time to finish the sentence. My magic rushed out of me in so much rage, I felt the hearts of all six Task Force members explode in their chests at the same time. Some gasped, but most just collapsed to the ground like rag dolls.

I'd felt guilty before every time I took a life. Now, I didn't feel a fucking thing.

A wretched roar shook the ship below our feet. I looked up. A dark creature towered over us. It had leathery skin and arms that were twelve feet long and ended in sharp claws. It walked on them like some kind of ape. The creature had no eyes, only a row of sharp teeth and a forked tongue that it licked menacingly.

I went to stop its heart, but the creature's magic rebelled against mine, and it didn't work. The thing was too powerful. It dove its teeth downward, mouth opening wide for a bite, and Imogen screamed. I rolled out of the way, and the monster's mouth tore open the floorboards, leaving a hole in the ship.

The monster wasn't alone. It was accompanied by a reptile-like creature that walked on its hind legs like a man, poisonous spikes protruding out of its body, and a spindly wyvern that was made of nothing but bone.

The reptile swiped its hand downward, grabbing for Luana. It grasped her in its hand, and she screamed as it lifted her toward its mouth.

I wasn't letting anyone else die tonight. No fucking way. I sprinted around the ape-like creature. Jake and Imogen were throwing everything they had at it with Sassy's help, while Cheveyo and Trace handled the bone wyvern. I summoned water from the vapor around us and created a blade with it. I sent the blade spinning outward, and it sliced off the reptile's arm at the elbow. The monster let out a giant screech, blood spurting everywhere, while Luana unfurled herself from its fingers and scampered out of the way. The reptile turned its vengeance on me, but I wasn't one for fucking around today. As it swept its poisonous spiked tail in my direction, I leapt to avoid it. I called the water blade back again, sending it spinning like a boomerang. This time, I aimed for the neck. The blade cut straight through the sinew, decapitating the creature. Its headless body fell, toppling over the side of the ship as its head remained gaping on the main deck.

Jake had created an Air shield to blow the ape back, while Imogen whipped stones at the creature's eyes. Sassy held its arms in place with her vines, doing her best not to let it move. The creature pulled an arm free and whacked Sassy to the side. The kitsune hit a lifeboat and cried out, getting Imogen's attention.

"Sassy!" Imogen yelled. She ran to her Familiar, leaving Jake alone. The ape burst through Jake's Air shield, and his eyes widened. He forced out a gust of wind to hold the creature back as the ape swung one of its arms wildly, nearly catching Jake with its claws and giving a guttural groan.

I could feel the blood pumping through the beast's body. While it was distracted with Jake, I called to the water in its bloodstream and turned it to ice.

The ape gave a gasp. It fell forward, teeth gnashing, and Jake took his chance. He sent a gust of Air hurtling toward the creature so fast, it was like seeing the power of a tornado. The wind slit the creature's throat, and Jake leapt out of the way. The monster created a massive hole in the floorboards, toppling below as it died in pain.

Trace and Cheveyo were still battling the bone wyvern. Cheveyo's stallion reared up and pawed its hooves at the creature, cracking off a piece of its leg. The wyvern hissed, bones clacking as it advanced.

That gave me an idea. I sent water into the spaces between the bone wyvern's crevices. The creature screeched in pain. I didn't even think twice as I made the water expand outward. Bone went flying in all directions as the wyvern exploded to pieces, sending bits of skull, ribs and other parts scattering across the hardwood and reducing the wyvern to dust.

Imogen stared at me in horror as I breathed murderously, hands shaking like a deranged madman. I was going on an all-out fucking killing spree. My wife had died, and if the Task Force could feel just a taste of the torture I was in because of it, they'd never recover. I didn't want them to.

As the last monster fell, Cheveyo waved his hand. "Hurry! If there are soldiers here, more are to follow!"

We ran. There were yells of Task Force behind us, though I didn't know where from. Cheveyo took us into a staff entrance, and we hurried after him down the hallway.

I panted. Luana reached out her hand, and I felt her touch my back as her healing magic flooded into my veins. I recovered a bit of strength, enough to keep me going, though the real thing that drove me on was the terror that we might be too late to save Jonah.

It resonated on Jake's face, too. I saw the fear in his eyes that we'd find

Jonah dead. Amelia hadn't been in good shape when we'd found her, and she'd said Jonah was worse.

We drew closer and closer to the boiler room, and I felt the temperature elevate. Sweat beaded across my brow as heat rose.

Then we heard it. A man's agonized wailing. It was a long, drawn-out sound that rattled my bones and made me feel like passing out. The screams continued, vibrating the walls.

Imogen's face went white. "That sounded like Jonah!"

It had to be him. I knew it was. My gut clenched with sickening certainty as his cries echoed down the hallway. I'd never heard him make a sound like that in his life.

Jake had to put an arm against the wall to steady himself. He'd turned green. I grabbed his arm and squeezed it tightly. "We're close. Let's keep moving."

Jonah's wails of agony penetrated the walls of the staff hall. We picked up the pace, moving as fast as we could without creating a disturbance, our steps in time to the sound of Jonah's screams.

I only had one small comfort in losing Sophia. At least she hadn't suffered like this.

Jonah's cries ceased abruptly. The change was so dramatic it staggered my steps. Had he...?

I didn't hear anything else. Imogen let out a muffled sob. The blood drained from Jake's cheeks, but Cheveyo insisted, "He's being questioned."

Jake's form relaxed. Cheveyo held out an arm to stop us as we came to the door of the boiler room. When he cracked it open, steam emitted from it and drifted by. It was dark in the boiler room, lit only by the fires that kept the ship's engine running.

From here, I could make out voices, whispers and shouts against the blackness.

"I'm so fucking tired of dealing with you, Chanee! Give me information about the resistance, and I'll let you live! Is that so hard to comprehend?"

I knew that voice. It was Haley. Imogen stiffened beside me, and Sassy gave a low growl. Jake had this murderous look in his eyes that I knew was going to erupt from him at any moment.

"I'll die before I'll betray my friends," Jonah replied. He sounded so frail. "You're going to have to kill me."

"This used to be fun, but now you're really pissing me off," Haley hissed. "I don't have time for this shit. I'm not stopping this time until you give in."

"Do it, then." Jonah's voice sounded totally hopeless.

I heard the crack of a whip, and Jonah's voice rang out in pain again. Jake didn't waste any more time. He burst through the door. Haley's mouth dropped open as she turned to face us. In her hands was a literal fire whip, with several strands like a cat-of-nine tails. It trailed down to the ground, flickering with flame. She was alone, her chieftess robes disheveled and her hair a mess, a madness in her eyes. I didn't see Anwara anywhere.

Jonah. Poor Jonah. He was hanging from the ceiling, suspended by chains. His clothes were in tatters, stuck to his body only by the blood pouring from his wounds. His back was a matted mess, skin hanging off of it in shreds, exposing the muscle. His hair hung loosely around his face, which was matted with bruises. He had two black eyes, so swollen he could no longer see. Several of his fingernails were gone. There was a puddle of blood on the floor that was his, shoes skimming the top of it. His torso was colored black and yellow, revealing the broken ribs and mangled organs within. The chains were the only thing keeping him aloft. Without them, he'd collapse.

"*You bitch!*" Imogen screamed. She sent several rocks whizzing toward Haley's head, but she ducked. The rocks embedded themselves into the metal wall behind Haley. Sassy charged forward and unleashed her vines, but Haley sent a burst of Fire rushing outward, and Sassy yelped. She withdrew her vines and whimpered as Haley made a run for it, stampeding in the other direction with her Fire whip in hand.

Imogen went to chase after her, but I grabbed her by the shoulder and yanked her back. "Forget about her!" I cried, with a deliberate look toward Jonah. Of course I wanted Haley dead— but I wanted Jonah to live more, and we couldn't afford to get separated right now.

Imogen paled. She ran to him, and Trace and Cheveyo gave chase after Haley. Jake was messing with the chains around Jonah's wrists, frantically trying to get them off with tears in his eyes.

The cuffs weren't even noxite. We could break them. They'd drugged Jonah so badly he wasn't able to use his powers to escape.

"Let me." I took the steam from the boiler room and forced it into the locks that held Jonah captive, freezing it. The chains broke, and Jonah dropped. Jake caught him before he hit the floor, though Jonah gave a whimpering cry of pain.

"I've got you," Jake said, voice quaking. He gently guided Jonah to the floor, away from the blood puddle. Jonah leaned against Jake's chest, trapped in a daze.

"I didn't beg," Jonah whispered, like he wanted us to be proud of him. "I didn't give in."

"Of course you didn't." A few tears dropped from Jake's eyes and onto Jonah's hair.

Jonah moved his head. "Squeaks," he whimpered. He looked to the side of the boiler room, which was cast in shadow.

There was a shuffling in the dark. My heart dropped as I saw Squeaks limp forward. Her front leg was broken. Her wings were clipped, so she couldn't fly away, and long gashes had been cut along her sides. Several long burns, like the ones Haley's whip provided, ran along her flank. So many of her feathers had been pulled out, leaving bald spots. An iron collar was clamped around her neck and chained to the wall, preventing her from breaking free.

Luana ran to her. She knelt by Squeaks' broken leg and began channeling her healing energy into it, mending the bone before she crossed to each cut and burn.

Sassy reached out. The kitsune gritted her teeth through the pain and broke the collar in two with her burned vines, setting Squeaks free. Squeaks quivered in pain, but her shuddering lifted as Luana's magic did her work. Color began to come back into her wings as they grew. Squeaks stood on her four legs, fully healed. The burn marks and cuts had become long scars along her body, nothing more.

"Heal him," Jake demanded of Luana, though it was more like a prayer.

Luana knelt at Jonah's side and lightly laid her hands on Jonah's thigh. She closed her eyes, and she and Sierra both glowed with white healing magic. I observed Jonah expectantly... but nothing happened.

Luana's face became panicky. She glanced at Sierra on the top of Jonah's head, silently communicating.

"What? What's going on?" Imogen screeched in a panic.

Luana signed quickly. *I can't heal this. There's too much here.*

Squeaks gave a shrill cry, and fear clenched my soul. I'd never seen Luana fail to heal someone before.

That meant Jonah was already dying.

He'd lost too much blood, sustained too much damage to his organs. Healing magic forced the body to do what it naturally would on its own. Her magic couldn't reverse what was too far gone.

Jake wasn't giving up. He lifted Jonah into his arms. "We have to get him back to *Hok'evale*. He might have a chance."

At that moment, Trace and Cheveyo returned, though it was without

Haley. I saw that Cheveyo carried with him a woolen blanket. He must've gotten it off one of the maid's carts lying around.

"Did you catch the bitch?" I asked Trace, hoping to the ancestors they'd killed her.

Trace shook his head. "We lost her before she got to the first floor."

"Fuck."

Cheveyo gave Jake the blanket. Jake wrapped it around Jonah, and the blood soaked through.

"Liam, go ahead of us. Make sure it's clear," Jake said.

"Take the main stairwell up," Cheveyo told me. "It's the quickest way."

I slipped on Jonah's blood as I got up. I winced, but forced myself to keep going. I took two stairs at a time, and didn't hesitate to fling open the door to the main deck once I got there.

I was alone. I didn't see any Task Force, but I gathered water from the air anyway and held a ball of it in my hand just in case. I crept around the corner, holding my magic aloft in anticipation. A figure appeared.

The water ball fell out of my hand and splashed all over my shoes. My mind went blank. *I've lost my fucking mind.*

Sophia stood in front of me, only a short distance away. She wore an equally shocked expression. Her shirt was torn to shreds and stained with blood, but her middle was untouched, void of any mark. Esis perched on her shoulder, and I felt a whisper of wind rush by, pressing against me as I sensed a spirit leave the area.

This was impossible. She was dead. I *watched* her die.

"Liam!" Sophia ran toward me, and her voice mended what had been broken only moments before. I opened my arms and wrapped them around her. My body quaked, shaken by the gravity of her love enveloping me. I almost buckled, but her arms squeezing me tight held me up, preventing me from falling into a pit of disbelief.

Esis squealed. He jumped and scurried up my arm, lying on my head and giving me a hug.

I cried into her hair. Couldn't think. Couldn't breathe. Couldn't talk, either. My shoulders shook. Sophia pressed her hands against my back, bringing me closer, but it didn't stop me from being any less of a mess.

She was being more of a comfort to me right now than I was her. I was a useless husband. I felt that same strange presence press in around us before it was gone, vanishing with the breeze.

"Oh my god, Liam." Her voice echoed with relief. She pressed into my shirt and took deep breaths. She wasn't crying— more or less relaxed.

Couldn't say the same for myself. "How... how did you...?" I stammered.

"I pulled the rod out. Esis healed me," she said. "Ancestors, I saw you go over the railing. I thought you'd died."

"I thought you did, too. Jake caught me. *Ancestors*, Sophia."

"We made it. It's all right," Sophia said.

It wouldn't be all right. Not until she was safe at home, and we were off this forsaken ship. To think it'd once been a happy place. I never wanted to set foot on it again.

She pulled back, but I didn't let her out of my arms. I kept her there. "Where are the others? Where's Jonah? You're... you're covered in blood."

My mouth ran dry. "It's not mine. Sophia, how did you find me?"

"It was Nashoma," she said. "He came to me, Liam. He protected me. He led me back to you!"

Tears sparked in my eyes. This was too much emotion for one day. "Nashoma? Where is he?" I looked around, wishing for a chance to glimpse him, just once.

"He left when you arrived," Sophia said. "I know you can't see him, but he was *there*. He took care of Esis and I when you were gone. He's protecting us."

It felt like my magic wavered within my body. "I could feel him. He was nearby."

"Yes. He wants you to know it's okay you have Julian," Sophia said. "He spoke to me and said he wants you to be happy. He's not upset with you."

Warmth flooded me. I'd always wondered that, but had been too afraid to ever utter it aloud.

But Nashoma knew my heart. He knew it'd be one of the questions I'd ask him, if I had the chance. And he'd saved my Sophie. Add that to the long list of things I had to thank him for.

Just then, the door opened behind us. Imogen was the one who saw her first. She let out a relieved noise and shouted, "*Sophia!*"

Imogen pounced on her, along with Luana. Both girls flung their arms around her and squeezed her tightly, crying tears of relief. Esis jumped off my head and ran to Sassy and Squeaks, who he greeted with tight hugs.

Cheveyo gave a kindly smile. "Good to see you're well, chosen one."

"In a way," Sophia said, before her eyes went to Jonah. Her mouth fell open, and her eyes widened in shock as she took in his appearance. She didn't think he was going to be that bad.

Jake hadn't even acknowledged Sophia's existence. He trembled as he held Jonah to his form.

Sophia plowed forward. "Esis, help me." She laid a hand on Jonah. Esis ran up Jake's leg to give her aid. Sophia's face knitted in concentration, until it clouded with a semblance of fear. Though they channeled their healing magic into Jonah, it had the same effect Luana's had, which was nothing.

Sophia sent a desperate look at me. "What do we do?"

My lungs were strangled of air. "We get him home."

Just then, the ship rocked to the side. Imogen and Luana both screamed. They collapsed upon the railing, and Trace caught them before they went over. I held on to Sophia, while the Familiars crashed into each other. Jake fell against the side of a wall, and took a hard hit instead of letting Jonah experience more pain.

"What's going on?" Trace called, looking at Cheveyo.

"We've changed course!" Cheveyo said, and his horse nickered. "We're sailing to the south."

"Why would they do that? The pattern they've taken is consistent every time!" Imogen cried out.

"They know we're here, and they can't find us," I growled. Plans were changing.

Cheveyo's face was ashen. He straightened up slowly and said, "They're going with the alternative plan."

"Which is?" Sophia yelped.

Cheveyo maintained a straight face. "They're going to steer the ship into the Anichi shield surrounding *Hok'evale*."

Luana gasped. She reached out for Imogen.

"But the veil guarding the town can't handle an explosion like that!" Sophia protested. "It'll crumble the shield, and take *Hok'evale* with it!"

"Precisely their plan," Cheveyo replied.

"They'd kill themselves for a chance to destroy the rebellion?" Trace asked, almost in disbelief.

"The Task Force will blow up this entire ship to prevent you from getting off of it," Cheveyo said firmly. "Their orders from Oleander are to kill the chosen one and her inner circle at all costs. They know we're here. The Task Force on this ship will be hailed as heroes for giving up their lives to stop you. Oleander has promised the families of those who kill the chosen one ultimate riches and safety. Many would kill themselves to get their loved ones in such a position, in times like these."

"So what do we do?" Imogen squeaked. "Even if we get off this ship, they're still going to steer it into the shield!"

Cheveyo's tone was resolute. "I will steer the ship as it goes down, and prevent them from crashing it into the rebellion."

My mind blanked out. "But... if you do that, you'll die."

Cheveyo smiled grimly. "It will be in the service of my tribe, for one of the greatest Toaqua chieftains that has ever lived."

Before we could stop him, Cheveyo mounted his horse. "I will buy you time. Go!"

Cheveyo and his Familiar galloped off, and blackness infiltrated my vision. I felt like I was sending Cheveyo to his death, even though he was the one who'd volunteered.

"We have to get Jonah out of here!" Jake barked. The rest of us snapped to attention, and Squeaks danced anxiously beside him.

I mentally counted. Sabor was gone, but Jake could fly Jonah down. Julian and Squeaks could carry the rest. I leaned over the railing and cried out, "*Julian!*"

I heard the pumps of his wings before I saw him. In moments, Julian was flying beside the side of the ship, yelping when he saw me.

There was a gate that opened up on the side of the railing. It was supposed to be for the crew when the ship docked, but it was our best way to climb on Julian without falling off. There was a lock holding the gate in place. Sassy's vines ripped it off, and the gate broke free.

Jake stepped through it with Jonah tucked to his body. They dropped downward for a hundred feet before Jake began levitating, flying them toward home.

Imogen and Trace climbed onto Squeaks' back, calling for Sassy. She jumped into Imogen's arms, and they took off.

Julian hovered by the gate, and we carefully maneuvered onto his back. Luana went first, sitting at the front, while Sophia took the middle. Esis and Sierra perched on Julian's head.

I slid myself on behind Sophia, clinging to her as I commanded, "Jules, go."

He took off like a rocket. Sophia and I pressed downward, and I heard the sounds of explosions behind me as the *Hozho* began to erupt. I smelled smoke that carried through the air, and knew the ship had to be on fire, though the thought that the crew was actually detonating the cruise liner was impossible to fathom.

We were just outside *Hok'evale*. I pulled Julian up. The dragon hovered in mid-air, and I dared to look back.

Sophia and Luana gasped. Esis gaped, and Julian let out a low moan as we watched the bow of the ship tilt downward, arching the stern nearly vertical toward the ground. There were screams— so many screams. A cracking sound ricocheted through the air like lightning as the ship collided at full speed into a nearby mountain range. It broke in half, avoiding *Hok'evale* several miles off.

Professor Cheveyo had kept to his promise. He'd gone down with his ship.

The *Hozho* crashed and exploded like the fucking Hindenburg. We shielded our eyes from the detonation of light, the *Hozho* going up in an eruption of thunder. I heard the cries of Elementai as the flames swelled and absorbed them, the screams eventually falling silent as the dawn of morning ended their symphony. Flames from the cruise liner flooded into the trees surrounding the area, setting the forest ablaze.

All those people. Not just Task Force— prisoners of the war, soldiers of the rebellion and Biyami victims. Gone in a fiery inferno, never to return.

Sophia let out a sob. I held her, putting my chin on her shoulder as we stared at the carnage. The *Hozho* had been a part of my childhood. My dad and I had sailed countless times together on the cruise liner, doing tribal business. So much of what I knew about being chief, I'd learned there. Sophia and I had our first meal together on that ship. It was where I'd told her all about our world for the first time. Barely a year ago, the four of us had taken a cruise on it to Europe, to get away from it all. That ship had been our sanctuary, a break from reality in the middle of hell.

And now it was gone. Along with thousands of Elementai— whatever side they happened to be on.

We had only one small consolation. Haley had died, too. No way she made it off that ship. The Fire chieftess was no more.

Esis squeaked and pointed. Jake was far below with Jonah, and Squeaks had caught up to them with Imogen and Trace.

Right. We couldn't stay here and grieve over the *Hozho*. We had to save Jonah.

Julian came in for a rough landing. Luana fell off as we hit the ground, though she waved at us to say she was all right when Sophia started. We leapt off the dragon and ran toward Jake, who was surrounded by Imogen and Trace.

We'd landed just outside the cave system in *Hok'evale*. Though now that we'd arrived, we didn't know what to do. Jonah had grown weaker now. His throat had developed a death rattle, breath wheezing weakly from his lungs.

"Stay awake, soldier!" Jake jostled Jonah in his arms. Jonah's eyes remained half-closed, his head lolling.

He was fading— we were losing him.

Jake looked at Sophia, as if begging her to come up with some kind of solution. "Sophia, what do we do?"

Sophia let out a breath. "What?"

"You're the chosen one!" Jake bellowed. "*Do something!*"

Imogen sobbed. Sophia gaped, and Esis' head fell. Luana put a hand over her mouth as she watched Jonah's breaths grow weaker and weaker.

Squeaks gave a low coo. She nestled Jonah's hair with her beak, and he leaned into her touch. If Jonah died, Squeaks would, too. I could already see the light fading from her eyes as Jonah approached the Ancestral Lands.

Sophia's eyes were blank, and I lost all hope. There were no more plans. There was nothing else we could do.

I was about to suggest we should take Jonah home, so we could say goodbye and he could die in peace. Until Sophia's expression lit up, and she said, "The underground river! The one in the caves— the water the Anichi survived off of!"

Jake's eyes cleared with hope. I knew what river Sophia was talking about. We'd used it to sustain ourselves and hide from the Task Force before Jake had brought us to *Hok'evale*.

That river was magical. It had healing properties blessed by the ancestors. We could get there. We still had time.

Jake rushed into the entrance of the cave. Luana and Sophia used their Anichi magic to light the way. Imogen and Sassy ran beside Squeaks as I followed, praying that Jonah would hold on.

"Ancestors, don't let me die in a fucking cave," Jonah pleaded weakly from up ahead. He'd come around just long enough to know where he was.

"You aren't going to die." Jake's voice was gruff. "Jonah, I command you to stay awake! That's a direct order! Keep with me, soldier!"

I caught up with them. Jonah's head bobbed, but his eyes remained slightly open. The blanket Jake had wrapped him in was matted with blood now.

"I'll hold on for you," Jonah said quietly, giving a *whoosh* of breath. Jake's lip trembled.

We had to slow down in parts of the cave, because they were hard to get through. I helped Jake transport Jonah through some of the narrower areas. Hot, sticky blood from Jonah flooded onto my arms and into my clothes, but I didn't care. I had to save my best buddy. I had to.

Cheveyo had died— so many had died. If I couldn't save Jonah, what good was I? Squeaks cried out in desperation as she squeezed herself through the tiny crevices with all her might.

Finally, I heard the trumpets of elepees up ahead. The little elephants scattered out of the way as we broke into the clearing of the cave. Other creatures in the cave included the dracaverns and giant blue moths, which flew out the hole of the cave ceiling as we entered.

The river was only a few steps away. Jake ran toward it, submerging himself in the river's flow. Jonah gave a final breath just as Jake placed him into the water.

Our hearts pounded, breath becoming shallow as Jake suspended Jonah in the water. Squeaks crashed into the river, sending water spraying everywhere.

Nothing happened. Jonah's chest didn't rise and fall, nor did he move. Jake's expression blanched, while Squeaks let out a song of grief.

Imogen and Sophia both sank against me. Luana fell to the edge of the river on all fours, head bowed like she was uttering a lost prayer.

I couldn't believe it. Why wasn't the river working? Were we too late?

The blanket floated away. I watched as the water rushed over Jonah's features and began to glisten, washing the blood downstream.

That's when the magic happened. The dark bruises on Jonah's chest faded. His fingernails grew back, and the cuts on his body knitted together. The swelling around his eyes went down, returning his face to normal.

Jake lifted him. The knotted scars and jagged whiplashes on Jonah's back had faded, leaving thin pink marks behind. The gnarled muscle and ruined skin had been mended together, giving Jonah scars that were a reminder of Haley's torture.

Color returned to Jonah's face, and breath filled his lungs. He opened his eyes, staring upward at the ceiling of the cave. Jonah startled, like he was terrified, but Jake held him close. Jonah relaxed when he realized where he was— or rather, with who.

Jonah blinked as he gazed at Jake's face. In a hoarse, still fragile voice, he uttered, "I really love you. You know that?"

Jake said nothing. Only held Jonah to his chest and wept.

sophia
SIXTEEN

melia shivered. She sat across from me at *The Falcon's Nest,* sipping on coffee. Only a few days had passed since the *Hozho* crashed, and I was worried about her. I'd asked her to meet me here for breakfast. I'd had no intention about discussing what happened to her on the *Hozho.* I didn't want to hurt her any more than she already was. But she apparently hadn't gotten the memo.

"Jill got what she deserved," Amelia stated. Her eyes were hooded with darkness. She'd had it out for Oleander and the Task Force forever, but it was nothing like it was now. If Jake gave the command to attack Kinpago, she'd have it buried beneath the sea in moments.

"They all did," I replied. I leaned over to Ava-Marie's high chair and spooned applesauce into her mouth. I wasn't particularly comfortable talking about this in front of my daughter, but I didn't see the alternative. The war was heating up, and we had to send her away soon. I wasn't letting her out of my sight.

Amelia drew another sip of coffee, then set her cup down on the table. "To be honest, Jill deserved worse. If I'd had any strength to fight back, I'd have carved the skin off her face."

I shifted uncomfortably. Amelia was getting really morbid after what happened to her. I wanted to call her out for it, but another part of me felt it was justified. Once she had a chance to process it, she'd cool down.

"I'm going to kill Oleander," she said simply— like we were talking about the weather.

It took me a second to realize what she just said. Even Esis, who had a face-full of French toast, did a double take. Kiwi kept on pecking at his bowl of nuts, like he hadn't heard her.

"Not if Liam beats you to it," I replied, if only to ease the knot in my gut. I hadn't wanted my sister to become a killer, too.

But that's what happened in war. We all became killers eventually.

"It's not just about what happened to me on the *Hozho*," Amelia said. "I've been part of the resistance for years— before you even knew they existed. I'm tired, Sophia. I'm ready for this fight to be over."

"It will be. Soon." My stomach twisted as I spooned another bite into Ava's mouth. She kicked in her high chair and looked so happy. *If only she knew*. I had to give her up before this war was over. But maybe when it was, she could come back to me...

That thought was the only thing that kept me from running away with her.

The bell on the door jingled, and I caught sight of red hair out of the corner of my eye. I looked up to see Doya stepping into the restaurant, her velvet dress billowing around her legs. Naomi held her head high as they walked over to my table.

Amelia shot her a glare. The two still weren't on good terms— not after Doya sent Naomi to spy on my sister all those years ago. Though they tolerated each other's company— for my sake, I was sure— they didn't quite get along.

"Excuse me a moment," Doya said. She was softer to Amelia than normal. I guessed it was because she heard what happened to her on the *Hozho*. "I need a word with Sophia."

My spine straightened. "Of course. What is it?"

Doya gestured toward the door. "Can we talk in private?"

I glanced to Amelia, who looked uncomfortable.

"It's fine," she said, though not without some bitterness entering her tone. "I'll watch Ava and Esis for a few minutes."

"Thanks, Am." It killed me to step away from my daughter, but whatever Doya had to say sounded urgent. I hoped it wasn't about Liam.

I followed Doya outside, and she led me a few paces down the street, so we couldn't be heard. "Is something wrong?" I asked.

"More or less," she sighed, turning toward me.

Naomi sat comfortably at her feet. Usually, the Fire lion remained alert at all times, so I guessed this wasn't as terrible as I was thinking. I relaxed my shoulders.

"I've received word that the Koigni within *Hok'evale* are seeking a new chieftess," Doya said.

I gaped a few moments. "Does that mean they confirmed Haley's death? Did they find her body?"

Doya pressed her lips firmly together. "I haven't heard confirmation, but it's unlikely we will. The resistance has very few spies left in Kinpago, from what I've heard. Whether Haley's death is confirmed or not is irrelevant. Her chieftess ceremony was kept very secret, and resistance members are questioning whether she truly completed it or not."

I furrowed my brow. It wouldn't surprise me if Haley cheated. "Do you think she did?"

"I cannot speak for the ancestors," she replied. "I do not know if they would give Haley their blessing. I do know she was never my first choice."

"I remember," I said, recalling the conversation we had a year ago. She'd said she didn't think Haley had what it took to lead her tribe. She wanted me to take the spot as chieftess. "You wanted me on the council."

"Yes," she confirmed. "Now that there's an opening, I want you to fight to get it."

"Why me?" I asked bluntly. I had no desire to lead the Koigni tribe. I was already the wife of a chief, and I had to be there for *him* and my family. I couldn't handle the task of leading both the Water and the Fire tribe. "You're much better suited to be chieftess than I am. Don't *you* want it?"

She tilted her chin upward. "I want what's best for the tribe, Sophia—as I always have."

At one time, I'd have thought she was saying that to manipulate me. Now I actually believed it.

"The Koigni will not have me," she stated. "Though I only joined Oleander's side to keep an eye on him, the others still question my loyalty. I could not lead a tribe that did not want my leadership."

"You think they want mine?" I nearly squeaked. "I didn't grow up in Kinpago. I've been an outsider since the day I arrived."

"You are the *chosen one*, Sophia," she reminded me. "Perhaps you are to end this war in the position of chieftess. The other Koigni are desperate for this war to end. I'm sure they'll see it the same way."

I shook my head. "But I'm married to the Toaqua chief."

"Exactly," she emphasized. "With you as chieftess, our alliance with Toaqua will be iron-clad. You and Liam shall rule the tribe together. Nothing will be able to stop you."

"That's the problem!" I cried. "If I became chief, Liam and I would own the tribe. We'd evolve into a dictatorship, and I won't allow that to happen."

"Why not?" Doya sounded shocked that I'd protest such a thing. "You would have the final say in everything. You could lead the tribe in any direction you choose."

"Which is how we end up with people like Oleander," I shot back.

"You will never be Oleander, Sophia," she promised me.

I pressed my fingers to my eyes. "I know that, but it still doesn't make stealing all the power right. The power belongs to the people, not to my family."

"It could belong to your daughter," Doya said, as if the idea should entice me. "Once you and Liam are gone, Ava would be in a position to take over."

"I don't want that," I snapped.

Doya recoiled slightly. "You don't think she'd do a good job?"

"Of course I think she would. But we can't leave the power to one voice, no matter how good that voice may be. Besides, I thought the Koigni and Toaqua wanted nothing to do with each other."

"This war is forcing them to change their ways," she reminded me. "Many are seeking unity in these tough times."

"They have a funny way of showing it, if my wedding is any indication." I hadn't forgotten about the fight that broke out between both sides at my reception. But then again, that was months ago. People could change quickly in desperate times.

"The Koigni need you, Sophia," Doya all but pleaded. "They're looking for a replacement immediately, and will choose based on a vote. I want you to put your name in for consideration."

I shook my head, my mind already made up. "I'm sorry, Mother. But I want the best for the tribe, too, and I don't believe that I'm the best choice."

Doya looked dumbstruck by my admission. "But how could you not!?"

"I'm irrational and emotional!" I shouted, as if proving my point. I hadn't meant to do that. I lowered my voice and said, "I'm the chosen one because I'm willing to do whatever it takes to bring Oleander down. But the Koigni don't need a military leader. They need a peacemaker."

"You can be both!" Doya protested.

"No, I can't," I shot back. "That is why we are in this war in the first place! The chiefs and chieftesses couldn't stop fighting for power! Don't you think there's a reason Chief Cauac isn't leading the Anichi into this war? He's not just their safety net if things go south— he's their respected leader. He has Jake to handle the rest. And we both know I'm a lot more like Jake than I am like Chief Cauac."

Doya gaped, like she'd never looked at the chief hood that way, before she smoothed her hair and said, "The Koigni *need* a chieftess, Sophia."

"They will have one," I promised. "It's just not going to be me."

I wish it could be, but it didn't feel right— as if the job had been reserved for someone else. I didn't believe this was what the ancestors wanted of me. And I had to follow the ancestors' will— no matter what they asked.

Even if what they asked for shattered my world.

❧

I ROCKED Ava-Marie back and forth in the living room. I tried to sing to her, but my voice broke with every note. I couldn't get the song out.

Though it wasn't even dinner time, Ava-Marie slept in my arms. The ancestors hadn't asked me to become chieftess, but they *had* asked me to give up my daughter. It was a horrifying thought, but they weren't about to offer me an alternative.

To be honest, I hated them for it.

The door opened, and Liam stepped inside. He looked wiped after a long day at work, but his shoulders fell and a smile lit up his face when he caught sight of us. Dropping his coat off on a kitchen chair, he came over to stand beside us. He pressed a kiss to my forehead, then looked down at Ava-Marie.

"I love you both, *pawee*." His voice was strained— like there was something on his mind.

He didn't get a chance to say anything before Esis was jumping up and down at his feet. He pawed at Liam's hand, and Buttercup thumped her tail on the ground. Liam sighed and said, "Yes, Esis, I brought you home a treat."

He opened his fist and showed the kurbles two foil-wrapped chocolates. He held one up out of Esis' reach. "But first, you gotta do a trick. Roll over."

Esis rolled on the floor like a dog, and Buttercup copied him.

"Now sit," Liam commanded. The kurbles moved in unison. "Stay. Shake."

Esis put his paw in Liam's outstretched hand, and Liam chuckled. "Good job, buddy. Here you go."

289

He tossed the chocolates to the kurbles. For a moment, his smile was pure bliss. Then he turned back to me, and the smile instantly faded.

"What's wrong, Liam?" I asked, sensing the worst.

Liam sighed and sat on the couch. "There's something I want to talk about."

I chewed my lower lip. "Me, too. You first."

Liam knotted his hands together. The clock on the wall ticked, and my stomach twisted. I felt like we wanted to say the same thing, and we were both too scared to say it out loud.

Finally, Liam breathed a sigh and spit it out. "Soph, we're out of time."

My chest compressed as I stared down at my sleeping baby. How could we be out of time so quickly? I'd only just met her. I couldn't give up my baby— not yet.

Liam took my silence as hesitation. "The incident on the *Hozho* happened so quickly. When Oleander launches his counter-attack, it will be the same. We'll have no warning, no time to get Ava out."

"I know," I said, my voice cracking. "And I want Ava far away from here when it happens. I just... I just—"

I hiccupped. My chest felt like it was being piled under a stack of cinder blocks.

Liam blinked away the tears rising to his eyes. "Sending Ava-Marie away is the last thing I want to do, but I think it's time. We need to talk to Bren and Vanessa tonight. We need to get our daughter someplace safe. Before shit goes down, and we can't do anything about it."

"I agree," I said. Safe was far better than dead— or worse, in the hands of Oleander and his people.

"You don't have to cook tonight," Liam offered. "We'll order takeout and spend as much time with Ava as we can."

I sniffled and nodded, though it felt like a knife to the gut. I stood from the rocking chair and joined Liam on the couch, where he wrapped me in his arms. "I just want to hold her," I whispered.

"We will," he said. "Until it's time—"

A knock came at the door, cutting him off.

"Fuck the ancestors," he grumbled.

Carefully, he stood from the couch, so he wouldn't wake Ava-Marie, and went to the door. I kept my eyes on him. When he opened it, I saw Bren and Vanessa standing there.

"Hey, guys," Liam greeted, though he didn't sound very enthused.

"What a coincidence. We were just talking about meeting up with you tonight."

"Good, because we have to talk to you, too," Bren said. "Mind if we come in?"

"Not at all." Liam opened the door wider, and the couple stepped inside. Kingston followed behind, his three heads sniffing the air in different directions to get a sense of the place. Aisha remained outside, cooing at Julian. Xavier wasn't with them.

"Please, have a seat." Liam gestured to the couch across from me, and they both sat. They remained rigid, though, like they didn't come for good news.

Liam must've missed that cue, because he took a seat beside me and started talking. He was used to being the first to talk, with being chief and all. "Look, Sophia and I were talking, and we think it's time to send Ava-Marie away. We don't know when Oleander will attack next—"

Vanessa held up a hand. "Sorry, Liam. I'm going to stop you there. We came to tell you we can't take Ava anymore."

"What!?" I gasped. Ava-Marie stirred in my arms, and I lowered my voice to hiss at them. "I thought you wanted to take Xavier away, too?"

"We did," Bren assured me. "But that was before..."

He shot a look at Vanessa. Her mouth was down turned.

"That was before the Koigni asked me to be their chieftess," she finished for them.

I gaped. I could hardly believe it. On the one hand, I was happy for her. I knew she was exactly what the Koigni needed. She was well-respected, since she came from a family of Elders. The one strike against her was when she blew up in the town square and talked shit about Chieftess Annette.

"Why'd they ask you?" I asked. "Wasn't your name... well... tarnished?"

Vanessa blushed. "Well... traditionally, chiefs and chieftesses have to come from the original bloodline of the first chieftains of their House. I'm Haley's cousin, and also the only living relative left eligible to take on the chief hood. Without my blood ruling over Koigni House, it's said that the ancestors will curse our tribe. It's just a story, but I think all of us are wary of angering the ancestors any more than we already have in this war."

Made sense, but Doya was obviously not one to follow tradition. She'd have no problem pissing off the ancestors to put me in charge, if she had her way.

"That would make your son the first ever chief of Koigni, if you succeed in your ceremony," Liam said in awe. "Are the Koigni willing to go along with that?"

Vanessa shrugged. "They don't really have much of a choice. If they want the bloodline to continue and the tribe to go on, I have to take Haley's place."

A part of me felt relieved the chief hood wasn't going to another crazy psycho. Vanessa was level-headed and strong. She would be a good chieftess. I knew she would lead the Koigni well.

And it meant we got to keep Ava-Marie a little longer.

"That's great," I said honestly. Liam shot me a confused expression, like he thought I'd be sad they weren't taking Ava-Marie anymore.

"We're really, *really* sorry," Vanessa said. "But there has to be someone else who can take Ava, right?"

"Yeah," Liam said quickly, though we'd never discussed alternatives. "We'll find someone. Congratulations, Vanessa. I hope to work closely with you to mend the relationship between the Toaqua and the Koigni."

Liam stood to shake her hand. He was speaking as chief, not as Ava's father, whose godparents had just abandoned her.

"We will," Vanessa promised, before turning to me. "In fact, I hope to work with *both* of you closely."

I furrowed my brow, unsure of what she meant.

"Sophia, I want to appoint you an Elder," she announced.

I gaped at her. I'd already refused my mother's suggestion of chieftess earlier. Now I was being offered the title of Elder? It felt like too much.

"You don't have to do that, Vanessa," I told her. "If it's to make up for not taking Ava—"

"That's not it at all," she said quickly. "You and I have been friends for years now. We work well together."

"Believe me, Vanessa, I'm not Elder material," I said. "I lash out and can't keep my mouth shut sometimes."

"Which is exactly why I need you," she pressed. "My problem is I don't speak out enough. Change is needed here, Sophia, and I believe you can help make that happen."

"Because I'm the chosen one?" I asked. I was about to explain how that wouldn't help on the council, but she spoke before I could.

"No. Because you're *different*," she said. "I need people on the council who will push me to see from other perspectives. You didn't grow up in Kinpago, which makes you uniquely qualified to see our tribe differently. You can offer a new vision the rest of us can't see."

I'd used the same argument with Doya to keep me off the council. It was strange that Vanessa saw those same reasons as assets.

"You went up against the Elders in your trial," Vanessa added. "You convinced everyone you and Liam belong together. I know that you can do this."

"I don't know..." I said, thinking it through. To be honest, I didn't know if I had the energy for this. I couldn't be making any other life-altering decisions for the tribe right now. I already had one decision to make, and it was killing me.

"It may be a good thing," Liam mused. "To show the Hawkei Toaqua and Koigni are united. An Elder has never been married to the chief of another House before."

"I just don't think this is what the ancestors want for me," I argued, though I didn't know if it was true. I think I was using it as an excuse to keep my distance.

"What is it they want?" Bren asked.

I hesitated and stared down at Ava-Marie, to avoid looking anyone else in the eye. I didn't really have an answer. They wanted me to end this war— to give up my daughter. That was all I knew. If we all survived that... well, I didn't know what I'd do with myself if Ava-Marie weren't here.

I didn't know if I'd be able to keep going. I wasn't sure I could hold on to who I was anymore without her. Liam wouldn't want to keep me around when that happened. And if it did... I'd only let everyone down.

But if I didn't do this, it was all more reason to give up. As much as I hated to admit it, I needed something to keep me going. At least it would make everyone else happy... for now.

"Okay," I said, before I really decided on it. "I'll serve on your council, Vanessa. I'll be a Koigni Elder."

THE FOLLOWING DAY, I still hadn't processed what I'd agreed to. I was going to be a Koigni Elder. I hardly even understood what that meant. I hadn't told Doya yet, because I knew she'd want to start training me immediately. I didn't want anything distracting me— not until we found a safe place for Ava-Marie.

First thing in the morning, Liam and I stopped at Lindsey and Miranda's apartment. I held Ava-Marie in my arms, and Esis rode on Liam's shoulder. Miranda answered in a full face of makeup and a bonnet covering her dark curls.

"Hey, guys," she said chipperly. "On the way to Vanessa's chief hood ceremony?"

"We are," I told her. "But we wanted to stop by on our way."

"Sure thing. Come in." Miranda opened the door wider, and we stepped inside. The couple lived in the same complex as Cade and Imogen. The layout was the same, but the decor looked as if a flower garden had puked on them. Everywhere I looked, there were pictures of flowers, flowers in vases, or floral prints on the fabric. I leaned over to sniff a bouquet of daisies. Esis jumped on the table and turned his nose up at them.

"Those are fake," Lindsey snickered as she stepped out of the bathroom. She wore a pretty red dress and had her hair up in a bun for the ceremony. Her basilisk Familiar slithered out of the bathroom behind her and went across the room to snuggle up with Evelyn, Miranda's kirin Familiar.

"Fake?" I asked.

She wrinkled her nose. "Yeah, I can't keep a plant alive to save my life, but I love to look at them. What brings you two by?"

"Well..." I took a deep breath and looked to Liam.

He sighed. "The truth is... we're looking for someone to take Ava away from *Hok'evale*," Liam spat out. He hurried to explain before either Miranda or Lindsey could protest. "This war is too dangerous for a child, but we have to stay and fight. We believe the prophecy may speak of Ava-Marie's death, and we can't wait any longer. Vanessa and Bren were going to take her, but with the chief hood, they've changed their minds."

Lindsey and Miranda shared a look I couldn't read.

"You know we'd take her in a heartbeat," Miranda added quickly. "But we can't. Not now. You already know we're helping Maddie decipher her visions, and I'm sorry, Sophia, but that has to come first."

Part of me was thrilled Ava-Marie would be staying longer. Another part of me feared for her. "There aren't many people we can trust with our daughter."

"There must be someone," Miranda said.

I chewed my lower lip. "There are a few others, but we'd really hoped it might be you guys. You'd be perfect parents."

Lindsey snorted, then quickly composed herself. "Once Oleander's taken out, then maybe. But until then, I've got a fireball ready to shove down his throat. And believe me, you don't want a baby around when that happens."

"Are you guys sure?" Liam pressed.

Miranda sighed, like she didn't know how to let us off easy. To be fair, what we were asking was a pretty big deal. "Look, the ceremony is soon. Why don't we get through that, and we'll talk more about this later?"

"Okay," I agreed— feeling *good* about putting it off. I was the worst mother ever.

"Perfect," Miranda said. "Let me finish up my hair, and we can all go together."

Vanessa's chieftess ceremony would take place on a cliff overlooking *Hok'evale*. It was within the boundaries of Luana's shield, but Jake's men had been stationed in the trees and the air to keep watch for the Task Force, just in case.

When we arrived, Liam and I were escorted to the front row, since he was the chief of another House and I would serve on Vanessa's council. Jonah, Imogen, Luana, and the rest of our friends stayed toward the back, as the first few rows were reserved for Koigni attendees. Jonah had a faraway look in his eyes, like he wasn't really present with us. Jake draped an arm around his shoulder and held him tight. I worried about him.

In front of us lay a hot bed of coals at least six feet long, though no one went near it. I wasn't sure what it was for. Doya was sitting in the front row when we arrived, chatting with two other Koigni beside her. The first was Bren, which didn't surprise me. He bounced Xavier on his leg and cooed at his son. It was the second Koigni that nearly knocked me off my feet.

It was *Kelsey*— Haley's sidekick. Her jaguar Familiar sat beside Naomi, and Esis shot him a look. Her Familiar didn't look well, as it had missing chunks of fur all over its body. Its tail seemed shorter than the last time I'd seen it, and one of its front paws was covered in a thick burn scar that was still healing. Looked like Kelsey's Familiar had been raising trouble. It deserved what it got.

I stopped dead in my tracks and shot a glare at Doya. My lip curled. I hated Kelsey. She was Haley's right-hand. She had no right to be in *Hok'evale*!

"What the hell is she doing here?" I demanded.

Kelsey finally stopped talking to Bren and looked my way. Her face fell. "It's not what you think, Sophia. I've come here in peace."

"You mean you lost your chieftess, and you came to gain favor with the next in line?" I accused.

"What? No!" Kelsey sounded offended. "I was already on my way to *Hok'evale* when the *Hozho* went down. I've been funneling information to the resistance ever since you blew up the Task Force Headquarters. It became too dangerous for me there, though, so I had to leave."

I furrowed my brow. She sounded genuine, but it took a lot to trust Haley's former minion. She'd been a bully while we were at school, and terribly cruel. "Why would *you* join the resistance?"

"Why not?" she challenged. "You don't know what I've seen. You don't know what happened to me. I saw what they did to those Familiars. I'd had enough."

Liam looked equally skeptical. "But you had power in Kinpago. You were Haley's second-hand girl."

Kelsey scoffed. "You think Haley needed me as soon as she became chieftess? She didn't even elect a council. She *tortured* my Familiar to make me do whatever she wanted. You wouldn't understand."

My heart sank for Kelsey. No one deserved for their Familiar to be tortured, and knowing Haley, it'd been horrible. My eyes roamed over her Familiar, until it occurred to me that she might be lying. Anyone could've hurt this creature, and she could be lying about Haley to get on our side.

"How can we know that for sure?" I growled. "You could be a spy."

"Sophia," Doya said, as if in warning. "Might I remind you others said the same about me, and it turned out to be untrue."

"We can't be too careful," Liam objected. "This is a war."

"Calm down, guys," Bren insisted. "Vanessa trusts her. If our new chieftess can do that, can't you?"

Liam and I hesitated. He didn't say anything more. He knew as Koigni chieftess, Vanessa would have the final say.

But I was the chosen one, and I wasn't buying it. "I guess so," I said, only to keep the peace. I didn't trust Kelsey, and would be sure to keep a very close eye on her.

I sat beside Doya, and Esis snuggled in beside me. Her eyes immediately went to Ava-Marie, and Doya held her arms out to take her.

"I've got her." I pulled her closer to my chest. "I didn't realize you'd be sitting by us."

Doya smirked. "Why not, when Vanessa has asked me to serve as an Elder?"

My eyebrows shot up. "She did?"

I couldn't say I was surprised. I'd have done the same thing. Doya had the experience for it, at least.

Doya nodded. "Along with Kelsey."

"Kelsey's on the council?" I balked.

"Yes, I am," she said proudly. "To ease your worries, I promise that I intend to play nice."

For now.

"So that makes three of us," I said, realizing that all the Koigni Elders were sitting right here. "Is there a fourth?"

Doya shook her head. "Not yet. Let's show the ancestors some respect during this ceremony."

That was my cue to stop bitching about Kelsey being on the council. It wasn't like I had much choice, since Vanessa had appointed her herself.

Liam set the diaper bag at his feet and pulled out a fresh bottle for Ava-Marie. He didn't look happy as he handed it to me, but we both resolved to stay quiet. I started feeding Ava as more Koigni and other Houses alike filed into chairs to watch Vanessa's chieftess ceremony.

"What are the coals for?" I leaned over and asked Doya.

"Each House has their own ceremonies they perform for their chiefs and chieftesses," she explained. "In the Koigni House, our chieftesses are to walk across a bed of hot coals and profess their intentions to the ancestors. If the ancestors approve of these intentions, they will rise from the flames and bestow upon you a blessing."

It sounded really cool. I couldn't wait to see it.

I glanced around the crowd and noticed more people from non-Koigni Houses filling into the back. "There are a lot of people here from other Houses," I remarked. "I thought this ceremony was for Koigni only."

"Vanessa invited them," Doya explained. "It's her first act as chieftess to unite the Houses."

And that was why Vanessa deserved to be chieftess.

It wasn't long before all the seats were filled. Drums began to beat, and the sound of a trumpet blared across the cliffside.

I caught sight of a flying creature in the distance. Her blue scales glittered in the sunlight. As she came in closer, I realized it was Aisha with a rider on her back. At the sight of her, I heard Julian coo at the back of the crowd.

Aisha dipped in the sky and came to land on the cliffside not far from the coals. Vanessa wore beautiful red regalia. The beads created a design of a dragon and a phoenix weaving together against a plume of flame. She had several feathers twisted into her braided hair. She slipped off Aisha's back carrying a large basket in her arms. It looked homemade, like something Liam would weave, but I couldn't see what was inside.

The sound of the trumpet died, and the drum beats were the only sound within the clearing. I felt like I was sitting on the edge of my seat as I waited to see what the ancestors would say. I hoped they would bless her. Vanessa deserved this.

Vanessa looked like a princess as she walked across the clearing and stopped in front of the bed of coals, but she said nothing. She nodded to Doya, and my mother stood to address the crowd.

"Koigni, Nivita, Yapluma, Anichi, and Toaqua— all that join us here today— it is my pleasure to present to you Vanessa Emberly," Doya announced. She gestured to Vanessa and stepped aside as the crowd broke into cheers. "Vanessa is the daughter of Coraline Thomas; granddaughter of Selma Westfenix, former Koigni Chieftess; and niece of Annette West-fenix, former Koigni Chieftess. You have elected her to serve as your chieft-ess. Today, she stands before you to pledge her allegiance to the tribe, and to seek the blessings of the ancestors required to serve in such a high role. If anyone shall see her unfit as Koigni Chieftess, you may speak now, or forever hold your peace."

Nobody moved.

Doya turned to Vanessa. "Vanessa Emberly, you may now step upon these coals. Call upon the ancestors, and speak your intentions for all to hear."

Vanessa looked to her Elder Council. I shot her a smile of encourage-ment. Her eyes settled on her husband and son for several long seconds, before she tore her gaze off of them and stared far into the distance. Her chest rose and fell, then she stepped forward onto the hot bed of coals.

She winced as the coals shifted and burned her feet. I heard her cry out beneath her breath, but she did her best to hide it. She could've used her magic to dull the fire beneath her, but she didn't. She had to prove to the ancestors she could withstand any challenges laid before her.

"Ancestors," Vanessa called out in a shaky breath. "For centuries, the Hawkei have been at war. The Koigni have used their power for destruction."

She reached into the basket and pulled out a bouquet of flowers. They were all different colors— blue, red, purple, white, and green. As she took another step forward, she dropped the bouquet onto the coals below her. She gasped as the coals shifted again, burning her feet. My heart hammered as I watched, wanting to stop it but knowing I couldn't.

"We have fought Nivita, and their plants have withered to nothing," she announced in a strong voice. As she spoke, the bouquet caught fire, and the flames ate away at them within moments, leaving nothing but the charred remains. Flower petals broke off and turned to ash. I was slightly shocked, having not expected a display like this.

"We have fought Yapluma and poisoned their air." She reached into her basket again, this time pulling out a purple scarf. As she took her next step, she beat the scarf through the air at her side. The coals beneath her glowed red-hot as she pumped oxygen toward them, and she visibly held back a flinch. Black smoke rose into the air.

I glanced around. Several people had shifted in their chairs, looking slightly uncomfortable.

"We have fought Toaqua and turned their water to steam," Vanessa announced. This time when she took a step, she pulled out a cup of water and poured it over the coals. The fire sizzled, and steam rose to the air. Tears beaded in her eyes as the coals continued to burn her, but she continued.

Vanessa's voice grew. "And we have fought the Anichi, decimating their tribe, destroying their souls, and stealing their magic and bonds!"

I was interested to see what Vanessa was going to use to symbolize the Anichi House, but never in a million years would I have expected her to do what she did next. Vanessa tossed her basket aside in the grass and began to pull off her regalia. She ripped her feathers out of her hair and threw them to the coals beneath her, then stripped off her dress. Underneath, she wore a white gown.

My jaw dropped. Giving up your regalia and your feathers was like stripping off your own self-identity— a piece of your soul. This wasn't just a show. Vanessa meant every word she said. Tears spilled over and began streaming down her face as her regalia caught fire beneath her feet, though her voice remained strong.

"To this, I say *no more!*" Vanessa shouted. "As chieftess, I will not stand by and allow my House to go down the path of violence. From now on, the Koigni seek truth over lies, peace over power, and *one tribe* above all else!"

My heart swelled as I listened to her words. I knew Vanessa was the chieftess we needed, but I didn't know *why* until that moment. Vanessa's intentions were pure. *She* was the one who would convert Koigni to peace instead of revenge.

Vanessa spread her arms wide and closed her eyes, tilting her chin toward the sky. Tears rained down her face, and sweat beaded on her brow from the pain. "Take me as your chieftess if you will, but shall you not, I will stand on the side of harmony, from now until the end of time."

Several moments passed. I swore the entire crowd was holding their breath. If the ancestors didn't take Vanessa to be their chieftess after *that*, I didn't know how much longer I could follow them. I would stand beside Vanessa as my chieftess even if no one else did.

Then, the most marvelous thing happened. Vanessa twisted her hands and commanded her magic. Flames shot up from the bed of coals so high that when I tilted my head back, I couldn't see the top of them. The flames twisted into a column, reaching as high as a skyscraper. It was her display for the ancestors to show her strength.

Heat rolled off the flame column in waves. Though the Koigni in the front rows were fine, Liam started to sweat immediately. Vanessa's magic was impressive, enough to take out the entire crowd in one go if she wanted to.

Flames jumped off the column of fire, swirling into wisps of magic around Vanessa. She breathed a heavy sigh of relief, and her features softened, as if the pain was no longer assaulting her. The fire column died down, and the wisps of magic transformed, taking the shapes of various creatures. A phoenix flapped its wings and flew in a circle around her, followed by a unicorn that galloped circles. Three separate dragons of all different sizes rose from the coals and grew to Fire creatures of massive proportions. They circled her in the sky above, flames licking into the air. Other creatures continued to appear, including a seven-headed wyvern, a flaming serpent twenty feet long, and a winged bull. I even saw a deer-like creature with a long, flaming tail and huge antlers.

The creatures landed on the ground and shifted to reveal the Koigni chieftesses of the past. Each was made of Fire, but the details in their features were unmistakable. There were so many that I could not count them. I tried to look for a face that I recognized— either Haley or Annette, but I saw neither. I wondered if that meant the ancestors had rejected them — that they would suffer in *Aiya Nocshun*. A woman stepped forward, and Vanessa's tears continued to stream down her face.

"Grandmother?" she asked.

Her grandmother did not speak. She simply stepped forward and placed a hand on her own heart, then reached out to touch Vanessa's.

Vanessa spoke softly so that only us in the front row could hear. "I understand, Grandmother. I will not let you down."

Her grandmother nodded, then gestured to the other chieftesses. In the blink of an eye, they shifted back into their animal form. They circled around Vanessa, closing in until their flames blended together. Vanessa's tears ceased, and she took a deep breath, as if breathing their spirits in. One by one, the ancestor's spirits shrank into a beam of light, each one radiating out of Vanessa's chest.

Her grandmother was the last to go. For several long seconds, the beam of light remained, then it faded, and I knew the ancestors were gone.

A silent beat passed through the cliffside, then Doya stood and announced, "We now welcome Vanessa Emberly, our new leader. *Hail to the chieftess!*"

"Hail to the chieftess!" the Koigni echoed.

We all bowed our head reverently in unison.

I thought that was the end of the ceremony, but Vanessa raised her hands and continued. "To my fellow Elementai, allow me to apologize as the chieftess of Koigni House. The Koigni have marginalized their fellow man for far too long. I am ashamed to say it was *my* tribe who orchestrated the genocide of the Anichi people. It was Koigni who rose to power by beating down the Nivita, Toaqua, and Yapluma. It was they who initiated the war between Defortai and Biyami. I refuse to lead this tribe with hate and anger. We are Fire, but there's more to us than rage. Koigni will no longer stand for power, but rather *unity*. Anyone who believes hate reigns above all else is not a member of my tribe, because my tribe is not Koigni. My tribe is Hawkei. We may not share the same element, but we share the same heart."

Tears pricked at my eyes at Vanessa's speech.

"I see you, Elementai," she continued. "I hear you. Teach me— teach the Koigni— how to treat you better— how to *be* better."

To my surprise, Chief Cauac stood. All eyes were on him as he crossed the gap toward Vanessa. He reached out a hand and said, "As the chief of Anichi, we accept your apology and honor your commitment to a better future."

Vanessa shook his hand firmly, and tears began to fall down her face in gratitude. I couldn't help but cry, too.

Liam stood to join the other heads of Houses. "Toaqua also accepts your apology, and we vow to work with you."

"As does Yapluma!" a voice came from the back of the crowd. Everyone turned to look, and I saw Jonah standing in the back. He looked like a total mess, with tears staining his cheeks, but Vanessa must've sparked something in him, because he looked determined.

"And Nivita," Imogen added, squeezing Sassy tight to her chest. She wasn't crying as much as Jonah was, but she looked close to her breaking point. I shook in my chair, trying to hold back sobs.

Jonah stepped into the aisle and marched to the front of the ceremony. Imogen was close behind him.

"I am no chief, but I *am* the Storm Lord," Jonah said. "I speak on behalf of Yapluma today. Your transgressions against us are forgiven, and we will join the other Houses in unity."

Jonah shook Vanessa's hand firmly.

"I have no authority over the Nivita," Imogen started as she glanced around the crowd. "But with their blessing, I would like to step in as a representative."

Several beats of silence passed. Then the first Nivita stood.

"You have my blessing," Trace announced, bowing his head toward his sister.

"And mine," her father added, followed by her mother.

Soon, more and more Nivita stood and bowed their heads reverently. The vote was unanimous to allow Imogen to be the voice of the Nivita.

Imogen turned toward Vanessa. "The Nivita accept your apology. We will do whatever it takes to make amends between our Houses."

Vanessa sniffled, looking touched by the support. Her voice, however, did not waver. "To the ancestors, I make a sacred vow to honor all Houses, and to fight for the equal rights and representations of all Hawkei."

"Anichi joins you in this sacred vow," Chief Cauac announced. He reached a hand out toward Vanessa, and she took it.

"Toaqua joins you in this sacred vow," Liam added, joining hands with Chief Cauac.

Jonah took Liam's hand and repeated the same phrase. "Yapluma joins you in this sacred vow."

Imogen was the last to join, taking Jonah's hand on one side and Vanessa's on the other. The five Houses formed a unified circle. "Nivita joins you in this sacred vow."

I didn't quite understand what was going on, until elements began to rise from the middle of their circle. I gasped. It began as a small flame licking up toward the sky, but the flame grew bigger and bigger. As it rose higher, elements began to swirl within it. Earth rose upward on all sides, and water droplets defied gravity, creating a glittering display around the flames. Air magic conjured a mini cyclone, encompassing the other elements inside. Finally, white wisps of Spirit magic rose out of the ground, entwining with the flames.

My jaw dropped as I took it all in. Higher and higher the elements rose, until a column stood twenty feet high. There was no clear dominant element. They swirled gently and effortlessly together in a beautiful display. The column of elements twisted around the circle of Elementai, until it closed them inside, binding them to their promise.

"I vow that from this day on, the Koigni will shed their ideals of the past," Vanessa announced. "We will no longer tear you down to raise ourselves up, because we know that when you rise, we rise. Koigni will be your equal. This I promise, as the chieftess of Koigni House. You have my word."

Kelsey shot out of her chair. "And my word as well. As a Koigni Elder, I promise to stand beside my fellow Elementai."

My heart hammered, and tears streamed down my cheeks. I couldn't take it any longer. I could not remain silent. Holding Ava-Marie tight to my chest, I stood beside Kelsey. "I, a Koigni Elder, vow to do the same— to uphold the moral standards that apply to *all* Elementai, and to support in any way possible the fair and equal treatment of all members of the Hawkei tribe."

My voice cracked at the last words. Elders from all Houses began to stand to show their support— including those from Anichi and Toaqua.

Doya was the last one left. Several moments of silence passed, and all eyes turned toward her. It was no secret that she had contributed to the marginalization of other tribe members, and most of the tribe hadn't forgiven her for it. I held my breath, hoping beyond hope that my mother had changed.

For the split-second she didn't react, I questioned my beliefs about her. Tears welled in my eyes, begging silently that she would use her voice for good.

To my relief, Doya stood. I hadn't noticed it before, but her hands were shaking. It was one of the very rare times when I witnessed her walls crumbling.

"As a Koigni Elder, I stand beside my chieftess," Doya announced. "I bind myself to this cause in mind, body, and spirit. The Koigni have wronged you for far too long, and I vow that we will do better."

Vanessa broke into sobs. "This is our sacred vow, in the name of the Great Spirit. *Akotee et veni.*"

"*Akotee et veni,*" a chorus rang out.

The swirling elements dissipated, and the Elementai stepped away from Vanessa. She swayed on her feet. Esis drummed his tail on his chair, eager to heal her. We would the second this was over.

Bren stood up. He walked straight to Vanessa and got down on one knee. Even Xavier in his arms bowed his head to his mother.

"Vanessa, my chieftess," Bren said breathlessly. "I serve you, now and forever."

"Bren, honey," she replied kindly. "There is no need to bow."

Bren looked a little uncertain as he got to his feet again. Vanessa reached out for their son, and Bren placed Xavier in her arms. Vanessa held him on her hip and slipped an arm around Bren's neck. It looked natural, but I saw it for what it was. Her face had gone pale, and she looked like she was going to pass out from the pain she'd endured. She'd held on to Bren, so she wouldn't faint in front of everyone. Vanessa was a fighter, and she'd wait until the ceremony was over to collapse.

Bren wrapped his arm around her waist, and Vanessa held her chin up proudly to the crowd, as if presenting her family.

"It is as my grandmother used to say," Vanessa said for everyone to hear. "*My heart is your heart, and together, we are one.* And this is how it shall be, for as long as the Hawkei survive."

I put my fingers in my mouth and blew a shrill whistle, cheering as loudly as I could for my new chieftess. Suddenly, the crowd burst into applause, and it was in that moment I knew— the Koigni had changed, and they would follow Vanessa's call for peace.

No longer did I feel like I was the only one destined to end this war. We were in this together, and we would end this as one tribe.

Liam

SEVENTEEN

Today was finally the day of the long-awaited cabaret. I was glad it was happening, because after today everyone would finally stop talking about it.

After a lot of pleading, I'd convinced Sophia to leave Ava-Marie at my mom's house so we could go on a date to the cabaret together. We hadn't had much alone time at all since she was born, and ever since Sophia had reasoned we'd have to give up our daughter to save the tribe, Ava stuck to Sophia's side like glue. She needed a little bit of a break, even if she didn't want to admit it.

Sophia was in the bathroom, doing her makeup while I slipped on a suit jacket. Jonah had *insisted* the cabaret be black-tie formal. I'd have bitched and moaned any other time, but after what he'd gone through on the *Hozho*, I was willing to give the guy anything he wanted.

Jake was the only reason this play was happening at all. Jonah had wanted to call it off once he'd gotten back, a sure sign he was getting depressed. I didn't blame him. He'd nearly died on the ship. The whole experience had to be traumatic. Though the river had healed his body, his mind was still wounded. He still jumped at loud noises and didn't turn his back to anyone these days. Jake had thought the cabaret was the one thing that might bring some light back into Jonah's eyes.

And maybe the rest of us, too. We needed a little happiness in the world.

"Do I look okay?" Sophia came out of the bathroom, looking nervous.

She wore a fringy black flapper dress with red lipstick and a birdcage veil to fit the 1920's theme, her hair in voluminous curls. Esis was at her feet, fiddling with a black bow tie around his neck.

"You're a total bombshell, babe." I put my arm around her waist and gave her a kiss. She never bothered with how she looked anymore— she was too worried. That made me worried about *her*.

"Well, as long as we hurry back." She chewed her lip nervously.

"Let's just try to have a good time." I took her hand and squeezed it tightly. I just wanted to give us a night off, a night without thinking about stuff. She had to at least try.

We rode Julian to town, where a large crowd had gathered. *Hok'evale* had its own theater, set into the side of a stone cave. It wasn't anything impressive, more or less just a place for school plays. The doors were big enough for Familiars to fit through, and Julian followed us in as we entered the auditorium.

The seats inside had been temporarily removed to make place for tables and chairs. The tables were covered in white cloth, the seats red velvet. They were gathered around a broad stage with a long red curtain, spotlights flashing across it. The tables themselves had bottles of wine chilling in ice, with candles lit in the center and baskets of rolls set out for appetizers. Above us hung long red draperies of fabric. White flowers, levitating in the air by Yapluma magic, danced above our heads. Elementai in 1920's attire conversed with each other and their Familiars, while the band played jazz music for ambiance in the orchestra pit.

Jonah had put *so much* effort into this thing. I was glad Jake had pushed him not to give it up.

I caught sight of Doya and Baine sitting at a table in the middle of the auditorium. Baine's hair had been dyed black, thank the ancestors, and he was wearing a black tuxedo that had to be new, as I'd never seen him wear something that wasn't tattered before.

This cabaret was totally Doya's scene. She wore a red velvet dress with fishnet tights, elbow-length white gloves and an ostrich feather in her curled hair. Naomi sat at her feet and purred, wearing a diamond collar. Doya laughed and threw back another glass of wine elegantly while Baine pined after her like a schoolgirl.

Vanessa and Bren were sitting nearby at a table with Ezra. They waved, and I gave a casual nod. Sophia and I sat at our VIP table at the front. Julian lay down, so the people behind us could see, and Esis hopped on the table, immediately reaching for the rolls. On the left side of us was Jake, at his own table with a bouquet of purple tulips.

"Hey, guys," I heard Sam say, and we turned. His arm was looped in Luana's, who was dressed in a long, glittering white dress that had an impressive slit all the way up her hip. Sierra sat on Zaria's horn. Julian grumbled a greeting to the alicorn and moth.

So he was Luana's date. Interesting.

Sam and Luana sat across from us. *This place looks amazing, doesn't it?* she asked.

"Pretty brilliant," I agreed, signing back. Waiters in tuxedos began darting between tables, filling water and distributing salads. We popped open the wine, and I drank a few glasses— because I knew I would need it to get through whatever Jonah had planned for this mysterious cabaret.

The lights dropped, and the chatter in the auditorium fell silent. The curtains opened, and the spotlights centered on a singular man onstage, the background around him darkened in shadow.

Jonah was wearing a red velvet suit, complete with coattails, a hat, and a jeweled cane. His outfit paled in comparison to his beard and eyebrows, which had been completely coated in red glitter.

His steps were a little more hesitant than they should've been. I tried to chalk it up to nervousness, but I knew better. Jonah loved being the center of attention. What had happened on the *Hozho* was still on his mind. I hoped it wouldn't be by the end of tonight.

Jonah wore a microphone. He bowed to the crowd. "Welcome everyone, to the Grand Cabaret! I am your host, Jonah Chanee. Tonight only, for your entertainment, we have a collection of very talented dancers and singers looking to excite, please, and titillate."

I rolled my eyes. I *knew* he'd throw that word in somewhere.

Jonah winked. "So please, esteemed guests, put your hands together for our opening act and the face of our cabaret, Miss Miranda Summers!"

As Jonah twirled off stage, the stage itself brightened, revealing a complicated set. Two sets of stairs were built in a curve, leading up to a high platform in the middle.

Miranda stood on this platform in front of a microphone. She wore a black feather boa with a glittering red dress. Her kirin, Evelyn, was beside her, wearing a feathered headdress that looked like it belonged on a Vegas showgirl.

Miranda's face was pale. She froze up when she looked at the audience, and it was quiet for a moment.

Evelyn kicked her. Miranda started, and the band jumped into a show tune before Miranda sang the first bar of a song that came from a popular musical.

As Miranda began to sing, Familiars flew out from behind the curtain and lined up in rows. All of them were birds, and they sat on the bannisters of the stairs. There were all kinds, from phoenixes to small songbirds. They began singing with her, creating a background choir.

Miranda could really sing. I'd never heard her sing before, but now I wondered why. She hit all the notes and could belt out a complicated tune better than anyone I knew. Sophia's mouth dropped open in awe as Miranda sang, clearly impressed.

Evelyn began to sway beside her. She used her kirin powers to amplify the sound of Miranda's voice, sending it out on quivering shockwaves that sent shivers down the back of my spine, causing the notes to waver and bend.

Why hadn't Miranda pursued a professional singing career? She had the pipes for it. I knew she wanted to be a Familiar hairdresser, but at the same time, her voice was one I wanted to listen to over and over, and I'm sure others agreed. She was being too humble when she insisted she wasn't any good. She was marvelous.

Toward the end of the song, Dyami waddled onstage, a black tie draped around his neck. He puffed out his chest proudly and joined in with the other birds. He sang along with Miranda in a warble, though it was painful to listen to.

I winced as Dyami sang off-key. The thunderbird's song was more like a croak than a trill, though Miranda's voice managed to save the act.

By the end of the song, the crowd was cheering enthusiastically. Ezra clapped loudly behind us. Dyami put a wing in front of himself and bowed, though I don't think the applause was for him. A few people threw roses onstage at Miranda's feet, and she blushed. Evelyn and the birds collected the roses before they rushed offstage, and the curtain was pulled closed.

The spotlights changed direction, rushing toward the ceiling. Several people gasped. Directly overhead hung Lindsey, suspended from silks that were tied to the ceiling. Her legs wrapped up in the fabric as she began to bend and twist. Medusa was wrapped around her body, snaking up her arms and legs slowly. Lindsey's red hair was free, and she wore nothing but thin red panties.

And she was topless.

Didn't know it was that kind of show, but okay. They did this kind of thing in Paris. I could appreciate *art*.

I knew aerial silk dance was one of Lindsey's hobbies, but I didn't realize how good she was at it until now. As the music played out a slow, sensual song, Lindsey twirled within the confinement of the silks, stretching out to do the splits. She did a variety of tricks, tying the rope around herself so she was suspended in mid-air by only her middle. A few times, she hung only by her legs completely upside down, letting go of the rope with her hands as she twirled in circles.

I felt a bit nervous watching her. She wasn't hooked to anything— there was no safety line. If she made a mistake, she and Medusa could fall and get seriously hurt. She was relying only on her skill to keep her safe. I don't know how she was able to wrap the silks around herself without breaking a leg. She was quick, doing so many twirls and flips.

But damn, she was good. And very entertaining. I found myself holding my breath just as much as I was gasping in surprise. As the music built and picked up speed, Lindsey moved fluidly within the ropes, before she let go completely and began to free fall.

The crowd gasped, and several people screamed. My heart leapt into my throat, thinking Lindsey had made a mistake. But at the last second, Lindsey wrapped her ankle around the silk and caught herself, finishing the dance in a spin that twirled her around at high speed, flinging her arms out wide.

The crowd completely lost it, cheering as Lindsey flipped herself upright. Medusa waved the tip of her tail in farewell, and the curtain opened again.

This time, it was Cade on the platform, sitting on a stool with his guitar in his lap. Miranda was next to him. Miranda sang a Spanish song that sounded familiar, but I couldn't translate.

As the song picked up, Stevie stepped onstage, wearing a red ball gown, and Ezra cheered obnoxiously. She was followed by Arabelle, her brother Teagan, and his canine Familiar. Teagan and Stevie began to ballroom dance together, while Arabelle and Teagan's dog mirrored their movements.

Teagan stepped on Stevie's foot once. She audibly swore, which drew a few laughs from the crowd. Teagan blushed and mouthed *sorry* before the song went on.

Other couples joined the ballroom dance, including Imogen. She was dancing with Trace, before the dance switched and they changed partners, so she could dance with Teagan. Imogen glowed onstage like she belonged there. Her smile was wide as she spun, and though Cade didn't miss a beat on his guitar, his eyes didn't leave her the entire time.

Ezra gave a loud whistle as the curtain drew and Stevie gave a curtsy. "Yeah! That's my baby!"

Stevie blew a kiss to him, then darted off stage. There were a couple more acts from people we didn't know, including a balancing act where a guy and his cat Familiar stood atop a high perch based on a very thin pole, and a hip hop act from James and Carter that felt very nineties.

Eventually the lights rose up, indicating intermission had begun. The waiters flooded back into the room and placed plates of salmon and filet mignon in front of us, with fresh vegetables and cheesecake for dessert. Conversation resumed as we tucked in.

Aw, it looked so good. I was starving. "So how did Jonah rope Cade into this?" I asked.

"Probably with sex from Imogen," Sophia quipped, and Sam laughed.

Sophia was eating instead of pecking at her food, which was something. She must be having a good time.

The lights dimmed again as our plates were taken away. This time, when the curtains opened, it was only Jonah and Squeaks onstage. Jonah had tap shoes. He began to move his feet, and Squeaks copied him, sending tapping noises throughout the auditorium. Squeaks was wearing brand new horseshoes on her hooves, to make her steps clap in time with Jonah's.

Jonah didn't miss a beat as the music went on, but as the music got faster and faster, Squeaks struggled to keep up. She floundered a few times, until eventually, she missed a step on the tap dance and fell on her face, right at the end of the dance.

I heard Sabor groan in the audience. Jonah wasn't looking where he was going and collided with Squeaks' backend. He went tumbling head over heels, careening across the stage and losing his balance.

The song ended right as Jonah fell on his ass. But instead of looking embarrassed, Jonah put on a big smile and threw his arms skyward, like he'd meant to do it.

I heard a big laugh from Jake, and the audience burst into applause. Jonah looked thrilled as Squeaks helped him to his feet. She chirped an apology, but he patted her on the back, and the hippogriff bristled like she was proud.

The cabaret went on, featuring everything from major songs in Broadway musicals to pop songs by Korean superstars. There seemed to be no rules in cabaret. Anything could happen, and I never knew what was coming next.

Toward the end of the show, cancan music blared from the band. Imogen came onstage, along with Stevie, Lindsey, Miranda, and a line of other girls. All of them were wearing matching red and black dresses that were little more than lingerie with bustle skirts, along with feathers in their hair. As expected, they began kicking their legs up in a very fast rendition of the cancan.

A line of Familiars joined them onstage and lined up behind, trying to copy them. It was very cute, and kind of funny, watching Sassy and Squeaks kick their back legs up, sending the skirts on their hindquarters flying. Evelyn kicked too hard, and her skirt came off completely, sailing into the crowd and hitting Baine in the face.

Sophia burst out laughing, and I grinned. It'd been too long since she had laughed.

Finally, there was a drumroll as the last song of the cabaret was played. The curtains drew back, and the spotlight focused on a singular figure on the platform onstage.

Oh. My. Ancestors.

Jonah had gone full speed ahead in all-out drag. He was wearing a purple curly wig, with a lavender corset dress that had huge puffy sleeves, and diamond earrings that were bigger than what Doya would wear. The train on the dress had to be at least ten feet long, with designs of lightning bolts stitched into the fabric. He didn't hold back, right down to the shimmering eyeshadow and purple metallic lipstick. The red glitter on his beard was gone, replaced by violet this time around.

Luana poked me and signed, *What a queen! Total Storm Lord vibes!*

Jonah lifted the microphone and began to sing as the band struck up. When he lifted his skirt to walk down the stairs, I saw he was wearing five inch heels. That he'd found a pair to fit him was a miracle in itself.

Ancestors, it was so over the top. It was so *Jonah*. I snuck a glance at Jake, to see his reaction. This was *definitely* his thing, because right now, Jake was looking at Jonah like he was a snack.

Jonah was a bass singer, so it was really something hearing him sing Barbra Streisand's "Don't Rain on My Parade" in a deep voice while wearing a corset. But shit, he pulled it off. Jonah transitioned from one song into the next, and people began joining him onstage. Miranda came on to sing a duet. Squeaks followed, her cancan costume gone and replaced with purple glitter edging her wings. The rest of the cast joined them, singing along as the show was brought to a close. Imogen, Lindsey and Stevie wrapped their arms around each other's waists and swayed on the last bar. As Jonah ended the song, fireworks burst from the end of the stage, and confetti fell from the ceiling, coating both the performers and audience.

As the show ended, the crowd leapt to their feet, giving a standing ovation. The cast had huge smiles on their faces. Jonah had tears welling up in his eyes. Miranda pulled a tissue out of her bosom and handed it to him, and he dotted at his eyelids gently. The curtain closed, but the audience kept clapping for a full five minutes afterward, even as the waiters began cleaning off tables.

As much as I complained about the cabaret, I appreciated it. It was fun, and it'd been a well-needed distraction.

That was a great show! Luana signed in excitement. I knew she couldn't hear the songs, but she could feel the vibrations, and she could appreciate the dancers and costumes. *Jonah outdid himself!*

"He really did," Sophia agreed eagerly. "Come on, we should go congratulate him."

There was a cocktail party at *The Falcon's Nest* afterward to celebrate. It took a while to squeeze through the crowd leaving the auditorium, especially with Julian's big ass, but we eventually made it to the restaurant.

Esis had eaten one too many rolls at the cabaret and was feeling sick. Julian took him back home, so Sophia and I could join the party.

It was already packed when we got there. Most of the cast was already here, though they'd changed out of their costumes. Some people were dressed casually, though I saw Jonah had changed into his third outfit of the night, a deep violet tuxedo. His hair was tied up, and the glitter from his beard was gone, though Squeaks still had it edged on her wings. He held the tulip bouquet that Jake had gotten him, shoulders seemingly lighter than they had been in days.

"Jonah!" Sophia squealed and jumped on him, giving him a hug. "You did wonderful!"

Jonah hugged her back. "Thanks, babe. It's about time you all acknowledged my musical genius."

I rolled my eyes. "You did a good job, man. Really."

Jonah gave a scoff. "I wasn't expecting high praise from *you*."

"You knew you weren't gonna get it." I laughed.

Imogen came up behind us and plumped her hair. "Wasn't it the best show?" she gushed. "Everyone says it was so amazing."

Jonah batted his eyelashes. "Well, you did have an excellent *director*."

He emphasized the word and dragged out the ending, making it sound totally annoying.

Imogen took the tulips from Jonah. "I think I'll take these," she teased. "You'll want someone to hold on to them."

"Excuse me, bitch? For what?" Jonah blinked.

Imogen jostled the bouquet. "You'll see."

My eyes edged the room for Jake. I saw him somewhere in the back with Sabor, waiting for the right moment. Squeaks chittered in anticipation, though I smacked her in the side to tell her to shut up. She grumbled and kicked at me, knocking me into the bar.

As Jonah sat down at a booth, Jake signaled Lani. She turned the music down, and Jake crossed the restaurant in a few strides. Conversation died down, and Jonah's eyes became wide as Jake stopped in front of him. Everyone in the room turned to observe Jake as the moment dragged out.

Jake cleared his throat. "Jonah, I'd like to congratulate you on your spectacular performance tonight. You've given everyone, including me, something to hope for in this war."

Jake paused, and Sabor gave an impatient click from his beak, as if pushing Jake to go on. "You've given all of us happiness tonight. But most importantly, you've given *me* happiness. I hope I do the same for you. I know we haven't known each other for a very long time. But I don't think time is important, when a man is truly in love and he believes he's found the one."

Jake got down on one knee. From his pocket, he procured a small black box, which he opened slowly. In the box was a silver wedding band lined with several large diamonds, set into the metal.

Jake took a deep breath. "Jonah Chanee, would you do me the honor of—"

Jonah gave a shrill squeal that broke the eardrums of everyone in the restaurant and plucked the box from Jake's hand. He held it up to the light and shouted, "Yes, yes, a thousand times *yes!!!*"

Squeaks clacked her hooves on the floor in celebration. Jonah jumped up from the booth. Jake slipped the ring on his finger, and Jonah took him in his arms, dipping him down so they could have a deep kiss.

Luana jumped up and down and clapped, while Sophia, Imogen and I all shared a smile. We all knew he was gonna do it. A week ago, Jake had sat the three of us down and talked to us about it. He wasn't so much asking permission as asking for a blessing. Jonah's parents weren't around and they didn't really give a shit about him anyway, so Jake wanted to ask the people who did.

Each of us said yes. After the *Hozho*, it was clear there'd never be anyone else for Jonah but Jake.

Jonah rushed over to us and screamed, "You guys! Did you know about this?"

"We might've," I said.

"You're all hos not for telling me. I was completely unprepared!" Jonah shouted. "I wanted to have this big speech planned and everything, and instead I went totally speech*less*!"

"That's how a proposal is supposed to go," Sophia said. "You're supposed to be dumbfounded."

"Forget about that. Now we can finally plan your wedding!" Imogen sang.

Jonah's eyes brightened. He puzzled as he put a hand to his beard and said, "OMG, there's so much to plan. Color scheme. I need a color scheme. What do you think, purple and white, or purple on purple? No, too gaudy. Never mind, there's no such thing as too gaudy."

"You have time for all that. Enjoy the engagement!" Sophia pushed Jonah into the crowd. He rejoined Jake. Jake put his hand on the middle of Jonah's back with a smile as they received congratulations from the crowd.

Jonah went around the restaurant, showing off his ring and his man to anyone who listened. I had a thought and groaned.

"What is it?" Imogen asked.

"We just got done with this cabaret," I complained. "Now he's never gonna shut up about his wedding."

"If he has one," Sophia said quietly.

That caused me to freeze. As much as I hated to admit it... she had a point. The Elders were growing bolder, and Oleander was running out of options. Another battle was on the horizon, and quickly approaching. This war was coming to a head soon.

If we lost— or worse, anything happened to Jake or Jonah— they'd never get to be together. The Elders would take their happy ending away.

"Don't say stuff like that, Soph. Of course it'll happen," I told her.

Imogen's face hardened. "I will *make* Jonah's wedding happen. Even if I have to march to Kinpago and shove dirt down Oleander's throat to do it," she pledged. She grabbed Sophia's arm and pulled her forward. "Now come on. Let's party."

Sophia danced with Luana and Imogen in the middle of the restaurant, but it was half-heartedly. I sat at the bar and had a drink. I hated seeing my wife like this, but I was out of ideas on how to make her feel better. To be honest, I didn't think I had any standing to do that in the first place.

Nothing could help having to give away your kid.

Imogen scowled and walked over. Sophia was distracted in a conversation with Luana, so she didn't notice. Imogen leaned on the bar. "Do you really need that? You had one before I left this afternoon."

"I'm fine," I said, which was a lie. I was kind of glad she'd caught me at it.

"You need to stop, Liam. You're going down a path you don't want to wander," she warned.

She was right. Nobody needed a drunk chief, so I ended on my current round and turned to water.

Imogen leaned in and dropped her voice. "You know, if you're looking to get away, there's some hot springs not too far from here. It'd be good for you and Sophia to loosen up. You guys need a mini-vacation."

That got my attention. "Where's it at?"

"Within the boundary. If you follow the main path to the north of town, you'll see the entrance. It's marked with a sign. It's closed after five, but nobody will notice if you sneak in."

"How do you know about it?"

Imogen wiggled her eyebrows. "Cade and I visited a few times. It's where all the couples in *Hok'evale* go to get some space."

Space sounded nice. Maybe I'd stop feeling like I was suffocating. "Thanks, Im."

She bounded over to Cade. I wandered behind Sophia and touched her on the arm. She was fiddling with a glass absentmindedly. "Huh?" she asked.

"Let's get out of here," I said. "Imogen suggested a place we should explore."

"What about Jonah?" She looked at him. He was currently surrounded by a gang of girls, flashing his ring and fawning.

"He's not gonna realize we're gone. He's too busy planning the wedding," I pointed out.

Her expression twisted. "We should get back to the baby."

"We won't be long." I tugged on her, and she reluctantly complied.

We left the restaurant out the back entrance and followed the main road to the north like Imogen had suggested. We stopped at home to change into jeans so we wouldn't get our nice clothes dirty, though I hardly cared. I had too many suits now, and was wearing them too often these days. Probably the worst part about being chief.

Finally, we came to another cave entrance. This one was noticeably smaller than the others in the area, only big enough for a few people to walk through at a time. There was a sign that said *Hok'evale Hot Springs* outside the entrance, as well as an indication of hours. The entryway was roped off, but I ducked under it, and Sophia followed. She took off her sneakers and walked barefoot on the warm stone as we entered the small cave.

The hallways were narrow, six feet across or so. But as we progressed into the cave, I saw overhead that the cave opened up to the starry sky, shining moonlight downward. The cave widened, and I felt the air around me become muggy and hot as steam rose around us.

We came to a wide room. Here, there were several round pools set into the stone, bubbling and swirling. There was laughter ahead of us. Stevie and Ezra were in one of the pools, fooling around. Both of them were naked, but their hips were submerged underwater. Stevie's chest was pressed to Ezra's front so we didn't see anything. Looks like they had the same idea we did.

Not that they were bashful about it. "Hey, bro-in-law," Stevie called out, like this was a family gathering. "Fancy seeing you here."

"We came to get some privacy," I said. Imogen was right about this being the stop for every couple in town. Should've known these two would be here.

"Well, you can't join us. There are more pools down the way," Ezra said. "Get your own."

"Geez, we're going," Sophia said in a teasing way. Ezra made the water rise up and splash her feet. She yelped and shot a fireball at him, which fizzled out before it reached his head.

"Those two screw like rabbits," Sophia commented as we headed down the next hallway.

"It runs in the family," I joked as I drew her close.

We entered another room, where magical creatures swam in some of the pools. Most of them were reptiles, like turtles with diamond shells, or iguanas whose skin reflected the moonlight like mirrors. They were enjoying the heat that the pools emitted. Most of them just blinked at us as we walked by, though a toad the size of a cat let out a disgruntled croak at being interrupted.

I didn't feel comfortable finding a pool of our own until Stevie's laughter had long faded. We came to a secluded room that had a huge ceiling, where we could see multiple constellations and the moon overhead. Sophia dropped her shoes by the biggest pool and slipped out of her clothes.

I tossed my clothes on a rock nearby and observed Sophia's naked body as the moon kissed her skin. Didn't matter how much time had passed or what changed in the world, she'd always be beautiful to me. Looking at her was like looking at the moon itself. She was something to be honored and revered.

Sophia stepped into the pool, and I followed her. The water was hot, to the point of being nearly unbearable. Yet in a way, it was almost soothing. Sophia dipped her head underwater and came up, giving a sigh. "It's perfect. Just the right temperature."

Course she'd think so. Sophia turned around and moved her hair. I noticed two new tattoos across from the daisy she'd gotten for Imogen. On the shoulder opposite the composite daisy, she had my name and Ava-Marie's tattooed in cursive. I'd seen them before, but hadn't mentioned them... and she hadn't either.

Sophia noticed my curious look. "I wanted something permanent."

"We're not going away," I said, before I realized my poor choice of words. I was an idiot.

"Sometimes it feels like it."

"Don't say that."

She looked away from me. "You brought me here to forget. Let's not talk about it tonight."

I didn't know if we'd ever talk about it. We hadn't discussed what we were going to do with Ava-Marie ever since Lindsey and Miranda turned us down. We were stalling, trying to buy as much time as we could... because we knew if we didn't have a plan, didn't make a clear decision, we wouldn't have to face the day when we'd have to give her up.

It was selfish. We couldn't keep doing this to our little girl. In war, you made sacrifices— sometimes ones that could break you.

But the thought of Ava-Marie dead was far worse than the thought of her being taken away from me. I wouldn't allow that to happen. I'd give up everything if it meant she could have one more day. We had to do something about this situation. We were running out of time.

Not tonight, though. Tonight was about us.

Sophia started kissing me— probably because she wanted me to stop talking. Or maybe it was because she needed me. I wasn't certain. Wasn't sure of much these days.

She tasted like the wine from the cabaret, red merlot. I drank from her, because she was the only substance I needed to keep moving forward. We sank low until our shoulders were submerged, and the only sound in the background was the water swirling in the pools around us.

We hadn't come together like this in a few weeks. Ever since the *Hozho* went down, we knew what we had to do. To be happy like this felt like a betrayal.

We couldn't live like this forever, though. We needed the escape sex provided. Even if it was just for a moment in time.

As Sophia kissed me, she wrapped her legs around my hips and pressed against me. I moved her upward, burying my face in her breasts. The water stirred against our bodies as I dove into her, my fingers running along her velvet skin, digging into her back as I fought against release. I could hear her breathy gasps as I came against her, my body shuddering. I put my face in the fringes of her wet hair as we moved, and smelled the scent of her perfume. Flowers, and a bit of sunlight. Sophia smelled like summer. Summer was nice to think about when you felt like dark winter was never going to end. Spring had come to *Hok'evale*, but it hadn't come for us.

Sophia fisted her hands in my hair and put her forehead against mine as she came. I let myself go at the same time, releasing my body, my spirit, everything, emptying it into her until I felt like a man who had nothing left to give.

Sophia didn't let me go even after we'd finished. She clung to me like I was her life.

We're not going away. It felt like such a lie.

For a long time, we just stood there and held each other. We were falling to pieces, but at least we were crumbling together as a unit, instead of apart.

We stayed in the hot spring until eventually, I could no longer stand the heat and we had to get out. I dried us off, and we got dressed. We explored the cave for a little while, voiceless, until I heard familiar voices up ahead.

Imogen, Jonah and Luana were wandering the hot springs. Sassy and Sierra were with them, but Squeaks was noticeably absent— she was too big to fit in these caves.

Sophia and I both plastered on masks and smiles. Neither of us wanted our friends to see us like this.

"We thought we'd find you guys down here," Imogen teased. "Have fun in the pools?"

"They're really nice. We'll have to come back," Sophia suggested. She sent a glance at Jonah. "What are you doing down here? Thought you hated caves."

"They're open to the air," Jonah said, pointing upward. "I don't mind it as much if there's not a roof."

"Shouldn't you be busy with your new *fiancé*?" Sophia asked in a toying jibe.

"Cade, James and Carter took him out for celebratory beers," Jonah said with a sigh. "Besides, I think it's best I'm with you guys right now. His proposal has me *so horny,* and I'd totally jump him if we were alone at the moment. We're so close to getting married now, I don't want to throw it all away and give up the purity vow."

"Kudos to you for sticking to it," Sophia said. "You're almost at the finish line."

"I know, right? Yay me!" Jonah gushed, before his voice took on a nervous tone. "Okay, to be honest, I'm kinda freaking out. I might've glimpsed it when he got out of the shower the other day, and I tell you now, it's *not* gonna fit."

"Let us know how you really feel," I said flatly.

"I'm serious!" Jonah whined. "His D has me shaking! Sophia, how do you handle it?"

"Lots of practice," she replied.

"And lube," Imogen commented. The girls cracked up.

I've come to these springs since I was little, Luana signed, before she giggled. *Though I've never snuck in before. How exciting.*

"You wanna bring *Sam* down here?" Imogen said playfully as she signed, and Luana turned pink.

"Yeah, what was that earlier?" Jonah asked, rounding on Luana with a hand on his hip. "Give us details, girl!"

Luana shook her head and signed, *I don't kiss and tell.*

"So you *did* kiss him," Jonah gasped. "How juicy."

Luana blushed even harder. I took pity on her and changed the subject. "I wonder how far these caves go," I said, peering down a long hallway. "We have to be getting to the end of them."

"I don't know, but let's find out," Imogen said curiously. Sassy led the way, and Sierra trailed ahead as we wound through the halls of the springs.

Eventually, the hot springs ended. We no longer heard the rushing of water. Jonah was complaining he wanted to turn around and go back home, until Sophia lifted a hand and said, "Hold up. I think there's something up ahead."

"What do you mean?" I moved closer to her. Sophia didn't respond, just slipped herself through a narrow slit in the cave wall.

The rest of us followed. We had to yank and push on Jonah to squeeze him through the tiny space, but once we did, my jaw dropped open in amazement.

We were in the biggest room of all in the caves. The moon shone down directly overhead, its light casting on five wooden chests in the center of the room that were collected in a circle.

"Ooh! Buried treasure!" Jonah gushed.

"It's not buried treasure if it's not in the ground," Imogen said in irritation.

Sophia proceeded toward the first chest. They looked old— decades, if not centuries. They were lined with a thin layer of dust. Sophia blew some off the lock and coughed. "I wonder what's inside..." she whispered.

I began wiping dust off the trunks. Each one had a lock that was forged with each of the House symbols— Koigni, Toaqua, Nivita, Yapluma, and Anichi.

"Um, you go opening that, you're gonna release a thousand-year-old Hawkei curse, I bet," Jonah swore.

"Things can't possibly get any worse," I argued, which was stupid to say, because they always could. But my curiosity outweighed my caution. I knelt by the Toaqua chest and clicked open the lock. The lid lifted without any hesitancy, though I had to push upward on it to break the rust coating the hinges.

"Wow," Imogen breathed as she looked inside. "Liam, do you realize what this is?"

I reached inside and lifted up a heavy leather garment, painted blue, the inside lined with white wolf's fur. The outside of the coat was layered with whale bone and turquoise for defense. There were beads and feathers sewn onto the fabric. Designs of sea creatures had been painted on the back in the traditional Hawkei style.

"Toaqua chief armor," I marveled. "I've never seen anything like it. So much of what we had was destroyed. This has to be at least a hundred years old."

And it was still in top shape. To experiment, I stood up and slipped it on. It fit perfectly, like it'd been made for me. Inside the chest were matching leather boots and pants.

Luana was the next to open a chest. She lifted the lid of the Anichi trunk and pulled out a long white cape. The armor was made of braided cotton and was in two pieces, the top a beaded breastplate, the bottom a long skirt that had slits for the legs on both sides, leaving the midriff exposed. Gauntlets that were the same color as the breastplate matched the beaded sandals that came with it.

Healer armor! She signed in triumph. *This is what the Anichi wore when they entered battle!*

Jonah's worry about a thousand-year-old curse immediately lifted when he realized there was stuff to get out of it. He rushed over to the Yapluma chest and tossed the lid open, letting out a dramatic gasp. "Storm Lord armor!"

Jonah yanked the armor out of the chest. He pulled out a purple silk shirt and pants, with several sections of flat silver metal that pieced together over the chest, arms and legs. The armor came with purple slip-on shoes, as well as a long violet coat embroidered with silver thread in a geometric shape around the edges. The coat fell all the way down to his ankles, and was honestly more like a cloak. The armor was Hawkei, but definitely had some Middle Eastern influences for Yapluma.

Imogen opened her trunk next. The armor inside was leather, painted green and designed in the shape of leaves, interlocking to connect over the torso and limbs. The breastplate was a laced corset, threaded with golden ties. The gauntlets were also leather, but designed to be in the shape of tree bark, with knee-high boots to match.

Nivita armor. Imogen's face twisted as she began to fit the pieces on her body. "This is getting a little weird."

Sophia was the last to open her trunk. She began lifting pieces of Koigni armor out of it, piece by piece. They were alternating colors of black and red, made of a combination of leather and cotton. The main piece was a red robe that was knee-length. Black beads and white bone were sewn into the heavy cotton, making a fire pattern. The gauntlets were designed to look like flames, while black feathers were sewn into the shoulders.

Sophia looked mystified by the Koigni armor as she turned it in her hands. She clutched the robe to her chest, while Jonah slipped his on and paraded around like he was some kind of king.

"Okay, doesn't anyone think it's odd we're finding ancient armor in the middle of some nowhere cave, and it fits us all correctly?" Imogen asked. "No offense, Jonah, but you're bigger than a horse."

"Excuse me?" Jonah gasped in outrage. He deliberately made a show of sweeping the coat behind him dramatically.

"Wait." Sophia bent down over the Koigni chest. In her hand was a yellowed note. Sophia unfolded it carefully and began to read aloud, her eyes widening with each word.

To my descendent,

By the time you read this, many years will have passed, and I will long be gone. I have prepared special armor for you and your friends, by the best craftsmen of each House. You will need it in the days to come.

Showana Harjo

My mouth fell open. "To my descendent... but Soph, that means—"

"I'm a descendent of Showana Harjo! She's one of my ancestors!" Sophia said in excitement. "She must be a relative of my Anichi grandfather, on Doya's line!"

Imogen tapped her chin. "You know what? *That's* why you were able to speak to Showana, at the Anichi temple! I thought Ancestors' Day would enable you to talk to any ancestor even if you weren't related, but you were able to communicate with her so easily. You must share her blood!"

She must've had a vision and put the armor here for us, Luana signed. *It's been waiting for years for us to discover it.*

"Makes sense," I agreed. It was a very *naderei* thing to do, to leave things behind to prepare the prophesied one for war. Maddie would do something similar.

"You must be related to Madame Wells, too, like a distant cousin," Jonah suggested to Sophia. "Both of you have Anichi ancestry. You two must come from Showana's line."

Optimism grew in Sophia's tone. "Does this mean I can reach out to Showana? Maybe she'll talk to us about the prophecy," Sophia said. "What if we got it wrong? What if we can keep Ava?"

I frowned. "I don't think so, Soph. When we spoke to Madame Wells, Showana made it pretty clear she wanted you to figure this out on your own."

Sophia's eyes blazed with determination. "It doesn't matter. I can't give up now. I'm still going to try. Maybe if I ask Showana myself, I can convince her we need answers!"

I hoped so. For all our sakes.

EIGHTEEN

I was surprised to learn Showana was my ancestor, but the more I thought about it, the more it made sense. I was part Anichi, and I *had* communicated with her easily on Ancestors' Day. Was that why I'd been chosen? And more, was that why I'd been asked to give up Ava-Marie — because my daughter was the descendant of a *naderei*, born in the middle of this war? I had to find out.

I waited until long after Liam had fallen asleep. It must've been past midnight by now. Ava-Marie slept soundlessly in her crib, and Esis and Buttercup snored in unison at the foot of the bed. I rolled out of bed quietly, tip-toeing across the room. I wore sweats and a baggy t-shirt. I slipped on my coat and left out the back of the house, to the gardens.

The caves opened to a large hole above my head, and stars twinkled in the night sky. Beautiful foliage surrounded me, but it was nothing more than shadows at this time of night. I could hear crickets chirping and the hoot of a Familiar in the distance.

I walked to the center of the gardens and knelt to my knees. Showana wasn't my spirit guide, and I couldn't summon her myself outside of Ancestors' Day. But she *was* my ancestor, and I hoped that if I prayed, she would hear my cry for help.

"Showana?" I whispered, but my voice cut harshly through the night. It seemed too loud in the beautiful garden. I bowed my head and cleared my throat. "Showana, are you there? I need to talk to you. I have so many questions."

A shiver traveled down my spine. "Questions about my daughter... about this prophecy," I continued. "Is this the path you intended for me— to give my daughter up, an innocent life for the tribe?"

No... the ancestors would not wish to sacrifice a baby. Perhaps that was why I'd held on to Ava-Marie so long, because deep down, I refused to believe the Great Spirit would allow anyone to hurt her.

And yet, so many Hawkei had perished before, including children. I was a fool to think they would not do this to me... to my family.

"Showana, I need answers." My voice cracked. "What do I need to do to win this war?"

I was met by nothing but silence. The thought of giving my daughter up chilled me to the bone. Frustration started to grow inside of me as I knelt there, waiting for an answer that didn't come.

"*Please*, ancestors. Somebody tell me what to do!" I begged. Tears began to streak down my cheeks.

And still, no one answered.

I waited, expecting a voice to come through in the wind. I glanced around earnestly, hoping a spirit would appear. But nothing happened. I was alone.

"How do you expect me to win this war!? I don't know what to do!" I cried. My voice echoed off the sides of the caves, and my chest compressed, as if a dragon was sitting on it. "I don't know how to use the *Azaimperiai*. I don't know how giving up my daughter will save us. I don't know what you want from me!"

Tears rushed out of my eyes faster. For so long, I'd gone along with what the ancestors wanted. I vowed to do as they asked. But without answers, I felt useless— hopeless. How could I do as they asked if they weren't clear with their requests? It was maddening.

"Showana, Viola, Great Spirit, *anyone*!" I screamed. "Help me! I will serve you, if you just tell me what to do!"

Sobs broke out in my chest, and I leaned over, pressing my forehead to the ground. I fisted my hands in the dirt as my tears soaked the soil. I couldn't accept this, yet what other choice did I have? I was suffering— my people were suffering— and those we prayed to chose to be silent.

Minutes passed, and nobody came to my aid. Part of me wished Liam would wake and come out here to find me— because at least if he was here, I wouldn't be alone.

But I was. And even when I had my family and friends around me, we were all alone— abandoned by the ancestors. It was like they didn't even care anymore, like they were happy to let us kill each other off. Were we all that big of a disappointment?

I wanted to go back to Liam. I needed him to hold me right now. I got up to head back inside, but I hesitated and turned to the gardens.

"You can't do this to me!" I burst. "You can't name me your chosen one and then leave me in the dark! What is this? A test? Because without your guidance, you'll make damn sure I'm going to fail. If the Hawkei perish, it's on *you*. Screw you, Showana. If you wanted to save the Hawkei, you could've done a damn better job."

I whirled around and headed back inside, wiping my tears as I went.

Liam stirred when I entered the bedroom. "*Pawee,* what are you doing?"

He couldn't see my tears through the darkness. I steadied my voice. "Just went to get some fresh air."

I crawled into bed beside him and laid my head on his chest. He wrapped me in his arms, and my shoulders relaxed, though the knot in my chest felt tighter than ever.

"Liam?" I whispered. "Do you think the ancestors still care about us?"

"Of course they do, Soph," he said sleepily. "The ancestors wouldn't abandon us."

He said it like it was an absolute— like there was no chance we'd ever be left alone. But he was wrong.

We'd been abandoned. Left to die.

&

I spent the better part of the next week cursing the ancestors, trying to get them to prove they hadn't left us. I called for Showana day in and day out to provide us with answers, but she never answered my prayers.

Without answers from her, I wasn't about to go making plans to give my baby girl up. If the ancestors didn't want to tell me what to do, then I wasn't going to do it— and that meant I wasn't going to sacrifice my daughter for their sick war.

In fact, I was seriously considering leaving the resistance altogether. It was selfish and heartless, and I knew that. But at this point, I wasn't feeling like the ancestors really needed us anymore.

I'd pretty much made up my mind about it. If the Great Spirit didn't want to help us, and neither did the ancestors, there was no point in sticking around. I was taking my husband and kid and getting the fuck out of *Hok'evale*.

I knew it was the frustrated Koigni in me that had made the decision. But honestly, what other choice did we have? Sit around here and wait to die? Wait to lose Ava-Marie?

No. I wouldn't go that far.

"Liam, can we talk?" I suggested on Saturday.

Maddie was over, playing with Ava-Marie and the kurbles. Liam watched them from afar, really taking in the moment.

"Sure," he said. "What's up?"

I glanced toward Maddie, who was tickling Ava-Marie's feet in the living room. "Not here. Can we go for a walk?"

Liam's face fell. He knew it was serious. "Sure. Hey, Mads. Can you watch Ava for a few?"

"Absolutely," she said, without looking up from Ava's adorable features. "You two go make more babies."

"Mads, that's not—" Liam started.

She waved him off. "Just go."

The air was warm when we left the house. Esis scurried along at our feet. It was a beautiful spring day, and *Hok'evale* was alive. Musicians played in the streets, and children danced to the beat of a drum. Julian, Eirakari, and Aisha led a dragon's dance in a clearing nearby. Familiars frolicked through lawns, and butterflies fluttered up and down the street, leaving trails of glitter in their wake. Flowers of all different colors bloomed throughout the canyon, and Esis jumped from one to another, skimming his paws along the petals.

I hated the thought of leaving this place. It'd become our home.

"What is it you want to talk about, *pawee*?" Liam asked as we walked.

I took a deep breath. Where did I even begin? "Do you feel like we've hit a dead end?"

Liam gazed ahead with a far-away look in his eye. "Every day. It feels like we're just waiting for Oleander to strike."

"We are," I stated bluntly. "Once he rebuilds his noxite arsenal, our waiting will be over."

Liam sighed. "I know we're running out of time to send Ava away—"

"We've run out of time for everything!" I pointed out. "There are no more prophecy pieces. Showana's not giving us any more answers. This is it — and I'm afraid we're not prepared to win this war."

Liam stopped and turned to me, brow furrowed. "We're as prepared as we can be. What are you trying to say, *pawee?*"

"I'm saying I think we should— ow!"

Something poked my ass. I whirled around to see Squeaks standing there, nudging my butt with her beak.

"Squeaks," Jonah scolded, though he was laughing. He carried three shopping bags and was flanked by Imogen and Luana, along with their Familiars. Each of the girls was wearing a headband with a unicorn horn on it. Esis squealed and jumped onto Squeaks' back.

Liam's features brightened when he saw the three of them approaching. He seemed to forget our conversation altogether— that, or he was glad to avoid it. "Hey, guys. Didn't think we'd run into you."

"We're wedding shopping!" Imogen said, twirling around so that her skirt billowed around her knees.

Jonah's considering letting the bridesmaids wear these to the reception, Luana signed, pointing to her headband. *We got you one, too, Sophia.*

I signed back. "That's really sweet, but—"

"Sophia! Liam!" Another voice called from down the road.

I rolled my eyes. "What does a girl have to do to get a private moment with her husband?"

I sighed and turned around to see Baine running our way, waving a thick tome in our direction.

"*Pataa?*" I asked. "Is something wrong?"

Baine stopped beside us and caught his breath. "Wrong? Not at all. Just wanted to catch you before I lost you. I was just on my way with some interesting news."

"What kind of news?" Imogen asked. She eyed the heavy book in his hand, looking interested. It seemed ancient and had Anichi writing on the front.

Baine glanced around the street, then gestured to us. "This way. It's something you all need to hear."

"Ooh, good," Jonah said. "We showed up just in time."

Yeah, perfect. Now I was going to have a hell of a time figuring out when to tell Liam I wanted to get the heck out of dodge.

Baine led us down the street, to a small alcove in the canyon where we wouldn't be overheard. Sassy trotted on ahead and curled onto a rock. Luana and Imogen sat beside her. Squeaks tried to sit next to them, but she practically squashed Imogen. Im slapped Squeaks' ass until she moved. I stayed standing with Esis in my arms.

"What did you find?" Liam asked.

"It's strange, really. I was going through my books for information on the *Azaimperiai*, when I came across this." Baine held up the huge book in his hands. "I've never seen it before. I don't know how it got into my house, but it has some valuable information in it."

"Can we trust it?" Liam asked.

"I have no reason to doubt it," Baine said. "It looks completely legitimate."

Can I see? Luana signed.

Baine handed her the book, and she ran her fingers over the cover. Esis hopped out of my arms and onto the rock beside her. He peeked over the spine of the book to get a good look.

It's a legitimate Anichi record for sure, Luana assured us. *Though it belongs in the Hall of Records. Are you sure you didn't get it from there and forgot?*

Baine furrowed his brow. "It's possible... but no matter. The information inside is useful."

"What does it say?" Jonah asked.

Baine's eyes brightened. "It's something I've been researching for a very long time, something I didn't have the answer to until now."

"Will you just spit it out, *pataa*?" I asked, getting irritated.

"This book tells us how to make an *Azaimperiai*!" he exclaimed.

I gaped. "So it could tell us how to use it?"

Baine chewed his lower lip. "Perhaps. I haven't translated it yet. But I believe there is something to learn from its creation."

"So, how *do* you make an *Azaimperiai*?" Imogen asked.

"It's a transfer of energy, much like transference," Baine explained. "But it's much more advanced magic. It takes so much energy, you must trade your life for it."

"Trade your life?" I balked. "You said Showana made our *Azaimperiai*. So she... she *died* to make it?"

How could a woman who gave up her life for this cause have abandoned us? It didn't add up.

"According to the text I translated, Showana would have indeed given her life to create this *Azaimperiai*," Baine said. "To create such a powerful object, you must die."

"So she put her life energy into the tomahawk and dropped dead?" Imogen asked. "I see why not many people create them."

"Not exactly," Baine answered. "Creating an *Azaimperiai* is not something all Hawkei can do. You must be incredibly strong. Showana had the power to create one because of her *naderei* strength. Performing the ritual would've taken years off her life, and practically stripped her of her powers. After the ritual took place, she'd have wasted away over time, much like if a cancer had taken over her body. She probably had a year afterward to get her affairs in order before she passed away of a painful death."

"That's worse," Jonah said. "Creating an *Azaimperiai* becomes a curse, a suffering."

Liam shifted uncomfortably at my side, and it made my guts churn. He'd already suffered so much. A year was nothing to him.

Baine nodded. "Yes, which is why even those most powerful refuse to create such an object. It's an example of the ultimate sacrifice."

Luana gasped, and we all turned to look at her. Her eyes remained fixed on the page she was reading. It took her a few seconds to notice we'd all stopped to stare. Esis' hands went over his mouth, like he too was shocked.

"What is it?" Baine asked, signing when she raised her head. "Can you translate it?"

My Anichi is rough, but I know enough, Luana replied. *According to this passage,* Azaimperiai *magic can be transferred.*

Baine furrowed his brow and signed back. "Yes, as I said, it is a transfer of magic from one person into the object."

Luana shook her head. *That's not what I meant.* Azaimperiai *magic can be transferred* after *an object is created.*

"You mean, to another object?" Baine balked. He took the book out of her hand and peered closely at the page, but I could tell by the slow movement of his eyes he struggled to translate.

Luana's eyes brightened. *This could be why the tomahawk doesn't work! Because the magic was transferred into something else. It used to be an* Azaimperiai, *but it's not anymore.*

"But the tomahawk was protected," Liam protested. "It *has* to be the one."

"Luana might be right," I said. "If the *Azaimperiai* magic was still there, I'd be able to use it."

Jonah groaned. "We're looking for *another Azaimperiai?* Ancestors, I don't think we can wait that long."

Jonah was fucking right. It felt like the ancestors were sending us in circles. Why couldn't we just get some answers already and stop playing this stupid game? Maybe they *wanted* us to give up.

I think we should talk to my dad, Luana suggested. *He may know something about this.*

We all agreed talking to Chief Cauac was a good idea. We walked through the village, until we came to the temple in the center of town. Luana led us to the Anichi Council quarters at the back, and Esis scurried up to the door to knock. He barely made a sound, so we let ourselves in. Inside, Chief Cauac was alone with his companion, meditating cross-legged on the floor. His eyes opened slowly when he heard us approach.

"Hello," he said brightly. "To what do I owe the pleasure?"

We have some questions about this book, Luana signed.

Chief Cauac tilted his head, and Baine handed the book over. Cauac studied it for a moment before his eyes widened. "Where did you find this?"

Baine opened his mouth, but he stumbled over his words. "I-it appeared in my home, Chief."

Chief Cauac furrowed his brow and stood. "Shut the door. Hurry."

Jonah rushed to shut the door behind us, leaving us in privacy.

Chief Cauac rounded the council table and sat at his chair. He plunked the book in front of him and started flipping through the pages. "I can't believe it! This is the *Anichi Book of Secrets*. It's been lost since the war."

My heart gave a start. How had this book shown up out of the blue like this?

A moment later, the answer struck. Perhaps Showana hadn't abandoned us at all. Perhaps she had placed this book in Baine's possession as an answer to my prayers. I felt a new sense of hope as I eyed the book.

Pataa, did you know Azaimperiai *magic could be transferred between objects?* Luana demanded.

Chief Cauac's jaw dropped, but he quickly signed back. "I may have some information that is privy to Anichi Elders alone."

"Why didn't you tell us this when we came to you about the *Azaimperiai*?" Liam practically growled. He wasn't happy we were just learning this now. I wasn't, either. We'd waited too long for valuable information like this.

"I believed the tomahawk *was* the true *Azaimperiai*," Chief Cauac defended. "I still believe it. The transfer of *Azaimperiai* magic is an Anichi secret alone, and a power no other House possesses. But Anichi hasn't *had* power since the war, not since the *Azaimperiai* was created. No one could have made the transfer."

I glanced over to Luana, who looked like she was thinking hard. "That's not true," I blurted.

Chief Cauac tilted his head.

"Luana has Anichi magic," I pointed out. "As did her mother, and her mother before her."

Luana's eyes were calculating. She turned to her father and signed, *What would happen to someone if they transferred Azaimperiai magic from one object to another?*

Chief Cauac took a long breath. "The effects would be similar to that of creating an *Azaimperiai*, depending on the person's magical capabilities. For some, it would drain their life energy. Others, it might rob them of their magic until their last days."

Tears beaded in Luana's eyes. Sierra fanned air into Luana's face, but it didn't seem to help. A sob broke out of her chest, and she covered her face as tears streamed down her cheeks.

"Luana!?" I cried, rushing over to her. I touched her gently on the shoulder, to let her know I was there.

She lowered her hands, but continued to cry. She signed to her father so fast I had a hard time keeping up. *You said Mom was sick before she died!*

"Yes, of course she was," Cauac stated. "It is natural for *memularti* to experience particularly difficult pregnancies."

Hers was worse, wasn't it? Luana demanded. *She knew she would die when she had me. It is the way with* memularti. *She had nothing to lose by transferring the Azaimperiai's magic to another object!*

Cauac gaped at his daughter. "She wouldn't do such a thing without telling me."

Luana cocked an eyebrow. *Except you would've stopped her if she did.*

Chief Cauac hesitated. Though his wife had been destined to die in childbirth, he'd have made her as comfortable as possible until the arrival of his daughter. He wouldn't have allowed her to suffer.

"But *why* would she do that?" Chief Cauac asked, as if trying to make sense of it all. "We have the *Azaimperiai*. To create a new one would only delay the prophecy."

"Unless the ancestors asked her to do it as a safeguard," Imogen said thoughtfully.

I agreed Imogen had a point. "That makes a lot of sense. Koigni was going after the *Azaimperiai* for years. If no one knew the magic had been transferred, they'd have been after the wrong item. Luana's mother must've put the tomahawk in the temple as a decoy."

"A good idea, but it makes no sense," Liam replied. "If the ancestors truly wanted to throw off Koigni and wanted *you* to find the *Azaimperiai* to end this war, then why didn't they leave us with any clues on where to find it? Hell, why didn't they just drop it into your lap if they wanted you to have it so badly?"

"I don't know," I admitted, chewing my lower lip. I could tell the frustration was getting to both of us. "Perhaps there's an answer in the book."

The room fell silent as we all fell into deep thought. Chief Cauac flipped through the book, and even Jonah held his breath in anticipation. Instinctively, my hand came upward to clasp the Spirit Totem beneath my shirt. I didn't even realize I was doing it, as if touching it might connect me to the ancestors and give me answers.

Liam was right. If the ancestors wanted me to use the *Azaimperiai*, why had they hidden it from us? Wouldn't it be easy enough to just give it to me, like they gave me the Spirit Totem—

I inhaled a sharp breath, and everyone in the room turned to look at me. My heart hammered. Esis became so alarmed he started shaking my leg, as if to make sure I was still breathing.

"*Pawee*, you okay?" Liam asked in a rush.

Slowly, I withdrew the Spirit Totem out from underneath my shirt. I'd gone so breathless, I could hardly speak. "Liam... I think you might be right."

He eyed the Spirit Totem but tilted his head in confusion. He opened his mouth to ask a question, but it halted on his tongue. Realization crossed his face.

"What?" Jonah demanded. "What is it?"

I whirled toward my friends. "What if the ancestors *did* give it to me!?"

Luana's eyes widened, like she couldn't believe what I was suggesting. Imogen squealed at the same time Sassy barked. Jonah looked in awe. Even Squeaks got a twisted look on her face, until realization struck.

Baine was the slowest on the uptake. "Even if they did, we have some research ahead of us."

I chuckled, though it was mostly in relief. The ancestors had been on our side all along, more than any of us ever knew. "No, *pataa*. It's here! *This* is the *Azaimperiai*."

"The Spirit Totem?" Baine looked totally unconvinced. "No. That's a separate relic."

Why can't it be both? Luana challenged.

I was so excited for the answer, I could hear my pulse in my ears. "This explains *so* much! The Spirit Totem was given to me by design. It was no accident we found it during the Elemental Cup."

"But it may just be a Spirit Totem," Baine argued.

"It can't be!" I cried. "It *acts* like an *Azaimperiai*. I just didn't realize it until now. Last year at the child camps, I summoned my grandparents. I didn't know how they appeared to me, because they're not my spirit guides. But the *Azaimperiai* has the power to control the ancestors, right? That's how I summoned them. It's the same way I saw Nashoma on the *Hozho*. I grabbed the Spirit Totem before he arrived. I called out to him with it. I just didn't realize! All I had to do was touch the Spirit Totem and ask for their guidance and protection, and they answered my call!"

Liam clutched at his heart— like the mention of Nashoma was both agonizing and touching at the same time.

I raked my hands through my hair. "Ancestors, it all makes sense now. Showana gave me a message through Madame Wells, and I didn't know what it meant until now. *All the answers you seek are close to your heart. You must translate that which you have into that which you wish to know.* She was talking about the Spirit Totem!" I held the totem out triumphantly. "She was trying to tell me I already had it!"

Jonah frowned. "Why not just come out and tell you, then?"

I thought about it for a few moments. I'd wondered that so many times. If she could send me a message, why talk in riddles? Unless she wanted to delay the answer for some reason.

Imogen realized it first. "Because if we'd have known this was the *Azaimperiai* back then, we'd have fucked things up already. We'd have rushed into the final battle without raiding the camps and saving the kids, and without saving the Familiars."

"This was all part of the design," I noted. All sense of abandonment had washed away. "The ancestors aren't *testing* us. They're *training* us!"

Liam wore a look of shock. Slowly, his features softened. "I-I can't believe we've had it all along."

Baine straightened his spine. "I suppose there was no reason to go exploring the temple, then. Though I have to admit, it was fun."

Liam scoffed. "If you call dodging boulders *fun*."

"Can you use it, Sophia?" Imogen asked eagerly.

I stared down at the Spirit Totem clutched in my hands. My heart fluttered at the thought that I had the true *Azaimperiai* with me all along. How had I not seen it? "I can try."

I closed my eyes and thought back to what I'd done to summon my grandparents and Nashoma. All I remembered doing was touching the Spirit Totem and calling out to them.

Grandma, Grandpa, I thought, my heart swelling in desperation. *This war is close to an end, and I know that I must be the one to end it. But I can't do it alone. I need your help, as the prophecy predicted. Please come to me.*

Gasps traveled around the room, and my eyes shot open. My grandparents stood in front of me in spirit form. They held hands and offered me a soft expression. Everyone else had gone wide-eyed, like they couldn't believe what they were seeing.

"Sophia," my grandmother greeted kindly.

"It worked," I breathed. I'd always thought using the *Azaimperiai* would take incredible magic— that I'd struggle with it. But this was so easy — like calling them on the phone. "I'm so happy to see you. You came when I asked."

"Of course," Grandpa said with a smile. "We will always be here for you, Sophia."

For a moment, I just stared at them, drinking in their presence... until I realized I'd summoned them for a reason. "Grandma, Grandpa, we need your help. The *Azaimperiai* is supposed to end this war. There's no need for anyone else to die! If the ancestors use their power to kill Oleander and stop the Task Force, the war will be over. Will you end this for us, before any more blood is shed?"

I expected my plea to be met with assurances— that they would promise me all would be taken care of. I *needed* to be told Ava-Marie would be safe, because if the ancestors ended this now, Oleander could never touch her.

But that's not what happened. My heart split into pieces when Grandpa's gaze dropped, and he shook his head. "This is not the way of the ancestors," he said.

I gaped at him. Tears started to bead in my eyes. "But this was part of the prophecy. It says the *Azaimperiai* will end the war. If I control it, the ancestors must do as I say. You must end this!"

Grandma's features softened— like she felt sorry for me. "The word *Azaimperiai*, or *ancestral control* in Hawkei, is a misnomer. The *Azaimperiai* does not allow you to strip the ancestors of their free will. We will not allow the *Azaimperiai* to be used for destruction— rather, it is a tool of healing."

"But we *can* heal— after this war is over," I insisted. "It's a sacrifice, like the prophecy says. We have to sacrifice one side of the Hawkei so the rest of us can survive!"

Grandma shook her head regrettably. "You're asking us to divide the

Hawkei, Sophia, but the purpose is to mend together, not break apart. That's why Showana sacrificed herself. She gave up her life to *heal* the Hawkei, not help them destroy each other."

Frustrated tears blurred my vision. How could I have the *Azaimperiai* and not be able to stop this? "That will never work with Oleander," I protested. "I can't make him agree to peace. He will kill every Hawkei who refuses to bow down to him. We've lost any chance to unify the Hawkei."

"You *can* use it to heal the tribe," my grandfather insisted. "But you cannot use it as a weapon. The *Azaimperiai* was made to create miracles, not to force the ancestors to fight for you."

"Nashoma fought for me!" I reminded them. "He appeared when I asked and killed that monster to save my life."

Grandpa nodded gently. "In certain situations, the *Azaimperiai* can be used to protect. But for the *Azaimperiai* to be used as a weapon of war defeats the purpose. Nashoma defended you so you could survive and fulfill the prophecy. But he wouldn't have killed anyone just because you asked."

My fingers curled tighter around the totem. "So the *Azaimperiai* is useless."

I glanced to my friends. They all wore a look of disbelief. Baine had a calculating look on his face, like he'd gotten it wrong about the *Azaimperiai*.

I turned back to my grandparents. "If we can't use this to fight, how do we use it to heal?"

My grandma crossed her hands in front of her. "It is the ancestors' *choice* to come when you summon them, and to do as you ask. It is imperative that you ask the ancestors the right questions."

"What about my daughter?" I begged. That *had* to be the right question to ask. "How do I save her? I can't sacrifice her. I can't give her up."

"The time will come when you will know what to do," Grandma said.

"No!" I protested. "I need real answers!"

Grandpa responded like he hadn't heard me. "Keep the *Azaimperiai* close, Sophia. There will come a time when you need its healing power most."

"What do you mean? That I'll heal Ava?" I asked.

But they'd already started to fade.

"No!" I screamed, clutching onto the Spirit Totem tightly. "No, come back!"

They were already gone.

Tears streamed down my face. Liam stepped toward me to take me in his arms. I curled into him, sobbing. "This isn't right!" I insisted. "The ancestors aren't being fair."

Liam ran his fingers through my hair. "I'm sure the ancestors have a plan."

I drew away and wiped my eyes. I wanted to believe him, but he sounded uncertain.

Jonah took a step forward thoughtfully. "So, we have the *Azaimperiai*, and we know it works... though not like we were hoping. What comes next?"

This was the part that made my stomach churn. I had to be strong for everyone, because if we gave up now, we were certainly fucked. Liam better be right. I could only hope the ancestors would be by our side, even if they didn't want to fight, because it was the only way we were going to win.

I straightened my spine and cleared my throat. "There's only one thing left to do— prepare for our final battle."

NINETEEN

"That looks gross."

Sophia and I met Imogen for ice cream at *The Blue Rabbit* the first week of May. It was packed inside with people looking to get their first taste of summer. We got our ice creams from a sweet girl behind the counter, whose name tag said *Jennifer*. Her black liger pulled boxes out of storage with his teeth and growled at us pleasantly as we took a table near the corner.

Imogen had picked three different flavors for her ice cream, including goat cheese, pumpkin, and lavender. She'd gotten a million different berries on them, with granola and pomegranate juice. It was as out there as she was. Very much a Nivita concoction.

Sophia had gotten... ugh... peanut butter with gummy worms and caramel drizzle. I watched in horror, wondering how they managed to eat that stuff.

"At least I'm not a basic ass bitch!" Imogen said, pointing to my cup with a laugh. "Good thing your sex life isn't as boring as your eating habits!"

I'd gotten vanilla. *Plain* vanilla, because it was the only flavor that was mildly tolerable.

"Doya always gets the red wine flavor with raspberries," Sophia said. "Or the chardonnay with mango."

"You've been in here with her?" Imogen asked.

"A few times," Sophia said. "You wouldn't know it, but she has a soft spot for sweets. She and Baine are always in here. They'll share the butter pecan, because it's his favorite."

"Yeah, I bet she likes his nuts," I said.

Sophia smacked me on the arm, and Imogen cackled. Sassy was on the floor, licking at banana ice cream in a cup while Esis and Buttercup shared an entire carton. Ava-Marie sat in a high chair next to us and munched on some berries. The juice had smeared across her face and all over her hands. She made tiny humming sounds as she ate.

Ancestors, she was so cute. My heart stalled every time I looked at her now.

Maybe it was a bad decision to give her up. Maybe we didn't have to do it. Nothing had happened yet, right? Who's to say it would? Wasn't she safer here with us, where Sophia and I could protect her? We were two of the strongest warriors in the tribe. Nobody dared to hurt her on our watch.

"Where's Jonah? I haven't heard from him in a few days," I asked. It was weird he wasn't here. He never missed a chance to get his nasty bourbon ice cream.

"I don't know. I tried to get a hold of him, but Sassy couldn't find him to deliver any messages yesterday," Imogen said thoughtfully. "We should head over there and check on him."

"Maybe he's just wrapped up in wedding plans," Sophia suggested.

Imogen snorted. "Probably. That man has been a total groomzilla, and they haven't even set a date."

"What about Luana?" Sophia reached down. She had to wrestle the empty carton away from Esis, who was clinging to it and wailing with all his might.

"I asked, but she's on another date with *Sam*," Imogen said with a wily smile. "I think it's getting serious."

I groaned. "No more weddings, please. I can only take one at a time."

Jonah hadn't stopped going on about how he was going to be flown into the ceremony on a chair suspended by hundreds of helium balloons. *Over-the-top* didn't come close to describing his plans. He was turning his wedding into a full stage production.

"So when's Cade gonna ask you?" Sophia said, eyebrows wiggling.

"Hey, that's Cade's deal, not mine," Imogen said. "Ask him when he's gonna get the show on the road."

I'd figure pretty quickly. Imogen and Cade had known each other the longest out of everyone. I think Cade was just waiting for the war to be over before he proposed.

And if Cade asked Imogen, then Ezra would feel like he'd have to ask Stevie, too. There were a host of people we knew who'd follow after. Then they'd all want kids, and so on and so forth.

Fuck. My life was going to be nothing but weddings and babies for a pretty long time. I needed to set aside a private fund for gifts.

When we left, I snagged Ava-Marie into my arms before Sophia could. She frowned, but didn't say anything.

I felt like I'd won some unsaid argument. Sophia was greedy with Ava lately. She didn't let anyone hold her, not even me, and I was her father. It was a little irksome. I knew Sophia wanted to hold the baby as much as she could before we had to give her up, but I deserved a turn.

We knocked on Jonah's door, but no one answered. It was dark inside—looked like nobody was home.

"Okay, this is starting to get freaky," Imogen said. She tapped her chin nervously. "If I don't hear from him today, I'm going to get very worried."

"Let's walk around town," I suggested. "He and Jake have to be somewhere."

We wandered through the crowded streets of *Hok'evale*. This time of day, it was packed. I spotted Wyatt and Mia together near a street vendor, with Mattias in a stroller. Wyatt's arm was around Mia's waist. Mia saw us and waved, giving a kindly smile.

"Are they a thing now?" Imogen wondered aloud as we passed.

"He's been coming into council meetings with a stupid grin on his face, so I'd say so," I said.

They weren't the only people we saw in the square. Maddie was looking through silk dresses at a nearby stand. She jogged over.

"Hey, you guys," she greeted. "What are you doing?"

"Looking for Jonah," Sophia replied. "We can't find him anywhere."

"Hm. I haven't seen him around." She tilted her head as she counted Familiars. "Where's Julian?"

"Probably getting some dragon ass," I said. He was always with Aisha. I was certain they were together, though he wouldn't admit it to me. He was my companion instead of my Familiar, so we didn't have a telepathic connection, but body language said it all. He was hiding something.

"I would think so," Maddie said. "Dragons gossip. Eirakari said Aisha's been sneaking out to see him nearly every night."

Ha. Caught him. He couldn't lie to me.

The sound of labored breathing caught our attention. We turned as a group and saw Jonah stampeding up the path. Several people got out of his way before they were trampled by his six-foot frame. He was by himself.

"Speak of the devil. We were just talking about you," Maddie said as Jonah came to a sliding stop.

"I'm always on everyone's minds, boo," Jonah said breathlessly, before he rushed to say, "I need your help. Jake and I just got back."

"Back from where?" Imogen lifted an eyebrow.

Jonah paused. He blushed, and confessed, "Um... Jake and I *might've* ran off and gotten hitched last night."

Imogen's mouth dropped open. "No. Freaking. Way. You guys eloped? How romantic!"

"Yeah. I'm sorry I didn't tell you, but it was a spur-of-the-moment decision," he said, and he scratched the back of his head. "I wanted you guys there, but we decided it should be a private thing."

"Are you still having the wedding?" Sophia asked.

Jonah nodded. "We are. We're saving the big ceremony and party for after the war. No way am I giving up *my* wedding. I just... we really wanted to be married, you know?"

"What was the hurry?" I wondered.

Jonah frowned. "Well... we all know a big battle is coming up. And if I'm incapacitated to the point where I can't make decisions for myself, I don't want my parents to have guardianship over me. I want my spouse to decide what's best. Jake will make the right decision. I didn't want my parents to have ownership of me anymore, and this was the only way they legally couldn't. We made sure to file that he's my next-of-kin, not them."

Wow. That was a smart decision. It bothered me that Jonah was putting his affairs in order, but at the same time, none of us wanted Jacen and Joyce Chanee making the choice to pull the plug if Jonah was in a dire state.

"Well, congratulations," Maddie said kindly. "But what is it you needed our help with?"

Jonah took another deep breath. "It's Squeaks. She's gone."

"Gone where?" Sophia asked. Esis' ears perked up.

"I don't know. Jake left for work this morning, so I slept in, thinking she was around. But when I got up, she was nowhere to be found. I've been looking for her since. She's *missing*," Jonah moaned.

This was serious. "Do you think someone might've taken her?" I said.

"I don't *think* she's been kidnapped. Or in any danger," Jonah said. "I can sense she's nearby. I reached out to talk to her, but she's ignoring me. It's like she's busy. She told me to go away."

"Is she mad at you?" Imogen questioned.

"I'm not sure." Jonah dropped his head. "I don't know why she's hiding, but I want to find her."

"We'll help," Imogen said, and Sassy yipped.

Sophia glanced at Ava-Marie. "If there's any trouble, we can't take the baby."

"I'll watch her," Maddie suggested. "You guys look for Squeaks while I take Ava back to your house."

I slowly handed off Ava-Marie.

Jonah led the way down the city streets, ranting, "I've searched every-where! She's nowhere in town."

"Do you think she might be in the woods?" Imogen asked.

Jonah shrugged. "I mean, probably, but why would she go there?"

"If she's not acting like herself, why not?" Sophia said.

Jonah made a face. "She was happy last night! She was dancing with Sabor and everything when Jake and I got married. I don't know what could've pissed her off."

Sophia's expression was sly. "So, how *was* the wedding night?"

Trust my *pawee* to want information on how good the sex was. Jonah's worried expression changed briefly into a smile. "Girl, it was *ah-mazing*. The best bang I've ever had. Jake totally blew my mind."

"And something else, I bet," Imogen said, and Sophia laughed.

"You have no idea. We were at it all night," Jonah gushed. "I didn't fall asleep until after the sun came up. That man has got *stamina*."

Jonah frowned. "Maybe that's why Squeaks is mad. I didn't give her much attention after the ceremony."

"She might be planning a surprise," I offered. "It probably isn't serious."

It was then we spotted Jake. There were bags under his eyes, and he looked tired. He obviously hadn't gotten any sleep. Yet he smiled when he saw Jonah, and waved us over. There was a silver wedding band on his hand now.

"Babe, I can't find Squeaks!" Jonah said. "She wasn't at the house this morning, and—"

"Squeaks is fine. She's with Sabor," Jake said gently. "They're together in the forest. We can go to them later."

"Later?" Jonah blinked.

"There's something we need to handle." Jake reached out a hand and took Jonah's, before glancing at us. "The rest of you can come along. Some support would be helpful in this situation."

That sounded bad. Jake began leading us in the direction of the Anichi government buildings. I thought he was taking us to see Chief Cauac, before he steered us toward the jail.

Going to that jail was never a good thing. Some people had probably shown up that we didn't want to be here.

I got my confirmation when we entered the main cell block. Jonah's parents were in the first cell. Jacen and Joyce's clothes were ripped and filthy. Both of them were covered in dirt, like they'd been on the run for days. For two people who were extremely vain about their appearance, it was odd to see. Neither of them typically had a hair out of place. Jacen's Tasmanian devil was curled up on one of the cots with Joyce's primate Familiar. Both were asleep.

Jonah's sister Jenny was in the cell next to them. Her wolverine lay on the floor, breathing listlessly. Jenny's clothes were just as mangled, and there was blood streaked across her face.

Jonah froze when he saw them. His eyes widened. Jacen looked up in hope. Jake put a hand on Jonah's shoulder and kept it there.

"Jonah!" Joyce wailed, and she flung herself at the bars. "Thank the ancestors. Now we can get out of this horrible place."

"Why are you here?" Jonah asked hoarsely. "You were working for Oleander."

"The man tried to kill us!" Jacen barked. "It turns out you were right about him all along. He only cares about himself."

Wow, that was a fucking shock. It'd only taken Oleander turning on them to get these *brilliant* people to change their minds.

"Sweetheart, we came here to get away. We wanted to see you," Joyce pleaded. Her voice was so patronizing it made me sick to hear.

"You never cared before," Jonah said flatly.

"Of course we care. You're our son!" Jacen replied.

Jonah made a skeptical noise. "Like that made a difference when you decided to disown me."

Jacen's face twisted. "You've always been ungrateful. We're your parents! The least you can do is let us out of here."

"Jacen," Joyce snapped. "That's no way to speak to our son."

I wasn't fooled. She didn't care about Jonah. She just wanted to save her own skin. And it finally looked like Jonah had stopped buying her crap, too, because he wasn't moved.

Jonah's hands tightened into fists. "You came here because you thought you could get something out of me. Mainly, my protection. You didn't miss me. You came here because you had nowhere else to go."

Joyce's lip wobbled. "I can't believe you think so lowly of us."

"From what I've heard, you don't deserve any of the respect he's given you," Jake growled. He was incredibly still. This was the deadly soldier coming out of him we were all afraid of.

"And who are you to involve yourself in family matters? It's none of your business," Jacen said.

"Seeing as how you're my in-laws, it is very much my business," Jake snapped. "Don't test my patience when it comes to Jonah, because you'll find I have very little."

There was a gasp of surprise from Joyce. "You didn't even invite us to the wedding?" Joyce sniffed and dotted at her eyes. "For shame, Jonah."

Jonah didn't even flinch as he said, "You didn't belong there."

Way to go, Jonah. I was so fucking proud of him for standing up to these assholes.

Jacen narrowed his eyes as he looked at his son, then at Jake. "This man is your *husband?*" he sneered. "I can't believe you'd stoop so low."

"Didn't know the leader of the resistance wasn't a prestigious enough position for you." Imogen had to interject. Her arms were crossed, and her tone was cruel. At her side, Sassy let out a low growl.

Jacen huffed. "Leader of the resistance, huh? Sounds to me like someone who doesn't have a *real job*. More like the leader of a bunch of thugs."

"A bunch of thugs that you're asking for help," Jonah said sourly.

"We wouldn't be in this position if the resistance hadn't risen up against the Elders!" Jacen shouted. "The Defortai would've remained in power, like it should be."

"And yet here you are," Jonah replied, and he flung his arms wide. "So let me guess. You want me to get you out of this cell."

"Well, it's the least you could do, seeing as how you couldn't let us know you were married," Joyce sneered. The nice act was fading as she struggled to hold it together. "We didn't come here to be disrespected."

I expected his sister to join in on the torments, but Jenny just stared at the floor.

"Your friends have poisoned you to hate your family!" Jacen pointed a finger at us. "You know I've never liked any of them. Bunch of little punk-asses."

"Damn straight," Sophia and I both said at the same time. Jacen gave us a glare that was about as intimidating as a bunny.

"My *punk-ass* friends have saved my life more times than I could count. I'd be dead without them. You'd have left me to the wolves," Jonah snapped. "The only reason I'm here is because they helped me survive. Not just the Elders, but growing up being raised by you."

Jacen shook his head and laughed. "You are so delusional."

"Your father is right. Your friends are trash. They have brainwashed you against us," Joyce said. She wrinkled her nose. "Stop this nonsense and come home to your family, Jonah. You don't know what you're getting into with this marriage. He's just not right for you. You deserve someone better, someone that's equal to your status."

Jake's face flushed in shock. It was then Jonah's temper erupted. He strode toward the bars and shouted, "Don't make me choose between you and my husband, because it's always going to be him! He's been there for me when you failed to. He picked me back up when you left me to die. So if I have to make a choice, I'm choosing him. *Every single time.*"

Jacen reared back from the bars that were dividing him and Jonah, like he was scared. He sent a wary eye at Jonah's fists, like he might reach through and grab him.

Jonah made a disgusted noise. "I'm not going to hurt you. I'm not like you."

Jake was *so close* to losing his shit. A blood vessel in his forehead twitched.

"I've known the truth for years now. I just didn't want to admit it to myself," Jonah said. "You two are narcissists. You can't love others. You can only love yourselves. And if you can't keep me within your control, you will bully, abuse and threaten me until I get back in line. It's happened a million times, and I've fallen for it a million and one, because I had the hope one day you would change. I always thought I wasn't worthy of your love, because that's what you taught me, so I hated myself. I hated myself *so bad* because nothing I ever did was good enough for you."

His voice grew strong. "But not anymore. I'm done being manipulated by you. I've learned you can't earn love. It can only be freely given. And you two will never give me anything for free. There will always be a price attached."

Jacen straightened. When it was clear Jonah wasn't going to attack him, he said coolly, "Well, looks like you've forgotten about us. It's clear your so-called spouse is more important than the people who gave birth to you."

"Dad, just shut the fuck up." Jenny closed her eyes as she leaned her head against the bars. Jacen's mouth fell open in shock. Joyce gave a dramatic gasp, and Jonah's eyes widened.

I'd never heard Jenny talk back to her parents, especially not to defend Jonah.

Jacen's teeth gnashed. "*What* did you just say to me? I'm your father!"

"If it weren't for you, Charity would still be alive." Jenny's eyes watered at the mention of her girlfriend. She wiped her face quickly and added, "As far as I'm concerned, you're no father of mine."

Jacen's face turned red. He gave no shits that Charity had died, only that his daughter had the gall to confront him.

Joyce's mouth contorted as she raged. "How *dare* you speak to your father that way! This is unacceptable! I don't care what happened to your little bitch of a girlfriend, that's no excuse for treating him that way. You and your brother both need to—"

"*No!*" Jenny yelled, cutting her off. "Jonah's right, Mother. *Enough.*"

Joyce gaped. It was like the woman was in shock someone had the balls to tell her off. Jenny turned her head away.

"There's nothing more to say here," Jonah said. "We're done."

He turned on his heel and left his parents behind him. It was safe to say that if I never saw Jacen and Joyce for the rest of my days, it'd be far too soon.

The oracle cards had said Jonah would have to make a choice, between his old life and his new one. I was glad he'd made the right decision.

When we got out of the jail, Jonah's strong reserve crumbled. He bent over his knees and took deep breaths, trying to calm down as his shoulders shook. It'd taken everything in him to stand up to his parents.

When Jonah straightened, Jake was right there for him. He took his face in his hands. "How could a beautiful person like you come from someone like *them?*"

Jonah's eyes glimmered. Jake wrapped him in a hug. They embraced for long moments, until Jonah gave a sigh and stepped away.

"What should we do with them? I'm leaving this in your hands," Jake said.

"You can set my sister free. She won't cause any trouble," Jonah said. "But my parents have to stay locked up, at least until the war is over. We can't trust them. They'll manipulate the situation to their advantage, whether it's our side or the Elders. If they think they can get a better deal by ferrying information to Oleander, they will."

Jake nodded. "Done."

Jonah rubbed his face. "I really want to see Squeaky."

Jake's face brightened into a wide smile. "She's got some good news."

"Really? How do you know?" Jonah asked.

"Follow me." Jake put an arm around Jonah's shoulder, and we followed him into the woods. We took a winding path into the trees, deep into the forest where only the wild animals lived.

Jake parted a few branches to reveal a clearing. We saw Sabor and Squeaks in the middle of it. Sabor was standing overhead, but Squeaks was lying down in a large nest the size of a horse stall. Sassy and the kurbles darted forward, sniffing at the nest curiously.

"Squeaks!" Jonah ran toward her and knelt by her side. "Where have you been, girl? I've been looking for you."

Squeaks chirped and moved her wings. Underneath them were three large—

"Eggs!" Imogen shouted. Nestled against Squeaks' side were three eggs, white and flecked with brown spots. Sabor puffed up his chest proudly, while Squeaks cooed.

Jonah gasped. His eyes got teary, and his lip wobbled as he flung his arms around Squeaks' neck and cried, "Oh, Squeakers! You're a *mommy*!"

Squeaks grunted. One of the eggs began to wobble. A crack appeared in the side, and we held our breath as a tiny beak poked through.

"They're hatching," Imogen whispered in wonder.

The other eggs began to do the same. Pieces of egg fell off as the newborns inside poked their heads though. The eggs shattered, and three baby hippogriffs fell out of them; two girls and one boy. The females were gray and brown, while the male was black. Their feathers were soft and downy. They were no bigger than my forearm, and had dark eyes that blinked at the world.

Squeaks used her tongue to start cleaning off the babies. Sassy sniffed at the gray baby hippogriff. She sneezed, and the fox went tumbling backward.

One of the newborns was trying to stand. His legs wobbled before he fell down, collapsing on his side with a *meep*. Sabor nudged him upward, and the foal tried again, stumbling before he caught his balance.

"Oh my gosh! They're so cute." Sophia laughed. The brown-feathered baby nipped at her shoelace, pulling the knot undone.

"Jakey, did you know about this?" Jonah put a hand on his hip.

"I might've. Hippogriffs show common signs when they're breeding."

Jake rubbed his chin. "Though it's a bit strange. Hippogriff mares usually nest in trees. It's odd Squeaks built hers on the ground."

"It's so none of your babies fell out, isn't it, girl?" Jonah scratched her head, and Squeaks cooed.

Squeaks had been pushed out of the nest by her mother as a child. We all knew that it was on purpose, as her mother never wanted her, but maybe Squeaks still thought it was an accident. Like Jonah, she always saw the best in others.

"You did such a good job, girl. You have the most adorable little foals," Jonah praised. He looked at Jake. "Should we take them back home? I don't want the babies to get cold."

"You won't get Sabor and Squeaks to move from this nest for a few days," Jake said. "Squeaks will keep them warm while Sabor hunts for them. They'll come back when they're ready."

Esis patted the head of the gray hippogriff, while Buttercup played with the tail. Sophia itched the baby under the chin. "We should go get Ava," Sophia suggested. "She'd love to see the babies."

She would. Imogen stayed behind with Jake and Jonah, while Sophia and I headed back to the house.

Though the new hatchlings brought a little light back into the world, something had been weighing heavily on my mind ever since we'd found the Azaimperiai. "Soph?"

"Hm?" Her thoughts were far off. She turned to face me on the path.

I was a bit embarrassed to ask this question. But I was desperate, too. "Since we know how the *Azaimperiai* works... do you think you could summon Nashoma? So I can talk to him?"

Her eyes widened in surprise. "Um... I can try."

Sophia wrapped a hand around the Spirit Totem and closed her eyes. Her brow furrowed in concentration. Long moments ticked by, drawing out like frozen molasses. *Come on*, I pleaded, but nothing happened.

After a few minutes with no appearance, Sophia let her hand drop from the Spirit Totem with a small frown. "I'm sorry, Liam. I don't think he's going to show up. My grandparents must've been right when they said it's the ancestors' choice to come to us when I summon them."

My gut twisted so painfully it almost made my heart stop. Was Nashoma unable to visit me because it was forbidden? Or because he didn't want to?

Sophia reached out and squeezed my hand. "I'm sorry. It's my fault. Maybe if I'd been more persistent..."

"It's not your fault. I knew it was a long shot, anyways." I couldn't hide how heavy my voice was. This felt like a refusal. Had he forgotten all about me?

We continued along the forest path. Esis skittered ahead of us, picking up stones on the ground and observing them in wonder.

"Liam? Can I ask you something?" Sophia said.

"I guess." My heart felt broken, but maybe conversation would get my mind off things.

Sophia chewed her lip. "What's it like to lose your Familiar?"

No one had ever asked me that question before. Not even her. "What makes you ask that?"

"I don't know. A part of me always wonders what you were like before Nashoma died. I know you were never the same afterward, but I'd like to understand how." She swept her hair back.

I contemplated the question. "It's hard to describe. Except... imagine you don't know who you are anymore. Your identity is wiped clean. Everything that's tied you to everyone in your life is different. No relationship is like it was before. That kind of loss taints whatever you have. You have to piece back together all the things you thought you knew about the world and look at it in a different light, because what was grounding you to the earth and your old life is gone now. Every belief you have is challenged. You realize even the smallest thoughts were the ones that held you together."

I took a pause. "I can remember getting up every morning and looking in the mirror, and not knowing who was looking back."

"That sounds horrible." Sophia's voice was troubled. "I don't know how you can lose yourself and still manage to get by."

"I had to rebuild it after I met you. Giving up was no longer an option. When you lose someone you love, a piece of yourself dies. But when you lose your soul, you lose yourself. The only option for survival is to become someone different. You can't go back to the way you were before. It's impossible. That's why losing a Familiar is the most painful loss an Elementai can have, because it erases everything you once were. It's like you're reborn at the beginning of life and have to start all over."

"How can that be true? You've always wanted to be chief since you were a child. That hasn't changed," Sophia pointed out.

"My motives for being chief *did* change, though. I always wanted to help people, but I wasn't that serious about it. Dad was always getting pissed off at me for screwing around. I'd constantly blow off responsibility." I took a moment to pause. "Once Nashoma died and the chief hood was taken away from me, I realized how much time I'd wasted. How many people really needed my help, and the opportunities I'd wasted when focusing only on myself. Before Nashoma died, being a leader was something I wanted. After he passed away, I *needed* to be that leader. I was dying inside without that role to fill. Even when I tried to shirk off being Captain for the Elemental Cup, I knew it was what I had to do— though it didn't feel like I deserved it."

"How did you find the strength to go on?"

I kicked a rock down the path, and Esis skittered after it. "I don't know. You have to remember, I was told I had an undiagnosed illness a week after it all happened, so my entire life was upended. I thought I was healthy, and that was ripped out from under me at the worst possible time. The option was either to die, or keep going. I didn't have any other choices. And I don't know if I ever *wanted* to die, even when I tried to kill myself. I just wanted the pain to stop. It was exhausting moving forward and feeling like I was getting nowhere."

"You tried to stop fighting."

"Yes. But you can't stop fighting when you have my disease. Once you give up, you die. Now and then, I still wish I had gone with Nashoma to the Ancestral Lands. But a bigger part of me is glad that I stayed here with you."

Sophia nuzzled into my front. "I'm happy you're here. I wouldn't have made it this far without you."

"Me, too." I stroked her hair. "Losing your Familiar is a curse I'd never wish on anyone. Not even someone like Oleander. It's a wound that's never going to go away. It's been years, but a certain song can come on, or I can see the wrong thing, and it takes me right back there. I have no control over it. You're just not the same after that."

"Well, you're a lot better than you were," Sophia said, and she gave me a kiss.

I smirked. "I try. Sort of."

"You're too humble. You don't take enough credit for all the work you do."

"I still feel like I have to make up for past mistakes. My head knows, logically, that Nashoma's death wasn't my fault. It was an accident."

I sighed. "My heart, though? I'll always carry that guilt. It's my penance."

"I hope someday you don't," Sophia whispered. "Because I know for a fact your Familiar is proud of you."

I had to smile then. The rest of our walk was quiet, but it was a warm and enveloping silence that made me feel heard and loved. Though I hadn't gotten to talk with Nashoma, I felt lighter. The conversation had helped me, in a way.

When we got to the main road, I saw my brother hauling ass down the way.

Oh, no. What now?

Ezra's voice came in a rush. "Liam, thank the ancestors. It's Ava."

Sophia's face drained of color, and my stomach clenched. We'd left her with Maddie for less than an hour. "Is she okay?" she asked.

"No time to explain. Come on!"

Ezra took off at a run. We kept pace, until we reached our home. The sound of Ava-Marie's crying gutted me— she was wailing.

I burst open the door. Our house was a mess. Furniture had been upended, and several things were broken. It looked like there'd been a fight.

I didn't stop panicking until I saw my child. Doya was holding on to Ava, bouncing her in her arms to calm her. It didn't do much good. She kept wailing, her voice a terrified screech.

Sophia immediately went to her. She yanked Ava-Marie out of Doya's arms and into her own. Against Sophia's chest, Ava calmed, though she hiccupped and looked at me with wide eyes.

"The bedroom," Doya said quickly.

I got there in seconds. Maddie lay on the bed, an ice pack to her face. Baine stood next to her, a water ball in his hands. He had his sights focused on two people kneeling on the ground— a Nivita woman and a Toaqua man. Both of them were bound, ice frozen around their torsos so they couldn't move. The crib was tipped over, and the railing on it had been snapped in half.

The scariest thing was the knife on the floor.

Ezra came in beside me, arms crossed. "I heard a yell and came running. These two broke in and knocked Maddie out."

"Eleanor and I had stopped by for a visit when we heard Maddie scream," Baine growled. "If we hadn't been here to stop them, they would've accomplished what they were after."

The Nivita girl kept her eyes down, though the Toaqua's stare was resentful.

"They had the audacity to try to steal from the Water chief?" I asked.

"They weren't here to steal anything," Ezra said. "They were trying to hurt Ava."

It took two seconds for me to go from shocked to deadly. *"Why?"*

The Nivita girl's voice shook. "Word has gotten around about the prophecy. Of the chosen one's sacrifice," she said. "She still hasn't given the baby up. We don't want to die because of one child."

How the information had gotten out, I didn't know. We'd all been very quiet about it, but we must've been eavesdropped on at some point, because now all of *Hok'evale* knew.

Rage flared. I barely kept it under control. "What the chosen one decides is up to her."

"The Hawkei will go extinct if the child does not die!" the Toaqua man burst. "A chief who cannot sacrifice his children for the good of his tribe doesn't *deserve* to be in charge! The tribe isn't worth one little *mopite* girl!"

Ezra moved before I did. He grabbed the man around the throat and shoved him against the wall. "What the *fuck* you just call my niece?"

"Ezra, enough," I said. I was a chieftain. I had to show restraint. Even if all I wanted to do was choke this fucker into oblivion.

Ezra backed off, but he didn't move an inch away from the Toaqua after letting him go. He was still coughing for air.

I turned my back on them. "I want them removed," I told Ezra. "Take them to a holding cell."

Baine and Ezra yanked the prisoners upward. I returned to the living room. Sophia hadn't been in the conversation, but by the stark look on her face, she'd heard every word.

"We're taking Maddie back to my mom's and staying there tonight," I said. "Pack some things."

"I'll get them for you," Doya said. "Just take your sister and go."

I nodded in thanks. I helped Maddie to stand. She was conscious, but weak. Julian had returned at this point, and he grumbled in worry.

Sophia hadn't said a damn word. She just held Ava-Marie tightly to her, white-faced.

By the time we landed on the beach, Jonah, Jake and Imogen were waiting there for us. I tried to help my sister, but she pushed me aside weakly.

"I'm okay, Liam. I can walk," Maddie said. She staggered as she slid off Julian and climbed up the porch steps into the house.

Sophia clung to Ava and rushed in after Maddie— like she was afraid to be out in the open and wanted Ava-Marie to be in a safe place. The kurbles skittered after her.

It was a real shitty day when not even *Hok'evale* was safe. And it wasn't even the Task Force this time. It was our own people.

"Stevie came and got us. We heard what happened," Imogen said in a rush. "What can we do to help?"

"You can help by taking care of Sophia. I think she's in shock," I said. I wished I could comfort her, but at the moment, I had orders to give. This situation needed to be handled.

Imogen nodded, and she ran into the house. Jake took a wide stance and asked, "What are your plans for the Toaqua man? He's in your jurisdiction."

"I want him executed. Immediately," I said. "What you do with the Nivita woman is up to you."

"Without a trial?" Jonah's eyes widened. Typically, the death penalty would have to be voted on and agreed by an entire House council before it was carried out. I was breaking tribal law by giving an executive order. It was something I'd recoil at doing in any other situation. It went against my moral code.

When it came to my daughter? Fuck the law.

"He doesn't need a trial. We caught him in the act," I spat. "Oleander will be here any day. We can't be wasting our time on traitors. He needs to be made an example of."

"You're acting just like Oleander," Jonah said. "You can't go around butchering anyone who—"

"We can't allow the daughter of the Water chief to be attacked without repercussions!" I bellowed. "What does that look like in a time of war?"

Jonah smoldered. "I know the bastard deserves death. I want anyone dead who tries to hurt Ava. But I don't want you to become a monster because of this war."

"I will become *anything* to keep my child alive," I snarled. "So help me."

Jonah fell silent. Jake crossed his arms and said, "How shall it be done?"

"I'll do it myself," I climbed back on Julian and grabbed his spikes. "I have no worth as chief if I can't take a man's life after I give the order to end it."

By the time I returned that night, Sophia had gone to bed. I didn't wake up until noon the next day. The weight of all the decisions I had to make were exhausting, and my body was struggling to account for it.

My mind felt weak. I'd worried about my daughter since she was born into the world. She wasn't even a year old, and already, someone had tried to kill her.

The world wasn't safe for those like her. Indigenous women were kidnapped and killed at rates far higher than most other demographics in North America. There was a genocide being committed against Native women in this country, and we all knew the government wasn't going to do shit to stop it. The latest statistics I'd looked at showed at least sixty percent of indigenous women experienced sexual assault at some point in their lives. That didn't even take in the prejudice she'd experience as a minority, let alone being female.

I'd wished more than once she looked more like Sophia and less like me, because she'd be safer. But she hadn't been born that way.

Growing up, I thought any children I'd have would be safe in the Hawkei world, because if we stayed within the boundaries of our reservation, they'd less likely come to harm. Then the war had broken out, and now my daughter was in more danger than ever— from her own people instead of outsiders.

I'd thought *Hok'evale* was safe, too, and it turned out not to be. Last night's actions had changed my way of thinking into something more permanent. I could live without my daughter in my life, but I wouldn't survive it if she died. A man could only take so much loss. I had lost my Familiar, but I would not lose her.

Sophia came in to put Ava-Marie down for her nap. I didn't want to say the hated words *we need to talk*, but Sophia knew what was on my mind.

"What?" The word was accusatory from her. It nearly woke up the baby.

"Let's not fight in front of Ava." I felt like this conversation wasn't one we could have without it dissolving into an argument. We left the bedroom, and went into the office next door.

When Sophia locked the door, I took a heavy breath. "Soph, you know what we need to do. She can't stay here."

Sophia bristled. "So we'll leave. We can take Ava and go."

The thought was so tempting, but I pushed it aside. "You know that's not an option."

"Why?" Sophia put her hands on her hips. "Why can't we run away? Leave the Hawkei to their fate."

"We've been working toward this for over two years. We have the

Azaimperiai. You're the chosen one. There are a million reasons why we can't just go."

"None of those are worth our daughter."

"Sophia, open your eyes! Do you really think people are going to stop coming for us? That we can just run off into the sunset and live happily ever after once we leave the tribe to their fate?" I asked. "No. They'll hunt us down. Not just Oleander, but the resistance, too. They'll hold us to our word and make us fulfill the prophecy whether we like it or not. We are never going to be free until this war is over for good, and I'm not going to force Ava-Marie into a life on the run. That's too traumatic for a kid."

"We shouldn't have left her alone. If she stays at our side at all times, we can protect her," Sophia argued.

"Are you going to bring her into battle? Fight Oleander with her on your back?" I gave a noise of disgust. "We're being selfish. This is not the right decision. When I became a parent, I promised I'd do what's best for her and not for myself, no matter how much it hurt me."

"She's in danger if we're not there."

"She's already in danger, with us or not. She's a mixed House child," I said. "Things have changed in our world, but not completely. The Hawkei still need time to accept the idea of integration. Her existence challenges that. Now that people know the wording of the prophecy, they won't stop coming for her to save their own skins. To some, she's the daughter of the chosen one, but to others, she's just a *mopite*, one who doesn't deserve to live. I didn't understand that, but now I do. And I have a duty to protect her from these monsters."

"We've already asked people to take her, and they said no. There's nowhere for her to go," Sophia said weakly.

"There are options, Sophia! We just haven't been looking at them because we don't want to do this!"

"So what do we do? Huh? Who do you want to give her away to, exactly? Who do you trust with our child?" Sophia's voice wobbled. "Because I trust *no one.*"

There was a knock on the door. Our argument paused. "Can I come in?" a soft voice asked.

It was Imogen. Sophia cleared her throat and unlocked the door. Imogen stood outside, wearing a wary smile.

"I have something for you guys," she said. "I was hoping you'd like to look at it."

We were in the middle of something, but Sophia was looking for an excuse to get out of this, so she said, "Sure. What is it?"

Imogen led the way into the kitchen. A wave of impatience rose within me, but I pushed it down, promising myself I'd pick it back up again later. I wasn't done with this conversation.

Jonah, Stevie and Ezra were gathered around the counter. They were looking at a scrapbook, turning the pages in interest.

"This is for us," Imogen said. She turned the scrapbook our way and started at the beginning. "Before we left Orenda Academy, I got all the pictures off Jonah's phone and put them into this book, so we could always remember the good times. No matter how bad things got."

Sophia turned the pages. There were a lot of pictures in here. The book started a few weeks before the Elemental Cup. There was a picture of Jonah carrying Imogen on his shoulders outside the greenhouse, and others of all four of us eating in the dining hall for the first time as Jonah snuck a selfie.

I looked pretty grumpy in most of them. But there was one where I was smiling. It'd been the week before the tournament. I was on my bike, and Sophia was sitting behind me. She had her arms wrapped around my middle while making a goofy smile.

That was before we started dating. Man, if it wasn't easy to see the puppy-love on my face. I'd been totally smitten.

The photos continued. There were pictures of us playing soccer, and of Jonah's first game with the school team. A few had been taken at parties, where we were too drunk to take pictures well. There were a shit ton of us in the Commons, just messing around and doing stupid stuff.

I hadn't known we'd taken so many photographs. We had to sneak them in order to avoid being caught. But I recalled these memories as if they just happened yesterday.

"Liam, you ducked out of half of these," Stevie complained as the pages turned. "You're always in the corner."

"He hates taking pictures," Sophia commented. The look in her eyes was far away, like these photos came from a different time. I guess they had. There were some from Christmas the year before last, just after Sophia and I had won our trial, and a bunch from our trip to Europe.

There was a significant gap from our trip to Europe to our arrival in *Hok'evale*. We'd been too busy sneaking people out of the castle to have fun our last semester. There were photos of Stevie, Cade and Ezra at *The Falcon's Nest*, Luana cliff diving, and all the Familiars dancing in the square. There were pictures of our wedding, and the cabaret. Some pictures I'd forgotten existed, until I remembered these events had really taken place and weren't something made up.

We'd come so far in two years. But even after all the shit we'd gone through... those had been good times. And I wouldn't have traded it for anything.

The last pictures in the book were of Ava. There was one Sophia had taken where she was cuddled on her side, and another of her with Esis. The kurble had his arms around her while Ava-Marie smiled.

It pained me to look at pictures of her. It'd be worse after she was gone.

The last picture in the book was the one we'd taken the night of the Elemental Ball— the selfie Jonah had hurriedly created, where Sophia was in my arms, and Jonah and Imogen were in the center.

I'd never tell anyone, but that was my favorite picture of us. We'd all been so happy.

"A lot can change in such a short time," Sophia whispered.

Imogen closed the book. "Everything, really."

There was a heavy silence that felt more like grief. Ezra asked, "Do you think things will ever get back to normal?"

We knew the answer. Things would never be the same again.

But none of us wanted to admit it. Until Jonah said, "Things will be a new normal. And we'll adjust. And then it'll be better than it ever was before."

"Ancestors, I sure hope so." Imogen blew a lock of hair out of her eyes.

"As long as I never have to go out to get pancakes at three a.m. with Ezra ever again," I deadpanned. It'd been a weird memory to have, but it just popped out at me, clear as day. I hadn't thought about such a thing in months, and it'd used to be almost routine.

Ezra laughed beside me. Stevie nodded in enthusiastic agreement.

"Is that a thing?" Sophia asked.

"Ezra *always* wants pancakes after he smokes," Stevie said, rolling her eyes. "Weed makes him hungry. And stupid."

"We have some pretty dumb conversations," Ezra admitted.

"Hey, that night after my high school graduation was pretty rad," Jonah said. "We had the *most philosophical* conversation over eggs and bacon after midnight, if I remember."

"Because you were drunk off your ass." I smirked. "The dumbest conversation in the world sounds intelligent when you've gone through a case of beer with your buddies."

"You act like you were a saint," Jonah said. "You begged me to help you hide some shit from your dad back in ninth grade."

"Please. I haven't smoked weed since I was a teenager," I scoffed.

"Is it because of your asthma?" Sophia asked.

"Yeah. But I don't lose brain cells. Unlike my brother."

"There's not much to lose there," Stevie cracked.

Ezra groaned. "Bro, you're such a buzzkill since you became chief."

"I became an *adult*," I shot at him, and he grinned. "You should do the same now that you're on the council."

"A little partying never harmed anyone. Right, babe?" Ezra asked Stevie, and he nudged her.

Stevie sighed. "I think my partying days are just about over."

Ezra threw his hands up. "I can't win! Jonah, *please* tell me you aren't done turning up."

"I'll be the old creepy guy hanging around at parties long after I'm supposed to be there, mark my words," Jonah vowed.

As the people around me shared a laugh, a strange sense of unease came over me. It was so bizarre we were standing around talking about parties and having fun when the past year had been nothing but fighting to survive.

None of us were yet twenty-five. Most of us would still be in college if it weren't for this damn war. It was hard to remember we were so young when we felt so damn old. This kind of stuff changed you.

We'd all been through far too much.

The front door opened, and Doya walked on through, Baine beside her. The woman never knocked. She walked into all places like she owned them, whether she did or not.

I thought she'd go to Sophia, but instead, Doya came to me and clasped her hands in front of her dress. "Liam, I must have a word with you."

Ancestors, what did I do this time? "What can I help you with?"

"There was a reason we stopped by yesterday," Baine said. "The attack on Ava-Marie gave us reason to hesitate, but Eleanor and I have decided that this cannot wait."

"We were hoping you would agree to marry us," Doya said. "You are Elliot's chief, and therefore, have the authority to officiate the wedding."

Sophia gaped. "Are you serious? You guys want to get married?"

"Yes," Doya purred. "I think it would only be proper, seeing as we have a child together."

Talk about old-school. I knew Doya loved Baine, but she also had some old-fashioned ideas about how things should be.

"We want to celebrate our love," Baine added. "And we'd like to do it before the battle begins, in case... well, you all know."

In case something happened. I sighed. "Well, sure. That's something I can do. What day do you want to do this?"

"Today, if at all possible," Doya said. "There is no time to waste."

"What, now?" I asked in surprise.

"I assume you heard me the first time. Tonight, on the beach," Doya said. "I think that should be sufficient time to get a wedding around."

This woman had some high expectations, but Jonah and Imogen pounced on the opportunity. "We can sort out everything," Jonah gushed.

"Yes, don't worry about a thing," Imogen added. "We'll make the decorations perfect."

Doya turned to Baine. "I suppose you can tell everyone the good news? I think sunset would be a beautiful time for a ceremony."

I opened my mouth to tell them that wasn't quite enough time, but my mother must've overheard, because she bustled in from the next room. "That leaves me just enough time to go grocery shopping. I'll call Susan Henley and see if she can lend a hand with the cooking."

My mom was creating a monster.

Doya fluffed her hair as she said, "I'm keeping my last name, by the way. I love you, darling, but I see no need to replace my own with yours."

"Whatever you want, my precious pearl," Baine cooed.

My mother's house turned into wedding central in zero to five seconds. Baine rushed out the door to invite people, while Imogen and Jonah ran to get decorations.

"So, when did *pataa* propose?" Sophia asked her mother once Baine had left.

Doya shrugged. "I asked him, actually. I was tired of waiting around. A woman has to take charge, you know."

That was so Doya and Baine. This whole thing was them, actually—putting a wedding together in less than an afternoon and expecting it to be perfect.

But then again, why wouldn't it be? We needed a little more happiness in the world.

It was one more distraction before the storm set loose.

Hours later, I stood underneath a white arch threaded with red roses— a last-minute creation of Jonah and Imogen's. Thalassa had slithered onshore and towered beside Baine at the arch. The sea serpent cast a shadow over the beach chairs from the setting sun.

A congregation of around twenty sat in them, plus Familiars. Doya and Baine didn't have many friends, but the ones they did have showed up to support them. Most of them, I had to admit, were our friends. Chief Cauac had come to be polite, along with the Henleys, but they were the few older adults here. Perot sat near the front with Baxtor at his side and stared wistfully at the arch, as if thinking of what he and Alric might've had.

Ava-Marie sat in Imogen's lap in the front row, wearing a fluffy white dress Jonah had found at the store on the way back. Imogen waved Ava's hand at me, and I smiled. Ava-Marie gave a wide grin and cried out, bouncing on Imogen's lap. Squeaks was absent, as she was at her nest, but Sassy was there, and she was pulling at the white ribbon in Ava's hair to try straightening it, as it'd gone crooked. Esis and Buttercup shared a chair, though they were nearly squished when Sassy climbed onto it beside them. Jonah ate a tub of popcorn on the other side of Imogen, like this was a movie for his personal entertainment and not a wedding.

As the beach was cast in an orange hue, people rose to stand. The bride began her walk down the aisle. Doya had her hair done in a sleek 1940's updo, lips accented with red. Her white dress was tea-length, and she wore a white fur shawl over her shoulders.

She'd asked Sophia to walk her down the aisle, which I thought was amazingly sweet. Sophia's smile was kind and warm as she walked arm-in-arm with her mother toward her father.

The sand below their feet had been coated with red petals, and the waves created the background music as Doya set her eyes on her future husband, which were hungry and wanting. Naomi prowled, purring with pleasure.

"Who gives this woman away?" I asked as they reached the arch.

Sophia went to speak, but Doya said, "I give myself away. As does my daughter."

Sophia shook her head in an amused way and took a step back to serve as Doya's matron-of-honor. As Baine and Doya joined hands, Thalassa reached her head down to nuzzle Naomi. The lioness happily rubbed her head against the sea serpent's nose, and the audience took their seats.

I was gonna make this quick and simple. Doya had been insistent there was no point in *wasting people's time with silly Hawkei wedding traditions,* and Baine had confessed he was too embarrassed to do them anyway in front of a big group. We were doing the vows and legalities, and that was what they wanted.

"Friends, family, and fellow tribe members, we have gathered today in the presence of our ancestors to unify this man and this woman under the light of the Great Spirit," I began. "Fire and Water will become one, equals instead of opposites, lovers instead of enemies. We will return to the ways of our forefathers by uniting this couple in marriage, proving that love conquers all, despite what differences we have created between ourselves— for at our heart, the Hawkei are one tribe."

Sophia's eyes gleamed at me as I spoke. This wasn't so different from our wedding not that long ago. I knew it was a secret dream of hers that her parents would someday marry, and now it was coming true.

Doya had specifically told me to leave out the part about objections, and swore she would smoke the first person with a fireball who stood up with one, so I skipped that part and replaced it with, "The couple will now exchange their vows, along with their rings. Elliot will begin."

I gestured to Baine, who fumbled in his suit pocket. A full minute passed. I raised my eyebrows, and the audience fidgeted uncomfortably. Finally, Baine pulled a box out of his coat, but he dropped it in the sand. He mumbled an apology before he opened it, and Doya audibly gasped.

Holy shit, that was a big rock! Sophia's eyes widened as Baine placed the diamond on Doya's hand. "Eleanor, my darling, I have loved you from the moment I set eyes on you. When you walked into my classroom the first day of your freshman year at Orenda Academy, I always knew you'd be the only one for me."

Okay, Baine, we don't need to know the embarrassing backstory. As cute as this all was, he had been her teacher when they'd gotten together, and it was more than a little weird.

Baine went on. "I have made many mistakes in my life, the worst being that I let you go. But I never regretted loving you. Our love created a child together, a child I have never been prouder of. As the saying goes, better late than never. And I promise to enjoy the twilight years of my life with you by my side, and to never forsake you again."

After the ring was on, Doya kept her hand aloft, though I didn't know how. Thing had to be at least five carats. Baine must've hoarded his professor's salary for years to pay for that thing.

Sophia slipped a man's ring into Doya's hand. It was gold, very traditional. She placed it on Baine's ring finger as she spoke. "Elliot, you were always my life. Even when we were apart, every decision I ever made has been for you and our daughter. The magic within me is Fire, yet it was clear to me since the first time we made love that Water was my true home. I missed you like a sailor misses the sea, gone away for too long. I promise to love you as faithfully as I have done all the days of my life, for the Fire that blazes inside my heart burns for you, and you alone."

Well, what do you know. Doya could even make me tear up. A couple of people in the audience dotted their eyes with tissues, while my mother cried full-on into a handkerchief, whispering *that was beautiful.*

I cleared my throat. "By the power vested in me as chief of the Toaqua tribe, I officially declare you married. Elliot, you may kiss the bride."

Baine placed a passionate kiss on Doya's lips, and cheers rose from the audience. People clapped as they walked down the aisle hand-in hand. My mother rose tearfully from her seat to begin distributing the dinner that was inside the house, while Ezra ran to play the stereo, so we'd have music for the makeshift reception.

"They look so happy," Sophia said. "I hope they get to stay together."

"Doya's tough, and Baine's no pushover when it comes to magic," I said quietly. "They'll be okay."

At least, I hoped so. It wouldn't be fair to them to have to wait this long to be together, only to be violently torn apart by the Elders during a battle none of us could control.

"Liam, Sophia, may we speak with you?" Robert Henley had approached the arch with his wife, Susan. Sophia's adoptive parents were arm-in-arm, and though their expressions were kind and friendly, I feared the intent behind it.

"What is it?" Sophia's words held a note of fear. "Is everything okay?"

Robert sighed. "Not really, Sophia. We didn't want to talk about this, tonight of all nights, but... well, things need to be done."

Sophia paled. My intestines felt like they were being squeezed to death.

Susan added, "We know you're looking for a home for Ava-Marie, and we want to open ours. We were waiting for you to ask us because we didn't want to pry. We knew you needed time. But after the attack on Ava-Marie last night, we hate to say there isn't time left."

Sophia swallowed. "What about your foster kids?"

"There's always room for one more, especially our own granddaughter," Robert said. "Your mother and I want to move back to Utah as soon as possible. It's no longer safe here, and after the last battle over Christmas, we've seen our final fight. We plan to leave in a week. We'd like to take Ava with us."

A week was only seven days. Practically nothing. Susan reached out a hand to stroke her daughter's arm. "You know Ava-Marie will have a good life with us. She'll want for nothing. I know this isn't what you wanted, and this is the most difficult decision a parent could make."

Susan's eyes welled with tears. "But trust me, Sophia. I had to give you up when you left for Orenda Academy, because it was the best choice for *you*. Now you have to make the same decision."

"War is imminent," Robert said. "If you want Ava-Marie far away from the chaos, she has to leave now."

Sophia bit her lip and looked toward the ocean.

Lowly, I said, "I agree. I think this is the only option we have."

Sophia looked at me as if I'd committed a betrayal, but that didn't stop her from agreeing. "Okay." She finally broke. "Ava-Marie can go with you. We'll get everything in order, and you can take her away from this war. To a place she won't get hurt."

That was the only thing we wanted, in the end. Ava's safety.

Even if it killed us both to let her go.

sophia
TWENTY

If I knew what was best for Ava-Marie, I'd have sent her away weeks ago. But I just couldn't let her out of my sight. To do so felt like a crime against motherhood.

And still... I knew we had to do it. Whether I liked it or not.

We'd gathered everyone at *The Falcon's Nest* one night to say goodbye. It wasn't something we'd planned, just something that sort of happened. No one talked explicitly about Ava's departure, but the atmosphere was melancholy.

This wasn't like the other parties we threw. There was nothing fun about it. The night felt cold. Though people chatted and passed Ava around, I didn't hear a word anyone said.

Liam and I returned home late that night. It seemed that no one had wanted to leave, as they all knew this would probably be the last time they saw our daughter. Ava-Marie had fallen asleep in Haloke's arms shortly after ten o'clock, and the party wound down after that. I was grateful, because Liam and I were both exhausted.

I didn't want to go to bed right away. Though I could hardly keep my eyes open, all I wanted was to stare down at my little girl and enjoy her with the few hours we had left. But I hadn't even taken a seat on the couch when the front door swung open. Liam and I both looked up.

Doya strolled in like she owned the place. She shot her heart-stopping gaze in my direction. "What the hell was that, Sophia?"

"Shh..." I hissed. "You'll wake Ava." I didn't even bother calling out her rudeness. She never knocked, anyway.

Esis scurried in front of me like he was protecting me from Naomi, who shared the same pissed expression as Doya. Both Familiars stood their ground and glared.

"Don't use your daughter as an excuse to avoid this conversation," Doya snapped, wagging a finger at me.

"I'll take Ava," Liam offered.

There was an unspoken message in his tone. We both knew this conversation with my mother could get ugly. She'd approached me several times already tonight, and I kept avoiding her. How did you tell the woman who gave you up that you were about to do the same thing to her granddaughter? It made me sick.

Ava-Marie barely stirred as Liam took her to the bedroom. Buttercup followed, leaving my mother and I alone with our Familiars.

I took a deep breath, knowing I couldn't avoid telling her the truth. "Liam and I are sending Ava-Marie away."

Doya crossed her arms. "And this is the first time you care to mention it to me?"

"You would've tried talking us out of it!" I protested.

"Of course I would!" she shot back. "She's my granddaughter. She's not going anywhere."

"That's not your decision to make," I stated bluntly. "We've been planning this for a while. We need Ava to go somewhere safe."

"And who might she *possibly* be safe with?" she asked with tight lips. "Leave her with me, and no one will touch her."

"What, so you can *protect her* like you protected me?" I snapped.

I hadn't even realized I said it until it came out of my mouth. Doya gasped— like I wouldn't possibly dare throw that at her. Esis' eyes widened.

I was so exhausted, I just didn't care anymore. I sank onto the couch and sighed. "That's not what I meant. We need you to fight in this war. That's why we didn't ask you to take her."

Doya narrowed her eyes. "Who *did* you ask?"

"My adoptive parents," I told her. Before she had a chance to protest, I added, "They took care of me when you gave me up. They'll do a good job with Ava."

Doya pursed her lips. "Where are they taking her?"

"Somewhere far away," I answered vaguely. "People are trying to kill her, Mother. Don't tell me you wouldn't do the same thing."

"I *did* do the same thing," she reminded me harshly. "And I've regretted it every day since."

"This is different," I protested. "You didn't even want me! I *want* Ava-Marie, but I have to do whatever I can to keep her safe."

"I wanted you, too!" Doya burst.

The silence that hung in the air was deafening. No, worse than that. It was choking me.

Doya's nostrils flared as she took a deep breath. "I wanted you, Sophia," she repeated in a softer tone. "Recall that people tried to kill you, too. You were a mixed-House baby. I only feared what they might do to you. I gave you to Betsy and Alan to protect you."

My tone soured. "That's not what it sounded like in your journal entry."

"I was bitter when I wrote that," Doya admitted. "I hated myself for giving you up, Sophia, and it was a mistake to turn that anger around on you. The truth is, I always wanted you. I don't want you to live through that same regret."

"You know what I'd regret more?" I challenged. "Keeping Ava here and getting her killed!"

Tears welled in my eyes. I pressed a hand over my mouth to keep from sobbing.

Something I said must've clicked with Doya, because her shoulders suddenly dropped, and her tone softened. She came over to sit by me on the couch and placed a hand on my back.

"Sophia, I understand how hard this is for you," she said.

"Then you have to know this must be done," I sobbed. "I just don't know if I can do it."

Doya gazed at me for several seconds, watching the tears run down my face. She looked like she was about to say something, but must've decided there was nothing she could say to make this better. Instead, she leaned over and *pulled me into a hug.*

That's right. Madame Doya— the woman who bullied me while I was at Orenda Academy and continuously humiliated me in class, the teacher who threatened me so I would summon the ancestors and act as a Koigni pawn— was hugging me. It was so strange how our relationship had shifted, and yet it felt natural. I needed her right now, because she was the only person who really knew what it was like to give up their daughter. Naomi purred and put her chin on our laps. Esis flopped over and hugged her head.

"H-how did you do it?" I asked as I melted into Doya's embrace. "How did you give me up?"

"It wasn't easy," she answered softly. "I know I made it sound like that, but it was the hardest thing I've ever done. I thought you'd be better off without me."

"That's not how I feel about Ava," I said, wiping at my running nose. "I want to be there for her, and right now I can't help wondering who needs me more— my daughter, or the rebellion."

Doya didn't speak for a long time. It was like she was mulling over what I'd said.

Finally, she took a breath. "I wish I could make this decision for you, Sophia. I wish I could tell you to keep Ava-Marie here with us, that we'll keep her safe."

Doya took a breath. "But I know you are right. Perhaps she is better off far away from the enemy— away from *anyone* who would hurt her. It is much better for her to live apart from us than to keep her here where she's in danger."

My heart sank at my mother's words, but at the same time, I felt a little better to have her support. "How do I let her go?"

"You don't let yourself think of it that way," Doya said. "You're not giving up on your daughter. You're giving her a chance. If I had kept you, Sophia, you'd be dead. Giving you up was the hardest choice I ever had to make."

She sighed. "Yet... it was the right decision. Because I made that sacrifice, you are here with me. You're alive. And I'd suffer a thousand times over if it meant we were together in the end."

I didn't know how much I needed to hear those words until that moment. All this time, I'd been worrying about abandoning my daughter— about leaving her without a mother. But this was not about what she might lose. Rather, it was what she might gain. If Ava-Marie stayed here, she'd lose her life. Right now, all I could give my daughter was a chance at survival.

I damn well hoped it was the right decision.

Ava-Marie clutched tightly to my shirt. My heart swelled and broke into a thousand tiny pieces all at once. If my chest could hold the world inside of it, it was blooming the most beautiful landscapes while earthquakes and volcanoes rocked its foundation. It was purely contradictory, and yet, I felt it all at once. Fire blazed through my chest, while my Spirit calmed my belly. It sent tremors of pain throughout my body, because such agony could not reside in a place of love.

Liam and I sat on the couch, snuggled tightly with Ava-Marie in my arms. This day had come too soon, and I wasn't ready for my time with her to end. I squeezed my eyes shut and pressed my lips to the top of her head. She clutched me even harder, like she could sense this was goodbye.

"I love you so much, little pumpkin," I told her, my voice cracking. "But this isn't goodbye forever. Daddy and I are going to win this war, and we'll bring you back, because this is your home, okay? It's *your home*, and nothing's going to change that."

Ava-Marie's eyes sparkled as she looked up at us. Her bottom lip trembled, and my heart shattered all over again. It felt as if a dragon was sitting on my chest, breaking my ribs and sending the shards straight into my heart.

"Don't cry, Ava," I squeaked. "If you cry, I'll cry."

Though she didn't shed a tear, I couldn't help it. Tears began streaming out of my eyes. Liam pulled me tighter to his chest and sniffled. He didn't say anything, but right now, I didn't think he could. We were both choking on our emotions.

Liam stroked Ava's hair. Esis and Buttercup sat on the back of the couch, swaying back and forth in each other's arms. It was sad and solemn and made me cry even harder.

"It's too soon," I whispered, because even though my voice was painful to hear, it was better than the silence.

Liam's chest heaved once, like he was trying to hold back a sob. Liam was good at hiding his emotions at times, but right now, he couldn't hold them back. It only made saying goodbye that much harder, because I never thought I'd see my husband crack like this.

"Here," I said, sniffling. I sat up straighter and placed Ava-Marie in Liam's arms.

He looked really surprised. "You never let me hold her."

Esis handed me a tissue, and I dotted my eyes. I wanted to argue that I *did* let him hold her all the time— but he was right. I'd been particularly possessive with her lately. "Well, now's your chance."

Liam kept his gaze on his daughter as he rocked her back and forth in his arms. Tears beaded at his eyes, but he wore a soft smile, too. I never knew my heart could feel so much at once.

"You're perfect, Ava-Marie," Liam said. She giggled, then grabbed his finger with her hand. His shoulders fell. "You're so goddamn perfect, and giving you up is the hardest fucking thing in the world."

I didn't care that he was swearing right now. The swear jar didn't even cross my mind. At the moment, harsh language seemed justified.

"Grandma and Grandpa are going to take good care of you," Liam promised her. "This will all be over soon, and you won't remember any of it. We'll come get you... if we make it."

A sob broke from my chest so loud it made Esis and Buttercup jump. Tears began to leak out of my eyes like freaking Niagara Falls. "Don't say that, Liam," I scolded through sobs. "We'll make it."

"But Ava— Ava—" He choked on his words.

As Liam went into a coughing fit, he placed Ava-Marie back into my arms and doubled over.

"Liam!" I cried. "You okay?"

"Fucking no," he spat. He coughed a few more times, then sat upright again. His eyes were rimmed in red. "Who knows when the next time I'll see my daughter will be? It could be in the Ancestral Lands!"

My tears fell onto Ava's onesie and soaked it. "Don't talk like that. We're going to see her again."

Ava-Marie hiccupped. We both looked back to her, our argument forgotten. It was almost like she'd intended it to distract us.

"You're right," Liam said, wrapping an arm around me again. "I *have* to believe we'll see her again. I can't go into this battle believing anything else."

"Me, either," I whispered so softly I wasn't sure he heard me.

Then Ava-Marie reached up with both hands and touched the side of our faces. The red-hot lava burning through my chest seemed to cool.

Liam placed his hand on hers. "I-I think she's trying to tell us everything is going to be okay."

I sniffled again. "I sure hope so. To be honest, Liam, I don't care if we die— as long as Ava is safe."

Liam ran a finger over her soft cheek. "Same."

Just then, the sound of a carriage approaching the house met my ears. My guts twisted, and I held Ava-Marie closer.

"It's time, Sophia," Liam whispered.

I gasped. "I'm not ready."

"We never will be," Liam replied solemnly.

A knock came at the door, but I hesitated to stand and answer it.

"*Pawee*," Liam pressed.

I finally stood with Ava-Marie in my arms, but I swayed on my feet. I didn't think I'd ever be ready for this. Liam and I walked to the door, and we answered it to find my adoptive parents standing there. Their coyote and bobcat Familiars were at their feet. Their carriage was parked behind them.

"Is Ava-Marie ready to go?" my mom asked.

"Almost," I answered, though I really meant; *No. She'll never be ready.* Yet this is what had to be done. I knew that, but couldn't bear it.

"Take all the time you need," Dad said kindly.

Ava-Marie had her eyes fixed on my mom and reached out for her.

"Looks like someone's eager to leave," Liam joked, but it sent a heavy rock to settle in the pit of my stomach. He must've sensed my unease, because he placed a hand on my shoulder and squeezed it tightly. It was his way of telling me I had to move on with this. It wasn't fair.

I took a deep breath. "I guess we should get her bags in the carriage."

Liam grabbed the bags we'd packed for Ava-Marie. Esis took one of her stuffed animals, which was practically as big as he was, and carried it down the stairs. Julian stood by the carriage, looking sad. Liam loaded the bags inside. I peeked in the back seat to see a car seat was ready for her, along with snacks, diapers, and toys my parents had bought to keep her entertained. My mom opened the door, but I couldn't move. Even though I tried to make my legs move, they wouldn't.

"How long will the trip take?" I asked, stalling.

"We can't tell you that," Dad said. We'd already discussed the plan at length, and I knew that. "We won't be heading back to Utah right away. We don't want to risk anyone finding us— after what happened with the break-in."

"I know," I sniffled. "I just wish I knew where she'd be."

"She'll be safe, *pawee*," Liam assured me. "She's in good hands."

"Hey, wait for us!" a voice called from down the street.

We turned to see Jonah waving in our direction. Imogen followed beside him with a huge bag over her shoulder. Squeaks and Sassy weren't far behind. Squeaks' babies trotted alongside her, but they were so tiny they kept tripping over each other. They'd certainly inherited some of their mother's personality traits.

Jonah approached and placed a hand on his hip. "If you thought you could let our little Ava leave without saying goodbye, you were wrong."

Liam rolled his eyes at him. "You're late."

"Fashionably," Jonah teased.

"It was Squeaks' fault," Imogen said. "She's super slow ever since the foals were born."

Her pitch grew higher as she reached out a finger to tickle Ava-Marie. "But we made it, didn't we? Yes, we did."

"Can we hold her?" Jonah asked.

I hesitated a second, until Liam nudged me and I handed her over. Ava-Marie cooed in Jonah's arms. I wrapped my arm around Liam's waist, because I had to do *something* with it.

"You are just the cutest thing, aren't you?" he asked in a baby tone. He tickled her stomach, and she laughed. "We're gonna miss you so much. But you know what? Uncle Jonah and Auntie Imogen brought you gifts!"

Liam groaned at my side, and I already knew what he was thinking. Knowing Imogen and Jonah, that bag was filled to the brim with inappropriate items.

But when Imogen opened the zipper and started showing Ava the gifts, I was surprised at how practical they were. "This is a picture of us," Imogen said, holding up a framed photo. "So you'll never forget your aunt and uncle."

She placed the photo back in the bag and dug out a cute pink dress. "I got you this in three sizes so you always have one to wear, even as you grow."

Next, she pulled out a rattle and shook it at Ava. It was made in the shape of a dragon, and Ava loved it. She reached out for it and laughed as she shook it.

"There's also a mobile, bath toys, teethers, bibs, and ointment," Imogen said.

"Show her the best part," Jonah nudged.

Imogen reached back into the bag and pulled out two different nightlights. One was shaped like a fox, and the other like a hippogriff. Imogen started to tear up as she showed them to Ava. "They're nightlights so you don't get scared in the dark, and so that S-sassy and Squeaks will b-be there when you sl-sleep."

Imogen started to wail, which made *me* cry, which turned into one huge crying fest. Even Julian started howling loudly, as if he intended to wake the entire neighborhood. Jonah handed Ava off to Imogen, who handed her to Liam.

The goodbyes must've gone on for an hour... but it felt like far too soon.

"I'm going to miss you every moment you're gone," I whispered to my daughter as I placed her in my mother's arms. My chest tightened to the point where I could hardly breathe, even though I knew this was the right thing to do. "I love you, Ava-Marie."

She cooed and kicked her legs. I assumed that was baby talk for *I love you, too.*

"She'll be safe, Sophia," my mom promised for at least the hundredth time. "We promise."

Dad clapped Liam on the shoulder and shook his hand firmly. "Everything will be okay, Chief."

Liam wiped his eyes. Far too soon, my parents climbed into the carriage. My breath hitched as the carriage began to drive away. I grabbed on to Liam, because I didn't think my knees would keep me upright. He nearly fell over, too, but Julian was right beside him to support the two of us. Esis and Buttercup climbed onto Julian's horns. Esis tilted his chin toward the morning sky and let out a mournful cry that Buttercup echoed. Squeaks had curled up on the ground, wrapping her babies under her wing. Sassy ran after the carriage, barking loudly.

I turned to Liam, sorrow thick in my tone. "I can't do this, Liam."

His look was sad, but he was staying stronger than I was. He took me by the shoulders and looked me in the eyes. "But you have, Sophia. The hard part is over. Now all we have to do is win this war... so we can see our daughter again."

By the Great Spirit's holy name, it was the only thing that kept me going. Ava-Marie was gone, and I would do everything in my power to make sure she made it home safe.

I COULDN'T FUNCTION the rest of the week. Every morning, I woke expecting to hear my daughter's cries, but there was nothing but silence. Her crib lay empty, as if she'd never been there in the first place.

It was so eerie. My whole life for the past five months had revolved around her— feeding her and changing her, putting her to bed and keeping her entertained. She absorbed most of my day. Now that I'd gotten that time back, I didn't know what to do with myself.

At times, it felt like I'd imagined her. But now was not the time to dig myself into a hole. Now was the time to be strong— to fight. Even though Liam and I sensed the emptiness in our home, we would not allow it to break us.

The following weekend, I accompanied Liam with chief duties. It was the only way to keep myself occupied when I wasn't practicing my Anichi skills with Luana or sparring with our friends on the beach. We'd been training extra hard lately, pushing our limits to see just how far we could take our magic in order to defeat the Elders.

And yet, it wasn't enough. We'd seen the kinds of Familiars they'd brought to our front door when they attacked *Hok'evale* last Christmas. We had to be able to defeat anything Oleander threw at us. Right now, even with the progress we'd made since then, I wasn't sure we could take them all out before the rest of Oleander's creature army took us down.

"We'll need every resource we have," Liam had announced several times.

I wholeheartedly agreed. It was why when Liam wasn't in council meetings and I wasn't training, we were infusing crystals with magic, to ensure every member of our army had an extra boost of power.

We sat in the square near the Anichi temple late one afternoon, working our magic into the crystals. Transference had become an entire community project. All who were able gathered with us to transfer their magic into the crystals. Chief Cauac and other Anichi worked on sorting the crystals into non-powered and powered, then placed them in color-coded wheelbarrows for each House's magic.

I didn't know why we'd chosen to operate near the Anichi temple. It just happened like that one day, and no one suggested any alternative. I swore I could feel my magic grow more intense near the temple, and I suspected others felt that way, too.

I worked quickly, transferring my Anichi magic into clear crystals and tossing them into a bucket nearby when I'd finished. I sat on a long picnic table beside Liam. Luana shared a bucket with me, as we were the only two who could infuse Anichi magic. Imogen worked quietly beside her, one of her hands laced in Cade's fingers. Jonah raced Jake to see who could fill their bucket first. Amelia was trying to keep Kiwi from swallowing the smaller crystals, while Trace struggled with transference beside her. He'd gotten half a dozen stones so far, but he wasn't very fast. Sassy chased Esis and Buttercup, who kept stealing crystals away from us and hiding them in holes they dug under the table.

At the end of the table sat Baine and Doya. Doya had complained earlier she was hungry, and Baine had left to get her takeout. He came back with a sandwich and soup from *The Falcon's Nest*. I tried not to laugh when he opened the soup container and spilled it all over her dress. To my surprise, she waved it off and gave him a kiss. She was like a totally different person around him.

Now Doya was working on transference while she ate, and Baine was skimming through the Anichi book he'd acquired. I didn't know what else he hoped to find in there. Chief Cauac had translated it fully, and Baine could hardly read Anichi himself. But he just kept adjusting his glasses and reading on, like he was fluent in the language.

Wyatt and Mia were watching a bunch of kids in the middle of the square, including Mattias, Jackson, and Xavier. Neither of them had mastered transference, so it was their way of helping.

I tried to keep my eyes off the kids, but it was hard. They just kept reminding me of Ava. Haloke had returned with her housekeeper, Beatrice, and she and the orangutan-like creature handed out snacks to the kids.

Ezra and Stevie were on the other side of Liam, but they weren't working on transference. Instead, they sorted through old war paints and used their water magic to renew the pigments that were dried out.

"This is a beautiful color," Stevie said, staring down at the blue. It matched the baby blue bow she wore in her hair today.

"I prefer yellow," Ezra said, reaching for a container of bright yellow paint.

"You do?" Stevie raised an eyebrow, then stuck her finger into the paint and smeared it on his nose. "Boop!"

Ezra laughed and wiped it off. "Yeah, it, uh... it matches Dyami's feathers."

At the sound of his name, Dyami looked over to us. He was by Vanessa, Maddie, and Drew, along with all the dragon Familiars, breaking apart larger crystals so they'd be easy to carry. Bren, Lindsey, and Miranda carried more over for them.

"War paints use Hawkei symbols, don't they?" Jonah asked thoughtfully.

"Absolutely," Jake answered. He sounded enthusiastic, like he knew a lot about war paints.

Jonah stared at him, completely forgetting about his race to fill his bucket. He was so star-struck with his new husband. It made me smile, at least for a moment.

Jake went on. "Certain symbols can enhance your magic. If everyone's got war paint and these crystals, the Elders are going to have one hell of a time out there."

I shifted uncomfortably in my seat, and Liam noticed. If the ancestors didn't want to show up for us, I didn't know how this war would end. Still, we had to do everything we could to level the playing field.

"How do we know which symbols to use?" Jonah asked, entranced by everything Jake said.

It was Ezra who answered. "I'm on it."

He pulled out a stack of papers from beside himself I hadn't noticed before. They all had strange writings on them that I recognized as Hawkei, but couldn't translate. "Liam and I learned the symbols as kids. Stevie and I created these cheat sheets for everyone."

Liam eyed him curiously. "You learned war symbols? When? You were always too busy fucking around."

Ezra frowned at him. "I paid attention."

"Until puberty," Cade cracked. "When you went totally *air headed*."

"Not fair!" Ezra protested, but he was laughing along. "It's not like I'm the only guy whose dick suddenly started thinking for him."

"It's true," Imogen added. "Your dick really does have a mind of its own!"

"Ancestors," Liam sighed, hoping to end the conversation. "Let me see those."

He took one of Ezra's cheat sheets and looked it over. His features softened the more he read, and he handed it back. "I have to say, you did a good job, bro."

"Told you," Ezra shot back as he nudged Liam in the shoulder.

"Come now, children," Imogen teased. "There's no need to fight."

"But *Mom*," Ezra complained.

Imogen scoffed. "If anything, I'm Aunt Imogen. Liam's the mom around here."

Liam's eyebrows got tight. "I'm not *the mom*."

Luana scrunched up her nose and signed, *Yeah, you kind of are.*

"I'm chief," Liam reminded them. "Call me Mom one more time, and I'll have you thrown in the caves."

I snickered lightly, but inside, my stomach sank. For the first time in what felt like forever, Liam was being playful. It felt nice, instead of being serious all the time. Yet right now, as we were preparing for war and our daughter was away, it didn't feel right.

"That's a serious threat," Jonah teased. "You *try* to throw me in the caves, and I'll rain lightning down on your ass."

Liam smirked. "I'd like to see you try."

"Oh, yeah?" Jonah challenged. He raised his hands toward the sky, and storm clouds began to brew.

"Touch my husband, and you're getting a fireball to the head," I added, only half serious.

"Aww, I can't play?" Jonah grumbled, lowering his hands. The clouds cleared quickly.

"Baine," a woman's voice said so loudly, we all turned to look. Madame Wells had been walking by. She stopped at our table when she saw Baine reading the Anichi book. She sounded slightly surprised.

Baine looked up at her and adjusted his glasses. "Yes, Madame Wells. May I help you?"

She shook her head. "No. I just noticed you received my book. Was it of any use to you?"

Baine gaped at her and looked flustered as he flipped to the cover and then back to the open page he was on. "This book is *yours*?"

Madame Wells smiled, but otherwise, didn't look like she understood his shock. "Yes, of course. I thought that was obvious? It was handed down my family line. I left it in your house, because I thought it would be helpful."

Doya's features darkened, and she stood to face Madame Wells. "This book contains critical information. Why didn't you hand it over to my husband sooner?"

Cade groaned. Doya had been calling Baine *her husband* every chance she got. It was starting to get a little over the top.

Madame Wells faced Doya without an ounce of fear in her features. Normally, others would cower under her gaze. "I simply listened to the will of the ancestors. Showana told me to wait until it was time."

I huffed under my breath, but all eyes were still on Madame Wells. Only Liam noticed. I stood from my seat and walked a few paces away from the table.

Liam quickly followed. "*Pawee*, what's wrong?"

I turned to face him, but I lowered my voice so no one else could hear. "I'm sick of Showana," I hissed. "*Just wait*. It's all she ever says. What kind of bull crap is that? Our daughter is gone, this war never ends, and Showana just wants us to wait around. For what?"

Liam took me by the shoulders. "I know it's hard, *pawee*, but you said it yourself— the ancestors are training us. If we'd tried to beat Oleander a year ago, even months ago, we wouldn't have been ready."

I crossed my arms. "What makes you think we're ready now? We'll *never* be ready. We might as well get it over with."

Liam sighed heavily. "What happened, *pawee*? You were so hopeful just a few weeks ago."

"We gave up our daughter is what happened," I snapped. "Liam, I wasn't lying when I said I wasn't sure we could do this."

"But we *have* to," he pressed. "We don't have any choice."

"Exactly," I emphasized. "My destiny has been written since before my birth. I never had a choice in any of this. The ancestors are using me as some sort of pawn, and I'm sick of it."

"I don't think that's true, Soph," he said. "You've always had a choice, and you chose to be the one the prophecy speaks of."

"Well, it doesn't feel like it." I turned my gaze away from his. My chest rose and fell in shallow breaths, and the air was hot and heavy. I knew Liam was right, but I couldn't say so out loud. Giving up my daughter had changed everything.

"Tell me this," Liam suggested. "If you had to do it all over again, would you change anything?"

I bit my lower lip and thought about it for several long seconds. If I'd known at the beginning that the ancestors wanted me to send my daughter away, I never would have agreed to it.

But if I hadn't followed my destiny, who knew if Liam and I would even be together now? Maybe not— but if I weren't the chosen one, we wouldn't have had to go on the run. Perot would've told us of Liam's true health earlier. Ava-Marie never would've been born. If I could choose a world where my daughter was alive— even if she wasn't by my side— and one where she didn't exist at all, I'd choose the one with her in it every time.

"I guess I'd still do everything the same," I admitted.

"You know how close I've come to giving up, *pawee*," Liam reminded me. "Sending Ava away... it damn near killed me, too. But I won't allow myself to see this as a sign to give up. We have to use it to spark hope— to fight as hard as we can."

I reached up to caress the side of his face. He stared back at me with a soft expression, and I felt like I could fall into his eyes and never stop falling. "When did *you* become the wise one?"

Liam looked a little shocked at the question. "I don't know. When shit got hard, I guess."

A few beats passed between us. I stared down at my fingers and poked at a loose hangnail. "I want to believe you, Liam. I want to be strong for everyone. I just don't know what that feels like anymore."

Liam glanced toward our friends and shifted uncomfortably. When he turned back to me, his face lit up. He took my hand in his and started leading me across the square.

"What are we doing?" I asked.

"We're getting out of here," Liam stated.

"But the war effort," I protested.

"The war effort is nothing if you're not motivated to fight," Liam said. "You need something to fight for, *pawee*."

Liam and I stopped beside Julian, and the dragon bowed his head to us. Liam hoisted me up on Julian's back, then jumped on behind me. Across the square, Esis noticed me, but he was so wrapped up in collecting rocks that he just waved.

"Liam, where are we going?" I asked, not sure if I actually wanted to leave or not.

Liam grabbed tightly to Julian's spines. "You'll see."

He kicked Julian's sides, and the dragon took off. My stomach lurched as we shot into the sky, and my heart didn't slow until we were high above the town.

Julian leveled out. The wind whipped through my hair, but I tossed it over my shoulders so I could look out over the ocean. The setting sun glistened off the beautiful blue sea. The skies were all shades of pinks, purples, and blues. For a moment, I forgot that we were fighting, because the sight was so beautiful.

"I know what we're fighting for," I told Liam, gesturing to the ocean. "This. Our home."

"But it's more than that," Liam said.

I was about to ask what he meant, when Julian shifted course. I yelped and held on tighter.

Liam's warm arms tightened around me. "We're almost there, *pawee*. Hold on."

Julian flew out far past the town, but within the boundary of the protection shield. I tried to watch where we were going, but I didn't like looking down.

After a few minutes, Julian started his descent. I didn't know where we were going, as I'd never been out this way before. As a nearby cliff came into view, my jaw dropped.

The rocky cliff touched the edge of the ocean, and waves sprayed sparkling water everywhere. Lush greenery filled the cliff, with vines hanging down over the edge and bordering a beautiful waterfall that rained into the ocean. But it wasn't the gorgeous scenery that got me. It was the dragons.

Hundreds of dragons swarmed the cliff, their scales glittering in the setting sun. There were fire dragons, earth dragon, air dragons, and ice dragons alike, and they were all different sizes and colors. As we came in closer, I saw that smaller dragons were perched in the treetops, while the larger ones were curled up in a huge clearing, all watching the sunset. Between them, little baby dragons wrestled one another. Fortune Fairies fluttered around the clearing, their luminescent bodies flickering on and off as if the cliff was glittering with magic.

Julian tilted in the air, circling the dragon clearing from above. The other dragons took notice, and a whole fleet of them created a formation, then took off to the skies. They circled around, following Julian as if he was their leader. Several baby dragons tried to follow, but they barely got three feet off the ground before their wings gave up. One of the baby fire dragons hiccupped, and fire shot out of his nose while he went flying back several feet. I snickered and pointed, and Liam laughed with me.

"They're so cute!" I beamed.

Julian landed in the clearing, and Liam and I slid off his back. Nearby, dragon mothers were nesting on their eggs, while a group of younger dragons swayed back and forth and cooed together in song. The larger dragons who'd followed Julian landed beside us. Each of them bowed their head and nudged it against Julian's, as if it was their way of greeting each other.

"Wow. This is beautiful," I said breathlessly. I couldn't take my eyes off all the shining scales.

Liam took my hand in his, and we walked toward the edge of the cliff. "It's a community, Soph."

My eyes traveled across tiny baby dragons, then out toward the ocean where others flew in formation. Liam stopped close to the edge of the cliff, and we sat in the grass to watch the sunset.

Liam draped an arm around me. "It's beautiful, because it's built on love."

"Like us?" I asked, squeezing his hand.

Liam nodded. "Exactly like us. Our people became united in a time of fear, but we stayed united because of love. That's what we're fighting for, *pawee*. We're fighting for Maddie and Drew, who were tortured by Oleander and his men. We're fighting for Bren and Vanessa, whose son was taken from them. We're fighting for Lindsey and Miranda, for Wyatt and

Sam, and everyone else who was held captive by Oleander. We're fighting for everyone who lost their Familiars, and all the kids we rescued from the camps. We're fighting for your parents, who were forced out of their home. We're fighting for Amelia, who was tortured on the *Hozho*, and for Trace and Cade, who were forced to fake their own deaths and leave their families behind for the cause. We're fighting for my mom, who lost her husband to the power-hungry greed of the Elders, and for my siblings who lost their father. We're fighting for Luana, who has never seen the world because she was born into the role of protector for these people. We're fighting for all of Anichi, who have never known the blessing of bonding to their other half."

Tears started to bead in my eyes, but they weren't angry or frustrated. I felt sorry for each one of the people he listed, and I knew I'd do anything for them.

Liam took a long breath before continuing. "We're fighting for our family— for Jonah, for Imogen, and most of all, for Ava. And as for me... *pawee*, I'm fighting for *you*."

I hiccupped, then tears started rolling down my cheeks. I placed my hand over my mouth to hold it back.

Liam leaned over to wipe the tears away. "We've lost so many people in this war— my dad, your grandparents, Alric..."

He trailed off before he could finish the list. We both knew it didn't quite have an end anymore. "We fight so that we don't have to lose one another. We fight for the people we love, to give them the future they deserve. *That's* what I'm fighting for, *pawee*. What about you?"

I couldn't contain myself anymore. Sobs rocked my chest, and I threw my arms around his neck. "That's what I'm fighting for, too," I cried. "I won't give up, Liam. Never. What you said just now... it means everything to me. I will do everything to fight for the people I love."

Liam opened his mouth to say something more, but he didn't get a chance. I pressed my lips to his and silenced his words with a passionate kiss.

Before long, we were totally making out. Liam's tongue slid inside my mouth, and his hand inched up my shirt. My fingers roamed through his hair, and I climbed on top of him, arching my back. My heart beat wildly in my chest. I wanted him so desperately right now.

"Touch me, Liam," I begged.

Liam drew away from me and glanced around. It was almost dark now, and the stars had started to come out. "You really want to fuck in front of all these dragons?"

I hesitated and bit my lower lip. "That's weird, huh?"

He scrunched up his nose and laughed. "A little."

I smirked. I always did love screwing around in new places. "Then I guess we're going to have to finish this somewhere private."

Liam pushed me off of himself and stood, reaching out a hand. "Come here, *pawee*. I have an idea."

I didn't question him as I placed my hand in his. Liam wrapped an arm around my waist. He smiled in the light of the quarter moon. Suddenly, a cold chill slithered around my body. I gasped and looked down to see that a column of seawater had risen from the ocean below and was swirling around the two of us.

"Hold on," he warned.

I wrapped my arms around him and closed my eyes as his water carried us out over the sea. We were flying high above the ocean, spinning as if in a dance. Along the cliff, the dragons started to hum a tune. The moment was so incredibly magical.

"Thank you for bringing me here, Liam," I whispered.

Liam pushed my hair from my eyes, and I looked up to him. "Thank you for being here with me, *pawee*."

There was more to his tone— like he didn't mean just here and now, but for all of time.

Liam's magic curled around the cliff, until the water spiral dropped us off a hundred yards from the dragons. We could still hear their song, but we could no longer see them. Liam led me into the trees, where Fortune Fairies lit up the forest. Above us, the stars twinkled in the clear sky. My feet sank into a soft, dry bed of moss.

Before I could tell Liam how beautiful this forest was, he scooped me up into his arms. I yelped in surprise, but his kiss silenced me. As he kissed me, he got to his knees and lowered me onto the soft bed of moss. He leaned over me, his hands roaming the curves of my body, until they reached my breasts. I grabbed for my shirt and pulled it up over my head, because I'd be damned if he didn't touch me like I wanted to be touched right now. Liam reached behind my back and used one hand to pop the clasp of my bra open. My breasts broke free, and Liam tossed the bra beside himself in the grass. I was so freaking wet right now, I nearly tore his shirt yanking it off of him.

Liam slowed when we were both topless, and he trailed gentle kisses down my neck. "You're so perfect, *pawee*," he whispered against my collarbone. "I can't imagine a life without you in it. I will fight for you until the day I die."

I didn't like that kind of language— as if he was prepared to sacrifice himself for me in this war. No way in hell did I marry Liam Mitoh just to lose him before our first anniversary. He'd survived losing his Familiar. He could survive anything.

Yet if he didn't... I couldn't handle the thought right now.

"Shh..." I said. "Don't talk."

I dragged Liam closer to me, and he seemed eager to let our bodies do the talking. Liam kissed me like it was the last time. I drank him in like he was the last glass of water I'd ever have. His hands roamed every inch of me, and I wrapped my legs so tight around him that he'd never escape my hold. I thrust my hands into his pants, and I got even wetter as my fingers curled around his hard cock.

Liam gasped, and his lips left mine to travel down to my breasts. He bit at my nipple, and I cried out in pleasure. I wanted him inside me *now*.

I pulled at the button on his pants, and Liam was quick to read my signals. He stood and threw his pants off in record time, then knelt beside me to take mine off. In moments, he was on top of me again.

"Fuck me, Liam," I begged.

He didn't have to be asked twice. In one swift hip movement, Liam was inside of me. The world spun around me, as if I was tumbling over and over again down a steep ravine. It was scary and exhilarating all at once.

Soon, my world could end. But right now, I was more alive than ever. Liam was right that we would fight for the people we loved. I'd be damned to *Aiya Nocshun* if I didn't fight until my very last breath for this man.

I thrust my hips up, and we went rolling across the ground. Liam drew heavy breaths as I climbed on top of him and rode him with everything I had in me.

"Fuck, *pawee*," he gasped. "Not yet. I want it to last."

"Then pleasure me," I begged.

Liam grabbed me around the hips and pulled me off of him. He tossed me onto the ground beside him, and it was anything but gentle. It was hot—animalistic. Just the way I liked it.

I writhed on the ground, begging for everything he could give me. Liam ducked his head and ran his tongue along my clit, then thrust his fingers up inside of me. His other hand reached up to fondle my breasts, squeezing my nipples. I gasped in pleasure, and my moans echoed through the forest.

"Liam," I cried as pleasure built up inside of me.

Liam licked me again, then paused to say, "Call my name, Sophia."

"Liam," I cried again. I could barely get his name out past the hammering of my heart. I'd gone totally breathless as he finger-banged me like there was no tomorrow.

The build-up of pleasure was unlike anything I'd experienced before. Liam and I had a *lot* of sex, but this was different. It seemed to last forever, that exhilarating high. Then just like that, I reached a peak, and I went spiraling into an earth-shattering orgasm that might as well have opened up the world and swallowed the two of us whole.

Liam jumped backward as I came, and it took me a full minute to come down from the high. I lay on the ground, panting and waiting for my heart to slow. When I finally opened my eyes, I saw he was sitting several feet away from me.

"What's wrong?" I asked, though I couldn't wipe the smile off my face.

Liam smirked and gestured to my hair. "Your Fire got a little carried away."

I reached up to where he was pointing. I realized my hair was on fire! I quickly pulled back on my magic, then ran my fingers through the strands. My hair was back to normal, except the surrounding moss had caught fire and was quickly turning to ash. I used my magic to stop it, then turned back to Liam. We shared a quiet moment, before the two of us burst into laughter.

"Well, that's a new one," I giggled.

Liam smiled. "There's always something new with you, isn't there?"

I beamed back. "It keeps things interesting."

"In that case, let's try something else new," Liam said with a hunger in his eyes.

I raised a curious eyebrow. "What's that?"

"Lay down," Liam instructed.

I did as I was told, eager to see what he had in store. Liam climbed on top of me, straddling me. Just as I thought he was about to get in position, he grabbed my hips and flipped me over. I gasped as I lay on my front and Liam smacked my ass playfully.

I snickered and glanced back at him. "You like that?"

He stared down at my ass eagerly. "Fuck yeah, I do."

"Then do it," I told him, shimmying my ass at him.

Liam couldn't hold back any longer. He forced my legs apart and thrust into me from behind. The two of us moaned in unison. At this angle, he hit pleasure centers I hardly knew were there. Liam rocked back and forth several more times, and I placed my hand between my legs to play with my clit while he moved inside of me. It didn't take long before that pleasurable sensation grew within me again.

Liam gasped, and together, we reached our peak. This time was— dare I say it?— even better than the last. Anichi magic bloomed from my chest, creating a huge shield around us in the forest. Out of the trees, I could hear the waves crashing against the cliff side fiercely. Liam's magic stirred the whole fucking ocean.

We fell to the ground together, panting. Liam couldn't catch his breath to say anything. Instead, he reached out an arm, and I snuggled into his chest. We stared up past the trees to the sparkling stars. I didn't know what would happen next, but I knew that tonight had been perfect.

After minutes of listening to Liam's heartbeat, I whispered, "What are you thinking about?"

Liam took a moment to respond. "I was... actually looking at the sky and thinking about Starbeasts."

"Starbeasts?" I asked. I recalled Lani mentioning them, but I couldn't remember what they were.

"I learned about them in Hawkei Legends," Liam said. "They're creatures made from stardust, and they can control things like meteor showers. Supposedly, they used to bond with Anichi."

"Mmm..." I mused. "I wonder if they're still out there."

"They are," Liam said. "I saw them once. Creatures of all different types came down from the skies— dragons and unicorns and sea serpents. Their form was black, but they were made of stars. It was incredible. I'm sorry you didn't get to see them. Legend has it, they once bonded with Spirit Warriors."

I took a deep breath, trying to imagine them. "Maybe you can introduce me someday."

"I'm not sure how Lopez summoned them," Liam admitted. "We can go back to where I saw them. Maybe they'll show."

"That sounds like fun," I said dreamily. I liked that we were making plans for after the war, if only to hold on to a bit of hope.

We lay there for what must've been an hour, until we could hear Julian outside the trees calling for Liam. The two of us got dressed and headed back toward the clearing, where Julian jumped like an excited puppy to see us.

"We're fine," Liam told him, scratching his nose. "We just needed a few minutes by ourselves."

Ancestors, I was still beaming. Julian reared his head, gesturing for us to get on his back.

"I guess we should get back," I said. "Esis is probably wondering where we're at."

Liam agreed, and we climbed on Julian's back and flew to *Hok'evale*. When Julian landed outside our house, I saw that Jake and Jonah were sitting on the stairs. Jake was tickling Buttercup, and Jonah was letting Esis braid his hair. Squeaks and Sabor were hacking up their last meal to feed their kids. Ew.

Jonah's eyes lit up when he saw us. He stood, though his hair hung down only half-braided. "Hey, guys. We didn't know where you'd run off to. We thought we'd wait with the kurbles until you got back."

Jake set Buttercup aside. Though Jonah sounded happy to see us, Jake looked a little solemn. My stomach sank, the high from earlier gone.

"Is something wrong?" Liam demanded.

Jake shoved his hands into his pants pockets. "As you both know, I've been sending spies to fly above Kinpago to track Oleander's movements."

"And?" I pressed, sensing this was anything but good news.

Jake drew a deep breath. "Our spies have just returned with word that the Task Force is preparing another strike on *Hok'evale*."

Liam's hands curled into fists. "We can't let them get here again!"

"That won't happen," Jake promised. "We're going to meet the Task Force halfway. We'll stop them before they get this far."

"Halfway?" I asked, hardly able to process what he was saying.

Jake nodded. "Our final battle has arrived. We march at dawn."

Liam

TWENTY-ONE

I had a restless night. Jake had told us to get some sleep, as we'd need it for the coming battle.

Sleep was the last thing my body wanted. Instead, it craved revenge.

A combination of angst and anxiety ate me up until it was time to rise. I awoke expecting to hear Ava-Marie's cries, but the house was silent.

She was a fussy baby. She cried more than she rested and was inconsolable unless she was held. She'd been difficult, but I'd give anything to have one more sleepless night listening to her wails, over experiencing the crushing silence as my wife tossed and turned, unable to get any peace herself.

Those bastards had taken my daughter from me. I wanted to make them pay. My body would live off nothing but hatred until she was back in my arms again.

Dawn came, and it was time to move. Soldiers were marching out of *Hok'evale*, climbing onto their flying Familiars and taking to the skies in formation. Those who could not fly had already left, to get a head start to intercede the Elders. The only ones left behind in town were women with small children, the elderly, and those too sick to battle. Everyone else who was of age and had magic was expected to fight.

Jonah and Imogen were waiting outside, along with Luana and their Familiars. Sophia and I joined them. We'd donned the Elementai armor and painted our faces with our respective House colors to match.

We'd all picked Hawkei symbols. My blue paint showed the rune of bravery. Julian was beside me. It'd taken an hour for me to paint his scales in a way that matched mine, but if I wasn't mistaken, he appeared fiercer than he had before.

Jonah had picked the rune of loyalty, and Imogen went with heart. Luana had gone with Anichi symbols, ones similar to those on the Spirit Totem that, if I was translating correctly, spelled *healer* across her nose and under her eyes.

Sophia had chosen the rune for sacrifice and painted it on both cheeks with opposing colors— red for Koigni and white for Anichi. Esis had copied her, a red line drawn down the middle of his forehead. My wife wore the *Azaimperiai* around her neck and had my mother's compass attached to her armor at the hip.

The Hawkei hadn't painted their faces for battle in decades. That we were doing it today made us feel a connection to the warriors of the past. We felt ready to fight, but were we really? People were going to die out there today— probably people we loved. How much more were we willing to lose in order to win this war?

"We look badass," Jonah said as he looked us over. Squeaks' wings had been painted with violet. "The Elders are gonna start running when they see us."

Squeaks chirped in agreement. Her babies were at my mother's house. They'd stay there until the fight was over.

"Where's Jake?" Sophia asked. Her demeanor was calm and collected. She'd drawn blood before and wanted to do it again.

"He's at the battlefield." Jonah began to levitate. "We should meet him."

Sophia and I climbed onto Julian's back, while Luana and Imogen got onto Squeaks. Sassy jumped and settled on Imogen's lap, while Sierra rested on Luana's shoulder. Jonah led the way as we flew through the orange-red sunrise, out of the boundaries of *Hok'evale* and into the wind. Esis— the only kurble who'd joined the fight— sat on Julian's head and faced the world with determination written on his face.

Hundreds of others flew alongside us on their way to join the rebellion. Were we leading these people to their deaths? Or to freedom?

Jonah began to descend, and Julian and Squeaks followed him. The trees broke, revealing a long battlefield. There were two sides— the one below us, where the resistance was gathered, and one a mile or so off, where the Elders had collected their army. Nothing had happened yet, but it was clear by the tension radiating through the air that the battle was about to begin.

I'd been here before. This was the forest where we'd completed the Fire task of the Elemental Cup, though most of the dead trees had been cleared to make way for a battlefield— something Oleander must've intentionally done. The caves where we'd found the Spirit Totem were in sight, though far off in the distance. Being here felt awfully like repeating the past.

Jonah landed on a cliff above the resistance side. Jake was waiting there for us, along with Sabor. As I slid off of Julian, I looked down. Nivita were creating trenches several feet deep, wide enough for Elementai and most Familiars. I couldn't see all the way to the other side from here, but I bet the Task Force was doing the same thing.

As we came beside him, Luana touched Jake on the arm. He started when she did so, as if deep in thought. He appeared relieved at the sight of us.

"There you all are," he said, signing. "I was worried we'd begin without you."

"And miss all the action?" Imogen said. "Nah. We're always there when the shit starts."

"Unfortunately." Jake said. "It seems the Elders have been preparing for our arrival. Their march was a preemptive attack to lure us out of *Hok'evale*. One I suspected, which is why we're giving them the illusion we've fallen for it."

Well, that's kind of a jackass move by them, Luana signed, and Sophia nodded in agreement.

"It doesn't matter. It was always going to come to this anyway." Jake frowned as he looked upon the battlefield.

"What's on your mind, babe?" Jonah asked, tilting his head. He put a hand on Jake's shoulder and squeezed it reassuringly.

Jake swallowed. "My parents always spoke of this day. But I didn't think it'd ever come. This war has gone on forever. I didn't see an end to it. I don't... I don't know what my life is going to be, after this. Being a general is all I know."

"That's not true," Jonah said. "You know who you are. And once it's all over, you'll get to be a hippogriffologist, like you always wanted. You'll never have to deal with war again."

Jake's mouth was thin. "You know that's not the only option."

"Then we'll be in the Ancestral Lands together," Jonah said. "And nothing will ever hurt us ever again. Either way, it's a win-win."

Jonah's optimism sure had a way of putting a spin on the worst of things. But it must've worked for Jake, because the thinnest of smiles had worked its way onto his face.

"So what's our strategy to win?" Sophia asked.

"We're not going to get to Kinpago. That's for certain," Jake said. "Luckily, I've been informed that Oleander is here, along with all of his Elders. We have to kill them first. Once Oleander doesn't have any support, we'll aim our sights on him. If we take him down, most of his followers will abandon the effort and give up. Then it'll all be over. Our priority will be getting across that field and into Elder territory."

"I don't see him here," I said as I scanned the clouds for Skylis. A creature that big should be easy to spot.

"He's hiding, but he's nearby. After what happened in the last battle we had, he no longer trusts his Elders to get the job done," Jake said.

So we just had to kill Oleander, and the battle would be won. Sounded easy, but far from it. We had to get to him first, not to mention he had a dracash to fight for him.

"It's a simple strategy. Kill the generals, and the soldiers fall apart," Jonah mused.

"Obviously, their Familiars will counter us, so we'll have to do our best to get as many over to the other side as possible." Jake sighed. For as confident as his voice was, I wasn't sure how truthful he was being.

"Sophia and I will go," I volunteered. "Julian's big enough now. He's one of the few Familiars that can take on Skylis."

Julian displayed his fangs. Jake hesitated. "I applaud your bravery, but you're the chief of Toaqua. We can't afford to lose you. It'd be better if you stayed back and gave orders to your tribe."

"My Elder Council will keep things in line for me. I've commanded them to direct the Toaqua army while I deal with Oleander," I said. "He's taken on the role that was meant for me. He's mine."

Jake raised an eyebrow. "You plan to challenge him to a chief's duel?"

"If I can get that close? Yes."

Jake rubbed his beard. "This might give us an advantage. He can't deny you a duel if you demand one. By ancestral law, he'll automatically forfeit his chief hood if he refuses. He won't look weak in front of his soldiers."

"Exactly. So leave Oleander up to me."

Jake crossed his arms over his chest. "I suppose the four of you are sticking together?"

He meant Sophia, Jonah, Imogen and myself.

"Of course," Imogen said. "Jonah can fly on his own. Sassy and I will ride on Squeaks. We'll find these Elders and kick their ass all the way to the Ancestral Lands."

"Then I'm coming with you. I'll lead the charge of our best soldiers over no-man's land," Jake said. "The other generals will stay behind and hold our position."

Jonah smirked. "You just wanna protect *me*."

"Well, there's that." Jake wrapped an arm around Jonah's side, and Sabor nuzzled Squeaks.

What will the Anichi do? Luana asked.

"Those crystals are our biggest asset. The Elders don't have Anichi to fight for them, which means they don't have shields. That makes a difference," Jake said. "The job of the Anichi is to keep the rest of us protected. As long as their shield holds, our trenches will be safe."

Then I'll help them do it, Luana said. *The Task Force won't get past our shields if I hold them up.*

Jake nodded briskly, and he started forward. "Luana, come with me. I must discuss this further with your father."

As Jake, Luana, and their Familiars left us, our little group stared toward the battlefield. Something lengthened between us, but it wasn't worry. It was more like... resignation. Like this was where we'd meant to be all along.

"You know," Imogen started, "all this happened because the Reject Team decided to fuck shit up."

Sophia sputtered, and Jonah gave a loud, humorous noise. Before I knew it, the four of us were laughing, because she was right. Ever since our Cup win, things had been leading up to this. Everything we'd done in the past two years— our trial, going up against the Elders, sneaking people out of the castle, joining the rebellion—had brought us to this moment.

And I don't think any of it would've happened if four misfits hadn't broken the rules and upended everything society told them to be. Our Cup victory had set off a chain of events that couldn't be undone. The rebellion had waited for years to challenge the Elders. It wasn't until a group of outcast kids had stood up to them that things started to change.

All of it had come to be because we never gave up on each other. We were from four different Houses. We weren't even supposed to be friends, and yet I'd die for any one of these people. Again and again, the world had tried to keep us apart, and we'd said no.

We were the most unexpected people, yet we'd all grown more

powerful than most Elementai alive. We'd gotten here together mostly by faith. More times than not, we'd hung on by nothing more than a prayer.

We were here today because we refused to accept what was, and demanded to see the impossible. Now our future was within reach. All we had to do was grab it.

"Before we do this... I just want you guys to know you were the greatest friends I ever had," Jonah said.

Squeaks cooed, and Sassy brushed her head against her leg.

Imogen choked up. "Me too," she whispered, giving a sniff.

"And me," Sophia added, lifting Esis onto her shoulder.

"The best years of my life were spent with you guys," I said quietly. "I really mean that."

"Wow, he finally admits it!" Imogen exclaimed through her tears. "It only took impending doom!"

"Shut up. I'm still an asshole," I said.

"And some things never change," Jonah quipped with a sigh. "Whatever happens, Liam Mitoh will always be a dick."

"*You'll* always be annoying," I added, though it was more affectionate than it was an insult.

"And all of us will always be weird," Imogen finished. "That's never going to change."

Ancestors, I hoped not. I wouldn't know what to do with myself if these people were normal.

Sophia swept a lock of hair back as Esis began braiding it. "No matter what happens, one of us has to make it out," she said. "For Ava."

I hadn't been scared before she said that, because I'd resolved myself to die this morning, if that was the way it was going to be. But to think of my friends going out that way... it was so much worse. There was a possibility that not just one of us would die... that *all* of us could.

I didn't want that to happen. I'd sacrifice my own life if it meant Sophia, Jonah, and Imogen got out. I'd planned to do the same during our tournament. Even in two years, that hadn't changed a bit.

Imogen shook her head. "No. I'm not agreeing to that."

"Ava needs us. If something happens to Liam and I, you guys are all she has," Sophia pleaded.

"Fuck that," Jonah said. "We have the same agreement we made when we went into the Elemental Cup. We all come out together, or we don't come out at all."

Sophia blinked, before she nodded. With tears in her eyes, she said, "Okay. Then we come out together."

I nudged Sophia. "Hey. Team motto on three?"

Imogen and Jonah's faces brightened with smiles. They stuck their hands in. I placed mine on top of theirs, and Sophia's warm fingers spread over my own. Esis reached from Sophia's shoulder, though he was far off from touching our hands. Squeaks and Sassy even joined in, putting a hoof and a paw in on the ground below us.

"Okay. One... two... three... *Let's not fucking die!*"

This time, we said it in unison. Yeah, it was a silly thing to do. We were going to war, not playing a sports game.

But this wasn't all that different from the Elemental Cup. And saying it made us feel better. It bonded us as one.

We wandered down to the trenches, where Nivita were still digging. Imogen spotted Cade and ran off to say some quick goodbyes— *for now,* Imogen had said.

"You got the *Azaimperiai, pawee?*" I asked Sophia as we headed down the stairs of the nearest trench.

"Yeah." She brought the Spirit Totem out of her armor before tucking it back in. "I'm ready to use it... whenever it's time."

"Your grandparents said you'd know. Just keep it close."

My brother was passing out canteens filled with water, which had belts to strap around the middle so Toaqua would always have a source to draw from. I took a canteen from him and attached it to my side. There wasn't much water out here, and everybody would be drawing some from the air, leaving not much to go on. It was best to be prepared.

Ezra had painted his face yellow, with streaks of black to match Dyami's feathers. Stevie was noticeably absent. "Where's your girlfriend?"

"She actually agreed to stay behind, for once," Ezra said. "I know, I'm as shocked as you are."

That was odd. She must not be feeling well today. Stevie was a good fighter, and we kind of needed her, but at the same time, she was one less person we had to worry about out here. If her disease was making it so she couldn't fight, maybe that was a good thing.

Someone had come to replace her, though. My mouth fell open when I recognized my mother, distributing supplies to other Toaqua. She was wearing leather armor that had been passed down from her grandmother. It was ancient Toaqua warrior armor, and meant to be ceremonial, though it'd once seen battle years ago. I'd never seen her wear it.

"Mom, what are you doing here?" I asked. "Where are the kids?"

"With Beatrice. I could not stand idly by when the people who killed my husband are still out there," Mom said fiercely. "This is my fight."

I wanted to tell her to go home— and as chief, I had the right— but even I was scared of my mother when she was pissed, and she was in a *mood*. I couldn't stop her from killing Task Force if that's what she'd come here to do.

Beside her was Maddie and Drew. I was surprised to see both of them. Neither had ever fought in any battles. Both were of age, but as a *naderei*, Maddie always insisted on sitting out fights, and Drew usually did the same.

When she noticed my curious look, Maddie tossed her hair back. "You're going to need me later. Trust me."

Maddie's expression was grim, which didn't bode well for the rest of us. Whatever she said was coming, it was happening soon.

I noticed other people among the trenches. Wyatt and Mia were here. I didn't think Mia would show up, as she had Mattias, but apparently she'd left him behind with someone to come here. Tuskin was missing— presumably in the ocean with other Water Familiars, but Taryn was dutifully by Mia's side. Bren, Lindsey and Miranda were working to keep the Fire wall around the trenches burning. Anichi held crystals in their hands and concentrated beside Luana, building the invisible shield. I counted others— Amelia and Trace, Riley and Isabella, Professors Perot and Amber, and Tabitha. Even Vanderbilt and his son, Sean, were all preparing for war alongside their Familiars.

Vanessa was giving orders to the Koigni tribe, but she was alone. Aisha was missing, along with a host of dragon Familiars. Where were they?

Well, besides them, the gang was all here. Time to see what we were made of.

James was pacing nearby. His dragon Familiar, like the others, wasn't nearby. He wore a path in the mud as he wandered back and forth nervously.

"This is impossible!" James burst, and several people looked his way. "How can we win this fight? How can we expect to survive?"

He stopped and shook his head. "It's hopeless. The Elders are so strong. All we can do is pray. Nothing's going to save us."

Many dropped their gazes, void of hope. My stomach knotted with anxiety and fear. James was right. We were expecting a miracle.

Carter strode forward, a determined look on his face. His lindwyrm,

Tiara, cooed as he left her side. Carter turned James to face him roughly and wrapped an arm around his waist, proclaiming, "Our love will save us."

Carter kissed James full on the mouth. A few people clapped and cheered, but myself, I was shocked. James' eyes widened in surprise— like he wasn't expecting Carter to do what he just did— then he fell into the kiss, throwing his arms around Carter's neck as they made out for the whole world to see.

Um, okay. Looks like I was wrong about them not being gay.

Jonah was giddy. He looked at me and mouthed, *I told you*!

"Geez. Everyone's hooking up at the last minute, huh?" Sophia asked.

"Better to tell someone how you feel now than to live with regrets," I said as we watched Carter and James sneak off to another part of the trench to get a private moment.

Baine and Doya were obviously proclaiming to the Elders they were together. They wore *matching* tactical outfits, for the ancestors' sake. Though Baine fumbled with attaching his water canister to his hip, Doya and Naomi certainly looked in their element. Both were cool and collected as they prowled to our side.

Doya crossed her arms as she stood in front of us. "I hope you're ready. This is the day we've all been waiting for."

"I'll do whatever it takes to stop Oleander," Sophia pledged. "I promise that."

"Leave Oleander to the rest of us. Your life is more important than anything else in this battle, Sophia, because this rebellion depends on you," Doya said.

Sophia stiffened beside me, and I squeezed her to my side for comfort. Doya's words rang true. Sophia was a symbol of the rebellion. As the chosen one, she couldn't fall.

I wasn't going to let that happen.

The sun came up over the battlefield, igniting the morning. Conversation fell dead as minutes passed. We waited in a line at the head of the trenches, holding our breath. Neither our side nor Oleander's had made a move. I didn't know why. It was like both parties were waiting to see what the other was going to do.

I had to fight off dread and worry as it threatened to swallow me whole. It was agonizing, dragging out the moment like this. It was practically worse than the fighting itself. The only thing that kept me from running off was Sophia at my side.

Voices began rising over the horizon. At first, I thought they were screaming madly at us, until I realized the Task Force was speaking words. What the hell were they chanting? I couldn't hear them. Silence fell over the rebellion, until the sound of their screaming broke through.

"*Strong survive! Strong survive!*"

The Defortai motto. My mouth soured as I heard it. *Only the strong deserve to survive.* It'd been shoved down my throat since this whole war had started, and I was sick of it.

"One tribe!" I heard Ezra cry out. Several people glanced at him. As the Defortai screamed their slogan, he screamed again, "One tribe!"

Others caught on. Mom was the second to lend her voice. Lindsey, Miranda, and Bren started shouting with them. Sophia and I joined in. Our voices grew louder and louder as the battle cry swelled across the trench. Eventually, the entire rebellion was screaming it, thousands of voices crying out our protest as the Task Force demanded our surrender.

"*Strong survive!*"

"*One tribe!*"

"*Strong survive!*"

"*One tribe!*"

My heart grew bold with our words. We *were* one tribe. And we were fighting so the Hawkei could be united forever, no longer divided by House lines. We had become a singular people. Unity was what the ancestors had planned for us all along. I fought today so my daughter could live in an integrated tomorrow. This battle was needed, if only for the sake of our children, so they did not have to experience the hatred and division all of us had suffered. I'd been so scared for so long— scared to love Sophia, scared to be friends with people from other Houses, scared of the Elders.

I knew I might die today. But I wasn't afraid anymore, because we had nothing left to lose. This was worth fighting for. It was worth *dying* for. And I'd bring that new tomorrow about for Ava-Marie on this day, no matter what it cost me.

With no warning, the battle cries ceased and turned into screams. Somebody must've let out a spell, because I heard it whizz by. A small explosion happened— probably a gust of Air slamming against the shield. It rocked the trenches, scattering dirt, before the Anichi rushed to repair the hole in the shield. The rebellion began firing.

I didn't know what side had attacked first, but it didn't matter, because the trenches broke into chaos. Elements flew overhead as people shot them off. Magic from the other side slammed into our shields, and Luana gritted her teeth as her powers took the blow.

Resistance members rose out of the trenches with their Familiars. They began running toward the enemy, but once they crossed halfway, explosions rocked the earth. Bodies went flying, and dirt hurtled into the air. Fear chilled my bones as the explosions left craters, killing everyone who was within a short distance.

Mines. They were using fucking *mines*. And we'd walked right into their trap.

People on the resistance side screamed. There was momentary panic, as the few soldiers that hadn't been unlucky enough to step on a mine turned back, being chased by elements that the Task Force cast. Only a couple made it back to the trenches alive, shaking and covered in dirt.

"That field is filled with Koigni mines!" Jake screamed as the realization hit. "We can't cross it on foot!"

That left only one option. We had to rely on our flying Familiars to get us to Oleander and the other Elders.

Fire rain from the Elders began to pour down from the sky. Sophia and the other Koigni concentrated their powers to make it fizzle out before it reached the shield. Jonah and Jake worked together, and the skies darkened overhead. Lightning ricocheted across the sky and struck several Familiars out of the air as a tornado began to form in the middle of no-man's land. The tornado traveled toward the Elders' side, but it began to lose energy the closer it got to the Task Force. Jake struggled to keep it going, but with the other Yapluma on the enemy's side, his magic was fading.

Imogen moved in unison with Cade as they summoned boulders from the earth. The boulders rolled toward the Task Force at a brisk speed, but shattered into pebbles once they came near the enemy Nivita.

I commanded rain to fall down upon the Task Force. I turned it into hail, and several large chunks of ice struck the Task Force on the head. There were screams as people went down. I was stronger than the others, so my magic lasted longer, but I felt the push of Water magic that was different from my own fighting against me. It took multiple Toaqua at once to overpower my magic. The rain stopped pouring completely until it was reduced to a drizzle.

Sophia sent a huge fireball across the battlefield, but it turned to smoke before it touched any of the Task Force members. All around us, other resistance members were channeling similar powers, but it wasn't working. Whatever magic we sent at the Task Force was canceled out and vice versa. Their magic couldn't harm us, because we'd end it once it got close. The distance between us was making it impossible for anyone to control their powers.

"We've got to cross that no man's land!" I cried out to Jake over the noise. This was getting us nowhere.

Jake nodded. He waved to a soldier nearby, who lit up his hand with Fire. The Koigni waved the fireball in the air like a signal, and from above, creatures swooped down.

It was the stingsailers— the magical flying manta rays. They soared over the battlefield, their great fins cutting through clouds. On their backs were multiple soldiers, shooting elements down.

"Let's go!" Jonah and Jake flew into the air, while others climbed upon their flying Familiars. I got onto Julian and pulled Sophia on after me as he spread his red wings to take to the sky. Imogen gave Cade a hasty kiss before she climbed onto Squeaks, summoning Sassy to her. Cade mounted Arabelle, following her lead. As they took off, Sabor followed with a screech, and we came after.

It was way worse in the sky than it was in the trenches. Lightning flashed around us, and it wasn't all from Jonah. The storm the Yapluma on both sides had created was wild and uncontrollable. I watched as a lightning bolt hit a stingsailer and took it out of the sky, sending its riders flying. Its body smoked as it slammed into the earth, and the other stingsailers let out screeches of grief.

The Task Force had wooden catapults, which the Nivita were rolling giant boulders onto. The catapults launched, and the huge rocks flew through the air. One of them was half the size of Julian. Sophia and I had to hold on tight as Julian lurched to the side and avoided the boulder. It hit a flying cheetah behind us and took him down with his Elementai. They both ended up on the ground, crushed underneath the boulder.

I watched in terror as the catapults began taking out multiple Familiars at once. A winged wolf and a pegasus were both smashed by a singular boulder before another took down a second stingsailer. Those that didn't hit anyone fell to the ground and set off the mines. The mines exploded, creating black, smoking concaves in the earth and destroying what bodies were near.

Imogen moved her hands, and she was able to shatter the boulders before they hit any of us, giving us time to get into the clouds. The rebellion had to fly higher, to get out of reach of the catapults.

So many were dying. It was happening so fast. But we had Esis. He stood on Julian's head and held his little arms out, creating a shield around

Julian that nothing could penetrate. Lightning bounced off the shield, and as we dove downward, nothing touched us. Even the boulders the catapults launched dissolved into dust when they slammed against his shield.

Esis didn't even flinch. Though so much magic was being thrown at Esis, he handled it without a problem.

"Way to go, little buddy!" Sophia called out.

The boulders fell uselessly to the ground as their projection failed to ascend to our height— but that didn't stop the lightning. It attacked relentlessly, frying one Familiar after another as the sky lit up. Jonah spun in the air, trying to stop it. As the catapults were being reloaded, he redirected the lightning so it struck one catapult, erupting it in flame. He sent bolt after bolt into the rest of the catapults, destroying as many as he could.

Yapluma on the ground redirected their powers, and tried to get Jonah to drop out of the sky by manipulating the air currents around him. Jonah faltered, but Jake was there to catch him. Jake held Jonah up by his magic as the Storm Lord continued his relentless assault on the Nivita, who no longer had time to load the catapults. Sophia moved her Anichi shields overhead to protect who she could as the lightning continued to ricochet across the skies.

When it was clear nothing could be done to harm Jonah, the Yapluma turned their attention on the rest of the group. They began manipulating the air currents there, and several Familiars began falling out of the sky. They were either blown away, or forced to crash against the ground as their wings couldn't save them.

A hippogriff let out a frail cry. I twisted around so fast it made my back hurt. Squeaks had been caught up in one of the failed air currents and was plummeting to the ground, taking Imogen and Sassy with her. My heart raced in fear as my friends fell to their deaths, but from here, we were too far away to save them.

"Imogen!" Sophia yelled.

Squeaks screamed as she pumped her wings to no effect. Imogen and Sassy held on for dear life. Jonah saw them falling and reached out his Air, but a rogue lightning bolt raced by. He jumped to control it before it hit both him and Jake, leaving him no time to save the girls.

Sabor let out a vicious cry and pawed at the air. He opened his beak and let out a gust of powerful wind, creating a strong tunnel. He swooped downward like a racing bullet, directing the tunnel at the Task Force.

The tunnel swept up several Yapluma in its path, sending them hurtling hundreds of feet. As Task Force bones cracked against the ground, Squeaks recovered. She flew upward to rejoin the rest of the rebellion, steadying herself in the air once more. Sassy's fur was all over the place, and Imogen clutched at her chest like she'd had a heart attack.

"We have to advance!" Jake screamed. "Move forward!"

The resistance swept down. Sophia's hold tightened around me as Julian sucked his wings to his sides and dove. Esis held on to Julian's horn with one paw, guiding a new shield with the other. As Julian leveled out, he opened his mouth and blew fire upon the Task Force soldiers below. Sophia grew the flames, so they began spreading over the Elders' camp. Task Force Toaqua rushed to put it out, but I pulled back their magic and forced the water to evaporate.

Familiars that fought for the Elders began rising out of their ranks. I watched as a herd of peryton launched itself on a massive eagle, forcing it to land. A griffin lunged for Squeaks. Sassy changed into a kitsune and lashed out with her vines to keep the creature at bay, while pegasi clashed in the sky.

My stomach clenched as a giant snake unfurled itself from below and slithered into the air. It was a basilisk, like the one Lindsey had, but this one was much larger and had wings. The creature was purple, and at least twenty feet long, with fangs as large as me. It was riderless, yet lack of an Elementai didn't make it any less formidable.

The basilisk flew in a circle around the rebellion, locking them in. It opened its mouth, and both animals and people screamed in terror as the basilisk began swallowing people whole.

I saw Carter and James hold on as Tiara soared at the basilisk, roaring a challenge. The lindwyrm sank her teeth into the basilisk's neck, and the monster cried out, venom spitting out of its fangs and spraying everywhere. Those who were unlucky enough to be hit by the projectile screamed in agony as the venom burned away at their skin and flesh.

A wyvern with white scales and autumn leaves for a mane soared at Julian. It spread its wings wide, swinging its body backward so its poisonous tail was directed at my dragon's throat. Julian spun until we were momentarily upside down, before Julian's claws lunged for the wyvern's throat. Esis' shield dropped as he clung to Julian's scales, trying to maintain his bearings.

The person on the wyvern's back was Nivita. As he raised his hands, the autumn leaves that made up the wyvern's mane detached a few at a time. He sent them at us like throwing knives.

Esis' shield was down, so one slipped by and grazed my face, causing a cut. I instinctively raised a hand to check the damage. He'd drawn blood.

Sophia focused her powers outward. The leaves sizzled and turned to ash at her command. The Nivita screamed in rage, but none of the leaves came close again.

The wyvern swept its tail back and hissed. It poised like a scorpion, ready to strike, before sweeping the mass of its body backward and aiming the stinger at me.

Shit. This was a fucking problem. Sickness welled in my gut as I braced myself, preparing to take the full stinger so the wyvern's poison wouldn't touch Sophia.

Julian growled, and the dragon sharply swung to the left. His tail came around in an arc, slapping the stinger away.

But it didn't stop there. Julian had used so much force that the stinger made a full circle, embedding it in the wyvern's forehead. The wyvern moaned in pain. His eyes rolled back in his head as he spiraled downward, the Elementai giving a dying cry before they both hit the ground.

Another mine went off. Several creatures were fighting with the massive basilisk, trying to help Tiara take it down. The basilisk bit down, crushing many before taking out others with its venom.

The basilisk sunk its fangs into Tiara's side. She moaned, but she didn't back down. She must've been immune to its venom, because the basilisk bite didn't slow her up. If anything, it only made her attacks more vicious.

More and more Familiars kept coming. Two hydras with six heads each flew into the sky and soared at Dyami. Ezra redirected the thunderbird, and Dyami ducked so the hydras ran into each other. As they were untangling their heads, Dyami channeled a storm. He whipped up the clouds so rain poured down upon the hydras, slowing them up. As the hydras sprang free, they chased after Ezra and Dyami. Dyami kicked it into high gear and flew as fast as his wings could carry him, while Jonah and Jake flew after to help.

I withdrew water from the canister at my side. I forged it into a long whip and lashed it out at the Task Force. I lassoed my whip around multiple riders, tossing them off their mounts and sending them to their deaths. Sophia sent out Fire columns that made me sweat, roasting the sides of Familiars who flew by. Even as we worked, it seemed where we took care of one Familiar, another sprang up.

We were outnumbered two to one up here. The Elders had more flying Familiars than we did. Without the help of the ground team, we were fucked.

"Hold our position!" I heard Jake cry, but I didn't think anyone was listening. Resistance members were dropping like flies. Panic overwhelmed my senses, causing alarm bells to ring in my head. Skylis hadn't even made an appearance yet, and we were losing ground.

The battle had just started, and we were already dying.

Then a space in the clouds parted, letting a halo of white light shine through that beamed across the mountains. Dots on the horizon grew closer and closer with the arrival of the holy sunlight, and I saw wings send rays jetting throughout the landscape.

"The dragons are here!" Imogen yelled.

Julian trumpeted a hearty greeting. Aisha led the pack. Hundreds of dragons soared in from above, breathing a combination of fire, ice, earth and wind. Eirakari flew by, freezing Familiars in their place and causing them to fall to the ground, where they shattered into a million fragments. James' dragon rammed his horns against one of the hydras, and it went down, crashing into a flock of hippogriffs before it smashed the Task Force underneath. A few dragons flew back toward the resistance side, to pick up riders and bring them to the battle to fight.

The Elders had their own dragons to fight for them. They abandoned their battles with the other Familiars and turned to face their own kind. Some dragons began dueling with their elements, while others smashed their horns together. So many roars broke out it seemed the sky itself was quivering.

Julian locked himself into a deadly combat with another fire dragon. Flames shot over our heads as the two males locked horns and fought viciously with their teeth. Julian's body rocked violently as the dragons hissed and sputtered.

I couldn't cast. I was too busy making sure I stayed on.

"Sophia!" I called out as a flame nearly singed my armor. This was more than a little dangerous. Male dragons more often than not killed each other during a fight. I watched as a flame began to build in the opposing male's throat.

"Hold on!" Sophia shouted. She flung her hand forward. The Fire in the dragon's breath halted. It couldn't move forward. The dragon gagged and coughed, trying to get it out.

Julian took his opportunity and sank his fangs into the enemy's neck. There was a hissing sound, like steam being set loose, and the other dragon moaned. As Julian bit down, molten lava poured from the dragon's neck. It ran down Julian's teeth as he deepened the gash he had made. The male dragon stopped squirming, and Julian let him go, dropping the opposer's body to the black earth.

Julian made a chuffing sound in his throat as he looked to Aisha for approval. As the dragons fought, Aisha hovered over the fight and gave guttural noises that vibrated in my core. The dragons created a formation and swept through the Task Force Familiars in a singular line. It was like the dragons were following her command. She must've become their alpha!

A sense of pride came over me as I watched Aisha order the dragons. I never would've expected it from a dragoness with a hurt wing, one who'd been rejected by the others. She'd once been the smallest, but now, she was the strongest.

There was a whizzing sound, and I heard an object make an impact. A golden dragon next to us moaned. My eyes widened as I saw he had a long, spear-like object sticking out of his chest. The Elementai on its back wore a fallen expression— expecting death.

More spears went whizzing through the sky. They took out multiple dragons, skewering them through the wings or embedding in their sides. Earthquakes vibrated throughout the land as the dragons' massive bodies toppled to the earth.

I looked to the ground, and disbelief ran throughout my core. Holy fucking shit, these assholes had *harpoons*. They loaded the gargantuan machines, putting another harpoon in its place the moment one had fired.

One of the harpoons struck the other hydra. It collapsed out of the air and died, though the Task Force didn't stop firing. They didn't even care if they shot their own. All that mattered was they killed us alongside them.

Aisha cried out a bugle, ordering the other dragons to fly out of reach. Jonah and the Yapluma were so busy trying to misdirect the harpoons from hitting the dragons, they didn't have time to destroy them. Sophia called a lightning bolt down from the sky, but it missed, striking the area beside the harpoons instead. It killed a few Task Force, but not enough to stop working the harpoons.

"Julian, go, go, go!" I ordered.

Julian tilted upward. Sophia and I flattened ourselves to his back as the harpoons sailed by. He had to tilt in the air several times to avoid getting hit. One harpoon sailed over my head, and it hit the rider behind us, gutting him through.

Esis puffed out his chest in rage as he watched the dragons around us die. He let his shield drop as he called a massive ball of light into his paws. It grew larger and larger, until it had swelled to the size of Julian's head and we couldn't see in front of us. Julian turned, and I knew he'd done that so Esis could aim at the harpoons.

Esis launched the light ball with a shrill cry, and it careened toward the Task Force. People screamed and dove out of the way, but not everyone escaped in time. The ball of light collided with the ground, making a huge crater in the earth. The harpoon guns went flying. Broken pieces of wood and iron scattered everywhere, leaving an array of bodies and debris behind.

"That's my Esis!" Sophia praised. Esis clapped, like he was proud of himself.

Esis' magic had given them a blow, but it'd left us defenseless. One singular harpoon gun was left, with a final shot in place. Aisha had stayed low to make sure the other dragons made it out. My insides tightened as I watched them redirect the gun her way.

Julian bellowed. He flew forward, knocking Aisha out of the way. Sophia tried to create a shield, but she didn't get it up in time. The harpoon soared by, creating a hole in Julian's wing.

Aisha gave a cry as we began spiraling toward the ground. Julian pumped his hurt wing, but to no effect. It would no longer hold us up. We were definitely going down.

"Brace for impact!" I shouted. The ground neared. Esis and Sophia made a collective shield just before we slammed into the dirt.

The shield broke our fall, but it was still rough. All three of us were thrown from Julian's back several feet. I hit the ground and rolled, wincing as my shoulder twisted. It took a few moments for me to gain my bearings.

That fucking hurt, but on quick inspection, I didn't think anything was broken, and I hadn't hit my head. I staggered upward. Sophia was on her feet, holding Esis.

"*Pawee*, you hurt?" I coughed as I got ash in my mouth.

"Esis and I are fine!" Sophia said. I barely heard her over the sounds of the battle.

Shit. We were on the ground. One false step, and we'd be blown to pieces by the mines.

Julian had the same idea I did. He remained frozen in place, frightened to make a misstep. He wasn't getting out of here unless he could fly again. One of his massive footsteps would surely set off a mine.

"Can you heal him?" I yelled to Sophia.

"I need time!" She was already working on mending Julian's wing.

I turned, taking in the immensity of the fight. Though the harpoon machines were gone, they'd taken out most of our dragons. We were defenseless out here.

There was a winged lion who'd been hurt nearby. It was still alive, but it needed help. The Elementai kneeling next to it saw Sophia. He broke into a run, waving at us to get our attention. He clearly wasn't thinking straight.

"Chosen one!" he screamed. "Help us!"

"Wait!" Sophia cried out. But too late.

The guy running at us stepped on a mine. My ears rang with the sound. It was far enough away it didn't damage my hearing, but near enough that I'd remember it forever. I closed my eyes in seconds, yet I'd already seen him get blown up. His body was ripped apart as the mine erupted, sending body parts and entrails scattering over the ground.

I forced myself not to vomit. As I looked to my wife, the sensation to gag got even worse. Sophia's lip wobbled. She nearly broke down in a sob.

"Soph, it's not your fault." I tried to block out the sounds of the dying lion crying out from beyond.

"He was asking for me."

"There was nothing you could do. Julian needs your help," I reminded her.

Sophia swallowed. She rushed back to attending Julian, until his wing was mended again. We hastily returned to the skies. Most of the rebellion was clustered in a section high above. Jake, Jonah and Imogen had regrouped in the center, along with Ezra. Julian flew to meet them. I heard the frays of a panicked argument as we grew close.

"Jake, we need to land," Ezra said. "We can't keep at it this way. We need the support of the ground team."

"How do you expect us to get past those mines?" Jonah yelled. "We don't know where they are. Even if I shot lightning at them, it could take all day to find them all!"

I had the thought to fly over and attack the Task Force from the other side, but that wouldn't work. We didn't have enough flying Familiars left to mobilize in such a way without taking out the rest of our army.

Jake's eyes were frantic. He didn't know what to do. His ashen face paled as he counted the numbers we still had of those left in the sky. It wasn't half of what we needed to find Oleander.

Sassy gave a bark, and Imogen's eyes glinted. "Everyone stay in the air!" Imogen said. "I've got an idea! Sophia, get that shield around me!"

"What are you going to do?" Jonah cried, but Imogen had turned Squeaks downward. Sophia cast out a shield that surrounded her fully.

Squeaks hovered about fifty feet over the ground. Imogen took a breath and closed her eyes— like she was meditating. She spread her fingers wide and hovered them forward, like she was splaying them over a map.

A few seconds passed. The Task Force pointed up at her, and several creatures flew upward in an intent to knock her out of the sky. Sassy and Squeaks both hissed, and Sassy raised her vines in a warning to stay back.

I was about to scream for Imogen to get out of there, but that's when her magic erupted. Several people gasped as the ground below us began to shake, then rocked violently. Imogen's power created a deep crack in the earth, one that spanned from this side of the battlefield to the other.

Her earthquake set off every remaining mine all at once. The battlefield became one big explosion. Dirt flew upward as the mines were set loose, scattering throughout the air. I took a breath in shock, amazed Imogen was able to pull off this kind of magic all by herself.

As the earthquake ended, Imogen sagged against Squeak's neck in exhaustion, her eyes lolling as she nearly passed out. Jonah flew forward to help her. Squeaks landed on the ground, and so did Jonah. Imogen would've fallen off Squeaks' back if Jonah hadn't caught her.

Now that the mines were gone, other resistance members began rising out of the trenches and running to help us. A line of unicorns with riders on their backs charged forward, their horns lowered. Creatures who couldn't fly stampeded at the Elders' army, creating a horde that would terrify Oleander.

We got Julian back on the ground. Imogen was coming around. Sophia placed a hand on her shoulder to heal her, and that's when Imogen's eyes brightened.

"You okay?" I asked. Sassy let out a croon.

"I am, thanks to Sophia's healing magic," Imogen said. "Come on, we have the advantage! Let's move!"

We ran forward. The rebellion had collided with a line of Task Force. Elements soared overhead and in every which direction. I had to veer to the side to avoid getting hit by a rock, and Jonah prevented a blast of air from slicing us in half as it ran by. I noticed the noxite guns were absent. They must've run out.

Something tripped me up. I fell, and Sophia cried out as Imogen and the others ran ahead.

I turned on my back. Micah was smirking at me. He'd shot out a rope of Water to trip me.

At his side, his disgusting reptilian Familiar hissed. The *malerta* hunched its back, and the sharp, pointed scales rose up in a threatening display.

This asshole again. I should've drowned him when I had the chance. I went to get to my feet, but a hand extended in my direction. It was Mia. I took it, and she pulled me upward. Taryn barked.

"You guys need to go," Mia said. "I'll deal with him."

"We can't leave you here to take him by yourself," Sophia protested. She had a fireball blazing in her hands, like she was ready to shove it into Micah's face.

"She has me." Wyatt came out of nowhere. He cracked his knuckles as he faced Micah, like he'd been praying for a moment like this.

Micah's smile washed away when he saw Mia. He flung out a spell, crying, "*You*! Where'd you take my son, you bitch?"

Micah's water slapped Mia across the face. Wyatt gasped, but Mia barely reacted. A snarl crept over her lips as she turned on Micah viciously, calling Water to her command from the canister at her side. It swirled around her form in rage as she cried, "You've raised a hand to me for the *last time!*"

Taryn growled and launched herself at Micah's *malerta*. She tangled herself in the monster's legs and bit down on the ankles. The reptile hissed and tried to bite Taryn with its jaws. Wyatt sprang in, using his Water to expand an orb around the reptile's face to drown it. The *malerta* broke free, but only for a few seconds to breathe before Wyatt's magic surrounded it again.

Mia and Micah were trading water balls back and forth. He hardened them into ice, aiming for her head. But Mia was not to be fucked with today, because she conjured her magic faster than Micah and flung her powers at him in a fury, releasing all the pent-up emotion she had for him in one blow.

Micah wasn't close enough for me to stop his heart, but I could get to him. I was about to spring in and lend a hand until a low croon tugged at my heartstrings, and my head swung to the side.

Eirakari had been injured by one of the harpoons. It stuck out of her shoulder halfway, creating an oozing gash that was exposed to the air. I tugged on Sophia's arm. Her eyes widened when she saw Eira limp across the battlefield.

Eirakari needed our help. If Wyatt and Mia said they had this, we had no choice but to leave them to it. We abandoned their battle with Micah to save the ice dragon. Sophia and I made our way to her, avoiding the mayhem of the fight.

Once we reached her side, Julian bent down and gripped the harpoon with his teeth, ripping it out. Eirakari gave a roar of pain. Sophia looked at the wound. Her face fell as she observed the matted tissue. Eirakari's leg was barely holding on by a few threads, bones sticking out from underneath her scales. She moaned and tried to move her leg with no success.

If we didn't heal her now, Eirakari would either bleed to death, or she'd lose her limb. Blood continued to seep out of the cut as Sophia put her hands over it.

"This is bad. I need time to fix it!" Sophia called. "Keep them off me!"

"Working on it." I panted as I took out multiple Task Force members at once.

Healing took time. Not even Sophia and Esis could fix wounds immediately, let alone reattach limbs. I summoned water balls and threw them at Task Force members and Familiars both. Anyone who stepped in my immediate vicinity, I stopped their hearts— I didn't think twice.

But Maddie had to survive, and if Eirakari died, she wouldn't. She wasn't just my sister, someone I loved— she was also a *naderei*, who'd said we'd need her later. I wouldn't bet against that.

Our group managed to clear the surrounding area of Task Force members long enough to give us a short break before more came swarming in. A sick cry rang through the skies, and a large shadow passed overhead. Julian hissed in distaste. The basilisk still wasn't down, and it was taking down anyone in the sky who challenged it. Tiara was on the ground nearby, trying to recover her strength as Carter, James, and his dragon fought off the Task Force. No one tried to stop it.

Julian crouched. He glanced at me, waiting for my order.

I worried about setting him loose, but Julian was a big boy. He could handle himself, and I knew that look in his eye. He was on the hunt. He wouldn't stop until his blood lust was satisfied.

"Take it down, Jules," I told him.

Julian spread his wings and launched into the sky, making a direct line to the giant snake. The basilisk didn't see Julian coming until the last moment. Their bodies smashed together, making a sound like thunder, and the basilisk gave a screech as Julian sank his claws in. The dragon shook him in order to break his spine, but the basilisk slithered out of Julian's grasp, flying in the other direction. Julian followed at high-speed, breathing Fire after the basilisk's tail.

As Sophia worked on healing Eirakari and Julian battled the basilisk overhead, two hated figures stepped through the smoke. Renar and Mallory.

They were flanked by Mallory's Familiar, the bunyip. The swamp monster curled its lips back, revealing awful teeth as it waved its curved horns in warning. The moss on its back was stained red.

I didn't see Alvarice— not at first. My blood ran cold as I saw he was feeding on the body of a girl that had fallen nearby. The cockatrice swallowed her entrails before moving on to the heart, blood slicked across his black feathers. The girl's eyes stared out blankly. Her head lay several feet away from her corpse, a sign the cockatrice had killed her in moments.

Renar snapped his fingers. Alvarice recoiled, then slunk behind him. The cockatrice clicked his beak as he observed Squeaks hungrily. She gave a low hiss in response.

More figures landed beside us. Jake and Sabor stood beside Jonah, while Cade and Arabelle flanked Imogen.

Mallory was the first to speak. "See you've come back from the dead," she told Cade scathingly. "Too bad it's not gonna last long."

"You shouldn't be talking, Mallory." Cade's fists tightened, and Arabelle gave a growl. The bunyip gnashed its teeth.

Renar's smile was so insulting. He looked over all of us like we were complete trash. "Looks like the losers are all here. You four never could leave your little gang-bang."

"Should've known *you'd* show up," Imogen spat hatefully. If looks could kill, Renar would long be dead by now. Imogen's face turned red, like she was contemplating strangling him.

Renar spread his arms wide. "I killed Chieftess Makawe. I'm the chief of Yapluma now, sweetheart. It's my job to put you Biyami in your place."

"You're Oleander's bitch," Jonah shot out. "Nothing more."

"Big words from somebody who was once mine," Renar hissed. "You find someone sorry enough to take your desperate ass?"

Jake's expression when he gazed upon Renar was full of the utmost hatred. He took a step in front of Jonah, and Renar laughed.

"Aw, baby, this your new man?" Renar thumbed at Jake. "That's cute. How long is this boyfriend gonna last, five minutes?"

"He's my husband, actually." Jonah's tone was full of malice. "And *don't* call me baby."

Jonah attacked first. He swept out an arc of Air, which Renar deflected. Everyone moved at the same time. Alvarice jumped for Jonah's throat, but Squeaks charged, knocking him onto the ground. She went to trample him under her hooves, but the cockatrice rolled away and hissed. Sabor moved in, charging at Alvarice with his head down. Jake went to help Sabor and channeled a wind tunnel at Alvarice. It slammed into him, but the cockatrice held his ground, giving a sharp whine.

The bunyip charged with its horns down. Sassy's vines whipped out and grabbed the bunyip around the horns, tossing it several feet. The bunyip landed on its side, and Sassy ran after it. Arabelle jumped to help, while Cade and Imogen turned on Mallory. Both of them summoned rocks to their command and threw them in her direction, but Mallory called roots upward and deflected the rocks, sending them soaring every direction.

Sophia was still working on healing Eirakari, alongside Esis. I had to protect them. I stood in front of Sophia with a Water shield up. As elements came shooting by, I held my ground and sent them skittering in the other direction.

I wanted to step in and help, but I couldn't do that without leaving Sophia and Eirakari vulnerable— and to be honest, this wasn't my fight. This was Jonah's. I stood back enough to give them space, but not so much I couldn't intercede if they got into trouble.

Jonah and Renar were locked into a deadly duel. They sent gusts of wind at each other in fast succession, one right after the other. Renar summoned a tornado, and it spiraled in Jonah's direction, but Jonah easily broke it apart. He thrust out his hand, and a wind tunnel went spinning in Renar's direction. Renar got caught up in it, and it slammed him against a boulder that had been tossed by one of the catapults. Renar crumpled, but only for a moment before he forced himself back upward. He hovered above the ground as he sent a gust of wind at Jonah. It knocked Jonah off his feet, but the armor prevented Jonah from sustaining any cuts. Jonah mastered a tornado of his own and forced it Renar's way. Renar threw out his hands and held back the tornado so that it spun in place. It veered in both directions a few feet, but didn't move otherwise. They struggled in a battle of will, each of them attempting to overpower the other.

Alvarice prowled between Squeaks and Sabor, as if choosing which to make his next meal. Jake sent out his power to knock the creature off his feet, but Alvarice jumped and took to the air. He spun above like a vulture, circling inward. His claws extended as he aimed for Jake's head, but Sabor got in the way. He reached out his beak and bit down on Alvarice's leg before he could touch Jake. Alvarice screamed, but Sabor didn't let go. He bit down harder, drawing blood. Alvarice reached out with his other claws and scratched at Sabor's eye. The hippogriff let go, wailing.

Squeaks gnashed her beak at her mate's pain. She flew into the air and gave chase after Alvarice— though it was a trap. As she followed the cockatrice through the skies, the creature turned abruptly and opened his claws, waiting.

Squeaks didn't slow her attack. Instead, she opened her beak, and a wind tunnel burst forth. It knocked Alvarice down, sending him tumbling out of the air.

The cockatrice gave a groan as it slammed into the earth. Jake advanced, seeing an opportunity— but as he got close, the cockatrice lashed out and struck Jake across the side with his claws.

My heart leapt into my throat, and Jake gasped. He fell to his knees, clutching his side.

He was still in one piece— good. He was lucky Alvarice hadn't sliced his torso in half.

Sabor charged forward vengefully, stomping his hooves. He stepped on Alvarice's tail, but the cockatrice rolled back onto his feet. Squeaks landed. The hippogriffs cornered Alvarice on both sides, but neither got close. The birds snapped their beaks at each other and sent warnings, spreading their wings in offensive maneuvers.

"Babe!" Jonah called. He sent Renar spiraling as a wind tunnel knocked him backwards, and desperately looked for Jake.

"I'm all right," Jake called, but he winced as he held his middle. Blood spread from his fingers as it soaked through his clothes. He was down for the count.

"Esis, go to him," Sophia ordered. "I'm almost done here."

I glanced back. Eirakari's wound had almost healed— just a few more minutes. Esis raced away, avoiding the battle around him and jumping from place to place to reach Jake.

Nearby, Cade and Imogen were locked into a vicious fight with Mallory. Cade controlled the boulders in the area and sent them rolling in her direction. Mallory darted around them, snaking her roots over the ground as she tried to bind both Imogen and Cade. Once, the roots wrapped around Imogen's ankles, but Imogen commanded them to let her go and caused them to turn on Mallory instead.

Mallory's face twisted in rage when she realized the roots were no longer listening to her. She took a deep breath, screaming in a primal way as her magic opened up a crack in the earth, one that plummeted hundreds of feet.

The battle field around Mallory became a cavern, and Cade fell. He slipped into the breach, and Imogen screamed— though he used a root to catch himself. He wrapped the root around his waist to hold him up, to avoid tumbling into the dark cavern below. As he struggled to climb upward, the cavern walls began moving inward, to crush him.

"Cade!" Imogen ran to him. She grabbed his arms and began pulling him out of the hole while Mallory laughed.

Cracks began to form in the ground where Imogen was. Mallory was opening up the cavern further, to plunge both of them in!

Imogen's eyes blazed red. She sent her roots racing toward Mallory. They snaked over the ground, and Mallory's gaze widened with fear. Her magic ceased as she ran in the other direction. Imogen bought enough time to pull Cade out of the cavern as the ground below her steadied.

Arabelle and Sassy scattered out of the way. The bunyip ran with its horns down, its large feet creating ruts in the earth. Sassy lunged away in time, but Arabelle was too slow. The bunyip rammed into her with its horns, sending her flying. She landed hard and slid several feet, skidding her wing against a few jagged rocks. As Arabelle fell, Sassy used her kitsune powers to send a few balls of light hurtling at the bunyip, though none of them made contact.

Arabelle shook her head and bounced back up. She moved with a limp, but didn't appear too hurt... unless she had internal bleeding we couldn't see. If she did, she didn't let it faze her, because she beat her wings and ran after the bunyip with exposed fangs. The bunyip charged again, but Sassy opened her mouth and sent out a beam of light. It blinded the bunyip, and the creature spun in place. Sassy lashed out her vines and grabbed the creature by the ankles, yanking it to the ground. The bunyip struggled to move as Sassy's vines snaked over its body. Arabelle growled and climbed on top of the bunyip, placing her fangs at its throat.

When Mallory noticed her Familiar was trapped underneath Arabelle, she raced to help it. But Imogen flung out a hand, and from the earth bubbled up sticky black tar.

The tar pits weren't far from here. It wasn't unreasonable to think that some still lay beneath the surface, and Imogen had been counting on that. The tar seeped over the ground, and Imogen widened a pit in the earth. The pit filled with tar, creating a black pool.

Mallory tried to avoid it. She skidded to the side, but lost her balance, falling face-first into the tar pit.

With her arms restricted and weighed down by the tar, Mallory couldn't cast her magic. She tried, but her powers wouldn't work on the tar. Cade gave a shudder. With a singular hand movement, he formed the tar over Mallory's body, so she was covered completely.

The bunyip squealed. It wiggled within the vines, trying to escape in order to save Mallory, but Arabelle delivered a final blow. She used her fangs to rip out the bunyip's artery, and the creature stopped crying out, its body ceasing to struggle as Sassy pulled her vines away.

With Mallory's death, Renar's gaze grew wide. He sent out quicker bursts of Air toward Jonah, yet Jonah dissolved them into wisps of breeze without even blinking. Esis had healed Jake, and he rose to his feet as Jonah advanced on Renar.

Then a piercing cry shot over the wind. Alvarice had Squeaks by the neck. He bit down, and Squeaks screamed, beating her wings in a struggle. She called out for Sabor, and the other hippogriff lunged. Sabor kicked Alvarice in the head, and the cockatrice let go with a long snarl. Squeaks staggered away, taking ragged breaths. Sabor stepped in front of his mate, pounding his hooves and warning Alvarice to stay back.

With Squeaks hurt, Jonah lost it. Jonah called lightning down. It slammed into the spot where Renar had been seconds before, and Renar screamed. Lightning struck again and again, and Renar dragged himself along the ground to avoid it, cowering like the rat he was.

As Jonah approached, Renar looked up. He was on his knees. Tears streamed down his face, and he pleaded, "Jonah, you know I didn't mean what I did to you, right? I was messed up. It was wrong, and I shouldn't have—"

"Shut the fuck up!" Jonah shouted. "The entire time we were together, you told me no one would love me! You said the world was a terrible and dark place, and that I didn't deserve to live in it."

Jonah's chest heaved. "But you know what I've found? The only terrible thing about this world is beasts like *you!*"

"Mercy," Renar begged. "Please, mercy! Don't kill me!"

Renar fell forward and pulled at the edge of Jonah's cloak, kissing his feet.

Jonah's nose wrinkled in disgust as Renar whimpered pitifully. Jonah ripped his cloak away and took a step back. "I won't kill a man when he's on his knees," Jonah snapped. "I'm not a monster."

Renar quivered. Jonah walked away, turning his back.

That was a mistake. When Jonah was no longer facing him, Renar threw his hand forward and cast a spiraling gust of wind.

"Jonah!" Several of us cried out at once, including me. Jonah turned, but he didn't have time to stop it. He was only spared when Jake stepped in

front of him, slicing his hand downward to cut the draft in two. It went around the both of them, blowing back their hair.

Jonah's mouth dropped open. Even with how horrible a person Renar was, he still couldn't believe he'd do something like that.

The rest of us weren't fooled, though— especially not Imogen. She knew how much of a backstabber Renar really was. Rage welled within her as she advanced upon Renar, breathing raggedly.

Renar's face went pale white. He fell backward and scurried away, but roots grew upward and locked along his legs, pinning him to the ground.

"You hurt Jonah," Imogen seethed. "Now I'm gonna hurt you."

"Please," Renar gasped, but his voice was cut off as the roots twisted over his body. They wrapped around his torso, constricting the air from his lungs. He gasped as the roots created a noose, tightening around his neck until his face turned blue.

Imogen didn't hesitate, and no one stopped her. She forced the roots into Renar's gaping mouth, where they burst out his eyeballs. The roots continued through Renar's body, erupting out his stomach and sending blood everywhere.

I would've gagged if it had been anyone else, but I hated Renar so fucking much this was almost pleasurable to see. It was wrong, sure. But this was definitely what the bastard deserved.

One massive root burst through Renar's chest, spearing his heart. At this point, he was long dead. Renar's head lolled, and the root grew until Renar was suspended over the battlefield. He hung there as an eerie reminder to anyone who dared join up with Oleander.

Well, that was gross. But it wasn't quite done. Alvarice was panicking now that his Elementai was dead. He frothed at the mouth, frantically pacing back and forth as he felt death encroaching upon him.

Sassy bared her teeth. She ran forward, and her vines lashed out. They wrapped around Alvarice's neck as the cockatrice gave a final screech. With one pull, Sassy tore the head from his shoulders.

Sassy let the head drop. Alvarice's body twitched and ran around headless for a moment, like a chicken's would, before his convulsing form fell to the ground and lay still.

Imogen and Sassy had gotten their revenge for the attack they'd endured years ago— and had avenged everything Renar had ever done to Jonah. We'd never worry about him again. Or Mallory, for that matter.

Jonah looked away. He didn't get any satisfaction from what Imogen had done.

"Are you okay?" Jake put a hand on Jonah's shoulder.

"It's done," Jonah said. "We should move on."

He went to Squeaks to check her over. The wound on Squeaks' neck was just a small cut. Esis climbed onto her back and healed it, leaving her good as new.

Eirakari rose to her feet with a groan. Sophia had repaired her leg, and she was back in action. She spread her wings and took to the sky to help with the fight above. Ahead of us, the Task Force was still battling the resistance, holding the line that was protecting the remaining Elders.

"We have a chance! Come on!" Cade cried.

We raced to the fight. Overhead, I heard a moan. Blood droplets poured from the skies like rain. Julian had wounded the basilisk. The giant snake crushed its own wings as Julian tackled it to the ground. Julian bore some small scars, but they were nothing compared to the gaping holes in the basilisk's side. Julian crushed the basilisk's head in his mouth, and the creature died instantly.

I dared to feel hope. The basilisk was down. That was easily one of the Elders' most powerful Familiars. We had a shot at this!

Then... cries rang out from the Task Force. I saw something sail through the air... something small and metal. Once it hit the earth, there was a *pinging* sound, and the hiss of gas being released.

Jake screeched to a halt before we reached the main line. He grabbed Jonah and Imogen and held them both back. "Stop! Turn around!"

I was going to ask what was going on, before I saw it. A green gas began rising over the members of the resistance. It started to rise through the air.

The people and Familiars who breathed the gas in began retching. Their eyes bled, and large sores formed on their faces as the poisonous substance ate away at their skin. Soldiers fell to the ground, tearing at their faces as they gasped for oxygen.

There was a metallic scent that I recognized. Noxite. Oleander had developed fucking *noxite gas*. No wonder they hadn't any left for their guns.

If that gas reached us, we were dead, and a large plume was coming toward us. Jonah and Jake used their powers to blow it in the other direction, but there was so much poisonous gas, it was nearly impossible.

I drew all the water I had out of the canister, ordering it to head into the gas. The droplets dissolved most of the gas, leaving only small traces.

I closed my eyes and tried not to inhale, but eventually, I had to. I immediately felt my powers weaken. They didn't go away completely, but the gas had done some damage. My lungs contracted, provoking a violent coughing fit. The gas burned my throat and itched on my skin.

I dug in my pocket for my emergency inhaler and took several puffs. Beside me, Sophia was bent over her knees, coughing. I passed the inhaler to her, and she used it before she gave it to the others. We backed away hacking, watching the carnage unfold.

All the water in my canister had been used to try to dissolve the gas, but it was only enough to save me and my friends. So many soldiers were being killed. The noxite gas was killing us all.

More gas canisters were tossed into the air by the Task Force. They burst, taking out anyone within a twelve-foot radius. The rebellion began panicking, stampeding backward to get away.

"Retreat!" Jake bellowed. "*Retreat!*"

What followed next was pandemonium. The rebellion turned and ran the other way. Creatures flew overhead, and some knocked us over in the effort to escape. I grabbed Sophia's hand and pulled her along behind me. She clutched Esis to her as bodies shoved us this way and that.

Then Julian landed beside us. He forced people out of the way, roaring in anger and opening his wings wide. I shoved Sophia onto his back before climbing on myself. Up ahead, Jake and Jonah were riding their hippogriffs, and Imogen had gotten onto Arabelle beside Cade.

Julian flew us back to the rebellion trenches. I looked down. My hopes were dashed as I watched the soldiers still on the ground be trampled or cut down by Task Force members, who were on the chase.

We were being slaughtered. We'd had the advantage for a moment, but that noxite gas had wiped out so many. We didn't have anything that could counter that kind of sick weaponry.

Julian landed behind the safety of the Anichi shield. Sophia and I ran into the trenches. Here, bodies lined the walls. Soldiers who had been injured cried out for someone to help them, and were ignored as the resistance members that could still fight battled the enemy.

Luana's eyes kept dancing from those holding the shield to the soldiers, as if contemplating who was more important to help. In the end, she chose the shield, though tears welled in her eyes as she kept it aloft.

Sophia and Esis went into action. They darted amongst the soldiers and tried to save as many as they could... but most were already dead.

More rebellion members slipped through the shield, collapsing into the trenches. I counted up numbers, and there were just far too few. Not enough that we could continue to hold our position.

The Task Force stopped at the beginning of the shield. As they weren't resistance, they couldn't get past it. Instead, they regrouped, forming battalion lines that were neat and orderly, as if waiting for the right opportunity.

I took a few deep breaths. Okay, so they couldn't trespass the shield. What did we do now— stand here and stare at each other all day?

The Task Force tossed more gas canisters. They bounced against the shield and went off. Green gas filled the area, but it created a dome around the protective defense the Anichi had made. The Elders' army backed off, keeping a distance of a hundred feet.

That was a waste. I didn't know what they were trying to do. No magic could get past a Spirit shield. Not even the noxite gas could penetrate it.

Several Koigni Task Force walked forward from the Elders' army, wearing gas masks. They stepped into the fumes, and sparks emitted from their hands.

Oh, shit.

"Get down!" Jake roared. Several people flattened themselves against the ground of the trench. I flung myself against the dirt and yanked Sophia beside me before the Koigni erupted flames into their palms.

Once the gas hit the flame, an explosion rocked the earth. The noxite gas detonated against the Anichi shield, and Luana gave a cry of pain, falling to her knees. The ground rumbled, and dirt flew into the trenches. I observed in horror as the blast created a hole in the Anichi shield. The noxite gas ate away at the Spirit magic, until the shield was completely gone.

There was nothing protecting us now. We were exposed to the Task Force.

"Luana, do something!" I cried out, signing as I did so.

Luana's face had fallen. *The Anichi students have used all their crystals,* she signed. *The explosion sucked what magic we had left. There's no Spirit energy left for them to use.*

"Can you get it back up?" I asked. Luana had sustained the shield over *Hok'evale*, right? This couldn't be any different.

Luana tried. She winced as she cast her spell, and I saw the edges of a shield flicker around the trench before it went out. *I cannot.*

It was hopeless, then. Luana couldn't sustain a shield to hold back an entire army when her magical reserves were running on fumes.

We had less than seconds to figure out what to do. Yet it seemed we didn't even have that, because the walls of the trenches began closing in.

Dirt filled in from all sides as the Nivita Task Force ordered the trenches to fill. Familiars and Elementai attempted to claw their way out as rocks and sand fell down from above, filling their mouths and eyes.

They were caving in the trenches, burying people alive! I was alarmed as I felt dirt being spraying from overhead. Cade and Imogen created stairs to get people out, while Jake and Jonah flew people up, but they were at least twenty feet away from us. We'd never make it in time.

I heard Julian's scared groans as he paced at the trench edge. He was too large— he couldn't reach in and get us out without causing the whole thing to cave in.

I had the thought that this was the end, before Dean Hestian stepped forward— the former dean of Nivita at Orenda Academy.

"You go! I'll hold them back!" he shouted. He flung up his hands, and the dirt splayed around him, protecting us from being hit.

"Use my roots to climb out. Hurry." Hestian made a ladder of roots in the opposite trench wall, his forehead beaded with sweat.

"You're a hero," I told him breathlessly.

"I am no hero," Hestian said. "This is what the Great Spirit wants me to do. Go, chosen one!"

Sophia's eyes watered. "Ancestors bless you."

She began climbing up the root wall, and Esis held on tightly to her back. I followed, and dared a glance behind. Hestian was still holding the dirt back, so more soldiers could climb out of the trenches after us. Sophia and I reached down and started helping people out of the pit. We pulled as many up as we could, but my arms shook with the effort. I was getting tired, and Oleander still hadn't shown. I wasn't sure if this chief's duel would happen at all.

Two of the people we pulled out of the trenches, I knew. It was Wyatt and Mia. Wyatt was filthy, but unharmed, and Mia had blood streaked across her face. I didn't think it was hers. Sophia lifted Taryn out of the trenches, who barked and licked her face in thanks.

"What happened to Micah?" I asked. Wyatt reached back to pull another person out of the trenches.

"I dealt with him," Mia said. "He'll never hurt another woman again."

A small consolation prize. The Task Force stormed toward what was left of our trenches. Jake flew overhead on Sabor, barking orders.

"Get to the mountains!" Jake yelled.

The trenches were abandoned as the rebellion left them behind. I heard a Familiar call overhead. Ezra landed Dyami in front of us and slid off the thunderbird's back.

Thank the ancestors he was all right. I'd been worried sick. "Have you seen Mom?" I blurted.

"She's made it out. She's leading a bunch of people to the mountain range," Ezra said quickly. "If we can regroup, there might be a chance—"

He didn't get to finish what he was saying, for at that moment, I cried out in pain. Sophia gasped, and my brother reached out to catch me. I fell into his arms, and blood spread across my armor as Ezra laid me on my back.

I was in too much shock to feel much, because I realized someone had sent a rock through the back of my shoulder, which had come out the front. Esis squealed, and Sophia dropped to her knees. I tried to breathe, and felt an immense pain in my lung. Absentmindedly, I used my fingers to poke at the wound, and felt it go clear through.

There was a hole in my goddamn chest. Great.

Sophia pushed my hand aside and began healing me. Ezra's eyes were frantic as they latched on to the hole while Mia and Wyatt stood overhead.

"Bro, you okay?" Ezra's voice shook. Some of my blood had splattered on his face.

"I'm okay," I breathed out as Sophia healed the wound in moments. Thank the ancestors she was here, though, because if she wasn't, I wouldn't be.

"It went through your lung, but you're okay now," Sophia said. "Try not to use that shoulder."

Yeah, because my right casting arm wasn't something I needed in the middle of a fucking war. Ezra sighed with relief when he saw the sinew in my chest knit back together. He helped me to sit up, and I looked to see who had literally stabbed me in the back.

Courtney. She'd been one of the people in my Hawkei Leadership class who'd insisted it'd be better for the tribe if I was euthanized. She was a *pleasant* individual. No wonder she was working for the Elders. Her rainbow colored bird hovered overhead. It was as large as Dyami and gave me a hateful glare from above.

Sophia pulled me to my feet. Ezra's hands tightened into fists as he rounded on Courtney. "You tried to kill my brother!"

"Yeah, and I'm going to try again," Courtney seethed. "What the fuck you gonna do about it?"

Ezra lashed out with a water ball. Courtney ducked to the side, and his magic missed. Courtney let out a nasty cackle as it went sailing by.

"Give up! We've won, Ezra, and you've lost!" Courtney shouted. "What are you even fighting for?"

Ezra's eyes narrowed, and his voice became strong as he rose up, summoning Water to his hands. "I fight for my chief."

Ezra's temper erupted. He sent dozens of frozen balls of water after Courtney, and they exploded overhead as she ducked. Her rainbow bird reacted in defense and flew toward Ezra, but Dyami was there to stop her. The two birds locked talons and bit at each other in a blind fury, feathers trailing from the sky.

Ezra didn't stop his assault. He flung water ball after water ball at Courtney, until one of them struck her in the face, giving her a long wound across her eyes. Terrified, she turned tail and headed for the trees. Her Familiar pulled away from Dyami and followed, though the thunderbird gave chase, emitting an eagle's cry. Ezra ran off after her, chasing Courtney further into the woods. Both of them vanished into the trees.

"Ez!" I cried out, but he didn't stop. Just kept going. I went forward, but Wyatt held me back.

"You're the chief. You help the tribe," Wyatt said. "We'll go after him. Come on, Mia!"

Wyatt and Mia hurried behind Ezra. I went to follow, but hesitated. The three of them could handle Courtney. I had to get the rest of my people out of here. Whoever was left to fight, we had to save. Otherwise, this battle was lost.

"Soph, come on. We gotta get to the mountains," I said. I rolled my shoulder, which still hurt. "I need to find a source of water. I don't have anymore."

"There's a river up ahead. It's not far," she said.

The battle had become more like a riot. Disorganization was everywhere, and wherever I looked, I was hardly able to tell who was the resistance and who was the Task Force. It was just too confusing.

"*Pawee*, whatever you do, you stay alive out here," I told her. "Don't stop. Not for anyone."

"We all make it out of here, or we don't make it out at all," Sophia insisted. "We promised. Now let's find the others. This war isn't over yet."

She said that with the utmost confidence, yet I struggled to believe her. To me, it felt like we'd already lost.

And I wasn't just being negative. Us losing was the reality, and unless something incredible happened, there was no way we could turn this around.

Ancestors help us. It'd take a miracle to get us out of this one.

sophia
TWENTY-TWO

I didn't let myself look back at the broken bodies of the people we'd lost. I placed one foot in front of the other and raced through the forest beside my husband and the resistance army. Right now, retreating was the only way to survive. Hesitation would only get us killed, and we had to hold on as long as possible. There were only two ways out of this war— and that was death, or victory.

Liam and I slowed at a narrow river. Other Elementai and their Familiars trudged straight through it, but Liam fell to his knees, panting. My breaths grew shallow. Now was not the time for Liam's illness to flare. Esis jumped out of my arms to lap a quick drink from the stream. I grabbed Liam by his good shoulder and channeled my healing magic into him as he gathered water into his container.

Liam shrugged me off. "Don't waste your energy, *pawee*. We're going to need it out there."

"I'm fine," I insisted. I was far from reaching my magical limits. I had crystals in my pocket to give me a magical boost, but I had yet to tap into my Anichi reserve. This battle had my emotions running full-steam, and as long as I tapped into the right emotions at the right time, my magic flowed through me with ease.

Liam shoved his canteen into my hands, and I took a huge drink of water. He chugged his own drink, then filled it again.

Above us, the sound of dragons screeching met my ears. I glanced upward to see Julian following the resistance from the air. A limb fell from the tree above us, and my heart leapt. A chimera roared from all three of its heads as it burst through the canopy. I threw my shield up, and broken branches slammed into it. The chimera landed in front of us, its curled ram horns lowered for attack.

"Drop your shield!" Liam shouted.

I'd learned not to pause on the battlefield, and I did as my chief commanded. The second I did, Liam summoned water from the river. He thrust it forward in six streams. The chimera charged, but reared backward as a stream of water entered each of its nostrils. The water filled its lungs, and the creature fell onto its back, sputtering. Esis shook his fist at the creature.

"Come on!" Liam screamed, grabbing my arm as I scooped up Esis. "The Task Force isn't far behind!"

Liam summoned more water balls as we crossed the river. He formed them into ice and shot them at the approaching enemy creatures, while I summoned Fire to the surrounding trees. The thought crossed my mind to use intrafusion to slow them down, but we were moving so fast I couldn't focus.

Pegasi and unicorns reared on their hind legs, and a herd of angry elk veered off in another direction to find a way around my Fire. Several Fire creatures charged straight through the flames.

We'd slowed a few of them down, but they were still coming. Liam and I kept moving forward. Finally, the trees broke, and we came to a valley at the edge of the forest. Resistance members scattered across the valley, rushing to find reprieve in the mountains far beyond. The land here was mostly clear, but there were broken tree limbs and debris littered in all directions. Most of it had been grown over, as if a tornado had ripped through here a few years ago.

That's when it hit me. I drew a quick breath. "Liam, this was where our third task was!"

Liam's lips curled into a sneer. "The fucking Elders are leading us back through the Elemental Cup. The sick bastards."

Toward the other end of the valley, Nivita were already working to create trenches for us to hide in. They weren't as big or elaborate as the last ones, but they'd provide much-needed shelter from the Elders' elements.

The race to the trenches seemed a mile long. Task Force Familiars flew overhead and killed as many of our people as they could. I created a shield around myself and expanded it outward, until it encompassed at least thirty resistance members running for cover. Elements exploded against my shield, but nothing was able to penetrate it.

My heart hammered in my ears. I glanced around the valley, assessing the damage— to see how many resistance members were left— but it was chaos. Nearby, I caught sight of an enemy dragon swooping down to capture a Koigni man and his hellhound Familiar. My stomach dropped when I caught sight of his familiar face. It was Professor Lopez, the man who taught Liam's Hawkei Legends class. He'd been one of the first Koigni to join the resistance.

His screams could be heard echoing throughout the valley, but there was nothing I could do. One second he was there, and the next, the dragon had ripped his body into two pieces. The dragon threw the professor's top half toward the trenches, and his bottom straight over my head. Blood splattered over my shield and dripped down the side.

My guts twisted, but I didn't let myself dwell on the sensation. All I could do was gather that disgust and anger into my chest and use it to fuel my Fire later.

We reached the trenches and jumped inside. Liam and I slid down the sloped side, landing on our backs. Resistance members flooded in beside us, but we just stayed there for a few seconds, hearts pounding and trying to catch our breaths. Esis splayed across my belly, heaving.

Liam grabbed my arm. "We made it, *pawee.*"

"Another minute survived," I replied in relief.

Above me, my shield was holding strong, so I pushed it outward to encompass most of the trenches. I could feel people and Familiars pushing against it from the outside. My Soul magic could sense the intent of their hearts. I let resistance members easily pass through my shield, while I kept the enemy at bay. It wouldn't win us this war, but it would help keep the Task Force at a distance while we gathered our bearings.

Julian landed next to the trench beside us, but he was too big to fit inside. He cooed happily at the sight of Liam.

"Glad you made it," Liam breathed.

I finally caught my breath and lifted my head. Not far from me, Imogen, Cade, and Trace were using their Nivita magic to widen the trenches. Amelia and Madame Wells were beside them, pushing water out of the trenches as it seeped in. My heart rate slowed in relief when I saw they'd made it. I spotted Sam beside Isabella and Imogen's parents further down, working their Nivita magic. Not far, Professor Perot was assisting Riley with summoning a storm overhead to use against the Elders.

"How many are left?" I heard Jake bark from down the trenches. I looked the other way toward him. Jake clutched the edge of the trench, like he was about to pass out. Jonah grabbed him and started shoving oxygen into his lungs.

"At least a third," Jonah answered. He didn't sound hopeful at all.

Jake finally caught his breath and sighed. "We better hope it's enough."

Luana came by just then, carrying a backpack. She shoved an energy bar into Jake's hands. *Eat,* she signed with a firm expression.

Jake ripped open the energy bar and scarfed it down in two bites. I didn't know how much time had passed since the battle started, but it had to have been hours. I was starving, too. Luana continued down the trenches, handing out rations. Her eyes brightened when she saw us.

Surprised? I asked.

She smiled, like she was happy to see us. *No, I felt your shield. I'm just happy. Eat.*

Luana gave me an energy bar, then handed one to Esis. She shoved two into Liam's hands and rushed away before he could protest.

Liam gave me a look. "I don't want to take someone else's rations."

"There's enough to go around," I told him. I didn't explain what I meant — that we'd lost more people than we'd anticipated, and we had far more rations than we needed now. But I could see in Liam's eyes that he knew it, too. "You need your energy, Liam."

He nodded in agreement, then bit into his energy bar. It wasn't much— barely a snack— but it was enough to keep my legs from quaking.

My shield, on the other hand, was another story. Elementai and Familiars alike were blasting magic at it. I wasn't sure how much longer it would hold. I threw my arms upward to keep it steady, and Esis helped at my side.

Jake and Jonah approached with their hippogriffs. They both looked wiped. I was just happy they were alive.

"Next move's your call," Liam said to Jake.

"It's nothing but chaos out there," Jake stated. "We have to be strategic. Our first move is taking out the Elders."

"Which Elders?" I asked.

"Does it matter?" Jonah replied. "We take out all of them!"

"It does matter," Liam said firmly. "Whatever elements we're fighting determines our plan of attack."

Jake pressed his fingers to his lips, like he was calculating. "There aren't many left, as Oleander hasn't been quick to replace them throughout the war. But I know for sure we're up against Elder Barron of Nivita and Elder Wallace of Yapluma—"

"We fight the Koigni first," a woman said.

My heart swelled at the sound of my mother's voice. I glanced behind me to see Doya strolling forward with Baine at her side. Naomi's teeth were bared. "You made it!" I cried.

Doya blew a strand of red hair out of her eyes. "Of course we made it," she said, without an ounce of humility. She turned to Jake. "The Koigni House is the strongest right now. There are still three Koigni Elders alive, and they're second in ranks after Oleander. If they fall first, the other Houses have little power to lean on. It will be easy to take the others out."

Jake thought about it for a second, then nodded. "Then we'll send in Toaqua— oppose their Fire with Water."

Baine shook his head. "No. I don't think that's the best call."

Jake furrowed his brow. "Why not?"

"You don't know the Elders like we do," Baine said, shooting a glance at Doya. "Koigni women are strong. They'll counter any attack by Water, Earth, or Air. In this case, our best option is to fight Fire with Fire."

Jake's expression turned hard. "Will this work?" he asked Doya.

"It's our best bet," she replied. "The Koigni Elders are overconfident, and it is their greatest flaw. Send Koigni in first to weaken the Elders— then send in the next wave to finish them off."

For once, my mother seemed to be talking rationally, and not just to bolster her own position.

"But we aren't as strong as they are. We need everyone," Jake countered.

"Our troops need a chance to recuperate," Doya reminded him. "Let the Koigni give them a chance to breathe."

Jake didn't speak for a few seconds, then finally nodded. "Okay, we'll send in our Koigni troops first. Sophia, how long can you hold that shield?"

"Not much longer," I admitted in a strained voice. I was itching to give those Koigni bitches what they deserved, and my anger was making my shield seriously unstable. "You've gotta send the Koigni troops in now, Jake."

Jake's nostrils flared, but he didn't take a moment to think about it. He turned and yelled down the trenches. "Koigni, to the front lines! All other Elementai, stand down!"

No one had the luxury of questioning him. If anyone defied his orders, it was a recipe for chaos and certain death. Perot and Riley pulled back their elements on the storm brewing above, but it didn't seem to help. The storm had taken on a pattern of its own now, and dark clouds swirled overhead.

Koigni Elementai rushed to where Jake stood, awaiting orders. A weight lifted from my chest when I saw Lindsey and Miranda approach hand-in-hand. Vanessa and Bren hurried close behind, followed by their Familiars. Bren was nursing a sore hand, and Vanessa's hair was in disarray. Soot and dirt covered her face. One of Kingston's three heads— the dragon head— looked like it'd taken a particularly hard blow to the nose. Dry blood was crusted all over the chimera's broken nose. Kelsey hurried over, out of breath, but she and her Familiar looked like they still had fight left in them.

"What's the plan?" Lindsey asked. Medusa hissed at her side.

Jake quickly explained. "Target the Koigni Elders. Our objective is to weaken their army. Take down the strongest first."

Miranda gave a salute. "You've got it."

The Koigni scurried out of the trenches and onto the battlefield. I was still struggling to hold my shield. Doya hurried out beside the others, but hesitated when she saw I wasn't coming.

"What are you doing, Sophia?" she barked. "Come on!"

"I need to hold the shield!" I protested.

Luana approached and placed a hand on my shoulder to get my attention. *I've got the shield. The Koigni need you. Go.*

I wasn't sure Luana was telling me the truth. I didn't think she could hold the shield herself, but she seemed to think the Koigni didn't stand a chance without me.

I shot a glance at Liam. Though his features were sullen, he looked conflicted. "She's right, *pawee*. You and Doya are the only ones with enough power to go head-to-head against the Koigni Elders."

"But what about you?" I asked, desperation twisting in my gut. I didn't dare leave my husband's side.

Julian let out a cry, and I recognized it for what it was— a plea to let Liam rest and recover before he led the Toaqua into the second wave of battle.

Liam stepped forward and took my hand firmly in his. "This isn't about us anymore, *pawee*. We have to save the tribe, no matter the cost."

Tears pricked at my eyes, and my Anichi shield shook overhead. I hadn't let myself hesitate in this battle for a moment, but as I stared at Liam, I did. How could I leave his side when this could be the last time we saw each other? Yet how could I abandon my fellow Koigni and stay back while they fought, knowing they needed me out there if we were to gain any semblance of the upper hand?

Liam was right. We had to save the tribe.

"I love you," I said, before grabbing Liam's shirt and pulling him into a passionate kiss. I felt my Anichi magic swell around me as his love filled me to the brim. But right now, the tribe didn't need my Anichi magic. They needed a flaming bitch.

Liam and I parted. "Take Julian," he insisted. "And Soph... come back to me."

The breath halted in my chest when I saw the sad look on his face. I forced the sorrow into anger— anger at the Task Force, at the Elders, and at Oleander, for putting us in this position in the first place. The heat in my body began to rise.

"I will," I promised.

I turned to Luana and pressed one of my Anichi crystals into her palm. She drew away and tried to protest, but I wouldn't take it back. "Take it," I insisted. Hopefully it was enough to hold the shield.

I crawled out of the trenches. Esis jumped onto my shoulder, and Julian bent at my side. I grabbed hold of a spine and jumped onto his back.

"Mother!" I called.

Doya had been waiting for me. She jumped onto Julian behind me, and Naomi followed. I gave the command, and Julian took off to the skies, following behind Aisha and Vanessa. I could tell the moment we broke out of Luana's shield, because the air pressure quickly shifted. Humidity was thick in the air, and it got hard to breathe. Wind whipped by us, and below us, the earth was visibly shaking.

Julian made it to the front of the Koigni line. I opened my mouth to tell Julian to attack, but I didn't get the words out before a creature swooped out of the sky and sliced a talon across the back of Julian's neck. He careened to the side, nearly knocking us off.

"Hang on!" I cried to Doya.

I yanked my head in the direction the attacker had flown. It was a griffin, and it was coming for another attack. Blood leaked from Julian's wound, dripping down onto my hands.

"Deal with that!" I yelled at my mother. Esis threw up a shield around us, while I worked on healing Julian's scales.

Just as the griffin swooped downward again, it caught fire in mid-air. The creature squawked so loud it made my ears ring. The smell of burning feathers and charred skin met my nose, and the griffin went spiraling out of the sky.

"Good shot," I called back to Doya.

She gave a proud huff. Another creature flew at us. Julian ducked, and we just barely missed getting knocked off by a wyvern. My heart leapt to my throat.

"Julian, get us to the ground!" I called over the roar of the wind. "Follow Aisha! We're going to get killed up here!"

Julian did as he was told and swooped downward. We landed at the front lines of Oleander's army, just as the rest of the Koigni approached from the ground. Vanessa led the charge, with Bren at her side.

"Attack!" Vanessa called.

Fire raged across the valley, lighting brush aflame. Huge billows of smoke rose above our heads. I slipped off Julian's back, and Esis let out a high-pitched shriek. I saw the giant fireball coming my way the same time he did, and I ducked, flattening myself to the grass below. Blood pulsed in my ears as it whizzed above my head, singing a few of my hairs. The fireball must've been five feet across.

Doya raised her hands to deflect it, but it split in two. One of the halves caught her shoulder, knocking her off her feet.

Naomi burst into flames and bared her teeth at the attacker. He was a middle-aged man with a beard and long hair. Doya jumped to her feet, and though a huge welt showed through her torn shirt, she didn't seem bothered by it.

"Do you truly think that was wise?" she snarled at the man.

"Someone has to take care of you, Eleanor," he snapped.

My guts sank when I recognized that voice. He'd let his hair grow out, but it was definitely Professor Curt. I'd known he'd been assigned Defortai, but it broke my heart that he'd stayed with them. He'd taught my Dragonology and Fundamentals of Familiar Magic classes. I always did like him. Shame that he'd stayed on Oleander's side.

Professor Curt's Familiar, a red dragon named Kalina, stepped forward.

"You really want to make this personal?" Doya shouted at him over the roar of the battlefield. She started toward him, fireballs crackling in her open palms. "Just because I rejected your advances?"

"You mated with a Toaqua!" he roared back. "You've polluted the Koigni bloodline! Killing you is the ancestors' will!"

Doya scoffed. "Is that the bullshit Oleander's been dealing out? You get one chance to beg for mercy, Curt."

I was shocked my mother was giving him a chance at all, but it sounded like they had history I didn't know about.

Professor Curt curled his lips back into a snarl. "Not a chance, Eleanor. You will drown a thousand times in *Aiya Nocshun* for your transgressions!"

Heat flared in my bones the way he spoke to my mother. Professor Curt lifted his hands to attack, but Esis and I were faster than he was. Esis threw out a shield around my mother. The urge to protect overcame me, and a blast of Anichi light shot out of my palms. It slammed straight into Professor Curt's chest and kept going, burning a hole straight through him so I could see the battlefield on the other side. Professor Curt's words halted immediately, and his eyes went lifeless.

Kalina let out a pained cry that made the earth shake as her Elementai dropped to his knees. She quickly turned her gaze toward us, like she intended to rip Doya's head off before she inevitably fell beside her Elementai.

But she never got the chance. Naomi leapt forward and sliced her strong claws across the dragon's neck. Blood spurted out of her throat, spraying hot red liquid over Esis and me. I shuddered. I was almost certain the energy bar I'd eaten was about to come back up, but I managed to swallow my disgust. The dragon stumbled a few steps forward, but flames were already crawling up her feet from where Naomi lit her on fire. The dragon's eyes rolled back into her skull, and she fell to the earth as the flames overtook her form.

Naomi licked her lips and returned to Doya's side with a proud look. Doya patted her on the head. "Good girl."

"One down, hundreds more to go," I said. "Let's find the Elder bitches."

"If I know Madame Benally— and I do— she'll be at the back," Doya said. "She'll be waiting for the Task Force to wear us down before coming in to show off her power and take all the credit."

"Then let's go!"

Doya and I began racing across the battlefield. The fire was so thick, smoke filled the skies and blurred out the sun.

Fuck. I was going to need that.

I stole a glance back at the resistance. Wind swirled around Luana's shield, as if the Yapluma were trying to clear the smoke, but it came in faster than their magic could handle.

Julian took to the skies again, blasting Fire out of his mouth at any Task Force members he could find. It was clear he was going to take his own path across the battlefield. He was a better fighter in the air anyway.

Vanessa and Bren were kicking ass with a Fire tornado they'd summoned, but still, we were falling behind. Everywhere I looked, resistance members were dropping dead. As soon as they fell, the flames would come by to burn their remains like an unforgiving monster from hell. I honestly wasn't sure hell was much different from what we were experiencing on this battlefield.

Doya used her magic to create a tunnel for us, where Fire couldn't touch us. Every time a Task Force member crossed our paths, I threw a giant fireball or whipped up a firestorm nearby to keep them at a distance until we found the Elders. Still, it wasn't enough. A rogue fireball clipped me in the calf, and I screamed as it seared my skin. Esis squealed and started healing me immediately, but the second that wound was knitted back together, another fireball whizzed by and slammed into my thigh. My nostrils flared as I glanced around for the attackers, but the smoke was too thick to see them. I trudged on through the pain, knowing Esis' power would deal with it.

"Esis, a shield!" I commanded through labored breaths. I couldn't work Fire and Soul together, so I had to choose one.

Esis threw up a shield, and we gained reprieve from the surrounding fight, but it only lasted a moment. A scream cut through the battlefield, and I whirled toward it to see a Koigni guy get knocked off his hippogriff by what looked like a flaming lance. A one-winged hippogriff reared on his hind legs, and I realized it was Baby, with his Elementai Nicholas. Nicholas writhed on the ground in pain, clutching his chest where the stream of Fire had caught him.

"We have to go help!" I cried.

"We don't have time!" Doya insisted. "Our mission is to find the Elders."

"Not at the cost of our people!" I didn't listen to my mother. I veered off course and went to Nicholas' side. He gasped for breath, and I placed my hands over the charred wound. "This will only take a second."

Baby squawked loudly, but he barely noticed Esis and me. Instead, he went charging forward, aiming his beak at the attacker. It was a thick-muscled Task Force member with an orange lynx at his side. I recognized the creature, and therefore the Task Force member. It was Brandon, the Koigni asshole from my Dragonology class. Figures he'd join the Task Force.

Brandon lifted his hands to attack Baby with Fire, but Baby was quicker. He beat his beak downward, and Brandon's helmet went flying off. Baby struck again, and his sharp beak bit into the flesh on Brandon's face.

His eye cavities turned to black holes, and I gagged. The lynx lunged to bite Baby's ankles, but the hippogriff kicked and caught the lynx in the face. Blood spurted from the feline's nose as it went flying through the air. Baby lashed out with his hooves and talons, while Brandon clutched his face and screamed. Baby grabbed Brandon around the throat, then spun around and launched him into the flames nearby.

Brandon's scream filled my ears, and I gave a shudder. I didn't watch as he burned in the flames, but I sure as hell knew he was gone. I could smell it from here. His lynx Familiar curled into a ball on the ground and cried out in agony.

Baby strutted back proudly, just as I was finishing up healing Nicholas.

"Thanks," Nicholas said.

"There's no time. Go!" I cried.

Nicholas and Baby hurried off toward another group of Koigni resistance members. I noticed Professor Ambika in the group, attacking a group of Task Force Familiars. Drew was beside her, creating an impressive Fire dragon that struck three Task Force members down at once.

But that was where the impressive attacks ended on our side. Task Force created Fire creatures of their own, and used their magic collectively to create firestorms a hundred feet tall. Professor Ambika got swept up in one and flung sixty yards away.

I knew by the sound of crunching bone there was no use in trying to heal her. She was already gone. I hadn't realized I'd gone still as a statue, the sounds of death echoing in my ears. My stomach felt empty and hollow. I was an Elder and the wife of a chief. I was supposed to protect my people, and they were dying in droves.

"Sophia!" Doya snapped. "Stop dawdling. Now is not the time!"

Doya yanked me forward, and battle continued to rage on around us. Professors battled students, but they were so far off that I couldn't help. A massive lump rose to my throat as bodies dropped around us. I spotted Professor Maynard and Professor Bates, who were both Defortai, battling Piper, a Koigni girl who'd been in some of my classes. Piper aimed her Fire at them, but Professor Maynard responded by throwing water the size of a wave at her. It knocked her off her feet, and she went flying backward through the air. Professor Bates summoned a huge root out of the ground, and it speared Piper through the heart the second she landed. I winced, the memory of her death searing into my eyeballs.

Nearby, a woman I recognized as Professor Azalea sent a boulder rolling across the battlefield. It caught up with Cordelia Swanson. She fell to the ground, and the boulder crushed her. Her raven Familiar wept at her feet.

My breath grew hot, and my skin was sizzling. Doya was right. I didn't have the luxury of healing anyone this time around. We had to kill the strongest of them all and force the others to give up. It was our only hope.

"There!" Doya shouted.

She pointed through the rising flames, and I noticed a woman who looked on with pleasure. She didn't move to attack, just watched the fight with a proud look on her face. A serpent slithered at her side, looking equally pleased. The bitch wasn't even in uniform. Instead, she wore her usual cheetah-print leggings and pursed her plastic lips.

Madame Benally.

Fire blazed in my chest at everything she and the Elders had done— how they'd hurt my friends during the Elemental Cup, voted against Liam and I in our trial, and killed others during the riots and the battle of Orenda Academy. She didn't get a chance to beg for mercy. This bitch was going down.

Flames grew around me as I conjured the most terrifying creatures I could— a Fire dragon the size of Julian, a sea serpent with foot-long fangs, and a six-headed snake. I commanded the Fire creatures to attack, and my flames swooped down at the Koigni Elder from behind.

For a second, I thought I had her with the element of surprise. But it was like she sensed my Fire coming at her. Madame Benally whirled toward my creations. She thrust her hands upward, and my Fire dragon sputtered to nothing more than a tiny dracavern. It spiraled to the ground and burst upon impact. I thrust my anger outward, and my six-headed snake split in two, until twelve Fire serpent heads were aimed at her. I commanded them to strike, but she twisted her hands, and my flames were sent in the other direction. Her magic wrapped around mine, yanking the snake from my hold. I could no longer control the heads, and the creature disappeared into thin air.

I gritted my teeth. In one final attempt, I sent the sea serpent after her. I aimed its head at her face, but at the last second, I spun its tail around, intent on knocking her on her ass. But she threw a six-foot fireball at it, and my magic sputtered, leaving nothing but a few flames.

I searched for her magic and tried to cut off the connection to her Familiar through intrafusion. It was easy when I'd done it to my friends while sparring on the beach. But today, I was worn down, and Madame

Benally's magic resisted me. My attempt at intrafusion barely weakened her magic a degree.

"She's fucking strong!" I cried to my mother.

Madame Benally spotted me across the battlefield. Her eyes narrowed as she realized I was the one who dared to attack her. She lifted her hands, and the soles of my feet burned in agony.

"Gah!" I screamed.

I jumped away from where I'd been standing, but Madame Benally had lit my fucking feet on fire! The flames licked up my legs, and though I tried to overpower her magic and kill the flames, it didn't work. I dropped to my knees, writhing. Pain seared my skin and settled deep in my bones. Esis quickly created a shield around my feet, and that provided much-need reprieve from the flames. I sighed in relief.

Even though Esis had begun to heal me, my mother was fucking *pissed*. A shadow fell over Doya's eyes, and anger became etched in every inch of her features. Doya still had burn marks marring her shoulder and soot all over her face— but none of that seemed to faze her. She was a total badass as she stepped in front of me, poised to fight. No one touched her daughter and got away with it.

"I'll deal with her," she snarled.

Doya bared her teeth and lifted her hands. The flames eating away at the battlefield followed her command and swirled together. The temperature rose around us, and red and yellow flames began to gather into a column nearby. A Fire tornado quickly took shape, and it was bigger than any I'd ever seen before. It was at least twenty feet in diameter and reached all the way to the clouds above. But that wasn't the most impressive part.

Doya lifted her hand to the sky and concentrated. A bolt of lightning blasted across the sky, but it didn't fizzle out. It kept on crackling, swirling into her Fire tornado until they became one— the flames blazing in a red-hot column while lightning crackled out the sides.

My jaw dropped. I'd never seen anything like it. I didn't even know it was possible. My mother was wielding incredible magic.

Doya sent her Fire tornado blazing toward Madame Benally, but there were other Task Force between us. The tornado swept them up like they were weightless feathers. Their screams could be heard echoing down at us from the skies. Several dragons flying by got caught up in the storm, and I could see their wings slowly shriveling to nothing as they were burnt alive.

Madame Benally thrust her hands out at the tornado. I didn't expect anything to happen. Doya's magic was incredible. No Koigni could counter her attack. But I was wrong. Madame Benally had been placed on the council for a reason, and it was clearly because of her power.

Doya gritted her teeth as their magic clashed. The Fire tornado slowed its advance, though it continued to swirl and crackle. Madame Benally thrust her arms to the side, and the Fire tornado split in two. Their eyes connected, and Madame Benally threw her head back in laughter.

"You think you can kill me, Eleanor!?" she shouted across the space between us. "You're pathetic! No wonder you joined the Biyami. You're as weak as they are."

That was *not* the right thing to say. Doya didn't take well to being called weak.

"You're the weak one, you bitch!" Doya spat back.

With all her strength, Doya melded the two Fire tornados back together. Esis had healed the pain in my legs, and I struggled to my feet, prepared for the impending victory from our side. But the second I stood, Doya's magic blasted backward. Madame Benally had created a Fire tornado of her own and mixed it with Doya's. She'd gained control of the tornado and thrust it in our direction. I was whipped off my feet by the strength of the wind passing by. My whole body shook as I tried to stand. The tornado swept up Doya and Naomi, and they were flung fifty feet in the air. Madame Benally smiled proudly as she watched Doya fall out of the sky.

I threw a shield up as quick as I could, but it wasn't enough to take the full impact. Doya crashed to the ground, and the sound of breaking bones met my ears.

But my mother wasn't about to give up. Though her leg was twisted at an odd angle, she sat up straight. Naomi limped at her side, unable to walk on her back leg. Doya grabbed her twisted leg and yanked the bone back into place, letting out a shrill cry as she did so. Esis threw up a shield around us, and I rushed over to my mother.

"Ancestors!" I cried.

Doya didn't even acknowledge her broken leg. She kept her murderous gaze on Madame Benally. "I'll distract her. You go in for the kill."

I couldn't let her sit here and wait to die. "Esis, stay here and heal her!" I demanded.

Esis crawled onto my mother's shoulder and began healing her immediately. I ran off, out of Madame Benally's sights. I planned to circle around to the back and attack her where she couldn't see me. My breaths came in shallow heaves, as it was difficult to breathe through the smoke.

I tried using my Anichi magic to turn myself invisible, but I couldn't summon it as my Fire blazed. I was so exhausted, I could only use one power at a time.

Doya tried a different approach this time. She formed a huge flock of Fire dragons, all with teeth bared at the Koigni Elder. Madame Benally laughed, then lifted her hands as a hundred Fire basilisks formed in the surrounding flames. The Fire creatures attacked one another, each of the armies trying to get past the other. Wherever they met in the sky, they burst into balls of Fire before forming back into their shapes again.

I doubled around and approached Madame Benally from behind. Fire blazed in my palms. I intended to give it everything I had to burn this bitch alive, but I hesitated. She knew how to overpower another Koigni's magic. If I attacked without delivering a killing blow, she'd retaliate. I'd be done for.

My next thought was to attack with Anichi magic, but as I watched her fight against my mother, red-hot rage burned through me. No way was I summoning enough Anichi magic to take her out. I had to play to my strengths, and right now, that was Fire.

I caught sight of Madame Benally's Familiar, a twelve-foot long serpent at her side. It slithered around her, leaving trails of Fire in its wake, but it didn't seem to be watching its surroundings at all. It was as Doya said— the Koigni Elders were confident to a fault. Her Familiar wasn't watching for threats, because it didn't anticipate anyone would be brazen enough to attack.

That's where it was wrong.

Anger swirled in my chest, and my Fire begged to escape, but I held it back until the last second. Madame Benally's Fire serpents flew into the hearts of my mother's Fire dragons, tearing them apart. A well of rage rose inside me, unbound. *Fuck you, Madame Benally. Fuck you for using me as your pawn. Fuck you for hurting my friends. Fuck you for attacking my mother. Burn in hell, bitch.*

Flames twenty feet high licked around me. I thrust my hands forward, and the Fire wall went seeping across the battlefield, eating all the grass and broken branches in its path. Madame Benally noticed the Fire approaching, but it was a second too late. She whirled around and threw up a hand to stop it, but it blasted forward.

Her Familiar didn't have time to react. Though the Fire split around Benally at her command and missed her entirely, it slammed straight into her Familiar. The serpent hissed loudly and tried to slither away, but flames licked up and down its body, melting the scales right off its flesh. I dropped my arms and drew a deep breath, feeling the victory wash through me.

"No!" Madame Benally screamed. She dropped to her knees and pulled her Familiar into her lap. Though my flames burnt her skin, she didn't seem to care. She raised a fist toward the sky and screamed at the ancestors, "*Strong survive!* You promised! Oleander said you promised!"

Her pleas fell to deaf ears. While Madame Benally was distracted by the death of her Familiar, Doya pushed herself to her feet— broken bone still on the mend and all. She lifted her hands, and Fire engulfed Madame Benally and her Familiar. The woman screamed and tried to counter the attack, but without the magic flowing through her Familiar to support her, it was no use. Her body crumbled to the ground, charred and ashen.

"We did it!" I cried as I rushed toward my mother.

She huffed, as if she wasn't satisfied with the kill. "We killed one Elder. There are plenty more to go."

My mother glanced around, and disgust filled her features. I followed her gaze, and my stomach felt like rocks. There were so many bodies— resistance members mostly. I could tell by what was left of their clothing, though it wasn't much. Most bodies were unrecognizable from the fire. We were losing far more people than we were killing. Even if we took care of all the Elders, I didn't know how we would even our numbers to a fair fight.

"Then let's get moving," I said. Our only choice was to keep fighting.

Doya controlled the flames in our path, sending smoke billowing to the sides of us. I heard a scream and looked to see a fellow resistance member on the ground, her sleek black hair spilling around her in the grass. A Task Force member had tackled her and was shoving a hand down her pants.

Sick bastard! And in the middle of battle, no less. I recognized the girl. It was Coco, the makeup artist who'd dressed Imogen and me for the Elemental Cup opening ceremony. A tiny chameleon-like Familiar stood on a rock nearby, crying out for help.

Witnessing the attack made my knees quiver. I stopped in my tracks, knowing I had to get to her.

The flames raged on around the man like he didn't notice. She tried to struggle away, but the guy flicked his wrist, and the surrounding flames swirled into a circle, trapping her in.

I started running toward them, Esis hanging tight to my shoulder. When I got there, I jumped over the flame circle he'd created and tackled him. He let out an *oof* as he rolled over in the grass, but he came to a stop before he touched the fire.

"Go!" I shouted to Coco. She scooped up her Familiar and raced off.

Flames licked up from my palms, and I was poised for attack. But the laugh that bubbled up from the man's throat stopped me. He reached up and yanked his helmet off his head, so I could look into his eyes. His piercing eyes, dark hair, and strong jawline were unmistakable. It was Landon Barnes, the asshole I'd met at the strip club before my trial— the one who'd testified against Liam and I and made up lies to get us executed. The unmistakable urge to kick him in the balls overcame me, but he wasn't close enough.

"So we meet again, Sophia." He moved toward me boldly, like he didn't view me as a threat at all.

"Can't say I was looking forward to it," I growled. I watched his every move, calculating my attack. He was a strong Koigni; throwing a fireball at his head wasn't enough to finish him off.

"It's a shame my testimony didn't get you locked away," he drawled. "Luckily for me, I get to kill your *mopite* ass."

The foul word hit me like a punch to the gut, and anger ignited in my chest. "Not if I kill your lying ass first!"

I struck, sending a jet stream of Fire straight at his face. It was huge, at least ten feet across. I thought for sure it'd catch him before he could retaliate, but he was fast. Oleander had trained him well. Landon ducked out of the way of my attack and rolled on the ground. In a mere second, he was on the other side of me. He threw out a hand and grabbed me around the throat.

"You're a weak breed, Sophia," he snarled. "And I'm gonna take you out."

I clawed at Landon's hand and gasped for breath that didn't come. His fingers ignited, searing my skin. I couldn't even scream. I forced my skin to heat in response, but Landon didn't seem to care. He could easily take the heat. The heavy weight of hopelessness swirled in my belly.

Esis scurried to the top of my head and beat Landon's face with his fists. Landon swatted Esis away, and he went flying. He landed with a squeak in the grass.

I shifted to protection mode quickly. *Nobody* touched my Familiar.

A shield formed around me, easing the heat on my throat. I pushed it outward, and though Landon struggled against it, he wasn't strong enough to break it. Confusion crossed his rage-filled features as an invisible force pushed his hand off my neck. I gained control and sucked in a deep breath, but I didn't end the fight there. I continued to expand my shield outward, until it encompassed only Landon.

Then I pushed the magic inward. Like I'd done to the Task Force before, I used my shield to crush him, squeezing tighter and tighter.

Landon went rigid. Veins popped in his eyes, and bruises splayed all across his face. Bones crunched under the weight of my magic.

Just like that, the life drained from his eyes. I released my magic, and he crumpled to the ground. Above us, the sound of a dragon's cry could be heard as his Elementai died. It shouldn't have felt so good to take his life, but I'd be damned if I wasn't relieved to see his dead body lying in front of me. The asshole deserved it.

Esis scurried over to me and jumped into my arms. I glanced around for my mother, but she was nowhere. *Shit!*

I quickly jumped back into fury-mode as I weaved my way through the endless flames. I calmed those in my path, but I could still barely see anything. Screams echoed through the air, and the sounds of dying Familiars could be heard from every direction.

I stumbled over something, and I gagged when I saw that it was a dead body. The woman was covered in so many vines, she was almost unrecognizable. Then I saw the chameleon lying lifelessly at her side.

Coco.

I threw my hand over my mouth. I'd saved her from one asshole just to get her killed by another. Fuck! This battle was a death sentence for the entire resistance. Something had to change, and *fast*.

Hot tears rose to my eyes, though they refused to fall. We needed to gain the upper hand, but we couldn't do it without help. I placed my hand on the Spirit Totem, but Esis tugged on my hair and pointed. I followed his gaze to see a firestorm swirling nearby. In it, I spotted Doya going up against Elder Wallace, the last remaining Yapluma Elder. She was trying to kill him with her Fire, while he deflected her attacks with his Air. Tabitha and Hudson were beside her, riding on the back of Gooby, the giant snail. Tabitha's golden bird Familiar flew overhead. Every time they got close to Elder Wallace, he'd knock them back twenty feet. Gooby had all sorts of bleeding wounds from being sliced by Elder Wallace's Air magic.

Naomi's form blazed a dark red, and she leapt at Elder Wallace. He thrust his hands outward, and she went flying backward in his blast of Air. As I rushed over to help, Doya was already working on sending her magic through the space between them. Fire licked up at his feet, but he controlled his Air and sucked the oxygen straight out of the flames, deflecting the attack quickly.

I shot fireball after fireball at him. Though Tabitha and Hudson were attacking from the other side, he deflected each of our hits. I skidded to a stop beside my mother, and Esis threw up a shield around us. It was just in time, because Elder Wallace had conjured up massive blasts of Air. They spun like giant disks at us, and were so powerful I could see the air being manipulated. Esis' shield rocked as the blasts connected with it.

"How the fuck do we fight a Yapluma Elder?" I screamed. "He'll just kill our Fire!"

Doya pursed her lips and narrowed her eyes at him. "We'll have to get creative."

One of Tabitha's fireballs hit Elder Wallace, drawing his attention away from us. He raised his hands to counterattack, but Doya already had her hands in the air. She conjured a bolt of lightning, and her aim was spot-on. It connected with Elder Wallace's outstretched hand, and he was blasted back several yards.

For a second, he just lay there. I thought that the lightning bolt might've stopped his heart. But the guy was only stunned, and he forced himself upward a second later.

"Any other ideas?" I asked in a rush. I was working on summoning Anichi magic, but switching off my Fire wasn't easy at the moment. I was too fired up.

Elder Wallace turned his gaze upward. Within seconds, a swirling tornado came out of the sky and touched the ground. It was so powerful that Tabitha and Hudson got caught up in it and were yanked right off Gooby's back. Doya thrust her arms outward while Elder Wallace was distracted, sending a Fire wall hurdling at him. He must've felt the heat coming, because he whirled around and pushed against it with his Air.

What he didn't realize was Gooby was *pissed*. The giant snail crept up behind him and opened his mouth wide.

Elder Wallace was gone in moments, swallowed up by the giant snail. I heard the crunch of bones as Gooby ate him with glee. It was both sickening and satisfying.

At Elder Wallace's death, his magic gave out, and the tornado fizzled away. Tabitha and Hudson screamed as they were thrown through the air. They landed with a hard *thud* in front of us. The two of them groaned in agony. I rushed forward to heal Hudson's dislocated arm and Tabitha's sprained ankle, along with the burns and cuts all over their bodies.

"We have to get to the rest of the Elders!" Doya shouted above the roar of battle.

Hudson pointed and stammered, "We saw Elder Barron head that way!"

The four of us, along with our Familiars, started in the direction Hudson had pointed. I expected to meet other fights along the way, but all we saw were dead bodies.

Up ahead through the smoke, the sounds of elements clashing and Familiars roaring met my ears. Doya cleared the smoke. I saw with horror that huge boulders were swirling in the air. In the center of them, Elder Barron stood with his huge python Familiar. Nearby, Kelsey, Vanessa, and Bren were throwing fireballs at the Nivita Elder, but he deflected them with his boulders. He threw one of them, at least six feet wide, at the trio and their Familiars. They jumped out of the way just in time for the boulder to land right where they'd been standing. The ground rumbled beneath my feet, though we were a good forty yards out from the fight.

Vanessa threw up her hands, and a ring of Fire formed around Elder Barron. Doya was quick to jump into the fight. She intertwined her magic with Vanessa's, making the flames grow so high I couldn't see Elder Barron anymore.

We reached the other Koigni. All seven of us worked together to create a fire that encompassed Elder Barron. The flames were bigger than anything I'd seen before, and the fire was so hot it nearly burned my skin from a distance.

Elder Barron fought back. Though he couldn't see us, he directed roots out of the ground. One of them wrapped around Kelsey's ankle and yanked her to the ground, and another huge one swung at Hudson. Gooby jumped in the way, and the root smacked into his shell. A sickening crunch sounded, and I knew his shell had been cracked. From out of the flames, huge rocks flew at us. I abandoned helping with the fire and turned to deflecting the rocks with shield magic. Meanwhile, Kelsey and Vanessa had teamed up to burn the roots before they could touch any of us.

"How much longer!?" Bren yelled.

"Any second now!" Doya strained.

The ground rumbled beneath our feet so fiercely I could hardly stay upright.

"He's deflecting our Fire!" Doya shouted, as if she could feel Elder Barron's magic working against hers.

"What do we do?" Bren asked.

"I have an idea!" Vanessa said. "On my count, pull back. The second our flames drop, we send our Familiars in. Target the python!"

"As you wish, Chieftess," Doya said. It was still strange to see her hand power over, but Vanessa had earned everyone's respect— including Doya's.

"One..." Vanessa started. "Two... Three!"

The seven Koigni dropped their hands, and the fire fizzled away. I caught a glimpse of Elder Barron on his knees, panting. His python was poised ten feet high and aimed its unhinged jaw at us.

"Attack!" Vanessa shouted.

Familiars flooded toward the python. Aisha attacked from above, while Kelsey's jaguar ran alongside Naomi. Kingston rushed into the fight in front of Gooby. All five of them met the python at the same time, using their sharp teeth to tear apart its body. Scales and blood went everywhere, and Gooby swallowed up the python's entrails.

Elder Barron's back arched. He cried out, as if he could feel the pain of his Familiar being ripped to shreds. The brutal way his python was killed seemed to accelerate Elder Barron's death. Within moments, he slumped to the ground. His face landed in burning grass, and the fire began to eat away at him.

I turned my gaze away and bit down hard on my lower lip. I didn't know how much more death I could handle, even if it was an enemy's demise. "That leaves only two Elders," I said to Doya.

"Madame Locklear and Madame Wright won't be easy to defeat," she replied.

"Well, we have to try!" I shouted.

The Familiars returned, and Tabitha and Hudson jumped onto Gooby's back again. I glanced to the skies for Julian, but I couldn't see anything. I prayed he could hold his own up there.

Vanessa turned to Doya. "How will we find the remaining Elders?"

"We find the biggest fire on the battlefield." Doya pointed. "There."

I looked to where she was pointing, and my jaw dropped. Across the battlefield, a wall of Fire at least a hundred feet high burned. Dark black smoke rose into the air, polluting the skies. No wonder the Yapluma couldn't clear it— the smoke cloud was fucking massive! Flying creatures could be seen ahead of the Fire wall, racing away from it.

Bren cracked his knuckles. "Let's kick some Koigni Elder ass."

We made our way across the battlefield. The sound of screams grew the closer we came to the Koigni Elders' attack line. We approached from the side so that we could see both sides of the fight. On the Elders' side, their soldiers were like shadows, blanketing the valley in dark uniforms. There must've been hundreds of them following behind Madame Locklear and Madame Wright. They were using their Fire wall to push the resistance back and force them to retreat.

Fireballs and flames shot out from the Elders' wall, and resistance members fell on the spot. It was like the Fire wall was alive and had a mind of its own. Its aim was always spot on. Koigni and their Familiars were the only ones able to tolerate the heat— anyone from another House who got close to the Fire wall was incinerated on the spot.

"How are we going to fight against *that?*" Hudson asked. He tilted his head back, barely able to see the top of the wall.

"We have to kill those flames," Doya insisted. "Weakening the Elders' element is our only shot."

"You work on that," Vanessa instructed Doya. "I'll get a team ready to attack the second that Fire wall breaks."

We hurried over to the resistance side and found Koigni lined up all along the length of the Fire wall. Lindsey and Miranda were at the front, deflecting any fireballs they saw aimed at resistance members. The battle was chaos. Every time someone tried to fight back, they were knocked down by a rogue fireball. The ground shook so violently most of us couldn't stand regardless. This fight was hopeless if we were all fighting our own battles. We had to unite as one.

"We have to work together!" I shouted over the crackling of the massive fire. Though many resistance members were distracted deflecting elements, others turned to listen. "Remember your lessons at Orenda Academy— if you *intend* to share your element, it will not harm your partner."

Doya smiled proudly beside me, like she was glad I'd taken her lessons to heart.

"We can intertwine our magic!" I continued. "Together, we can overpower the Elders!"

Lindsey and Miranda ran to me, dodging fireballs and trying to stay upright on the shaking earth. Their Familiars were close by, which was a relief, but they both looked worse for wear. Their hair was matted to their heads, and their faces were covered in so much soot they were almost unrecognizable. The bottom of Miranda's shirt was torn, and a huge burn mark marred her belly. Lindsey's arm had a deep gash in it, like she'd been hit by a rock. Blood dripped from it, but she didn't seem to care. She just kept on fighting.

"We're here," Lindsey said in a rush. "Whatever you need."

"We need to act as a single unit," I said, reaching out for Lindsey's hand. She glanced down at my hand, but a moment later, a proud smile tugged at the corner of her lips.

She grabbed Miranda's hand, and I took Doya's on my other side. The other resistance members saw what we were doing, and one by one, they came to line up beside us. Esis stood proudly on my shoulder as I gathered my magic and aimed it at the fire in front of me. I could feel the magic from the others sizzling up and down our joined row of hands. We pushed outward, entangling our powers into the fire.

The Fire wall resisted our control, pushing back and heating my skin. Doya's hand grew hot in mine as she pushed harder. Lindsey's skin was nearly boiling. The Fire wall advanced, coming closer and closer. Sweat broke across my brow.

"More!" I screamed down the line of resistance members. "Draw from your crystals, your Familiars, anything!"

I channeled magic from my crystals, then reached out further across the Fire wall. I searched for magic I could steal, and sensed a high-frequency buzz of a nearby Fire unicorn. I wrapped my magic around it and tugged back, performing intrafusion like Liam had taught me.

I searched for more sources of magic and found them with ease. I drew from the enemy creatures, tugging on their magic until it became my own. I kept on pulling until I drained their magic so much I felt their life energy give out. Familiars and Task Force members began to drop at my command — at least a dozen at once. I redirected the magic into the flames, commanding them.

The flames began to die, but they only dropped halfway. They continued to tower above our heads, eating away at the battlefield so quickly we had to walk backward to keep our distance.

The more I performed intrafusion, the harder it was to do. Magic swept through me so quickly it was hard to keep up. I tried to seek out the Elders' magic, but when I found it, their magic resisted me. It was almost like they'd prepared for this. I wasn't surprised— not after Liam used intrafusion to kill Poole and Malison. They wouldn't fall for the same trick the second time. I was growing weaker by the second.

Elements continued to fly around us, and resistance members were dropping out of our line one by one. Screams echoed as mounds of dirt were flung upward by Nivita on the other side, launching Koigni resistance members yards from where they'd been standing. Creatures flew above the flames and ducked downward, grabbing people and Familiars straight out of ranks. Blood sprayed across the battlefield, and people were tossed into the fire.

Bile rose within my throat. I used it as fuel to drive my anger, knowing the only way to win this was to kill this Fire wall and slay the two Koigni Elders on the other side. Doya squeezed my hand tighter, and I bit my lip hard.

"Keep going!" I screamed.

The flames died more, until I could make out the silhouettes of people on the other side through the flickering of flames. Madame Locklear and Madame Wright were directly across from me. They wore matching smirks of satisfaction, like they knew they'd win regardless of our attempts to stop them.

We'd almost gained control of the Fire wall, but our Koigni numbers were falling. We were quickly losing our momentum, and the flames started to grow higher.

"It's not working!" Doya growled. Wind whipped by my ears so fast I could barely hear her. We had to shout to communicate.

"We have to keep trying!" I replied.

"If we try any harder, we'll reach our limits," Doya protested. "We'll kill ourselves by drawing too much magic."

My hand shook in hers, and I knew she was right. As much magic I was drawing from crystals and intrafusion, it wasn't enough. The other side was just too strong.

"I know what to do!" Lindsey said from beside me. "You have to trust me."

"We'll do anything," I told her. "We have to get this wall down."

Lindsey didn't answer right away. Instead, she got a sullen expression on her face. She shared a look with Miranda I couldn't quite read. Miranda nodded, and Lindsey turned to me, blinking back tears. "I'm sorry, Sophia, but we have to."

My stomach plummeted to my toes, and I went rigid. "Have to—? Lindsey, *no!*"

It hit me what she was planning. I could hardly wrap my head around it. Tears began to fall down Lindsey's cheeks, and Miranda shook.

"You can't!" I cried in a broken voice.

My protests went ignored. Lindsey and Miranda had already made up their minds. Lindsey let go of my hand and stepped away from me. Someone might as well have sent a boulder straight through my stomach, because my guts went totally solid.

"Stop!" I demanded. I grabbed her shoulder and tried to yank her backward, but Doya's arms wrapped around my middle. She wouldn't let me go after them.

My throat tightened, and it felt like I was choking on my own grief. Lindsey took Miranda's hand firmly in hers, and they stepped toward the wall of Fire. Medusa and Evelyn followed bravely at their sides.

"N-no!" I sputtered, barely able to get the words out. I struggled in Doya's arms but couldn't break free. My mother had a strong grip.

"Now is not your time, Sophia!" Doya hissed. I knew she was trying to protect me, but it barely registered. Lindsey and Miranda were about to sacrifice themselves; I didn't care about protecting myself.

Lindsey and Miranda both turned to me. They'd wiped their tears and wore matching expressions of resolve on their faces. They didn't look fearful at all. Instead, they looked as if they were at peace with the decision — like they'd already decided long ago that they would die for the tribe if they had to. They were both ready for the Ancestral Lands, and nothing I could do or say would stop them.

"It's okay, Sophia," Miranda said soothingly.

"We'll be all right," Lindsey added. "Once this is done, you end this thing, okay?"

"Don't!" I sobbed. I didn't think this war could break me more than it already had, but I never expected to watch two of my friends walk to their deaths. I broke right then and there, clutching my stomach as tears poured from my eyes.

Doya's hold on me tightened. Esis screamed protests from my shoulder, but Medusa and Evelyn just shot him a look of goodbye.

Fire rose to my skin, and I ignited in flames. I didn't realize what I was doing until I did it. I was trying to burn Doya so she'd let me go. Doya gave a loud gasp. She sucked in a pained breath through her teeth, but she rode out the pain and held me in place, refusing to let me move.

The battle seemed to happen in slow motion. All sounds were distant, like my head had been dunked under water. I might as well have been drowning, because I couldn't breathe. My vision blurred, until all I saw was the brave Koigni couple as a silhouette against the red-hot flames. In the distance, I swore I could hear the sound of a flute playing and a woman's song— like the ancestors were calling Lindsey and Miranda home.

Magic rolled off the two of them in waves. I could see it distorting the landscape beyond. I kicked my feet outward and tried to escape my mother's grasp, but I couldn't find the strength.

"No!" I screamed again, but the word seemed to last for minutes, echoing in my ears and shaking my bones. The tears streaming down my face seemed to have no end.

"Lindsey! Miranda!" I cried. They continued forward like they hadn't heard my earth-shattering screeches.

Watching my friends step into the Fire wall was like being crushed beneath a landslide. Every inch of my body ached as my Fire burned to escape— to *help* them. But just like a landslide hurtling down the mountainside, there was no way to stop this.

The Fire wall raged, twisting and contorting to Lindsey and Miranda's demands as they worked to rip control from the Elders' grasp. The crystals in Lindsey's pocket grew so hot they literally burned a hole through her clothes and fell to the ground. Beside my friends, Medusa burst into flames — and it wasn't because she was a Fire creature. Medusa couldn't create Fire like that naturally. Lindsey had drawn too much magic from her Familiar, and it was killing her. A moment later, the same happened to the kirin, Evelyn. Her single antler lit first, then the fire began to consume the rest of her body. Though they were on fire, the two Familiars continued walking forward, blazing heroes against the darkness of war.

My chest felt like it was being burned alive with them.

Lindsey's hair ignited, but she didn't scream out. Together, Miranda and Lindsey gained control of the Fire wall. I knew when the moment happened, because the flames dropped to almost nothing. For just a split-second, I saw the shocked looks on Madame Locklear's and Madame Wright's faces. It took them a moment to realize what happened. By the time they did, it was already too late. Lindsey and Miranda controlled the Fire and sent flames licking a hundred feet in the air. The wall was equally long. The two of them advanced toward it, until the wall followed their command and shifted in the direction of the Elders.

"Retreat!" someone yelled from the other side, but it was nothing more than a faint scream I barely processed. Footsteps could be heard beneath the cry of terrified Familiars.

"Do something, you useless twat!" I heard Madame Locklear shout.

"Me?" Madame Wright responded. "You're the one to blame!"

That was all I heard before the echoing screams masked all other sounds. The screams were so loud and so many— there must've been hundreds of people caught up in Lindsey and Miranda's magic.

The Fire wall continued to advance on the enemy soldiers and swallowed them up. Shadows within the flames raced around for escape, but found none. Hundreds of people dropped where they stood, burning to embers.

I should have felt victorious as the flames swept over Madame Locklear and Madame Wright, but I only felt loss. Grief curled its ugly fingers around me, turning my limbs to water. Lindsey and Miranda stepped over the Elders' burnt remains, and the two dropped to their knees at each other's sides. The flames began to die as they drained every drop of magic in their reservoir.

The couple turned toward each other, and Lindsey swept Miranda into her arms. I sank to my knees as I watched one final kiss play out between the two of them.

Then the flames licking across their bodies consumed them. They fell to the ground in an ever-lasting embrace, their bodies molded to each other's in the flames. Medusa and Evelyn finally collapsed at their sides. One last twitch of Evelyn's leg, and all four were dead. All it took was a breath, and they dissolved to nothing but ash.

Tears streamed down my cheeks as I stared at their lifeless forms, unable to believe how fast it all happened. I'd never seen anyone die by using too much magic before, but it seemed to consume their entire bodies, until there was nothing left. I couldn't believe they were *gone*— not even a body to bury.

I knew Koigni turned to ashes once they went beyond the boundaries of their magic. But seeing it happen before my very eyes was too much to bear.

My entire form shook as I stared at where my friends had fallen. Battle continued on around me, and I barely heard it. I thought that I'd prepared for this. I'd seen so much death, and I was ready to fight in this war no matter the cost. But I never thought I'd see my friends make such a heart-wrenching decision. To witness it was torture I didn't wish upon my worst enemy.

"Sophia!" Doya said, though I couldn't respond. I was still in her arms. She shook me. "The fight isn't over!"

I didn't process her words. Who cared if the fight went on or not? Two of my closest friends had sacrificed themselves in this war. Who else was I going to lose?

"Sophia!" This time, her voice sounded closer. My eyes snapped in her direction, and my senses started to return. Though Lindsey and Miranda had given their lives to kill the Elders, it had barely made a difference. I could still hear the sound of death around me, and smell the burning of flesh.

A shadow flew above us, and my heart lurched. I glanced upward to see it was Aisha. She let out a victorious cry, and the Koigni around us started to cheer. It was a signal to Jake, to let him know the Koigni Elders were gone and now was the time to send in the rest of the army.

"Sophia, we have to move!" Doya snapped. She grabbed me by the shoulder and yanked me to my feet. Esis was clutching my shoulder tight, like he too couldn't believe what just happened. Doya and I stumbled behind a huge boulder for cover. I collapsed with my back to it, trying to catch my breath. Naomi pressed her head against my side to keep me from falling over.

I grabbed my stomach, as if trying to hold my insides where they belonged, though I hadn't been injured. I stared out into the valley, though it was all just a blur.

"Listen to me!" Doya grabbed me by the shoulders and shook me. Her broken tone suggested she was nearly half gone herself. "If we grieve on the battlefield, we die. We have to keep going. We can mourn later."

I blinked a few times, still trying to understand what she was saying.

Doya must've noticed she wasn't getting through to me, because she sighed and wrapped her arms tightly around me. I wanted to cry into her shoulder, but the tears wouldn't come. Right now, I was just a girl who needed a hug from her mother, to keep from falling apart.

"Sophia," she whispered, "don't let Lindsey and Miranda's sacrifice be in vain."

That snapped me back to attention. She was right. There was nothing I could do to bring them back, but I sure as hell could make sure their sacrifice was worth it. My limbs felt like noodles, but I had to keep fighting.

"I won't," I promised, swallowing the lump in my throat. "We have to finish this."

Doya pressed a kiss to the top of my head, igniting my strength again. "That's my girl."

Though grief was still churning in my gut, I knew I couldn't let it consume me. I had to transform it and use it against the Task Force. It was the only way.

As I looked down, I realized Esis was healing Doya's arms. They'd been horribly burned by my Fire when I was trying to get her to let me go. Her skin repaired itself at Esis' command, but I realized Doya hadn't even mentioned the damage I'd done to her. She'd taken the pain without complaint.

It was the best proof I had she really did love me.

I glanced around, my stomach hollowing. Though Doya said we had to finish this, the only way out was the same way Lindsey and Miranda had gone. There were only a handful of Koigni left, and now that the Fire wall was down, Task Force members were advancing fast.

We couldn't lose anyone else. My heart wouldn't take it.

Resistance soldiers swarmed the battle field. Liam raced out of the trenches toward me, panting. "*Pawee!*"

We connected in an embrace. Sobs racked my chest as I tried to explain to him what happened. "L-Lindsey and M-Miranda—"

"We know," Liam said, smoothing my hair down. "We saw."

Baine had followed Liam, and he swept Doya up into his arms. "My love!"

The two kissed like teenagers, until she drew away and slapped him in the chest. "We can make love later. Right now, we fight."

Jonah and Imogen approached beside Liam with their Familiars. Imogen's eyes were stained with tears, but Jonah looked fucking *pissed*. He cracked his knuckles. "I'm going to suffocate those motherfuckers. They killed my best performers!"

I wiped the tears from my cheeks. Grief swirled into red-hot anger within my chest. "Save your Storm Lord powers. Right now, I need you to part the clouds. I need some damn sunlight."

Jonah lifted his hands to the sky and started working his magic. Jake wasn't far behind and came over to help, along with Perot and Riley. With the Koigni Elders gone, the Yapluma finally gained traction with the smoke. The storm clouds parted, and a ray of sunlight streamed down onto my skin. It was already late in the afternoon, but I could feel its warmth radiating through me.

I turned my gaze on the approaching enemy, and my spirit flared with unimaginable rage. "You all might want to stand back. This is going to get fucking deadly."

I barely caught a glimpse of Liam's wide eyes and Imogen's fearful expression before I turned away. I approached the Task Force alone. Esis threw up a shield around me, and elements bounced off it as I walked forward. My skin glowed with the magic from the sun, lighting me up like a blinding star. My magic burned so hot that as soon as a Task Force member got within twenty yards of me, their bodies disintegrated to nothing but ash in two seconds flat. They barely had a chance to scream before they were silenced, and their cremated remains were whisked away into the wind.

Now that the clouds and smoke had parted and I could channel power from the sun, I was unstoppable. After what happened to Lindsey and Miranda, I had no fucks left to give. There was no mercy— just unadulterated, burning rage. I fucking hated the Task Force. I hated Oleander. They'd taken so many people I loved from me and destroyed my home. I didn't care that I was a mere Elementai and not the Great Spirit. Today, I was their judge, and they would burn in *Aiya Nocshun* for their crimes.

I didn't feel like myself as I surged forward with murderous intent. The enemy caught sight of me, and Task Force members started running in all directions, rushing to escape my wrath. Others tried to attack from a distance, but their attacks could hardly shake Esis' shield. As my Familiar's shield bloomed bigger, so did my range of magic. Soon, Task Force up to fifty yards away were dropping dead under the power of the sun as I channeled it through me.

I thought of Lindsey and Miranda— of their sacrifice and how much they'd given to our cause. As my pain mounted, my magic ignited. I was Fire. I was death. And I was going to make every single one of these monsters pay for laying a finger on the people I loved.

Power welled within me so strongly, I couldn't hold it back. I sent my magic out in a burst of impenetrable flame. My screams filled the air, echoing a piercing cry of loss all across the valley. My magic was so strong I felt it burning me from the inside out, but I didn't care. I wanted *justice*.

My flames killed a hundred Task Force at once, bursting their bodies into ash, before it became too much and my knees buckled beneath me. The glow across my skin dimmed, and I fisted my hands in the dirt as I gasped for breath.

I'd almost pushed myself too far. Apparently, I did have a limit.

I gritted my teeth and begged for the tears to come. They welled up inside of me, pressing like angry beats of a drum against my chest, but they refused to flow freely. It was as if I was cursed to this grief, as if I may never overcome it. I didn't understand how I could kill a hundred people and still not feel any better. It was maddening.

Liam rushed to my side. His voice came out in a shaking rasp. "*Pawee?*"

When I looked up to him, I saw he wasn't alone. My mother and *pataa* stood by his side, along with Imogen, Jonah, and Jake. All five of them stared down at me like I was a bomb about to go off. Even Doya clutched at Baine's shirt, looking terrified of me. It was strange, because Doya wasn't scared of anything. Imogen took a cautious step back when my eyes met her. She looked at me like I was possessed— a monster. And maybe that's what I was.

Nausea rolled around in my belly as the reality of what just happened hit me. I couldn't believe what I'd just done.

"Soph, how'd you do that?" Liam balked. He looked so uncertain of me. Even his hand on my shoulder was shaking.

I shook my head, as if trying to toss out the images from my mind. So many bodies had burned at once. "I don't know. I'm just trying to survive this."

That's what I told myself, but I knew it went far deeper than that. I wanted the tribe to live in peace, yet how could we do that when I was out here massacring Hawkei like a rogue demigod? It went against everything I believed in, and I felt utterly sick at what I'd just done.

And still, my people were being killed. Retaliation was the only way to save them.

I resolved to deal with my transgressions later. If we didn't move, we'd only lose more people.

I struggled to my feet. I was a little lightheaded and had to grab Liam to keep upright.

"Come on, everyone," I said. "We have a tribe to fight for."

Everyone looked a little wary of me, but we didn't have time to stand around and discuss it. Esis encompassed us in a shield, protecting us from whirlwinds and fire. We advanced on the Task Force and retaliated with our elements.

Suddenly, the dirt exploded like a bomb had gone off— it was a Nivita attack. My heart hammered as my friends and I were flung into the air. We landed several yards away, and the wind had been knocked out of me. I didn't have time to catch my breath before dirt and rocks were raining down on us, splaying bruises all over my body. I threw my hands up to conjure a shield, but my magic sputtered.

Sassy barked and leapt to her feet, her vines snapping at huge rocks and breaking them apart. Imogen reacted and controlled the Nivita attack. Huge clods of dirt bigger than cars hung in the air, and her arms shook as she fought against it.

"Everybody move!" Imogen shouted.

Liam was beside me on the ground, groaning. A sharp rock had sliced into his side, embedding there. Adrenaline surged through me, and I jumped back into battle mode. I grabbed Liam and dragged him backward. Meanwhile, Jonah's leg had been pinned under a rock, and he was crying out in pain. Squeaks and Sabor worked on moving the rock, while Jake yanked Jonah out from under it. Baine and Doya had sustained minor injuries, but there were cuts all over their faces, blood dripping out of them.

As soon as we were all out of the way, Imogen dropped her hands. The giant pieces of dirt slammed to the ground, sending up giant clouds of dust.

I didn't have a second to catch my breath before I heard an alicorn whine from behind me. I whirled around to see Zaria, Sam's Familiar, rearing on her hind legs. She aimed her hooves at a unicorn with a Task Force member on its back. Sam was on her back, controlling rocks above his head that he aimed at the Task Force.

The horse-like Familiars attacked each other. Zaria landed a hoof to the unicorn's face, but the unicorn ducked its head and brought its horn upward. The sharp black horn caught Sam's leg, before slicing into Zaria's side. Blood dripped from both of their wounds, pooling into the mud beneath them.

I flipped to protection mode and created a shield around Sam and Zaria. The unicorn attacked again and hit my shield, but it couldn't break through.

And still, I hadn't been fast enough. Zaria fell to the ground, and Sam rolled off of her, screaming as he writhed in a mud puddle.

"Esis, heal!" I commanded. My emotions had turned stone-cold. It was the only way I managed to keep on fighting.

Esis ran for Sam and Zaria first, since they were worse for wear than Jonah. I aimed Anichi orbs at the Task Force. The first hit the unicorn square in the side of the head, but it was only strong enough to stun it for a moment. I shot another one, and the unicorn reared on its hind legs. Its rider fell off, and I shot another orb at him. It missed entirely, whizzing above his head.

The whole time, I was advancing on him. When I reached him, I didn't give him a chance to fight back. I jumped on top of him and grabbed him by the shoulders, shoving him deep into the mud. I drew his life force out of his body, ripping the very spirit out of him to protect my friend. He barely made a sound— just slumped lifelessly. The unicorn toppled over and let out a final breath before it died.

Liam wasn't far from me. As soon as I crawled off the Task Force member, my eyes connected with his. He didn't blink, just stared like he couldn't believe how I'd just twisted my magic against this man.

Fuck! I'd done it again. But I didn't exactly have the luxury of questioning my morals in the middle of a battle.

Tears pricked at my eyes. "I'm sorry, Liam. I-I didn't mean to scare you."

He stepped toward me and shook his head, though he couldn't take his eyes off the Task Force member. "You didn't," he said, though it sounded like a lie. "That just... wasn't you."

A sob broke from my chest, and I threw my hand over my mouth. "Yes it was. I've done it before."

I was on the verge of a breakdown.

"Soph, Soph!" Liam sounded very worried. He rushed over to me and grabbed me by the shoulders to shake me. "*Pawee*, listen to me. I know this war is hard. I know how death can change a person. But we are *not* Oleander."

Fuck, is that what he thought of me? That I was becoming *Oleander*? It sickened me.

"Remember who you are, *pawee*," Liam said. "That's the only way to win this war."

His words echoed in my mind as blood pulsed through my ears. Liam didn't want me stooping to Oleander's level, and yet we had— all of us— time and time again. And it was only getting us slaughtered. I didn't know how to win apart from fighting Fire with Fire, but Liam was right. We had to try a different approach.

I just didn't know what it was yet— but I resolved to find out.

I sniffled and wiped my nose. "I will."

Liam relaxed, but it barely lasted a moment before the sound of a rock blasting into the ground startled us. I turned to see that Cade had arrived. Three Task Force were advancing on him, and he was sending rocks flying in the air to counterattack.

"We have to keep fighting," I said to Liam.

He nodded firmly, but there was something in his eyes. I had to fight like Sophia, not like Oleander.

I ran toward Cade, while Liam took off in the opposite direction. My friends and I were backed into a tight circle, merely twenty yards across. There was so much happening from every angle that we each had to fight our own battles. I shot Fire at the Task Force, but it barely slowed them down.

"We have to work together!" Cade shouted.

"On it!" I called back. *That* kind of attack was Sophia, I realized. Oleander didn't operate under unity— only fear mongering and threats. I worked alongside my friends as one, and that's what made us different from Oleander and the Task Force.

As Cade's rocks whizzed through the air, I concentrated on them, working to heat the surrounding air with my magic. I focused on the power of the sun, and it flowed into my body effortlessly. All at once, ten rocks the size of my fist melted into molten lava. They whizzed straight through the Task Force's elements and pummeled through their bodies like bullets. The Task Force dropped immediately.

A scream filled the air. I turned to see Sean Andre on the back of his golden doe. A rogue fireball had caught him in the shoulder. Vanderbilt was nearby, and rage marred his features. He thrust Fire outward toward a fire-breathing lizard the size of a car— the one who'd hurt his son. The lizard skirted around his attack and jumped for Sean. His doe leapt out of the way, but the lizard caught her by the hind legs. She went down, and Sean got pinned beneath her.

"*Not my son!*" I heard Vanderbilt shout.

I summoned my Fire, ready to attack the fire-breathing lizard, but Vanderbilt got there first. He shoved his hands into the eye sockets of the lizard, while his hound bit the lizard's tail and ripped it off.

Vanderbilt started screaming, and he drew away. His hands were blackened and charred when he pulled them out of the lizard's eye sockets. My guts twisted. It didn't look like it was burned from Fire, but from a poisonous chemical. His skin turned black and started falling off his body in chunks. The lizard bled a thick, tar-like liquid from his eyes, and I realized that its blood was venomous. Vanderbilt's hound howled as the deadly blood filled his mouth.

The lizard thrust its head into Vanderbilt's middle, and Vanderbilt went flying. Blood covered him, and his skin was gone in seconds. His screams ceased.

"Cade!" I shouted as the lizard aimed its jaw back at Sean.

Cade lifted another rock with his magic, and I turned it to lava. He thrust it forward, and it burned a hole straight through the lizard's head, killing it.

Sean survived, but he was visibly shaken. His doe had to support him as they raced for cover behind a mound of dirt. His eyes stared in disbelief at his father's corpse.

I felt sickened by Vanderbilt's death. He'd been our lawyer— he was one of the few reasons Liam and I had won our trial. We weren't exactly close, but he had saved our asses at a time we needed him most. He'd stuck up for us when no other lawyer wanted to put their neck on the line.

And now... like so many others, he was gone.

Good people were dying in this fight. And there was nothing I could do to stop it.

Nearby, Bren, Vanessa, and Maddie were fighting a herd of magical creatures. All sorts of animals charged, from bulls to elk to moose. My friends weren't alone, though. They were surrounded by at least twenty other resistance members, all trying to thwart off the Familiars' attacks. A dozen people stood in a row and joined their elbows in a human chain.

Elements swirled around them with incredible magic. The Nivita formed a huge rock wall to protect themselves from the herd, while Toaqua pulled water from the ground and sky to create streams of water that sliced straight through Familiars. Koigni burned others at a distance, and Yapluma sliced Familiars in half with their magic.

It hit me who the twelve people were. They were the ones we'd helped escape from Kinpago on one of our first missions— the ones the Elders had labeled as dangerous. And dangerous they truly were.

But we still were no match for Oleander's army. Tornados swirled out of the sky— more than I could count— and picked up resistance members like they were sheets of paper. The tornados twisted and swirled, flinging people into huge crevices in the earth created by Nivita enemies.

Screams met my ears, and I whirled back toward my friends. Doya and Baine were working on taking down a massive wyvern, while Jake and Jonah were fighting against a team of Task Force Yapluma. Jonah couldn't even stand— it was taking a serious toll on him. Liam and Imogen were nowhere to be found.

I glanced around frantically, searching for my husband and my best friend. I spotted them not far away. They'd gone to Trace and Amelia's aid, but all four of them were trapped in a Nivita attack. The dirt had turned to mud, and my loved ones were sinking up to their chests. Liam and Amelia were trying to loosen the mud with water, while Imogen and Trace were attempting to push the dirt aside. The Task Force fought against them, and they gained no leeway.

Julian swooped down. Liam and Imogen grabbed on to his feet, but even as he tried to drag them out of the mud pit, they were stuck.

Esis was almost done healing Sam and Zaria. "Esis, get to Jonah next!" I cried.

He gave me a firm nod, and I hurried off to save my husband. I came to a skidding halt at the edge of the mud pit. I couldn't work with Earth or Water. My elements were useless here.

Then I spotted the Nivita Task Force on the other side of the pit. There must've been six of them, all laughing hysterically as they watched my friends sink deeper and deeper with no escape.

Anger bubbled up inside of me, and I let my Fire rage. I screamed as flames came shooting out of my palms. They shifted into various creatures— two phoenixes, a unicorn, and three hippogriffs. I aimed them at the Task Force, and my Fire creatures flew over the pit and struck. It happened so fast the Task Force never saw it coming. All six of them went up in flames, screaming as my magic burned them alive.

My friends gained the upper hand, and they were able to push the dirt and water aside. Julian dragged them out and back onto solid ground.

Jake and Jonah approached with their Familiars, along with Esis. Thunder rumbled above us, and huge gusts of wind whipped my hair back. It was so strong, I could hardly stay upright. The winds had the strength of a Storm Lord behind them.

"Jonah, stop that!" I cried, but I could barely be heard over the sound of the wind.

"I'm not doing anything!" he shouted back.

The ground continued to shake, and water began to seep up through cracks in the earth.

Fear began to take over my insides. What was going on? If Jonah wasn't controlling those winds, who was?

"We have to keep moving!" Liam shouted.

We didn't even make it a step before the earth cracked. Mud from the pit went splaying everywhere, and a shadow passed over us. I looked up in horror to see a hydra rising out of the mud pit. Each of its nine heads were covered in black tar, but its terrifying green eyes stared down at us with murderous intent.

Hydra were water creatures. This one had apparently been traveling through an underground water system, because it came up out of the earth like it'd been lurking there the whole time. The serpent was huge, with nine heads and necks a dozen feet long.

"Run!" Liam shouted.

Liam jumped onto Julian's back and yanked me on, along with Esis. Jonah and Jake mounted their hippogriffs, while the others started running at record speed. Julian spread his wings and took off, but we barely made it three feet off the ground before one of the hydra's claws swiped at us. The sickening sound of bone crunching met my ears the same time an ungodly pain shot up my leg. Julian cried out and fell back to the ground. The hydra had caught both me and Julian at once.

Julian rolled to the side, and Liam and I fell off. I nearly crushed Esis beneath me, but he wiggled free. My heart was hammering so hard, I could barely breathe. I was losing a lot of blood from my leg— and fast. All around me, the sound of my friends screaming echoed across the battlefield.

The hydra had struck each of its heads at a different group. Squeaks had been ripped out of the sky, and she lay on the ground with her wing twisted. Jake writhed, his arm bent in the wrong direction. Imogen and Sassy were both unconscious, while pieces of Cade's skin hung off his body in chunks.

Trace leaned over Amelia as blood poured out a huge gash in her stomach. Furthest from me, Doya's face was almost unrecognizable, as it was covered in a thick mask of blood. Naomi's tail had been ripped right off of her, and Baine's hand was missing fingers.

Streams of Fire erupted from Doya's hands as she aimed her magic at one of the hydra's heads. But it wasn't enough to injure it. All nine hydra heads reared backward, poised for a second strike— the killing strike.

I didn't have a moment to think. All I knew was that this was the end. There was no way we were taking down a hydra with the injuries we'd sustained. One last strike from those razor-sharp teeth, and we were done for. Oleander had won.

He can't! I thought. That wasn't how the prophecy was foretold. I wouldn't let it happen.

In a last-ditch effort, I raised my fingers to the Spirit Totem. My vision blurred, but I could see the shadow of the hydra's head racing toward me, going in for the kill.

Ancestors, please, I begged one last time.

I squeezed my eyes shut, expecting the blow...

But it didn't come.

My eyes shot open, and I glanced around, half expecting the ancestors to be there in an answer to my prayers. But there were no ancestors within view. Instead, the hydra above our heads reared backward when its nine noses slammed into an invisible barrier.

Was it the ancestors? Had they created a shield for us?

No, I realized as my eyes landed upon Esis. He stood close to me, his paws lifted to the sky. His eyes were knitted in concentration. The hydra struck again, but Esis' shield did not waver.

Esis' nose twitched, and sparks flew out of his palms. They were small at first, until they grew into huge Anichi light balls. The balls flew straight through his shield and smacked the hydra in its various faces. The nine-headed serpent cried out in pain as the orbs seared wounds into its skin.

It was clear Esis' urge to defend us had never been stronger. Esis' orbs transformed into straight beams of light. They sliced through the hydra's heads like lasers, decapitating each one in turn. The hydra screamed and twisted, but it could not escape my Familiar's attack.

Blood spurted over top of us, and all nine heads fell to the ground. The serpent's body slumped into the mud, sinking slowly.

Pride mounted in my chest. I'd never seen Esis pull off such a feat of magic. I didn't even know he *could*.

"Esis, you saved us!" I cried. I leaned over to pet him, but I sucked in a sharp breath when pain shot up my leg.

Worry etched in Esis' features. He quickly assessed the damage to my legs, then glanced around the battlefield at all the other injured Elementai and Familiars, including our friends. Tears beaded in his eyes, and his bottom lip trembled. Hopelessness settled in my gut when I realized he may not be able to get to all of us before one of us died.

"Save the others first," I whispered to Esis.

Esis turned his gaze back to me. He shook his head, then placed his paw in my hand. I wrapped my fingers around it, and tears streamed down my face.

Perhaps this really was the end. To be honest, I was surprised we'd held on this long. Giving up seemed inevitable at this point.

Then something amazing happened. Esis' horns started to glow. They became so bright it was blinding. I squeezed my eyes shut, and even then, I could still see the radiance of his Anichi light behind my lids. Incredible, pure white light filled my vision, and then...

Kaboom!

Esis' Anichi magic exploded, expanding over the battlefield and wrapping it in a beautiful light. Warmth seeped deep into my bones, and the pain in my leg was completely forgotten. For a moment, I was so warm and comfortable, I forgot we were fighting at all.

Then I opened my eyes, and I saw that storm clouds were still swirling above me. The sounds of elements clashing against elements was almost deafening. I lifted my head and was surprised that I could move my leg. A moment ago, I was bleeding, but now the skin was smooth and unharmed.

I glanced around and saw that all my friends had been healed, too. The gash in Amelia's abdomen was gone, and she ran her hands over her smooth belly in amazement. Naomi's tail had grown back, as had Baine's fingers. Even Squeaks' wing had straightened out. Jake rubbed his arm, and Cade's skin was smooth. Arabelle's wounds had knitted back together. Imogen and Sassy rubbed their heads and sat up.

It was incredible. Everyone's injuries had healed in moments. Liam and I shared a jaw-dropping look, then stared down at Esis in amazement.

"Esis, buddy," I gasped. "How did you do that?"

Esis just shrugged, then bounded over to Julian to make sure he was okay. The gash across his side was nowhere to be seen.

Liam and I had both gone speechless. Years ago, everyone said that Esis was useless— nothing but a ball of fur. *Weak*. But they were fucking wrong, because Esis was the strongest Familiar I ever knew. He'd proven that long before today— I just didn't truly see it until now. Tears pricked at my eyes, and for the first time in this battle, they weren't from grief. If there was a word that went beyond *proud*, that's how I felt about my Familiar. He was everything everyone said he'd never be. He was amazing.

"The Task Force is wiping out our troops!" Jake shouted. He pointed in the direction of a battle raging nearby. "We have to get to them."

"We'll be slaughtered!" Doya protested.

"We have to sneak up on them," Amelia suggested.

"But how?" Cade asked.

An idea suddenly struck, but I didn't know if I could pull it off. After watching what Esis had just done, anything was worth a shot.

"Let me try something," I told them.

I lifted my hands and pushed my Anichi magic outward. At first, it was just a shield, but I manipulated light around it.

Come on, I thought. *This has to work.*

If it didn't, I wasn't sure what else we could try. But I wasn't going to give up hope. I continued to seek out the sun. My Fire flared when I connected with it, but I changed the energy within me, transferring it from my heat into my healing magic.

All at once, we went invisible.

"Holy crap!" Imogen screamed. "Where'd I go!?"

"I made you invisible," I told her.

"*Pawee*, this is incredible," Liam said. I felt him reach out to me, but I couldn't see him.

There wasn't time to revel in my prowess. "Let's get a move on!" Baine called.

As we moved, I shifted the light and shield with us. I got us close enough to the Task Force that they didn't see us coming. My friends attacked while I held the shield, and elements went flying at Task Force members and Familiars. Some of them whirled around, as if searching for the source, but they found nothing. Even so, they retaliated chaotically. Elements slammed into my shield, and my invisibility sputtered. We blinked in and out of visibility.

A couple of Task Force caught on and launched direct attacks. Above us, a twister started to form, and a crack in the earth appeared between us.

"Watch out!" Jake shouted. The crack widened, separating our group in half as my magic failed and we went visible all at once.

Jonah conjured lightning from above, and it cracked down against the earth. The bolt spider webbed out and struck three Task Force members at once. Another bolt sizzled against my shield, but it felt like nothing more than a tickle.

"Jonah!" I called to him across the crevice widening between us. "Do that again. Aim a lightning bolt at me!"

"What?" he gawked. "No way."

"Do it!" I called. "I have an idea."

Jonah conjured up lightning from above. I dropped my shield just in time for a lightning bolt to crack through the air right in front of me. As the blinding light blinked on, I thrust my shield outward, encompassing it inside.

My shield hovered in my hands as a sphere not much bigger than a basketball. Inside of it, the lightning was trapped, sizzling and trying to escape.

With a proud smile, I drew my hands outward, expanding the shield above my head. The lightning raged, pounding its electric power against the sides of its container. The shield grew to the size of a house. I thrust it forward, and it went flying into the middle of the Task Force's ranks.

It exploded. Tendrils of lightning bolts blasted outward, connecting with dozens of Task Force all at once. They were all electrocuted simultaneously, stopping their hearts.

Unfortunately, it caught the attention of the rest of the army, and many were distracted from their fights to turn on us. The ground shook once more as Nivita attacked. The earth split beneath my feet.

I jumped to one side, and Liam jumped to the other. I realized in horror a second later that we'd been separated. Esis screamed from my shoulder as the earth started to crumble beneath Liam. My heart leapt to my throat as

Liam slipped on the crumbling rock. He caught himself on a root, and Julian quickly came to his aide before he could fall into the pit.

I opened my mouth to call out to him, but I was cut off as a fireball whizzed by my head. I whirled around at my attacker, a fireball ready in my palm. My. Heart. Stopped.

At first, I thought I was seeing a spirit, but she was there in the flesh, summoning Fire like she fucking owned the battlefield.

Haley.

Her face was marred with burn scars, and her dark hair stuck up in disarray around her face. Anwara flew above her, flames licking off her tail. My flames burned higher.

Haley threw her head back and laughed maniacally. Her eyes widened, making her look positively insane.

"Surprised, Henley?" she snapped.

"I see the ancestors had mercy on you," I stated coolly. I had the urge to slam a fireball in her face, but I burned to know how she'd escaped the *Hozho.*

Haley chuckled as she paced in front of me. "The ancestors had nothing to do with it. I saved myself. The ancestors can go fuck themselves, for all the mercy they've shown me."

"Maybe you don't deserve it," I suggested, unable to stop myself.

That really pissed Haley off. She attacked, shooting fireball after fireball at me while she screamed. "I didn't wrestle a dragon to fly me off the *Hozho* just to come here and be insulted by a filthy *mopite!*"

I countered each of her attacks, but I only narrowly escaped them. With all the power I'd used today, I was exhausted and drained. Haley, on the other hand, seemed to have been saving herself for me.

"I'd rather be mixed blood than a selfish bitch like you!" I cried back.

A guttural scream erupted out of Haley's lungs, piercing my ears like hot rods. Flames blasted out of her hands, and I threw up a shield to protect myself. I drew magic from the crystals in my pocket, but my shield became unstable. There was hardly any magic left in the crystals. The heat from her flames burned a hole through my shield, and the air quickly heated around me. Esis whined, and sweat broke out across my brow.

"You started this, Henley!" Haley screeched. "Everything changed when you came to Kinpago. This war is your fault!"

"And yet you're still fighting!" I snapped back.

Fire blasted out of my palms, and flames licked high above her head. Haley lifted her hands and drew the flames back, ripping my magic from my grasp like it was a child's play thing. Holy shit. I took a cautious step back, heart hammering.

"I have to!" Haley screamed. "You've taken everything from me!"

Haley created a swirl of Fire around me, trapping me inside a ten-foot circle. The flames were so high, I couldn't see past it, save for a small opening where I could see her shadow advancing on me.

"I've taken nothing from you," I countered. I threw an Anichi battle orb at her, but she dodged out of the way.

Haley's flames grew higher. The air was heating so much that it was getting hard to breathe. Red welts started to break out across my arms.

"If it weren't for you, my mother would still be alive," Haley accused with a snarl.

I thrust my magic outward, and I caught a portion of her flames. They raged back in her direction, but didn't touch her. "You're the one who killed her! Anwara attacked."

"You don't get it!" Haley shrieked. "Anwara wouldn't have done that if you didn't pull your little stunt at the execution. Anwara was stupid to kill my mother."

"But she's your soul," I argued. "Some part of you wanted her dead!"

"Don't tell me what I want, *mopite!*" Haley screamed. "I hated my mother, but I never wanted her dead. You don't know what it's like having to be perfect *all the time!*"

I felt a twinge in my chest, and was surprised to find that a part of me actually *felt sorry* for Haley. She was fighting for her home, same as I was. She was right. When I'd come to Kinpago, everything *had* changed. I didn't blame her for hating me.

Haley twisted her hands, and the heat around me intensified. Hot air swirled, and though I threw up my shield, it became unbearable. Esis aimed Anichi battle orbs at Anwara, but she dodged each one of them. After his feat of magic earlier, we were both running low on power.

"I hate you!" Haley shrieked at me. "You're nothing but a curse upon the Hawkei."

Haley went in for the kill, but I reacted quickly. I thrust my flames outward, and our Fire clashed. Flames burst toward the sky between us, skimming along the bottom of the clouds. My arms shook as I struggled to use my Fire against hers.

Haley threw her flames to the side, and mine fizzled out, but Fire continued to rage on around us. When our magic clashed, it created a Fire storm. Fire tornados swirled into the sky, and flames ate away at the earth at record speed.

Anwara swooped down from above me to attack. I ducked, but she caught Esis on my shoulder and knocked him off of me. Esis shot orbs at Anwara as she flew overhead, retaliating with fireballs. An orb and a fireball met in the sky and exploded like a firework.

Haley advanced on me, and I knew I had to run. I didn't have the energy left to fight her. I yanked Esis off the ground and ran to the side, jumping over the ring of Fire she'd created around me. Hot air assaulted me, and the flames burned my skin. Esis and I both screamed as we made our escape. Haley just laughed while Anwara circled ahead.

"You can't run from me, Henley," Haley threatened.

A blinding flash of light burst in front of me, and my whole body rocked with electricity. I was shot backward like I'd just run into a brick wall. I landed on my back, gasping, while Esis swayed on the ground beside me. His hair stuck up in every direction and was singed on the ends.

Holy shit. Haley had just conjured lightning and *struck* me with it.

This bitch wasn't messing around anymore. She'd said her peace and was ready to kill me. Haley was a mere shadow on the other side of the flames, but her body came into focus as she stepped right through them. They didn't hurt her at all.

Haley took one look at me and my Familiar on the ground and started laughing again. "You're weak, Sophia. I can't believe the ancestors chose *you*."

"Well, they did," I snapped. I raised my hands to her, but my magic wouldn't come. I'd overexerted myself, and if I pushed any further, I'd end up like Lindsey and Miranda. The only thing I could do was talk my way out of this. "I'm supposed to unite the tribe, and you can be a part of that. We want the same thing. We can help each other."

Haley's lips curled into a sneer. "I'll be the one to win this war, by getting rid of you once and for all."

Haley raised her hands to go in for the kill. My heart leapt, and for a moment, I thought she might actually overpower me.

I threw up my hands to protect myself. I didn't call upon Anichi or Koigni magic specifically. I just let everything I had flow out of me— and I was shocked by what I saw. Flames erupted from my palms, but inside the streams of Koigni magic were glowing white tendrils of Anichi magic.

The blast was so powerful that when it hit Haley, it sent her tumbling head over heels a hundred feet backward. My heart leapt in my chest when her shadow disappeared into the crack in the earth. Anwara let out a worried cry.

"Ancestors!" I screamed, scooping Esis into my arms. I hadn't been trying to hurt Haley. I was just trying to counter her attacks and protect myself.

I ran over to the crack in the earth and looked over the side. To my surprise, Haley had caught herself on the edge and was trying to climb back up. The crevice had to be fifty feet across now, and twice as deep. Tar bubbled at the bottom. One wrong move, and Haley would fall to her death.

I couldn't explain what came over me. I should have been happy to see her die. But I was sick of this war— sick of the bloodshed. Another life lost on either side was another loss for the Hawkei as a whole.

Liam's words came back to me. I had to fight like Sophia, not like Oleander. I didn't want to be a monster. We'd already lost so many Hawkei today. Slaughtering each other couldn't be the answer. Our tribe would never heal. Not unless we started with forgiveness.

I flatted myself onto my belly and held my hand down toward her. "Haley! Let me help you!"

Haley's top lip curled back. "So you can throw me to my death? No, thank you!"

"Haley, please!" I begged. Beside me, Esis was pacing back and forth frantically, as if searching the battlefield for help. "I can help you! You're going to fall!"

"Because of *you*!" she spat.

Haley reached for another rock to climb the side of the broken earth, but it broke off the steep face and tumbled into the pit below. Haley nearly lost it, but held on with one hand. Fury deepened in her features. An earth-shattering scream erupted from her lungs, and Fire burst out of her with such heat and intensity that I had to jump backward. Her flames filled the crevice and shot upward, expanding across the battlefield.

Esis and I worked together to create a shield around ourselves to stay protected, but others were not so lucky. Down the battlefield, Task Force members and their Familiars lit aflame. Haley's own army screamed out in agony. Some of them threw themselves into the pit just for reprieve from the pain.

Anwara circled overhead. Her cries echoed over the battlefield as she watched her own people burn to death, but Haley wouldn't listen.

I saw the moment Anwara made her decision, because her features changed— her eyes narrowed, and her wings became rigid. She set her sights on Haley, who had just reached the top of the pit and was crawling to safety. Anwara's entire body became outlined in flames. She dove for her Elementai.

For a second, I thought she was going to save Haley. I never could've anticipated what happened next.

Anwara *attacked*.

She thrust her talons into Haley's eyes. Haley screamed like I'd never heard her scream before. Anwara pecked at Haley's chest, ripping flesh clean off her ribs. I became a statue, watching in horror at something I never thought possible.

"Anwara, stop!" Haley shrieked. She scrambled to her feet, but Anwara followed. Her feathers burned brighter, and she shoved her wings into Haley's face. Haley's hair went up in flames, and the deadly Fire continued to consume the rest of her body. No matter how much Haley screamed, or how much magic she tried to use to stop it, she couldn't. Anwara wouldn't let her access it.

"I hate you!" Haley shrieked as the flames consumed her, the Fire roaring ten feet tall around her form. "I can't believe I bonded with you! I hate *myself*!"

Haley fell to her knees, the raging Fire on her skin too much to bear. One last scream tore across the valley, and then— nothing.

Haley's body slumped to the ground, Fire licking across every inch of her. Anwara circled overhead one more time before swooping down and flying straight into the deadly Fire she'd created. Anwara shrieked as her own flames consumed her, until there was nothing left of the phoenix but ash.

I trembled, unable to tear my gaze off Haley's burning body. I couldn't believe what I had just seen. Haley's own Familiar had slaughtered her. How was that possible?

Anwara had seen what Haley had done. She'd decided it was better to sacrifice Haley, and sacrifice herself, than it was to allow Haley to keep hurting people.

As much as I wanted to save Haley, in the end... some people just didn't want help. They'd rather cling to their hatred than step into the light. And though I'd tried... Haley had refused to be saved.

Esis grabbed me tighter. He was as equally shaken up as I was. A dragon's cry sounded overhead, finally snapping the two of us out of it. I recognized the cry as Julian's, but I couldn't see him through the thick smoke. I raised my hand and shone an Anichi light above me as a beacon.

Julian landed, and Liam jumped off his back. He had a look of terror on his face and was heaving shallow breaths.

"*Pawee!*" he cried, rushing over to me.

We fell into each other's embrace, and he kissed me on the top of the head. "I thought I'd lost you," he whispered.

I drew away, but when I opened my mouth to respond, nothing came out. My feet rooted to the ground, and my hands shook in his.

"What happened?" he demanded.

"H-Haley," I stammered. I pointed in the direction where her charred body lay. "Anwara killed her. How's that possible? Were they truly bonded?"

Liam looked as shocked as I did, but he composed himself quickly. "I don't think Haley allowed balance with her Familiar. Haley became corrupted, and when she held on to the darkness, Anwara took the good."

That's why Anwara became enraged when Haley started killing her own side. She knew it was wrong.

"Haley had betrayal in her heart," Liam explained. "Turns out, she could even betray herself."

Esis shuddered, like he couldn't imagine such a thing.

"I'll never let that happen to us," I promised Esis. Just the thought made me sick. I quickly turned back to Liam. We didn't have time to stand around talking about Familiar bonds. "Did everyone else make it?"

Liam's features fell. "As far as I saw. We were attacked on the other side, but I left to come looking for you. The truth is, we're still being slaughtered."

Just as Liam said it, the sound of a horn blowing sounded across the battlefield. It was deep and so loud, it cut through all the sounds of battle and elements around us.

I stilled. The air pressure seemed to change instantly, and a gentle breeze swept by us. The smoke around us cleared. The sun was starting to set, but there was enough light to see across the valley. On the far end of the battlefield stood a flag lined in each of the four House colors.

Relief flooded through me as the battlefield quieted. "Ancestors, did we win?" I gasped. "Is it a truce?"

Liam's lips tightened. He looked like he knew what it meant, but he seemed conflicted about it. He shook his head. "No, *pawee*, we didn't win. The dragon horn and flag are a call for a ceasefire."

"That's good, right?" I asked breathlessly. We needed time to recuperate.

"Yes and no," Liam said stiffly. "Oleander's giving us a chance to collect our dead, but he's also asking us to surrender."

"We can't!" I cried, heart pounding. I'd rather die than surrender to Oleander. This whole war was to stop him from leading the Hawkei.

Esis pulled on his ears from my shoulder. He wasn't willing to let Oleander rule, either.

My breaths came in shallow heaves. "How long do we have?"

Liam's jaw tightened, like he might go find Oleander himself and butcher him right where he stood. "We have until dawn to surrender. Otherwise, he'll slaughter us all."

My stomach dropped. That didn't feel like enough time. We had to do anything but surrender, and we barely had time to form a new plan.

Liam took my hand and led me back in the direction of the resistance trenches, where we could take refuge for the night while Oleander gave us time to consider surrender. I barely felt my feet beneath me, and I could hardly focus. My energy was completely drained, but I wasn't the only one. What little resistance members were left walked like zombies. Liam and I leaned against each other, forced to hold each other up.

We could've ridden Julian back, but there seemed to be an unspoken agreement between myself and my husband— we wanted to assess the damage. We had to walk through the battlefield to see what had truly happened.

Dead bodies were scattered so heavily over the valley, we had to step on charred remains to make it back. Though many were Task Force and enemy Familiars, the battlefield was mostly dead resistance members. My stomach sank further and further the more we walked. I felt hollow inside— like Oleander himself had reached into my stomach and yanked out my insides. We'd lost so many people; I knew there was no coming back from this. We'd hit our limits today. Oleander had granted us a moment of reprieve, but it wouldn't be enough to regain our strength and win. Right now, surrender felt like our only option.

No one had the energy to pick up the dead, to give them proper honor for their sacrifice. It was horrifying.

Tears streamed down my face, but I didn't have the strength to reach up and wipe them away. Beside me, Liam slowed and took in the devastation. The expression of disbelief in his features was staggering. We'd seen so much death these past few years, yet nothing like this.

"Liam, say something. Please," I whispered. I couldn't take the harrowing silence that had settled over the battlefield.

Liam's tear filled eyes met mine. "There's nothing to say, *pawee*, because the truth is just too—"

Liam choked up, unable to finish his sentence. "We... we've lost. There's no way we can fulfill the prophecy after this."

Sobs rocked my body. "I-it's not too late to contact the ancestors."

Desperately, I clawed at my shirt, until I reached the Spirit Totem under the fabric. I clutched it tightly in my hand and closed my eyes. I'd tried several times throughout the battle to call upon them, and they hadn't shown. But we hadn't ever been more desperate than we were now. Surely they'd come to save us.

Ancestors, please, help us. Now is the time we need you the most. You said I'd know when to contact you, and I know it's now, when we are most hopeless. Help us win this war.

I opened my eyes, but I saw nothing. The silence was deafening.

Liam reached out and placed a hand on mine, gently pushing it away from the Spirit Totem. "It's no use, *pawee*. Look at what the Hawkei have done. We've destroyed each other. The ancestors have given up on us."

My shoulders shook. I refused to believe they wouldn't come, but my own two eyes couldn't lie to me. The ancestors weren't here, and they weren't coming. The prophecy was a lie, and the resistance had lost.

The only light among all this darkness was knowing I had a few more hours left with my family and friends— to say our goodbyes.

I spotted Jake and Jonah not far away, each of them riding the backs of their hippogriffs. Imogen and Cade followed behind, along with Doya and Baine. I quickly counted Familiars and saw that they'd made it, too. Amelia and Trace had gone further ahead with Sam toward the trenches. I quickly scanned the battlefield for others, and saw Vanessa and Bren helping Kelsey, who looked injured, back to safety. Perot looked totally lost as he took in the dead. Maddie and Drew hugged each other tightly, while Tabitha and Hudson wept over the dead bodies.

Liam and I met up with Jake and the others near the edge of the trenches. Luana jumped out of the trenches and rushed to our sides.

Thank the ancestors you all made it! she signed. *Who needs healing?*

Madame Wells approached, along with Isabella. The two of them dragged Riley over. Blood poured from a wound on his head, and he was unconscious, but I didn't think he was dead. Luana immediately went to him and started healing.

"What's our plan, Jake?" Liam asked. The hopelessness was evident in his tone.

Jake's shoulders slumped. He was so pale, he looked on the verge of vomiting. "We have to surrender."

"No," Jonah protested immediately.

"We can't give up!" Imogen cried.

"We *must,*" Jake argued. "We can't lose any more people."

Jonah's eyebrows knitted. "If we surrender, we become Oleander's slaves! Do you know what the Hawkei *do* to prisoners of war? I'd rather die than be a Biyami again."

Jake pressed his fingers to his eyes. "This isn't an easy call to make, but it's what has to be done."

"Isn't there anything we can do?" I asked. There had to be *something*. And yet, I wasn't holding my breath. Jake was right— we couldn't lose any more people.

"If we keep fighting, the Hawkei will wipe each other out," Jake said. "If we surrender, at least the tribe has a chance to go on."

"The tribe isn't worth it if they follow Oleander," Liam spat.

"Let's just think about this," Imogen said. "We're not ready to make a decision immediately. We all need to eat and rest, and we'll discuss our options rationally."

"There are no other options," Jake growled.

"Im's right," Jonah added. "We need to rest and at least consider if that's true. We have until dawn. I'm not surrendering a moment sooner."

Jake sighed. "Okay. Let's all take a moment to process this before we decide."

It sounded like Jake was just trying to make everyone happy for a moment. I didn't think he'd change his mind.

Jake turned and headed for the trenches, and Jonah and Imogen followed. Doya and Baine walked by. Both nodded to me, but they were both so winded they couldn't manage to speak.

Liam and I just stood there like statues in indecision. It didn't seem right to rest when so many of our people were dead. It felt like we should be out there on the battlefield beside them.

Without hardly realizing it, Liam and I began to walk aimlessly over the battlefield. I didn't know what I was looking for— perhaps some sort of sign, an answer to an unasked question. Esis shivered on my shoulder, horrified by the mass destruction.

The sun began to set, and darkness started taking over the battlefield. I didn't know how long we'd been walking. It could've only been minutes, or it could've been hours. All I knew was that when Liam stiffened beside me, time altogether halted in its tracks.

My eyes had been locked on my feet. As I lifted my gaze, my stomach plummeted. We were nearly to the edge of the battlefield, and the trees rose high in front of us. Just through an opening between two pines was a cluster of figures. They were mere shadows against the night, but their silhouettes were unmistakable.

Wyatt and Mia sobbed over the limp form of a dead body. Just inside the tree line, a huge thunderbird lay splayed out, his wings spread-eagled on the ground beside a still body.

"*Ezra!*" Liam's gut-wrenching cry sounded far off, yet it tore across the battlefield in a piercing wave.

Liam ripped his fingers out of mine and ran forward, but he stumbled on his way to his brother. My heart crushed into a million pieces at my husband's agony, and I fell to my knees. Julian must've felt it, too, because he raised his head to the sky and howled out in pain. Esis did the same, matching Julian's tune to a higher pitch. It was a song of heartbreak and loss.

Liam staggered to his knees and crawled the remaining few feet toward his brother. Mia wept, while Wyatt held her in his arms.

"It was Courtney," Wyatt managed to say.

Ezra's still body was surreal, unbelievable. His eyes were closed, like he was at peace— or merely sleeping. It was like this entire war was just a dream, because I didn't know how the ancestors could take Ezra from us. He was too good, too kind. Ezra had the sweetest heart, and was the most loyal. Out of all the people we could've lost, why did it have to be him?

Liam grabbed Ezra and pulled him onto his lap. He cradled him so close that Ezra's yellow war paint bled onto Liam's armor.

I finally found my feet and followed my husband. I knelt at his side and placed a hand on his shoulder, but he didn't seem to notice I was there. Liam rocked Ezra back and forth, and his shoulders shook heavily in sobs that broke my heart.

Liam's eyes desperately caught mine. "Soph, heal him! Use your powers, fix his wounds. *Please!*"

Esis' ears dropped, and I remained silent. There was nothing I could do to heal Ezra.

He was already gone.

Liam ceased to beg me again when the inevitable reality hit him. Instead, he turned toward the immobile body of his brother. "*Yellow!*" Liam wailed. "Ezra, you idiot! Yellow's for warriors ready to give up their souls to the Great Spirit! You know that... you— you—"

Liam's breath caught in his chest, and it ripped my spirit to shreds. I wished I could say something to him, but there was nothing that could be said. All we could do was grieve for Ezra— for everyone.

Ezra went into this war willing to give himself up as a sacrifice. The Great Spirit had listened to the will of his heart.

But would He listen to those of us who survived, and have mercy on our souls?

I wasn't so sure anymore. We'd lost everything.

TWENTY-THREE

I didn't want to fight anymore.

I wanted to give up.

I carried Ezra's body through a crowd of resistance fighters. People parted to make a path and bowed lowly, whispering condolences.

Sophia hung back to give me some space. There was a small clearing in an outcropping of trees nearby where the dead were being placed. Most of the bodies had been left on the battlefield. Our soldiers were too exhausted to gather the fallen. Only those that had died close enough to the trenches were brought in.

Julian walked behind, Dyami cradled carefully in his mouth. No one followed me into the clearing, save for Wyatt. I found a peaceful spot underneath a tree and laid Ezra down beside it. Julian placed Dyami beside Ezra's form, and the two of them rested beneath the fronds of the willow.

Ezra. My little brother.

I was aware of Wyatt's footsteps as he came to a halt. My shoulders hunched. The pain of grief had given me a mortal wound, one I thought I'd die from. My soul was bleeding out, pouring everything I thought I was into the earth. The weight of my pain was so heavy I felt like I'd be crushed by the loss. I thought it'd hurt when I lost my father, but this...

"What. Happened." My voice was so broken. And underneath it, a tsunami of rage.

"We chased Courtney all the way to the mountains," Wyatt began in a whisper. "By the time we caught up, she was waiting for us. Dyami had her

Familiar in his talons. We thought we had her, but she commanded a tree. A branch whipped out... broke Ezra's neck."

I swallowed, but didn't say anything. I was memorizing the features in Ezra's face.

Wyatt continued. "Dyami fell out of the sky. It all happened so fast... Mia and I tried to stop her, but once Dyami was dead, she took off on her Familiar. We lost her over the mountains."

My throat felt so thick, my tongue heavy. This was hell. It was absolute hell. There was nothing like this bitter agony on this earth. I'd trade a lifetime in *Aiya Nocshun* to avoid the reality of my brother's death. A hole had caved within me and was devouring everything that was alive. I was thinking of everything Ezra had ever done, everything he'd never get to do.

I wished it had been me. I was the sick one. He was healthy, had been full of life. It wasn't fair that I was still walking around and Ezra was gone. I wanted the Great Spirit to take my life and put it back into him. If only things worked like that.

"He didn't feel anything, Liam," Wyatt said. "I don't think he realized what had happened. I saw the light leave his eyes. He was gone before his body hit the ground."

I wasn't sure if Wyatt was lying or not. But I chose to believe him. If Ezra had died painlessly, it was the only blessing in this.

"It's my fault," I said heavily. "If I had gone after him—"

"If you had saved Ezra, others would've died in his place," Wyatt said. "The Toaqua were dying out there. Had you left, hundreds would've died in the trenches. You made the right choice as chief to lead them out."

"It's not the right choice to put the tribe over my own *family*. My father made the same decision one too many times, and it ruined us. Now I've done the same thing. I killed my own brother!"

"You didn't murder Ezra. He knew the risks. He was wearing yellow paint. He was ready to die."

"He was twenty fucking years old. He didn't understand the implications."

"Yes, he did," Wyatt said, kneeling beside me. "You don't want to hear this, but Ezra would've wanted you to save the others over himself. And you know that's what he'd ask you to do."

"I don't care." I didn't care about the rest of the world, about the lives I'd saved, because I'd lost one so precious to me. The tribe could be damned. I'd give them up now if I could return Ezra to me. This was wrong. This whole fucking war was wrong.

We'd lost people today. Lindsey, Miranda, so many others. And now one of the people I loved the most.

Let Oleander win. I just wanted my brother back.

Wyatt stepped aside and drew back into the trees. I heard soft footsteps behind me. Stabbing emotions raged through my chest as I saw Mom. Her face was paler than a ghost, and she was covered with dirt and blood from the battle. Her braid hung loosely over her shoulders. Tears began to trail from her cheeks to the ground, too numerous to count as her eyes settled on Ezra's body.

My mother fell to her knees and wailed as she flung herself over Ezra's chest. The weight in me got even heavier and dragged me down to the bottom of the ocean. Hearing her screams was worse than hearing my own. Mom put her face into Ezra's chest and wept openly, shaking with heavy sobs as she stroked his black hair.

Torture would've been far preferable. Nothing Oleander could do to me would hurt more than this, watching my mother sob over my brother's dead body. We didn't even have time— or a safe way— to take him to the burial mounds in Kinpago and lay him to rest. We had to leave him out here.

As darkness approached, my mother got to her feet. She stumbled, but I reached out to catch her. It took all I had to hold her up, because if I didn't, she'd surely collapse.

My mother looked at me. No words were spoken, but in those few seconds, Mom's expression changed from unfathomable sorrow to complete and murderous rage. She yanked her arm away from me and turned her back on Ezra's body with a shaking form. It appeared like it took all her strength as she rounded her shoulders and stomped forward, eyes blazing with a hatred I'd never seen in her before.

I didn't know what my mother would do now. But I feared for anyone who got in her way.

I stayed with Ezra's body for a while longer. It felt wrong to leave him, even though he had Dyami. It got darker, until the only light in the area was from the camp nearby. I stared at Ezra and thought about things. Mostly stuff from when we were kids, you know? I ruffled his hair. I cried a lot.

Didn't matter. He didn't get up.

Eventually, someone came and sat beside me. It was Maddie. Tears stained her face, while Eirakari let out moans of grief. Julian threw his wing around her to comfort her as Maddie handed me a blanket. "Here. It's one of the few we have."

I took it, but instead of wrapping it around myself, I laid it over Ezra's body. I kind of tucked him in. It was cold.

"He's not there. He's already gone."

Didn't mean I wanted to abandon him out here. Maddie hugged her legs to her chest and stared at Ezra's body. Maddie's face was wracked with grief, but she didn't seem surprised.

Then I knew... she expected this.

I remembered the violent vision Maddie had received on the beach months ago. How pale she'd been when she looked up and saw Ezra's face.

"Did you know?" I asked her. "Did he?"

Maddie sniffed. "I tried, Liam. I told him not to fight."

My guts twisted. *Why, Ez? Why?*

"You should've told me. I would've made him stay home," I said roughly.

"There were a thousand scenarios in my visions. All of them led to this," Maddie said. "He was going to fight no matter what."

"And what about the others?" I asked. "Could any of them be spared?"

"Why do you think I asked Lindsey and Miranda to help me interpret my visions?" Maddie asked thickly. "I needed people on the other side... in the Ancestral Lands... who could pass on the information to other Hawkei in the future. I foresaw their deaths years ago. They were the only people I could depend on."

Grief welled within me and threatened to spill over. I only managed to keep it together by placing a hand on Julian's scales. "Is that why they sacrificed themselves? Because they knew this was the end?"

"I never told them they were going to die." Maddie dropped her gaze. "I only told Ezra because I thought I could change it. And it didn't matter. He wouldn't listen to me. He wanted to stay by your side and help defend the resistance. He thought if he died, it might save the life of one of his friends."

Damn you, Ez. He was loyal to a fault. And that loyalty had cost him his life.

Sometimes people were too good for this world. I wished Ezra was more selfish, more of a jackass. Even more of a coward. He'd be alive if that was the case.

Not him, though. Ezra was brave. And I knew if he had to die, he'd be okay dying to give the rest of us a chance to go on.

Even if I wasn't okay that he was gone.

"And what about the rest of us?" I managed to ask.

Maddie chewed her lip. "It's all up in the air from this point out. Whatever decisions you guys make are going to affect us all."

That gave me a little comfort, if only to know we were in charge of our own fate, instead of being subject to a prophecy that left no room for error.

Then Maddie added, "But if you want my honest opinion, I don't see how we're going to make it out of this one."

That caused my heart to drop. "You said that winning this war would be worse than us losing."

"Yes. That still stands."

"So what are we supposed to do?"

"I don't know. If I had answers, I'd give them to you."

Eirakari nuzzled Maddie, and Maddie said, "Jake is asking for you. Don't worry. I'll stay with him until dawn."

I didn't want to leave. Just needed to sit here and turn to stone. I wanted to say I'd died with my brother.

But that wasn't true. I was a chief. And I still had people who needed me.

Maddie raised her head. As she did, she waved her hand. The tears drying on her face circled over Ezra, and water rose from the ground. It settled around him in a thin sheet of ice, covering him and Dyami both until their bodies were coated in a shroud of diamond.

Now the elements wouldn't ravage him. Until we got back, at least.

And we *would* get back to bury him. I wasn't dying out there. Not today. My mother had already lost a husband and a son. She would not lose another child.

It took everything I had to leave Ezra behind, but I did. Julian had to push me with his head to get me out of that clearing. I left a piece of myself behind, and when I stepped out of those trees, there was yet another part of my soul that I'd never get back.

Nothing could hurt more than losing Nashoma, but Ezra's death rivaled even that. I never wanted to do this again. This fight wasn't over yet, but I refused to lose anyone else.

Mia was waiting there for me. She fell to the ground before me and bowed, weeping profusely.

"I'm so sorry, my chief. I've failed you *again*." Mia sobbed. She beat a fist into the earth, like she felt responsible.

I reached down and gently pulled her to her feet. "You didn't, Mia. You did all you could. What happened was because of... *her*."

I couldn't even say Courtney's name.

Mia wiped the tears away. "I want to do something that matters. I keep screwing up."

"You did do something that matters. You killed Micah. Now there's one less Defortai in the world," I said. "When dawn comes, resolve to finish off the rest."

Mia nodded slowly. I heard a ruckus somewhere in the crowd. The pit within me grew bigger as I recognized Stevie's voice, calling for Ezra.

"Ezra? Ezra, where are you?" Stevie asked, looking everywhere. "Has anyone seen Ezra?"

No one responded. Sophia followed behind, at a loss for words. She didn't know what to tell her. Esis sat on her shoulder, pulling nervously on his ears as he waited for the worst to happen.

I wasn't sure why Stevie was here. She'd opted to stay behind. The reasons hardly mattered, because her entire world was about to collapse.

Stevie ground to a halt when she saw me. I didn't have to speak. Her face paled as she took me in. When my eyes connected with hers, I started crying again.

"No," she said, shaking her head. "No."

She pushed past me and ran into the trees. Sophia grabbed my arm. Several heads looked up as piercing shrieks rang throughout the night. They were the most devastating sounds I'd ever heard. Faces fell amongst the crowd, like people wanted to rush in and comfort her... but didn't know how.

I couldn't take hearing Stevie scream. It was too much, and Sophia knew it. She pulled me along. "Come on. We need to find the others."

Stevie's wails of grief faded into the background as the noises of the resistance welled around us. People were trying to eat, or get some rest, or making fires. Mostly, though, people just stared and talked quietly, like they were waiting for their execution. Esis jumped from Sophia's shoulder and sat on mine, giving my head a hug.

"Thanks, buddy." I scratched his ears.

Imogen, Jonah and Jake were gathered around a small fire. Imogen stood, while the other two had taken seats on the ground. Blood smeared all of our armor, some ours, some not. Jake's face was haunted— like he felt responsible for every life we lost out there. Squeaks and Sassy were exhausted. They lay curled against each other as Sabor prowled nearby, handing out what was left of the food from saddlebags on his back.

Everyone looked up when Sophia and I approached. Imogen was the first to react. She faced me and opened her arms. "Hey."

Imogen knew what this felt like. She'd lost two brothers.

I still couldn't speak. I fell upon Imogen and just sobbed. She wrapped her arms around me in a tight embrace. It felt like she was trying to squeeze all the hurt out of me.

I can't say it worked, but it felt a little better. I never noticed, but Imogen gave the best hugs.

When she let go, I sat next to Jonah. He'd been crying, too. "I'm so, so sorry bro. Ez didn't deserve that."

"Don't just feel bad for me. He was practically your brother, too."

Sophia sat beside me. She didn't touch me, but she was here, and her presence was enough.

"I just... I can't believe Ez is gone," Jonah said. "Will you give him a *banahi yuelrah?*"

"Yes. Along with Lindsey, Miranda, and all the rest of them." I'd force myself to survive just to give my brother that much, and every soldier who'd died here today.

"What's that?" Sophia asked softly.

"A warrior's burial. Reserved only for the greatest of Hawkei braves," I said. And Ezra was a warrior if there ever was one. He had a fighting spirit.

Jake cast a stick into the fire and watched it burn. "It's obvious we have no other choice. We have to surrender."

"Jake, no," Jonah pleaded. "We can't."

"I refuse to sacrifice any more lives," Jake replied. "I'd be no commander if I led us all to our doom."

Jake stared at me, waiting on my answer. It was obvious why Jake had asked for me. He wanted me to back him up.

I wouldn't do it. I wouldn't surrender. Not just for the people we lost, but for the people we had left. Toaqua was a proud tribe, and I refused to be its last true chief. We'd go out on our dying breath.

Jake saw my expression and made a harsh noise. "You're as bad as Vanessa."

I'm guessing she wasn't willing to throw in the towel, either. Not that Jake's request was unusual. Logic said that surrender was the only way.

When no one responded, Jake lost his shit. He slammed a fist into the ground and snapped, "The writing's on the wall. We're going to lose this battle. I don't know how we can pull out of this."

"Slavery isn't a better option," Jonah argued. "Do you want to be serving Oleander and his kind for the rest of your life? I'd rather die than be treated like Biyami dirt again!"

"You might feel that way, but I'm trying to save lives," Jake said firmly. "We still have resistance children back in *Hok'evale*. If we don't surrender now, they'll be slaughtered when we lose. I will not allow that to happen."

"So you're going to let them be enslaved. Do you know what Oleander's going to *do* to those kids?" Jonah asked.

"I'm well aware. But at this point, life is better than death," Jake replied.

"For you," Imogen mumbled, but Jake didn't seem to hear her.

"And what about us, huh?" Jonah asked angrily. "You just gonna give up and let them imprison us? We'll never be together again!"

"I refuse to be taken as a prisoner of war," Jake shot back. "When the time comes, I'll end my life before I allow them to separate you and me."

Jonah's face fell. "Jake."

"It's decided." Jake got up and walked away. Jonah threw his hands up. Sophia continued to stare into the flames without comment.

"We need a new plan," Imogen said quietly. Sassy raised her head and yipped, while Squeaks nodded.

"It's obvious what we're doing isn't working." I rubbed my face tiredly.

Our little group had done this so many times— pivoted when something went wrong. When all hell broke loose, we stood as one and found a way to stay alive. If I thought any different— if I gave up now, even for a moment— we'd lose. I was a cynical bastard through and through, but in the darkest moments of our lives, we pulled together and pulled through.

I had to keep the faith, as did the rest of us. There could be no wavering in belief from this moment out. Not if we wanted to live.

"So what now?" Sophia asked. "What do we do?"

"We do what we do best. Pull a solution out of our ass," I suggested.

"The four of us haven't been beaten yet," Jonah offered, before he frowned. "Though... this looks pretty bad, guys."

"It always looks bad. But we find a way. This is no different." Imogen bit her lip as she thought. "We can't stop now."

"Yeah. I'm not about to let my husband off himself a few days after we got married," Jonah said sourly.

"We've killed all the Elders. That only leaves Oleander," Sophia said hopefully. "The Defortai *have* to be thinking of giving up, too."

"But they have the numbers," I said. "They can overpower us. That's what they're counting on."

"So... what? When dawn comes, we go searching for Oleander and wreck his shit?" Jonah asked.

"Maybe." I doubted Oleander would come out unless he absolutely had to, and seeing as we were outnumbered and at a disadvantage, he had every reason to sit back and watch this go down without lifting a finger. He was a coward. He wouldn't fight until he was backed into a corner, and the resistance had no way to make that kind of move.

Not with the people we had left.

"We have to make Oleander come out," Imogen said. "It's the only way."

"And what if Jake surrenders? We can't fight him without an army," Sophia objected.

"I'll do what I can to convince him." Jonah got to his feet. "He's just in a rough spot right now."

Jonah jogged off, but to be honest, I didn't have a lot of hope. Jake seemed to have his mind made up.

We tried to sleep, but it didn't do much good. Most of the resistance was up all night, fearing that Oleander wouldn't honor the temporary truce and slaughter us all when we slept.

I was scared of that, too, and my mind was too full with thoughts of Ezra for me to get much rest. But I dropped off for a few hours and awoke again sometime around midnight. Sophia lay beside me, but she wasn't really sleeping, though Imogen was out of it against Squeaks on my other side. Esis was in the distance, running from person to person to heal their wounds.

Esis appeared to be at his peak. Kurbles had good stamina. One of the reasons they ate so much was to store up energy to use in situations like this. Out of everyone, Esis was the only one who didn't appear tired, but invigorated.

There was a nudge at my feet, and I felt something land against my legs. It was a rabbit. Affection brightened when I saw Sassy's wagging tail.

Sassy had gone hunting. She'd brought a rabbit for all of us to share.

"What a good girl," Imogen cooed, pulling Sassy onto her lap.

Jonah stirred sleepily. He must've been unsuccessful in convincing Jake, because he wasn't here.

I figured we'd better eat. Sophia didn't look away this time when I skinned the rabbit like she had during the Elemental Cup. It was a bit unnerving.

Other Familiars had also gone hunting for their Elementai, bringing small animals in and whatever they could find. The smell of cooking meat rose throughout the camp. The four of us shared the rabbit, and I felt a bit of strength come back into my body. It was a poor last meal, so I resolved it wouldn't be. The little reprieve we'd gotten was enough to give us some energy back.

Sophia put a hand on my back. "How are you feeling, Liam?"

I savored the touch of her pressing against me. "I'm good as long as the moon's out. It's giving me back my strength."

The moon shone above us. I was pulling power from it, and had been all night, to bolster my energy. I felt its cool, smooth magic drift into me and pulse through my veins, making it feel as though I'd gotten a good night's rest.

I was lucky. No one else had the power to do this. Sophia wouldn't be able to pull from the sun again until it had risen, and the rest of the army had to rely on getting magic from their Familiars, who were already tired. I was planning on siphoning as much energy from the moon as possible until the battle began again, because I knew we'd need it.

A lone figure wandering the camp caught my eye. Luana weaved between bodies, her form weary. She appeared on the verge of collapse. Sierra sat weakly on her shoulder.

Sophia got up and grabbed Luana. "What are you doing?" she asked, signing as she did so.

I've been up healing people, Luana signed. *There are so many who need my help.*

"You need rest." Sophia's gestures were firm as she signed the words. She forced Luana to lie down. Sierra fluttered to the top of her head and lay in Luana's white hair, wings drooping.

Luana gave a noise of protest, before her head settled on Sophia's lap. She was out within moments.

The moon left me feeling recharged. I could stand now without nearly falling over. I got up and said, "I need to check on the rest of the tribe. I'll be back."

Sophia nodded. I wandered throughout the battlefield, looking for Toaqua. There weren't very many— a lot of them had run out of water in the mountain ranges and been killed when they could no longer defend themselves. Julian flew overhead, making small circles as he looked down upon our sorry state.

Most of the Toaqua were gathered together on the edge of the camp. Their eyes brightened when they saw me, but only slightly. My mother was within their ranks, being comforted by a few women. She stared ahead with that same deadly expression she had when she'd left Ezra's body earlier.

Then I saw Stevie. I knew she still had a Familiar— still had a soul— but she didn't look like it. All the life had been vanquished out of her. Her face was ashen and gray. Her shoulders slumped like a permanent burden had been placed on them.

And her eyes. There'd been light in them before, but all the life that had boldly resonated from within had gone, like a smoldering candle blown out in the wind. There was so much emotion there it was hard for me to swallow.

Her glassy gaze reminded me of a corpse. It was like she was dead inside.

I gravitated toward her. She saw me coming and headed toward the tree line. She didn't stop until we were far enough away for privacy.

Stevie turned her back on me. "I'm sorry. It hurts to look at you."

I spoke hoarsely past the hard knot in my throat. "I understand."

Stevie's voice was choked. "He was acting so weird yesterday morning before he left. He kept saying, *I got a bad feeling, Stevie.* Just repeating it over and over."

She hugged herself and kept her back turned to me. "Maybe he knew. That's why he didn't want me to come with."

I didn't tell Stevie about what Maddie had seen. How she'd tried to warn Ezra. She didn't need that kind of information haunting her for the rest of her life.

"He wouldn't have wanted you to come with him, anyway. He wanted you to be safe," I said.

"I should've been out there with him. I might've been able to do something."

"No, Stevie. It would've done you no good to watch him die."

"But I could've stopped it."

"Could we have stopped all this?" I motioned to the battlefield, to the many bodies that were still lying forgotten. "We did our best. There were still sacrifices."

Stevie shivered. "I should've fought. I know I should've. I just... I thought it'd be safer if I stayed behind. For the baby."

My eyes widened. Stevie turned to face me. "I found out a little while ago. It's still pretty early."

I was so floored I couldn't speak. Stevie was pregnant? I didn't understand how this had happened. She and Ezra had been so careful.

Stevie's lip trembled. "It was the hot springs. I know it was. I was sick not that long ago, remember? Couldn't get over it. Perot gave me antibiotics, to get me through the infection... told me it would make my birth control less effective and to be extra careful, but I forgot, and we were in the water, so we obviously didn't use a condom..."

Stevie gasped and put a hand over her mouth to hold in a scream. "It's my fault."

"No one's perfect with this disease, Stevie." My senses were going haywire as the feeling of being overwhelmed crashed in around me. A new life was coming into the world, just as one had ended.

And Stevie would have to be a parent without Ezra. Poor girl.

"Did Ez know?"

Stevie sniffed. "I was going to tell him after the battle was over. I didn't want him to be distracted."

If possible, my heart broke even further. Ezra had no idea he was going to be a father. He'd gone to the Ancestral Lands without knowing.

What a sick and cruel world this was. It was so horrible I almost hated living.

Stevie put her head in her hands. "The chances are *fifty percent*, Liam. I can't damn this baby."

"You aren't damning this child. Remember what you told me before Ava was born? There's no guarantee if she has our disease, and even if she does, it'll be okay. The same thing goes for your baby."

"But how can this child grow up without a father?" Stevie raised her head. Fresh tears fell from her eyes. "How can my baby be happy if Ezra isn't in their life?"

"Because they'll be loved. They'll have a family that will take care of them, no matter what happens."

I reached out to her, but Stevie flinched away. The movement was like driving a jagged knife into my heart. I looked too much like my brother.

I took a breath and steadied myself. "Stevie... if you want this baby to live, you have to get out of here."

"You need me. Our fighters are down. I'm still fresh. I can fight, baby or not. I should've in the first place," she said.

"Jake's going to surrender."

Stevie's gaze was horrified. "What?"

"He wants to give up. We've tried to convince him not to, but he's not listening. If he does, we'll all be taken prisoner. You've gotta be far away from here before that happens. So your baby won't be born a slave."

Stevie's eyes flashed. I could tell her mind was working fast as she took a few gasping breaths.

Then she tugged resolutely on her ponytail, pulling it tight. "Who killed Ezra?"

I could hardly say the hated name. "Courtney. You've never met her. She's Nivita. Our age."

"How will I know it's her?"

My mind worked. "She has a cut over her eye that Ez gave her. Extends from her hairline past her nose. I saw him do it before he chased after her. It was the last time I saw her. She has a rainbow bird Familiar. Same size as Dyami."

Stevie took out a blue hair bow out of her pocket. She pinned it into her ponytail before she said, "Ezra gave me this bow. And I'm going to be wearing it when I take that bitch's life."

Stevie stomped past me, on a mission. I hurried behind her, but ceased to follow when Stevie walked up an embankment that overlooked the camp. She stood at the top, peering down on the survivors. What was left of the resistance was gathered below. Heads looked up as she took an offensive stance at the top of the hill. Julian landed next to me and tilted his head as he wondered what she was doing.

Sophia, Imogen, Luana and Jonah were nearby. I stood with them and recognized the faces of those we had left. Vanessa, Bren, Cade... a few others. Jake was standing alone on the other side, head down in a submissive position.

Stevie bunched her hands into fists and threw her shoulders back. "I need everyone's attention," she shouted, and her voice echoed over the field.

The surrounding conversation quieted. People fell silent, a bit perplexed, as they waited to hear Stevie speak.

Stevie's voice held true and didn't tremble. "Most of you don't know who I am. But to be honest, that doesn't really matter. All you need to know is that I loved someone who you would recognize— Ezra Mitoh. He was an Elder on the Toaqua Council, the brother of the Water chief, and the love of my life."

Stevie's words began to tremble. "Ezra was the best person I'd ever met. He embodied everything the resistance stood for. Kindness. Compassion. Loyalty. Traits that so many of our fallen gave their last breaths to defend, and we cannot fail them now! The resistance fights for love, for peace! Are we really going to back down and give Oleander the satisfaction of knowing everything we've sacrificed for was worth *nothing*? Will we let him get away with separating people from their families and loved ones without one last final protest?"

Jake's eyes flickered away guiltily. But Stevie continued. She pushed past her agony and said, "Ezra loved me. He loved me how every girl deserves to be loved, and so much more. He was faithful to his tribe, willing to do anything to protect the Elementai. And that went beyond the Toaqua tribe. He considered everyone Hawkei, no matter what House they were from. Even before he knew about the resistance, before the war began, Ezra treated everyone the same. He was a friend to all. To him, we truly were one tribe."

Stevie took a quivering breath. "But as close as Ezra and I were... and as much as he adored his tribe... I think we all know there was one person on this earth Ezra loved more than anyone else."

All eyes looked to me. I heard a few people whisper my name. Sophia slipped her hand into mine as tears rose back to my eyes. Jonah put a hand on my shoulder, and Imogen pressed in behind me. The tightness in my chest was so thick I couldn't do anything but force myself to breathe.

Stevie went on. "Ezra adored his brother. From the moment he was born, he worshiped his chief and followed him wherever he would go. Ezra laid down his life for our cause and our tribe. And all of us should be ready to do the same, without objection, gladly taking the sacrifice. We've lost friends today. We've lost family. We've almost lost everything that makes our lives worth living."

Steel hardened her tone. "But we haven't lost the war. And I refuse to lay my magic down until the second it's stolen from me. To give up today would bastardize the memories of our lost. Oleander and the Task Force can take my freedom when they pry it from my cold, dead hands. And when I enter into the Ancestral Lands, my ancestors will welcome me with a battle cry. Because I chose to go down fighting. I will *die here* before I surrender. I will *die* before I surrender my tribe. I will give Oleander such a fight, he'll have nightmares for years to come about what we did today."

Sophia ripped her hand from mine. She strode toward the hill Stevie was standing on. She was ablaze as she took her place beside Stevie and grasped her hand. Esis reared up on her shoulder and puffed out his chest.

"I know I'm not the chosen one you all expected. I don't even know if I'm the chosen one you deserve," Sophia said. "But the more I fight in this war, the more I realize there's really no such thing as a chosen one. One person can't change the world. Not on their own."

Sophia stood tall. "But together, we can make a difference. It takes a whole tribe to make the world a better place. It takes people like you. And if we band together, nothing can stand in our way. I'm supposed to be special

— but if we don't go down in history making a stand against Oleander's tyranny, I don't matter. In fact, *none* of us matter unless we come together as a community and tell the world we're united once and for all!"

Cries of agreement rang throughout the camp. I caught Doya in the crowd and saw her eyes shining with joy. Baine was sobbing tears of pride.

"A society is only strong if it cares for its most vulnerable members!" Sophia yelled. "A society that only provides for the people at the top will fall apart if met with any sort of resistance, and *that's* why Oleander is going to fail! Because he only cares about himself, and we care about each other!"

The resistance began cheering. I felt a wave of passion move through me like never before for my wife. That was *my* Sophia.

The speeches must've lit a fire under Jake's ass, because he strode forward. He climbed the hill and stood next to the two girls. His voice cried louder than the rest as he said, "We will not surrender on this night! Or any night after! We will continue to fight until Oleander and his army are done, or until we draw our last breath. If we are to die, let it be with honor!"

Everyone jumped to their feet. Fists shot into the air as the resistance army gave a unified war cry. Jonah sighed, clearly relieved, while Imogen cheered beside him.

Hope against hope, I began to believe again. We had a chance. This might not be the end. And if it was... we were giving Oleander one hell of a fight.

Then the cheers of unity dissolved into screams of terror. I heard a whizzing sound. Sophia and Stevie gasped at the same time as an arrow flew out of the sky and landed in Jake's chest.

Jake fell to his knees, a dazed expression on his face. The arrow stuck out of the middle of his chest, and blood leaked from the wound. Jonah gave a cry of misery. He charged forward, and Squeaks followed, putting her head down and butting people out of the way.

More arrows began hitting resistance soldiers. They went into the backs of our people, or into their necks, delivering killing blows before our army could even defend itself.

I looked up. Yapluma Task Force were hovering above us, hiding within cloud cover and shooting with bows. Approaching from the east was a line of Task Force members from other Houses, elements at the ready to kill us all.

I knew it. The bastard couldn't hold a truce. He was just waiting for us to get our guard down.

Julian roared. He took off and opened his mouth to fry dozens of Task

Force members with his fiery breath. Charred bodies began dropping out of the sky, and just like that, it started up all over again.

I raced forward. Luana and Imogen matched my strides as we ran up the hill. Jonah was cradling Jake in his arms as Jake blinked at the sky, confused.

Sophia wrenched out the arrow. Luana put her hands over the wound, and the muscles knit back together. The hole in Jake's chest healed with the help of Luana's magic, but he still looked stunned.

"Babe, are you okay?" Jonah asked.

"I'll be fine," Jake rasped. "We need a plan of defense!"

"Defense isn't going to work. If we don't get on the attack *now*, we're done for!" Imogen shouted.

My thoughts grasped at straws to find a solution. Oleander had to die if we were going to win, but he wasn't here. We had to do something so drastic that Oleander couldn't hide anymore. We had to force him to confront us.

The light of the moon shone downward, and the answer snapped into my head like it was delivered by the ancestors themselves. "The ocean," I told Jake. "We have to get to the ocean. It's our only chance."

Jake didn't ask any questions. He got to his feet and cried out, "The ocean! Quickly, we have to get to the sea!"

The resistance members began running or flying, on Familiars or otherwise, to the west, in the direction of the ocean. Stevie and Jake led them ahead, and I whistled for Julian. He came down, shaking the earth as he landed roughly beside me. Sophia and Luana raised their hands. A shield bloomed from their fingertips, blocking out the rest of the arrows, but the damage had already been done— we'd lost at least a dozen more people in a matter of moments.

"What are you planning?" Imogen yelled over the noise.

"Oleander's most likely in Kinpago, which means we have to do something to get him out," I said. "Imogen, you and Cade need to make a land bridge with the other Nivita once we get to sea, so the Task Force can't box us in. Get as many people as you can to a safe place, but leave the Toaqua and Yapluma behind. Make sure you're nowhere near the city. Luana can go with you, heal those who are hurt. Sophia, you're with me."

"What am I going to do, exactly?" Jonah asked dramatically.

I smirked. "That depends. You want to help me make a hurricane?"

Jonah grinned slyly. "Oh, *fuck yeah*."

"Then follow me." I got onto Julian's back, and Sophia slid on behind me. As he took off, Jonah climbed onto Squeaks and followed. We soared ahead of the group, while Imogen, Jake and the others moved on foot. Sophia and Esis created a shield around the resistance escaping toward the beach. Their shield merged with Luana's, creating a defensive barrier that the Task Force couldn't get past— for now, at least.

"What are you thinking?" Sophia asked as the ocean appeared on the horizon.

"We direct the hurricane toward Kinpago. Make it so strong, it threatens to destroy the city," I said. "He'll have to confront us then. If we level the place, there's nothing for him to rule over. He's not going to let that happen."

"This is the craziest fucking idea we've ever had!" she shouted.

"Well, crazy seems to work with us. Let's go!"

I flattened myself to Julian, and he beat his wings faster to get us up to a high speed. We landed on the beach ahead of the resistance. I got off of Julian and began directing people who came in from the trees.

"I need every Toaqua and Yapluma available!" I cried. "Nivita, follow Imogen! The Koigni, with the chosen one!"

The Nivita diverged as Imogen waved her hand. She ran to the shore-line and began forming a land bridge with Cade's help. The rest of the Nivita aided them, building the bridge as fast as they could in order to escape. It stretched out to sea and curved back around to a far-off beach to the south. The Task Force blocked escape on land, so the only way around them was to move forward, then double back.

"What do you need me to do?" Sophia asked as she faced me.

"We're gonna have to split up. Don't give me that look, there's no other way."

"But bad things happen when we're not together! I have to stay by your side!"

"You can't be out on the water, and I need you and as many Koigni as possible to stop the Task Force from helping Oleander. They can't aid him if they can't get to him," I said, pointing to the trees. "Once he's isolated, he's vulnerable. You hold the line until I get him down."

"Well, what are we waiting for?" Doya came striding in, Naomi with her.

Baine was behind her, breathless. "We have to divert our strengths. It's our last hope."

"The Task Force won't get through me," Doya said, and she played with strands of flame with her fingertips. "I'll enjoy watching them burn."

"We will help you." Chief Cauac was there at an instant. His white warrior's robes were stained with blood. In his hands, he dual-wielded two weapons— a stone club and a jade ax.

The Anichi behind him, who were all wearing similar robes, carried bows, spears, and stone daggers. Some of my Anichi students, who'd run out of crystal magic, had also taken up arms and were ready to fight hand-to-hand combat. They'd been fighting with us the whole time, but I hadn't seen them until now.

The noise increased as the Task Force approached. They were starting to break through the trees and onto the beach. As they did so, Chief Cauac and his warriors became total badasses. They ran toward the Task Force with a war cry, dodging elements and retaliating with heavy blows. Chief Cauac swung his weapons above his head before bringing them crashing downward on two Task Force members at once, ending their lives in one blow.

"I'll stop them. Summon Oleander!" Sophia ran to help Chief Cauac, flanked by Doya, along with what Koigni we had left.

Vanessa and Bren were at the start of the line, and Vanessa was shouting orders. The Koigni threw their hands out simultaneously and created a Fire wall that prevented the army from getting through. A couple of Task Force members slipped past, but once they did, Cauac struck them down.

That should hold them for a while. I swung myself back onto Julian, while Baine ran into the sea. He called out Thalassa's name. The giant sea serpent rose out of the waves, and Baine climbed onto her head before she surged back into the churning ocean. As I flew, Stevie followed me, riding her cypher Familiar.

The storm overhead still hadn't stopped from earlier. We could use that to our advantage. Julian flew us out to sea, and the Yapluma followed, with Toaqua surfing the waves below us. We flew until we were miles offshore, so far away we could no longer see land. I pulled Julian up. The group halted, waiting on my instruction.

Jonah used his Air magic to amplify the sound of my voice as I shouted, "I need two circles of Elementai! One in the skies, and one in the water!" The Yapluma began forming into a circle, and the Toaqua underneath it did the same, until hundreds of Elementai and their Familiars were in formation, waiting on my command.

"We need to make a hurricane and direct it toward Kinpago! If we work together and infuse our powers, we'll stand a chance!"

Several faces paled in horror at my suggestion. No one had ever wielded that kind of magic before. It wasn't considered possible— especially in this part of the country, where hurricanes were unheard-of.

"This is our only shot!" A voice shouted behind me. "We cannot afford to make mistakes. Let's make it count!"

It was Professor Perot. He was hovering nearby, Baxtor at his side. He gave me a firm nod, and I smiled at him, appreciating his show of support.

"If you're a Yapluma, follow my lead!" Jonah cried. Lightning cracked across the sky at Jonah's command, and the Yapluma moved as one. They began channeling the warm air upward, creating an area of low pressure on the ocean's surface. The wind picked up around us, and flying Familiars, including Julian, were almost steered off course.

"You okay, Jules?" I asked. His big wings were acting like parachutes in the breeze, weaving us back and forth.

Julian had his fangs bared, and grunted lowly. He could keep aloft, but the effort of making the hurricane was dragging all of us further out to sea. We barely had control.

Meanwhile, the Toaqua in the ocean created rain. Water poured from the skies, soaking my armor clear through to the bone, churning the ocean into an angry rage. Water evaporated rapidly from the ocean's surface, and the Toaqua began swirling the clouds to make a funnel overhead.

Water Familiars had to hold on tight as the waves surged. I felt the light of the moon on my skin and drew from it, putting everything I had back into the ocean. The storm grew in moments, becoming more violent. The rain became a downpour, and Jonah's lightning crackled within the swirling cloud torrent, becoming a dangerous display.

My eyes widened with surprise. I'd hardly figured we'd pull this off, but together, we were doing it! Jonah shouted something, but I couldn't hear him over the noise of the storm. I got his meaning, though— we had to steer the hurricane toward the shore.

I motioned to direct the hurricane toward Kinpago. The Yapluma and Toaqua followed my lead— but despite our best efforts, the storm was stuck in place. It refused to move, gathering momentum and power from its place deep in the ocean waters. I pushed against the hurricane, pointing it at Kinpago, but the hurricane just pushed back.

It wouldn't listen. We didn't have enough energy, even with me channeling from the moon. We were almost there, but fell short just enough so the magic wouldn't take. Our plan wouldn't work. Not unless we had a bit more power. We needed more magic to fuel the hurricane, but what we had here was all we could draw from... unless someone sacrificed themselves, and pushed their body beyond the boundaries of their magic to get the hurricane moving.

It was clear. One of us would have to die.

We all knew it, too. I saw the look in everyone's eyes. They flickered from left to right, waiting to see who would make the sacrifice.

I was seconds away from giving my all and letting the hurricane take my life, before the storm suddenly gave a burst of power. It knocked me against Julian and temporarily winded me. The storm began to move of its own accord in the direction of Kinpago. The rain slowed to a slow drizzle, and the waves settled beneath us as the hurricane surged onward at an unnatural speed.

I glanced around to see what had happened, until Jonah pointed. As the storm passed and the waters became calm again, I saw a body in the water, beside the floating corpse of a feathery peacock.

No. I dived off Julian. I swam toward Perot and took him in my arms, trying to keep his head above water. Perot's face was pale— his dark eyes were losing light.

"Professor, why'd you do that?" I gasped.

Perot gaped upward at the stars as he uttered, "I have repaid my life debt. It is time for me to join Caspian. Let me go, Liam."

"I can't." But as I said the words, Perot gave a final breath. His body, along with Baxtor's, dissolved into the wind— just like Lindsey and Miranda's bodies had turned to ash. His body floated out of my grasp, vanishing into the air as he became the sky.

I knew people who extended themselves beyond the abilities of their magic became their element as they died... I'd just never seen it up close. Not until Lindsey and Miranda.

Not until Perot.

Hopelessness welled within me and crashed over my spirit so heavily, it felt like I was being crushed from the inside out. Perot pushed himself past the limits of his magic, and gave himself up so the hurricane would have the power to move to shore. He'd died for us. He hadn't just been my doctor, or my teacher. He'd been my friend. He'd given me a diagnosis for my disease, and hadn't given up on treatment when things looked terminal. He was one of the few people who'd helped me when everyone else had turned me away.

I gave a cry of rage and smacked the water. How many people were we going to lose in this fucking war!?

"Liam!"

Someone put a hand on my shoulder and yanked me around. It was Stevie. Tears ran down her face from the loss of Perot. "We can't grieve now! We need to help the people we can!"

I knew she was right. It was the only thing keeping me going, thinking of saving those we had left. Julian dipped down to grab me. I pulled myself up his leg and perched on his back again as Jonah flew down to meet me.

"What do we do now?" he asked.

"Now we wait," I said. My heart felt heavy. If I knew I had to destroy my home to save the tribe I loved, I probably wouldn't have joined the resistance. But I knew I had no choice.

And wait we did. For what felt like forever. We soaked up the rain and battled the wind and waves as the edges of the hurricane battered our forms.

As time passed, it became evidently clear my plan had failed. Perot had died for nothing. Oleander wasn't coming.

Jake's stare was heavy as he hovered toward me. "Our soldiers can't stay out here. We're dividing our forces. It's your call."

"Get the rest of the Yapluma and the Toaqua back to shore," I ordered. "We're done here."

Jake nodded. He began barking orders, and the Yapluma and Toaqua traveled out. They went in the direction the land bridge had been built, on the other side of Kinpago.

Me, I stayed behind. Just in case. Only Baine, Stevie, and Jonah were with me.

Jonah guided Squeaks my way and shouted, "Bro, I think we'd better head back. Oleander's not gonna show."

I felt my jaw tighten, but I relented. Oleander was a bigger coward than I thought. "All right. Let's just—"

There was a high-pitched screech that hurt my ears, and Julian stiffened. A shadow loomed against the clouds. As lightning struck the ocean, a formidable monster emerged from within the storm. Skylis came down from overhead, his multiple heads baring teeth while his collar glinted against the light from the stars.

Upon his back was Oleander. He wore white and silver robes, which symbolized him as High Chief. Leather armor adorned his lithe form, and he wore an intricate headdress that— no shit— looked like it'd been forged from the bones of his enemies.

Ancestors. This guy had issues.

I could feel the hatred radiating from Julian as he focused his reptilian gaze on Skylis. Dracash and dragons were natural enemies. They fought for territory and food, typically to the death.

Julian didn't like Skylis coming on his turf. His nostrils flared as he took in the other reptile's scent, emitting sparks. Skylis was larger than Julian, but that didn't stop my dragon from flicking his forked tongue hungrily like Skylis was prey. His body heated underneath my legs as he prepared to use his Fire.

"You're as disruptive as your father," Oleander said spitefully as his gaze landed on me. He continued hovering Skylis above us, pretending to be the god he thought he was. "I should've eliminated your whole family when I had the chance."

I didn't take the bait. Instead, I raised my voice and shouted, "Elder Oleander, as chief of Toaqua, I challenge you to a chief's duel."

"It's High Chief Oleander now, *boy*." Oleander wrinkled his nose in distaste. "And you have no authority at which to call yourself chief. I am the sole supreme ruler of the Elementai."

"Prove it." I moved before Oleander did, because I knew he wouldn't fight fair. I launched a water tunnel out of the ocean, and it streamed upward, knocking Oleander off Skylis. Julian surged forward with a roar. I jumped off his back, and a column of water caught me, suspending me above the waves as Julian locked his claws onto Skylis.

Oleander had caught himself with a wave and was surfing it with a vicious expression. He raised his hand, and three spiraling towers of water rose up behind him, large as pillars. He threw them at me in quick succession, but I swept my column aside to dodge them. The towers went spinning down like spears and crashed into the ocean, sending water spraying everywhere.

Jonah, Stevie and Baine rushed forward to help. But before they could, two giant sea serpents rose out of the ocean, blocking their path. They were red and black, and towered hundreds of feet over the sea. I didn't think Oleander was controlling them with magic— but they were on his side nonetheless, as they swam around him protectively. Oleander must've paid off their Elementai, to have these creatures act as his personal bodyguards.

Jonah and Stevie hung back, but Thalassa sneered and dove forward. She locked her jaws onto the black sea serpent's neck and shook viciously, but her opponent pulled free and slammed himself onto her front. The two sea serpents engaged in deadly battle, twisting around each other and ripping into scales with open jaws. Baine summoned water, freezing it in place to create a formidable ice spear. He jabbed it at the sea serpent's eyes, trying to blind it while it attacked.

Jonah and Stevie teamed up to take on the red sea serpent. Jonah flew Squeaks around the head, while Stevie stayed in the water and steered her half-griffin, half-hippocampus around the sea serpent's middle. Squeaks let out a shock wave from her beak, which slapped the serpent in the face. It snarled and raised its giant tail, smacking Stevie and her Familiar down into the depths of the ocean. My breath caught, but Stevie soon resurfaced. She brought up her hands, forming the waves into frozen pointing spikes that were twenty feet long. The sea serpent had to be careful as it outmaneuvered the spikes. Stevie had turned the entire surrounding area into a treacherous icy waterscape.

"I've brought friends!" Oleander sneered.

He summoned a water ball and threw it at me. It almost hit my head, but I turned it to snow, and it dissolved in the air before that could happen. I sent a wall of spinning ice daggers at Oleander's front, but he caused a wave to rise up like a shield and block my attack.

The wave turned my way, but I weaved my hands in a circle, and it overpowered Oleander's magic, changing into a water spout. I spun the water spout at Oleander, hoping it would pull him in, but Oleander rose up on the wave he rode and smashed it to nothing more than droplets.

Dammit. He was good. I ordered the water column to surge me forward. It did, but Oleander pulled his wave back and surfed to another, keeping his eyes on me as he maintained a steady distance.

He wasn't that stupid to let me get close enough to stop his heart. I had overpowered his last spell, so perhaps I could take his magic using intrafusion. I reached out. I felt a temporary shock as my magic recoiled against Oleander's. There was a lot of strength there. Almost more than I'd ever felt in any Elementai before. I tugged at it, ordering his energy to flow into me instead, but it rebelled. I was blown backward by the force of the push back, and slammed into the surface of the sea. I righted myself with another water column, but didn't dare to try that again.

For the first time, intrafusion hadn't worked. I couldn't take his powers away. His real Familiar wasn't here, and he was pulling from that creature from miles away. I couldn't interrupt that connection from such a distance.

Oleander gave a mad laugh. "Never fought anyone who's your equal, have you, boy?"

No, I hadn't. Nobody had ever been able to best me on the water. The ocean was where I belonged.

Oleander still wasn't my equal. I was better than him, and I was going to prove it.

I let out a yell as I flung my arms forward with all the strength I had. A water column fifty feet wide gushed out at Oleander, but he pushed his hands apart. The column split, sending the water in two directions without even touching him.

I took a few hard, deep breaths. I was throwing everything I had at Oleander, and he was brushing it off. How much more could he take?

Above, I felt droplets of blood fall against my face like warm rain. Skylis and Julian were still tangled up in each other. Julian's claws dug into Skylis' belly, but it was all he could do to hold on as Skylis' five heads attacked. He was able to fend off two of them with his tail and the other three with his wings and head, but he looked stressed. It was too much going on at once for him to handle. Skylis bit down on Julian's shoulder, and he cried out, his screams shaking the skies and making the clouds tremble.

Julian needed my help. Oleander laughed and watched, entertained, as I blasted myself upward to save my dragon, a large water ball trapped within my grasp. Knowing this was a stupid idea, but hardly thinking anyway, I wedged myself in between Skylis and Julian. I channeled energy from the moon and put as much energy into the water ball as possible as I forced it toward Skylis, demanding the two reptiles break apart.

The blast sent both of them careening backwards from each other. I fell against Julian's middle, but he caught me, and he slung me back on his shoulder as he became level in the skies. Once he did, he opened his mouth to breathe fire at Skylis. The dracash did a loop and opened its mouths in retaliation. Out of two of its heads spouted ice, while the others blew fire. The elements merged together in one stream, creating a deadly combination. Julian swung to the side. I heard a sizzling sound on the end of his left wing, and Julian gave a bellowing cry.

As Julian righted himself, I looked at the tip of his wing. It was black—like it'd been frostbitten, or touched by dry ice. He moaned in pain, but shook it off. Skylis' middle head reared back and began shooting balls of green venom that exploded like grenades when they reached the ocean. Julian dodged the attack, but with his hurt wing, he was slower than usual. I smacked the venom balls away with streams of water as we flew, gathering them in my hands to use them like giant whips. As Julian faced Skylis, I lashed the ropes out around his legs and wings, trying to hold him in place. I gritted my teeth and pulled back; Skylis was suspended before he ripped free, shattering my water ropes to little more than vapor.

Both Julian and I paused to take a breath, before Skylis or Oleander could attack again. My mind was working overtime, trying to figure out openings and seeing none. It was like these two were unstoppable.

"You have no idea who I am, do you?" Oleander bellowed. "I was no one! I was worthless, just like you, until I forced myself to do impossible things! I was once the weakest Toaqua alive, and now, I've earned my place as High Chief. The ancestors never noticed my potential, but they'll see it now!"

Oleander clapped his hands together. Water began rising, collecting into a tidal wave. A shadow fell over me, and my gut sank as I watched the wave grow greater and greater. At its utmost height, it was hundreds of feet.

"Get out of the way!" I shouted.

Jonah and Stevie turned. They began racing in the other direction as the massive tidal wave charged toward them. Baine and Thalassa didn't move— merely braced themselves as they planned to dive into the wave, instead of run from it. The other two sea serpents rode Oleander's wave, hissing with delight as it chased us down. Julian took a ninety degree angle, and I had to hold on tight as he flew us vertically over the wave. It skimmed the bottom of his tail and nearly knocked him off course as he swerved to avoid it. I looked down to see how the others fared.

The tidal wave had hit Thalassa and Baine first. She was able to weather it, because of her massive size, but it'd knocked Baine off her head. Thalassa groaned as she called for Baine, searching for him everywhere.

My heart stopped, but after a few moments, Baine floated to the top of the sea, stunned. Thalassa helped him as he slowly clambered back onto her head, dazed.

Squeaks had flown Jonah above the tidal wave, but I didn't see Stevie anywhere. Panic set in my gut, until I saw a familiar blue bow floating on the surface.

Oh, no. She hadn't...

I felt suffocated, until a great splash caught my attention. Nihoni had struggled to the surface, Stevie on her back. Stevie choked and sputtered. She took a few gasping breaths before she righted herself on Nihoni's back, eyes glowing red with rage. Her teeth gnashed as she set her gaze on Oleander.

"You're going to pay for that, you *fucking asshole!*" Stevie screamed.

Oleander's mouth dropped open in shock as Stevie summoned a tidal wave that rivaled his in size. She sent it hurtling at Oleander with a brutal cry that shook me to my core. The sea serpents went underneath the wave to avoid it, but Oleander didn't move in time. The wave smacked into him, sending him downward into the ocean.

Minutes passed, and neither Oleander nor the serpents surfaced. Hope began to rise within me. Had Stevie done it?

Then Skylis let out a roar and flew downward. A hand reached out to grasp a claw. My yearning to see Oleander dead was destroyed as I watched him climb Skylis' leg, swinging himself over to sit in the area between Skylis' wings.

The blow hadn't killed him, unfortunately, but at least it'd left him stunned. The two sea serpents rose to the surface, unharmed. They surged at Stevie, Jonah, and Baine, and the three of them along with their Familiars began battle all over again.

This was impossible. How could one Elementai be so hard to kill? Oleander gave me a callous look from the back of Skylis, and rage welled inside me so strongly, it was almost inhuman.

I wasn't going home until this bastard was finished. Once and for all. I summoned the water whips again, though they were more like chains this time. I swung them forward, intending to knock Oleander off of Skylis' back again. Oleander responded with water shields, blocking my every move. Julian and Skylis began circling each other instinctively, waiting for the right moment to get an opening and strike.

One of my whips broke through Oleander's shield, but he brought another one up again before I could grab him. Frustration grew, and I had to fight against it so it didn't turn into carelessness. I couldn't afford to get sloppy. One wrong move, and Oleander would kill me. But at the same time, this was madness. With that big-ass dracash defending him, it wasn't a fair fight. I needed help.

Then out of the waves came a giant killer whale. The orca gave a shrill cry, and my heart leapt as I saw Madame Wells riding the back of it. She moved her hands in a circle, creating spiraling strands of water that weaved over her head.

"Your wife told me you might need help!" Madame Wells called to me with a sly smile. She sent the spinning strands at Oleander like arrows. He deflected them with another water shield. As she did so, a hint of alarm came into his eyes.

He couldn't fend us both off at once. I increased my speed, lashing my chains out with vigor while Madame Wells surged out arrow after arrow. When one shield was down, another had to come up.

Oleander started to panic. He looked like a cornered animal as Madame

Wells and I continued to advance. We moved so quickly, he couldn't keep up.

My water burst past his shield just as Oleander was warding off another water arrow from Madame Wells. My chains bound Oleander, wrapping around his middle and forcing his arms to his sides. Fear paled his face, and I felt the triumph of victory. We had him! I went to squeeze the chains tight, to suffocate Oleander and crush his organs, so we could end this thing for good.

Then Skylis moved. He wrenched his wings back, so that he was nearly vertical. The movement broke my chains and ended the connection, sending the water back to the ocean in torrents.

Before I could do anything, Skylis dove downward. Julian gave a warning cry, but it was too late. One head bit down upon the orca— the other, Madame Wells.

"Don't!" I cried out, but I knew my pleas would go unheard. The orca gave one last call before Skylis tore it in half. Blood spilled into the sea, and Skylis let the body drop, watching as the head and the tail of the orca floated away from each other.

Madame Wells let out a horrible cry of grief before Skylis' jaws clamped down. I couldn't hear the crunching of bones, not from here, but my mind still imagined them. Madame Wells went silent. As Skylis opened his jaws again, her broken body fell into the sea, landing beside the two halves of her killer whale. Both of their corpses were dragged downward into the deep by the churning waves, never to be seen again. The blood sat on the surface of the water, creating a stain that appeared so heartless here at the edge of the world.

Oleander gave a remorseless laugh that was chilling and savage. I closed my eyes and tried to block out the sound. My hands dug so tightly into Julian's scales they bled, and I was grateful for the distraction, for the pain. Madame Wells had been one of my best Elders. Now we'd lost her.

I'd promised to make Oleander pay for everything he'd done to me, to my family, to my friends. My vows were falling flat. I was failing *everyone*.

I wiped my hair out of my face and forced the tears back down. Okay. No more fucking around. It was time to fulfill my promises.

I inhaled as I called upon the moon's power. Her magic poured into me as a gift, like I was her son and she was giving me life. Her power filled up my lungs, gifting me with love and light. The energy that cascaded into me was so strong, it was like standing in a gushing stream that threatened to make a dam break free. It overflowed and pooled over within my spirit, like the time when I'd taken Elder Malison and Elder Poole's magic. Back then, I'd lost control. I was barely able to hold it back.

But this time, I knew I could master it. All I had to do was master my thoughts. Julian growled as he felt the power flowing through me, and I rooted it to him like a conduit, to keep it contained until I could set the moon's powers free. People had called me one of the greatest chiefs in Toaqua history. I had centuries of the most powerful chieftains alive running through my veins. I could do this.

I kept my breathing steady and calmed my mind. I forced Oleander and the battle out of my head as I centered myself on the process of creating the spell. This was any other day. I was just doing magic. No more, no less.

Oleander's eyes grew wide as he watched my calm and steady movements on Julian's back. With one arm, I created a giant eagle out of the ocean, like the one I'd made during my chief hood initiation. With the other, a massive Water wolf crashed from the sea and gave a howl, setting its sights on Oleander.

The Water eagle spread its wings wide and soared at Skylis with an open beak. The eagle crashed into Skylis' side, veering him off course. Oleander clung on, unable to do any magic while attempting to keep himself on Skylis' back. As Skylis hurtled to the side, the Water wolf was there to greet him. The wolf sank its jaws into Skylis' shoulder, and the dracash cried out as blood ran freely down its leg. The eagle hovered in place and attacked the dracash with its beak, while the wolf continued to gnaw and bite. Oleander's body was tossed from side to side as Skylis took each blow. Dozens of cuts opened up on the dracash's scales. The five heads were kept busy attempting to fend off the creatures, though their jaws only met water whenever they went to take a bite.

Julian hissed and clenched his teeth. He went to go forward, but I said, "No, Jules. Wait."

Julian hung back, though smoke furled from his mouth with the effort. My body shook as I concentrated on keeping my magic alive. The moon was channeling the spell, but as I was casting it, I couldn't hold it forever. My magic wavered, and eventually, the eagle and wolf grew weak, retreating back into the ocean as I let the spell drop.

My shoulders ached. It felt like I'd been bench pressing the entire ocean for ten minutes. Julian moaned, to ask if I was okay.

"I'm fine, Jules." And I meant it. I was exhausted, but I wasn't on the verge of passing out. Not yet, anyway. I attempted to pull from the moon again, but found her power had weakened.

The skies above were igniting, and a thin orange line had appeared at the edge of the sea. Dawn was breaking, and the rising sun was blocking my connection to the moon.

Which was bad. I didn't think I had anything left in me after that magic. Jonah and the others were too busy fighting the sea serpents to help me. Julian and I had to do this on our own— yet I was so weak.

I'd been fighting more or less for two days straight. I couldn't keep this up. I was pretty much done for. At this point, we needed a miracle.

Skylis had been worn out by the fight with the wolf and the eagle, and was hurt, cuts gushing blood. He was still breathing, but the wounds he'd been dealt would slow him up. We had a chance.

Julian and I needed to end this now, before he recovered. I searched Skylis, looking for an opening— for anything that might bring him down.

My eyes settled on the middle head, and the metal collar at the base of his neck. The collar. We had to break the collar. Oleander couldn't control Skylis without it.

"You know what to do, bud. Go for the throat," I told Julian.

Julian bound forward the moment I gave the okay. Skylis didn't see him coming. Julian slammed into Skylis, and I felt his body quiver. Skylis gave a note of alarm, and Julian made a guttural sound that vibrated in his belly. Julian clenched his jaws around the metal collar, and in one ferocious movement, ripped it clean off.

"No!" I heard Oleander cry.

Julian kicked away, flying us to a safe distance. As the collar sank to the bottom of the ocean, Skylis' five heads shook slowly, as if coming out of a trance. His dark eyes turned red, and I watched the monster seethe as he came around, realizing where he was.

Skylis bucked, sending Oleander flying. Oleander fell into the ocean with a scream. He barely had time to catch himself with a wave before Skylis turned on him. The creature gave a bellowing scream, lashing out its five heads. Oleander ducked and spun, avoiding the heads as each one reached down to crush him within its grasp.

"Stop! You obey me!" Oleander cried. He slapped one of Skylis' heads away with a wave, but it did nothing to deter the creature. Skylis' moves only became more violent, and all of Oleander's attention was taken up trying to fend the creature off.

When the sea serpents saw that Oleander was in trouble, they abandoned the fight with Jonah, Stevie and Baine and swam toward him to help.

The sea serpents planted themselves in front of Skylis and hissed, waving their fin tails in a threat.

Skylis drew back, eyes calculating. Instinct should've told the creature to fly off, but he didn't. It was like the only thing he cared about was killing Oleander; he was just wondering how to do it before the sea serpents killed him.

Then I heard the sound of hoofbeats coming from the east. The light from the sun warmed my face, and with the rising dawn emerged a woman, riding on a kelpie's back.

It was my mother. She was clinging onto Menilly's seaweed mane, her head thrown back and her hair free. She was alone, only the music of the kelpie's hooves slapping against the surface of the sea to accompany her as she rode upon the dying night.

Mom raised both hands. As she did so, hundreds of kelpies, made from her Water magic, rose from the waves and charged toward Oleander. The music of the thundering herd grew massive, making my ears ring. Jonah, Stevie, and Baine urged their Familiars to get out of the way as the kelpie herd ran full out in Oleander's direction, led by my mother and Menilly at the head.

The sea serpents reared back and groaned. They went to dive under, but the kelpie herd was faster than they were. They stomped the sea serpents into the ocean, smashing them underfoot and completely destroying them. Blood spurted, and the sea serpents let out singular cries of pain as their lives ended at the kelpie herd's violent trampling.

Skylis faced the oncoming herd, surrendering himself to the stampede. The kelpies overwhelmed him almost immediately, and the dracash went down into the sea without protest. He gave a dying moan of relief, as if he had waited for this moment for ages and it had finally arrived.

Oleander's cries grew hysteric. He seemed to have forgotten he could use magic as he paddled at the waves in a pathetic attempt to escape, pleading with the ancestors to save him from his demise.

The ancestors had turned their backs on Oleander. I took my chance to make a final move. I formed water into an icicle and aimed it directly at Oleander's heart. The ice dagger went soaring through the air, and as the kelpie herd approached, Oleander didn't have time to brace himself.

The icicle sank into Oleander's chest, and I felt his heart stop. He looked up at me, a vague expression of shock on his face. He fell backward onto the waves, and his body floated there for a moment as the wound in his chest oozed blood.

Finally, after all this time... the bastard was dead.

Oleander's body went under as the kelpie herd trampled over him— the first of them being my mother, who urged Menilly to drive her hoof into his head. His skull cracked open. A singular hand floated over the waves as the water kelpies smashed into his corpse.

That was the last thing I saw of him.

My mother flung her hand out in a command, and the kelpie herd carried Oleander's body— as well as the sea serpents— downward, dragging them to the pit of the ocean as if carrying their souls to hell itself.

All was quiet. Mom pulled Menilly up. She sat upright as she stared downward at the ocean, receiving her revenge.

Everyone rushed to her at once. "Holy shit!" Stevie screamed. Nihoni swam forward, and Stevie threw her arms around my mother's shoulders. "That was incredible!"

Mom patted Stevie's back gently with a smile. "Nothing to boast about, dear."

Yeah, okay. My mom was a freaking goddess of the sea. And I'd never known. I thought my talent had come from my dad, but obviously, I'd been wrong.

"Now I see where Liam gets it from," Jonah said in awe. "That was amazing, Mom!"

Mom swept her hair back.

Baine was open-mouthed. "Mrs. Mitoh, that was very powerful magic. I never knew you had it in you."

"I preferred to let Liwanu handle things," Mom said with a shrug. "Though I was quite formidable, in my day."

"Looks like you still have it," I commented.

"As do you. Well done, my son," Mom said. "We've achieved victory."

Realization crashed against my thoughts like an unexpected wave. She was right. We'd *won the war*. Oleander was done for, which meant the Task Force no longer had a leader. Against all odds, we'd finished him.

The bloodshed could end. It could all cease here and now.

"Oleander is done. It is time to tell the Task Force to surrender," Mom said, and she turned Menilly toward the beach. "There's no time to lose."

Our group traveled back toward Kinpago with a renewed hope. Julian carried one of Skylis' heads in his mouth as we flew back to shore, as proof of Oleander's end.

"Where were you all this time? Could've used you earlier," Baine said over the sound of the falling rain.

"Getting Maddie to safety. I came as soon as I could," Mom replied. "I would've been by earlier, but I knew Liam could handle himself. The kelpie herd could've never vanquished Oleander had he not weakened him first."

"You came at just the right time. I was about out of magic." I sagged on Julian's back, feeling more tired than ever. I was so sore I could barely move. I longed to take a warm bath and crawl into bed.

And... ancestors. I could see Ava-Marie again. The war was over. I could get my little girl back. Tears rose to my eyes when I thought of her. Our family could be together again, and be safe. I wanted to fly to Utah right now, just so I could have her back in my arms. The only thing standing in my way was finally bringing this thing to a close.

The hurricane was still raging, and the last verges of a fight were still taking place on the beach. People were being swept away by the wind, or killed by flying debris, but no one seemed to care about the surrounding weather. Koigni and Anichi were still fighting the Task Force, killing each other without mercy as the storm raged on overhead.

Though the numbers looked much more even now. Many Task Force had been killed, and their bodies littered the beach alongside resistance members. For the first time since this battle began, we had the upper hand.

Sophia caught my gaze, and her eyes lit up when she saw Skylis' head in Julian's mouth. By the relief that crossed her expression, she knew it was over.

I was about to call for a ceasefire, before Stevie's eyes set on someone still fighting on the beach. Courtney had killed an Anichi warrior, but she was hurt. She limped along the beach with a long cut gushing blood on her leg. Her rainbow bird Familiar gave a low croon as it lay against the ground, both of its wings broken. The scar on Courtney's face was more prominent than ever, marred by the deadliness of battle.

Stevie charged up the beach, and I didn't stop her. She stood over Courtney, breathing raggedly. Courtney stared up at her with a bewildered expression, completely lost.

"*You*," Stevie seethed. "You took away my reason for breathing."

Courtney didn't have a chance to respond, because Stevie had already cast her magic by the time she finished her sentence. Courtney gargled. She grasped a hand around her neck as redness began bubbling past her lips as she choked on her own blood. Courtney's eyes rolled backward as Stevie commanded the blood in Courtney's body to rush so quickly to her heart, it blasted a hole in her chest.

The rainbow bird let its head fall back in death. Stevie stared at Courtney's body, shaking. There was something in her eyes that told me she was surprised that taking Courtney's life hadn't made her feel any better.

It wouldn't. No amount of revenge would bring Ezra back. Though I'd be lying if I said the sight of Courtney's still body didn't give me a gratified sense of comfort.

The Task Force had begun to stop fighting as they noticed Skylis' head in Julian's teeth. My dragon dropped the head upon the shore of the beach, and all eyes looked to me.

"Oleander is dead!" I cried. "There are no more Elders to follow, no more dictators to submit to! Surrender now, and your lives will be spared!"

One Task Force member broke off, in a last ditch attempt to win. He drew back his bow and shot it at me, but I whacked it away with a stream of water. He cowered before me.

"*Stand down*," I demanded. "It's over."

The Task Force members glanced between each other. Most of them had lost their helmets in the fight, and now looked just as scared as the rest of us felt. They laid down their bows and put their hands up slowly in defeat.

There was a cry of joy from the resistance army. Celebrations began— people began embracing, or crying from joy. The Task Force members kept their heads down and stared at the sand, expressionless. Some of them were calculating... as if wondering what all of this had been for.

As I walked up the beach, Sophia flung her arms around me and embraced me tightly as Esis cheered from her shoulder. "Oh my god, Liam, we've won! *We won!*"

I squeezed her back. We had won, and what was more, we were both alive. I was aware of the pounding of hippogriff hooves beside me as Sabor and Squeaks reunited. Jake and Jonah held one another close.

"I... I can't believe it," Jake said. "After all these years... the war is finally over."

"Yes! You can be a hippogriffologist, like you wanted!" Jonah said. "Isn't it great?"

Jake blinked, like the idea was still impossible to him. Then a crackle of lightning split across the sky. Several people screamed. Others ducked, and the lightning bolt struck a group of trees, igniting them into flames.

"Jonah, cut it out," I said in irritation. "We won. There's no need to gloat."

"That wasn't me!" Jonah protested.

He was kidding. It *had* to be him. No one else could make a lightning strike that big. But then another lightning bolt just as large ricocheted across the sky, and another, and another. Rain began pounding down upon the earth in giant droplets. I figured the hurricane would be dying off by now, as no one was still funneling energy into it. But that wasn't the case. If anything, it only appeared to be growing in power, picking up speed despite being over land.

"Call off your elements!" I shouted. "The fight is done!"

"We're not doing anything!" a Task Force member said. The group had pressed themselves together, looking terrified.

"We're not either!" The resistance members turned their palms upward, showing they weren't casting any magic.

Anxiety churned in my gut. I told the rain to stop— should've been an easy enough task to do, even considering how weak I was. It was First Year level stuff.

Didn't happen. If anything, the rain only increased, falling harder than before. By the look on my mom and Stevie's face, they'd attempted to do the same thing to no effect.

I stuffed down the growing horror that threatened to make me lose my mind, praying this wasn't what I thought it was. "Jonah, try to call off the hurricane," I told him. "Or at least weaken it."

Jonah nodded. He raised his hands to the sky, and Jake followed his lead. The two men concentrated their attention on the storm, commanding their Air magic to slow the hurricane's funnel.

Nothing happened. Jonah paled. He shook his head at me as he pulled his hands away from the skies, looking confused. Jake's eyes narrowed, jaw working as he tried to end the hurricane, and failed.

Something was wrong. Something was very, very wrong. The burning trees began falling over, down the embankment and crashing onto the beach. People screamed and dove out of the way.

"Are the ancestors punishing us?" I heard someone scream over the chaos.

"We need to go to a safe place! Somewhere sacred, where the ancestors won't hurt us!" another shouted.

"Follow the land bridge to the Anichi temple!" my mother cried, taking command. "We'll be safe there!"

Task Force, resistance, it didn't matter— people ran side by side to get away from the severe weather. Julian opened his wings to shield us from the heavy rain, which was almost painful as it slammed against our sides. I wrapped my arms around Sophia and held her close as we hurried down the land bridge. A resistance member ahead of us fell down and sprained her ankle. She cried out, and a Task Force member yanked her upward, carrying her in his arms as they ran to safety. One Task Force was hurt, bleeding from a cut on his side, but two resistance women flung his arms over their shoulders and dragged him ahead.

Defortai, Biyami, the labels didn't matter anymore. Not at a time like this. No one's magic was working, and we couldn't figure out why. That was enough to make every Elementai bond together, just for the sake of staying alive.

Fire began falling from the sky. Elementai screamed and ducked as the flames smashed into the land bridge, killing some and wounding others. Doya flung her hand out to stop one fireball from hitting her, but it ceased to veer off course. Her mouth fell open in shock as the fireball continued on its path, ignoring her command. She was only saved from being struck at the last moment as Naomi pushed her to the side, and Baine pulled both of them out of the way.

Sophia's mouth was thin as she pulled out of my arms. She cast her hands at the sky, but though she yelled at the fire to stop, it didn't. It mingled with the rain, making a sizzling sound. Esis tugged at her hair, and I pulled her under the safety of Julian's wings. The fireballs rolled off his scales ineffectively, though my dragon grumbled worryingly at my side.

The flames didn't listen. Not even to *Sophia*.

Just as we got off the land bridge and onto another beach, the earth split in half behind us. Several people fell into the massive hole to their deaths, and water poured in from the ocean, filling up the gap. A Nivita beside us tried to force it back together, but the dirt didn't even shift.

It was clear. Our powers were futile. We no longer had the elements under our control.

I didn't think I could run anymore, but panic forced my body to produce adrenaline, so I moved fast. Elementai screamed in horror as we ran through the forest, the earth bubbling up beneath us, swallowing trees whole. Animals, both Familiars and wildlife, stampeded mindlessly ahead, like they were fleeing some natural catastrophe. It was as if the earth was rebelling against the Hawkei themselves, protesting at the mistreatment it'd experienced at our hands.

Did we deserve it?

The Anichi temple was up ahead, and the drawbridge into it had been lowered. Imogen and Cade stood outside the temple, watching helplessly in horror as the earth continued to split and crack.

"Thank the ancestors you guys are alive," Imogen said. "What's happening?"

"I don't know," I roared. "Let's get inside!"

We charged inside the temple. Julian was too big to fit, so he remained outside the temple with the other large Familiars, turning their backs to the wind. The inner hall of the temple was packed, with only torches to light the way. Task Force members and resistance fighters clung to each other, screaming as the ground trembled beneath us. Small stones fell from the temple walls, though the building more or less held strong.

I thought about our tribe. There were thousands of people still in Kinpago— civilians, children. How was the city holding up against this onslaught? Would it still be standing after this was over?

Chief Cauac and the other Anichi had made it inside the temple, but they appeared as bewildered as the rest of us. The only magic that seemed to work anymore was Anichi. Luana and Sierra rushed from person to person, healing all without discrimination. Sophia and Esis went to help, and I watched as Sophia's healing magic mended the broken leg of an alicorn nearby.

Their powers worked, but it was obvious all other elemental magic was gone. The rest of us were useless.

Imogen and I stared hopelessly at each other. My eyes searched the temple, until I sought out Maddie. She was pressed against the wall with Drew, who was holding her. Drew had a hooded expression, like he was simply waiting to die. Maddie appeared to be having a panic attack, shaking in Drew's arms while tears ran from her eyes. Ace lay at their feet, his paws over his eyes, while Eirakari drooped her head and crooned sadly. They acted like they were at a funeral, not hiding from a storm.

I ran toward them. Imogen and Jonah followed. I grabbed Sophia just as she had finished healing a fallen dove, and hauled her over. We came to a stop as Maddie lifted her defeated gaze to meet us.

"Maddie, what's happening?" I cried over the raging winds battering the outside of the temple. "When will this end?"

"It's not going to end, Liam." Her foreboding tone caused a shiver to race across my spine.

"What do you mean? It has to end. This is madness."

Maddie closed her eyes and quivered. "Nature demands a balance. When that balance is upset, nature will do something to correct itself. Even if it requires the death of a species."

Jonah gave a strangled sound. Imogen gasped, and Sophia went utterly pale.

"No," I protested. "That can't be what this is."

"Since we were children, we were told that an Elementai's power must be regulated. That it remains in control," Maddie said. "There's a reason why Elementai aren't supposed to mess with the weather. It's because of situations like this. Do you think you can cause a hurricane in Northern California and it won't ruin our ecosystem? We're not just playing with elements now. We're playing God."

Maddie cast her gaze upward. "But the battle caused us to lose our heads. We used our elements without regulation, without thought. We used our powers to hurt each other instead of for the greater good, and now nature is stopping us before we kill the earth. We've caused an ecological catastrophe. And now that it's been let out of the box, there's no stopping it. Or putting it back."

"There must be something," Jonah pleaded.

"Don't you understand?" Maddie yelled. "We've fucked up the climate, our *atmosphere* during this battle! We've fucked up *everything*. Now, to save itself, the earth is going to deal with the damage. By getting rid of us."

The pieces of the prophecy clicked into place as the storm outside echoed our doom. *This* is what Maddie had foreseen. What Showana had foretold. The extinction of the Hawkei, forever.

And it was at our own hands.

We'd run out of options. With the elements refusing to bend to our magic, we couldn't stop the storm. It'd continue to rage until it killed all of us, without mercy.

"I told you all that us winning this war would be worse than us losing," Maddie said in a finite whisper. "You didn't want to listen."

Maddie was right. This was the end. With no way to stop the weather, and no other options left, we had to accept our fate.

There wasn't anything left to do but wait to die.

I thought the war was over, but as the ground shook beneath our feet, I realized we'd been fighting more than Oleander all along. Our elements were meant to be in balance— to be unified— and we'd defied our very nature.

Now nature was fighting back.

Jonah turned from Maddie and squatted. He fisted his hands into his hair, curling into a ball. He rocked back and forth in a way that twisted my chest into knots. I knew tight spaces terrified him, and with so many people in here, we were cramped. With the elements raging outside, there was no escape.

"Jonah!" Jake cried, kneeling at his side. He ran a comforting hand down Jonah's back. "Let's move. We'll find an open room with more space."

"I'm not scared of the goddamn temple!" Jonah roared. He dropped his hands from his hair, and his face turned red. "Don't you see!? What's happening out there is *my* fault. The whole Reject Team!"

The accusation was like a knife to the gut, but it was true. If Liam, Jonah, Imogen, and I hadn't won the Elemental Cup... if Liam and I hadn't gone to trial... this war never would have happened. The prophecy mentioned me because *I* was the one to set off a string of events that led to the Hawkei's demise.

When the tribe divides in two and war has begun
The Hawkei have reached the point of no return.

Smoke will Blaze through the sky and signify the Hawkei's extinction.

Maybe the Air piece had never been referring to the Battle of Orenda Academy like we thought. Maybe it was referring to *this* battle— the sign of our extinction.

"That's not true." Imogen argued with Jonah, but I wasn't sure she believed it.

Liam reached out for me, and the two of us held each other tight. My hands shook in his. All hope was gone.

Liam shook. "Jonah's right. Everyone's going to die because of us."

"We'll get out of this!" Imogen protested. "We always do. That's what the Reject Team does."

Jonah shook his head. "Not this time, Im. Look around you!"

Jonah gestured around the temple. Task Force and resistance members alike had collapsed in exhaustion. They just sat there watching the temple shake, waiting for the elements to claim them.

"Without our elements, we're done for!" Jonah cried.

My heart hammered wildly. I wanted to agree with Jonah. Logic told me there was no way out of this, that we'd done all we could.

But deep within my chest, a fire continued to burn. It swelled until I couldn't ignore it. Something about this battle had left me unsettled, but I couldn't put my finger on it. There *had* to be a way to save everybody.

Luana had seen the distress on Jonah's face and came over. *It's going to be all right*, she signed.

"We're all going to die," Jonah said weakly as he signed back.

Why is death something to fear? Luana questioned. *It is not the end. We'll be with our ancestors in the Ancestral Lands. Is that not the goal of this life? Life on earth will go on without the Hawkei. The earth will be healed once we are gone.*

Nausea rolled around in my gut. Luana was trying to soothe us, to ease the impact of what was going on. But I refused to believe her. There was more to this life than just living and dying. We had a purpose— *all* of us. And the ancestors had chosen me to preserve that purpose. Had I failed them? Had I failed *everyone*?

Esis' eyes darted toward the doorway. A huge *boom* sounded outside as thunder cracked above. Esis tugged on his ears, then jumped off of my shoulder.

"Esis!" I cried.

He ran across the temple, bounding over people and their Familiars. I abandoned my friends and followed after him as he raced toward the entrance. My blood chilled. For a moment, I thought he was so disoriented he was going to run outside. Instead, he skidded to halt at the entrance and just *watched* down the long hall.

Rain whipped by the entrance, and air whooshed past us. The sound of thunder and rumbling earth was practically deafening. I stopped beside him and bent to scoop him up, my heart hammering.

"Esis, no!" I scolded. "We have to stay away from the door. The storm could kill us!"

Esis squealed and tried to jump out of my arms again, but I held him close to my chest. "Esis, stop!"

My Familiar managed to squeeze himself out of my arms. He went tumbling toward the floor and reached upward, scratching me across the arm. His tiny little paws swiped across the compass on my belt, making it clink against my armor. I stopped dead in my tracks.

Esis righted himself and looked up to me. My gaze flickered from him to the compass. It was the one Haloke had given me before my wedding— the item she said would always guide me onward in the right direction. I'd nearly forgotten I'd brought it into battle.

"You want me to use it?" I asked him.

Esis nodded.

I wasn't sure what good it would do, considering it hadn't worked for me in the past. To be honest, I wasn't even sure why I'd brought it along. For good luck, I guess? But when Esis suggested I use it, my heart finally slowed. My fingers trembled against the fastenings as I untied it from my belt, but everything else around me seemed to quiet. The thunder overhead and the wind whistling through cracks in the temple barely registered.

I knelt beside Esis and held the compass up in my palm. Closing my eyes, I opened the hinge and whispered a prayer to the ancestors. "Please, ancestors. Show us how to save the tribe."

I opened my eyes, and the spinning needle slowed until it came to a stop. It pointed directly in front of me.

There was nothing there except for Esis.

My breath halted in my chest. Before I could process what the compass was trying to tell me, Esis chittered and jumped forward. He bounced onto my knee, then jumped on my shoulder. He thrust his little paws beneath the collar of my armor and dragged out the Spirit Totem. He waved it in my face, and the ice in my belly seemed to melt.

I knew now what had left me unsettled on the battlefield. The *Azaim-*

periai hadn't worked, yet I was supposed to use it to end this war. The ancestors kept saying I needed to start asking the right questions.

I thought I knew what questions to ask. How could we win the war against Oleander?

But the *Azaimperiai* was never designed to win any war. It was as my grandparents had said. Wars only brought destruction, and the *Azaimperiai* was a tool for healing.

The real question was not how to destroy Oleander, but how to *heal* the tribe.

The Air piece wasn't the last piece. The Hawkei would not see extinction if I had anything to say about it. And I did— all I had to do was accept my fate the ancestors had written for me long ago. The Soul piece ran through my mind.

Should the Koigni child accept her fate
An innocent soul must be freely given
The tribe will be reborn
With the chosen one's greatest sacrifice.

Saving the Hawkei was never going to happen through destruction and war. I knew that now. We could only heal through means of selfless love.

Gravity fell upon me as the entire weight of the universe settled upon my shoulders. The very air was sucked out of my lungs, leaving me suffocating.

I knew what I had to do now. I knew how to save the tribe.

The knots in my chest eased, but tears filled my eyes. "Is it the only way?" I whispered to Esis.

His blue eyes sparkled with tears, and he dropped his head. His tiny chin bobbed up and down in confirmation.

What I was being asked to do was unthinkable. But it was the only way for the Hawkei to survive. I didn't *have* to do it. Showana had assured me many times that I had a choice. But by the Great Spirit, I would not bring any further destruction upon my people. I would be the chosen one I was always meant to be.

I drew myself upright and pushed my shoulders back. I had to be brave for the Hawkei.

"Earth, Water, Fire, and Air... Gifted to us by the breath of a prayer..." The tune of the Hawkei's song drifted through the temple as resistance members and Task Force alike joined in. I'd heard so many versions of the

song before. This time, though, nobody argued about the lyrics. They just sang in unison.

I moved in what felt like slow motion as the song carried me back to my friends. Everywhere I looked, tears were streaming down people's faces. Familiars reared their heads in agony, and Elementai clutched one another.

The Reject Team was huddled together, weeping. Cade held on to Imogen, and Luana was wrapped in Sam's arms.

"It seems symbolic, you know?" Jonah wept. "Dying on Ancestors' Day. It's the anniversary of when they gifted us our powers— and now we've lost them... lost everything."

Liam's eyes were fixed on mine, like he'd been watching me the whole time. "*Pawee*, what is it?"

He reached out to take my hand. When I touched him, an electric shock went up my arm. It killed me to think of what I was about to do. I didn't think Liam would let me go through it, and yet I wanted him— no, *needed* him— to be there with me.

"I know what we have to do," I said, my voice thin.

Imogen wiped her eyes. "You have a plan?"

I nodded confidently. "The prophecy isn't over. We must finish this, before it's too late."

Luana's knees shook, but she was the quickest to ask, *What do we do?*

I took a deep breath. "Follow me."

My friends didn't question me— they just followed. My gaze traveled over faces as we made our way to a nearby tunnel. I could hardly make them out behind the tears, but it brought comfort to my heart to know I had one last chance to save them all.

Soon, our small group moving through the temple caught the attention of others. Doya and Baine quickly rushed over, followed by Amelia and Trace. Wyatt and Mia were holding each other next to Vanessa and Bren. The four of them saw us leaving the main room and followed, too. Chief Cauac knitted his brow and came over to speak with Jake. His companion prowled at his side. Though Jake didn't have an answer for the chief, he followed us. Maddie had gone to comfort Haloke and Stevie. They, along with Drew, were the last to join us. I could hear them in the back asking what was going on, but nobody really knew, and they didn't answer.

The Hawkei's song echoed through the tunnels as over a dozen Elementai and Familiars wove through the temple and climbed toward the highest point of the pyramid. None of the obstacles that had been in our way the last time had been reset, so we were met with no resistance. It was as if the ancestors themselves were welcoming us to our final trial.

The song of the Hawkei faded into the distance, but our footsteps continued like drum beats. They were not the beats of battle, as I'd grown so accustomed to over the last few days. They were sad and melancholy, like we were marching to the beat of a funeral procession. It felt frighteningly appropriate.

We reached the highest point of the temple. Nothing but a door separated us from the Summoning Room, where I had spoken with Showana two years ago. I pushed at the door, but it wouldn't budge. The wind was so strong it was forcing it closed. Liam came beside me and pressed his shoulder against the door to help.

"*Pawee?*" he asked. "What's going on?"

I opened my mouth to tell him, but I choked up. "Just trust me, okay?"

Liam didn't question it. He trusted me wholeheartedly. Imogen and Jonah stepped up beside us, and together, the four of us thrust the door open. I stumbled out onto the highest platform of the temple. It was covered by a roof, but there were no walls— only columns carved in the shapes of Familiars. Cold air whipped through the Summoning Room, chilling me to the bone. Esis clung tightly to my shoulder to keep from being thrown off.

From this vantage point, we should've been able to see for miles, but the clouds were so thick and the rain came down in sheets. I knew the sun must've been rising, but it looked dark as night. The only light came from fires raging near the beach, and bolts of lightning sizzling through the sky every few seconds. Thunder cracked overhead, and though we were high up, I could still feel the earth shaking beneath our feet.

The Summoning Room looked as I remembered it. There was a huge offering table in the center, which sat below a carved hole in the ceiling meant for channeling magic. Rain poured in through the opening, spilling across the ceremony table.

I stepped up to the table. A faded blood stain remained from my last summoning. Everyone else gathered around, shivering. I saw anger, fear, and sadness written across each of their faces. As if their emotions were my own, every ounce of regret permeated deep into my bones.

Imogen wrapped her arms around her middle, and her hair flew in wild waves around her head. Sassy was curled around her leg. "Sophia, what's going on?" she asked over the roar of the wind.

Rocks settled in my gut. I tried to force out an explanation, but it felt like I was choking on my words. I might as well have been swallowing needles as pain entered my throat. If I told them, they'd try to stop me, and there was no time for negotiations. But they had to know what I was about to do. It was too painful a burden to bear on my own.

"I know what the prophecy means now," I told them. "I know what sacrifice has to be made."

Liam's face paled. I could hardly hear him over the roar of the wind. "What do you mean? I thought *Ava* was the sacrifice the ancestors needed. She's not here!"

"It was never her," I replied, trembling. "Ava would be a sacrifice I could not bear, but she was never meant to be the *ultimate sacrifice* the prophecy speaks of."

Haloke was the first to catch on. "The ultimate sacrifice? Sophia, you don't mean—?"

"I have to!" I cried. My jaw tightened, and I could hardly draw in a breath. "It's the only way to end this."

Liam stepped forward, his eyebrows knitted in fury. "This war ends in death! We all die now. That's how it has to be, because I'm not letting you give yourself up!"

"I'm not—" I started to say, but a sob broke in my chest. I threw my hand over my mouth as the agonizing cries escaped involuntarily. If I meant to give myself up, it'd be easy. I was ready to lay down my life for the Hawkei as so many of my fellow Elementai had done before me.

But this... this was like having my guts removed with a rusty fork while I watched.

Tears streamed down my face. "I'm not giving myself up," I managed to choke out.

"Then what—?" Liam's face fell. All the blood drained from it as I reached up to take Esis off my shoulder. I cradled him in my arms. I swore Liam was about to pass out. I personally didn't know how I'd remained standing this long. Realization crossed Liam's face.

"The ancestors asked for an innocent soul," I said, my voice cracking. My tears dropped into Esis' fur. He was surprisingly calm in my arms, but I shook like I was being rocked by a typhoon. "They're asking for *Esis*."

"*No!*" Liam wailed, his cries cutting through the storm. Sassy growled and tried to leap forward, but Imogen yanked her backward and clung to her fur. It took Jonah, Jake, and Cade to all hold Squeaks back.

Liam rushed over to me and tried to grab Esis from my arms. I turned away from him, though I really wanted to let him take Esis far away from here, to make the choice easy for me.

"Sophia, you can't!" Liam protested.

Doya and Baine were equally furious. "If you sacrifice your Familiar, you sacrifice yourself!" Doya barked.

"You can't do that!" Baine yelled.

"I have to!" I screamed. My knees trembled beneath me. "I'll die either way. This way, the Hawkei will live on."

Amelia's nostrils flared. "You don't even know if this will work!"

"And so I shouldn't try?" I growled. "The elements are going to kill us! *All of us!*"

Then we die together! Luana signed.

"No!" I yelled at them. "You will all live on. You will restore the Hawkei. The Anichi will be welcomed back."

Vanessa stepped forward, raging. "Sophia, as your chief, I forbid you to do this."

"You can't do that," I cried. "You must understand, I'm doing this to save the Hawkei. This is our last chance! Maddie, *tell them!*"

All eyes turned to Maddie. She had both hands over her mouth, and her eyes were bloodshot with tears.

Slowly, she lowered her hands and nodded. "I never saw this," she sobbed, biting down hard on her lower lip. Maddie looked on the verge of a breakdown, and I didn't know how much longer she could stand to watch. "But Sophia's right. This is what the prophecy meant. This is what the ancestors wanted."

"That's absurd!" Liam shouted. "How could they ask such a thing!?"

"I don't know!" I screamed, harsher than I meant. To be honest, I hadn't figured out why the ancestors wanted me, either. But I knew that it had to be done. "All I know is this is how we save our people."

"Esis can't be the one. He's not innocent!" Liam argued. "He's killed others."

"Only to protect me," I reminded him. I knew Liam was only saying it to convince me to reconsider, but I didn't. I knew Esis was the innocent soul the prophecy spoke of. There was no doubt in my mind.

Esis wasn't a child anymore. He'd seen far too much and knew how cruel this world could be. He wasn't innocent in the ways he used to be. There'd been a time when his innocence was so pure that he didn't understand the permanence of death.

I think I understood now why it took him so long to figure it out. It was because Esis' own death would not be an end, but a beginning. His death was meant to usher in an era of healing.

And though he'd learned that not all deaths were the same, Esis continued to embody innocence and purity. He never acted out of selfishness. He didn't seek vengeance or thirst for revenge. He was a protector through and through, filled only with love. Whereas I was the part of our soul that reacted in fear and retaliated with Fire, Esis was the part that put love first and knew healing was the answer to conflict. He was everything good the tribe had lost... and he would bring it back to them.

"Ancestors!" Imogen breathed like she'd just realized something. "Esis' tarot card reading! He got *The World*. He was always going to be the one to save it!"

Liam barely seemed to hear her. "You don't know what you're getting yourself into, *pawee*. You don't realize the kind of pain you're bringing upon yourself."

He placed a hand on my shoulder, but I shrugged him off. "It is a pain I will welcome. We are chiefs. We are Elders. We must do *everything* to save our people, or we are *nothing*!"

My chest heaved in sobs, but I continued. "I *need* you, Liam. I need you to let me do this— to *support* me. Otherwise, this war was all for nothing."

"I won't let you become a martyr, Sophia," he said with firm conviction.

"Better to be a martyr to save my people than to let them perish," I argued. "Liam, you want to know why you're still alive— why you didn't die with Nashoma? It's because we all have a purpose here on this earth. The ancestors brought us together, because I *needed* you in this war. I need you now... because I can't do this on my own."

Tears poured from my eyes like a broken dam. The thought of giving up Esis, no matter if it saved thousands of people, was unbearable. Sobs rocked my entire body, sending a chill from my head to my toes. I couldn't see through the tears. All I could do was break down into uncontrollable sobs. I felt Liam come up behind me and place an arm around my shoulder, but it barely registered. It was Esis' paws stroking my arm that were the true comfort.

"I'm here," Liam whispered in my ear. "I'm here, *pawee*. Tell me what we have to do."

I didn't know what I'd said to change Liam's mind, but I must've convinced him. My husband was ready to fight for me, no matter what I asked. The weight on my chest eased slightly.

My breath wavered. "I-I don't know exactly. Esis, what do we do?"

Esis' ears drooped, but he blinked up at me like he was content— like he was *ready* for this. Esis reached out, and his paw touched the side of my face. When it did, the chill left my body, and I was filled with a peaceful warmth— like healing Soul magic.

It will be okay, Sophia, a voice rang in my mind. It was a young male voice, soft and smooth like a song.

My jaw hung slack in disbelief. Esis was speaking to me!

My sobs grew, and I threw a hand over my mouth, but ended up biting down on my knuckles to calm my breath. The sound of his voice was so bittersweet I could melt right then and there. He'd never spoken to me before— but now his voice was coming to me at the time of our greatest need, sealing our bond forever.

You have nothing to fear, Esis explained. *I have always known this was how it would end. It is why the ancestors led me to you— why we bonded.*

"W-what?" I gaped.

I knew I would have to leave you one day. That's why I pushed you and Liam together. I wanted to leave you with someone who could understand what this was like, so you could help each other. Esis' eyes blinked innocently.

"Wait..." I said aloud. Everyone else must've noticed Esis and I were communicating, because they all just froze and watched. No one tried to interfere. "I'm not going with you?"

Esis shook his head, and his big blue eyes glittered like stars. *You have the power of the sun to sustain your life energy. You and Liam will be each other's souls now.*

"But why *me*?" I asked in a broken voice. "Why do *I* have to give you up?"

Esis stared at me for a long time. *The ancestors chose you for many reasons, Sophia. Your Anichi blood makes you unique to bond with a crea-ture like me. And it is only I, a bonded Anichi creature, that can complete what needs to be done.*

"What about Luana's family?" I protested. "She's bonded, too."

Esis shook his head. *She has a calling of her own, and you know as well as I that she'd never give up her Familiar. You were chosen because you are willing to give up your own soul to save others. This is what the ancestors ask — for the Hawkei to prove they have changed. And that change comes through you.*

"I don't want to!" I wailed through shallow breaths. "I don't want you to leave, Esis."

Esis stroked my cheek, wiping the tears away. *Fear not, Sophia, for I will not be far. I am your soul, and I will always be with you.*

I stared into Esis' eyes, as if waiting for something. What I was waiting for, I wasn't sure. Perhaps for him to tell me it didn't have to be this way, for him to offer up another solution. But it never came.

It is time, Sophia, Esis said. *You must let me go.*

I squeezed my eyes shut tightly and wrapped one hand around the Spirit Totem. I hesitated for only a moment, unable to fathom what I was about to do. But with another deep breath, I took the terrifying plunge.

"Ancestors, I know what needs to happen now," I whispered. "Please... help us heal the tribe."

As I spoke the words, the surrounding wind stilled. The storm continued to rage on outside. Rain whipped behind the pillars, and thunder cracked loudly. The sound of breaking earth and falling trees could be heard in the distance. But here in the Summoning Room, it was like a switch had been flipped. The wind was calm, and the rain had stopped pouring in through the opening in the ceiling. It was like we were in the eye of the storm.

Barely a second passed, then a blinding white light lit up the entire Summoning Room. At first, I thought it was a crack of lightning, but it lasted far too long. I shielded my eyes a moment before lowering my hand.

A beam of light shone down from the sky. It was a mere foot across and came down through the hole in the ceiling, shining onto the offering table. It was like a beacon— magic sent straight from the ancestors. I knew it was meant for Esis.

I didn't let him go right away. Instead, I pulled him closer to my chest. I took a deep breath to control my voice, but my words came out in broken sobs. "Esis, you've been here for me since the very beginning, ever since I came to Kinpago. You were there for me when I got sick, to brush my hair and comfort me. You were by my side in every class, and helped me through every study session. You must've gifted me a thousand shiny rocks by now. Without you, we never would've made it through the Elemental Cup. You stood beside Liam and I when we went to trial. When the war started, you fought beside me in every battle. When I almost died giving birth to Ava-Marie, you were there to save me."

Esis' eyes connected with mine and never faltered. My breath wavered, but my tone became even. "I needed you back then, because I didn't know who I was or where to call home. Kinpago became my home, and then *Hok'evale.* I used to think home was a place, but it never was. Home was wherever you were, because when you're there, everything feels calm and peaceful. I feel like together, we can conquer anything."

I sniffled. "You taught me the power of healing, Esis— not just with Anichi magic, but for myself and my family. You mean the world to me. Letting you go is the hardest thing I've ever had to do."

My arms shook as violent sobs rocked my shoulders. Though Esis was calm, his body trembled in my arms. I pulled him closer to me and shoved my nose into his fur. Letting my Familiar go was torture unlike I'd never experienced before. Nothing could measure up to this— not watching my loved ones be mutilated in front of me, not coming inches from death in childbirth, not thinking Liam had died on the *Hozho*... not even sending Ava-Marie away. It could all happen a hundred times over, and it wouldn't be as painful as letting Esis go.

The earth might as well have opened up right then and swallowed me whole, because it felt as if a pride of manticores were dragging me to the depths of *Aiya Nocshun*. It was torturous.

And yet, I welcomed the torture. I couldn't explain how my Fire seemed to sear me from the inside out, and yet my Spirit soothed me. My elements raged war, and for the first time, my Spirit won. Saving the tribe was bigger than me, bigger than Esis. And so I would do as Esis asked and ensure the Hawkei survived.

A sense of clarity overcame me, and for the first time, I truly understood what Showana had been training me for— it was *this* moment. Had she told me before what had to be done, I never would have agreed to it. I'd had run halfway around the world with Esis to save him from his demise, because I never would have been able to withstand the grief. It would have been selfish of me.

But I knew grief now like I knew my elements. I knew that it was a necessary part of life, that it kept us going and inspired us to do better— to *be* better. Showana had trained me to understand my grief and learn how to navigate it— even become *comfortable* with it.

I knew now there was no way the Hawkei were walking away from this grief-filled war the same tribe we started as. Showana had been right... this war had doomed the Hawkei to extinction. But that was the old tribe. With Esis' sacrifice, we would rise as a *new* tribe.

Fractures cracked within my heart until I couldn't hold it together any longer. I set Esis on the offering table, and my heart crumbled into a million tiny pieces. He looked hopefully at the pillar of light, then turned to face me one last time.

Goodbye, Sophia, he said.

Tears rained down my face. "I love you, Esis."

All around me, the sound of sobs grew. My friends and family wept for my Familiar, but there was only one person who truly knew how heart-wrenchingly painful this was. Liam wrapped an arm tightly around me, and I felt his body tremble against mine.

Esis turned away and slowly stepped toward the beam of light. I wanted to reach out for him, to yank him back into my arms, but I couldn't. We were out of time.

"*Esis!*" I cried. My voice echoed across the temple. The storm seemed to pick up my voice and carry it through the clouds, my Familiar's name echoing all across the Hawkei's land. It was the saddest sound I'd ever heard.

Esis took another step, and I couldn't hold myself upright any longer. My knees buckled, and I dropped to the floor, clutching the edge of the offering table. Liam knelt beside me, holding me close as I cried. I wasn't sure I could watch what was about to happen, but I couldn't tear my gaze away, either.

Esis stopped at the edge of the light and tilted his gaze up at it. The confidence in his stance was undeniable. Esis was ready for this... he always had been. He was not just my protector, but the protector of the entire tribe. He welcomed his calling with bravery I dearly admired.

Esis stepped into the beam of light. A mere moment passed...

Then his body wavered, and he slowly collapsed into a heap on the offering table.

Though I knew it was coming, I couldn't believe my eyes. My heart hammered wildly as the agony consumed me, but at the same time, it felt as if time stood still. Esis' chest did not rise and fall, and his tail didn't twitch. He just lay there in the beam of light... lifeless.

No matter how much I tried to breathe in, the air wouldn't come.

I'd wondered so many times what it was like to lose your Familiar, as I'd tried to understand what Liam had gone through when Nashoma died. None of the scenarios in my head came anywhere close.

Watching your Familiar die wasn't just about the grief— which was agonizing enough in its own right. When your Familiar died, you *felt* it tearing you apart from the inside out. My soul was being ripped in half. One half was pulled onto the ethereal plane, and the other remained in the physical realm. There was no physical pain, but the emotional turmoil couldn't compare. The ancestors could've ripped me limb from limb with the powers of the elements— pulled my flesh straight off my bones while I watched— and it wouldn't have hurt this much.

I understood how people died moments after their Familiars. When your soul was ripped away from you, there wasn't any reason to keep going. As an Elementai, you followed your Familiar anywhere— even to death. A death with them was far preferable to a life without them.

The only thing that kept me holding on in that moment— that kept me from just giving up and dying right then and there from sheer agony— was Liam's arms. Esis wanted me to stay, and I'd fight tooth and nail to honor his wishes.

I still couldn't believe what had happened. In the blink of an eye, Esis was taken from me. My wails pierced my ears. I hardly recognized them as my own.

I didn't realize what I was doing. I ripped myself from Liam's hold and scrambled on all fours onto the offering table. Cold rain water seeped between the spaces in my armor, but I barely felt it. I crawled across the table until I reached Esis. I took his tiny little body in my arms and curled him close to me. His cold, limp form was confirmation he was dead. I couldn't wrap my head around how fast it had happened.

Esis' body stirred in my arms. I yanked away, holding my breath. Had he come back to me?

Esis wasn't moving at all, I realized. Tendrils of ancestral light twisted around his form, pulling his body away from me. My jaw dropped. The light was warm and reassuring, as if promising Esis would be okay in the hands of the ancestors. The light cradled Esis and carried him out of my arms. It tore me to pieces, but I let him go. I couldn't take my eyes off the magnificent scene in front of me.

Esis' body returned to the pillar of light, but he hovered mid-air, as if attached to a harness. His tail swayed limply, and his big ears drooped at the side of his face. Though he was gone, his features seemed peaceful.

Little beams of light began to emit from his fur, like miniature stars gathering around every inch of his form. The light beams glittered, but soon became so bright I couldn't continue watching. I shielded my eyes as the light grew in intensity, filling the temple with blinding whiteness.

Whoosh!

A blast of warm air swept across the temple, blowing my hair all around my face. My heart beat pulsed in my ears. The light faded enough that I could open my eyes again. I went speechless when I saw what had appeared.

The beam of light was gone, along with Esis' body. Instead, a million tiny little stars had burst outward, lighting the temple like the night sky. It seemed like someone had projected an image of a galaxy across the room, except the drops of starlight looked solid.

The stars were visible from every angle and swirled around us all like a kaleidoscope. Sassy batted at one of the bits of light, and it rolled through the air. Nobody spoke as we took in the light display. I wanted to ask what it meant, but by the look of wonder on everyone's faces, I didn't think they knew.

All around me, the little drops of light began to swirl faster, until they came to rest on my skin. The comforting warmth of Spirit filled me like an embrace, and it was in that moment that I realized what the starry lights were. They were *Esis*.

I gasped, and the lights jumped off my skin and swirled above me. They came together to form a miniature galaxy, shifting into the form of a kurble.

Esis' spirit drifted down from above, until he was standing on the offering table in front of me. He wasn't solid anymore, but he wasn't like the watercolor spirits I'd met. His outline was black, barely visible behind the layers of sparkling stars. His entire spirit twinkled, like he was made of galaxies.

It hit me. Esis *was* made of starlight!

"Esis, you're a Starbeast!" I cried. Liam had told me about Starbeasts only days ago. They were Anichi creatures made of starlight. They bonded to Spirit Warriors and could influence the cosmos.

Esis nodded his sparkling head. *It is why you were chosen, Sophia. Only a Starbeast has the power to save the tribe.*

I didn't think that I could cry anymore, but tears rolled faster down my cheeks. I wasn't sad for Esis. I was *proud*.

"Esis, you're amazing," I told him.

Esis reached out to me. Though he was merely spirit, I could feel the warmth of his paw on my hand. His big eyes sparkled up at me. *Not as amazing as you are, Sophia. You have made incredible sacrifices in this war. You were always there for me. And now, I offer you a gift of gratitude.*

Esis raised his hands. I didn't know what to expect, but I was surprised when beams of light shone down through the opening in the ceiling, as if Esis was creating some sort of spell. The sound of flutes began to play, and I quickly realized it wasn't a spell at all. It was a *summoning*.

Each beam of light transformed into a different animal. There must've been over a dozen. I noticed the one straight in front of me first. It was a wolf— Nashoma. He bowed his head lightly to Liam, in a way that was both affectionate and respectful. Overcome by emotion and still on his knees, my husband began to sob.

Next came a second kurble. It was bigger than Esis and had huge horns. The kurble shifted into the form of a woman with a long braid down her back— Showana Harjo.

Tears beaded in my eyes once more. My jaw hung slack, and my eyes darted around the room at the other spirits. An eagle shifted into the shape of a tall man that reminded me of Liam. I didn't have to ask to know it was his grandfather. On one side of him, a huge bear shifted, and I recognized Liwanu. A thunderbird flew in an arc above our heads, then landed beside Liam's forefathers. The thunderbird shrank and became a young man— Ezra. He stopped in front of Stevie, and though he didn't speak, the two shared a heart-wrenching gaze that was both melancholy and filled with love. Stevie had gone speechless, though sobs rocked her chest. She looked like she wanted to say something, but she couldn't manage. Maddie squeezed her hand tightly, and Stevie dashed away tears. I choked up when Ezra reached out and pressed a spirit hand to Stevie's stomach. Stevie lost it at the gesture.

"I love you, Ezra," she cried.

Haloke's sobs echoed through the Summoning Room as she took in her husband and son. Maddie cried, and Liam completely broke down. Ezra turned from Stevie and gave Liam a comforting smile as the two brothers faced each other for the final time.

My breath stalled as more and more creatures came down from the heavens. As each one appeared, the sound of flutes intensified. A ram and a cat became my grandparents, while a basilisk and kirin shifted to reveal the faces of Lindsey and Miranda. A peacock landed beside them, becoming Perot.

It was so painful to observe the figures of all those we had lost. And yet it was soothing. Wails mixed with sounds of awe filled the Summoning Room as more and more of our ancestors came down to greet us. They formed a circle around the outer edge of the room, surrounding us.

I caught a glimpse of my friends. Liam's eyes darted from spirit to spirit, but they kept going back to Nashoma. Imogen, Cade, Jonah, and Jake were all watching the spirits in awe. Even Squeaks had backed down to take in the magnificent sight. Amelia and Trace held each other, as did Wyatt and Mia. Vanessa and Bren were both calm, while Maddie's features softened as Drew held her. Baine and Doya wept in each other's arms, which I'd never witnessed before.

Chief Cauac stared slack-jawed. I wasn't sure he'd ever seen an ancestral spirit in his life, but his eyes were locked on a white-haired woman— Luana's mother. Luana reached her hand upward, and a killer whale swimming through the air touched its belly on her fingers. Her eyes sparkled as she felt the spirit pass through her.

The killer whale landed and shifted into the form of Madame Wells. Beside her, a giant dragon became Head Dean Alric, who reached out and took Perot's hand in his. A hydra and a unicorn flew down from the heavens beside each other. For a second, I forgot who they might be, until they shifted and I saw they were Professor Costas and Professor Fawn— the two professors who'd been murdered in the riots.

Next came an arctic fox and a gray fox. I didn't know whose ancestors they were, as I'd never seen anyone with those Familiars before. Both foxes swooped down and circled around Sassy. She yipped and batted at them playfully. The foxes ducked away from her, and the sound of their playful barks filled the Summoning Room. They ran over to Maxwell, Trace's Familiar, and circled him as well. When they reached the outer edge of the room and took their spot beside the other ancestors, they shifted, and the wind was knocked out of me. It was Soren and Roland, Imogen's brothers. Imogen and Trace both let out sounds of grief and welcoming.

The ancestors continued to flood down from the skies for a final goodbye. A hound shifted into Vanderbilt, and a stallion became Professor Cheveyo. A hummingbird tweeted as it flew beside a scorpion. The two landed beside each other and shifted into the form of Luca and Miss Evangeline.

I was so overwhelmed, I threw my hands over my mouth. I couldn't believe this was real. Finally, a wyvern, a firebird, a hound, and a griffin flew into the room and swirled around me. I knew without watching them transform that they were my spirit guides. Warmth filled my chest as they landed and completed the circle.

For a moment, I thought that was all the ancestors that would appear. But to my surprise, another beam of light appeared. At first, I couldn't make it out. The soul was blindingly bright and beautiful, but I managed to keep my eyes on it. As it drifted down from above, the light faded, until I made out the shape of a tiny elepee. It landed in front of me on the offering table and titled its head, as if studying me, though it wouldn't look me directly in the eyes.

There was something about its features that reminded me of someone I once knew. I couldn't put my finger on it until...

The elepee shifted and grew to the shape of a young boy. I gasped, but the air caught in my chest. Soul magic swirled in my belly, mixed with the heavy pain of loss. He stepped forward and knelt beside me, and though I wanted to say something, I couldn't find the words. I could only cry.

"Adriel?" I managed to choke out.

Adriel dropped his head, then reached out and placed his spirit hand on mine. "Sophia," he whispered back. "I missed you."

The flute music swelled, reaching a peak and playing a tune of pure bliss.

I totally lost it. Tears streamed down my cheeks, though I didn't know it was possible to cry any more. My whole body shook, but it wasn't out of fear. The Spirit magic all around me built within my soul, filling me up with so much love and reassurance. I'd never felt so comforted in all my life. It was then I knew with unwavering certainty that everything was going to be okay.

Showana stood beside Nashoma on the offering table. She stepped forward and crossed her hands in front of her. "You've done well, my child."

Relief washed through me, but I couldn't stop the tears from coming. "You were right all along," I cried. "I really did have the answers within me."

Showana nodded. "You chose well, Sophia. I could not be prouder of you."

I swallowed. The storm continued raging outside, and though I was thrilled to see all my loved ones here, I knew there was work to be done. "What happens now?"

Showana stepped aside and gestured to Esis. "That is up to you."

Esis drew his shoulders back and puffed his chest out. With the slightest of smiles on his face, he walked over to Nashoma. The wolf bowed, and Esis climbed onto his back. He tangled his paws into Nashoma's fur and kicked his sides to guide him forward.

Nashoma stepped closer to me, but I was not his target. Instead, he turned to Liam. Liam was only a few feet behind me. He'd gone absolutely speechless, staring at his Familiar like he couldn't believe his eyes.

"Nashoma," Liam breathed. He opened his mouth to say more, but he couldn't get the words out. Nashoma simply nodded, like he seemed to understand Liam's unspoken words.

I have always been here, Liam, Nashoma said for all to hear. *Your heart was not always open to hear me. Now that it is, you can rest assured you will hear me always. Remember we will be together again.*

Nashoma's head turned to observe everyone in the Summoning Room. *All of us.*

Tears leaked from Liam's eyes. He reached forward, and Nashoma bowed his head. Liam's palm pressed into the air where Nashoma was standing. Though Liam couldn't touch Nashoma's spirit physically, I saw him shudder, like he felt something pass through his body.

The temple shook violently, and Liam fell to the side as he was knocked off his feet. I grabbed on to the edge of the offering table, so I wouldn't fall over. My friends yelled and held each other to stay upright.

Esis' ears perked up. *There is no more time. We must act now!*

No one had a chance to respond as the temple continued to shake. Esis raised his hands to the sky. From out of the clouds drifted all different types of creatures. At first, I thought they were more ancestors, but they did not glow with spirit. Instead, they were formed from an inky black color and glittered with white light. As dragons, griffins, and unicorns galloped out of the sky, they left behind trails of black wisps.

Starbeasts!

Esis had summoned his brothers and sisters, and he had become their commander. Pegasi, chimeras, and phoenixes circled through the sky, surrounding the temple with starlight. There were kirin and hippocampi, along with hundreds of other creatures, all who appeared to be created from the night sky.

Esis threw a fist into the air and let out a high-pitched battle cry. Nashoma lifted his chin and howled. Nashoma ran in a circle, then barked, as if sending a message to the ancestors. In turn, they each shifted back into their animal forms. Nashoma ran toward the edge of the room and leapt past the pillars. He floated in the sky, following the Starbeasts around the temple. The ancestors followed, until ancestral spirits and Starbeasts alike were swirling through the sky around us. Larger Familiars who couldn't fit in the temple took to the skies to join them. I spotted Julian flying alongside Nashoma and Esis, looking proud. Aisha and Eirakari were there, too.

I reached out for Liam, and we clung tight to each other as we watched the magnificent scene before us.

The ancestors and Starbeasts moved as one unit. The sound of flutes returned, and the creatures began to sing along to the tune. The shaking earth calmed, and the howl of the wind died down. The rain became nothing more than a drizzle. Above us, the dark storm clouds thinned until they cleared completely from the skies.

The scenery from up here was incredible. In the eastern sky, the sun was rising. To the west, we could still see the stars dotting the darkened sky.

"Sophia!" Liam pointed to the north, and I gasped. In the last bits of night, we could see Northern Lights gracing the sky, following the path of the ancestors as they calmed the storm.

Imogen and Jonah took hands, and they stepped toward us with their Familiars. Imogen wrapped her arm around my waist on one side, and Jonah draped his arm over Liam's shoulder on the other. We stood there, watching the Northern Lights as they faded with the rising sun.

Complete and utter peace overcame me. The storm calmed. Though we could still see fires below, trashed areas of forest, and crevices in the earth, it finally felt like it was all over. I could finally breathe again. We all could.

Which was why I was surprised when Showana appeared again. She stood in spirit form over the offering table, waiting for me.

I bowed my head to her. "Is it over?" I asked, a little wary that there was still more to come.

"There is one thing left to do," she said.

I held my breath.

"Years ago, the ancestors took away the Anichi's ability to bond, in order to protect them and their magic," Showana said. "The ancestors agreed that only when the Hawkei were united again would their power be restored. You, Sophia, have proven the Hawkei have outgrown their hatred. You showed what you're willing to sacrifice for others, and the ancestors believe that the Hawkei are ready for this change. And so, it is time for the power of healing to return to the tribe."

Showana lifted her hands, and the sky began to glow with spirit magic. It was so blinding that it shone brighter than the sun, creating a white sky that spanned as far as the eye could see. The sheet of Spirit magic began to lower across the landscape, giving the appearance that the sky was coming down to crush us. But it didn't crush us at all. The sheet of Spirit magic passed straight through us, as if blessing us with complete immersion in Anichi healing. All of my aches and scratches healed instantly, and Liam seemed to stand a little taller beside me.

The Spirit magic continued downward through the temple and toward the earth. I barely had a second to process it, because my attention was stolen by the sight of Chief Cauac before me. While the Spirit magic simply passed through everyone else, pieces of magic clung to the Anichi chief. His skin glowed bright white. He flipped his hands over and over, trying to make sense of what was going on. Beside him, his white jaguar companion glowed, too. The ebbing blue lines through his fur glowed with such intensity it was almost blinding.

Luana gasped and reached out for her father, as if she might be able to heal him, but he held up a hand to stop her.

"There is nothing to fear," Chief Cauac said as he signed to Luana. "I have bonded, and I am finally whole."

A tear streaked his face, and the glowing Anichi magic finally dimmed. Luana stared at him a few moments, then threw her arms around his neck. The two embraced. When they drew away, Chief Cauac smiled, then lifted his palm and conjured an orb of light.

You have magic! Luana signed enthusiastically.

Chief Cauac couldn't contain himself. He threw his arms into the air and gleefully cried to the ancestors, "The Anichi are free!"

Everyone in the room erupted into cheers of salvation and wonder. Where there was once grief, now there was celebration. The tribe had finally been saved.

"Ancestors!" Jonah squeaked. He threw himself in front of me and placed a hand on either of my shoulders. "You did it, Sophia! You fulfilled the prophecy! You restored glory to the greatest House!"

I'd gone breathless. I could hardly believe it was done. Before I could say anything, Jonah grabbed my face in his hands and planted a big, slobbery kiss right on my lips.

"Ancestors, Jonah!" I cried as I wiped my lips.

"Did you really have to—?" Liam started, but Jonah cut him off by kissing *him* next. "Bleh! What the fuck!"

Liam coughed as Jonah pulled away.

"The tribe is saved!" Jonah sang. "The Reject Team made it!"

"Anichi's magic is back!" Imogen squealed. Jonah grabbed her around the waist and hoisted her up over his shoulder. He twirled her so fast she couldn't stop laughing. Imogen tried to smack his ass, but she couldn't reach. "Put me down!"

Sassy barked, and she and Squeaks started dancing around the Summoning Room in celebration. Jonah caught sight of Jake and dropped Imogen on her ass. He rushed over to his husband and swept him into his arms. The two made out like they had a private room.

Imogen sucked a breath and rubbed her butt. "*Someone's* excited."

"He should be!" I said. "I can't believe we did it."

Imogen walked over and pulled me into a tight hug. "Did you ever doubt us?"

I scrunched up my nose. "A little."

Imogen swatted my shoulder. "Never again, you hear me? The Reject Team can do anything."

I smiled. "Yeah... I guess we can."

Imogen left to go celebrate with Cade, leaving Liam and I in private. Though we were in a room full of people, no one approached us, and it felt as if we were alone. It felt eerie to be totally alone with him. Neither of us were holding Ava-Marie. Esis wasn't circling my legs or trying to jump in Liam's hair. Julian wasn't nudging Liam for his attention. It made me really sad.

Liam reached up and pushed a strand of hair out of my face. "You're very brave, *pawee*. I never could've done what you did."

"But you did," I reminded him. "You just didn't have a choice when Nashoma died."

Liam stared down at me in a way that made my heart flutter. "Sometimes I wish I had the choice. But if I did, I never would've been around long enough to meet you."

I blinked back tears. "I love you, Liam. From the moon to the stars, to the sun and back. If it weren't for you, I never could have made the decision. This has been really fucking hard, but I know everything's going to be okay... because you're here."

Liam wrapped his arms around me and placed a gentle kiss to the top of my head. I shuddered under his touch, but it was a good shudder. "As long as the sun keeps chasing the moon through the sky, I will be here for you, *pawee*."

My heart warmed. I tilted my head up, and Liam's lips swooped down to meet mine. Kissing him now was like the first time all over again. The coolness of his lips met my hot skin. Where Fire and Water shouldn't mix, they swirled together as one. Because we were one now— one soul, one being... one tribe.

"You guys have to see this!" Amelia burst through the door to the Summoning Room. I hadn't even realized she'd left, but she was breathless, like she'd raced all the way up here.

I exchanged a glance with Liam, but Amelia's voice sounded pretty urgent. Everyone rushed to follow her downstairs, but Liam and I hesitated. The ancestral spirits and the Starbeasts had spread all across the landscape, many of them mere dots now. In the distance, I could see Julian flying with a group of dragons.

I held my breath, hoping for one last glimpse of Esis. Liam paused too, as if he thought the same about his Familiar.

Just as I was about to give up and head inside the temple, Nashoma and Esis appeared. They came from above the temple and flew downward. Nashoma's spirit was transparent against the rising sun, and Esis' form glittered on his back.

Nashoma gave a firm nod toward Liam. I was sure it meant something to Liam, though I wasn't sure what. Esis smiled proudly and offered one final wave. I waved back.

Then Nashoma turned, and he ran off with Esis toward the Starbeasts, disappearing into the morning sun. I didn't take my eyes off Esis until the last moment, when his glittering form eventually faded into dawn.

Already, I longed for his presence. But he had completed his destiny.

And so had I.

Liam wrapped an arm tight around my waist. "Come on, *pawee*. We should go."

Though I hoped to see Esis again, I knew he wasn't coming back. He was already gone, on his way to the Ancestral Lands with Nashoma. Taking a deep breath, I grabbed for Liam's hand. We were the last to leave the Summoning Room, but when we did, we left in peace.

Liam and I wove our way through tunnels back to the main entrance of the temple. As we got closer, we could make out the sounds of Familiars and Elementai alike. It was hard to tell what was going on, as each voice drowned out the next. At first, I thought there might be an argument. When we broke out of the tunnels and into the main cavern, however, I saw that the Hawkei were *celebrating*.

Anichi lights and shields were visible from every angle as Elementai tested out their new-found abilities. Some of them clung to creatures in tight embraces, like they'd finally bonded with their Familiars. Yapluma celebrated the end of the war by levitating themselves and doing flips in the air. Koigni shot huge flames into the air like fireworks, and Nivita made leaves fall from vines like confetti. Toaqua drew water from the damp walls to create fountains in celebration. Glitter rained down from alicorns flying overhead. Elementai sang, and Familiars danced.

Elementai flooded out of the temple to view the aftermath of the storm. Liam and I followed behind Amelia.

Outside, the aftermath was devastating. The trees that once concealed the temple had all toppled over. Huge crevices split the earth in horrifying fractures. The closest one had stopped mere yards away from the edge of the temple. Smoke billowed in the air from nearby forest fires, and the dirt had turned to thick mud from flooding. While Elementai inside the temple were celebrating, the atmosphere turned melancholy when we saw the devastation.

Haloke threw her hand over her mouth. "Ancestors," she breathed.

"No," Imogen protested. She looked from one sad face to the next. "No, you guys. Don't give up."

Chief Cauac frowned. "The reservation has been destroyed. Thousands of years of growth... gone."

"But we have our elements back!" Imogen reminded them. "The Anichi are the head House. *You* are the Spirit of the earth. We can heal it!"

Luana's eyes brightened. *She's right, pataa. Now is not the time to become hopeless. Let's do what our magic was meant to do.*

Chief Cauac stared at his daughter a moment longer before drawing himself up. He took a deep breath, then climbed onto the back of his companion. "Anichi," he said, his voice booming across the Elementai gathered. More and more continued to flood out of the temple. "My daughter has said it best. Today is not the day to become hopeless. Today marks a new era. Anichi's magic has been restored, but we must use it to restore our earth, and our tribe. Who's with me!?"

Though Chief Cauac addressed the Anichi, all the Elementai broke out in cheers. It didn't matter what House you belonged to, because we were one now.

Chief Cauac let out a victory cry, and his massive jaguar took off running into the decimated forest. Elementai followed as a sense of hope surged inside of them.

Liam squeezed my hand tightly. "Come on, *pawee*. What are we waiting for?"

I smiled. "Nothing."

I aimed my Anichi magic at the ground, and tendrils of light seeped into the dirt. I didn't know how I was still controlling the magic, since Esis wasn't here to draw from, but I found that it worked regardless. The Spirit magic was within my blood, and so, I'd carry it always.

All around me, Anichi followed my lead. Healing magic filled the earth, and fallen trees stood themselves back up. Crevices began to close in the earth, and the last bits of remaining drizzle ceased. Sunlight poured over us, warming my skin as we moved in the direction of Kinpago. Though other

Elementai helped, I could feel the pulse of Spirit magic beneath me, and knew that the earth would not heal without Anichi's blessing.

Toaqua used their magic to draw water out of the flooded earth and direct it toward nearby rivers that led to the ocean. Nivita repaired broken plants and forced the crevices in the ground to close. From a distance, I saw that the smoke from the burning fires were clearing as Koigni put out the flames. Yapluma calmed the winds and used their magic to assist Nivita. They blew dirt into the crevices to help close them up.

The march of the Hawkei continued across the reservation as we healed the earth. We could've been walking all day and it wouldn't have mattered, because we were working together and restoring our home.

Soon we came to the outskirts of Kinpago. We stood along the edge of a cliff, where we could see everything from this vantage point. Orenda Academy was far in the distance, but only a single tower remained standing. The hurricane waters had flooded the streets, and we could see hordes of women and children rushing for higher ground along the trails leading toward the Koigni village. The trees in the Nivita village had all been knocked over, the homes crushed beneath them. In the Yapluma village, houses had fallen from the sky, demolishing the buildings beneath. Out in the ocean, we could see rubble floating from what remained of the Toaqua village that was once laid out undersea.

"I'm taking a group to the Koigni village to speak with those who are left," Vanessa announced. Hordes of people followed her, but they weren't just from her tribe. There were people from every House willing to help.

"We'll fly to the Yapluma village," Jonah added, and Jake nodded in agreement. "We'll search for survivors."

"And we'll take the Nivita village," Imogen said, holding Cade's hand.

Liam's gaze was distant as he looked over the wreckage out at sea. He shook it off and went into chief mode. "I need Toaqua with me. We'll draw the hurricane waters from the town and push them back into the ocean."

Baine hurried to his side, along with Doya. "I will help wherever you need me, Chief," Baine said with a nod.

"And I will do whatever I can," Doya added. For the first time, Naomi bowed her head to Liam, surrendering to him as her chief.

That must've given Liam a boost of confidence, because he threw his shoulders back. A moment later, Julian swept out of the air. He landed just beside Liam and I. Liam jumped onto his back, then reached down to help me on.

Liam turned back to the tribe and threw a fist into the air as Julian reared on his hind legs. "One tribe!"

"One tribe!" they echoed back.

Even as Julian took to the skies, we could still hear the echoing of chants in the distance. Julian circled around Kinpago, and I got a full view of everything the Hawkei were doing to help each other. Though buildings were smashed and Kinpago was merely a pile of rubble, the tribe worked as a unit to restore their home. Yapluma used their Air magic to move away debris in a rescue mission. Toaqua evaporated the water flooding the streets, while Nivita cleared fallen trees and moved bricks and rocks. Koigni put out any remaining fires, then offered food and blankets to one another. The Anichi continued to funnel their healing magic into the earth, until I swore Kinpago was brighter than ever before.

Today, we'd truly become one tribe.

WHISKERS TICKLED the side of my face, and something wet wiped across my cheek.

"Esis," I groaned as I stirred awake. When I opened my eyes, however, it was not a white kurble staring down at me. She was brown. Buttercup licked me again.

"Hey, girl," I said, stroking her ears. She stopped licking my face and purred.

I glanced around the room, almost forgetting where I was. I had drifted off while resting on the couch in our home back in *Hok'evale*. The fireplace burned in my living room, and Ava-Marie's bouncer stood in the corner.

It'd been only a few days since the war, but already, it was starting to feel like a dream. Sometimes, I swore I heard Esis shuffling through the fridge or chittering in the next room.

Until the hollowness of grief struck, and I realized he was no longer here.

My heart sank as I was once again reminded of the loneliness growing inside. I placed my hand on my aching heart and inhaled a deep breath. I was grateful to be alive, and that the Hawkei were saved. My heart settled.

Someone cleared their throat across the room. I looked up to see Liam standing there, gazing down at me. "You okay, sleepyhead?"

I sat up on the couch. Buttercup curled up on my lap. She was still unbonded and had taken a particular liking to me. She never left my side. In a way, I guess she'd become my new companion.

Which was very helpful. I needed someone to help fill the cavern within me that'd been left since Esis had died.

"I didn't mean to fall asleep," I said. "How long was I out?"

Liam checked the clock on the wall. "An hour?"

"Ancestors! My parents will be here soon!" I cried, suddenly alert.

Liam crossed the room and sat beside me. He draped an arm around my shoulder. He took a deep, calming breath. "What do you say we visit the beach afterward?"

"I think that sounds lovely," I agreed.

Liam shifted on the couch and winced. Instinctively, I reached out and placed a hand on his chest. He didn't protest— just took deep breaths under my palm. I used intrafusion to summon Anichi magic from Buttercup, and I funneled the healing magic into him. Liam sighed, and his muscles relaxed.

"Better?" I asked.

He nodded. "Better."

I drew away from him and gazed down at my hands.

"What is it, *pawee*?" he asked.

I shrugged. "I just don't get how I'm still able to heal you. Esis is gone, and the Spirit Totem doesn't work anymore."

I gestured to the totem around my neck. Ever since I used it to summon the ancestors, the power didn't work. I still wore it out of habit, though the Spirit magic was drained completely out of it. The *Azaimperiai* was now useless.

"You still have Anichi magic in your blood," Liam pointed out.

"Yeah, but so does my mother, and she can't do Anichi magic. I thought I could do it because of the totem, and because Esis is Anichi."

"Well, we inherit our magic like any other genetic trait," Liam said thoughtfully. "Some genes are dominant over others, while other genes lie dormant— like how someone can have brown eyes but carry a blue-eyed gene. I imagine it's the same with magic. Doya carried the Anichi gene, but it's dormant in her, while your Koigni and Anichi genes are codominant and your Toaqua genes are dormant."

"Mmm..." I mused. "That makes sense."

A knock came at the door, and Liam and I both stiffened. After a beat, we stood and went to the door. Baine and Doya were standing there, Naomi between them.

"Hey," I said brightly. "Come in."

"To what do we owe the pleasure?" Liam asked as my parents entered.

Baine took a deep breath. "Well, we have some news."

The two joined hands, and I furrowed my brow. What sort of news could they possibly have to share?

"Ancestors," I breathed. "Are you pregnant?"

Doya shot me a glare. "Don't be ridiculous, Sophia. We're going on an expedition!"

Doya sounded really happy about it. Baine was smiling so big it looked like he had a hanger stuck sideways in his mouth.

"An expedition?" Liam sounded impressed. "But we already found the *Azaimperiai*. What else is there to search for?"

"Oh, lots!" Baine's eyes lit up. "There are hundreds of miles of tunnels in the cave system that are still unexplored."

"You're going spelunking?" I asked.

Baine tilted his head in confusion, like he didn't understand where I got that idea. "Ancestors, no. I'm ready to expand my horizons. I've decided to write a textbook about the Great Supernatural War."

"We'll be traveling all over the world and immersing ourselves into various supernatural cultures," Doya explained. "I'm very excited to meet the Midnight Gathering."

Of course she was enticed by vampires and succubi. It was like her to take interest in some of the most dangerous creatures on earth.

"I can't wait to find Atlantis," Baine said. "Mermaids have always fascinated me."

Liam winced. "Maybe start with something a little more tame?"

"Oh, we will," Baine replied chipperly. "We'll be starting in Connecticut. I have some connections from my time as a professor that should get us through the coven's protection spell."

"The Miriamic Coven?" Liam balked. "The witches who gave us the Omnimotus Curse and sold us nightshade?"

Baine fumbled with his words. "W-well, yes. But I'm sure they're not *all* bad. After we visit the coven, we'll be headed to Malovia in Europe."

Liam tilted his head. "Aren't the fae in a war with their monarchy right now?"

"We'll be fine," Baine said, like it was no big deal. "Malovia is a tame country."

Doya shot him a glance. I got the sense that Baine was underestimating the conflict in Malovia. The fae didn't exactly have a reputation for being nice.

"How long will you be gone?" I asked.

Baine shrugged. "Could be a few months. Could be up to a year. We don't know for sure."

That was typical of my *pataa*. He was always so unorganized.

"Well, in that case, take this." I reached up and pulled the Spirit Totem from around my neck. I handed it to Baine.

He blinked down at it, looking touched. "But Sophia... this is—"

"The *Azaimperiai*, I know," I said. "Its magic is gone. I want you to have it for good luck."

Baine placed his fingers to his mouth and looked like he was about to cry. I hadn't realized it when I handed it over, but now I knew how much an artifact like this meant to him— even if it didn't have any power left.

"Thank you, my daughter," Baine said, sounding choked up.

I turned to my mother. "Are you sure you'll be all right on your travels?"

Doya held her nose high. "Yes, of course. I've made all the arrangements."

Doya sounded eager to leave. I didn't think it'd be easy for her to stay after everything that happened. She wanted a break from the Elementai world.

"Well, I hope you guys have a lot of fun," I told them honestly.

Just then, the sound of a carriage pulling up outside caught my attention. I practically jumped on the couch to look out the window. My heart leapt in excitement when I saw who had arrived.

"They're here!" I cried. I rushed outside, and the others followed. Buttercup scurried so close to my feet that I nearly tripped over her.

My parents' carriage stood parked out front. It was a beautiful day at the end of May. The air was crisp, and the sun was shining.

"Ancestors, there she is!" I cried as my mother pulled my daughter out of her car seat. Ava-Marie's eyes glimmered, and she made a loud noise of joy when she saw me.

I took Ava-Marie tightly in my arms and began bawling. She looked like she'd grown so much in the short time she'd been away. She laughed as I nuzzled my face in her hair. I inhaled her familiar scent and let peace wash over me. Ava's hands curled around my hair, and she tugged hard, but I didn't care. Holding her again was like taking the most precious magical artifact the world had ever known into my arms. She was incredible and fragile, and I'd be there always to take care of her.

"She missed you two so much," my dad said.

"But she was a trooper," Mom added.

Liam wrapped an arm around me and the other around Ava as he kissed his daughter's forehead. "We missed her, too."

"I'm so glad to have her back," I whispered.

Doya came up to me and held her arms out. "Can I hold her? I'd like to say goodbye before we leave."

Though it was difficult, I wiped my tears and placed Ava-Marie in my mother's outstretched arms. Baine baby-talked to her and waved the Spirit Totem in front of her like a rattle. Ava reached for it and laughed. She seemed so happy to be back. I felt so blessed that we'd gotten her out of *Hok'evale* in time. She'd never know the destruction that passed through our home.

I turned to my adoptive parents. "Thank you guys so much for taking her."

"It was our pleasure," my dad said.

"We'll take her anytime," Mom offered.

Doya and Baine took their time saying goodbye. Eventually, my adoptive parents decided to check in on their foster kids, while Liam and I dressed Ava-Marie for the beach. Liam carried her down the path, tickling her and humming the Elementai's song to her. Ava-Marie stared up at him in awe, totally at ease in his arms.

We passed by Jake's house and spotted him out on the porch. He and Jonah were lounging on matching beach chairs beneath the natural rock awning carved into the side of the canyon. They each had a cold beer in their hands, and were watching Sabor and Squeaks teach their baby hippogriffs how to fly. I expected to see Jake barking orders like normal, but it was clear the guy really needed some time off.

Jonah waved us over, glee on his face. "*Oh em gee*, Ava's back!"

He drew a sip of beer and smacked his lips as he set it down. He ran down the porch steps and reached out for Ava-Marie.

Liam drew away. "Not while you've been drinking."

Jonah rolled his eyes. "It's not like I'm *drunk*."

"Don't listen to my husband," Jake teased. "He's toasted. Can't stop talking about getting the D every five seconds."

I snickered. "Isn't that normal?"

Jake shrugged. "Touché."

"What are you guys up to?" Jonah asked.

"We were just hanging with Sophia's parents," Liam said. "Now we're taking Ava to the beach."

"Sophia's parents?" Jonah asked. "Which ones?"

"All of them," I said. "Baine and Doya stopped by before my other parents came with Ava-Marie. Apparently, they're leaving on vacation soon so Baine can do research for his new book."

Jonah's eyebrows shot up. "Baine's going to write a book? Where are they going?"

"Everywhere," Liam said. "At least, anywhere supernaturals live. They're headed to Connecticut first, then Malovia—"

"What a coincidence!" Jonah squealed. "Jake and I were *just* talking about honeymooning in Malovia, weren't we, Jakey? Maybe we'll run into them."

Liam shrugged. "Maybe. Are you guys up for the beach?"

Jonah took a long breath and stretched out on his chair again. "Nah, we've got a case of beer to finish up. Gotta drink 'em while they're cold. We're hitting up the hot springs afterward, though."

Liam frowned. "Uh, spare me the details. We'll see you guys later."

"Yeah, see ya," Jake said with a wave.

We continued through town toward the beach. Liam kept pointing out various Familiars to Ava-Marie. She really loved animals. Buttercup followed along, picking flowers and weaving them together into a crown. She placed it on her head proudly.

We passed through the town square. All around us, people were dressed in white t-shirts with an emblem showing all the House colors and symbols in one design. On the backs of the shirts read *#OneTribe*. Some were sitting at tables, while others rushed this way and that. I couldn't make out what was going on. I noticed Amelia and stopped her.

"Hey, Am, what's happening?" I asked.

Amelia was carrying a stack of water bottles. Kiwi was perched on top of them. She looked a little surprised to see me. "Liam didn't tell you?"

She glanced to Liam, who got a guilty expression on his face. "I wanted to give her a few days off."

Amelia winced. "Whoops. Cat's out of the bag. Trace and I started a humanitarian aid group called One Tribe. Liam approved it, and we got everyone in on it! We're distributing as many supplies as we can to those in need. Once everyone's taken care of, we'll be working on rebuilding Kinpago, then the *Hozho*."

I glanced around at the volunteers. I caught sight of Vanessa and Bren in the distance. They stopped a carriage packed with supplies at someone's door and approached the house in person to deliver supplies to the tribe. Nearby, Imogen and Cade were seated at a picnic table, studying what looked to be blueprints of the Orenda Academy castle. They were planning on restoring it.

My jaw hung slack. "Wow, Am. That's amazing and... ambitious."

She shrugged, like it didn't bother her one bit. "Someone's gotta do it."

"I want to help," I offered.

Amelia frowned. "I see why Liam didn't tell you right away. You *just* got Ava back. You can start helping tomorrow, but today, you're taking the day for your family."

Amelia was bossy, like always. She wasn't giving me a choice.

"Fine." I sighed. "But first thing tomorrow morning, I want one of those shirts."

Amelia chuckled. "I'll save you one. In the meantime, I've got places to be. See ya, sis."

Amelia hurried off, and Liam and I continued through the square. The sound of music caught my attention, and Ava-Marie cooed when she heard it. The music was soft and smooth, like the sound of wind chimes. I looked over to see Professor Amber's Familiar playing the flute, while Professor Amber played a singing bowl. Luana and Sam were next to them, dancing slowly and deliberately. A group of at least twenty people followed their lead. It looked like some sort of meditation.

Liam noticed me watching curiously. "Looks like Luana's picked up a new healing method."

I eyed the class and noticed that most of them had been people who'd been severely injured in the war. Anichi magic had healed them, but it only went so far. Luana was helping them learn to heal themselves.

"It looks really peaceful," I said, almost wanting to jump in.

"We'll have to try it sometime," Liam offered.

"I'm sure Luana would love to teach us."

We left the square and made it to the beach. *Hok'evale* had been untouched by the hurricane, so the beach was spotless. There weren't many people there, though. I liked to think it was because so many were helping with the clean-up, but I knew the truth. We'd lost so many people in the war that houses now lay empty and most public places were bare.

Down the beach, I could make out Haloke's house. Beatrice was balancing Jackson on her shoulders, and the orangutan-like companion was working on corralling other kids for lunch. Most of the children were orphans, though I noticed Wyatt and Mia helping out, Mattias on Mia's hip.

At least twenty dragons lay in the sand, including Julian, Eirakari, and

Aisha. They were the few lucky ones who hadn't been severely injured in the war. Haloke walked from dragon to dragon, giving them water and ensuring they were all well taken care of.

Not far from the house, Maddie and Drew stood with their feet in the ocean. Drew held a huge basket that looked like it was woven by hand. Maddie reached into the basket and pulled out flowers. Each was different — roses, daisies, and tulips. She placed each flower in the waves and watched as they were carried out to sea.

"Is Maddie okay?" I asked Liam as we found a spot to sit in the sand.

Liam glanced down the beach at his sister. "It's going to be harder for her. She'll always think she could've done something to prevent it."

"But she'll be okay, right?" I asked hopefully.

"I think so." Liam sighed. "She just needs some time."

"We all do," I said as I spotted another woman.

She was on the opposite side of us, all the way down at the end of the beach where an outcropping of rocks began. Stevie sat at the highest point, running her hands over her belly. The air gently passed through her hair as she stared out at sea. Even from here, I could see the sorrow in her features. Her bird-fish hybrid jumped out of the water and slid across the rocks toward her. Stevie reached out to pet Nihoni's scaly feathers.

"It's not easy for any of us," Liam admitted. "We all lost a lot. Some of us more than others..."

Liam gazed down at Ava-Marie. He set her in the sand, and she ran her fingers through it. She laughed when the waves came up to tickle her toes. Liam's features had never looked so soft. It was very clear he didn't take Ava-Marie nor I for granted.

"How are you holding up, *pawee*?" Liam asked.

I didn't answer right away. I took a deep breath and stared out at the calm ocean, really considering the question. Esis was gone, and that made me really sad, but my insides weren't twisting like I thought they should.

"To be honest, I feel at peace," I admitted. "I mean, if I had the choice to bring Esis back, I would. But..."

"But you're okay if he never returns," Liam finished for me.

I smiled sadly. He understood exactly. "I know it all had a purpose, and that Esis did the right thing. He gave himself up so that we could start over. A new beginning— a genesis."

Liam and I both stilled at the same time. Ava-Marie kept on playing in the sand, but Liam and I exchanged a look.

"Gen-*esis*," Liam emphasized.

"Holy shit!" I threw my hand over my mouth when I let the curse slip out. "I didn't name Esis, Liam! When I bonded, I asked what his name was, and he made this sound that I thought was *Esis*. I missed half of it. He's *Genesis*. He's origin— he's the beginning of something."

Liam's features turned calculating. "So he really *did* know all this time."

"That's what he told me. It's still hard to believe. I'm going to miss him so much. Do you think it's true he's always there? Or do you think he's off doing work in the Ancestral Lands?"

Just then, a wave came up and tickled the bottom of my toes. As the wave receded, something hard stuck under my foot. I pulled away to see a shiny rock had been swept out of the sea. I picked it up and laughed.

"What is it?" Liam asked.

I held out the rock to show him. "It looks like something Esis would give me, doesn't it?"

Liam nodded. "Sure is."

"I think it *is* from Esis— a sign. He's out there watching over me." I clutched the rock tightly in my fingers and held it to my chest. My fingers touched the key I always wore— the one Liam found at our waterfall and gave to me on our wedding day. I wanted to keep the rock close to that, to hang it off the chain. I couldn't help but smile.

Liam watched me. "You look happy."

Happy was a stretch. "I'm... at peace."

I closed my eyes and took a deep breath to let the words sink deep into my heart. They felt fitting. When I opened my eyes, Liam swept his hands in front of me. Like a painting across canvas, colors began to bleed from the sky. Water droplets rose from the ocean, creating a magnificent rainbow over the water.

"Liam," I breathed. "It's beautiful."

"That's how our world should be now," he said. "Beauty, peace... nothing else."

I gazed down at Ava-Marie. She embodied perfection. "I agree. I don't want Ava to ever go through what we did. I want to build a better life for her."

"We will," Liam stated. "That's why we're here, isn't it?"

I turned to him. He had a contemplative look on his face, like he still wasn't sure why we'd been left behind without our Familiars.

"I've been thinking a lot about that," I admitted. "Like Luana said in the temple, there's life after death, so what were we afraid of? We could've given up and gone to the Ancestral Lands. But I don't think the Ancestral Lands serve us in the way we need."

Liam tilted his head. "What do you mean?"

"In the Ancestral Lands, there is no hardship, only peace," I pointed out. "But we can't know the light without the dark. We're here on earth for the ancestors to teach us. We're here to learn what appreciation and gratitude are, to learn the value of serving others— to experience and become deeply comfortable with love and passion and all these wonderful things that contrast the bad. The ancestors left us without our Familiars because we have a purpose, Liam, and I think I finally know what that is."

His features were soft, like he welcomed the idea. "What's our purpose, *pawee?*"

I clutched Esis' rock in my hands and stared out at the rainbow. "*We* become teachers now. You're chief, and I'm an Elder. We must share these vital lessons— not just with our daughter, but with the tribe. It's our duty to lead the tribe into a new age."

Liam took my hand. The two of us stared down at Ava-Marie as she gleefully crawled through the sand, happily slapping at the calm waves whenever they came close enough.

"We will, *pawee,*" Liam promised. "We'll teach the tribe a new way. Together."

I knew that promise was true. After everything we'd been through— the Elemental Cup, the trial, riots, battles, and more— there was only one thing left for the tribe to do.

Heal.

EPILOGUE

One Year Later

Life was different now in a way I could've never conceived before. The days of war and tyranny amongst the Hawkei were over. Instead, there was peace.

The harmony our ancestors had always told us about was finally here. It seemed a fairy-tale land— like heaven. If you had asked me years ago if people could change, if they could get past their prejudices to form a bright future, I would've been cynical.

But miracles did happen, because I'd seen one take place before my very eyes. The Elementai truly were one tribe now. House lines and divides didn't seem to matter anymore. The only thing that did was the fact we were all a family now. And we were willing to work toward a brighter future together.

As the spring sunlight filtered in through our window, yellow and warm, I turned into Sophia. The early morning felt like a new beginning as I pressed myself against her, tangled up in the white sheets.

Every day was like that now. Full of hope. There was a time when every morning left me with a feeling of dread and despair. I never thought I'd ever be happy like this. I'd wanted my life to end.

I'd been foolish. I would've missed all this.

I pressed my nose into Sophia's hair and began kissing down her neck.

Sophia shifted and let out a tiny moan. Her eyes fluttered open. She eyed my bare chest in approval as she said, "Someone's happy to see me."

"I'm always happy to see you." I continued kissing her collarbone, over her breasts and down her stomach. Sophia giggled, before she hitched a breath as my mouth trailed over her hip bones. I took off her panties and pushed her nightgown up, so I could taste her. Sophia's back arched, and her hands fisted in the blankets as I pleasured her with my tongue, savoring the sound of her heavy moans.

A high-pitched wail broke the soft silence. I lifted my head, and Sophia turned to listen.

"Baby's crying," she whispered.

"I got it. Stay in and rest." I shifted upward from the bed. "We'll have to continue this later."

Sophia entwined her arm with mine. "I hope that's a promise, Chief Mitoh."

I squeezed her elbow. "It's a fact."

Sophia grinned. "Jonah and Imogen would say we're addicted to making more kids."

"And what do they know?" I kissed Sophia deeply, before I left her to drift back into dreamland. My steps were quiet as I closed the door behind myself.

Sophia and I had moved our family back to my family mansion in Kinpago. My mother had offered it to us voluntarily. She was staying behind in the beach house in *Hok'evale*, to raise my siblings there. She said though she loved our old house, she could never go back— too many memories, though she insisted the place was fit for a chief.

I didn't mind being back home. It was comforting raising my children in the home where I'd grown up. My mother had enlisted the help of Beatrice to watch Jackson and the other kids while she worked a day shift as a dragonologist once again.

It was nice she was getting back to something she loved. She'd missed her career, and her return to it was one of the few things keeping her going after my dad and Ezra had died.

I passed Ava-Marie's room, which was my old bedroom. She was still silent inside. I went to the next door and opened it.

"Hey, little man. What are you crying about?" I hushed. I reached into the crib and picked up my newborn son. His wails dulled to a soft whimpering. I brushed down his black hair, which was all over the place, and wiped a bit of drool away from his tan skin. He hiccupped, and my heart softened.

Already, he looked so much like my brother. Sophia had said she wanted to name him Ezekiel... our little Ez.

Yeah, I'd broken down when she told me that. Though this past year had been full of peace, there were still wounds to heal. Ezra was a loss I'd never get over. And I was reminded of his death every time I looked in the mirror.

But once we discovered Sophia was pregnant with Ezekiel, that loss had ebbed somehow. Sophia had a flawless water birth in our home, and I'd been the one to catch him when he came out. There'd been no complications with her labor this time, and she was able to recover quickly, though Ezekiel had been a bigger baby than Ava-Marie.

Ezekiel fussed in my arms and gave a soft noise. Unlike his sister, Ezekiel was the easiest baby on earth. We'd quickly learned that Ezekiel cried when he was hungry, and slept the rest of the time. After I changed him, I took him down to the kitchen and fed him a bottle. He sucked on it greedily, going cross-eyed.

The sound of closing cabinets got my attention. Buttercup was rifling through the kitchen, looking for food.

"Sophia will be down in a minute," I told her. Buttercup gave an impatient sigh. It should've irked me, but it only made me grin. I was glad to have a kurble around, even if Buttercup couldn't replace Esis.

I really missed the little guy. Watching Sophia give up her Familiar was even more painful than losing Nashoma had been. I didn't want my wife, the love of my life, experiencing the same dreadful agony that I had, carrying around the same dead weight that would never go away.

Yet Sophia took it all in stride. Even on her bad days, she carried herself with a grace and acceptance I could never achieve, surviving her grief.

And I had helped her through it. I pampered Sophia endlessly since she'd lost Esis. I desired to make this easier than it had been on me.

Sophia kept herself busy with the kids and school. Orenda Academy had been rebuilt, and she'd returned to finish up her education. Once she graduated, Sophia planned to open up a photography and graphic design business, alongside being a stay-at-home mom.

I supported her every decision. It would keep her preoccupied. And her mind off what she'd sacrificed for us all.

I heard footsteps coming down the stairs. Sophia had wrapped herself in a robe and was carrying Ava-Marie. Sophia set our daughter down, and Ava's smile brightened when she saw me. "Daddy!"

"Hey, sweetheart." I smiled as she came running over. Her eyes glittered as she set them on Ezekiel, and affection bloomed in my chest. That was my favorite thing to be called now. Daddy.

Ava-Marie was a year-and-a-half, and she was so smart. She could almost speak in full sentences, and insisted on picking out her own outfits. Today, she'd had Sophia put her hair up in two pigtails, and had chosen a pink unicorn shirt, a purple tutu, green polka-dot tights and mismatching tennis shoes.

Her outfit resembled a rainbow. Ava *hated* wearing matching colors. She'd definitely gotten her sense of fashion from Imogen and Jonah, not from us.

"*My* baby," Ava-Marie said, laying a gentle hand on Ezekiel's forehead.

"No, Ava. We've been over this. *Our* baby," I said.

Ava-Marie made a face. Since Ezekiel had arrived, she'd made him her own personal doll, and didn't want to share.

Sophia began pulling boxes out of the cupboard to make pancakes, and Buttercup clapped eagerly. I set Ezekiel in the playpen on his back, and Ava-Marie watched him carefully through the netting. "I can help."

"You've had a long week at work. Let me," Sophia said.

I was grateful for her offer. My work as a chief never ended, and even small breaks were to be cherished. I'd been pulling long hours with Vanessa and the rest of the chieftains, to restore Kinpago and get the tribe back to a sense of normalcy. We'd come a long way, and our efforts had paid off. The city was rebuilt, and the tribe had recovered. All there was left to do was lead the Hawkei into a new future.

As she cooked, Sophia fiddled with the stone around her neck— the last gift Esis had given her. Sophia's eyes were far off this morning. I could tell she was thinking about Esis.

"It's been a year today," she whispered. "But it only feels like yesterday. Even after all this time, I still can't believe he's gone."

I dropped my voice. "You handle it much better than I did," I said. "I was a mess."

"I had you," she said. "That's the only reason why. I can't imagine how you survived, doing this on your own."

"I nearly didn't." I squeezed her shoulder. "But then you guys came along. You saved me just as much as I saved you."

Sophia's voice quivered as she took a breath. "I don't know if I'm ready for this."

"You'll never be ready." I wrapped her in a hug. "But it's time to say goodbye."

Ava-Marie's eyes were watching us. She didn't understand what was happening.

We hadn't had a formal funeral for Esis. There wasn't a body to bury after he'd left. But Sophia had determined she wanted a memorial for him, and I agreed. We were to meet up with Imogen and Jonah soon, to put it in place and give our final farewells.

Sophia wanted to do it on Ancestors' Day. Now that the day was here, it almost looked like she had reservations. Like she was still holding on to a small piece of him she didn't want to let go.

But she would let him go. And her healing would continue, as mine did.

Ava-Marie *insisted* on having sprinkles on her pancakes. Damn, the kid was bossy. She must've learned it from Amelia. She and Trace were putting the final touches on constructing the *Hozho II*, and were planning on sailing off into a permanent vacation. They didn't want kids and had chosen to spend their lives traveling. It helped they'd both been employed as co-captains of the ship.

Hey, it paid to know the chosen one.

Once breakfast was done, Sophia and I got ready while Ezekiel gurgled and Ava-Marie shouted at us to hurry up. When Sophia emerged from our bedroom, her hair was curled, and she was wearing a blue dress— one of her favorites and one of Esis', too.

She still made me breathless. Probably would for the rest of my life. Sophia fitted a bag around her shoulder, indicating we should be off.

"Daddy, hurry!" Ava-Marie yanked on my hand, though she didn't know where we were heading, only that we were going somewhere. As we stepped outside, Julian groaned. He was lying on the beach, and several tiny dragons were hopping up and down on his stomach. He looked exhausted.

Recently, Julian and Aisha had mated and had eggs. Their babies were constantly playing with Squeaks' hatchlings, who liked to romp on the beach. The baby hippogriffs jumped in the ocean and splashed Julian in the face. He didn't do anything, just took it in stride.

"You look as worn out as I feel," I told Julian with a laugh. He gave a weary puff of smoke.

We took the boat to shore while Julian, his babies and the hippogriffs flew overhead. Imogen and Jonah were waiting for us on the docks. Squeaks gave a chirp as her babies soared, while Sassy twirled in place to greet us.

Ava-Marie screeched when she saw them. She barely gave me time to tie the boat off before she ran at Imogen and Jonah full-speed, jumping into their arms.

"Hey, you little monster," Jonah said. He and Imogen held Ava-Marie between them as she hugged them tight. "Love your outfit today."

Ava-Marie tugged at the bows in her hair. Imogen set her down. As she did, a new sparkling engagement ring shone on Imogen's hand— a square-cut emerald on a gold ring.

Cade had proposed to Imogen after she'd returned to Orenda Academy last fall. Alongside her studies, Imogen had been hired as the head of interior design at the academy, and was busy redecorating the new castle. She planned to divide her time between cryptozoology and design once she got her degree, as she and Jonah were developing a fashion line together. Cade was working as a manager at the unicorn stables, and had clearly never been happier.

"Look what I got you." Imogen revealed a tiny hairbrush, which was covered in pink rhinestones.

Ava-Marie squealed with glee as Imogen placed the brush in her hands. Imogen looked at us. "I knew she'd love it, seeing as how she likes to play with hair."

That was an understatement. Ava-Marie was *obsessed* with long hair. She wanted to mess with mine and Sophia's constantly. "She's never going to put that down, you know," I said.

"Let her be happy." Sophia's smile was wistful. She adjusted Ezekiel against her as she started forward. We began walking up the path, winding into the woods.

"I haven't seen you two around," I said. It'd only been a few days, but still— I missed them whenever they were gone. We got together for dinner every Sunday at my house, but sometimes, I wanted more than that. We all had responsibilities now and couldn't see each other every day.

Still. I wished we could.

"Cade needed my help at the stables. Wedding planning has been driving us nuts," Imogen said.

"*Nobody* saw me yesterday but my husband. Jake bought new ropes. It was very Fifty Shades of *Gay*," Jonah purred.

"Jonah," Sophia scolded, with a look at Ava-Marie. But Ava wasn't listening. She was running after Buttercup, trying to comb her hair with the new brush.

"Hey, I'm busy now!" Jonah countered. "We don't get time to mess around like we used to."

Jonah's wedding had been wild. I'm shocked we survived. It was as over-the-top as we expected it all to be. The reception had gone on past four in the morning. We'd been thrown out of the venue before we wandered up the street to another bar, and been tossed out of that one, too. I might've woken up in a field somewhere after I'd passed out from one too many drinks.

I watched Ava-Marie carefully as she rode on Squeaks' back to Kinpago. I knew Squeaks wouldn't let her drop, but still.

"Lighten up, man," Jonah said as he walked by Squeaks' side. "I got her."

I scowled. "You know I'm overprotective."

"I'm a father now. I know how that goes," Jonah said.

As the trees broke into the entrance to Kinpago, we saw Jake. He gave a wave. Tucked in his other arm was a tiny bundle, a baby only a few months older than Ezekiel.

Jonah hurried ahead. He bent down to gush at the little girl. "Oh my gosh! Who's the cutest baby ever! Who's my little Josee? Come to daddy!"

Jake handed Jonah the infant. Jonah cooed as he cradled the little one. I was happy to acknowledge Jonah had gotten over his fear of babies; because he kind of was forced to.

"How's she been sleeping?" Sophia asked. She came closer to observe the small baby, who had dark hair and tan skin.

"Like a dream," Jake responded. "Hardly any trouble."

My throat tightened, and I had to look away. Jonah caught the look on my face. "You want to hold her, Liam?"

"Not yet." I would someday. But I couldn't now.

We continued our walk through town. Imogen said, "So, did you and Jake stop by the maternity ward yet? There's still things you need to pick up."

Jake bristled, and Jonah shook his head. "We haven't been there. Not since Stevie..."

Jonah's words drifted off, and nobody said anything more. Josee gave a squeal in Jonah's arms, and he soothed her.

I hated to say I'd won the death bet. It wasn't a game I ever desired to win. After Ezra died, Stevie lost the will to live. And you couldn't do that with our disease— give up. Because it would kill you. Stevie had fought as hard as she could, but she'd died hours after giving birth. Sophia and I were ready to take her child in, but before we could do so, she asked Jonah and Jake to give her daughter a home.

They'd accepted her with open arms. Jonah had chosen the name. Luana had tried to heal Stevie, but there was nothing that could be done to save her, and she passed away shortly after.

I knew Stevie was with Ezra now, but I still wished she was here with all of us. Even if only for Josee's sake.

There'd been quite a bit of money in the death bet pool from both of us. After she'd passed away, I'd taken the money and donated it to rare disease research. As much as Stevie and I had joked about blowing the cash once one of us had died, I knew that's what she would've done if I had gone first.

Stevie's brother Teagan and I were the only ones left now that were still alive with our disease. It felt lonely. And scary. He'd been devastated after his sister's death. But he knew our home was open if he ever needed to talk, and Josee would know that, too. She was my niece, our family. Jake and Jonah would raise her as their own, and we'd tell her stories about her parents, so she'd never forget them.

"Anyway," Jonah said with a sigh. "I've been working on wrapping up my thesis. It's nearly done!"

"You should take a break," Jake said, with slight disapproval. "I know it helps our schedule when you stay up to study with the baby, but you're pushing yourself too hard."

"Babe, how do you expect me to become a *dean* if I don't impress the board?" Jonah protested, and the rest of us held back a groan.

After the war, Jonah had been offered the open position of Dean of Yapluma— *after* he graduated with his master's. He'd shoved it down our throats almost as badly as the Storm Lord crap. He and Jake had moved up to the Air Kingdom and were renovating the palace there to live in.

Because obviously, Jonah wouldn't take anything less than a throne.

The Yapluma village had been destroyed in the war, so most of the Air tribe was moving back up to the Air Kingdom, where they felt they belonged. Jake was working with the Yapluma tribe to get the village in order, but once that was done, he had a job lined up working at the stables. Cade had expanded them to make a hippogriff area, and Jake was chomping at the bit, literally, to get there to start breeding them.

Yapluma had taken to calling Jonah *My lord*, which was already really fucking irritating. When Jonah wasn't taking graduate classes at Orenda, he was prancing around in his palace doing what he called *general Storm Lord shit*.

With all that and a new baby, I didn't know how he had time to breathe, but every so often Jonah popped by to annoy us.

And yes, I loved him for it.

A green luna moth fluttered in front of our faces, holding a tiny note. "Hello, Sierra," Sophia said kindly. She handed Ezekiel off to me, then unrolled the note from Sierra's tiny feet. Sierra fluttered away, and Sassy danced on her back legs to give her a goodbye.

"Luana sends her love," Sophia said as she pocketed the note. "She'll be by tomorrow to see all of us."

Luana still lived with the Anichi tribe, teaching her people how to use their newfound healing powers. But she visited often, and people traveled so frequently from Kinpago to *Hok'evale* they were one city now. Even with the distance between us, it seemed you couldn't break the unification between our people. We'd learned our lesson from the war and were ready to move forward, not back.

Sam was there with her. They were taking their relationship steady and slow. A few others had remained in *Hok'evale*. Isabella and Riley were together now, along with Tabitha and Hudson. Mr. and Mrs. Henley had retired on the beach, in a house not too far from my mother's. They'd all agreed there was nothing left for them in Kinpago and wanted to continue on with simple lives in the Anichi village.

We passed Carter and James, who were sitting at a café table nearby. They were holding hands, and their reptile Familiars lay around them in a circle. Carter raised a hand to me, and I waved back.

For the few people that had stayed behind in *Hok'evale*, most had decided to come back home. I'd hired Sean Andre, Vanderbilt's son, to be my own personal lawyer after he'd gotten a position working for tribal law. Never knew when you were gonna need a lawyer around here.

I saw Vanessa and Bren passing out boxes in front of brand new houses. Since the war, she'd started the Koigni Outreach Initiative, a group that was dedicated to help the Koigni make reparations to the other Houses, especially the Anichi tribe. Relations between Houses now were more important than ever before, and Vanessa was doing her best to make up for the mistakes of Koigni's past.

A woman stood at the edge of a construction site nearby, holding a clipboard. As she turned, I recognized Mia. Taryn barked and wagged her tail at Mia's side. She gave a nod to us before she went back to work, giving instructions to the builders.

Mia was opening up a women's shelter in Kinpago. She and Wyatt were married now, and she was expecting her second child— a daughter. While Wyatt was busy serving as an Elder, Mia had her hands full building a place where victims of assault and domestic violence could recover. She'd grown a lot in the time I knew her. She was a new person.

As were we all.

Jonah sighed as he took in our surroundings. "Everything's changed now. The city is almost back to the way it was. Looks like the tribe is tying up all the loose ends."

"Not everything." Imogen's tone was surly. I knew what she was getting at.

Jaymin Riske had never been found. We weren't sure if she was dead or alive, and to be honest, we didn't care. So long as she stayed the hell out of our lives.

Sophia placed a hand on Imogen's shoulder. "The past is in the past," she said gently. "We have to let it stay there."

Imogen nodded slightly. She knew, as all of us did, we couldn't go digging up old grudges. If we continued to carry around all the wounds the war had given us, we'd die from them. As the seasons changed, we had to continue to move on.

"Yoo hoo! Sophia!"

A woman waved up ahead. Sophia's face broke into a wide smile. "Mother!"

Sophia ran. She flung herself at Madame Doya and squeezed her tight. Beside her, Professor Baine was heaving for air after carrying a million bags. He set the suitcases down and wiped his brow.

"You're back!" Sophia said. Naomi purred and brushed her head against Sophia's leg.

"It was a very long trip," Doya said sourly. She looked at Ezekiel and immediately brightened. "I haven't met *you*, little one."

I knew I didn't have a choice, so I handed him off to Doya. Doya took Ezekiel in her arms and kissed him on the forehead. He blinked and spat up a bit of drool.

Baine gave Sophia a hug, then leaned over Ezekiel to observe him. "He looks just like—"

Sophia elbowed him, and Baine gave a quick glance at me. "Yes. Well. He's a fine baby, Liam."

"I can clean him up," Sophia offered as Ezekiel continued to spit all over the front of Doya's dress.

"It's nothing." Doya took her sleeve and wiped his mouth— something I'd never thought she'd do. "We're sorry we missed the birth, Sophia."

Doya narrowed her eyes at Baine. "We were *delayed*."

Baine blew out a breath that made his lips sputter. "Don't look at me! It wasn't my fault!"

"Yes it was," Doya snapped. "The sirens tried to eat us! They put you on a roasting spit while I did my damndest to get us out!"

"I was looking for *mermaids*, my dear. How was I to know Atlantis was in the other direction?" he asked.

"How did the rest of your trip go?" I said, trying to break up the quarrel.

"Oh, simply *splendid*, if you don't account all the times we nearly died," Doya said scathingly.

Sounded like a typical trip with Baine. Yet he wasn't willing to let it go. "It was an *adventure*," Baine whined, like that made up for all the mishaps.

"An adventure! Let me count all the ways we almost perished." Doya handed Ezekiel off to Sophia and began counting on her fingers. "First, we went to the Miriamic Coven, where we were nearly *hanged* by religious fanatics. If it wasn't for Nadine and Lucas, or whatever the hell their names were, we would've perished. Then we visited the Midnighters, which I was *very much* looking forward to—"

"Until you were seduced by a vampire," Baine finished, and he crossed his arms in a pout. "And forgot all about me."

"By the ancestors, Elliot, it was *magic*. I didn't sleep with the vampire, I just flirted with him!" Doya flung her arms skyward. "He compelled me. And for the last time, nothing happened."

Baine stuck out his lip. He was the jealous type. "You can't say it was a wasted trip. The Celestials were very welcoming," he countered. "Angels are by far the politest."

Doya slapped a hand to her face. "I didn't feel that way when the bastards almost drowned me."

"Why'd they do that?" Sophia asked.

"They may have caught your father and I together in one of their sacred temples," Doya said as she rubbed her forehead. "It was his idea."

"I take it you weren't sharing a kiss," I joked.

Doya gave a groaning sound. "Hardly. They accused us of desecrating the temple with carnal lust, and demanded we be baptized to cleanse us of our sins. I must've swallowed a gallon in that river they dragged us to."

"You're exaggerating." Baine's eyebrows knitted together. "I for one had a very peaceful meditation underwater."

"You can hold your breath for ten minutes! I was sputtering for air!" Doya shouted. "Then we met those sexist pigs, and I could not tolerate it."

"The Astromancers?" I guessed.

"Yes. The male enchanters are horrible over there. They despise women who have magic," Doya seethed. "I lit one fireball, and we were chased out of town."

Baine nodded in agreement. "Yes. Their city was beautiful, and their magical prowess with astrology is fascinating, but they are quite discriminatory."

Sophia frowned. "I'm sorry you didn't have a good time."

"Oh, it wasn't all that bad." Doya gave a fond look to Baine. "We did get to spend a lot of time together, and the things we studied were fascinating."

Doya's mouth became thin. "Just don't ask me to ever do it again."

"No need. The book is done," Baine said. "And I promise, next time we'll take a nice, relaxing vacation. To Tahiti, or something like that."

Doya huffed. "So long as you don't take me back to godforsaken Malovia."

"What happened there?" Imogen asked curiously.

"What didn't happen? Those fae cultists were seconds away from making us a sacrifice to their pagan gods!" Doya burst.

"We escaped," Baine protested.

"Only by the generosity of others," Doya snapped. She saw our curious looks and explained. "Some sweet shifter boy named Ethan lent a hand. He risked his life to set us free, though we only left the country by the skin of our teeth."

"We had a wonderful honeymoon in Malovia, didn't we, Jakey?" Jonah asked. "This little red-headed girl was super nice. Emma, I think it was? She helped us out of a pinch."

"Yes, after you got us lost." Jake smiled tenderly.

"I was *not lost*," Jonah insisted.

I rolled his eyes. I bet he was.

Ava-Marie held up her arms to Baine and danced at his feet. "Grandpa!"

He burst into a wide smile and hefted her into his arms. "There's my girl! You're getting big, aren't you?"

Baine had sent countless artifacts back for Ava-Marie to play with while he was on his adventures. She rested her head on Baine's shoulder, while Doya turned to us. "Where are you all off to?"

"We're having a memorial," Sophia said, before she added in a whisper, "For Esis."

Doya's expression softened, and Naomi let out a small mew. "Do you want us to take the children?" Doya offered. "I know this must be hard for you."

Sophia shook her head. "I want Ava and Ez to be there. Even though they're so young, I want to start teaching them what people had to sacrifice."

Doya placed a gentle hand on Sophia's arm. "Come by the house tonight. All of you," she said, looking between us. "Your father and I will cook the Ancestors' Day meal."

"What?" Baine yelped. "I've never cooked a thing in my life!"

"You'll learn," Doya said warily.

I appreciated the offer, though I worried I'd get food poisoning if Baine was involved. The man barely knew how to use a microwave. But at least his house was clean now, since Doya had moved in and made everything organized.

Doya kissed Sophia on the cheek and stroked Ava's hair before her husband put her down. "No matter what tries to separate us, I will eternally be here."

"Take care, child." Baine embraced Sophia again, though he held her a little tighter this time. "This is just the start of everything, not the ending."

Sophia's eyes watered as she drew away and took Ezekiel back into her arms. "I know, *pataa*."

We said goodbye to Baine and Doya, and ventured on. The city ended as the tree line loomed ahead, and Jake paused.

"I think I should take Josee home," he said, and he lifted the baby from Jonah's arms. "This is something the four of you should do alone."

"I won't be long," Jonah promised. They gave a parting kiss, and we continued onward. We followed a slim path through the woods, one we'd wound through so many times. I was discovering it all over again as I traveled down the path Nashoma had originally shown me long ago.

We broke out into the welcoming clearing that felt like home. The waterfall, magical as ever, poured down into the sapphire pool, creating ripples that caressed the stones. The clearing was tranquil and beautiful. Exactly as I remembered, as if this was one heavenly place that hadn't been touched by all the pain.

Ava-Marie squirmed, wanting to be put down. I set her on her feet, and she broke through the brush with a yell. It warmed my heart to see her play somewhere that meant so much to me.

This was the place where Sophia and I had fallen in love, where I'd found the key that looped around her neck and the place where our initials were engraved. I'd proposed to her here. Ava-Marie had been conceived here. This place was endlessly special to us, and as such, we knew it was the only location that could be Esis' final resting place.

It felt wrong to be here without Esis. Sophia hadn't been in this clearing before without him.

If only we'd known that day would've been the last time. We might've stayed longer.

Ava-Marie had a laugh like a super villain. Her maniacal giggle traveled through the clearing as she chased butterflies, Squeaks and Sassy in her wake. The fox and hippogriff danced as Ava-Marie spun through the flowers, Buttercup hot on her heels.

Julian's shadow, as well of that of the dragon hatchlings and the baby hippogriffs, spanned over our faces as we approached the pool. I kept an eye on Sophia as she came to the water's edge, but it didn't look like she needed me. Not yet.

Ava-Marie crouched by the edge of the pool. She reached out her hand to caress the multi-colored fish swimming within. "Daddy, fish!"

"Be careful, honey." I knelt beside her, so she wouldn't fall in. Her eyes were mystified by the fish. I rose an orb out of the water, containing a koi within it. Ava-Marie clapped and squealed as the koi swam in front of her, transfixed by my magic.

Sophia took a deep breath. She gave Ezekiel to Jonah to hold, before she lowered herself to her knees. "Imogen, it's time."

Imogen nodded. She weaved her hands, and as she did so, a beautiful, glittering stone began to rise out of the earth. It was rounded, like a grave marker, and had been carved with Anichi symbols that spelled out Esis' name— as well as a secret prayer that Sophia had asked me not to read.

I couldn't decipher the symbols on the stone, but I didn't need to. That was for her. As the stone set into place, white lilies began to bloom near the stone at Imogen's command. They wrapped themselves around the marker, until the stone was covered in intricate vines with pure, blooming petals.

Sophia reached into her bag. She'd brought incense as an offering, and lit it with her Fire as she set it into the glass holder. She placed more things next to the stone— shiny shells from the beach that Esis would've liked, and the bow tie he wore at our wedding. She'd cooked a hamburger this morning — Esis' favorite— and laid it on the edge of the stone like she was giving it to him herself.

Sophia's face fell. She put a hand over her mouth as she began to cry. I longed to reach out to her, comfort her, but I knew it wouldn't do any good. She had to experience this pain if she was ever going to get past it. And I couldn't take it for her. No matter how badly I wanted to.

Ava-Marie looked up at the sound of Sophia's weeping. Her eyes knitted in confusion, before she looked down at the hairbrush.

She tottered forward. She reached out her new hairbrush. She deposited it at the base of the stone. "Esis, Mama."

Okay, *that* made me tear up. Along with everyone else. Ava was willing to give up something she loved to try to make her mother feel better. Imogen gave a sob, and Jonah put a fist to his mouth to hold it in. Sophia gave a watery smile to Ava-Marie. Ava wrapped her arms around her, and Sophia held her tight.

A weight had fallen off Sophia's shoulders as she released herself from Ava's hold. Sophia stood up. She picked up Ava-Marie and cradled her as the four of us gathered around the stone. Ezekiel had fallen asleep and slumbered peacefully against Jonah's chest as a butterfly landed on Esis' stone. Squeaks pressed around us, while Sassy lay across our feet.

We were definitely missing a piece. Buttercup came up and hugged Sophia's leg, which made things feel a little better, but not quite.

"All right, guys. Show's about over," Jonah whispered, choked up.

"It *can't* be over," Imogen said as she wiped away tears. "It just can't."

I felt the need to lift the mood, if even a little. "Hey, at least we didn't fucking die," I offered, though my chest felt tight.

There was a cross between a laugh and a sob that echoed between us all. Most of us hadn't died, but not all of us.

Imogen frowned as she took in the lilies. "Our work's not over. Rumors are already flying around Kinpago from dissenters. People are trying to deny the Biyami genocide ever happened."

"There will always be deniers. But we know the truth," I said firmly. "It's our job to make sure the next generation knows, too."

Jonah tilted his head. "You know, sometimes I look back at everything that happened, and I just can't believe it. It just doesn't seem real. I mean, can you guys believe we really survived all of that?"

"It doesn't matter if it was real or not," Sophia said. "It was real to us."

Truer words had never been spoken. Long moments passed, before Jonah said, "Hey, Im? Will you walk me home? I don't... want to be alone. And I'm not, when you're with me."

Imogen lifted her gaze with a smile. "Always, Jonah."

Jonah handed Ezekiel off to me, and Imogen squeezed our arms to reassure us before walking away. We'd see them later, and at the moment, one more goodbye was too much to bear. Jonah and Imogen quietly left the clearing— as quietly as they could, with clumsy Squeaks tripping through the brush and Sassy giving joyful barks behind.

Once they were gone, Sophia took a heavy breath. "Do you think it's time?"

I nodded. "Yes, *pawee*. It's time."

Sophia put Ava-Marie down. Our daughter looked up as Sophia tied her hair back into a ponytail at the base of her skull. Sophia reached into her bag, bringing out a pair of scissors. She handed them to me. I cut until the ponytail was free and her hair ended in an even line at her chin.

I handed the hair I'd cut to her, and Sophia tossed it in the water. She watched as it floated away and was eventually swallowed up by the torrent of the waterfall, letting one more piece of her grief go.

Sophia stood tall. She rounded her shoulders back as she said, "Come on, Liam. Let's go home."

Home. It was right here. At this waterfall, within our tribe... within our children...

Within us.

❧

When we arrived back at the mansion, the door was slightly ajar. My senses went into overdrive. We'd locked it before we left.

Sophia's eyes went wide. I handed her Ezekiel and put a finger to my lips, to tell Ava-Marie to be quiet. She placed a hand over her mouth and didn't make a sound.

I summoned a water ball and proceeded slowly into the house. I prepared to attack, before I saw that the figure sitting on the couch was someone I knew.

"Maddie." I let out a breath of relief, and the water ball evaporated. It was only my sister.

I couldn't help myself from being overly cautious. The war had given me traits that would never go away. One of them being ever vigilant that someone was trying to harm my family— though we hadn't been attacked since the day the battle ended.

Maddie rose to her feet as I approached. Sophia heard me speak her name and entered curiously. Maddie was still. The scars on her arms had faded, and as far as I knew, her visions didn't haunt her anymore. As much as they had a year ago, anyway.

It was weird Maddie was here alone. She usually didn't come by unless she had Drew in tow.

"I need to talk to you guys," Maddie began. She gave a glance to the children, like this was a conversation we needed to have without them.

Sophia and I took the kids upstairs and put them down for a nap. When we came back down, Maddie was pacing. It looked like she had bad news to deliver and was worrying about how to tell us.

"Sit down, please," Maddie offered. Sophia and I took a seat, and Maddie sat across from us. She took a deep breath as she said, "I have something to tell you. I'm not returning to Orenda Academy."

"What?" Sophia asked, shocked.

I gave her a stern look. "Maddie, you have to finish your education."

"I will. Just somewhere else," she began. "There's a school for prophets that's offered me admission to their academy. It's a place for seers— for people like me. I *need* to go."

"I've never heard of such a school. Does it really exist?" I said skeptically.

"Yes. Mom and I have looked into it. It's legit," she said. "And the only place where I can learn how to use my powers without hurting myself."

"What about Drew?" Sophia asked.

Maddie's eyes watered, but she said, "Drew supports me. It's really going to suck having a long-distance relationship, but I'll come back home once I graduate. We'll move in together then. He's willing to wait. Ancestors, I don't know what I did to deserve a man like him."

"If you're set on going, you don't need our approval," Sophia said. "You know we'll always support you."

"I don't just want to attend this academy for myself," Maddie said tentatively. "I have to. For Ava."

The color drained from Sophia's face. In a hoarse voice, I asked, "What do you mean?"

Maddie frowned. "I'd been putting off telling you this until the war was over, because I didn't think we'd survive. But we did, and I can't wait any longer. For the past three years, my visions have been about Ava-Marie, and everything she's going to do."

"You can't be serious." Sophia was as white as a ghost. She put a hand to her chest, like she was willing her heart not to erupt.

Maddie's expression became gentle. "There's a prophecy—"

"No!" I leapt up from my seat and turned my back on her. "No, *no*, don't come at me with that shit again!"

"You can't stop it, Liam! You have to accept what is!" Maddie insisted.

I paced around the room. Ancestors, if my temper had been what it once was, I would've started throwing things.

But I was more mature now— and much more tired. As badly— as *achingly* as I wanted this to be a lie, I knew in my spirit that it wasn't.

Maddie's visions were never wrong.

"You're telling us our daughter is another chosen one. Like I am," Sophia breathed.

"Not necessarily," Maddie began. "My visions are hard to interpret. That's why I'm going to this school. To figure out what they mean, so Ava can understand them when the time comes."

"Lindsey and Miranda knew. Didn't they?" Sophia asked.

"Yes. But besides them and Drew, they're the only ones, along with you." Maddie's voice was short. It was taking everything out of her, to be honest like this.

"What do you know? What have you seen?" I asked.

"Fragments. Just bits and pieces," Maddie said. "They're difficult to piece together. I can't truly know what my visions mean unless I have more time to decipher them."

"Do you know anything?" I was begging her now, praying that my sister had a way to get my daughter out of this.

Maddie nodded. "All I can tell you is what I've managed to work out on my own. There will be a great battle within Ava-Marie's spirit, between the light and the dark. She must balance the two sides; otherwise, her choices will throw the world into peril. Whatever path she walks will decide the fate of all supernatural kind."

Sophia ran her hands through her hair as she tried not to crumble. I myself was struggling to comprehend the vastness of this new prophecy. "*All* supernaturals?"

"Yes. What's on the horizon is far greater than the Hawkei Civil Wars were," Maddie said. "In the end, Ava will determine what will happen to the Great Spirit, and bring to the earth a realm of gods."

I nearly gagged. Sophia sat back against the couch cushions. Unlike me, she had forced herself to calm and was taking in Maddie's every word, calculating.

"Are you sure of what you're saying? There isn't any doubt?" Sophia questioned.

"Yes. Madame Doya was right about her. Ava will be far more powerful than either of you," Maddie said. "And you need to temper that power before it gets out of hand and destroys us all."

"What the hell are you saying? My daughter's not evil," I snarled.

"*Listen to me*, Liam. This prophecy scares me, because I don't know what Ava will do!" Maddie said. "In my visions, she's insane. She's uncontrollable. And the power she wields is enough to bring down whole civilizations. If you don't teach her how to manage her emotions, how to fight for what's right, the magical community could be gone. She could level the world easily, in the blink of an eye."

Maddie snapped her fingers, and I flinched. Sophia chewed nervously on her lip. There was a sound from upstairs. We all jumped, but it must've just been Ava-Marie crying out in her sleep, because after a moment, all went silent again.

Maddie reached out to squeeze my hand. "I'm not saying Ava-Marie's a monster. I love her. She's my niece, and she's a sweet little girl. I know she's got good in her."

Maddie's tone became low. "But she has darkness, too. And in my visions, she can't escape it. She can only manage it. Which is why I'm depending on you guys to raise her to do the right thing. Especially when doing the right thing is the hardest thing *to* do."

"What kind of suffering is she going to face?" I asked. "What is she going to experience, being a pawn for a prophecy of gods?"

Maddie made a face. "You know I can't tell you that. You'll get in the way."

"Dammit, Maddie." I rubbed my face. I'd watched my wife suffer as a chosen one for years. She'd lost everything due to the prophecy. I'd do anything to prevent that from being my daughter's fate as well.

"How much time do we have before the prophecy starts coming true?" Sophia leaned forward and crossed her arms over her knees. "Tell us."

Maddie held her breath. "Twenty years."

"Twenty years? She'll barely be an adult by that time," I said scathingly.

"Sophia managed. Ava will, too. She's strong," Maddie insisted.

"It doesn't matter. There has to be a way to stop this," I pressed.

"Prophecies can't be stopped, only altered and changed by the choices of those who are impacted by it," Maddie said patiently. "You know this, Liam."

I dropped my gaze. Yeah, I knew. The events of the past few years had beaten that into me.

Wish it didn't have to be true for my kid.

"Are there any more details you can tell us? Anything important?" Sophia asked, as a final question.

"All I know for sure is there will be another conflict. A second Great Supernatural War, one Ava-Marie will be at the center of," Maddie finished. "And whatever choices she makes will decide what will happen to magic. Forever."

Another world war, between supernatural races. Our kind had hardly survived the last one. Who's to say we would make it through another?

Maddie reached into a backpack at her side. She pulled out a small leather journal and pressed it into Sophia's hands. "This is the wording of the prophecy I've created, along with a few notes from my visions. The pages are full. Give it to Ava-Marie once she comes of age. Promise you won't read it. These words are only for Ava, and whoever she chooses to share them with. The contents inside will only bring you pain."

"We won't," Sophia vowed. "We'll keep it safe."

Maddie nodded. "I'll try to find out more once I'm at the school. And for the ancestors' sake, keep your daughter close. She's really going to need you."

Maddie rose and left without a goodbye. Once she'd flown away on Eirakari, I turned to Sophia.

"We should have a look at that book," I said, reaching for the journal.

"No." Sophia swung it away. "Maddie's right. This is only for Ava-Marie. We shouldn't be tampering with it. We *can't* look at it unless Ava chooses to show it to us. Swear to me on our marriage, Liam."

I scowled. "Fine. But we need to lock that thing away. I don't want Ava to see it a moment before she's eighteen."

And maybe not even then.

"We'll put it in the safe." Sophia got up. I followed her to our bedroom as she put the journal into a lock safe we had in the closet, and closed it up tight. The ominous journal was shrouded in darkness as Sophia closed the door and changed the combination.

Twenty fucking years, and there'd be another war. To think I'd seen the last of the fighting... though this time, it wouldn't be my job to stop it.

It'd be Ava's. Ancestors have mercy on us all.

Later that day, before we left for Doya's house and the Ancestors' Day celebration, Sophia and I watched as Ava-Marie played on the beach. Ezekiel was swaddled tenderly against Sophia's chest, and I had my arm around her, holding both of them close. Julian put his wings over his eyes as Ava played peek-a-boo. Her laugh was a trill as Julian peeked at her, clapping her small hands in delight.

This felt perfect. Perfection couldn't last forever. But it'd have to do... at least for another two decades.

Sophia rested her head on my shoulder. "Whatever happens next... I love you, Liam."

I kissed the top of her head. "I love you too, *pawee.*"

There was a wail. Ava-Marie had scraped her knee. Blood trickled from the small cut, and she came running to me with tears streaking down her face. "Daddy, Daddy!"

I took her into my arms. "It's not that bad, sweetheart. Let's get it cleaned up."

I carried her to the kitchen and set her on a chair. She sniffled as I cleaned the cut and browsed the cupboard for bandages. Even though it was a mere bruise, her tears tugged at my heartstrings. The smallest little pain Ava experienced was enough to rip my feelings apart.

I couldn't handle a scraped knee, for the ancestors' sake. How was I going to comfort her when the real agony hit? When the war came and her friends started dying?

I knew the answer intuitively. I would soldier on through it, because the pain she'd come to experience wasn't about me. It was about her. And no matter how hard she fell, I'd always be there to catch her.

Ava-Marie noticed I was getting emotional. Her tears dried up in concern for me as she straightened. "Okay, Daddy?"

"Yeah. Daddy's okay." I knelt to put the Band-Aid on and brushed back her hair.

Ava-Marie leaned in to give me a hug. I held her as long as she would permit me to, because I knew this moment would be all too short. She wouldn't be a little girl forever.

But she would always be my little girl.

"Daddy, don't leave," Ava-Marie said as I got to my feet. She held out her arms to me.

I boosted her up and set her on my hip. I gave her a kiss on the head before vowing, "Never."

Our story had ended. But our daughter's?

Hers had barely begun.

END OF BOOK SIX

Thank you for reading the Academy of Magical Creatures series. We hope you've enjoyed this emotional adventure!

Continue the magic with Ava-Marie's story. Flip the page to read a special excerpt from book one in the Prison for Supernatural Offenders series: *The Villain Institute!*

HIDDEN LEGENDS

Read more from the Hidden Legends universe! Each Hidden Legends series takes place within the same world, but in separate and unique societies. Every series stands on its own, and they can be read in any order.

&

SHIFTERS, FAE, & SORCERESSES

University of Sorcery by Megan Linski

&

WITCHES, DEMONS, & REAPERS

College of Witchcraft by Alicia Rades

&

SUPERNATURAL PRISON

Prison for Supernatural Offenders by Megan Linski & Alicia Rades

&

Never miss a new release! Join our newsletter at
www.hiddenlegendsbooks.com/fanclub/

THE VILLAIN INSTITUTE
CHAPTER ONE

Ava-Marie

The day I was born, the world went mad.

And I went mad with it.

The pounding of the hippogriff's hooves beneath me was like a war drum beating a prayer song. I could feel the music that resonated through the earth as it sent power flowing through my blood. The valley ahead of me was green and open, welling with sunlight on a fresh August morning. The hippogriff herd pressed around me as the mountains of Northern California rose in the distance, redwoods like soldiers standing tall against the blue sky.

I could feel everything that was alive, smell the resonance of life as energy ricocheted through the air. I could see the entire universe, spread out like a map that was mine for the taking. I rode upon a euphoric high, feeling more powerful than a god and never wishing to come down as the colors began to bleed together into a watercolor painting.

I dug my hands into the creature's feathers and held on tight, pressing myself to the bird's neck and urging it to go faster. The half-horse, half-eagle creature let out a low whinny, enclosing its wings around my legs. I laughed along, giving a sound that was shrill and ignited the world.

Eventually, the valley came to a close as the mountains grew higher above us. The hippogriff slowed, until it jogged to a stop by the opening of a cave entrance. I slid off and patted the hippogriff's neck as the colors of the world bled away and became normal once again. "Good girl. Thanks for the ride."

The hippogriff snorted, blowing back my hair before taking off into the sky. The herd followed, spreading their wings to follow the lead mare into the clouds.

I looked back. My brother was clinging to the back of the slowest hippogriff, who rounded up the last of the herd. His black hair was wild and stuck up on one side, and his cheeks were bright red.

"Ava-Marie, wait up!" he complained. His hippogriff skidded to an abrupt halt. Ezekiel yelled as he was tossed forward and sent sprawling into the ground, tearing a hole in his jeans.

I put a hand over my mouth and laughed again as Ezekiel spat out dirt. The hippogriff huffed and kicked up its hooves, flying into the sky with the rest of them.

Ezekiel gave me a sour look. "You could wait for me every once in a while."

"You wouldn't fall behind if you were a better rider." I reached out a hand to pull him to his feet. Ez and I often raced hippogriffs, but he rarely beat me. He could never tell which ones would be the fastest. I could.

We turned toward the cave entrance. Ezekiel's mouth fell open as he gazed upward, taking in the sight of the cave— and the various signs around the entrance warning that further venturing would be trespassing on government property. As this cave was outside the Hawkei reservation, whatever was found within it was free for anyone to take— as far as the colonizers were concerned.

"Are you sure we should be doing this?" Ezekiel asked. "It definitely counts as illegal activity."

"Stop being such a baby." I reached into my backpack and took out a headlamp, fastening it before clicking on the light. "It's the weekend. No one's at the worksite."

"If we get caught here, it's a federal crime," Ezekiel said, pointing at the cords roping off the entrance.

I rolled my eyes. "What, like the colonizers committed a crime by *stealing our land*? Those artifacts are Hawkei property, Ez. They belong to the tribe. Now we're going to get them back. Do you really want the colonizers to put our heritage in one of *their* museums? It's not right."

"No, but—"

"Then what's the issue?"

Ezekiel's tone was flat. "I don't feel like going to jail."

"You're such a goody-two-shoes. Let's go."

"Ava-Marie!"

I'd slipped under the ropes before he had a chance to stop me. Ezekiel fastened on his own headlamp and hurried in behind, like I knew he'd always do. The sunlight vanished as we wandered further into the cave.

I got that Ez was nervous, but he needed to chill. This was the *right* thing to do. The supernatural world had suffered enough from humans in the past— the Hawkei being one of their greatest victims.

The Hawkei were an indigenous people who'd lived in California for thousands of years. We'd nearly been exterminated when the colonizers came to our territory and began terrorizing our tribe. We'd pleaded with the ancestors for help, and they'd answered our prayers, and gifted us our powers— the magic of the elements.

We became the Elementai— elementals— and grew strong enough to defend ourselves from the humans. We separated into five Houses for each of the five elements— Koigni, for Fire; Toaqua, for Water; Nivita, for Earth; Yapluma, for Air; and Anichi, for Spirit.

Though we had to keep our magic a secret, I wasn't about to let some colonizers get their filthy hands on what belonged to us. I was doing the right thing. They were trying to steal our culture. Now I was stealing it back.

The headlamps didn't provide enough light, so I lifted my hand. A ball of fire burned within it, illuminating the path ahead with light.

Ezekiel looked on in awe. "I'm so jealous. I can't wait to get my powers."

"You're seventeen. They'll show up soon."

Supernaturals got their abilities when they came of age, but Ez hadn't shown any magic yet. I was almost two years older than him, but I'd gotten my Fire magic the day I'd turned eighteen.

Though Ezekiel's powers would be different from mine. Our parents were from separate Houses. My mother was Koigni. My father was Toaqua. Elementai always inherited their powers from their same-sex parent, so Ezekiel would have Water magic instead of Fire like me.

Ezekiel scowled as the walls of the cave began getting narrower. "You could at least tell our parents where we're going. I don't like lying all the time. If he finds out we're here, Dad will be madder than when you got your tongue pierced."

I waggled my piercing at him. "Well, someone's gotta be the rebel."

"Not all the time. Can't we have a *normal* day for once?"

"I do what I want."

I held my arm out as the cave path came to an abrupt halt, leading to the edge of a cliff. I sent the fireball sailing downward. It landed on the cave floor twenty feet below, where it shone light on piles of pick axes, shovels, and wheelbarrows full of dirt. The fireball fizzled out, leaving the area below in darkness.

"There's the excavation site." I slipped off my bag and began pulling out my gear. I pounded an anchor into the floor and strung a rope through the safety clips before slipping on my harness. I was rappelling down the side of the cliff before Ezekiel even had his harness on. I landed on the ground safely and unclipped myself while Ez clumsily— and fucking *slowly*— descended.

Ezekiel got tangled up in his climbing gear a foot above the ground. He struggled with the ropes and glanced at me helplessly as he spun in circles against the rock.

"Um, can you help? This harness is strangling my balls," he whined.

"Ancestors, Ez, you're so clumsy." I got Ez loose, and he staggered against the wall. I had to resist rolling my eyes again.

"Hey, I'm a fat kid. I don't do things like this."

"You're not fat, Ez, you're fluffy."

"Easy for you to say. You can't weigh more than a hundred pounds."

"Shut up."

I called another fireball into my hand as I observed the excavation site. There were footprints in the dirt, and a lot of tools, but I didn't see anything of value.

"They must've not found it yet," I reasoned.

"Do you hear that?" Ezekiel tilted his head. There was a trickling sound. I followed the source of the noise across the area until my boots splashed upon mud and water. The fireball in my hand displayed a river ten feet wide, and probably just as deep.

"It's an underground river," I said. "How fascinating."

I reached into my bag and pulled out a leather guidebook. I scribbled a few things down while Ezekiel groaned. "Ava, can we go? I don't want to get caught down here."

I snapped my guidebook shut. "Look. When you're navigating ruins, you're supposed to document *everything*. Otherwise, you could miss a crucial clue that's important later. I have to practice, otherwise I'll never be—"

"*A real explorer*," Ezekiel echoed for me, like he'd done a million times. "I get it. Where is this thing, anyway?"

"Grandpa said the artifact would be down here." I followed my instincts and began navigating the river. Ezekiel nearly slipped into it, before I caught him.

"Grandpa's wrong about a lot of things," Ezekiel grumbled, but I ignored him. We moved ahead, leaving the excavation site behind us.

We walked for half a mile in silence. The walls of the cave narrowed. Eventually, the river ended, but not before I noticed a small slit in the cave wall near my feet. I'd fit through it, but not Ez.

I had a feeling there was something lying beyond. Ezekiel frowned when he noticed it. "You can't be serious."

"Where's your sense of adventure?" I asked. I had already dropped to my knees and began squeezing myself through the hole. "I won't be long."

Ezekiel danced nervously by the gap as I pushed myself through the claustrophobic space. For a moment, I did get stuck— momentary panic struck me, but I shoved it aside. Fear was a useless fucking emotion. It wouldn't get me what I wanted.

I finally slipped through. As I did, I was able to stand and light a fireball. I stood in a small circular area, and lying on the floor was exactly what we'd come here for.

I reached out and picked up a small gold sculpture in the shape of a person. It was as big as my hand, and depicted each of the five elements throughout. The face showed half the face of a man, and half of a woman. It was meant to be a carving of one of the Hawkei gods— a piece of the Great Spirit we worshiped alongside our ancestors.

After a quick inspection, I rendered it had to be authentic. A piece like this was invaluable. To the colonizers, such an item would sell for millions at auction, but to our tribe, it was priceless.

I wriggled out from underneath the gap, and Ezekiel sighed in relief. His smile brightened when I showed him the figurine.

"Finally. Let's head out." We turned to go, but as we did, the idol in my hand started to burn. I let out a gasp. Being Koigni, it shouldn't have hurt, but the statue was actually able to singe my skin. Both of our mouths dropped open as we realized the idol was glowing bright red. From the mouth of the idol streamed black smoke, which formed into a transparent man with a malicious grin.

Shit. The idol was a piece of Spirit Art. Grandpa had told me about these things. If a supernatural cared about their creation enough, they could actually seal a piece of their soul inside it, preserving their spirit forever within an item they treasured here on this earth. Usually, people who made Spirit Art were benevolent and kind beings, meant to help others.

But whoever had made this piece of Spirit Art was a fucking asshole, because this spirit was obviously not here to help. Dark magic like whips began gathering at his sides as the entity readied to attack. I saw fire flickering on the spirit's form— this man had been Koigni in his former life.

"Ava, run!" Ezekiel cried. He grabbed my wrist, but the dark entity lashed out, knocking him to the ground. His headlight went out, and I heard glass crack.

The spirit smacked me across the face. My helmet went flying off, and the light broke against the stone.

We were locked in darkness. I threw a fireball in the direction I thought the dark spirit might be. It sailed right through him. I saw with horror that the monster was advancing on Ezekiel, who was scampering backwards trying to get away from it. The evil spirit reached out its dark tendrils, wrapping them around Ezekiel's form and squeezing him tight. He gasped, pulling at the tendrils around his neck as they suffocated him, his feet kicking at the water of the river as he tried to escape.

When I saw that my brother was in danger, I didn't think. I reacted. I flung out my left hand, expecting flames to shoot out my fingers at the entity, though I knew it wouldn't do any good.

That's not what happened. A shiver ran from my core all the way out to the tips of my fingers as I felt my skin turn cold, not hot. I'd never experienced such a chilling feeling before. When I cast Fire, there was anger, passion, exhilaration— nearly on the bounds of being out of control.

This magic was different. It was calming. Cool. And had an ancient power within it that scared me.

The water in the river rose upward. The riverbed drained. Ezekiel gasped. The spirit just had time to look up before the wave crashed into him. The dark entity gave a wicked cry as the water smashed into his body, putting out the flames licking his form. There was a sizzling sound, and the spirit dissolved, leaving the idol silent and immobile on the ground. The water trickled back into the river, and I was left completely dumbfounded.

What did I just do?

Ezekiel shook, but it wasn't because of the entity. "Ava, you— you just used Water magic!"

I clambered to my feet. "No... it isn't possible."

"It has to be." Ezekiel got up, and his feet splashed on the stone. "I saw you do it. You're not just Koigni. You're Toaqua, too."

Denial flashed in my mind. I was a Fire caster, through and through. I had the fiery temperament for it. The ability to call upon Fire was as easy for me as breathing.

And yet... I'd told the river to protect Ezekiel without any effort whatsoever, and it'd obeyed.

I wouldn't accept it. It wasn't real. I couldn't have inherited my father's powers, too. This had to be a fluke.

I wouldn't have one more thing that made me more different than I already was.

"Ez, you can't tell Mama and Daddy about this," I said as he approached. "It has to stay between us."

His face fell. "If you're both Houses, it's important for them to know."

"No! I want to be Koigni— I want to be normal," I pleaded. "I'm already a fucking freak."

Ezekiel's eyes turned sad. "You're not a freak, Ava."

I let out a snort. Yeah, right. I'd been the weird kid at school. And weird was putting it lightly. People were afraid of me.

It was exceptionally rare— nearly unheard of— for an Elementai to have the ability to cast more than one element. Most could only cast the element of the House they were born into. Sure, there were exceptions, like my mother, who could use both Fire and Spirit magic.

But there'd never, in the history of all the Hawkei, been an elemental who could use both Fire and Water. The elements were total opposites. And I didn't want to be the first anything.

I picked up the idol and shoved it into my bag. "Come on. Let's go."

"Ava!"

Ezekiel protested all the way behind me— even as he struggled to climb the wall that led back out of the cave. When we burst out into the sunlight, he grabbed my shoulders to stop me.

"This isn't something we can hide," he said. "Nor should you."

Ezekiel was stubborn. He wouldn't give up.

"Let's just drop the idol off at Grandpa's," I said with a sigh. "Then we'll talk about it."

Or like, never.

Ezekiel's shoulders sagged. "Okay. We can stop by on the way home."

"Like hell! I *need* makeup." I could deal with jeans just fine if I was running around in a cave, but any other time of day, I wanted a dress on. Crawling in the mud was no excuse for not looking fabulous— and I was *not* walking through town with my hair like this.

"Ugh. Fine. I guess I'm hungry, anyway."

"You're always hungry."

The hippogriff herd had returned by this time. They were grazing in the valley beyond. The lead mare lifted her head as I walked toward her. I pulled myself onto her back, and Ezekiel climbed onto the same tawny stallion he'd fallen off of earlier. I nudged my heels into her sides, and the hippogriff spread her wings, taking off into the air.

There was nothing like feeling the wind on your face while you were flying on a hippogriff. I looked down, and as the valley shrank beneath me, I turned my gaze toward the city beyond.

Kinpago was my home, and always would be. I admired the beautiful skyline as the hippogriff tilted in the air, directing us toward an island that sat surrounded by the crystal clear ocean.

The two hippogriffs landed on the sandy beach of the island. Ezekiel and I fed them treats before bidding farewell and walking up the brick pathway to the grand stone mansion beyond.

I loved our house. It was open-concept, decorated in white and blue tones with a crystal chandelier hanging in the main entrance. The kitchen connected to the living room, and the porch doors were open, letting in the breeze from the beach. Some would say it was too big, but I had such a large family, it always felt warm and welcoming to me.

My younger sister sat on the couch, reading, like usual. Her red mane of hair fanned out behind her on the pillows. She looked up as we entered.

"Where've you guys been?" Alana asked. She was only fourteen, but she was fucking sharp— nothing got past her. She got off the couch and threw her book aside as Ezekiel began rummaging through the cupboards to make a sandwich.

I took the idol out of my bag and set it on the counter. "Getting this."

"No way. You found it?" Alana's eyes widened as she took in the statue.

"Yeah. It only took vanquishing an evil spirit out of the statue," Ezekiel said with a mouth full of food.

"Really? How'd you do that?" Alana asked.

I glared at Ezekiel, and he shut up as Alana inspected the idol.

I could hear swear words coming from the garage. I poked my head in.

My eleven-year-old brother, Maverick, was sprawled on the floor, surrounded by tools as he messed around with an old motorbike. The bike was an antique. It had been my grandfather's, passed down to my dad, then passed down to me. I took it to the mainland sometimes to ride it around. Maverick was itching to be old enough to drive it. I'd told him he could tinker with it. He was good with mechanical things. His brown hair was matted with oil as he tightened loose bolts.

"You got it, Mav?" I asked.

Maverick threw a wrench down. "Stupid chains are busted."

"Well, if you need help, ask."

Ez and I took after our dad— Alana and Maverick our mom. Ezekiel and I had tan brown skin, while Alana and Maverick's was lighter. Ez and I looked native, and the other two didn't— even though we had the same Hawkei blood running through our veins.

I returned to the kitchen. "Where are Mom and Dad?" Ezekiel asked Alana before he chugged a glass of milk.

"Dad's at the office," Alana said. "I guess Mom went with him for some reason."

Thank the ancestors that Mama and Daddy weren't home. Ezekiel had a big mouth.

"If they're both there, it must be important," Ezekiel said.

Alana shrugged. "Maybe."

Daddy was the chief of Toaqua, and responsible for everyone in the Water tribe. Mama was on the Koigni Elder Council, working alongside him to maintain peace amongst the Houses. During the Elementai Civil War twenty years ago, there'd been a prophecy about my mother and how she would save the tribe. I'd only been a baby then, but according to my parents, it'd been a terrible time of war and suffering amongst the Houses. As the chosen one, my mother had led the tribe into a new age of peace— but not without a lot of sacrifice.

Because I was her firstborn, I was expected to live up to her incredible story. And I'd thoroughly disappointed everyone.

As if being the daughter of the Water chief wasn't enough publicity. My parents were tribal heroes. Me being able to cast magic from two different Houses would cause more undue attention to our family.

Like I hadn't done that enough already.

While Ezekiel ate, I ran upstairs. I showered, dried and curled my hair before flinging open my closet door— which was packed to the brim with poofy dresses, bedazzled jean jackets, and six-inch pumps.

I stood at the door and tapped a finger against my chin. What was I in the mood for today?

I had this fabulous pink tulle skirt I'd sewn myself that fell around my knees, with a cut-off cream shirt. They'd go perfect with a white pair of heels. I slipped them on, then sat at my vanity and began applying primer and foundation before working on contouring my cheekbones. I tossed lipsticks and eyeliner around my messy room carelessly, looking for the right one.

I was nothing more than thinly organized chaos. Everything in my room was pink— I *loved* pink— though you could barely tell under the piles of clothes I had lying around. My bedroom had a theme; unicorns. I had a unicorn bedspread, unicorn posters, and unicorn lamps.

I collected unicorns. I was fricking obsessed with them. I even wanted a unicorn tattoo one day. It was all so pink and girly, and it made me feel fabulous. Anyone who thought my room looked like a five-year-old's could suck a dick, because I liked it, and that's what mattered.

I had a wardrobe full of makeup products. I didn't need them as much anymore... not since I quit my beauty vlog, but it felt like a sin to throw them out.

Mama and Daddy wanted me to pick it back up again. But I hadn't made a video since Monica died. It felt like a betrayal to make one without her.

Thinking of Monica always made a pang run through my chest. I threaded my fingers over the bracelet she'd woven me, which I never took off. Red and green, for Koigni and Nivita.

It was the last piece I had left of her. Sometimes, I still heard her laugh echoing through the house. The memory of her smile got me through my bad days. I had a lot of those.

I rummaged through my vanity drawer, looking for the final touch. If Uncle Jonah had taught me one thing, there was never enough glitter. I dusted a tiny bottle of it over my arms and cheeks before I posed in the mirror.

I looked *so hot*. Looks were everything. People judged with their eyes. I loved makeup, because there was nothing you couldn't hide with it.

Ezekiel was messing around with his guitar when I came downstairs. "Finally."

He put his guitar aside. Alana gave a wave as we headed out. We'd asked her to come with us, but she was an introvert and liked her alone time.

We took the motorboat into town. I watched as dolphins and whales swam between hippocampi— half-horse, half-mermaid creatures. Their scales sparkled in the water, making me wish to reach out and brush my fingers over their spiny manes. Everything about my world was magical, and I savored each moment of it.

We docked the boat before walking up the winding path to Kinpago. As we entered the city, another invigorating sense of *home* struck me. I watched from the streets as dragons flew overhead, twirling with griffins and birds with rainbow feathers that were bigger than buildings. The streets were packed with Elementai walking side by side with direwolves, basilisks and three-headed animals like chimeras.

The perytons were always my favorite. The winged deer had such spirits as they bounded through the streets, bobbing their antlered heads.

The Elementai had the most important job in the world— protecting and defending magical creatures. We were their caretakers as designated by the ancestors themselves, and the creatures depended on us for survival. Every magical creature imaginable that existed in the world had a species based here in Kinpago. More often than not, we were the only thing that prevented them from going extinct. As a result, many of them became our Familiars.

A Familiar was an Elementai's soul, the part of their spirit that existed outside of their body. Every Elementai was bonded to one, and you usually met them sometime after you got your powers. Elementai couldn't live without their Familiars, as they were the source of our magic, our life energy. If you died, so did they.

I hadn't gotten my Familiar yet. I'd desperately looked for one the first day I could cast my element, but I hadn't found them. Somewhere, I knew my soul was out there waiting for me, and the longing to join the pieces of myself together was almost like an obsession. What would they be, and what would my Familiar mean to me?

There were so many colors in Kinpago— streamers hung from buildings, and Hawkei music played as people danced in the streets beneath the skyscrapers and shops. I smelled fry bread, cinnamon, and freshly baked pizza. Vendors on the street sold beads for making jewelry, white sage and woven baskets.

I wanted to stop and look— shopping was my favorite activity— but Ezekiel pulled me along in the direction of my grandfather's house. He knew once I went on a shopping spree, I wouldn't stop until I was flat broke.

In the distance, I saw the spires of a white castle rise into the clouds, and my heart thudded with just a little bit of magic.

Ezekiel nudged me knowingly. "Are you ready? Just a few more days now."

Excitement welled in my chest. I couldn't wait to attend Orenda Academy of Magical Creatures. I'd heard so many stories from my parents about how amazing it was when I was growing up. I wanted to have those incredible experiences, too.

"I'm glad I'm going with you," I told Ez. I'd taken a year off after graduating from high school and postponed my enrollment because... well, Monica.

And something else I didn't want to think about.

But now I was ready. I was sure of it. And Ez would be there, right alongside me in the same grade. I could handle it.

Ezekiel came to an abrupt halt. I nearly slammed into him, but held myself back at the last minute.

An annoying laugh caused a twinge of irritation to pass me by. I saw the bleached blonde mane of hair before anything else. Ezekiel's mouth became thin, though I felt the hints of desperation oozing out from him.

I grabbed Ezekiel's arm and steered him in a different direction. "Just ignore her. She's not worth it."

His eyes remained glued to the back of blondie's head. I took another glance back. When I saw who she was talking to, my mouth ran dry.

I *really* didn't like Rosary, but it was the sight of the person beside her that churned my gut. I took a short look before I set my eyes forward. The small movement was just enough to make a smirk cross John's face.

Fuck him. I *hated* him.

I forced my hand not to shake on Ezekiel's arm, and we took a different path. Even when we were well out of John's sight, I still felt sick to my stomach.

I wouldn't acknowledge it. I'd forgotten. That was that.

Ezekiel hadn't noticed my momentary panic. He was still miserable. "Do you think there's a chance she'll take me back?"

I focused on the conversation with Ezekiel, to redirect my nauseated feelings. "You've gotta let her go, Ez. She's no good for you."

"I know." His shoulders slumped. "Just wish things would've turned out different."

Rosary had completely broken my brother's heart. He'd never been the same after she dumped him.

Good riddance. I thought of wrapping my hands around her neck and squeezing, and a smile crossed my face. "She was abusive. You can do so much better."

Rosary had hit my brother once. I'd made sure she'd never do it again. The burns were so bad she still had a scar on her arm. *Nobody* fucked with my little brother.

"I'm sure things would've worked out." He dropped his head. "If the baby would've survived."

Okay, Ezekiel was a goody-goody until it came to one thing— girls. He thought with what was in his pants instead of in his head. I guess the condom broke one time. Not gonna lie, it was kind of nice when Daddy and Mama found out. They'd grilled Ezekiel's ass instead of mine, for once. He and Rosary were set to become teen parents— until Rosary had lost the pregnancy last year, and dumped him right off the bat.

My brother had taken the miscarriage harder than Rosary had. Ez had such a sweet heart— he'd cried for days. My whole family had just managed to bring him out of it. And as much as I despised her, I felt sorry for Rosary. No one should lose a baby, but the way she'd treated Ez after the fact was just plain cruel.

I felt the tension in the air alter as Ezekiel changed the subject. "Maybe you should try talking to Johnny again. I know you guys had a falling out after Monica died, but you two were really close. It's sad you don't talk anymore."

A pit in my stomach opened up and devoured me. He wasn't Johnny anymore. He was John. And Ezekiel didn't know what happened between us. Nobody did.

Thoughts came rushing back. I tried so hard to push them out of my head, but they kept coming, pouring over me like an endless waterfall. I literally felt the color from my face drain. I let go of Ezekiel's arm, so he could no longer feel my hands quiver.

"Ava, are you okay?" Ezekiel noticed my pale expression. "Did you take your pills this morning?"

"I always take my pills." Not that they helped. I was still three fries short of a Happy Meal.

Ezekiel watched me carefully. "Are you sure you'll make it to Grandpa's? Maybe you should go back home."

"You're probably right. I'm not feeling great," I mumbled. I reached into my purse and gave him the idol. "Take this to Grandpa's. I'll meet you later."

He eyed me up and down. "It might be a good idea to walk you back."

"I'm fine, Ez. I promise."

I was not fine. Yet Ezekiel knew I hated it when people hovered over me, so he stepped back to give me some space. "Okay. You can take the boat back. I'll grab the ferry. See you."

Ezekiel started down the road. I turned the other way, though I didn't go back the way we came.

I needed to take a different path. I had to be alone.

As I wandered down the city streets of Kinpago, I felt a burst of energy fizzle through my brain. It felt like I could run a hundred marathons without breaking a sweat. I wanted to run right now— get all these eyes off of me. Dozens of people were passing me by, and it felt like all of them were staring right through me.

They're spying on you, Ava.

They're following you.

You're not safe.

Run!

"Shut up," I whispered under my breath. I shut my eyes for a few moments to make the voices stop, but they kept coming, so numerous I could no longer make out what they were saying. It was like an entire auditorium was screaming at me all at once, amplifying the volume with every word.

I could taste metal. I could smell blood. It was so overpowering it made me want to vomit. All those eyes were still on me. The buildings were leaning inward and threatening to topple over. I diverged from the main street and began jogging down a deserted alley, trying to escape the ringing in my ears.

"It's just a hallucination. Ignore it," I told myself.

Yet I couldn't. Voices. So many voices echoing in my head. There was no way of escape—

I was thrown off balance as someone slammed into my side. I thought it was another part of the hallucination, until I felt a strong hand on my arm keep me from falling over. I tottered on my heels and my purse slipped off my arm, falling onto the pavement. The voices abruptly stopped as I turned to face the person I'd accidentally run into.

"Easy there, pidge," a cool, smooth voice said. "Don't want to scrape up those pretty little knees."

I caught the flash of a remarkably cocky smile, and for no reason at all, it instantly put me at ease. My eyes roamed up and down the man who'd caught me. He had to be in his early twenties. He was a few inches taller than me, around six foot two. His dark hair fell into his murky eyes. We were so close together I could see the emerald flecks within the hazel tones, which appeared to be honey pools I could dive into. His skin was brown, darker than mine, and his body was corded with muscle. His ripped jeans and tight t-shirt was like something straight out of a magazine.

A bad boy. I liked bad boys. At his side, a gray husky with a star marking on its forehead sat panting in the sun.

I tried to place what ethnicity the guy might be. He had to be Hawkei, like me— he had a Familiar after all— but besides being an indigenous North American tribe, the Hawkei had been intermingling with other races for centuries. I thought I could place him as Latino, but I could see some Middle Eastern features as well, mixed in with African traits.

Hey, I liked multicultural guys, and this dude looked like a world tour. For my vagina.

Then I noticed something— how the man's gaze didn't quite connect with mine. The dog eyed me with a shining expression, one that was confusing to put together.

The man was blind. I felt stupid for not noticing sooner. Should've paid more attention instead of ogling over him like the god he was.

Which is why what came out of my mouth next was just as stupid. "How... how can you tell I'm a girl?" I asked. I didn't know if it was a rude question, but he couldn't see me, right?

The man smirked again. This time, I noticed he wasn't actually looking me in the eye— he stared in my direction, but his gaze went right through me, confirming my theory he was blind. "Most men don't wear perfume, pigeon. Or dresses that make that much noise. Your heels click on the stone."

His hand was still on my arm. The feel of his touch smoldered against my skin. I knew he couldn't see me, but when I looked into his eyes... I don't know. I felt a powerful connection, something that drew me in and absorbed my thoughts, making everything in my universe center upon this one man.

I didn't like being alone with guys, but this was different. I had an immediate knowledge that this stranger wouldn't hurt me. I noticed there was a jar on the ground, filled with a collection of coins and a few dollars. He'd been panhandling.

Sympathy filled my chest. I came from a rich family, so I'd never known what it was like to suffer financially. And however this guy had ended up in his situation, I didn't feel he deserved it.

"You dropped your purse." The guy took my purse from the husky's mouth. The dog must've fetched it, but I hadn't seen.

I took my purse back from him, still fixated on the sight of this guy. What was it about him that drew me in? "Thank you."

"No problem, pidge."

I felt like doing backflips. "Why are you calling me that... pidge?"

"Short for pigeon." He flashed another attractive smile. "Old timey slang for a hot dame."

He thought I was hot? I mean... he couldn't see me, but he had to be attracted to me all the same, to say something like that. Butterflies fluttered in my stomach. I *loved* vintage movies. I'd grown up on black and white films from the 1940's my Grandmother Eleanor loved. I thought the nickname was cute. "You new around here? I've never seen you before."

"Charlie Wahkin, ma'am," he drawled. "And you?"

"Ava-Marie." I knew better than to give him my full name. And yet we were like two magnets, drawn together as if by fate. Charlie. I liked it.

"You might want to be a little more careful next time," he said. "There are worse things in these alleyways than me."

I laughed. "Now why do I doubt that?"

He cocked his head a little. "Just mind what I told you, pidge. The back parts of any town are no place for a lady."

Charlie's smile smoldered, and my eyes went immediately to his lips. I had the thought of pressing mine against his... just to see what he would taste like. Gunpowder and lead came to mind. It would be explosive. I mean, it was insane to think of kissing a homeless guy, even one that was really, really cute. Hot damn, this guy was a full-course meal with dessert on the side. Could I put in an order for delivery? Because I'd totally eat him up.

I brushed off my skirt— it'd gotten some dirt on it when Charlie had grabbed me. "Well, Charlie, I hope I see you again soon."

"Don't count on it, miss. I don't stick around."

He inclined his head. The tiniest movement he made was sexy. I smiled back, though I realized he couldn't see it, so instead I said, "Thanks again, Charlie."

When I was at the end of the alleyway, I dared to turn around. Charlie was gathering the few things he had, stuffing them into a backpack before he and his husky wandered the other way.

Once Charlie was out of my sight, cold deadness settled back into my chest, bringing my heart down with a heavy weight. As I left the man behind me, the hallucination came pouring back into my thoughts. If I hadn't run into Charlie in the alley, and stopped the hallucination, no telling how far I'd fall into it this time.

I suffered from psychosis. Often. It was a symptom of my bipolar disorder. Not all people with bipolar saw and heard things that weren't there, but I did. I'd talked to invisible people long after it was appropriate to have imaginary friends, and described things I could see that other people couldn't. Sometimes, it happened in school and I'd scared my classmates. By the time my doctors had put together a medication regimen that lessened the severity of the hallucinations, my reputation had already been tarnished. Crazy Ava-Marie. That's what people called me.

Growing up, the response to that would always be I *wasn't* crazy, but now I wasn't so sure they were wrong. I'd been in and out of therapy all my life. I wasn't going now, because I'd been crafty enough to convince my parents I didn't need it. The truth was, I'd just given up hope, and didn't see how talking to someone would help me now if it hadn't in the past. The hallucinations had been under control, before Monica died.

Ever since? They were worse than they ever had been.

I got back on the boat so I could head home. I rummaged through my purse to find the boat key. I found it, but not much else. My guts bottomed out when I realized my wallet was missing.

What the hell? How did I lose it? My mind raced. I hadn't touched my wallet once since we'd left the house. I had no idea how it could be missing.

Then I pieced things together. My purse had fallen off my arm when I'd stumbled into Charlie. His Familiar was the one who retrieved it for me. The dog must've snatched the wallet before Charlie had given me back my purse! I'd had over a hundred dollars in there. This was bullshit!

I let out a huff and rolled my eyes. What the fuck ever. I never carried my credit cards with me, anyway, so those were safe. If that guy was lousy enough to steal, he needed the money more than I did.

Geez, what a loser. I thought that guy was hot. I had the shittiest taste in men.

I drove the boat back to the house in a bad mood.

It was a Sunday, so like always, my giant family was here, getting ready to have our afternoon get-together. My Uncle Cade was at the grill, while my Aunt Imogen was doing the hula to tropical music that played on the radio. Her fox Familiar, Sassy, rose up on her hind legs to sway to the beat. Four of their boys, all various ages, were playing football on the beach. Their fifth son— the oldest, same age as my younger sister, was talking to Alana as he swam around the pool. Alana never swam— she was afraid of water. She sat on one of the lounge chairs and screamed as Luis tried to splash her and missed.

"Ava, my darling!" A wet kiss was placed on my cheek as I felt arms the size of tree trunks wrap around me and squeeze.

"Can't breathe," I gasped. I fell several feet as my Uncle Jonah let me go. He was a giant of a man, but he had the biggest heart.

"You'd better be taking my dance class this semester," Uncle Jonah said as he waggled his finger at me.

"I've already signed up." Jonah was the Dean of Yapluma at Orenda Academy. He mostly taught Air magic and psychology classes, but his dance class was not to be missed. His Familiar, a hippogriff named Squeaks, trotted up to me and nudged me with her head.

Her offspring were a part of the hippogriff herd I'd gotten a ride from that morning. I scratched her shoulder feathers, and she cooed happily.

"Don't expect to get by so easily because you're my niece. I fully expect you to shake that booty until it falls off," Uncle Jonah teased, and his eyes sparkled.

I laughed. "Yes, Auntie."

Whether we called Jonah auntie or uncle depended on what personality he'd decided to put on that morning. He was fine with either. He crushed the beer can he was holding against his head and ran down the beach, screaming, "Save a touchdown for me, boys!"

His husband, Jake, was tossing the football. Jonah hurtled toward him and tackled him onto the sand, where they wrestled for dominance. Squeaks danced around them awkwardly, until her tail swished and knocked a tray of hot dogs off the picnic bench and onto the ground.

Jonah's daughter, Josee, was messing around with a soccer ball like always. She kicked it to Maverick, who tried to navigate it around her to score a goal. He failed when she snatched it out of the air effortlessly.

Josee was a total tomboy. All she cared about was sports. Not me. I liked looking pretty, thank you very much. She waved me over to join them, but I shook my head no and continued onto the porch.

Mama was there, taking pictures with her professional camera. The cutest little creature sat on her shoulder. It had big eyes, with fluffy brown fur, a poofy tail and long ears like those of a fennec fox. Her name was Buttercup, and she was a kurble— a type of marsupial. Buttercup trilled when I climbed the porch steps, and Mama looked up.

I always thought Mama was one of the prettiest women alive. She had long brunette hair with eyes that were always welcoming and kind, and she held herself in a dignified way I never thought I could imitate, or achieve. My mother radiated power like the sun radiated heat, and people respected her for it.

Mama put the camera down and smiled as I came by.

"Did you and your brother have a nice hike?" she asked.

"Yeah," I lied. "He's still out there. Wanted to stop by Grandpa's for a minute. What did you and the council talk about?"

Mama's smile faltered for a brief moment. "It was nothing important."

Nothing, huh? I wasn't the only one telling tall tales.

Just then, a dragon's roar rang across the wind. I looked up. A ruby red dragon, with scales glistening in the sunlight, spiraled down from the sapphire skies. The dragon was massive, and was almost as large as our house. As the dragon landed, shock waves resonated across the beach, and a man slid off the dragon's back.

"Watch your tail, Julian," Daddy said. "You nearly knocked down the house."

Julian grumbled and curled his tail the other way. It hit Squeaks and sent her flying into the water. The hippogriff made an angry sound, while Julian grumbled an apology.

Daddy was tall, with long black hair and a strong jawline that made him appear proud. The chief of the Water tribe always looked strong, even when he was at his weakest.

I wished I could emulate that kind of confidence. My dad had never been a fish out of water.

Unlike my Mama, Daddy was very sick. I could see it clearest when he was trying to hide how he really felt. Daddy suffered from a rare disease that caused his magic to weaken his bodily systems, his immune system getting the brunt of the illness. It was genetic, but so far, neither me nor my siblings had developed it.

And I hoped none of us ever did. It was tough growing up, watching your dad be in and out of the hospital. A few times, he'd barely pulled through. But I'd never have it any other way, because I really loved my Daddy, and I didn't care if he was sick, so long as he was here.

As he drew closer, I noticed the bags under his eyes, and the way his steps faltered slightly on the sand. He could smile, but I wasn't fooled. He was tired today.

Still, he put out an arm and drew me into a hug. "There's my peanut. I missed you this morning."

My stomach wiggled uncomfortably. I'd left before Daddy had gotten up, to retrieve the idol. "Ez and I wanted to get a head start on the hike."

"See anything interesting?"

I swallowed. Lying to Daddy was always the hardest. "Nah. Nothing out of the ordinary."

Daddy gave me a warm smile. Before he could ask anything else, I said, "You and Mama were gone for a long time. You don't work on weekends. Is something up?"

He frowned slightly. "You know tribal business can happen at any time. It's nothing to be worried about."

I knew exactly when Daddy wasn't telling the truth. He blinked twice.

It was strange Mama and Daddy were being shady about the Elder meeting this morning. Why didn't they want me to know about it?

I decided I didn't care. I trusted Daddy with everything. If he was keeping something from me, it was for my own good. He wouldn't lie to me about something important. He never hid secrets from me that mattered.

Mama's bit her lip as she took in my father's appearance. "You look tired, Liam. Come inside."

"Only for a moment." Daddy's eyes crossed to Aunt Imogen and Uncle Jonah, who were shaking their butts on the beach to the music. It was very typical of them. That was my crazy aunt and uncle.

Daddy shuffled slowly up the steps. I walked behind him, to catch him just in case he fell.

"I don't need to be nannied, you know," Daddy said crossly as he sat on a kitchen chair. He sent a surly gaze to me as Mama placed a glass of water on the table.

"What kind of daughter would I be if I didn't?" I asked. I hovered beside him, but not too close. Buttercup perched beside the glass of water and tilted her head before Daddy took a sip.

Mama sat across from Daddy and laid a hand on his chest. As she did, a white glow emitted from her fingertips and spread over Daddy's body. I watched, entranced by the silvery strands that wrapped around Daddy's form.

Mama could treat Daddy's disease with her Spirit magic. She couldn't cure him, but she could heal him partially, and treat his symptoms. Her powers were the only thing that kept him going most days. Watching her use her magic on him was always beautiful. Spirit magic came from love, and I could really tell that Mama loved Daddy.

All at once, the color in Daddy's face brightened, and he sat taller. It was like I could see his illness visibly ebbing away from him as Mama's Spirit powers worked their magic. When she was done, the glow faded and Daddy's voice was stronger.

He turned toward me. "So, what path did you and your brother take today?"

Before I could answer, the door burst open and slammed against the wall. I heard footsteps run into the kitchen as Ezekiel screamed, "Ava's got Water powers!"

Fucking dammit. Couldn't trust Ez to keep a secret to save his life.

Ezekiel skidded to a halt. The color drained from his face as he realized I'd gotten back first. My lips formed into a sneer. Mama and Daddy's mouths dropped open at the same time, looking from me to my brother in surprise.

I pounced. I jumped on Ezekiel's back and locked my arm around his neck. "You little snitch!"

Ezekiel grabbed my arm as he fell to his knees. We struggled violently before he wrenched me off. I went tumbling to the floor. I went to launch myself at him again, but Daddy held me back.

"Ow! You kicked me in the face!" Ez complained, holding his eye.

"Good, you probably look better," I shot back at him.

"Enough," Daddy said firmly. "Ava, what's this about?"

I took a few ragged breaths and refused to answer. But Ezekiel, who went to pieces under any sort of interrogation, blurted, "Ava and I were at the dig site, and—"

"You two went to that excavation?" Daddy leapt up from his chair. "I specifically told you not to mess around in those caves— don't roll your eyes at me, young lady!"

He'd caught me at it, but come on. This was stupid.

"Forget about that," Mama said quickly. "Ezekiel, you said Ava used Water powers."

"Uh-huh." Ezekiel's head bobbed like he was a little boy. "We found the idol, but it turned out to be a malevolent Koigni Spirit Art. It was going to kill me, until Ava commanded the underground river within the caves to attack it. I watched a wave rise up and destroy it."

"Honey, is this true?" Mama's eyes were wide. Buttercup mirrored her expression.

"I mean..." I shrugged. "Yeah, it happened, but it must've been a one-off thing. I don't have Water powers. I'm Koigni!"

"That's not what she asked," Daddy said. I was trying his patience.

"Look, I just did it to protect my brother! I don't know if I could do it again!" I said.

Mama nodded. She'd first discovered her powers doing something similar, defending her sister from an attacking lion years ago.

I fisted a hand in my hair. "Maybe we shouldn't have gone to the caves.

But whatever happened this morning, it won't happen again. I've never felt partial to Water. I like Fire. I'm a Koigni through and through, and—"

As I was rambling, Daddy purposefully knocked over the glass of water that was sitting on the table. I gasped and reacted instinctively. My left hand shot out. The water that was about to hit the floor suspended in the air, hovering at my command.

I was so shocked that the spell broke, and water splashed all over the hardwood. Nobody moved to clean it up. Everyone stared at me, like I was some sort of freak animal.

Daddy took in a breath. "Ava, you're incredible." Daddy was fit to boasting. He was proud I'd inherited his side of the magical spectrum. But why were they all so happy about this? I didn't feel like it was anything to celebrate.

There was no denying it. Or hiding it. I did have Toaqua powers. I just didn't understand why.

"How could this have happened?" I asked. "I thought Elementai always inherited the powers of their same-sex parent."

"Ava, you have multiple generations of Fire and Water running through your veins. The same-sex parent rule must be canceled out once your genetics become diluted enough. Fire and Water are both dominant traits in your genes," Mama said, marveling at her own words.

"Does this mean I might get Fire powers, too?" Ezekiel asked in excitement. He was thrilled about becoming a dual-caster, but he didn't get it. It wasn't a gift to be different. It was a curse.

"It depends on what traits are dominant. My traits are from my Spirit and Fire side, but they can co-exist peacefully. But I've never heard of Fire and Water traits being dominant at the same time," Mama said.

"Exactly. It's never happened before." I couldn't keep the bitterness out of my voice. This was just one more thing that would set me apart from everyone else.

"Ava, the ancestors chose to give you this gift," Daddy said. "Why not use it for good?"

"Because I just want to be normal, that's why!" I burst. "People already think I'm crazy. What are they going to say when they find out I'm a dual-caster? The press is going to go nuts!"

As the daughter of the Toaqua chief and the chosen one, I'd been the subject of Hawkei tabloids multiple times. Most of the articles weren't very kind. I couldn't imagine this one would be, either.

Mama's eyebrows scrunched together. "You're not crazy, sweetheart. You have bipolar."

I blew a lock of hair out of my eyes. "Big difference."

Ezekiel came close to me. This time, he looked a little bothered. "Are you okay, Ava? I was worried about you when you left earlier."

"I told you I was fine." Did he really have to bring this up in front of our parents? He could've asked me later.

"I just... I don't know." Ezekiel shrugged. "You had that look in your eyes you used to get when you were hearing things."

Daddy and Mama went rigid. I suppressed a groan. "You're hearing voices again?" Mama's eyes narrowed in concern.

"No," I lied. "I haven't heard anything. I was just tired earlier."

"Ava, you'd better be telling the truth," Daddy warned.

"Not a single sound."

I couldn't let them know the voices were back. They'd give me a kiss and ship me off to the loony bin before I had a chance to pack my designer heels. I'd told them the voices had stopped years ago, to keep them from worrying, when in reality they never had.

Ezekiel gave me *the look*. It was a secret gesture only we understood, and he was telling me I was full of shit.

"Ava, whatever happens, we're here to help you," Mama said gently. She took my hand, like she was good at doing, and squeezed it tight. "If you're hearing voices, or if you don't understand your magic, we can work it out. There's nothing we can't do together as a family."

Tears started to bead at the corners of my eyes, but I pushed them back down. I didn't cry. "You guys don't understand. I'm tired of being different. My magic was one thing that felt safe. And it doesn't feel like that anymore."

I turned away from them and ran. My parents called after me, but I ignored them. Everyone on the beach looked up as I bolted to the shoreline.

I didn't think about what I did. Just like my Fire, my Water magic erupted from me by feeling. I didn't know how I did what I did, but one moment, I was on the sand, and the next, a wave had risen up to catch my feet. I continued running, and the Water crashed upward to support my weight. I fell into the water and surfed across the waves like I would on my board. People gasped when they saw me riding upon the water. I heard more cries, but I pretended like I didn't hear them, keeping my eyes on the horizon.

Soon, the island was long behind me. I collapsed on the shore of the mainland on all fours, breathing heavily. My shoulders shook. My clothes were soaked, but I didn't care.

I felt like I was going to crack. If I didn't maintain control, I *would* crack, and everything I was holding inside would break free. I had to get it together. I forced myself to stand and slicked back my wet hair, eyeing the span of the empty beach.

I was so empty inside. The hollowness just wouldn't go away, and I didn't know how to fill it.

I was Toaqua now. Maybe I could drown it.

As the dark thought crossed my mind, I heard a rustle in the trees coming from the forest beyond the beach. I stood up slowly as a creature emerged.

By the ancestors, she was beautiful. The creature was a tall and slender unicorn, with a coat dark as night and an obsidian horn rising out of the center of her forehead. The mare's eyes were black, and her mane and tail burned with flame, sending embers to the ground as the fire that made up her hair trailed over her neck and withers.

A Fire unicorn. I'd heard of them, but I'd never seen one before. She was looking right at me.

I advanced toward the Fire unicorn. As I drew near, my clothes and hair dried automatically at the presence of her heat. The air around her was hot, but I didn't mind at all. The unicorn was completely still as she faced me head-on. In the middle of her forehead was a singular white mark— a seven-pointed star. She nickered as I dared to reach out a hand. I placed it on her velvety nose.

The moment I touched her, the entire world opened up. I saw so many colors at the edges of my vision, colliding together in a gorgeous rainbow. The purpose of my life entwined together with this creature, sucking me in and holding me in an embrace that was welcoming and home. I felt the fires of her passion burning away at me, taking away anything that was bad and leaving behind only what was right. This wasn't like the visions I experienced during psychosis. This was real, and it was comforting. I smelled sandalwood, the ocean, and the remnants of a burning fire. I heard my brother's laughter and the sound of Monica singing. The song continued, wrapping around me as I felt Daddy's hug and Mama braiding my hair. I imagined sunlight hitting my face, and the glow of a candle in the dark. Images flashed before my eyes, like they would if I was experiencing my last moments before death; but instead of death, this was a new awakening.

The unicorn placed her nose to my chest. When she touched my heart,

I felt such a powerful wave of emotion that my knees buckled beneath me and I cried out.

As the music faded and Monica's voice ebbed away, I knew immediately that I had bonded. I didn't need to question it. This unicorn was my Familiar. My soul. Familiars always came to you at your weakest point—and she had known I needed her now.

"Who are you?" I whispered. I was completely enchanted by her.

The mare blinked. She didn't speak to me, but I felt a strong feeling in my heart, and a name popped into my head... *Oberi.*

"Oberi." That was her name. I reached out and wrapped my arms around her neck. The unicorn turned her head inward and nuzzled me, as if hugging me to her chest.

The hollowness inside me went away, and I reveled in the feeling of touching my Familiar for the first time. I had found who I was. I'd discovered myself. Everything in my life tied me to this creature, and I knew then that I wasn't alone.

As I pulled away, the unicorn turned to me, offering me her back. I reached up to take her mane in my hands. Though it was made of Fire, the flames didn't burn me. I pulled myself onto the unicorn, and Oberi gave another knicker. She bounced a few times on her hooves before giving a tiny rear, then bolted forward.

Her feet kicked up sand as she galloped down the beach. My hair was blown backward by the wind, and I gave a cry of joy. This was entirely different than riding the hippogriffs. It was like Oberi and I were one, a singular being with no start and no end. Her flames blew by as I twisted them in my hands. It was like my spirit left my body as I felt her powerful strides pound the earth, creating a song in my heart as we splashed against the waves. As we ran, I saw other unicorns made of Water rise out of the ocean, charging alongside Oberi as we ran.

I had done that out of my emotion. My magic. Maybe being Toaqua wasn't such a bad thing after all.

Oberi slowed to a halt, and I took deep breaths to stabilize my shaking form. I slid off her back, still winded. My mind calculated the possibilities as I stroked Oberi's midnight coat.

I'd bonded with a Fire creature. This proved I was Koigni, right? Maybe I could hide my Toaqua side. Nobody needed to know about it, right? They'd never guess, not with a Fire unicorn at my side.

As I was still taking in the incredible moment, an angry cry rang out across the beach. "Get away from my Familiar!"

I turned around. My stomach bottomed out when I realized who was shouting at me. It was Charlie— the blind man I'd run into earlier. The one who'd taken my wallet. He was stomping up the beach, his bag thrown over his back.

Anger rose within me. This guy was a piece of work. What the hell was he doing, bothering me and Oberi? How did he even know where we were? He couldn't see us.

"You're going to get a fireball to the face," I snarled. I conjured one and drew back my hand to throw it.

Before I could, Oberi gave a high-pitched whinny. She ran toward Charlie, tossing her head. The fireball dropped out of my hand and fizzled on the sand as I watched Oberi change. In seconds, she'd morphed from a female Fire unicorn... into the same male husky I'd seen with Charlie earlier.

The husky barked and wagged his tail at Charlie's side. Shock twisted my guts when the husky turned to look at me. I noticed the same seven-pointed star on his forehead that Oberi had.

This was impossible. How could Oberi have two different *genders*? Two different *forms*? I'd never heard of such a Familiar before.

Then my heart twisted sickly as I watched Charlie pet the husky. His blind gaze rose to stare in my direction. When my eyes connected with his, I knew.

I wasn't just bonded to this creature— to Oberi. I was bonded to *Charlie* as well. His Familiar was also my own.

My spirit was split into two pieces. And the other half belonged to him.

I shared a soul with a complete stranger.

Continue Ava's story behind bars in the Prison for Supernatural Offenders series.

BONUS OFFERS

Find coloring pages, games, quizzes, and bonus content at www.hiddenlegendsbooks.com

Join *Orenda Academy of Magical Creatures* on Facebook to talk to other Elementai about upcoming books in the Hidden Legends Universe!

Never miss a new release! Join our newsletter at www.hiddenlegendsbooks.com/fanclub

Check out the *Academy of Magical Creatures Official Playlist* on Spotify!

ABOUT THE AUTHORS

Megan Linski (left) and Alicia Rades (right) are two best friends and the authors of the *Academy of Magical Creatures* series. Both are USA TODAY Bestselling Authors and award-winning novelists for teens and young adults. Megan Linski is a disabled author who loves laughter, adventure, and fantasy worlds. She is a proud member of Koigni House. Alicia Rades is a mother who enjoys exploring paranormal realms and trying new recipes. She is a champion from Toaqua House. Both girls love nature, animals, sexy romances, and eating cheese.

www.ingramcontent.com/pod-product-compliance
Lightning Source LLC
Chambersburg PA
CBHW060936190726
48286CB00005B/1294